BATTLELINES

BATTLELINES

LtCol DAVID B. BROWN, USMC (Ret)
TIFFANY BROWN HOLMES

iUniverse, Inc.
New York Lincoln Shanghai

BATTLELINES

Copyright © 2005 by David B. Brown

All rights reserved. No part of this book may be used or reproduced by any means, graphic, electronic, or mechanical, including photocopying, recording, taping or by any information storage retrieval system without the written permission of the publisher except in the case of brief quotations embodied in critical articles and reviews.

iUniverse books may be ordered through booksellers or by contacting:

iUniverse
2021 Pine Lake Road, Suite 100
Lincoln, NE 68512
www.iuniverse.com
1-800-Authors (1-800-288-4677)

Cover, maps & art by Henry Garrou

ISBN-13: 978-0-595-36695-8 (pbk)
ISBN-13: 978-0-595-67407-7 (cloth)
ISBN-13: 978-0-595-81118-2 (ebk)
ISBN-10: 0-595-36695-3 (pbk)
ISBN-10: 0-595-67407-0 (cloth)
ISBN-10: 0-595-81118-3 (ebk)

Printed in the United States of America

ACKNOWLEDGEMENTS

Our deepest gratitude goes out to more than one hundred Fox Company Marines and corpsmen, the heroes who shared their personal wartime experiences with us at reunions, in telephone calls, and in letters that included personal diaries, copies of citations, photos, and correspondence from their Fox Company friends. Their efforts in reviewing chapter drafts and the encouragement they have given us to complete this, their book, remain the principal reason for which Battlelines was written.

We want to acknowledge the men who recorded the war in radio transmissions, incident reports, situation reports, and those who compiled them into their monthly command chronologies. They have been instrumental in the historical specificity of the combat actions. We thank the Marine Corps for providing us with a copy of the 2nd Battalion, 5th Marines' command chronologies.

We also want to share our deep appreciation to two very wonderful friends, Henry and Jesica Garrou, who were responsible for the graphic design of the cover and the majority of the maps created for the book. Their "can do" spirit eliminated technical problems.

Three great books provided a broad perspective on portions of the war in which Fox fought. Those books are: Keith Nolan's Battle for Hue: Tet 1968; Eric Hammel's Fire in the Street: The Battle for Hue Tet 1968; and R. J. Brown's A Few Good Men, The Fighting Fifth Marines: A History of the USMC's Most Directed Regiment.

To our family and friends who were forced to be patient during the past three years while we researched, strategized, and wrote, we would like to express our tremendous thanks.

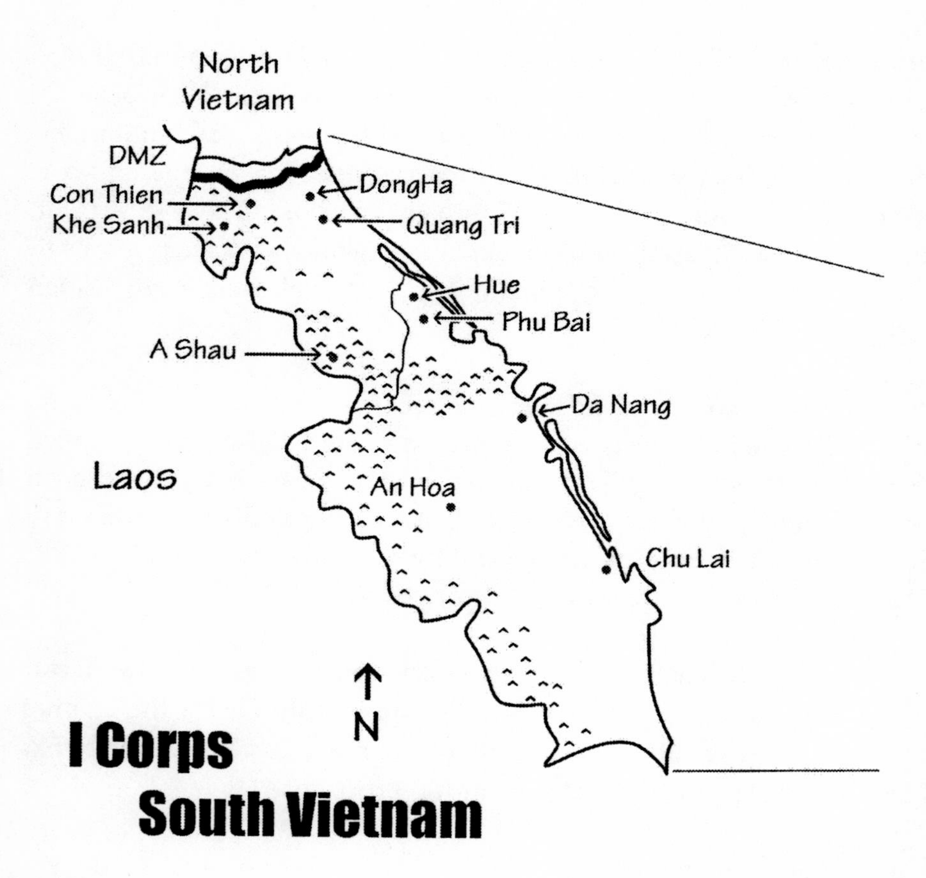

From March 1966 until March 1971, Fox Company, 2nd Battalion, 5th Marines fought from Chu Lai to the DMZ.

South Vietnam

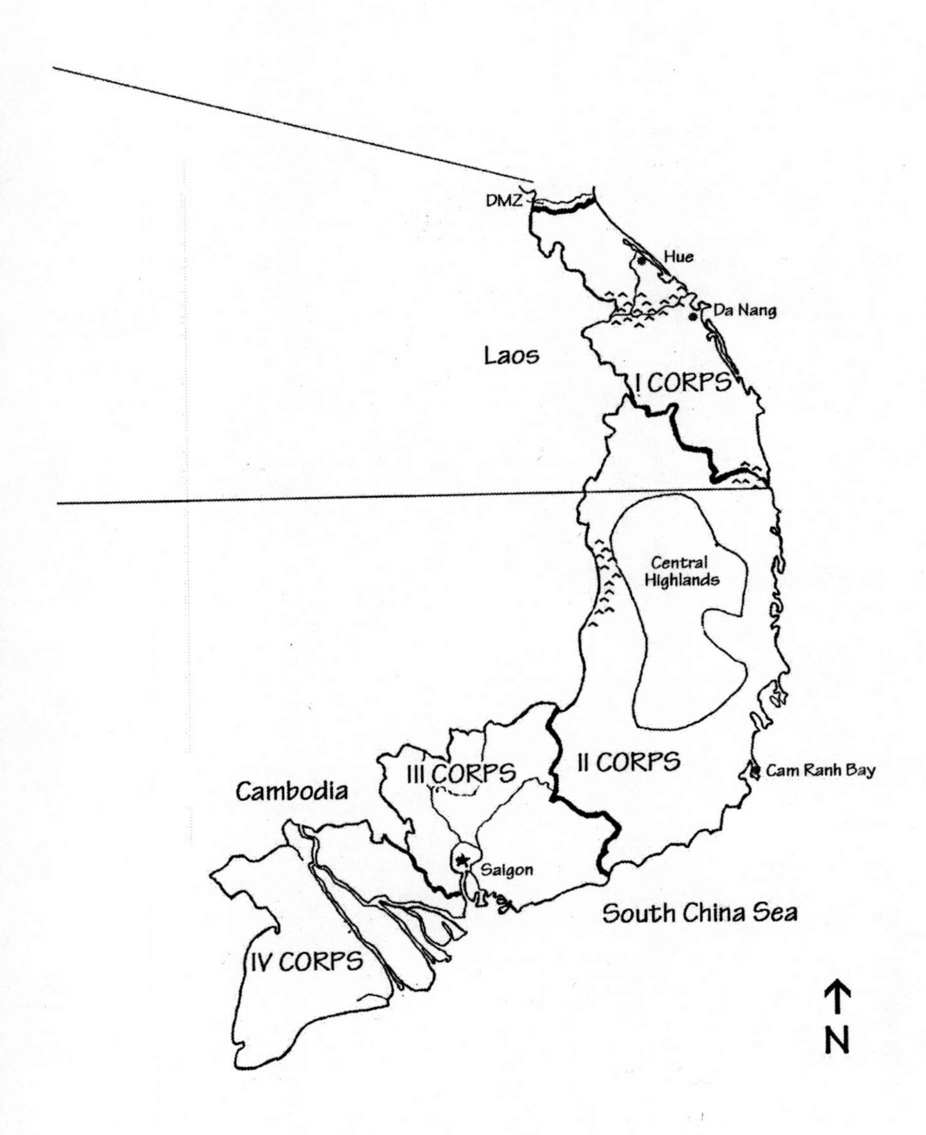

TABLE OF CONTENTS

PREFACE

What is it that makes a Marine extend his combat tour of duty an additional six months in lieu of accepting stateside orders and rejoining his family? The answer probably is quite varied, but in my case I simply wanted to be able to command a Marine Corps rifle company in combat. It was a passion. I had to taste it. I had to smell the gunpowder. I would never be a whole Marine unless I fulfilled this passion.

My destiny was Company F, 2nd Battalion, 5th Marines. Fox Company. And for men of Fox Company, their destiny was me. I knew a lot about the responsibility a commanding officer would have before joining Fox in July 1968. The men, their dreams and wishes, and their hearts and souls would teach me the rest. So much so that I have never let them go.

Over 200 Purple Heart Medals would be awarded during the six months we were bound together. Of them, twenty-seven truly wonderful men died. We were shot at by the NVA and Viet Cong, blown apart by endless mines and booby traps, napalmed by an F-4, and mortared by our own battalion. We spit in the enemy's eye, and Hanoi Hanna cited us as a targeted organization. We starved together. Our health would deteriorate from jungle rot, malaria, and leaches. Yet, through it all, we laughed. We played practical jokes on each other. We bonded. We were one.

When I left the company in January 1969, I thought the Fox Company experience would end. I believed that, with the exception of bumping into a few other career Marines who had served with Fox, I would have no further contact with this heroic band of men. I was right, at least in part. While I did run into Mike Downs, a former Fox Company commander who preceded me, and Bill Melton and Woody Lott, a couple of my platoon commanders, for the next nineteen years I did not meet any of the troops.

Things changed in June 1988. I was invited to attend a gathering of the 2nd Battalion, 5th Marines who were celebrating their gallant victory twenty years earlier over a vastly superior NVA and Viet Cong force in Hue City, the ancient capital of Vietnam. Their victory during the "Tet Offensive" would earn the battalion, and a couple other commands, the nation's premier unit award: the Presidential Unit Citation. When I joined the Fox Company five months after Tet, a few Hue City vets were still with the company. I accepted the invitation as I thought that it would be great to meet the Hue City vets after all those years.

The banquet was a lot of fun. Almost 200 people attended. I didn't know any one of the eight from Fox Company with the exception of Mike Downs. I shrugged off the low attendance of Fox vets as incidental. I had no idea, however, how the poor representation affected others.

Dan "Arkie" Albritton, a sergeant twenty years earlier and a senior US postal official in 1988, was incensed. He expressed his feelings in a brand new Fox Company newsletter written right from his "Chigger Ranch" in Arkansas. Arkie's writing style combined country wit and straightforward talk. While his style perhaps mirrored that of Mark Twain, his purpose was absolutely clear. Never again was the best company in the in the Marine Corps going to be shamed. Fox had always been first among all others and he would prove that they would be so again. Forever.

Chris Brown, a New York City insurance executive, had been a squad leader in Hue City. Chris immediately filled the role of recruiting lieutenant in "Arkie's Army". Chris badgered the Marine Corps Headquarters for unit diaries of Fox Company. He used "other" federal government contacts to correlate unit diary data with current mailing addresses and phone numbers. Chris contacted all of them, no matter where they were.

Fox Company held its first reunion in 1989. Arkie asked me to address any topic I wanted to at an afternoon meeting. I chose to discuss the time the company was accidentally napalmed and the results of the follow-on investigation. Two of the burned men came up to me later to thank me for the information on just how their bodies had become so heavily disfigured years ago. Mike Downs, then a Brigadier General and still on active duty, gave a day-by-day accounting about the battle of

Hue City. I was so impressed with his detailed recollection. No doubt, I thought, he had to have kept a personal dairy. Just why didn't I do that?

The two most moving speeches came later at the grand Saturday night banquet. They both dealt with the final minutes of the life of Medal of Honor recipient Captain Jim Graham. The story of his selfless sacrifice for his men by this Fox Company commander was told by his radio operator, Brent Mackinnon, and one of his platoon commanders, Tony Marengo. Both had been with Captain Graham until he left them to rescue his men trapped by the enemy. I was overwhelmed by Graham's story. Afterwards, the vets talked about the "coalmines", where a month after Captain Graham perished, Private First Class Newland earned—also posthumously—the Medal of Honor.

I had never been to a Veterans Day parade before 1990. Several Fox 2/5 vets told me that they would be marching. "Would I accompany them?" "Would I help organize the men?" "Harry Albert, a Fox Company vet and an officer with the Vietnam Veterans Association, was arranging for our company to march independently down the parade route, Pennsylvania Avenue, in Washington, DC." "Would I make a large poster identifying Fox Company?"

"Yes, yes and of course." By this time I was hooked. I loved it.

Thus, on Veterans Day 1990, I preceded to the Capital Mall accompanied by my nineteen-year old daughter, Tiffany, who delighted me by accepting my somewhat "tongue-in-cheek" invitation. The parade made me feel more proud of having served than I had ever felt before. "Go, Fox Company, Go!" the crowd would shout all along the route. Tiffany began to bond with one wheelchair bound Marine and his wife, Bill and Pat Nichols. Tiffany loved the whole thing. Our shared experience on that day was the seed of this book.

By July 1991 when the USS Hue City, a guided missile cruiser named in honor of the battle, was christened, the Fox membership totaled more than 200. Not unexpected, Fox had the best attendance at the ceremony. Still, not having served with Fox until after Hue City, I did not to attend. Arkie gathered the attending Fox Company vets together after the ceremony and, in absentia, elected me president of this new organization. I accepted by phone and held this position for five years.

I attended Fox's 1992 reunion in Reno, NV, by myself. Since Post Traumatic Stress Disorder, PTSD, still flourished and many west coast vets were meeting for the first time in years, I scheduled a "Tell Your Funniest Vietnam Stories" session. One by one the storytellers would go to the lectern and recant their stories. They were hilarious.

In 1994 Tiffany wrote her first novel, a historical romance set in England in the 14th Century. It was quite exciting, had lot of compassion, and captured many of the historical customs. I proofed it often, focusing more on the action parts and a lot less on the romantic segments.

I asked Tiffany to accompany me to the Wisconsin Dells reunion in 1994. By this time our list of members exceeded 400 and we had adopted a "family" orientation for the reunions. The theme for this reunion was PTSD. Perhaps half the Fox Company men returned from the war with a measurable amount of PTSD. While on active duty until 1982, I would have not believed that fact. Later, after being with the Fox vets for six years, I knew of its reality. Together, I wanted the men to stare the disorder square in its eye as they had the enemy years earlier and watch it retreat. Dr. Dennis Cadigan gave the keynote address. Tiffany loved the reunion as she began to identify with many Fox Company vets, their wives and now the children in their early twenties. I believe Sam and Donna Henderson wanted to adopt her. I could see her love for the company growing.

Sometime shortly after the Dells reunion, I learned that one of the Fox Company stalwarts, who had embarked on writing a book on the company exploits in Vietnam, was not going to be able to complete it. I resolved that this book must be written.

I could think of no better person to accomplish this than my daughter, Tiffany.

At this point it is most appropriate to turn the rest of our Preface over to Tiffany.

* * * * * * * * *

Shortly after my father's resolution, I stood watching not one, nor two, but four spectacular fireworks displays that 4th of July. Earlier in the day I had excitedly announced that I was "such a patriot," and my friends affectionately laughed at me. I did not take offense.

Not many people can claim my past, my experiences, or background. I am, however, a fortunate participant of a small, elite group, of which I am immensely proud. This group is comprised of patriots. I fondly think back to my many 4th of July holidays spent in my hometown of Washington, D.C. I recall my friends wrapping themselves in the American flag on our way to "The Mall" celebration. Growing up, the 4th of July has always been my favorite day of the year. My eyes still tear up when I watch fireworks.

I get misty every time I hear the National Anthem.

I ascribe my profound pride in my country to my culture. I grew up with a father who taught me to be brave when I thought it impossible, to "gut" things out, to be honest, and behave honorably. I have an admiration for my father that goes beyond the simple love of a daughter, and I esteem no other person higher than he. I am grateful to him and respect him. He is truly one of the "few good men"—a Marine.

When my father approached me with the intention of writing this book together, I was dumbfounded. I knew virtually nothing about the Marine Corps or their operations in Vietnam.

As always, he had faith in me.

Over the past four years I have researched and pieced together the history of Company F, 2nd Battalion, 5th Marine Regiment. It is my greatest honor to help my father provide this elite company of fighting men, their history, their memories, and their families with a record of their days in Vietnam.

Fox Company, with a mailing list exceeding 575, has one of the largest active military reunion groups for company-size units in the nation. Their reunions run every two years and each time, the location is different. The company spreads its gatherings across the country: east coast, west coast, and finally central U.S., in order, to ensure that their many members have as many opportunities to participate as possible. By moving each reunion site, it also keeps the visit fresh and exciting for all.

The reunions that led into this work started with eight men in 1988 and now have nearly 250 people in attendance including spouses and children. I was fortunate enough to have marched in a Veteran's Day Parade on the Mall in Washington, D.C. nearly ten years ago. I cannot describe my pride as I walked beside and behind these valiant men. The walk through the crowded streets of onlookers was impressive in its own right; but nothing compared to the moment when we passed a company of active-duty Marines. Not many people understand why Marines yell things like "Ooh rah," but when I was on the receiving end of those cheers the sheer magnitude of pride was overwhelming. There was a sense of brotherhood, unity, and yes, power. The thought that together, anything was accomplishable permeated my mind, and my body. The walk was long and near its end the temperature suddenly plummeted, but I gained strength from those Marines. I had been given something I now hold priceless…a glimpse inside the Corps.

Few civilians can claim a moment like that, but I, for just one moment, was able to share a camaraderie with some of the finest Marines in history. I was a part of Fox Company, 2nd Battalion, 5th Marines, Veteran group that surrounded me, and I was humbled by the experience.

Since that day, I have become a repeat participant of the Fox 2/5 reunions. Indeed, I look forward to Doc Connelly's Saturday morning sickbay, where the Bloody Mary's flow and the stories flow even more swiftly. The huge, raucous dinners, and excellent together time is made even more special by the healing that seems to go on at each gathering. The friends I have made there make the years between reunions run too long, and each day of the reunions flies by too quickly.

Approximately one to three percent of this book has been augmented or enhanced to provide continuity for the reader where the history records were vague or sparse, giving the book its fictional characterization. The remainder of the work has been recanted as faithfully as possible. We chose the title Battlelines, because this work is a compilation of their stories, in other words, lines from their past. We hope that we have done their outstanding war record justice. Our dream is that their families might share this important piece of history.

To the men of Fox Company, 2nd Battalion, 5th Marine Regiment—here are your Battlelines...

CHAPTER 1: FOX GOES TO WAR

1600 Hours. Four miles south of the Demilitarized Zone, DMZ. The date was the "13th" of October, 1966. Captain George Burgett did not consider himself a superstitious man even though many considered thirteen an unlucky number. 1600 was the time for all platoons to be back in camp as darkness would soon follow; the men needed chow; listening posts, LPs, needed to be manned, and bunker patrols would have to be set. Bunker patrols were crucial to the survival of the company, because the North Vietnamese Army, NVA, had been hitting them hard at night.

As usual, while Fox's platoons patrolled near the DMZ, Burgett, Gunnery Sergeant Sam Jones, and the reserve platoon for that day had moved 200 meters out of the main entrance of the somewhat fortified Hill 158, known later in the war as Con Thien. They established a defensive position on either side of the dirt road that ran from the main gate toward the DMZ. From there they could react quickly should one of the patrolling platoons become engaged.

1st Platoon hadn't returned yet.

As time dwindled away Burgett finally walked over to Lance Corporal Arthur Jarrett, his radio operator, and said, "Jarrett, how 'bout getting Staff Sergeant Schlader on the horn? I need to talk to him."

After a brief conversation with his anxious commanding officer, Staff Sergeant Charley Schlader, the commander of the 1st Platoon, turned to Staff Sergeant Sam Henderson, his platoon sergeant, and growled, "Skipper passed the word to get our 'butts' back to base camp."

"And what did you inform the good captain?" Henderson asked in an inquisitive, if not playful tone. Henderson's humor was winning him fast friends in Fox Company.

"Just what do you think I informed the skipper?" Schlader shot Henderson a sharp look.

Henderson merely raised his brows to pretend ignorance. He stayed quiet until Schlader affirmed, "I told him we would hump it back double-time and report in ASAP."

"Did you mention the bell?" Henderson asked.

Schlader's eyes found the item in question. They had moved three klicks up to the DMZ and back. Each day they followed a different route. Their mission: search-and-destroy. About an hour before Burgett's call while on the way back to the base camp, the platoon discovered an old stone chapel. Its walls were crumbled into heaps of large, jagged-edged stones, although the front wall of the chapel appeared to still be intact. From the look of it, this was clearly once a French structure that had been abandoned for decades.

"Hey, Sarge," Sergeant Rhodes called back to the platoon command group trailing his squad. "Come up here and check this out!"

"What you got, Rhodes?" Schlader asked.

"My guys discovered something."

The chapel had hidden its secret for many years. No weapon or rice caches here. When searched, its structure revealed that the chapel's bell tower remained intact, and inside, rested a bell complete with the date "1913" inscribed in it.

"Damn," Schlader muttered softly while studying the sixty-pound bell and wondering just how in the hell they were going to get it back to the base camp. They had nearly 1000 meters to go; yet this discovery would be worth the morale boost when they brought it back to the base camp to display it for their buddies.

Sergeant Rhodes interrupted Schlader's musing. "We'll hump it, Staff Sergeant."

"All right, damn it. I'll move Corporal Roller's squad up front, and you take up the rear." He paused only momentarily, "Harris's and Ronje's weapons will be with me behind Roller. Just don't let that thing slow us down. We're running late already."

Rhodes found his two biggest Marines, and with the aid of two sturdy sticks used as a carrying device, the squad began their movement back toward Hill 158. The hike back to base camp turned eerily quiet, and while no one mentioned that uncomfortable fact, all were aware of the potential meaning behind the forest's stillness.

When Burgett gave them "notice" that they were to force-march back to camp, Schlader thought little of it. 1600 hours was the time to report back. He and the men in his platoon were aware they were running late. The fact that they were returning with such a prize made their tardiness more justifiable.

Schlader and Henderson ordered the troops to get a move on. They made good progress on the small dirt road designated for their return trip and finally reached a point about one hundred meters below the spot where Schlader expected the company command group and men from Staff Sergeant Ken Sprimont's 2nd Platoon to be.

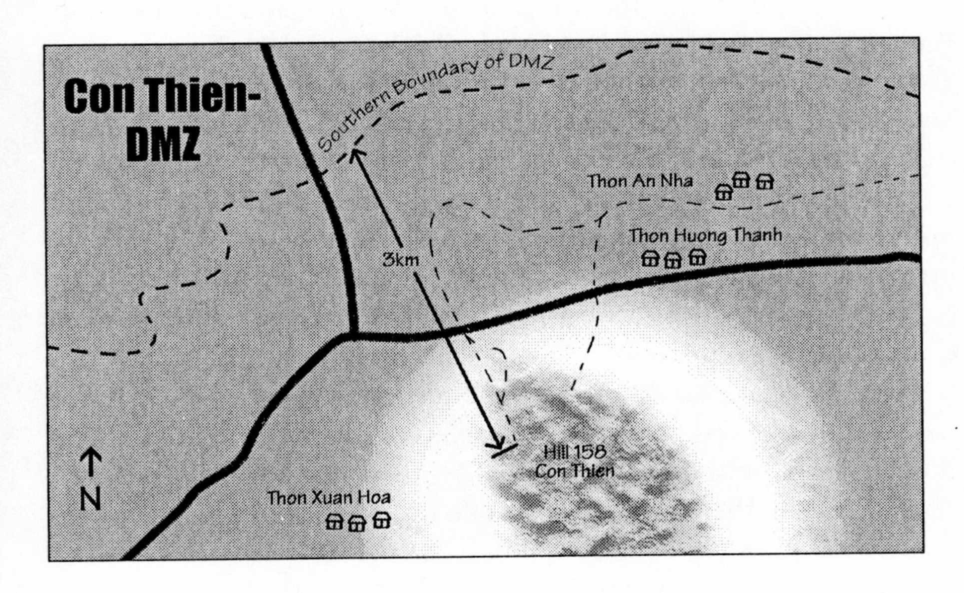

Abruptly, Corporal Robert Roller's squad held up.

"What's going on, One Charlie?" Schlader asked Roller, his 3rd Squad leader, over the company radio net.

"One Actual, we have a couple of tanks here." Roller responded. "One lost a track and the crew almost has it repaired. The other is covering, over."

"Roger, One Charlie," Schlader continued smiling, "I'll be right up there. Hold them up long enough for us to strap the bell on to one of them."

Then calling for Sergeant Rhodes, his 1st Squad leader—the one with the bell—Schlader said into his radio, "One Alpha, this is One Actual, over,"

"One Alpha, go."

"Alpha, get the bell on the good tank, and you and your humpers go back in with it, over."

Fox's security forces were waiting for the 1st Platoon one hundred meters up the hill from Roller's squad and the tank. Monitoring all the radio chitchat they knew the squad was almost back. Sprimont had the 2nd Platoon "saddle up" and get ready to move back into the base camp. Burgett's command group stood ready to follow the 2nd Platoon.

Rhodes loaded the bell with his three troops and departed on the tank for the main gate. The crew of the second tank got into the now-repaired vehicle and started its engine.

Although they were seventy-five meters behind Schlader, Henderson ordered the remaining squad with their attached weapons sections to get up and ready to go.

Schlader grabbed his radio handset. "Fox Six," he communicated using Burgett's radio call sign, "this is One, over."

"Err…Roger, One. Go," Jarrett responded.

Aware that he was talking to Lance Corporal Jarrett and not Captain Burgett, Schlader said, "Tell Six Actual, we're on our way in."

"Roger that," the thin Georgian, radio operator acknowledged.

Instantaneously, from a tree line sixty meters on the left, four AK-47 automatic weapons began firing on Roller and his men near the tank.

The tank's hatch slammed closed.

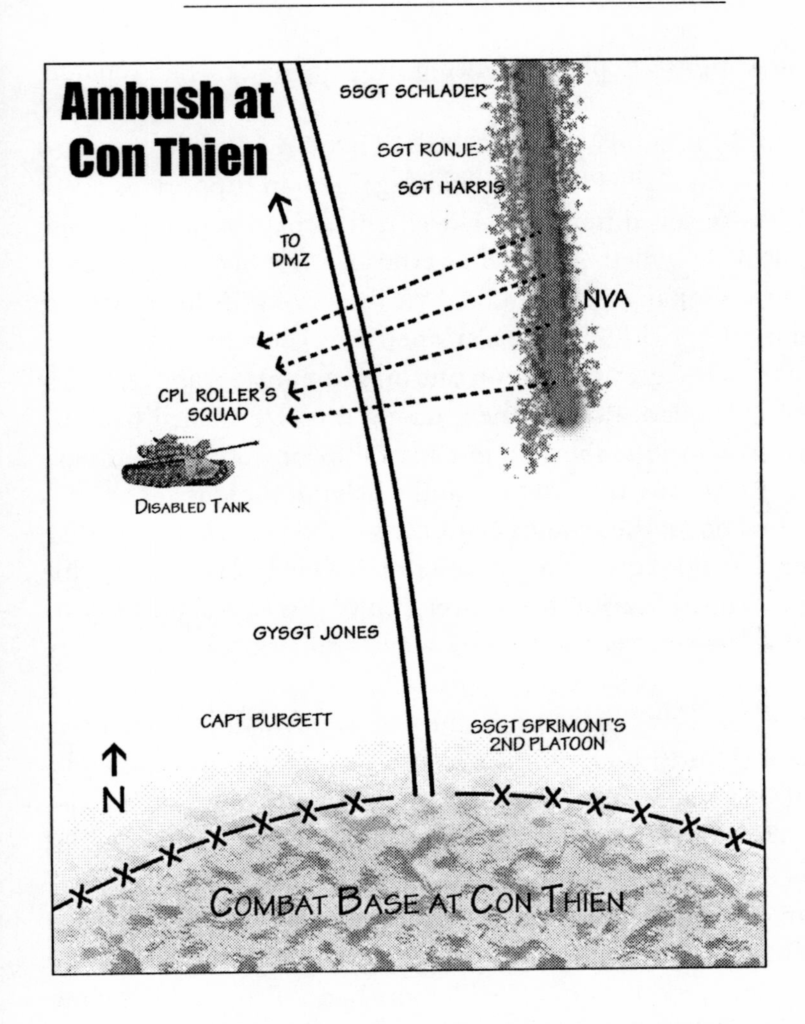

Roller wheeled and was immediately shot in his left hand and arm. Two other Marines were hit with the initial spray of bullets and went down.

"Marines! Take cover! Return fire!" Schlader yelled at the Marines around him who shot blindly into the tree line hiding their attackers.

"Harris, Ronje! Over here!" Schlader's bark gained his machine gun and anti-tank assault leaders' attention while he clipped orders over the noise of the rifle and machine gun fire.

"We got no options!" Schlader hollered over the noise. "Be prepared to counter-attack."

Schlader heard his radio operator, Private First Class Rubin, communicating with Fox Six. "2nd Platoon is moving down in support, Sir!"

"Okay," Schlader yelled in acknowledgement. Schlader and his radio operator ducked as bullets snapped overhead. "Tell Six," he ordered referring to the company commander, "We're moving in for a frontal assault. We'll meet up with 2nd Platoon when they get here."

With the command group less than one hundred meters above, Jones witnessed the 3rd squad, Roller's men, taking hits. He turned back to check on his captain, but Burgett and his radio operator had disappeared. "Shit!" he ground out, "Where in the hell did those two go?"

Jones sprinted down the road to assist the wounded men. He spotted the 1st Platoon's senior corpsman, Hospitalman Third Class, HM3, Phil Foxx, with a wounded Marine. Foxx crouched on his knees, his back to the enemy, and leaned over the Marine while applying pressure to his chest.

The 1st Platoon seized on what seemed to be their only chance for survival: take the North Vietnamese in a hard-charging frontal assault. Schlader and the younger sergeants, Dennis Harris and Joe Ronje, moved in on the left. Henderson who had been in the rear with the 2nd Squad, closed in behind Schlader.

All of them could hear the Fox's initial engagement with the NVA up the hill. Sprimont's 2nd Platoon attempted to distract the enemy. By now, Schlader realized that the 2nd Platoon had engaged the enemy inside his platoon's line of fire. He motioned silently for his sergeants to slide left, then, attack the enemy's left flank.

Fearlessly, Schlader, Ronje, and Harris assaulted into the tree line. Before Schlader had a chance to take one step, a maelstrom of suppressing fire blasted them. He watched numbly as Harris and Ronje fell dead at his side. They seemed to fall in slow motion, their limp forms spraying blood in every direction at once. Life drained from each young man; their faces bleached into a grayish-white. Instinctively, Schlader turned toward them to offer assistance. Within a millisecond a bullet hit his shoulder and tossed him onto his back like a rag doll. Schlader rolled out of the tree line. The sounds of the battle surrounding him seemed to fade in his ears until the only sounds he could hear were his own dull breath and muted heartbeat.

On the hill, Jones reached Doc Foxx, the corpsman. "Doc, what can I do?" Jones asked.

"Hold his feet, Gunny!"

As Jones's hands grasped the ankles of the young Marine, the enemy opened up again. In less than five seconds, Foxx was shot thirteen times in the back. One round passed through the front of Jones's flak jacket nicking his left shoulder, and passed through the back of his flak jacket finally coming to rest in his suspender straps.

Immediately, the once-silent tank hammered out its own suppressing fire. Jones twisted around to catch Burgett out of the corner of his eye and realized the skipper had rushed to the tank's outside phone, used by the infantry in order to communicate with the tank's crew.

Henderson and the 2nd Squad finally pushed into Schlader's position. He and another Marine tugged and slid Schlader, Ronje, and Harris backward fully out of the tree line, while the rest of the squad laid down a withering storm of fire. The enemy, firing from a trench line only fifteen meters away, suddenly ceased their attack. Regaining their composure shortly, the North Vietnamese began blasting away again. However, from their dug-in trench-line firing position, the NVA rounds harmlessly cracked over the heads of the Marines assisting Schlader.

Schlader's breath now echoed in his head, deep and fast at first, and then shallow, as though he were drifting off to sleep. Vaguely, above him, Henderson's face loomed into his line of sight. It was only then that Schlader realized he lay on the ground, wounded, next to the two men he'd watched die. His hearing returned as abruptly as if he had pounded water out of his ears.

"Sarge is down! Corpsman up!" Henderson was shouting. "Harris! Ronje!" Henderson's right hand held firmly onto Schlader as his left hand alternately shook the two men next to him trying hopelessly to bring them back to life.

Schlader finally comprehended he had taken a round hard to his right shoulder at the same time Harris and Ronje went down.

Peering up at Henderson and trying to get up on his left elbow, Schlader looked into the wide-open eyes of his platoon sergeant and gasped out, "It's all yours, Sam. I'm out of it."

Assuring his friend, Henderson whispered softly, "Lay down, and don't be moving around."

Turning away from Schlader, Henderson barked again, "Corpsman up!"

The new platoon corpsman, Hospitalman Third Class Danny Garland, hollered back, "Coming, Sarge!"

Henderson waited until he could be certain Schlader was safely in their corpsman's care. Schlader was now bleeding from his mouth; the hit was in his shoulder, but the bullet had pierced his lungs. At that precise moment, Henderson realized that after ten years in the Corps, the past thirty seconds had thrust him into a leadership position. He was next in the chain of command.

Captain Burgett and his radio operator, Jarrett, moved away from the tank when an urgent message was passed through the net.

"Six!" Henderson's radio operator shouted into the handset, "Sergeant Schlader's been hit! Ronje and Harris are down!"

At the same time, while the wounded Roller and the 3rd Squad began evacuating any injured men to the medevac site, Burgett jumped into action. He pointed and yelled, "Corporal Roller, Sergeant Henderson needs you and your squad down there!"

Ignoring his two wounds, Roller rushed into battle to help his new platoon leader, Henderson. He called for the remaining men in his squad to move out.

Jones, holding his left shoulder, caught up with Burgett and Jarrett. "Skipper, where the hell were you at? Don't ever run off like that!"

Burgett blew off the gunny's steam and looking at Jones's shoulder asked, "How bad is it, Gunny?"

"Ahhh, nothing but a nick."

"Stay here, Sam, and get a Priority One medevac. I think Schlader and a couple of Roller's kids are in pretty bad shape. Jarrett and I are going down to join Henderson."

"Aye, aye, Sir."

"Jarrett, tell the 2nd Platoon to hold where they are while the 1st Platoon attacks across their front," Burgett called out as he sprinted in trace of Roller toward Henderson's position.

By this time Roller and his men had covered half the distance to where Henderson readied the 2nd Platoon Marines for a second and final assault on the trenches inside the tree line. In horror, Schlader, head cocked to the side, watched Roller get shot a second time. A round plowed its way into the fleshy part of his left hip. Pausing only briefly, he further amazed Schlader by joining the right flank of Henderson's assault. He covered his new injury with his left hand as he ran by the wounded. Without hesitation, Roller, now seriously wounded two times, attacked through the tree line, his pistol in his right hand.

The Marines fired and yelled as they assaulted the trench line. Their rounds cut through what was left of leaves, branches, and tree bark. The men continued to advance; their attack squelched the enemy's return fire. When they finally achieved the trench, it revealed only seven dead enemy and their weapons. The rest had vanished.

Burgett reached Schlader's position after all weapons had quieted. "How's he doing, Doc?" the captain asked Garland.

"He'll be okay if we get him out of here soon, Skipper."

Burgett stood up. A light rain began to fall. He looked down at the young men, Harris and Ronje, now bloodied and still. Tears formed in his eyes, but they refused to fall…not then.

The company evacuated their men killed and seriously wounded. The two, now battle-tested and somewhat exhausted platoons, returned to the base camp at Hill 158. The bell they had recovered remained safely stowed aboard the M-48 tank. There wasn't a scratch on it.

1800 hours. That night the rain splattered on the slick surface of the makeshift tent. Who cared? It rained most of the time. Two men huddled beneath the meager protection and did their best to remain as dry as possible. They failed to notice the fact that they sat on wet ground; at least it wasn't cold. Hill 158 was unusually quiet. The men who had lived through the firefight, shared as much with their silence as they would normally with their conversation. This was the case inside the small shelter that covered Captain George Burgett, the "skipper", and his buddy, Gunnery Sergeant Sam Jones. The Marines of Fox Company had never before experienced a heavy firefight like they had earlier that afternoon.

Shaken by the battle, Burgett and Jones contented themselves to snap their individual poncho liners together to form something that resembled a tent, they called a "hooch." Any cover from the rain in Vietnam was good cover. The captain, gunny, and Fox's core group were unusually close. In the summer of 1964 had they traveled from California to Okinawa. They landed in Vietnam in 1965, went back to California, returned to Okinawa, and finally ended up in Vietnam again in March 1966. In doing all this, they had developed the deep-felt professional and social bonds characteristic of a nomadic tribe of warriors. For the men of Fox Company, every man in the company was "we", everyone else was "they".

Burgett blinked back a sudden memory of his immense pride in Fox Company as they sailed into port at Pearl Harbor on board the ship that transported them from Camp Pendleton to Okinawa, their final stop before Vietnam. As they sailed in he could see Marines lined along the docks cheering them as if they were on parade. How did they know Fox would arrive on board this Navy ship? That they would be on board at all? Then he spotted a large cloth sign secured by ropes hanging from a two-story building behind the jubilant Marines. The sign read, "Welcome to Hawaii Charley!" Burgett had laughed aloud, of course! They knew Staff Sergeant Charley Schlader.

The surprise didn't end there. As soon as the gangplank was lowered, none other than Lieutenant General Victor H. Krulak, Commanding General, Fleet Marine Force, Pacific, marched up onto the ship. Krulak, small in stature, was a man with a reputation of being one of the toughest and most demanding Marine commanders. He was also referred to as "The Brute". Burgett had thought to himself, now what?

Standing at attention with his staff non-commissioned officers on the narrow weather deck of the amphibious transport ship, Burgett braced himself for an admonishment of some sort at the very least. Why else would Krulak greet them? Instead, "The Brute" came up to the captain and welcomed him and the rest of Fox Company to Hawaii. When he moved on to Schlader, the two shook hands as though they were the closest of friends who hadn't seen each other in years. Then, Schlader and the general disappeared below so that Krulak could meet the rest of the men.

Liberty that night was restricted to the base, but no one from Fox could buy even one beer. They might have tried, but they were going to war; the Marines and sailors stationed at Pearl Harbor treated Fox all night.

It had been seven months after Hawaii since—the then First Lieutenant George Burgett—had landed in Chu Lai, Vietnam, bringing his company "in country". Now, Sergeant Dennis Harris and Sergeant Joe Ronje were dead. Lance Corporal Chmiel and Doc Foxx were dead as well. Staff Sergeant Charley Schlader had been seriously wounded. The heroic Corporal Robert Roller was wounded. Six others were wounded and evacuated. Burgett shook his head, wanting to erase the memory of their deaths, an impossible desire.

The rain began to let up.

Captain Burgett, deep inside his poncho-roofed cave, failed to be bothered by the cramped three-foot high space that confined Gunny Jones and him now. As he sat hunched over, his head touched the top of the shelter. It was hard to believe that they were fighting a war he didn't quite comprehend against a people that he absolutely did not understand. Self-doubt consumed the young, compassionate captain. What could he have done better? Differently? Did the North Vietnamese Army outsmart his men? Was there something missing in their training? What? What? What?

Equally silent, was his companion, Jones. A large, muscular man, who cleared six feet tall, Jones had joined Fox 2/5 at Chu Lai that spring, and had immediately approved of his captain. Jones was the epitome of the gunnery sergeant, tough, cool under fire, and fiercely loyal. Though not finished with high school, he decided to enlist in the Corps at the tender age of seventeen. He gained his initial combat experience in Korea at the Chosin Reservoir fifteen years before his tour in Vietnam as a rifleman with Easy Company 2/5: the battle of the Chosin Reservoir was the most arduous and definitive for the Marines in that war. The chill from the rain that October night near the DMZ paled dramatically from the sub-zero, snow-covered terrain he had fought in as an eighteen year-old.

Tonight, he worried about his captain who was totally consumed in thought. Burgett had to come to grips with what happened today.

Leaning back in order to rest his "nicked" shoulder, Jones relaxed. He thought of the unique position he held with Fox Company in Vietnam.

With nearly sixteen years as a professional Marine his company commander, Burgett, considered him the "finest field gunnery sergeant he's ever seen." Jones acted as the principal logistician for the company: ordering chow, water, and ammo for the troops; he also provided invaluable advice for the skipper on battlefield tactics. His job was to keep the boys alive, and he took his job seriously.

Burgett sat forward silently, suddenly occupied with another task. Jones saw him unholster his pistol. After watching him for a prolonged moment Jones deduced that the captain had resolved to clean his .45 caliber pistol over and over.

Jones remained noiseless in their tent, listening to the sound of water dripping from the trees. He rested as his captain busied himself with his pistol. They were hardened warriors, Marines, and now their company had the battle scars to prove it. Tomorrow, the captain would be better, Jones concluded. No more cordon and search missions; no need for 'experience'. They'd already been in battle. Jones closed his eyes. After today, the men would brandish their battle scars, know this war is real and not something others talked about. Their training was over!

An explosion ripped through the small hooch.

At 1845 hours, a .45 caliber bullet whizzed under Jones's nose and passed harmlessly through the poncho on the gunny's side of the hooch. "Big George", as the troops called him, feeling not so big now, had been lost in thought. He had, absent mindedly, inserted his magazine and chambered a round thinking that the weapon was clear.

The startled eyes of the captain told the gunny that he hadn't meant to fire the weapon. Jones calmly inspected the hole in the hooch just over his shoulder. They could hear the men running toward them.

The Marines carefully searched the area around the small hooch for possible enemy. Finally, they found the bullet hole as Jones's index finger protruded through it and swirled outside in the air. "Captain Burgett! Gunny!" men yelled, concern evident in their voices.

"Are you all right, Sirs?"

The tense atmosphere was broken by Jones's gruff voice, "Jesus, Skipper, just get your pistol qualification?"

By then, Burgett mustered an admonished smile for the gunny. The rain slackened enough for Jones to move out of the hooch and leave the skipper alone. He spotted Staff Sergeant Sam Henderson, newly in charge of the 1st Platoon since Schlader's wounding, lurking nearby with Staff Sergeant Tony Marengo, obviously keeping an eye on the captain.

Sergeants refused to acknowledge their feelings, if they have any at all, but this concern was not only genuine; it was something Henderson had trouble hiding. His response to Burgett's leadership had been immediate, complete; his concern for their captain was openly apparent. Jones remembered when he and Henderson first arrived in Vietnam.

Henderson and Jones had arrived together in June. That was almost six months ago. Their "processing," through Da Nang, went a little more quickly than either of them expected. Processing was designed to help orient new personnel with Vietnam and transition the old troops out of the country and back to the States. Jones arrived as a gunnery sergeant. Henderson was a staff sergeant. While they lingered for the next orientation class to begin, Jones and Henderson waited near their tin-roofed

Quonset hut, observing the activities in their sector of Da Nang. As they inspected their surroundings they noted a rapidly approaching jeep.

Gunnery Sergeant Hiram J. McDaniels, Fox's senior enlisted man, raced the jeep over to the processing area and achieved a sudden, tire-screeching stop in front of the two men. "Are you two Jones and Henderson?"

Without knowing the man he addressed, Jones answered inquisitively, "Sure are, Gunnery Sergeant."

"My name's McDaniels. My promotion warrant is at Division." He nodded toward the gunny. "I'm your first sergeant. Put your butts and gear in the jeep!" he commanded.

Jones turned to Henderson only momentarily before he replied, "But, First Sergeant, we ain't had our indoctrination yet!"

McDaniels growled back at Jones as he jerked his head in an easterly direction, "You don't need any friggin' indoctrination. I need you at the beach!"

Shrugging jointly, the gunny and the staff sergeant tossed their gear into the back of McDaniel's vehicle, loaded their butts in the jeep, and south they drove to Chu Lai.

The M151 jeep stayed at the speed limit within the 1st Marine Division compound and the air base area. Henderson and Jones took in the sights—all new to them—while stealing an occasional glance at each other as they simultaneously raised their eyebrows. Both agreed on the question that couldn't be asked aloud: what in the world had they gotten themselves into?

Once outside of the Da Nang suburbs on National Highway 1, McDaniels pushed the jeep to fifty miles per hour. The fresh air cooled the sweaty new arrivals. McDaniels was not sweating. In fact, even in his green utilities, he looked like he was ready for a Commanding General's, CG's, inspection. Fresh air perhaps, but it sure smelled rotten, something of a mix between water buffalo dung, beetle-nut breath, and the rotting fish being used to make "nuc mam", the favorite all-purpose local food sauce.

Black pajamas, dirty black pajamas, covered most of the indigenous population walking along the road or gathering near small homes built along the highway. The majority wore sandals. All the older males and females wore cone-shaped straw hats to block the sun. The men were thin and most bore gray goatees. The women ranged from thin to slightly stocky. Many of childbearing age had an infant strapped to their backs. Occasionally an older woman would smile at the passing jeep only to expose her blackened, beetle-nut stained teeth. The kids were a happy lot. All wore short pants. Most of the boys gave the "thumbs-up" sign, the same way their stateside peers clenched their fists and pumped their arms high in the air to get truck drivers to blow their air-horns. Some of the boys hustled to attention and attempted to salute. As they did, their buddies doubled up laughing at them.

About twenty-five miles into the trip, half way to Chu Lai, McDaniels announced, "Sam Jones, we just had Gunnery Sergeant Franklin transfer to the battalion S-4 to be the logistics chief, so you're the company gunny as of now," he paused letting that information sink in. "Henderson, I'm putting you in the 1st Platoon. You'll be the platoon sergeant there. You'll be working for Staff Sergeant Charley Schlader who is the acting platoon commander."

Both passengers listened and learned as their new "first shirt" provided the only orientation they would receive. McDaniels explained that Chu Lai consisted of a military compound, complete with an expeditionary airstrip constructed of Marsten matting, which had been erected from the ground up and placed on a sandy beach.

Fox Company was charged with defending a portion of the airfield in this key location. Their skipper was a young first lieutenant by the name of Burgett. "Actually, Burgett has been selected for promotion," McDaniel's said after a minute.

"He's a nice fellow. Single. Quiet. Intelligent," he continued cautiously describing his company commander, as accuracy was imperative.

"Burgett had been the company's executive officer, XO. He and about thirty-five of the men extended to take the company to Vietnam." McDaniels concentrated on the road for a moment. Then glancing over to Jones said, "Sam, Burgett's long suit is his compassionate concern for the troops' well being; his short suit is not having any combat experience. You men have to teach him that. 'Big George', as the men call him, is a fast learner; so don't be hesitant to get right in there with your ideas. He'll listen to you. Trust me on that."

Thirty minutes later the three of them plowed into Chu Lai. The two newcomers were immediately issued their .45 caliber pistols, flak jackets, helmets, canteens, and the rest of their "782"gear. McDaniels took Jones to meet the skipper. Sam Henderson slipped off to the staff non-commission officer, SNCO tent, which the men called the "staff hooch", and began stowing his belongings.

Besides the Corps, Henderson's other love was his wife, Donna. Henderson and Donna decided to purchase a tape recorder prior to his deployment. This would be the easiest, fastest, and most effective method to keep in touch with one another. So, his first order of business was to find the recorder. "Now just where is that darn tape recorder?" he mumbled as he dug into his sea bag. "Ahhh, got you!" Henderson whispered to himself as he grabbed the shoebox-sized recorder. "Okay, let's record!" he mumbled out loud. He checked the machine until he located the red "record" button. His large, heavy finger pressed it. Nothing happened. He thought for a moment. Then he pressed the red record button and the black "play" button next to it at the same time to make it record.

The snap of the tape wheels sounded out. Henderson cleared his throat, "Ah-hum," he allowed his eyes to dart across the hut assuring himself the rest of the staff non-commissioned officers were nowhere nearby to witness his message.

Just then the entrance to the SNCO hut opened to admit a staff sergeant, who otherwise served as platoon commander. The unlit cigar that hung diagonally out of his mouth and his wrinkled uniform did nothing to take away from his dark, olive-skinned good looks or his quiet, gentleman-like behavior.

Henderson snapped the machine off.

"Excuse me," a staff sergeant said as he pulled out the company's fire-support plans from under his cot. "My name's Tony Marengo."

"Henderson, Sam Henderson. Nice to meet you."

Marengo looked around the tent and took note that, with the addition of Jones and Henderson, the cots in their hut were finally full. "Good to meet you too. My lieutenant needs these plans. I'll talk to you later," and with that he was gone.

"Honey," Henderson started the machine again. The roughness in Henderson's voice seemed to seep away, and was suddenly replaced by a sweeter, slightly higher pitched tone. "I'm here and safe and sound. The trip was good, but man, is it hot here. I…"

Interrupted by a faint, high-pitched whistle, Henderson paused for a moment. That sounded a lot like…"Shit!" he yelled.

An explosion rocked the compound.

A second mortar round dropped out of the sky and blew out the ground a few yards from his hut. The unmistakable snapping of small arms fire opened up around the base as it came under attack from nearby VC. Henderson grabbed his helmet, flung it on his head, and snatched up his rifle. The air around his hut sounded like a Rice Krispies commercial. Everywhere he turned, it snapped, crackled, and popped.

Henderson evacuated his hut and dove into the nearest bunker. The Marines returned fire into the surrounding hills and rice patties. Platoons were dispatched to hunt down the errant Viet Cong and gradually, the firing stopped.

Henderson went back to the staff hooch anxious to get his hear stowed and ready before any new challenge occurred.

Jones followed him almost immediately, opened the tent flap more than the tie-tie could hold it open, and bellowed, "Henderson! You in here?"

"Yeah, Gunny."

"The skipper wants to meet you during chow. C-rats, of course"

"Roger that, Gunny."

"About 1800 outside the CP," he said referring to the company command post that housed a joint office for the company commander, first sergeant, and three admin clerks.

"I'll be there."

With that, both Henderson and Jones went about their business as though the prior attack had never occurred.

At 1800 hours Jones and Henderson, joined by Burgett, McDaniels, Schlader, Marengo, and Sprimont, began opening cans of C-rations outside the company admin tent. The three lieutenants with the company were eating elsewhere. Cans of meat, ham and lima beans, and beans and franks were placed on two or three one-inch locally-found stones for cooking. Blue heat tabs were slipped under the cans, between the stones and lit. McDaniels passed around a small bottle of hot sauce. Jones removed the piece of plastic covering the onion he took from a Da Nang mess hall; he flipped open his K-Bar snap, drew the knife, and cut a thin slice of the onion so that it dropped on top of the warming food before passing it on.

"Where'd you get the onion, Gunny?" Burgett asked starting the "getting-to-know-you" conversation.

"Ran into one of my cooks at the Da Nang PX, Sir. We were on a Med float with my old outfit. He's with the Wing now. I figure Fox'll get taken care of when we can get to Da Nang."

"Sounds good to me, Gunny," Burgett retorted. "By the way, how was your trip down here to Chu Lai with the first sergeant?"

Staff Sergeant Charley Schlader broke out in a raspy, boisterous laugh. "Hey, Sir, first let me tell him my story with the 'Top'," he broke in. "A few months ago, I'm standing on the beach in Chu Lai. When, out of nowhere, First Sergeant McDaniels almost runs me down in a jeep. 'Get over here Schlader!' he yells. I hustle over and he says to me, 'Do you know your enlistment ended yesterday?'

Staff Sergeant Charley Schlader in Chu Lai
(PHOTO COURTESY OF KEITH BYRD)

"So, I'm thinking, 'Well, what am I doing here then?' But before I get the words out, the first sergeant says, 'Sign here!' So, here I am!" He finished with a "can-you-top-that?" chuckle.

Henderson, a fairly newly promoted staff sergeant with ten years in the Corps, cleared his throat to join the conversation. He turned to McDaniels, "First Sergeant, on the way driving down here this afternoon you mentioned that the skipper and about thirty-five others extended to come to Vietnam. Who are they, and are any of those men in the 1st Platoon?"

The men laughed. McDaniels smiled humbly, "Tell you what, Henderson. I'm not the one to answer that question. The skipper can answer that."

Modestly, First Lieutenant Burgett smiled while looking down and shaking his head as a response to McDaniel's deferment. "First Sergeant, you're too kind."

"Well, Skipper," McDaniels spared Schlader a meaningful look, "you know it best and tell it best."

"All right," Burgett allowed as he grabbed the lid off of his beans and franks and inserted a plastic spoon into the bubbling contents.

He gathered his thoughts before replying. Burgett started by explaining that each platoon had about ten men who were with them when they left Camp Pendleton in California. Approximately thirty-five men in Kilo 3/9 extended to come back to Vietnam together.

He filled in some personal history for Henderson as he went back even further. In 1964 Burgett left The Basic School as a raw lieutenant and reported into Kilo 3/7 when the company was building up for a WestPac tour. The company went to Okinawa that summer and immediately became Kilo 3/9. Within days, the Tonkin Gulf incident had Kilo 3/9 afloat in South China Sea for sixty-eight days.

Eyeing Henderson, Burgett asked, "You follow me so far?"

"Yes, Sir, no problem."

"Well then, in December, January, and February we trained, first in Japan and then in Okinawa," Burgett detailed. He explained that by March of 1965, the battalion, 3/9, landed at Da Nang as the first complete US combat organization in country. Previously, only advisors and logistic support elements were present in Vietnam. These Marines were watched on the news by the world coming ashore to be met by girls who placed flower leis around their necks. "You saw that in the papers, didn't you?" Burgett asked.

They all silently acknowledged his rhetorically asked question. 3/9's landing had been covered heavily in the press as the most significant development in a brewing war. Unfortunately for the Marines who were prepared for potential enemy resistance, the "leis of flowers" ended up being somewhat of a joke. The press hadn't missed the irony.

Burgett continued to tell of Kilo 3/9's redeployment to Pendleton that July, at the end of its WestPac tour. When the Marines arrived in Pendleton, the company became Fox 2/5. The battalion asked if anyone wanted to go back to Vietnam with the company. "Thirty-five of us said

'Yes.' And, after a bit more training, we arrived here in Chu Lai in March 1966. Did I get you confused?"

Henderson offered a half-hearted "Ahhh...No, Sir." Those with him laughed slightly as Henderson tried to track it all.

The five of them talked pleasantries for the next hour and a half before breaking up.

After they ate, Henderson rested on his bunk in the SNCO hut. He reached for the tape recorder and pulled it on top of his chest, so he wouldn't have to disturb his reclined position. Once again, he found himself alone; and once again his large fingers found the "record" and "play" buttons. Only this time, the tape wouldn't start. Instead, silence met his action.

Sitting up, Henderson inspected the machine. It hadn't been touched during the attack and the tape was still inside. Henderson had used brand new batteries, so he knew that couldn't be the problem. He stared at the tape inside the machine and concluded that "rewind" would be the pertinent button to select this time. Sure enough, the tape hissed as it sped through the rewind process. When it was finished, Henderson remained perplexed as he pressed the "Play" button. Had he pressed "fast forward" by accident when the fighting broke out? Were some of his fellow staff sergeants playing a trick on him already? The possibility astounded him. Then, he heard a slight sound humming from the tape and a very familiar voice clearing his throat. More noise resonated from the speaker on the small machine. Henderson smiled. It was working. "Honey," a slight pause, "I'm here and safe and sound. The trip was good, but man, is it hot here. I...Shit! KABOOM! Snap! Zing! Pop, pop, pop, pop, crack!" Then listening closer, Henderson could here shouts from outside the hut, "Get down! Return fire! Over there!"

The sounds of the ensuing fight continued, including Henderson's banging around his hut in pursuit of his helmet and rifle, and slamming his way out of the tent. The entire fight had been recorded. Henderson's smile vanished. His eyes opened wide. Visions of Donna listening to his tape filled Henderson's head, making him blink rapidly.

He drifted into unconsciousness at the end of that first night with a letter to Donna clenched in his large fist. His words reassuring her that he was safe and sound were written clearly on the white paper. A slight smile rested on Henderson's lips, even in his sleep.

The ranks of Fox's junior enlisted were filling up at the same time of Jones's and Henderson's arrival into Vietnam.

One of the newly arrived enlisted Marines to enter Vietnam and join Fox in Chu Lai was Private Terry Klein. There, Fox's time was consumed by cordon and search operations: defining an area of operations and reducing the cordon in an ever tightening circle in order to search for rice and weapons caches as well as enemy troops. That's when Klein came "in country." Generally, the menial and lesser demanding tasks were assigned to newly arrived troopers. The average age of the fighting combat soldier in Vietnam was nineteen. True to form, newly assigned nineteen-year-old Klein joined Fox at the airfield at Chu Lai just before the company was ordered to the DMZ.

Klein was a native of LaVista, Nebraska. He was used to hard work, but not in a hot and steamy location like Chu Lai. Klein filled sandbags, carried supplies, and performed a multitude of equally un-invigorating tasks reserved for newcomers. He didn't mind. Many of the Fox veterans "in-country" considered Klein "wet behind the ears". After two weeks he felt like an old timer. He had his routine down pat. This was an eye-opening time for Klein who learned a great deal from his fellow Fox Marines. Klein couldn't speak for anyone else, but when he found out Fox was headed for the DMZ to partake in Operation Prairie and to engage the North Vietnamese Army, he had one single reaction: fear.

Now, following his and the company's first major firefight on 13 October, Klein confirmed the validity of his initial apprehension. Other emotions, with the firefight concluded, ranged from exhilaration to "being scared shitless".

1905 hours. Tonight, nearly six months after his arrival into Vietnam and his joining Fox, Jones walked away from the hooch, now punctured by a bullet hole just above his pack courtesy of his captain. He approached Henderson and Marengo who sat nearby but out of earshot. Despite the day's tragic events, both men were chuckling.

"What are you two laughing about?" Jones demanded.

"Oh, we were just remembering when the skipper thought we were lost," Henderson answered.

"What do ya' mean?" Jones snorted.

"Remember, Gunny? Right after we got here we were operating up at the DMZ on a company-sized patrol. It was the thickest jungle I had ever seen, let alone imagined. You know, we were in a column with the 1st Platoon in front, and you and the skipper were following."

Jones stared blankly back at Henderson so he went on explaining that the 2nd and 3rd Platoons trailed in the back of the tactical column as Fox weaved around tall trees that day—trees that seemed to be almost on top of each other.

Henderson paused when Jones still looked lost. "Geez, we looked like a line of ants marching around blades of grass in an overgrown lawn!" Henderson reminded the gunny of the jungle's thick patchwork pattern of vines, leaves, stumps, and logs. "1st Platoon had to literally hack our way up there."

"Wait a minute," Marengo countered. "My platoon had the point most of the time!"

"Well, maybe." Henderson continued without pause, "Anyway, it was really bad! There was no breeze available. And you know the temperature was flirting with, shoot, it had to be a hundred! Hell, we were at each other's throats from about noon on. Visibility was limited to no more than ten meters. Some friggin' liberal tree hugger would probably be talking about 'the natural beauty of that lush, green forest'. We sure didn't see it that way!"

Henderson retold the story, lost in the memory. Fox had been out for hours that seemed like days. Morale was down in a hole. "I heard more cussing from the troops that day than I'd heard in a long time. It was so dark we thought it was almost night." The fact that it was still daylight outside the canopy hadn't even occurred to the Marines. Jones nodded as his memory was triggered, but Henderson went on, too wrapped up to relent now. "The 'enemy threat' was a joke. They couldn't find us; we couldn't find us; hell, no one could find us!"

Shaking his head for emphasis Henderson continued, "As you know, we 'highly skilled' map readers and navigators," he added, "...were confident we could maintain any 'straight' line we wanted to.

"But, unfortunately, not then. We really weren't too sure where we were. And worse than that, Skipper didn't know either."

"Yeah, yeah, that's right," the gunny agreed, pointing his finger. At this point, the gunny picked up the story. "Big George decided his best option wasn't on the jungle floor, but up a tree." Jones said in a muffled chuckle. "And that is exactly what he did, climbed the nearest tree that'd hold him!"

The three men smiled as they recalled the scene.

With a twinkle in his eye and a chuckle Henderson continued, "About that time...remember? The radio buzzed and we heard, 'Fox this is Cassandra.'" Henderson pointed at the gunny. "Jarrett yelled out, 'Sir! It's the battalion commander.' You told Jarrett to, 'Answer him.' And, he said, 'Cassandra, this is Fox,' so innocently."

"And," the gunny added, "they came back, 'Fox, this is Cassandra Actual. Let me speak to Fox Six! Jarrett looked around him for help before he said, 'Lieutenant Colonel Airheart wants to talk to Captain Burgett.'"

Henderson took over the story telling once more, "None of us wanted the battalion commander, particularly since he was brand new, to know that Fox Company had no clue where we were. So, you told Jarrett that the skipper was "not available at the moment.'" Henderson started to laugh again. "Jarrett looked up. The look on his face was too much! All he could see was part of the captain's boot and his ass hanging out of that tree! All he could do was clear his throat and stare back at the radio."

"Yeah," the gunny resumed. "Then he said, 'Cassandra,' in the most serious voice, 'Fox Six is not here right now.'" Jones paused for effect before continuing. "'Where is he?' The good colonel asked immediately."

"Then Jarrett told him, 'Well, Sir, he's up in a damn tree!'" Henderson finished. "I," he started.

"We," Marengo corrected.

"Sorry, we," Henderson went on, "did all we could do to not bust out laughing. Then, and he did not sound happy, the colonel finally said, 'Well...Fox...tell him to call me when he gets down.'

"Needless to say, Big George was grave when he responded to Lieutenant Colonel Airheart. In his most serious tone," Henderson emphasized the word "serious", "he informed the battalion commander that his "stint" up the tree had afforded the necessary coordinates and that Fox would be reaching our destination in just a few short klicks. We'll never know whether or not the battalion commander heard the sound of us laughing in the background."

Jones said, "Yeah, that was pretty good. I still believe the colonel didn't know we were lost."

The firefight earlier and the subsequent evacuations of their wounded men including Schlader had thrown the gunny's schedule off. He began frowning again. He missed his nightly coffee, and now dark, it was too late to light up a heat tab.

"What's a matter, Gunny?" Marengo asked sensing the gunny's discomfort.

"Ahhh, nothing, Tony. Staying with the skipper, I missed my coffee. No big deal."

"Well let me see, what I can do," Marengo suggested, as he turned and walked away.

Henderson looked at the gunny and said, "That darn Tony can scrounge anything. If you put him in the middle of the damn desert with no clothes and no money, its guaranteed that within two hours he'd come back fully clothed on a camel with a harem of women."

Jones nodded his head in agreement and said, "I ain't never seen anyone like him!"

"You know, Henderson," Jones went on, "Fox has come a long way since we arrived. The skipper's leadership allows us the space to run the company the right way. I'll admit he's a bit complex: a big easy-going

Arizona cowboy, but he's serious and a deep thinker. You know, ol' First Sergeant McDaniels is right; he really does care for the troops."

"Tell you what I mean, Sam," Jones continued. "Fox is a disciplined outfit, more so than others. Three days ago, we had engineers and demolition men attached; you know that team of guys under that short corporal? What's his name, Rucker? I told them that we were going to be moving out at 0600 tomorrow. Rucker said, 'The other units say that, but they don't leave until two hours later.' Next morning we had our formation at 0530. We started marching at 0545. When we passed the main gate I saw the engineers waiting for us. I said, 'What time is it?' He said, '0600, Gunny.' When we say we'll go, we'll go."

In the dark Jones and Henderson paused to listen to someone coming down the path from the arty battery that shared the hill with Fox Company. It was Marengo. He was carrying a half-loaded Marine Corps issued, one-gallon coffee jug and some paper cups.

"Don't ask," Marengo said as he joined his friends.

1925 hours. "You three having a good time out here?"

"Skipper!" all three welcomed the captain as if Big George had just awakened from a three-day coma.

"How 'bout a cup of hot coffee, Skipper?" Marengo offered.

"Yeah sure, that'd taste good. What are you three talking about?" Burgett asked, shrugging off the day's events.

Jones answered, "We've been talking about how proud we are of Fox Company. We have solid leadership and great troops."

"Hey, speaking of that, I've got to tell you guys about Klein," Marengo interrupted and began telling a story referring to the nineteen year-old Nebraskan in his platoon. "Since we'd been operating up at the DMZ, I've been preaching to the troops that the NVA, which I had to explain to a few of them was the North Vietnamese Army, up north were way different than those mine-laying, harassing Viet Cong we'd encountered down south at Chu Lai. 'They are actually hunting for us Marines. We have to kill or be killed,' I said.

"Some time in the afternoon on our fifth day up near the DMZ, the time had come for my platoon to head back here," Marengo explained. The 3rd Squad had the lead and was followed by the lieutenant and the 1st Squad. Marengo had been in front of the 2nd Squad who was bringing up the rear. They had taken a road that led to small hamlet, that wasn't identified by any name designation. Most men would've considered it a large path; it was relatively narrow, and was covered in bushes.

"Private First Class Terry Klein was in the 2nd Squad. I'd seen him adapt to the combat up north pretty fast. He turned out to be the last man in the entire column." Marengo explained that the other two squads in front of the column had reached a small hamlet. They were already out of sight while searching the village.

Klein wasn't afraid of being the last man in the tactical column. He wanted to prevent any danger from threatening his new buddies. His senses had improved during his one month in Vietnam. Now, he could identify every whistle in the wind, or snap of a twig. "…And you know that ignoring sounds like that can get a Marine killed," Marengo stated. Every man sitting with Marengo nodded his head, a fact that had become too evident that same day.

Even with the threat, Klein was convinced that that wasn't his day to die. Looking forward, Klein could see that some of the men in his squad, as well as the entire 1st and 3rd squads, had reached the hamlet. He could see parts of the hamlet through breaks in the trees on his right. Klein looked and listened to his left. On that side the tree line was completely quiet; not one branch or blade of grass seemed out of place. Klein looked behind him at the road expecting nothing. After all, it had been empty since we'd started marching back to base camp. But then, out of nowhere, Klein thought he saw two NVA soldiers walking directly behind him!

Klein's mind caught up with his senses and he realized two enemy soldiers were approaching his position just as calm as they could be! Klein could even see their faces. He thought they looked like children.

Klein was stunned! He watched the two North Vietnamese soldiers realize that they were walking right toward a U.S. Marine. They froze in a sort of surprised fear like a deer caught in a car's headlights. "Klein's training took hold of him, and even though he thought it took a long," and Marengo drew out that word, "time, it was really only a few seconds until he reacted."

Klein lowered himself to his knee repeating in his mind, kill, or be killed. Kill, or be killed. But then, he wasn't sure whether the words were coming out of his mouth, or if they were in his head. Luckily his aim was better than it ever was on the firing range.

He fired and hit one of the enemy soldiers; he didn't know where exactly, but the force of the round jolted his enemy backwards. Immediately, both NVA sprang to their feet and raced through the trees that had been on Klein's right to what they thought was safety. "But they chose poorly," Marengo added, "because they didn't know that almost all of the 3rd Platoon, nearly thirty of us, were now inside the very place they were trying to hide!"

The enemy stumbled blindly into the village, seeking defensive positions where they could turn and fire at Klein, who was still crouched down at his post. "Of course, we all heard Klein's gunfire, and opened up on them. All hell broke loose, and the action was over in seconds." Marengo continued, "We all laughed at their bad luck. They could've escaped and given us a run for our money had they run into the trees that lined the other side of the road."

Marengo's tone became serious, but he went on after his companions' quiet laughter had subsided. "Later that night, back here at Hill 158 our spirits were high because of our successful, though limited, encounter with the NVA." He recanted that the men had hearty appetites and enjoyed each other's company. Only Klein stayed away. His emotions had been surging and reeling from the events earlier that day.

He wondered if he'd he done the right thing or if they would have surrendered had he'd given them the opportunity. They were dead; was it because of his actions? He was facing the same guilty conviction all Marines go through after a first kill. So many of the Marines' enemy were faceless, always hiding in tunnels or exposed tree lines leading into deeper jungles.

Klein close his eyes while the image of those two scared and childlike faces appeared before him. He knew they weren't children. But like so many of them, they seemed too young to have been his enemy. Klein sat on his helmet, never touching his C-ration dinner, and stared blankly at his dirty boots.

Marengo, looked at Jones, the captain, and his buddy Henderson, and said, "I asked him if he was okay. He jumped. I guess I startled him, and he gave me a lame, 'Yeah.'"

Klein was lying. He wasn't okay. He'd performed as the Corps had expected him to, but he wished he could stop replaying the incident over in his mind. Klein didn't know he sounded as down as he felt. He also didn't know that Marengo knew how he felt.

Turning to Burgett over his coffee Marengo said, "Lieutenant Scuras had just passed along a complement to me for the platoon's action that day. So I said to Klein, 'Come on. Let's go see the lieutenant.' We got there, and Scuras said he had been informed of Klein's actions."

Before Klein said anything, First Lieutenant Scuras spoke up, "Excellent work PFC Klein. Congratulations on your first successful enemy encounter. You showed no fear and, as a matter of fact, a lot of bravery. You are a fine Marine. So, again congratulations to you." Then he nodded his head toward Marengo and said, "…And to your platoon."

Klein thanked him. He felt clear, and confident, now that he had been congratulated and reassured on his actions. Then the lieutenant told him he was fairly certain that Klein had better things to do than hang around his tent, and he dismissed the two men.

"Lieutenant Scuras was great, Captain," Marengo said looking at Burgett and then the others. "He knew just what to say. Klein was walking and talking when we left the lieutenant. He went right up to his buddies and told them all the details about talking to the lieutenant. These days I just have to keep both his feet on the ground instead of floating in air."

Burgett laughed quietly. "That's a good one. You're right, all three of you. We have a great company."

Private First Class Conley approached the group. "Sirs," he said awkwardly in his New York accent.

They all smiled waiting for Conley to talk.

"Staff Sergeant Marengo. The lieutenant wants to see you. I think he wants to go on another ambush with us tomorrow night."

"All right, Conley, tell the lieutenant I'll be there in a couple minutes, and we'll watch Simpson," Marengo replied, obviously referring to something Conley knew and the rest did not.

Conley started walking away and Marengo said, "Wait a minute, Conley."

Conley turned back, "Sarge?"

"Conley, tell the gunny about the last time the lieutenant went with us on a night ambush."

Happy to be included, Conley began his story without hesitation.

"The 2nd Platoon had an ambush one night near the DMZ, Sirs. As we sat there in position, an enemy force began moving into our kill zone. We watched what seemed like dozens of them pass by on the road. Then, when the last of them were walking by, we here this loud, drawn out, 'BLHHHH.'" Conley peered at the officers expectantly after making his odd noise. "The NVA on the road start looking around, and we're all looking around like, 'Who farted?' But, luckily, the enemy withdrew and nothing more happened that night."

"You sure this is all right, Sergeant Marengo?" Conley asked.

"Sure, go on."

"Well, the next morning we marched back to Con Thien. First Lieutenant Scuras, called the platoon together and, in the highest traditions of the Marine Corps, lined us up. And you all know we all stand tall when the lieutenant tells us to.

"Standing in front of the platoon, and I swear he was so mad his voice sounded like it had been raked over gravel or something. He demanded, 'I want to know who farted!'"

Conley went on, "Lance Corporal Simpson jumped forward and said, 'I farted, Sir.' Simpson paused for a couple of seconds then said, 'And, Sir, I'll tell you why I farted. It's because of what you give me to eat. You give me baked beans and meatballs, baked beans and franks, and ham and lima beans.'

"So he goes on," Conley explained. "'Sir, I did not fart right away! For ten minutes I held my ass cheeks together. Soon I knew that wouldn't be successful. So I decided to pull my ass cheeks apart thinking that would be quieter. Little did I know that that it would be louder!'" Conley laughed. "So, from then on the platoon has a special order for Simpson. On days when there is going to be a night ambush, Simpson is only allowed to have ham and eggs!" With the captain, Jones, and Henderson covering their mouths in order to muffle their hysterics, Conley, with a straight face, looked a Marengo and asked, "Okay, Staff Sergeant?"

Marengo, having heard the "Who Farted?" story several times, replied, "Yeah, thanks, Conley. Thanks. Tell the lieutenant I'll be right there."

Staff Sergeant Henderson, still laughing, said, "Well, I better check on my herd as well. See you all in the morning."

Burgett and Jones were left standing alone. "'Nother cup of coffee, Skipper?"

"Sure. Why not?" Burgett answered holding out his empty cup while the gunny turned the tap. "Say, damn near shot you…Really sorry about that. I was in such a funk, I wasn't thinking."

"Don't worry about it, Skipper."

1945 hours. The night was starting to clear. The two men sipped their coffee in silence. Five minutes passed.

"Skipper? Gunny?" the battalion radio operator quietly called out.

"We're over here," the gunny replied.

Finally seeing them the radio operator walked over and said, "Sir, there's a big meeting over at battalion tomorrow at 0830. The colonel is sending a bird over for both of you at 0800. Something about us going to a place called An Hoa…"

CHAPTER 2: GUNNY JONES

27 November 1966. Gunnery Sergeant Sam Jones and Captain George Burgett were strapped into nylon-webbed bench seats on board a USMC C-130 aircraft. The men sat facing each other as they flew south from the DMZ to Da Nang. Fox's ultimate destination was An Hoa. In Da Nang they would split up: Burgett continuing west to An Hoa by USMC helicopter, while Jones remained behind to coordinate the transportation of the rest of the company by US Air Force cargo aircraft.

Burgett stared across at Jones. The gunny's facial expressions usually ranged from "no expression at all to down right mean". Right now, Jones's face remained a blank slate. Burgett knew that the gunny really hid the fierce compassion he held for his men—all his men—including the troops, non-commissioned officers, staff non-commissioned officers, and officers. Jones's Korean War combat experience had fashioned an image pickled with an aura drastically different than any other man in Fox. Somehow he carried an enormous stature and so far, seemed totally detached. The company depended on him so much: his orders were carried out without hesitation, without question. Thanks to Gunny Jones, Fox just didn't make the same mistakes other companies did. One minute the gunny might be teaching the troops how to dig a foxhole, the next minute he would be working with the lieutenants and forward observers planning their night defensive fire plans, only to turn around and share insight with the captain.

Burgett released a muffled laugh. Everyone in Fox paid one hundred percent attention to what Jones was saying, even him! Burgett crossed his arms in the turbulent air as the plane continued to climb to its cruising altitude, still studying the hardened gunny sitting across from him. The troops worshipped Jones. Despite his tough demeanor, he acted as a father figure to them: stern, unbending. Yet they knew that their best chance to stay alive in this war depended on following his instructions absolutely.

The aircraft climbed higher and the temperature dropped as it did. All passengers became slightly chilled, but as Burgett watched Jones's mind was far away from this battlefield Vietnam. Instead, he was back in Korea, a radio operator in the 3rd Platoon, Easy Company, 2nd Battalion, 5th Marines. He saw himself as he was then: a four-year Marine Corps vet and twenty-one years old—older than the "kids" are today.

1 December 1950. The temperature reached forty degrees below zero. The 1st Marine Division, which included the 5th Marine Regiment, had been cut off, surrounded by ten Chinese Communist divisions, while it fought its way fifteen miles south from the Chosin Reservoir to Hagaru-ri. Hands, feet, and noses froze. Only the seriously wounded and dead rode; all the rest plowed their way through on foot. At night while the enemy blew bugles to frighten them, the walking wounded brought coffee to Marines on the lines. They were exhausted, but charged on. For four solid days they battled. His company commander, Captain Sam Jaskilka, in his eternally calm manner, gave them the confidence to know that they would make it. Jones's officers and non-commissioned officers made the troops clean their weapons, check their ammo, and stay alert. Jones, who quit high school a year early to join the Marine Corps, was exhausted beyond belief. In spite of it all, they bullied their way through the enemy entrapment.

The cargo plane's engines increased in pitch as Jones's mind continued to wander back in memory. As a young man, this traumatic experience had changed him forever. He embodied the expression "Once a Marine, always a Marine." No wonder he never wanted to return home. He had been home—in the Corps—for the past twenty years. A smile, ever so slight, spread across Jones's face.

The plane began its descent. Burgett glanced up at Jones who now stared out the window. He wasn't sure, but had he just seen the gunny smile?

8 December 1966. At the Hoa Combat Base, Quang Nam Province, Lieutenant Colonel W. C. Airheart and his 2nd Battalion, 5th Marines' staff had just completed briefing the company commanders and leaders of the battalion's attached units on the enemy situation in the area. Orders had been issued to begin conducting search and destroy, S&D, operations.

By the end of November, the battalion began participating in Operation Mississippi under the operational control of the 9th Marine Regiment. At 1730 hours on the 7th, 2/5 was "chopped" from the 9th Marines to the 1st Marine Division gaining full control of the An Hoa operating area. This was the first opportunity Airheart had had to brief the battalion's leaders since their return.

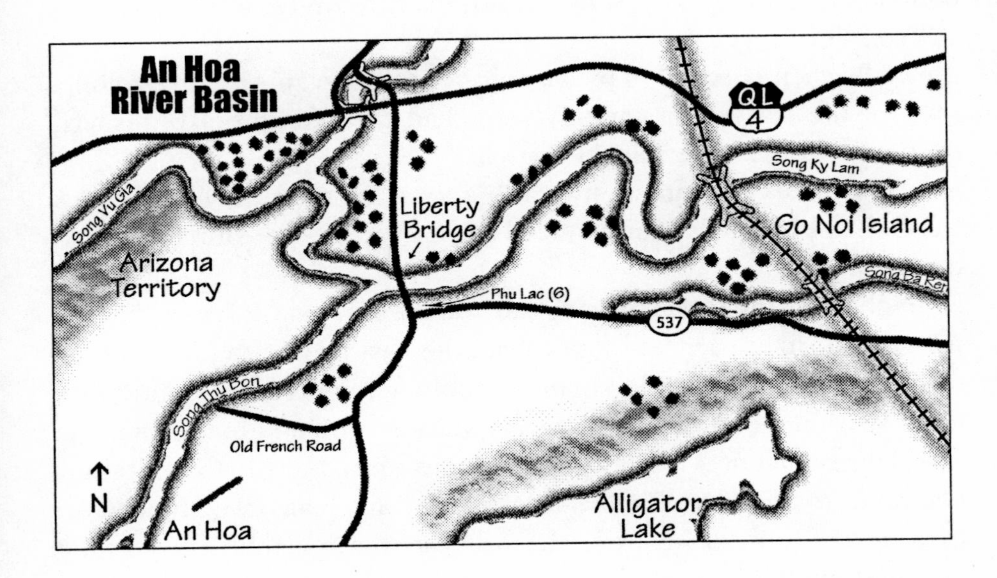

"George," Airheart singled out the Fox Company commander as the men were leaving the battalion's 16'x32' general-purpose tent. Burgett, at the tent's entrance, turned around and returned to answer his boss. Airheart casually moved to one of the tent's corners to allow for a private conversation.

"Yes, Sir?" Burgett asked softly not knowing what to expect.

"Good to see you back here in An Hoa."

"With all the rain we're getting, I'm not sure it's that great, Sir."

Airheart chuckled quietly, "George, I'm pretty impressed with Fox Company."

"Thanks, Sir."

"I have to share a story with you about Gunnery Sergeant Sam Jones."

"Sir?" Burgett responded somewhat defensively as the "Colonel" was about to talk about a man who Burgett believed was the finest gunnery sergeant in the field. Now grinning as he began telling his story, Airheart summarized, "Remember when we were flying back from the DMZ? You continued to An Hoa and left Jones at the Air Force terminal in Da Nang with orders to bring the rest of Fox Company to An Hoa?"

"Yes, Sir."

"Well, when I arrived to pick up a ride with Fox, an Air Force colonel read me the 'riot act'. Apparently, Jones had tweaked off one of his tech sergeants and then the colonel himself."

"This one's a new one to me, Sir. I only asked the gunny how things went when I was in Da Nang, and all he said was, 'Okay.'" Burgett replied carefully.

"Not according to the colonel," Airheart continued. "It seems that the Air Force load master told Jones that…he…was going to put so many troops in one aircraft and so many in another. Jones, rather bluntly, told him, 'We don't load aircraft that way; Marines load and maintain some semblance of tactical integrity.' Then Jones turned to the tech sergeant and said, 'You tell me which planes and how many men we can load on each, and I'll embark my troops.' As you can imagine, this pissed off the tech sergeant who complained to the colonel. The colonel came out, and Jones told him the same exact thing."

Burgett began smiling ear to ear. He rolled his eyes as he listened. He knew just how very direct and blunt his principal field deputy was. It was that very bluntness that the captain relied on so heavily in the field

Smiling as well, Airheart continued. "The colonel then appealed for help from a Marine aviator major standing nearby without any success. Finally, I came along and the colonel commenced to describe Jones's offensive and insubordinate conduct. I asked him, 'Are you sure he said that?' The colonel said, 'Yeah.' To which I looked the colonel in the eye and said, 'Colonel, that's what he should have said. He's loading the planes like he is supposed to. He gets paid to do this. In fact, when we're out marching in enemy territory, I ask him where…he…wants me in his column, not the other way around!'"

Both men laughed and shook their heads. Airheart had wanted to share that story, since only a couple of ranks ago he too, then a captain, had been a company commander. He knew that the only real way to be a successful company commander was to have a strong gunnery sergeant. Fox had every bit of that.

"Funny thing though, George, I bumped into that short staff sergeant of yours who took over the 1st Platoon after Staff Sergeant Schlader was wounded in October," Airheart squinted reaching for a name. "Henderson?"

Burgett nodded his head in agreement.

"I bumped into Staff Sergeant Henderson last night at the staff and officers' mess. When I asked him what he thought about his gunny, all he said was that he'd 'go anywhere with him because he was the meanest damn gunnery sergeant' he had ever seen. According to Henderson, Jones was probably the best 'at keeping your ass out of trouble in a combat situation.'"

"He's right, Sir."

Burgett left the tent after their conversation and returned to the Fox Command Post in especially good spirits. There he met the gunny and said "Gunny, at the meeting, we found out that the new sergeant major and some Headquarters troops are going to be selling beer at 1300 today. Twenty-five cents per can. The colonel's put a limit of two cans per troop. The sergeant major wants to sell the beer only to the companies and detachments and not to individuals."

"Aye, aye, Sir," Jones said without intonation. "I'll take care of it."

Jones marched over to the staff hooch and said to platoon sergeants Henderson, Marengo, Sprimont, and Rose: "Okay, we're getting beer this afternoon. Two beers per man. Staff non-commissioned officers can buy what you want. Have the right guides report to me here at 1230 with the money you collect from your Marines."

Immediately, they all scattered.

At precisely 1200, Gunny Jones yelled into the staff hooch, "Where the hell are you guys?"

Henderson stammered, "But, Gunny, you said 1230!"

Jones snarled, "Henderson, I'll tell you what time it is. It's Company Gunnery Sergeant's time, damn it! For you it is 1230!"

After the squad leaders collected the money, the right guides, who take care of the logistics at the platoon level, and Jones went to get the beer. From two trucks, the battalion sergeant major scurried to issue the beer to individual troops and squad leaders from other companies. Since Jones and the sergeant major hadn't met prior to that moment, Jones growled, "Sergeant Major, I'm from Foxtrot, and I'm here to pick up our beer."

Abruptly the irritated sergeant major announced to all present, "Stop everything! I passed the word to the company commanders this morning that I'm selling beer to companies, not platoons, squads or individuals! Since Fox did like I instructed, they get their beer. No one else gets any beer unless they are representing their company. I don't care if we run out!"

Later in the staff hooch, Jones, Henderson, Marengo, and Sprimont sat at one end of the tent and Echo's staff non-commissioned officers occupied the other. Quickly, the two-can rations ran out for the Echo Company staff non-commissioned officers. Soon they were asking, "What gives with you guys getting all that beer and we only get two cans each?'

Jones gave them a couple of cases and said, "Why don't you staff non-commissioned officers learn to run your company instead of having your officers take control? Stand up for yourselves and do your job; then you won't end up with two cans of beer apiece."

On the whole, Jones had no patience with lieutenants and they knew it. Besides Captain Burgett, the company had only one officer at this time. As a result First Lieutenant Scuras, the 3rd Platoon commander, would sometimes act as executive officer. Jones and Scuras were often at loggerheads over issues of who ran the company and who controlled the 3rd Platoon. In either case, Jones did not believe any lieutenant was necessary. He was comfortable dealing directly with Staff Sergeant Marengo, the 3rd Platoon Sergeant.

In one incidence, a distraught A-4 pilot assigned as the company's forward air controller, FAC, was not at all happy to be with Fox and wanted to be back with the "Wing", referring to the 1st Marine Aircraft Wing. This first lieutenant felt that there were vastly superior accommodations in Da Nang to those at the An Hoa Combat Base. He did not mind professing that fact to anyone who would listen. The men snickered at him as he continuously complained about wanting to use a "porcelain potty". Repeatedly, he would say, "Had I known I had to crap in the woods, I would have gone into the Navy!"

On one occasion Jones called a lieutenant aside and said, "Lieutenant Brady, with all due respect, Sir, you are far too friendly toward your radio operator. Over here, anything can happen to anybody. You're here one day and gone the next. As close as you are to that lance corporal radio operator of yours, you'll be emotionally devastated if something happens to the kid!"

Moving into and conducting operations in the An Hoa Tactical Area of Responsibility, TAOR, was a change for the men of the 2nd Battalion. They had to adjust to the monsoon rains that flooded the rivers and rice paddies, inhibited cross-country pursuit of the enemy, made them dependent on helicopter resupply, caused immersion foot, and wore out their personal combat equipment. Never before had they experienced the daily devastation that was caused by mines and booby traps. They quickly learned that on each path, at each break of a bamboo hedgerow, under each box or loose can, and in any area, a Marine would logically sit to rest there were explosives that would kill and maim. The men of the 2nd Battalion came to respect the regular and local Viet Cong soldiers who sustained themselves quite well in firefights, almost vanish in front of Marines chasing them, and were supported by most of the indigenous population. The enemy maintained the upper hand and dealt it to the battalion in an imbalanced way throughout this first month.

In this environment, during the constant rains of December, Foxtrot Company conducted search and destroy operations with Echo and Golf Companies in the An Hoa Tactical Area of Responsibility. At first, Fox searched near the An Hoa combat base; by 15 December they were six kilometers north of An Hoa; and by the 20 December they had traveled to Go Noi Island, fourteen kilometers northwest of An Hoa. On that date, Echo Company became heavily engaged in a firefight on Go Noi Island and sustained two Marines killed with five wounded. Thirty minutes later one of the CH-34 medevac birds was shot down while lifting out Echo's wounded.

Go Noi Island, an area that begins three kilometers east of Liberty Bridge, was well within the range of the USMC mortars and howitzers located on the high ground overlooking the bridge. About four kilometers by thirteen kilometers in general size, its long axis ran east and west. The island was dubbed so because the Song Ky Lam, in Vietnamese "song" translated to "river", bordered its northern side and the Song Ba Ren, which to the east becomes the Song Chem, bordered its southern side. The waters came from the mountains north and west of Liberty Bridge and were carried to them by the Song Thu Bon. Boats were required to cross the Song Thu Bon west of Liberty Bridge. However, by the time the Song Thu Bon split east of the bridge, the terrain flattened and Go Noi Island's northern river widened from 200 meters to 400–500 meters forming numerous small sandy islands. The southern river was mostly a dry sand bed except for the two-month monsoon season that occurred in November and December.

With the exception of an old French-built railroad berm that rose twenty feet off the loamy soil, the island was flat. The berm ran north and south splitting the island almost in half. A few, mostly unpopulated hamlets existed on the uncultivated island. During the period of 1966 up to the end of 1968, the island was a safe haven for NVA and VC soldiers transiting the area or seeking refuge after attacking Marines,

Vietnamese popular forces, or civilian population centers. As roads did not exist, the island was free of land mines, and there were few booby traps in and around the unpopulated hamlets.

20 December 1966. The monsoon rains had flooded the once-dry riverbeds with the exception of a few sandbars. At 1545 hours on that afternoon Lieutenant Colonel Airheart, after Echo's engagement and the loss of the CH-34 helicopter that was shot down, ordered Golf and Foxtrot companies to link up with Echo. Those companies were needed to help Echo secure the helicopter.

Fox was just south of Go Noi Island along an elevated east-west road that had been used by the French as a railroad bed. They were also seven kilometers east of Liberty Bridge. Its 2nd Platoon remained in An Hoa serving as the battalion reserve and was ready to fly out on a "Sparrow Hawk" mission to block an enemy's escape or reinforce the rest of Fox as necessary. To accomplish the linkup with Echo, Fox had to attack through Tho Son, a hamlet heavily populated with VC. Burgett, who wanted to complete the linkup by nightfall, shortly after 1900 hours, cautiously called for prep fires prior to attacking. Following the prep fire, Fox moved unopposed through the hamlet. If any enemy had been present, they had retreated toward the center of the island in the direction of Echo Company, the same direction Fox Company would follow.

As they left the hamlet the men began wading across the once-dry riverbed Song Ba Ren that was at one moment ankle deep and the next waist deep. 3rd Platoon was on the right of the company formation and the 1st Platoon on the left. Private First Class Mike Meldrum, who had joined Fox as soon as they returned from the DMZ, was assigned to Corporal Chuck Conley's squad in the 3rd Platoon. His squad was in the front of the platoon on the right flank of Fox. Conley, a young man over 6'3", led his squad across the streams cautioning them to walk exactly where he walked, remarking that he didn't want any of them to get dragged away like the kid from Echo had. Echo's missing man hadn't been found after disappearing under the water two days earlier. "Hey, Corporal Conley, you have a couple of leaches on you!" Meldrum yelled.

Conley didn't answer, and instead, plodded onward.

"Leeches, that's all I need," Meldrum mumbled to himself. Taking his mind off the leeches for a moment, Meldrum reflected on everything Conley had taught him in the three weeks they had been together. Conley's first lesson, however, Meldrum would not forget: Do not say anything when Gunny Jones was nearby. In fact, don't even get near him. Conley had simply said 'Do your job right, and you won't have to interact with him at all.'

One hundred meters after crossing of the Song Ba Ren, the lead elements of Fox started taking automatic weapons fire from enemy soldiers hidden in a line of trenches ahead. The ground seemed to explode around them and the elephant grasses began dancing their warped bullet dance. The rest of Meldrum's squad, who were busy doing just what Conley was doing, immediately followed suit when he dove for the ground.

The company command group had yet to enter the river when the bullets came skimming over the ground at knee level. Unaffected by the potential danger surrounding him, Jones was mesmerized with the fact that he could actually watch the bullets passing by him.

Burgett, amazed at the gunny's inexplicable calm as bullets zinged and zipped past the unflappable man, yelled, "Gunny, don't just stand there. Get out of the way!"

The gunny turned back toward the captain, and immediately both sought the safety of a nearby mound of dirt five meters away.

Across the river, Conley's squad returned fire with some degree of success. Without reason, the enemy slowed their rate of fire, which allowed the other two squads in the platoon to maneuver forward parallel with Conley's squad.

"Conley," Lieutenant Scuras yelled just as an 82mm mortar round landed harmlessly seventy-five meters behind them to the right. "Get ready to move out! Pass the word on to Ellis," he directed referring to Corporal Hank Ellis of the first squad now positioned on Conley's right in Fox's farthest right unit.

"Johnson, your squad ready?" he yelled, this time to the squad on Conley's left.

"Yeah, Lieutenant!" came the reply.

"Tony, follow Johnson's squad," Scuras shouted to Staff Sergeant Marengo, his platoon sergeant, while standing up. Then calling out for all to hear, Scuras projected, "All right, let's do it!"

Simultaneously, the platoon fired at the trenches and maneuvered in fire team rushes toward the line. With three fire teams per squad there was a constant and suppressing base of fire from each group of three-to-five fire teams alternately standing up, running toward the enemy for ten meters while firing, then hitting the ground. The enemy counter-fired with their AK-47s.

In an instance Scuras groaned, crying out while falling.

Meldrum's voice rose above the din, "Hey, Corporal Conley, the lieutenant's been hit in his leg!"

"You okay, Lieutenant?" Conley called out.

Hearing no response, Conley turned back to assist the lieutenant. He saw Scuras binding his bleeding right thigh with the sand-colored dressing from his medicine pouch. Conley, turned to his squad, pointed his finger in the air, and with a flip of his wrist pointed it toward the now-empty trench line before yelling, "Let's go!"

As the platoon ran through the trench line, Scuras, now limping heavily, joined his men. "Get in defensive positions," he ordered, "and take cover!"

As soon as the words left his lips, automatic weapon fire began cracking overhead. The enemy, who had previously withdrawn, had achieved new firing positions.

Burgett and Jones soon moved the command group across the river. On the far side, they too started maneuvering forward trying not to bunch up as well as they could. Staff Sergeant Rose, the newly appointed Weapons Platoon sergeant hailing from the hills of West Virginia, was near Burgett. Rose was never without a wad of chewing tobacco in his mouth and a rather pronounced drawl. During the rush, Rose hollered to Burgett, "Gol damn, Capt'n, I just swollered my chew tobacci!!" Even while enemy rounds continuously snapped overhead, not one person within the command group could contain themselves. Their raucous cackling lasted until they caught up with the 3rd Platoon at the trench line.

Jones immediately radioed for a medevac chopper as soon as he and the skipper arrived. Between the intermittent rain and harassing enemy fire, the bird finally showed up at 1845, more than two hours from Jones's initial request. Its blades thumping the air, the CH-34 touched-down softly. Jones, Scuras, and a sergeant who took a round in his fore-arm made their way toward the chopper. Scuras assisted the sergeant into the open side door three feet off the ground. Scuras then turned with his back toward the open door and placed his hands behind him in the floor of the aircraft. His first attempt to spring up onto the plane failed. His wounded leg, now stiff, made it impossible for him to board.

Jones placed one hand under Scuras's good leg and the other under his armpit readying himself to lift the lieutenant up and in through the open door.

Defiantly, Scuras muttered, "You don't have to help me, Gunny."

Equally defiant, Jones growled, "That's not your call!"

He hoisted the lieutenant into the chopper before running out from under the craft while it lifted off. As the chopper disappeared into the dark sky, Jones murmured under his breath, "Well, I don't have to put up with him no more!"

By 1925 Fox had reached the battalion command group, Golf, and Echo Companies, and tied into their lines.

At 2130 Jones returned from checking the lines. He sat down near the captain and announced, "All secure, Skipper."

Upon receiving no response from his captain, Jones recognized that his caring commander was again deep in thought. "You okay, Captain Burgett?"

Wholly ignoring the "all secure" message, Burgett squinted over at the gunny through the inky blackness of the night. His manner passive, he remarked, "Gunny, Scuras is gone. If something happens to me, you'll have to take the company. You know that don't you?"

Jones's soft acknowledgement belied any vestige of the gunny's true emotions in that moment, "I do, Skipper."

The chopper secured, the wounded evacuated, their mission completed, the company returned to An Hoa.

Once there, Jones made sure Scuras's paycheck was mailed to the lieutenant who was recovering from his wounds in Japan. Despite any clashes they may have had in the past, Jones cared for all his men, even the lieutenant. "First Sergeant, make sure First Lieutenant Scuras gets his pay check. You know that he'll need some money soon as he starts getting better, and I want him to enjoy his recovery."

The remainder of the year sped by for Fox. Shortly, Fox, Echo, and Golf Companies received orders to return to base.

Christmas came without peace.

Apparently, the National Liberation Front and the North Vietnamese failed to notify the An Hoa valley VC about the truce as they went on with their business of attacking every aircraft, truck, and individual Marine they could find. Their efforts, however, did cost the attackers at least nine killed and twenty-two wounded on Christmas Day.

While they were most successful in getting wet and staying wet, during the month of December, the company was the target of VC attacks on eleven occasions: sustaining three Marines wounded, netting six enemy KIA/WIA, and capturing one drunken VC who claimed to have been a former VC village chief.

As if the battalion's TAOR was not considered large enough, on 30 December it suddenly became larger by nineteen square kilometers. The added area of responsibility went as far south as the Nong Son coalmines, nine kilometers southwest of the An Hoa combat base, and from there, southwest to include Antenna Valley. For many NVA soldiers traveling the Ho Chi Minh Trail and wishing to go either to Da Nang or the villages just south of Da Nang, the best route was to leave the Que Son Mountains, go through Antenna Valley and as best they could, skirt the An Hoa area.

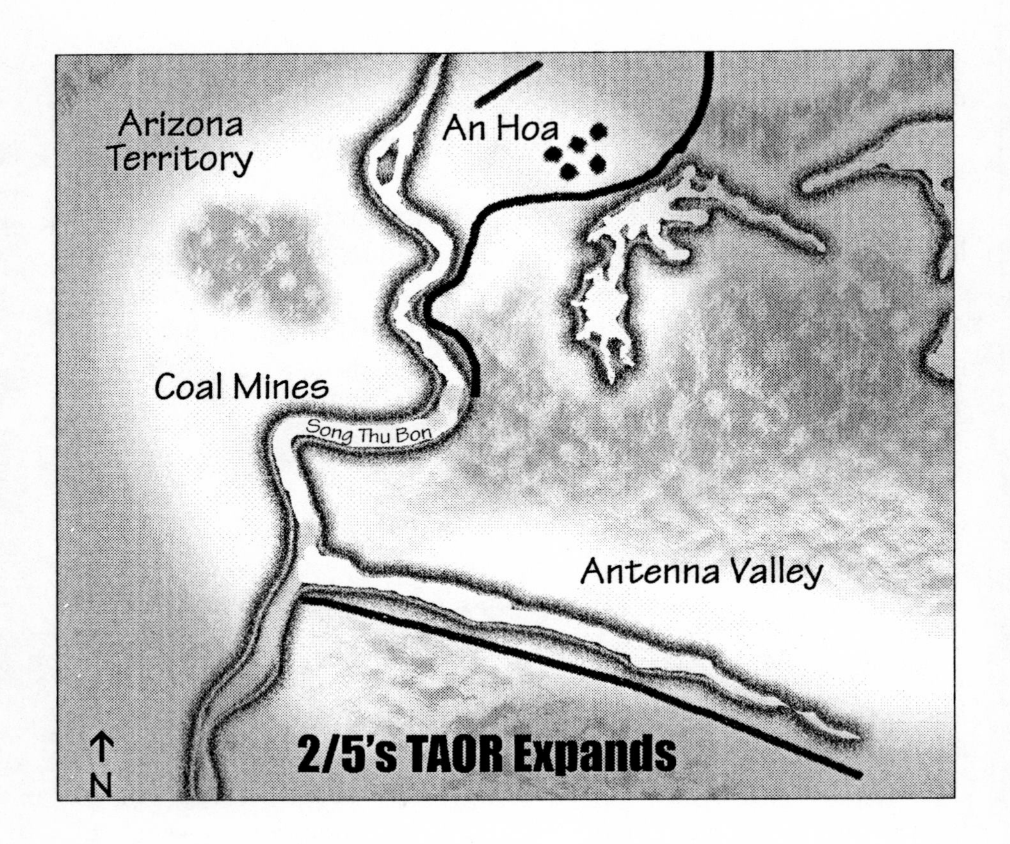

Perhaps a secondary reason for the expanded TAOR was the fact the Nong Son coalmines, situated directly across from the western end of Antenna Valley, were the only active mines in the country. Economically, the coalmines were insignificant; however, the general belief was that the country would appear to be a productive one if the mines still were functional. Hence, this façade augmented the importance of the coalmines. Notwithstanding, until that time no American force had operated in the vicinity of the Nong Son coalmines.

On 30 December Lieutenant Colonel Airheart selected Fox to conduct a search and destroy mission near the coalmines at Nong Son. At a company meeting the night before, Burgett notified the officers and staff noncommissioned officers of the fact that they would be moving out at 0800.

Reveille call went at 0530. By 0600 First Sergeant McDaniels, who had picked up Jones and Henderson upon their arrival into Vietnam and remained in An Hoa while the company was on maneuvers, approached Jones and said, "Here's my list of the men you're taking to the field."

Jones glanced at McDaniels and grumbled, "First Sergeant, here's my list. These are the men we are taking to the field!"

After comparing the two different lists, Jones pointed out why his list was accurate and the first sergeant's was not. McDaniels said, "Goddamn, Gunny, you know more about the men than I do!"

"Well, I should, First Sergeant. I get my information from the platoon sergeants, not the company clerks!"

Fox departed promptly at 0800. The plan was to replace a company of the Army of the Republic of Vietnam, ARVN, infantry at the Nong Son compound. After hiking for six hours east of the Song Thu Bon, Fox arrived at the small hamlet of Khuong Thuong, directly across the swollen river from their objective: the Nong Son coalmines. After getting off the trucks, Jones and Burgett walked to the edge of the rapidly flowing river. "Skipper," Jones announced, "I may be rated as a First Class swimmer, but this river is making me a bit nervous."

After a brief pause, the captain remarked, "Well, Gunny, the villagers look friendly enough, so we may as well try out their sampans."

The local craftsmen built small river crafts otherwise known as sampans. Both pointed ends of the boats swept upward. Each was constructed with a type of reed woven together and covered with a tar-like pitch, and could hold three to four Marines. To propel and guide the boat, the operator would move the aft rudder left and right.

For many the transit turned out to be even more dangerous and frightful than it looked. The raging and swollen river tore at the boats and rocked them from side to side, but somehow they all made it to the western side.

Safely across, Fox's 2nd and 3rd Platoons immediately occupied the bunkers fortifying a small compound. The compound was constructed at the bottom of a long terrain finger that ran to the top of the nearly 300-meter hill overlooking the river. It had French-built houses, some with generator-powered electricity, which were used to house the multinational engineers working the mines. Burgett sent the 1st Platoon up to secure the top of the hill.

Since the terrain was unfamiliar and the company was separated from the battalion, Fox searched for the enemy without straying far from each other's direct support. Resupply to Fox was nonexistent for the first three days due to the constant monsoon rains. But the local populace kept their guests fed with cooked rice and peppers, French bread, fruit, and—out-of-site of company authorities—whiskey, and beer for a New Year's celebration.

The orientation to the area lasted until 5 January when Fox began its participation in Operation Lincoln with Lieutenant Colonel Airheart's Command Group and Golf Company. Lincoln was conceived to flush the enemy from Antenna Valley and gather refugees from the valley. All remaining civilians would be considered VC supporters. Once accomplished, 2/5's rifle companies would have the freedom to operate in the valley without fear of harming friendly civilians. The concept of this operation was for Fox to cross the river by sampan again, meet up with the battalion command group and proceed eastward into the valley to meet Golf Company which was moving south from An Hoa.

Monsoon rains had flooded the valley heavily, restraining movement. The men stayed soaked at all times. Immersion foot, trench foot, or "jungle rot" as the troops called it, became a concern. This medical condition, where skin dies due to the constant exposure to water, crept up on the Marines with a horrible persistence.

6 January 1967. At 0945 on the second day Fox received automatic weapons fire from enemy occupying a small hamlet as they maneuvered eastward while still attempting to link up with Golf Company. Staff Sergeant Sprimont of the 2nd Platoon who led part of the counterattack during Fox's very first engagement at Con Thien was the only casualty. Jones had grown quite close to Sprimont as he had with his other two platoon sergeants, Marengo and Henderson. Sprimont had been badly wounded.

"Captain Burgett, I'm going back to check on Staff Sergeant Sprimont," Jones announced.

"Okay, Gunny. The colonel should be back there somewhere. I'll be back with you in a few moments."

Jones left and found Sprimont with the attending corpsman. As a few enemy rounds passed harmlessly ten feet overhead, Jones asked, "How is he, Doc?"

"Not sure, Gunny. He was shot up pretty bad. The worst round is lodged in his back. And he's hit in his wrist. Here," the corpsman added pointing to a small circular wound, "the bullet went out through his arm. I have him fairly well doped up at this point."

The gunny looked up and ordered a nearby machine gunner, "P.J.", referring to Lance Corporal Perry Jones, "Lay down a base of fire on those gad damn gooks." For good measure he added, "What are you sitting around here waiting for?"

"You two," he yelled at another two Marines crouching nearby frozen by the sight of their favorite, now wounded, platoon sergeant. "Make a temporary stretcher out of your poncho and some sticks. With this rain, we ain't getting any medevac birds in here soon. So we'll have to take Sprimont along with us 'til it clears some."

The two Marines jumped into action saying, "Okay, Gunny."

Because the machine gun's counter-fire had quieted the enemy, Fox and the battalion command group continued their sweep. By 1100 the rain had stopped and the Helicopter Support Team's radio operator ran up to announce to the gunny and the men carrying Sprimont that, "The bird's inbound and should be here in fifteen minutes!"

One of the staff non-commissioned officers from the battalion command group, sensing Jones's highly uncharacteristic compassion for his wounded mate, offered to coordinate the evacuation.

With Sprimont's color draining from his face, Jones was uncertain if his friend would live or die. "No thanks, I'll get my own wounded out," came Jones's curt reply, though all around could sense a sorrowful choking in his voice.

At about that time First Lieutenant Brady, the FAC who Jones had warned earlier not to become to attached to his men, came over to

Gunny Jones and said sarcastically, "Hey, I thought we weren't supposed to get attached to these people!"

The gunny, four inches taller and far more massively and powerfully built than the lieutenant, spun on Brady. When Jones's face reached Brady's, he fired out the word, "Fuck!" grabbing everyone's attention nearby. "You get the hell out of here!" Jones ordered the lieutenant.

Brady, aware that Airheart was in the crowd, turned around and asked the colonel, "Did you hear what he just said?"

Airheart replied in a quiet tone, "If I were you lieutenant, I'd get the hell out of here and leave him alone!"

Golf and Fox Companies linked up at 1600 on 6 January. Until 1450 hours on 7 January, the operation went as planned with Golf Company sweeping east on the north side of the valley. But at 1450 they learned that their resupply bird had been shot down and the crew rescued by a second helo. From that point forward, the operation took on added mission: locate and possibly destroy the downed CH-46 Sea Horse.

Operation Lincoln ended at noon on 9 January. One enemy had been confirmed killed and eight were "probably" killed. Twenty-nine refugees were moved to the district headquarters at Duc Duc.

On 10 January Burgett, Jones, and the 2nd and 3rd Platoons went to Antenna Valley to conduct search and destroy operations. On the first day, they found the downed helicopter, seven kilometers away from where it had been reported shot down. Fox destroyed the helicopter as directed.

By 18 January, the company had been pulled in closer to An Hoa and operated both near "Football Island" along the Song Thu Bon and near the industrial complex adjacent to the An Hoa combat base. The company returned to the base on 20 January to be briefed on Operation Tuscaloosa at 1000. This new operation was based on intelligence reports identifying a main force VC company in the Go Noi Island area. Those reports changed to a "main-force VC battalion-sized organization" shortly afterwards.

Burgett was to rotate out of Vietnam in ten days along with ten to twelve of his non-commissioned officers who had come in country with him some ten months earlier. Burgett anticipated a circuitous trip home via Sweden with his buddy Captain Jerry Doherty, commanding officer of Hotel Company. He was also anticipating his next assignment to the Marine Corps' glory post at Marine Barracks, Washington, DC.

On 22 January, two days before the operation, Fox's staff non-commissioned officers were eating supper at their favorite table in the staff and officers' mess. That mess with a separate entrance was part of the same large structure as the troops' mess hall. While the food was the exactly the same, the ambiance was a half-click higher. Henderson asked, "Hey, First Sergeant, who's that squared away looking captain over there at the milk machine?"

McDaniels leaned over so as not to project his voice and said, "His name is Graham. He's assigned to Hotel Company and will take command when Captain Doherty rotates in about ten days."

"Man, he really looks like a Marine," Jones offered.

"Yeah and, word has it, that he's been selected for the Astronaut Program," McDaniels offered.

"Wow," Marengo and Jones responded softly in unison.

Thirty minutes later Burgett and Doherty came in, having just finished their paper work prior to their planned departure on Operation Tuscaloosa at 0630 the next morning.

"Jerry," Burgett said while filling his plate. "You leaving shortimers back tomorrow?"

"A few. Why?"

"Hell, I'm letting ten of the guys that came with me from California last year stay back. I just don't they think should go. They've been through enough. Trouble is, it's wiping out all my junior leadership."

The two friends sat down at a table in the near-empty mess. "Well, what about yourself? You're short."

"Well, so are you," Burgett responded.

"We have less than a week, and I am going to take my replacement, Jim Graham, on this operation. That way, I'll be ready to turn over Hotel."

"I wish my replacement was here. If he was, I'd think twice about going." Shaking off a strange foreboding feeling, Burgett added, "Speaking about going, Jerry, I just had my flight to Stockholm confirmed. We'll be on the same flight."

"Great, I'm really looking forward to it. It will be fantastic to get out of this mud hole!"

"You hear anything about your fiancé lining up any dates for me?" Burgett teased.

"George, you just have no idea how many good-looking available woman are over there in Sweden. You'll see," laughed Doherty.

"Hey, let's get some cake and coffee and get out of here. We have to be moving in the morning way too early," Burgett suggested. Doherty nodded in agreement before grabbing the largest piece of cake he could find.

Corporal Rick Barnes, the machine gun section leader, was filling in as the second-ranking enlisted man after the gunny got Sprimont safely evacuated on the first outgoing chopper during the company's search for the downed CH-46. Barnes woke the men of the 2nd Platoon at 0330. All went to chow at the mess hall.

While dining on "SOS", a military delight consisting of cooked hamburger in spicy white gravy on toast, Lance Corporal John Golbrecht said to his gunner who the gunny had ordered to lay down a suppressing field of fire after Sprimont was hit, Lance Corporal "P.J." Jones, "P.J., you know yesterday morning 'they' said I didn't have to go on this operation since I'm slated for R&R on the 26th. By 1700, after we cleaned the gun, Barnes said he needs me. The captain is letting two corporals and one sergeant back because they are short. What's wrong with me staying back? I'm slated to go on R&R!"

"Life's a bitch, John, you gad dang slacker from Hanover, Pennsylvania," Jones remarked sarcastically with his best rendition of a Pennsylvanian accent which came out sounding more like President Johnson speaking than that of Gobrecht.

Chuckling and letting some steam out, Golbrecht countered, feigning his best deep Southern drawl, "Weeell, at least I'm not from gah daaamn Black Creeek, Geeeorga." Pausing, he added, "I just better get out on my

R&R by the 26th, that's all I have to say, or you're gonna have to put up with some pissed off Gi-rene!"

The weather was damp and overcast when Fox humped out the main gate at 0630. After three miles they left the main service road that led to Liberty Bridge and cut through the Phu Nhuans. On the way, they discovered and blew five booby traps. Fox continued directly to its Line of Departure, LOD, that ran along the same road, near the jump off spot where they began their effort to link up with Echo and Golf Companies a month ago.

The concept of operations was for Fox to cross the leech-filled Song Ba Ren to a location near where First Lieutenant Scuras had been wounded in the leg. Once across they would join up with Hotel. Together they would conduct S&D operations on Go Noi Island with Fox searching the center sector and Hotel searching the northern sector.

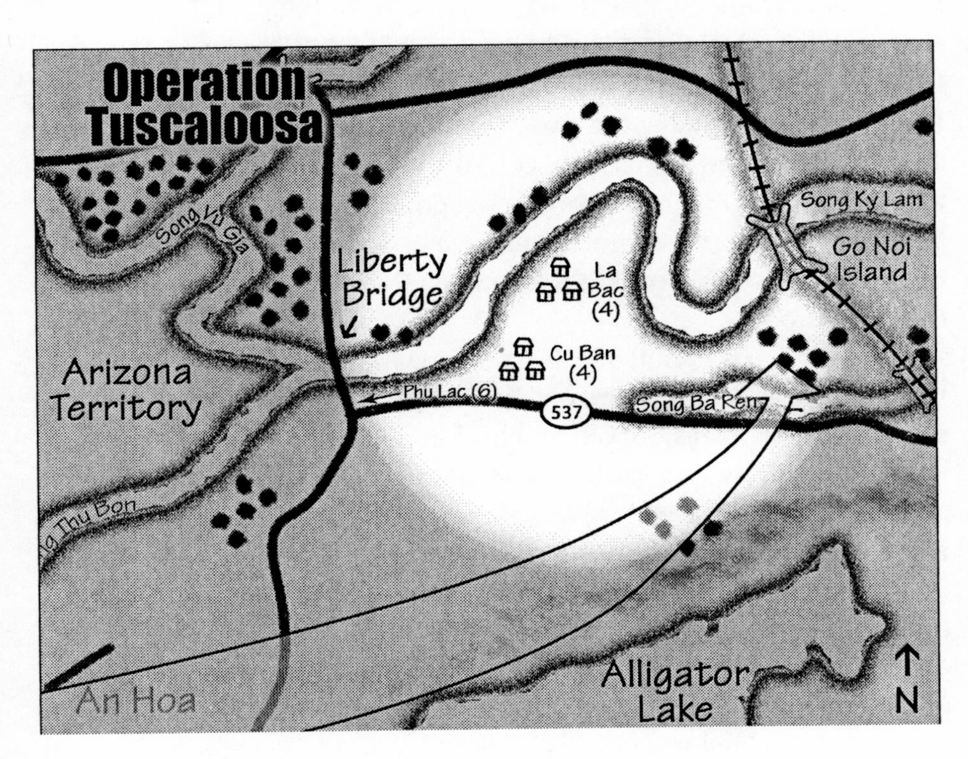

With one exception, the night of 23 January was generally quiet. One of Fox Company's ambushes was attacked early in the evening resulting in two Marines wounded.

At 0730 on 24 January, the company crossed the line of departure on time. That next day, 25 January, resulted in enemy sightings at a distance, finding a VC printing machine, two cases of C-rations, and numerous booby traps. Golbrecht even found a Buddhist flag to take with him on R&R and then home to Hanover.

By 0600 on 26 January only two enemy had been killed. The absence of enemy contact caused Lieutenant Colonel Airheart to request the termination of the operation on 26 January at 1800 hours. As a result, Fox was ordered to continue searching, but move in the direction of Phu Lac 6, the high ground overlooking Liberty Bridge.

Fox's route was to first move south from the center of the island, cross back over the Song Ba Ren, then travel west straddling the elevated road, Route 537, that had been an old French railroad berm, towards the junction of the main service at Phu Lac 6. By 0900, as the 2nd and 3rd Platoons began crossing the river, Fox started receiving sniper fire from the west somewhere in the vicinity of the village of Cu Ban. Soon, a multitude of small arms and automatic weapons fire opened up on the company, which found itself more out in the open than not. Two enemy 81mm mortars splashed into the Song Ba Ren, 400 meters to the east of the two platoons.

Hotel, on Fox's right flank, began taking mortar and heavy automatic weapons fire as well. The fire on both companies temporarily halted the mutual support plans Burgett and his buddy Doherty had worked out.

With ten junior non-commissioned officers back in An Hoa, Burgett and his cadre of trusted senior staff non-commissioned officers had to assume the roles of the missing squad leaders.

"Jarrett, tell the 2nd and 3rd Platoons to get across the river!" Burgett called out as he moved into action.

"Corporal Cox," Burgett yelled over to his 81mm mortar forward observer. Put some HE over there," he directed referring to high explosive rounds and pointing to a large grassy mound four hundred meters to his right. "That's where they're shooting from." Next, he demanded, "Jarrett, I need to speak to Staff Sergeant Henderson!"

After a quick conversation with the 1st Platoon's radio operator, Jarrett gave the handset to Burgett, "William B," Burgett used his nick name for Henderson, "hold where you are and get some machine gun fire on that grassy knoll to your right where the firing is coming from. We have to get the 2nd and 3rd Platoons across the river before we can cross. Be prepared to move your platoon and establish a blocking position on the far side of the river in that tree line to your front. Hotel will be driving the enemy into your position. Any questions?"

"None, Skipper. Out"

"Ouch! P.J. What the hell was that?" Golbrecht yelled holding his neck.

Attached to the 2nd Platoon, the machine gun team of P.J. Jones and Golbrecht had just reached one of the few dry sand bars left in the monsoon-flooded riverbed. An NVA soldier had fired at the gun hoping to render it inoperable or wound the gunner.

"Damn," Jones said as he looked over at Golbrecht now showing his neck so his buddy could assess his wound, "that gook tore a hole in your collar! You're okay, you lucky ass. Let's get the hell out of here!"

Jones and Golbrecht grabbed the gun and ammo can and leaped into the waist-deep river to catch up with the rest of the 2nd Platoon.

"With a brief "81" fire mission and the heavy base of fire put on the VC regulars by Henderson's machine guns, the 2nd and 3rd Platoons reached the safety of the raised road bed. They set into positions covering for Burgett's command group and Henderson's 1st Platoon.

Without knowing the exact direction Henderson's 1st Platoon was moving, the 2nd Platoon began firing 60mm mortars into the same area.

Seeing this, Burgett called out for Gunny Jones, who happened to be five feet away. "Sam!"

"Sir," Jones acknowledged.

"Get over there to the 2nd Platoon and tell them their 60's are landing right where the 1st Platoon will be going. We'll follow as soon as you bring the mortars under control."

"Aye, aye, Skipper," Jones, said as he turned and began running toward the river.

"Corporal Cox, I have to coordinate with Hotel! Tell Staff Sergeant Henderson to hold up firing their guns on the enemy, or he'll be without any gun ammo soon."

"Roger, Skipper."

"Hotel, this is Fox Six, over" Burgett began his exchange with Hotel's skipper.

The two captains quickly reassessed their positions and launched a counter-attack. Fox would fire into the enemy from its position on the left flank while Hotel attacked from the north. Together, they would drive the enemy west and gain the upper hand.

On Burgett's orders, the 60mm mortars ceased firing. Burgett looked around at Cox and the three radio operators with them and said, "All right, it's our turn! Jarrett, make sure the 1st Platoon is moving as well."

Under the blanket of automatic weapons fire provided by the 2nd and 3rd Platoons, the five-man command group began to make its dash to the protection of the raised roadbed and the rest of the company. After a few yards, an enemy mortar round exploded fifty meters to their right. No casualties. They continued across wet ground still short of the river. Their pace increased. Another exploding mortar round detonated, this time, twenty meters to the left flank of the group of pistol-packing radio operators, forward observer, and one short-time commander. Burgett felt shrapnel sear into his left arm. His pace quickened in response.

Only one thought, the thought that the command group had been bracketed flashed into Henderson's mind as he began running as fast as possible toward Burgett.

Burgett, still short of the river, continued trying to escape. From there, he couldn't tell the enemy had determined their position.

The third round slammed into the middle of the group. Its concussion blew Burgett to the ground. He knew he'd taken more shrapnel.

The battalion radio operator lay in a crumpled heap near the captain. Jarrett, his company radio operator, was sprawled on top of the other radio operator. The captain could tell Jarrett hadn't been killed because he was moving ever so slightly. Both radios were lost. Cox, unconscious or dead—Burgett didn't know which—was trapped under both of the radio operators. Bleeding profusely, Burgett simultaneously attempted to assist the badly wounded Jarrett while searching for any operational radio. After crawling the distance between them, he located one on Cox who now seemed semi-conscience. He dragged himself toward the radio, and painfully, switched it to the company frequency.

"Fox Three, this is Fox Six. Let me speak to your 'Actual', over," Burgett struggled.

"This is Fox Three Actual," Marengo responded.

Motioning the towering gunny to come over, Staff Sergeant Marengo in charge of the 3rd Platoon held the handset away from his ear allowing Jones to hear.

"We've been hit. Can you come back?" Burgett gasped.

Jones grabbed the handset out of Marengo's hand demanding, "What do you mean, can we come back?"

At once Jones's stomach knotted into solid steel. He didn't need to hear the answer; he knew what had happened—could hear it in his captain's failing voice.

Jones and Marengo charged back to the riverbank. By the time they arrived at Burgett's position the enemy had completely stopped firing at Fox and could be heard directing its firepower on Hotel Company. Henderson was already leaning over the captain.

Burgett was a sorry site. "Gunny, he's tore up pretty bad," Henderson synopsized. Burgett had been hit in both legs and in both arms, his flack jacket shredded.

As his three disciples gathered around their wounded leader, Jones kicked into gear, breaking their fixation, "Henderson, set up your platoon facing where that enemy was firing from! Marengo, get some Marines over here to evac these men. Oh, and tell Lieutenant Kelley I want his platoon to set up an LZ for the medevac about one hundred meters east, where its good and secure."

Jones continued reorganizing and giving directions. Looking at Cox, who had miraculously escaped shrapnel and now had regained consciousness, he said "Cox, give me the radio so I can give a SITREP to battalion and call in a Priority One medevac. I'll also get the scoop on what Hotel's intentions are. So, get going!" he ordered Henderson and Marengo.

By 1030 the medevac chopper was seen circling at 3000 feet as it began its decent toward Fox's LZ.

"Fox, this is Cobra One, over."

"Roger, One. We see you coming," Jones responded.

"Looks like you're pretty hot down there, Fox."

"That's a negative, Cobra One. Just stay away from the center of the island; Hotel's getting pounded pretty badly."

"Roger that, Fox. I think we see you along the road, but better pop your smoke."

Thirty seconds later the pilot confirmed, "Fox, that's a green smoke, over."

"Roger, Cobra One. It's green."

The pilot's next radio transmission was laced with panic, "Fox, we're being fired on! Jesus, my co-pilot has been hit!"

The silence after his transmission lasted only another thirty seconds. "Fox, I'm coming into your position. I'm not sure if this thing will lift out again under this kind of fire," the pilot announced.

Immediately, Jones directed all of Fox's firepower toward the AK-47 that shot out the right front window of the CH-34 helicopter, now hovering, one hundred feet above the spot where they had popped their smoke. "Cobra One," he radioed, "you're looking good. You're clear to land."

"Hey, Fox, I changed my mind. I'm coming in, picking up your wounded, and then leaving. So, get those casualties onboard as soon as we touch down; then we're getting the hell out of here!"

Now wrapped in a poncho and on a stretcher, Burgett's men carried him to the waiting aircraft. He pointed his limp finger at the gunny, who stood among the circle of men loading the seven casualties aboard. His message was clear: Fox is yours now, Gunny. Fox is all yours.

Fox launched a full barrage of small arms and mortar fires in front of Hotel Company, allowing Doherty's men to fight their way through the enemy. Finally, at 1430 Hotel arrived at the elevated roadbed next to Fox.

Standing by for a "Frag" order from battalion, Jones had the platoons set in a defensive perimeter, ready to move out.

With utter calm, one extremely sharp looking Marine officer walked up to what Jones had assembled as a functioning command group. "Are you Gunny Jones?" he asked.

Jones spied the parallel silver bars on his collar immediately recognizing him as a captain. "Yes, Sir. I am."

"My name is Captain Graham. I am your new company commander."

CHAPTER 3: DEMANDING COMMANDER

With utter calm Graham gave his first order, "As a result of this morning's air strikes, I don't believe we'll be getting any more 82mm mortars from the enemy battalion," he paused to eye each of the men with him. "And now with Golf attacking in our direction from An Hoa and the battalion inserting the two Sparrow Hawk blocking positions, we have the enemy trapped. They'll be desperate and will fight to the finish. Be prepared for some heavy engagements." His head nodded as he spoke, "Are there any questions? Lieutenant Kelley?"

The gunny had gathered Fox's available personnel together and they now received their orders from their new captain in a tight, huddled group. "Captain Graham, when my platoon comes on line with Hotel Company on our right flank, can I tie in directly with their left platoon and do you have that platoon's frequency?"

Graham shook his head slightly before answering, "For the time being, you'll have to come through me, and I'll coordinate with Hotel Company. If the situation dictates direct contact later on, I'll give you that frequency. In the meantime, we're tied into Hotel so you'll have a half hour to make direct liaison with their platoon before we move out." Not sure his earlier combat order had been fully comprehended by the lieutenant, he clarified, "Remember, Mr. Kelley, first, we are going to arc south away from Hotel. We will tie up with them at the Sparrow Hawk #1 blocking position later this afternoon."

Gunnery Sergeant Jones heard and noted the first of the many "Misters" he would hear from this new captain, filing the word in the back of his mind. Jones sized up the man as he did.

"What's your name, Corporal?" Graham asked the 81mm mortar forward observer with his hand in the air.

"Cox, Sir," the corporal responded crisply. "Sir, do you want me to plan fire missions for the 105s at Phu Lac (6)?" Cox asked referring to the howitzers placed there to support Tuscaloosa. Cox had to lean forward to hear the company commander's answer since the only thing he was certain he could hear, after the enemy mortar had knocked him unconscious, was a constant ringing in his ears.

"Go ahead, Corporal Cox. Then give them to me before you before you submit them."

Graham surveyed his assembled leaders and stated, "All right, then, I have 1402 hours, be prepared to move out in twenty-eight minutes."

Graham's order passed through the ranks and at 1430 on the mark, the 3rd Platoon, under the dauntless leadership of Staff Sergeant Tony Marengo, leapt off. Tense minutes ticked by: one—the point squad under Sergeant Carey crept forward...two—the signal was passed for the remainder of the platoon to advance...three—most of the platoon had covered approximately twenty meters from their jump off position...four—their pace increased until...a solitary shot rang out in the air. Carey held up his fist, temporarily stopping the forward movement. Simultaneously, Carey dropped to his knees as another bullet pierced the silence, felling Lance Corporal Guise, a Marine in his 1st Fire Team. The shots seemed to come from opposite sides of Carey's squad. As the 3rd Platoon took up defensive positions, Doc Zimmerman crawled forward, attempting to reach the Guise. As he neared the critically wounded Marine, the snipers opened up, killing him immediately. Rapid sniper fire pinned the men in place, and as Marengo reached for the PRC 25's radio handset, six more Marines hit the ground, wounded.

Marengo squeezed the PRC's handset, "Fox Six, this is Fox Three, over,"

"Six, go."

"Six, we have three Kilo India Alphas and six Whiskey India Alphas that need an evac. Recommend you select a landing zone back near the stream away from the enemy fire," he informed the command group. "We've started receiving incoming from small mortars, over."

"Roger Three. Can you get the casualties out of the kill zone?"

Marengo waited until the concussion from the last mortar quieted, "That's affirm, over."

Graham took instant control. "Gunny, they have three killed and six wounded. Get the evac started." He moved closer to the gunny, "Fox Three was talking about small mortars. I take it those are their "knee mortars" which have a range of about 400 meters, so make sure you have that LZ back far enough." He turned, pointing a finger, "Cox, grab a couple of men and see if you can help with the casualties. I'll be up near the 3rd Platoon."

"Staff Sergeant," Cox shouted to Marengo whose combat boots pounded the ground while carrying the mortally wounded fire team leader on his shoulder. "We'll take him to the LZ!"

"Yeah," Marengo panted lowering Guise's body to the ground. "Handle him with care, Cox," the platoon commander directed, staring Cox square in the eye.

"Don't worry about that, Sir."

Marengo spun, darting back to his other two squads to direct their counter-fire on the enemy. Once done, he set off to retrieve the other casualties from his lead unit. Marengo advanced a mere twenty meters when the enemy fire intensified just as he entered the kill zone. His remaining squads opened up allowing him the opportunity to get two more wounded back to where Cox and his crew waited.

A CH-46 chopper spun dirt into the air in a leaf-riddled cyclone as it hovered inches above the ground. A second bird was descending from 1000 feet. Fox lifted their wounded onto the waiting craft and as quickly as the first helicopter departed the second one landed. Within minutes, the casualties were on the way to the 1st Medical Battalion in Danang.

Graham and Captain Doherty from Hotel Company drove their companies into, through, and over the retreating enemy. By 1830, the enemy resistance, with the exception of occasional sniper fire, ceased.

Hotel and Fox tied into the defensive perimeter established by the Sparrow Hawk #1 blocking force.

The night hushed.

Delta Company, 1st Battalion, 26th Marines, became attached to 2/5 on 26 January. On 27 January the four rifle companies: Delta from 1/26 and Fox, Golf, and Hotel from 2/5, combed the battlefield to assess the results of Tuscaloosa.

Operation Tuscaloosa was finally terminated at 1700 on 28 January. Seventeen Marines had been killed and fifty-two were wounded. The VC lost seventy-nine confirmed killed, sixty-four probable killed with approximately seventy-three wounded.

Fox returned to An Hoa that same afternoon. To his immense relief, Private First Class Golbrecht departed for R&R that very same night.

31 January 1967. After two days in An Hoa, Fox prepared to participate in Operation Independence. First Sergeant Cleo Lee, who had taken McDaniel's place, approached Jones in the Staff hooch as the gunny readied his own equipment. "Sam, the captain wants to move the lieutenants down to your hut after this operation."

"First Sergeant, that ain't gonna happen!" the gunny barked back at him.

"What do you mean?" Lee asked stupidly.

"You know I don't get along with lieutenants. Hell, if we're down here relaxing with a couple of beers after an operation and one of those college fellas start pulling some of their fraternity pranks, I'm just likely to pick him up and throw him right through the screen door!" Jones growled. "And, First Sergeant," his voice lowered menacingly, "you know how hard it is to get screen down here in An Hoa."

Lee glared at Jones.

"But, I'll take care of the captain," the gunny offered with a shrug.

As soon as Lee departed, Jones turned to Marengo, "Tony, get the new company supply non-commissioned officer, Corporal Hollins, to come on over here. I want to talk to him about building the captain a one-man addition to the company office."

The concept for Operation Independence had been simple. Three companies drove an estimated main force VC battalion and local VC guerrillas from the Song Vu Gia east, through a portion of the Arizona Territory, to the Song Thu Bon. Fox and Hotel, who had been so heavily engaged in Tuscaloosa, were there to block their escape.

The operation was successful in that the enemy sustained thirty-eight KIA and twenty-one WIA. Eight POWs were taken. The Marines sustained three killed and fifteen wounded.

Fox's actions were minimal and, by 9 February, they returned to An Hoa where Graham moved into his new quarters.

Graham immediately went to the company office to sign unit diaries—the official company records that contained the names and social security numbers of newly joined Marines, KIAs, and WIAs—and other documents "Top" Lee had prepared for him. Gunny Jones and his staff compatriots marched immediately to the officers' hooch, knocked on the door, and entered announcing to any lieutenants who were listening, "We're taking the company commander's gear."

The next day, while Fox prepared to go to the Nong Son coalmines Lee stopped by to wish them well. Jones asked, "Any word yet on the skipper?"

"Skipper's recovering," Lee answered, knowing Jones was referring to Burgett. "But, it'll be a while..."

"Top, did the new captain say anything about his new quarters?"

Lee said, "When I asked him about that, the captain said, 'They're fine. Thanks a lot.'"

"Can't exactly figure that he'd share his quarters with the lieutenants like Captain Burgett did," the gunny mentioned, growing quiet.

"You know how religious Captain Graham is?" Lee started, "Well, I've seen him praying in that addition, and I don't blame for wanting some privacy. Do you, Sam?"

"He rates it. He's always finding time to read that Bible he carries 'round with him. Darnest thing I ever seen."

Lee then looked Jones in the eye, "Now don't forget, Gunny, I want to go to the field sometime on one of the operations."

Instantly the gunny said, "Sure, Top, I'll keep that in mind" even while he knew that it would never happen as long as he was the company gunnery sergeant. With a new CO, Jones didn't need anyone else looking over his shoulder.

On the hump to the coal mines that afternoon Private First Class John "Hanover" Golbrecht called up to his gunner buddy, Lance Corporal Perry Jones, and said, "Hey, P.J., did I tell you that that I met this good looking gal in Taiwan who really loves me?"

Jones looked over his shoulder and grumbled, "Hanover, if you tell me one more thing about your friggin' R&R, you Pennsylvania asshole, I'm going to turn around and beat the crap out of you."

Golbrecht smiled recalling his fond memories of Taiwan and kept trudging along.

Graham was not new to command. After six years in the Army Reserves, National Guard, and Marine Corps Reserves, he was commissioned a Second Lieutenant in the Marine Corps on 1 November 1963. He commanded Company M, 3rd Battalion, 6th Marines, as a lieutenant and was promoted to the rank of captain in less than three years of commission service. Many of his peers believed he was on the fast track to becoming a general officer.

After a day at the coalmines, Graham, who had gone to the Army's Ranger School and the Corps' Mountain Warfare Training Center, felt anxious to get to the mountains. Thus, on the morning of 12 February, he led the 2nd and 3rd Platoons above Nong Son to search for thirteen NVA elite snipers. This was planned to be a one-day event so they left their packs, most of their ponchos, and rations at the base camp. As they ascended, Golbrecht and P.J. Jones switched off carrying the heavy M60 machine gun. When he wasn't carrying the gun, Golbrecht was learning more about Sergeant Weldon, who had rejoined the Marine Corps after one year of separation, now was the father of two and attached to Fox from the battalion's Intelligence Section for his field orientation.

"Hey, Sarge," Golbrecht asked, "Why in the hell did you come back in the Corps?"

"The war," the out of breath sergeant replied. "And what made you join the Marine Corps, Golbrecht?"

"Oh, to hump this M-60 up hills with my good buddy from Georgia here," he said referring to his gunner, Jones, with a twitch of his head.

"Pass the word back we're stopping to take a five minute break," Weldon ordered.

Not thirty seconds later a bullet flew overhead and snapped the air above them.

Instinctively, Golbrecht and Jones leapt into the bushes.

"Son of a bitch, P.J., that was close. You okay, Sarge?"

When no response came, Golbrecht slithered five meters on his stomach up the path only to find the sergeant lying on his side. "Hey, P.J.," Golbrecht called, "the sarge took one right behind the ear. He didn't even have a chance to write home. Damn snipers!"

Jones responded, saying, "I'll pass the word up to the lieutenant."

The snipers who controlled the mountains kept the Fox Company Marines on the run. They were located on the same ridge and on the same trail as Fox. The Marines found themselves two to three hundred meters below the enemy. Fox pursued the enemy upward. Beside the trail were large boulders the snipers used for protection. Fox ran in and out of the boulders and up the trail all day. The moment the Marines stopped to catch their breath a bullet would impact so close that they ran some more. The men of the 2nd Platoon had it the worst. They frequently shifted the burden of carrying Weldon's body wrapped in the only poncho brought with them that day among different sets of four men. Weldon's body fell out of the slick rubberized material a half dozen times while they ducked bullets.

Finally around 1600, a chilling rain began saturating the high ground precluding the snipers from seeing Fox Company. The lull allowed a medevac chopper to lift out the body of Sergeant Weldon from a rocky high ground next to the ridge they had been on in the afternoon.

By 0300, drenched and shivering, Golbrecht whispered to Jones saying, "Not only am I starved and frozen, but those gooks below us slipping and sliding on the rocks are really starting to spook me. I hope Captain Graham is enjoying his day in the mountains."

"He is. And, like you said Hanover, the 5th Marines aren't the same as your old regiment. We're out to find the enemy and destroy them."

In the morning the patrol descended off the backside of the mountain and found a friendly village that provided two bananas per man. This curbed their appetites until the men arrived at the Nong Son base camp. Graham immediately gathered the men of the two platoons around him and began asking questions.

"What did you learn? How many enemy soldiers were shooting at us in the morning? How many enemy soldiers were below our position last night at 0200? The shot that killed Sergeant Weldon came from what weapon? What was the mood of the villagers who gave us the bananas? If enemy were hiding there, where would they most likely be?"

After his prodding, Graham explained the value of hard training and the discipline Fox would gain from it when they became engaged in a big battle.

Fox remained at Nong Son for the remainder of February and the beginning of March. During this time frame they improved the defensive configuration of the outpost, participated in planned and reactionary patrols, and stood post on the night defensive perimeter.

Graham quickly gained the reputation of being a most demanding commander, a "professional's professional", and possessing an ability to give the best tactical orders the staff non-commissioned officers had ever heard. He neither smoked, drank, nor swore. He rarely showed anger; in fact Jones thought the captain had a good sense of humor. The gunny also knew by this time that when Graham used the word "Mister" preceding a last name instead of a rank that that person had most likely erred and was in trouble. "Misters" he reserved mostly for lieutenants.

Blessed with these characteristics, Graham pushed the men harder than they had ever been pushed before. The importance of Nong Son's strategic position near the Ho Chi Minh Trail coupled with the growing enemy presence in and around An Hoa, Hoi An, and Danang became a major factor in totally reconfiguring the outpost. A road had to be cut from the base camp up to the top of the hill. The top of the hill had to be cleared. A defensive trench line on the top of the hill had to be dug. Large, reinforced, permanent bunkers, constructed of sand bags, had to be built. The importance of these activities could be measured by the number of visits by general-grade officers inspecting the progress. The totality of these tasks did not fall on Fox to accomplish alone, but on occasion when the men filled sand bags after 0100 hours in the morning, troop morale wasn't at its highest. Graham was the only new factor in the company equation that had changed, so the troops blamed the extra work on him. Jones, who supervised the execution of the filling the sandbags, remained intentionally oblivious about troop sentiment and believed the midnight filling of sandbags would only strengthen combat discipline as the captain had explained.

On 10 March Fox was relieved at the Nong Son outpost by Golf Company and returned to An Hoa to assume the mission of defending that combat base. Unfortunately for the men, their assignment was not restricted to base-only activities.

Their first new mission was to participate in a three-day civic action operation dubbed, "County Fair 5–14". At 0030 on 13 March, Fox surrounded the hamlet of Phu Nhuan (3) to ensure no VC were attempting to "mingle" with the locals and, if they were, to collar and capture them. The Duc Duc District commander, the Phu Nhuan village mayor, and Marines living and fighting with the local friendly forces participating in the Combined Action Platoon, CAP, program worked to improve relationships with the hamlet's population. The battalion's surgeon, Dr. Vidi, a dentist from Danang, and several corpsman came to provide medical and dental treatments. Actually, had the aircraft slated to carry the 1st Marine Division Band from Danang to An Hoa not broken down, the live music would have added to the county fair atmosphere. Fox Company Marines guarded the perimeter of the town nestled along the Song Thu Bon and enjoyed watching pretty young Vietnamese women who dressed for the occasion.

While no VC were found in Phu Nhuan (3), the county fair did not go unnoticed by the jealous enemy on the northern side of the river. On each of the three days, snipers wounded Fox Company Marines. Marine

Corps snipers and air strikes on the second and third days lethally countered the enemy trying to spoil the spirit of the county fair.

Fox conducted an amphibious raid without contacting any enemy on 20 March. The raid was as a prelude for Operation New Castle that took place in the Arizona territory during the 22 March to 25 March timeframe. The battalion encountered no enemy.

From a military point of view the operation was insignificant. The most salient event, at least to one Marine, was when Graham appeared out of nowhere before the young man. "Marine," he started.

Lance Corporal Thom Searfoss's head jerked up as the captain presented an open can of C-ration pound cake and said, "Today's your 18th birthday…I've been told."

Searfoss looked up in disbelief that his captain was actually addressing him, and sprang up, "Yes, Sir. It is!"

"Well, congratulations. You are the youngest man in my command. It's a pleasure serving with you." Then, Graham smiled, gave Searfoss the cake, shook his hand, and walked away.

Searfoss turned to his best friend, Lance Corporal Bob Bowermaster who had been eating a can of C rations, and said, "Man, do you believe that!"

On 27 March, Fox became the first rifle company in the 2nd Battalion to draw the M-16 rifle. "Fam", familiarization, firing took place on 28 March.

The war tempo increased in April when the company was assigned to the Phu Lac (6) outpost. That hilltop position, overlooking Liberty Bridge and the Song Tu Bon served as the gateway out of the An Hoa valley onto Go Noi Island. Contact with and sightings of the enemy surged to an average of three to four times a day. More often than not, chasing the enemy through rice paddies and trails resulted in men falling into punji traps, which were pits laced with sharp dung-covered bamboo stakes. Men tripped booby traps consisting of wires anchored on one side of a path to a grenade's loosely attached safety pin on the other side.

As the battalion's Tactical Area of Responsibility grew, Lieutenant Colonel "Mal" Jackson, who had taken Airheart's place as battalion commander, wanted to get further away from battalion and company level operations, and more toward platoon and squad sized patrols that would saturate 2/5's operating area.

Graham did not feel comfortable with this change. He felt especially bad when troops engaged the enemy and, worse yet, sustained casualties. Squads on their own in the field did not know all the required frequencies for medevacs, close air support, and artillery support. As each day in April passed, he grew more and more agitated.

Finally, Jones approached Graham, "Capt'n, the problem we're having is one of communications. The troops require a better and more complete briefing before they go out. Patrol leaders don't know to ask questions prior to their patrols. We assume they know some things such as frequencies and fire support. We just have to brief them better."

"All right, Gunny. You're probably right. Let me give it some thought," came the captain's careful reply.

Surprisingly, the gunny was quite pleased with the return of the newly promoted First Lieutenant Jim Scuras. Whether it was his leg wound sustained three months earlier or just the return to Fox Company, Scuras's demeanor had changed. He treated the gunny with a new and profound sense of respect. The lieutenant and Staff Sergeant Marengo worked well together. Jones could sense that the 3rd Platoon troops were happy for his return. Scuras stayed his distance and perhaps that was because Jones hovered nearby the highly demanding company commander. All in all, Scuras's return was welcome.

"Anderson, PFC David Anderson," Lance Corporal Tommy LaBarbera, Fox's unit diary clerk, called out to the new arrivals.

The lanky, twenty-two year-old, former Federal Police Officer who had worked to prevent drug smuggling in Panama, lifted his head and asked in a low, slow Arkansan twang, "You looking for me?"

"Anderson, the first sergeant is looking for you."

"What's he got in mind, LaBarbera?"

"Don't know," the short man said with a pronounced Brooklyn accent. LaBarbera retreated into the company office.

Moments later, after reporting in, Anderson stood at attention in front of First Sergeant Cleo "Top" Lee and uttered, "Sir."

Lee asked Anderson a few questions completing his checking-in progress and then asked, "While you're in An Hoa, Anderson, would you like to do battalion duties, such as mess duty, or would you like to duties to directly support the company?"

"Fox Company duties, First Sergeant," Anderson snapped. He'd heard of Fox's rising reputation back in Danang.

"Well, good. I want you to report to Corporal Hollins, the company supply non-commissioned officer, and tell him I want you to burn the shitters while you're in An Hoa."

Anderson always undertook all tasks assigned to him seriously, while never losing his sense of humor, and made a sport of it. In this case his task was passing the time in An Hoa in order to become acclimated before going to the field. Graham was wholly intolerant of Marines in the field getting heat exhaustion or heat stroke, so until Anderson grew accustomed to the weather, he was going to intellectualize burning shitters into a pleasant game.

After two days Anderson wrote to a friend of his still in Panama.

Eddie:

Our outhouses are small, enclosed little wooden affairs with seating arrangements for one, two, or three. Beneath each potty hole is half of a 55-gallon drum. When it gets about two thirds full we simply pull the half barrels out from their strategic placement and away from the wooden structure, stir in a couple of inches of diesel fuel, then burn off the fuel until only super-ugly, charred ashes are left in the bottom of the barrels. Talk about your "bottom-of-the-barrel" situation. We then lift the horizontal door located at the rear of each outhouse and slide the burned out barrels back in, which by now have been refilled with fresh fuel.

Sound like fun? Well I'm here to tell you that the stench, which is produced by a combination of burning diesel fuel and human wastes should be contained in some fashion, and used against the Viet Cong! I burned a bunch. Yep, Top Lee didn't let me become bored.

Stay well my friend.

Dave

On 10 April a 6x6 truck came to a stop at the top of the Phu Lac (6) outpost. Anderson and five other replacements jumped off.

The "Top" had assigned Anderson to the 3rd Platoon. As Anderson's foot hit the ground, he spotted a raggedy Marine and asked, "Hey, Marine, where's the 3rd Platoon hiding out?"

The Marine never took the cigarette out of his mouth, pointed and mumbled, "Them bunkers."

With that Anderson and another "newbie" by the name of Gerrard walked over to a nearby, medium-sized bunker. A staff sergeant was standing at the bunker's entrance. The staff sergeant, who looked a close second to Al Pacino, sauntered toward them. "Tony Marengo," the staff sergeant said.

Anderson replied, "Dave Anderson."

"How ya' doing, Andy?"

A smart-ass remark like, "Just fine, Marine," jumped to his mind, but one look into the coldest eyes he had ever seen, told Anderson not to be frivolous at all. Levity would have its place in Vietnam, but this was not the place. Instead, Anderson mustered a wimpy, "Okay."

Marengo pointed to a large bunker closer to the perimeter wire, "That's your place down there."

The three walked together. Along the way, Marengo introduced Anderson and Gerrard to Mike Nutt, the squad leader; "Professor" Lindstrom, the M-79 rocket man; "Waterbu" Haley, the 3.5 rocket Man; Doc Wodja, the platoon corpsman; and fellow grunts Dale "Mac"

McCauley, a Marine who simply went by the name of "Reed", "Tunnel Rat" Rizzo, and Bud Groch.

Anderson dropped his gear inside the large bunker, which housed the other Marines in his squad. It smelled the dank and musty.

"You two ready to meet Lieutenant Scuras, our platoon commander?" Marengo asked Anderson and Gerrard.

They both nodded silently, then followed Marengo back outside.

After his recovery, Scuras now appeared to be a slight man about a year older than Anderson, balding severely for his age, and held a similar look in his eyes to those Marines had who had far outlived the odds of the being killed. Scuras was soft-spoken but the voice of authority was definitely present in his demeanor. Like Marengo, he was all business.

Assigned to sandbag working parties at that defensive stronghold for the next three days, Anderson's face and body became brown from sun and dirt and he soon blended with the other Fox Marines.

From Phu Lac (6) the companies went on many patrols. The Marines developed a common hatred for the enemy and for their living conditions; yet they grew an uncommon bond for one another. They enjoyed the music on the Armed Forces Radio Station, candy bars, cigarettes—inside the wire—and some crazy concoction of C-ration coffee and cocoa. Occasionally they would receive a newspaper or magazine, a warm beer, and soda pop from a convoy passenger coming to An Hoa from Danang. The men reminisced about "the world", or USA, and made grandiose plans for uncertain futures.

Anderson met Jones. He rapidly attempted to master the art of staying away from the gunnery sergeant. As with the other Marines in Fox, he was unsuccessful. Collectively, the troops knew the gunny had eyes in the back of his head. In fact, most believed he had eyes growing out of every pore of his skin. Anderson became convinced Jones hated him more than anybody else in the company.

At Phu Lac (6), Anderson met Graham's company radio operator, Brent MacKinnon. MacKinnon was far more than a radio operator. "Mac", as he was known, was an intellectual from Northern California. He could read a map and call artillery and air support whenever needed.

His rapport with the company commander was exceptional. The two fit like a hand and a glove. As far as Anderson was concerned, Mackinnon was Fox Company's resident genius, matched only by his likeability.

Corporal Mike Nutt, their squad leader who Marengo had taken Anderson to meet on his first night with Fox, assigned Anderson and Dale McCauley to man an open foxhole on their third night in Phu Lac (6).

"Where are you from, Dale?" Anderson asked.

"I'm from Uhrichsville, Ohio. How about you, Andy?"

"Oh, I'm from a little place in Arkansas, no one's ever heard of. But the last few years, I was down in Panama chasing drug smugglers." Anderson paused, then added, "Man, that was pretty exciting. Damn drug runners are pretty slick in figuring different ways to bring that crap from their country."

"Wow, that must have been exciting!"

Even in the dark, Anderson could see the outline of McCauley's handsome young face, though he couldn't see McCauley's broken front tooth he had seen earlier in the day. He wondered why McCauley never had it repaired. "You're a tall guy, did you ever play any sports in Ohio?"

"Well, last year I was the leading scorer on my high school basketball team."

"That's cool, Dale. What are you going to do when you get out all of Nam? Are you going to play basketball in college?"

"Tell you what, Andy, when I get home the first thing I am going to do is to get married to my sweetheart."

"What's her name?"

"Nancy, but we all call her Nan," he smiled to himself.

"Way to go, Man," Anderson approved, nodding his head.

"Andy, how about me taking the first watch?" McCauley asked.

"It's okay with me."

"All right, I'll wake you at midnight," McCauley remarked easily.

"Yeah, I haven't had my first adventure outside the wire. Corporal Nutt says we're taking off about 0700. Wake me at midnight."

The planned departure did not take place as scheduled. Instead, at 0700, the captain assembled Nutt and his squad. Graham took extra time and care to brief them. He had them remember all the frequencies, wanted to be sure they knew exactly how to call in air strikes and artillery, and reviewed medevac procedures.

Finally at 0735, Nutt made his final inspection. "I know we're running a bit late, guys," he corporal explained. "But it will be worth it. I haven't had as thorough a briefing from any officers or staff since I've joined the company."

McCauley led the squad out of the Phu Lac (6) outpost and down the dirt road leading to An Hoa. Anderson followed McCauley; Groch was right behind him. Anderson felt good, safe almost; he was in the saddle with two in-country veterans on either side.

After marching two kilometers the squad abruptly exited the road in a southeastern direction and moved into a tree line. There was a break in the tree line after seventy-five meters that exposed an enormous rice paddy complex. Anderson spied the rice paddy dykes that the other Marines had been talking about. This rice paddy complex contained numerous islands, the closest one over one hundred meters away. Each island had palm trees and two to three thatched roof huts. Nutt spread the squad out along the tree line. He told a couple of men to watch for any movement behind them. "This is strange," he murmured as if to himself, "so far we haven't seen any Vietnamese in the hooches along our tree line." His words triggered an uneasy quiet.

"Fox Three, Fox Three, this is Three Alpha, over," he called over the radio.

"Three Alpha, this is Three, over."

"Roger Three, we're at Check Point 2, over. Moving to Check Point 3, out."

Nutt pointed to McCauley, Groch, and Anderson. He gestured for them to move forward to his position. When they arrived, he filled them in, "I want you three to move to that closest island out there and that check out those hooches." They nodded. "Stay fifteen meters apart in case there is any VC out there to greet us," he directed.

McCauley sprinted ahead, then Anderson, and finally Groch. McCauley took a prone position, searching around the edge of the island by the time Anderson reached the island. After a moment or two, McCauley felt confident enough to crawl, low, over to the first hooch. He ducked his head quickly in and out of the entrance, then back in again. He flagged the other two Marines over to him. "Andy, take a look in that hooch over there. Bud, show him how to search a 'slope' hooch."

"Slope" was the troops' term for those Vietnamese who were in between "villagers" or good guys and "gooks" the bad guys. Slopes would support the VC, but the government was always trying to win their "hearts and minds". The rules of war that the Marines followed were: shoot gooks, but not slopes. Trouble was, they all dressed in black pajamas, and seemed to look alike. The hardest part to identifying the differences occurred when a gook wasn't carrying a rifle.

Most small hamlets contained numerous below-ground bomb shelters. "Lai de. Di di mau." Groch yelled in Vietnamese. "Come here. Come quickly," he had called into the bomb shelter. McCauley explained that the locals understood Marines would not hurt them if they came out of the shelters. After eliciting no response, Groch threw a frag grenade into one of the shelters. The depth of the shelter muffled its explosion, revealing only a large cloud of red dust. McCauley returned to the edge of the island and waved for the rest of the squad to join them.

Once the squad had joined McCauley, Anderson, and Groch, Nutt ordered them to continue to the next island another one hundred meters away. McCauley led with Anderson and Groch behind him. The three traveled about fifty meters when a machine gun and several semi-automatic weapons opened up on them spraying water and mud around them. The enemy attacked from a lone tree line 150 meters on their right flank. Having observed the Marines' entire movement, they had waited until the entire squad had placed itself on the first small island. Now the squad was trapped there. They could not move without openly exposing and endangering themselves.

Anderson dove into the muddy water behind a protective bank, as did his two buddies, Groch and McCauley while the rest of the squad opened up with return fire from the small island. Nutt shouted to them, "Get back here! Get back here with the rest of us!"

Groch and Anderson slithered through the muddy water as rounds cracked over their heads and ate into the other side of the bank. Anderson twisted back to check on McCauley. His tall body lay halfway on top of the dike. The dike gripped his feet preventing McCauley's lame attempts to free himself.

"Shit!" Anderson grunted, his voice reaching an unusually high pitch. McCauley had been hit bad if he could hardly move his feet. Groch and Anderson reached the clump of huts. Anderson crawled close to Nutt who was already on the radio explaining the situation. Nutt made short work of their situation: there were an estimated twenty to thirty enemy firing on them; the enemy's rounds were hitting the dirt and the top of the huts around them; Private First Class Reed had been wounded in the thigh and was bleeding badly; Doc Wodja had been hit in the arm and calf while kneeling to patch Reed up. Two others were wounded. Disregarding his own wounds and Nutt's cautionary warnings, Wodja crawled from one wounded Marine to the other assisting them where he could.

"Andy, can you get out there and bring McCauley in?" Nutt yelled.

"You bet!" Anderson responded automatically. He took off his helmet, flak jacket, and web belt, laid down his rifle and two LAAWs, and looked out at McCauley with whom he shared a foxhole the night before and who now seemed like 1,000 meters away.

As fast as he could while bending down attempting to duck the rounds flying over his head, Anderson ran. Within eight meters of McCauley he dove, landing in the muddy water just a couple of feet from McCauley's body. At once, watered-down blood that appeared to be pumping out from an area directly below McCauley's right armpit saturated Anderson. McCauley eyes opened. Upon seeing Anderson, McCauley looked surprised, as if had been awakened from a deep sleep.

"Andy, let's do Detroit city," he murmured calmly, quietly.

Anderson had only moments to perceive how out of it McCauley was, "How about let's get the fuck out of here, Mac!"

Anderson rose, slung McCauley's lanky body over his shoulder, and ran. Ran, ran, ran while all around him the noise of enemy bullets swooped like swarming bees that zipped through the air surrounding them. McCauley seemed amazingly light. In record time, Anderson was back in the small hamlet, gingerly laying McCauley onto the ground. McCauley never spoke again. He sort of blinked. His skin grew ashen. He had run out of blood.

Doc crawled over to assist, looked over at Anderson and shook his head. Trying to save McCauley was useless. He was already gone. Anderson stared mutely into the wide-open eyes of the first dead Marine he had ever seen. That sight etched itself in the back of his mind…forever. He crawled over to the rest of his squad and began to return fire on the enemy.

Announced by the tremendous rattle of rotating tracks one hundred meters behind the stranded Marines, three tanks barreled through the tree line that Anderson's squad had moved through earlier. Within a minute the noisy tanks passed by Nutt's squad while firing angrily at the enemy positions. Fighter jets dove from the sky onto the invisible enemy. The squad stood up and cheered as the balance of the 3rd Platoon followed in trace of the tanks. Marengo marched by the once-trapped men in the front of the Marine column that followed the center tank.

Anderson hollered over to Nutt, "Damn if Staff Sergeant Marengo doesn't look like John Wayne!"

Nutt nodded back to Anderson, saying, "Good job, Andy. I'm really proud you're in our squad." Peering down at the M-16 rifle in Anderson's hand, his voice laced with squelched laughter, Nutt reminded him, "But it's time to put in a new magazine."

Anderson's smile vanished as looked down and spied a bullet hole in the center of his magazine.

Within thirty minutes, Graham and the 1st and 2nd Platoons arrived at the tree line. By this time the 3rd Platoon successfully completed the helicopter evacuation of Reed and Wodja as well as McCauley's body. Two wounded Marines refused evacuation and were allowed to stay with the squad.

By this time, the enemy had begun its escape to the northeast attempting to reach the safety of Go Noi Island. Graham sent the 3rd Platoon and the three tanks back to the elevated main service road. From that location the tank's crew had a view of all the rice paddies for about five miles toward Go Noi Island. The tanks sat ready to seal the enemy's escaped to the northeast. 3rd Platoon could react in any direction with the three tanks there for mobility if needed. Immediately, Graham led the rest of the company in the pursuit of the escaping enemy. With lightening speed they moved in a southeastern direction cutting any escape to the foothills that ran from An Hoa to Go Noi Island.

An aerial observer, AO, called in air strikes directed on three enemy he spotted fleeing east. He reported two VC probably killed and one VC confirmed killed.

Now cut off from any hope of reaching their Go Noi sanctuary, the enemy split into two groups, each group consisted of eight to twelve VC. In separate directions both attempted to escape to the northeast across the Song Thu Bon. Fox swung back on the two groups in their attack. F-4 Phantoms arrived on station. Graham called in 105mm artillery support from Phu Lac (6) and had his own 60mm mortars fire on the now confused and disoriented enemy.

By 1700 Fox clamped down on one group and had killed five VC. The AO flew over an area where the 105 rounds impacted and reported another 10 VC probably killed.

In desperation, four VC from the other group broke out in a run across the rice paddies right into the face of the tanks. Within seconds .50 caliber machine guns cut them down confirming four more VC dead.

Fox continued chasing the last of the second group until 1800 when one Marine tripped a necklace grenade booby trap that detonated four M-26 grenades and wounded nine Marines. Once the medevac was completed, the light of day was nearly extinguished. The company was ordered back to Phu Lac (6). Fox and their combat support team had killed eleven VC and approximately ten more while suffering one killed and nine wounded.

From that day forward Fox's unity jelled under the demanding leadership of Captain Jim Graham. The officers, staff non-commissioned officers, and non-commissioned officers shared one common purpose: to aggressively destroy the enemy. The troops no longer harbored ill feelings about filling sand bags and somehow figured even that had a purpose. With each passing encounter, they felt more like racehorses, anxious to get out of the gate, fully confident that they would bag some enemy that day. Fox had distinguished itself as a supremely confident combat organization. In fact, the battalion commander wrote in his command chronology at the end of the month, "The aggressive spirit of the Marines in 2/5 was demonstrated by two members of Company F, who, although wounded, refused medical evacuation until the completion of their mission. The seriousness of their wounds made later evacuation necessary."

CHAPTER 4: UNION II

By the end of April, Fox had gained a significant edge over the enemy in the An Hoa valley and western portion of Go Noi Island. As a result, their enthusiasm to go out on platoon- and squad-size search and destroy patrols grew exceptionally high. As a matter of fact, for their aggressive performance during the 14 April engagement, Lieutenant Colonel Mal Jackson sent the company to China Beach for two days of in-country R&R.

The company, less the rather unfortunate 2nd Platoon, which remained on guard at Phu Lac (6), flew by helicopter to Da Nang. Trucks took them directly to China Beach. The men were wholly unprepared for such a luxurious experience. The white sand sparkled like diamond dust and the rippling South China Sea warmed and eased even the most war-torn souls. The escape from the war was immediately evident. They slept in beach cabanas with racks and mattresses, one for each Marine. And there was beer, an endless amount of beer available to the troops who attempted to make up for all the nights they didn't have beer while in the field.

On the first night, before Gunnery Sergeant Jones put a stop to it, some Marines even snuck out of the beach compound to enjoy the nightlife in downtown Da Nang. Those men, however, guarded the tales of their raucous adventures from the rest and no one but they knew what really happened that night.

Corporal Melvin Long, a squad leader with the 3rd Platoon, had plotted Staff Sergeant Tony Marengo's toss into the South China Sea ever since he'd heard they were headed to China Beach. The sly Marengo was potentially difficult to corner, but Long had his mind made up. The men of the 3rd Platoon knew that physically, Corporal Long would have no problems handling Marengo alone. Quite simply, Melvin Long was the biggest, strongest, and baddest man in the entire company. With a reputation of being an all star football player in high school, absolutely no one would even think about challenging this gentle giant. But Melvin did not want to go it alone. He first instructed Corporal Pat "Water Buffalo" Haley, "Meet me over by the end table in the shade. Over there, Water Buffalo," he said pointing that long arm of his.

CORPORAL MELVIN LONG
(Photo courtesy of Pat Haley)

"Anything you say, Boss."

Long had another thought, "No wait. Go get that new guy Anderson. Bring him along too. I'm going to get 'Big Eyes.'"

"What's going on, Corporal Long?" Haley asked when the four gathered around the table.

Long sat down with a solemn look on his face, "We're going to make hit on Marengo."

Eyebrows went up.

"What the hell do you mean?" Lance Corporal "Big Eyes" Ken Reynolds demanded.

"We need to get that old man's body separated from the staff and officers long enough so that we can snare his butt and toss him in to the South China Sea. Are you men with me?"

...And so the plotting began.

Marengo, unaware of his soggy fate, resisted at first, but then felt honored to join the volleyball team consisting of Long, Anderson, Reynolds, and Haley. It would be a game for pride: the 3rd Platoon against the 1st Platoon and Company Headquarters. "Okay, I'm all for showing that 3rd Platoon is the best at anything!" Tony Marengo naively agreed.

The game took place in the sand fifty meters from the water's edge. The 1st Platoon and Headquarters team consisted of Captain Graham, Second Lieutenant Charles Shultz, Sergeant Gerry Ackley, Corporal Lloyd Woods, and Lance Corporal Brent McKinnon

Little did the great platoon sergeant, Tony Marengo, know about what was to happen at the precise moment his team scored their fifth point. Amazingly, it seemed that the rest of the company did, because by the time the game had reached a 2–2 tie, all Fox men had circled the volleyball court, Gunnery Sergeant Jones yelling the loudest. To no one's surprise, most were cheering for the 3rd Platoon's team. Boos and heckling calls were spat out when the other team dared to be competitive. After Lloyd Woods won a point, one heckler yelled, "Hey, Woods, you don't have to try that hard. We're on vacation!"

The fifth point came. Marengo grunted in surprise and alarm when his own team turned, tackling him mercilessly. Soon each conspirator held an arm or a leg. Marengo fought like a wildcat but to no avail. When Long yelled, "Should we throw him in?" the entire company agreed with a boisterous cheer. With a giant splash and a stream of explicatives slipping out from the man himself, Staff Sergeant Tony Marengo was unceremoniously plopped into the shiny sea. When

Marengo emerged, sputtering and spitting in surprise and disbelief, Captain Graham, known for his straight-laced personality, burst into laughter. Marengo had no choice but to forgive his wicked jokesters and join in the enjoyment his dumping had provided all. Then, as per China Beach custom, Fox partied on, way into the night.

The fun at China Beach ended too quickly. Before the men could dream up any more practical jokes, Fox boarded choppers, and flew back to An Hoa.

Upon their return from China Beach, all the "mud-Marines" were ready to go back to the field. But they weren't alone. First Sergeant Lee continued pestering Jones whose answer was still, "Not this time, Top." Lance Corporal John Painter, the unit diary clerk and a college graduate, wanted to get out and "kick butt" with the rest of them. Additionally, Private First Class Tommy LaBarbera, the admin clerk who kept begging to go to the field, had already requested a change in his occupationally specialty from "administration" to "infantry".

Fox's hard-charging-war-machine reputation became well established within the battalion. From 11 May to 20 May, during smaller-sized search and destroy operations, Fox ripped up Antenna Valley, netting twenty enemy killed, three POWs captured, and thirty-eight detainees collected, without sustaining any casualties. While Fox was slugging it out in An Hoa and the Antenna Valley, Operation Union, later known as Union I, took place thirty miles southeast of An Hoa from 28 April through 12 May.

Union I was a battle for control of the Que Son Basin, a triangular-shaped flat land with Hiep Duc Village at its western apex and National Highway 1, QL/1, at its wide end. The Que Son basin was an agriculturally rich piece of land containing some 60,000 Vietnamese residents. The basin had been under the control of the Communists for twenty-five years. This was the final destination for many NVA soldiers traveling south, down the Ho Chi Minh Trail and also served as the home of the NVA's 2nd Army Division.

Lance Corporal John Gobrecht, who had been wounded for the second time on an operation in mid-April, this time in the elbow, was aboard the hospital ship, Sanctuary, when casualties from Operation Union began arriving at the ship. A friend of his from boot camp, who had been wounded during Union, told him that his battalion had a seventy to a ninety percent casualty rate. In fact, while the enemy suffered 865 killed and 173 detained during the operation, the friendly forces suffered 110 killed with 473 wounded, plus two missing in action. After Gobrecht departed the ship and returned to An Hoa, Corporal Perry Jones greeted him at the entrance of the Weapons hut. Perry had become the machine gun team-leader in the 3rd Platoon. "Welcome back, Hanover. How's that elbow?"

"Hey P.J.! Great seeing you! Oh, the arm's a bit stiff, but I can move it. See?"

P.J. Jones smiled, "John, you know Corporal Rick Barnes. He's going to be the section leader that you'll be supporting in the 2nd Platoon. You're taking my place as the team leader for the guns and I'm gonna' to be the section leader for the guns with the '3rd Herd.'"

"That's great. I've been waiting to be team leader," Gobrecht smiled an endearing, lopsided grin. Then, turning, commented, "Nice seeing you, Corporal Barnes."

"Sure…likewise, John," Barnes nodded. "Hey, call me Rick."

"You guys hear about Operation Union?" Gobrecht asked.

"Well, the Sea Tiger and the Stars and Stripes've been saying Marines kicked some ass," Jones noted in his sincere Georgian drawl.

"P.J., I have only one thing to say about Operation Union, and that is: I'm glad Fox wasn't on it. We would have got'n torn up, too!" The men agreed heartily. 110 Marines killed was a staggering number, even for the most seasoned Marines.

However, soon after the completion of Operation Union, two separate Marine Corps reconnaissance patrols reported seeing between 3,000 and 4,000 NVA soldiers in the Que Son Valley. After studying these reports, the US and South Vietnamese governments concluded there was a need for a follow-on operation. With that, the planning for

Operation Union II began. The principal Vietnamese forces for the operation were the 6th ARVN Regiment and 1st ARVN Ranger Group. The 1st Marine Division was the principal maneuver force and would use the 5th and 7th Marine Regiments during this operation.

Colonel Kenny Houghton, a World War II hero, commanded the 5th Regiment. Houghton had his 1st and 3rd Battalions available for Union II. The 2nd Battalion would remain in An Hoa. The 3rd Battalion, 3/5, had three rifle companies available for the operation. On the other hand 1/5, commanded by Lieutenant Colonel Hilgartner, only had Alpha and Delta Companies and needed a third company in order to maneuver and to employ a reserve force if needed. Houghton turned to Lieutenant Colonel Jackson, the 2/5 commander, to nominate his most aggressive company, filling the needs of the 1st Battalion. Fox Company was nominated.

"Jones, I don't care what you want to do, you are not going on this operation," Graham responded to the raspy voice of his company gunnery sergeant. "Dr. Tom Viti told me that you have walking pneumonia. Now, I don't even know how a tough old Marine like you could even catch a cold, but the Doc said he didn't want you to go. Besides that, with Gunny Green's arrival, I'm lucky enough to have two top field leaders. It's your turn to stay back and get ready for the next operation."

"Skipper, you know Green's new in country," Jones protested weakly.

"I know," Graham responded quickly, as though he anticipated the gunny's argument. "He'll do just fine. Gunny, you'll have this place to yourself. I'm bringing Top Lee along. Top will assist Green if he needs it. And I'm taking Lance Corporal Painter and PFC LaBarbera, so they can stop bugging the first sergeant about not getting out to the field. An Hoa will be all yours."

"I don't know, Sir," Jones relented, shaking his head.

D-Day for Union II was 26 May. On that day, Lima and Mike Companies of the 3rd Battalion engaged a large, entrenched enemy force north of their landing zone as they entered a battlefield three kilometers west of Vinh Huy village. The enemy halted their progress, and the

Marines' casualties mounted. Lieutenant Colonel Esslinger maneuvered India Company into the fray and successfully outflanked the enemy. During the first day's battle 118 enemy were killed. However, 3/5 suffered thirty-eight killed, including Lieutenant Colonel Esslinger, and eighty-two wounded. Blocking forces were set in place to trap the enemy but as usual, they vanished. Colonel Houghton's gut feeling was that the NVA headed south out of the Que Son Basin and into the bordering foothills. He resolved to flush them out and into another decisive battle.

Fox's operational control, OPCON, was passed from 2/5 to 1/5 on 27 May at 1830 hours. On the next day, the company, all 154 of them and their attachments, waited on the An Hoa airstrip for a helo lift to get them to Union II.

"John," Private First Class LaBarbera said to Lance Corporal Painter, "you ever been on a helicopter before?"

"Yeah, I had a couple rides at LeJeune. Nothing like this. I just took the mail out to the guys who were on two-week exercises. There surely wasn't any hot LZ to worry about!"

"Right," LaBarbera agreed wondering why he'd asked the question. He hadn't thought about whether or not the LZ would be hot until this point. LaBarbera recalled the warnings he'd received when he arrived in country three months ago: "You'll be fine as long as you don't get assigned to the 5th Marines," someone had said. Of course, he was assigned to the 5th Marines.

When that happened, someone else said, "Just don't get to the 2nd Battalion." Predictably, he reported into the 2/5.

Then he heard his last warning, "Just don't get assigned to Fox Company!" So, here he was, flying out with Fox on a big operation, which he somehow volunteered to go on, and the LZ maybe hot. He must be nuts!

The first wave of choppers, picked up the 1st and 2nd Platoons, along with their Weapons Platoon attachments. They flew to a landing zone between Highway 535 and the Song Ly Ly to join forces with the rest of the 1st Battalion. The remainder of the company, including LaBarbera, waited for the second wave.

The birds came back, but landed near some waiting trucks across the runway. Large green items were being thrown out of the choppers. Initially, some Marines thought that the items were body bags, but it turned out to be flak jackets. The 1st Battalion was not wearing them, so Captain Graham decided his company wouldn't wear them either.

LaBarbera's first helicopter flight, by most accounts, was uneventful. But for a young kid from the Brooklyn, this was more than exciting. He peered through the small CH-46 windows at the mountains below as the bird flew south about twenty miles from An Hoa. So captured by the experience, he hadn't noticed that he had been sitting on his right leg for the entire flight.

As the rear wheels of the chopper touched the ground, the crew chief began his customary, "Get off! Get off!" Private First Class LaBarbera, combat equipment and all, stood up facing the opened rear of the plane with his left leg fully functional and the right one retaining absolutely no feeling at all. He made one step towards the exit and fell flat on his face as the "dead asleep" leg crumbled beneath him. First Sergeant Lee and Lance Corporal Painter looked down at their now, very humble admin comrade, laughed, and dragged him down the ramp.

On 30 May, the 1st Battalion, with Fox, flew from its more central position in the Que Son Basin to the highlands in the basin's southeast corner. By 31 May, 1/5's three companies, Alpha, Delta, and Fox, began maneuvering around the mountains to the north and then went westward toward the village of Vinh Huy. This village was just three kilometers east of location where 3/5 fought on D-Day on 26 May. Beyond that were the blocking forces from the 3rd Battalion; this time they would trap the elusive 3rd NVA Regiment.

For the next two days, enemy patrols and snipers engaged the 1st Battalion along the way to their final objective near the village of Vinh Huy. In the evening the NVA probed their night defensive positions.

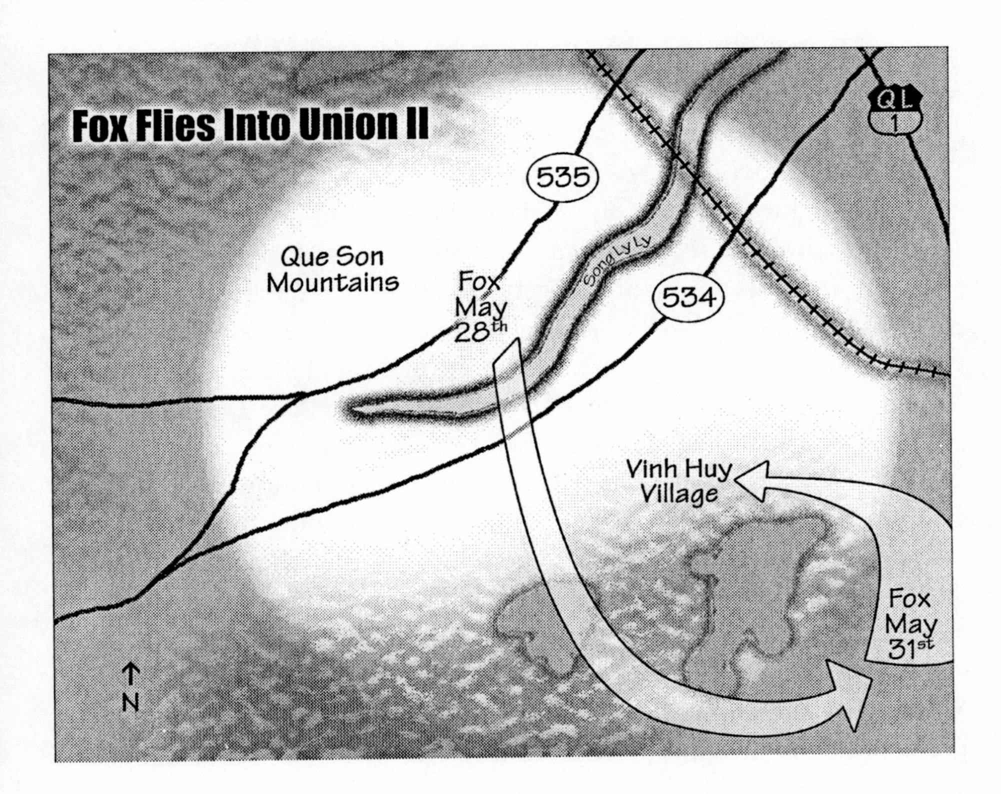

On 2 June the battalion was in a classic two-up and one-back formation. Fox and Delta Companies were forward, and Alpha Company was in reserve. Delta Company was 800 meters north of Fox; their final objective, Chau Lam (5), lay at the junction of an unmarked dirt road and Highway 534. Fox's final objective was the hamlet of Vinh Huy (2), part of an old, destroyed French village split by the same unmarked dirt road that stretched two kilometers between the objectives.

On 3 June, the battalion was on the move by 0600. At 0620 and at 1030 hours that morning, as Fox moved, they began receiving small arms fire from NVA soldiers who attempted to delay their advance. The company returned fire and continued their forward push.

At 1050 Fox held up briefly when a helicopter dropped off a "Kit Carson Scout" to join them for the day. Thruong Kinh was prematurely wrinkled at the age of thirty-five. Fox's interpreter, who had been with them since they left An Hoa, reported that Kinh had defected from the Viet Cong last July. After training, he had been designated a Kit Carson Scout for the Marines. "What the heck are we going to do with him, Skipper?" First Sergeant Lee asked.

"I'm going to pass him on to Marengo, Top, but keep an eye on him 'til we get a hold of Tony," Graham murmured hesitantly.

At 1130, Delta Company began sweeping a large rice paddy 600 meters in front of its final objective. From a dozen Viet Cong they began taking automatic weapons fire. They returned fire, killing four of them. Bracing themselves, the men of Fox prepared to face the same large enemy force that had vanished after 3/5's battle a week ago. Lance Corporal Dennis Sheehy, the 2nd Platoon radio operator, asked his new Platoon Sergeant, Gerry Ackley, who when promoted to sergeant was transferred from the 1st Platoon, "So tell me, Sarge…how does it feel to finally be out in the field on this your last day of your six-month extension?"

"Pay attention to where you're going, Sheehy. Oh, and tell Lieutenant Shultz that the company CP Group has just caught up with us. I'm going back and give this piece of comm wire we found to the skipper to see what he makes of it."

Captain Graham needed only one look at the communications wire, which was used by the NVA in their defensive positions. Fox's enemy was waiting for them! Knowing his lead platoon was about to enter the same rice paddy in which Delta was engaging the VC, he ordered his radio operator, Lance Corporal MacKinnon, to have the company hold up. From his vantage point through breaks in the trees, Graham could see to the far side of the rice paddy. Wisely, he called for air and artillery support before moving across the paddy.

"Sir," Corporal Cox the forward observer barked, "Battalion said that air and artillery support would not be available. They've already prepped the area."

"That's bull. You call Tam Ky directly for prep-fire," Graham bit back defiantly.

On their right flank, the sounds of rapid rifle fire and munitions increased measurably as Delta Company's battle with the enemy intensified.

Turning to his battalion radio operator, Graham said, "Corporal Dirickson, let me speak to Millbrook Six," referring to Lieutenant Colonel Hilgartner.

"Getting him now, Sir."

While waiting, Captain Graham turned around to the 3rd Platoon's point man and asked if "Water Buffalo" Haley was close by. Haley, one of the company's most experienced 3.5" rocketmen, dashed forward.

"Sir!"

"Water Bu, do you think you could hit a tree across the rice paddy with a 3.5?"

"Yes, Sir. You want me to fire one now?"

"No, just checking. We may be needing them before the day is out. Thanks," Graham answered, nodding his head.

"Sir, I have Colonel Hilgartner on the radio," Dirickson offered.

The men gathered near Graham listened intently to his side of the communiqué.

"Millbrook Six, this is Fox Six, over," he began. "Roger, Sir. I can't send my company across that large rice field unless I prep the area first. I need air or arty support, over," Graham insisted.

The Marines of Fox shared surprised, slightly angered looks as Graham pleaded his case. "Maybe so, Sir, but that prep fire was a long time ago, over."

Hilgartner's response was quick in coming.

"In that case we need to get up on Hill B to set up our own machine guns to provide cover, over," Graham countered. His Marines exchanged stunned glances with one another. Why wouldn't the Battalion give them air support?

"I spoke to Delta Six before he came under fire, and he said he didn't get this far south," Graham argued. "Yes, I know Delta's getting beat up over there, but unless we get some support right now we'll get beat up as well, over."

Graham was silent for a moment. “Well, at least let me have one round of arty to register,” he remonstrated. If the artillery battery was able to hit its objective accurately with one howitzer then, when called to do so, the other howitzers could also act immediately and accurately by using the same registration data.

“Aye, aye, Sir,” came Graham’s final, tight-lipped reply.

Gunnery Sergeant Green and Lance Corporal MacKinnon registered the disgust in Graham’s tone.

Graham stared at nothing, managing his frustration. To no one he blurted in disbelief, “He just gave me a direct order to move out.”

Green and MacKinnon understood the captain’s frustration. Direct orders were given only to subordinates when they did not understand or were tending to refuse the direction of the senior. Not complying with a direct order had the most serious consequences. However, there was no question in the minds of the three of them that complying with this direct order without prep fires was tantamount to suicide. Never the less...........Graham turned, “Mac, get me the actuals,” he said referring to his rifle platoon commanders: Second Lieutenant Shultz, 1st Platoon; Second Lieutenant Kelsey, 2nd Platoon; and Staff Sergeant Marengo, 3rd Platoon.

“Here you are, Sir,” Mackinnon said handing the captain the handset.

“Fox One, I’ve asked for arty and air support and it’s been denied. You’ll have to be cautious going across that field. Keep alert for anything that moves; the enemy are experts at camouflaging. As you can hear, Delta Company is heavily engaged with at least one company of NVA, over,” Graham directed.

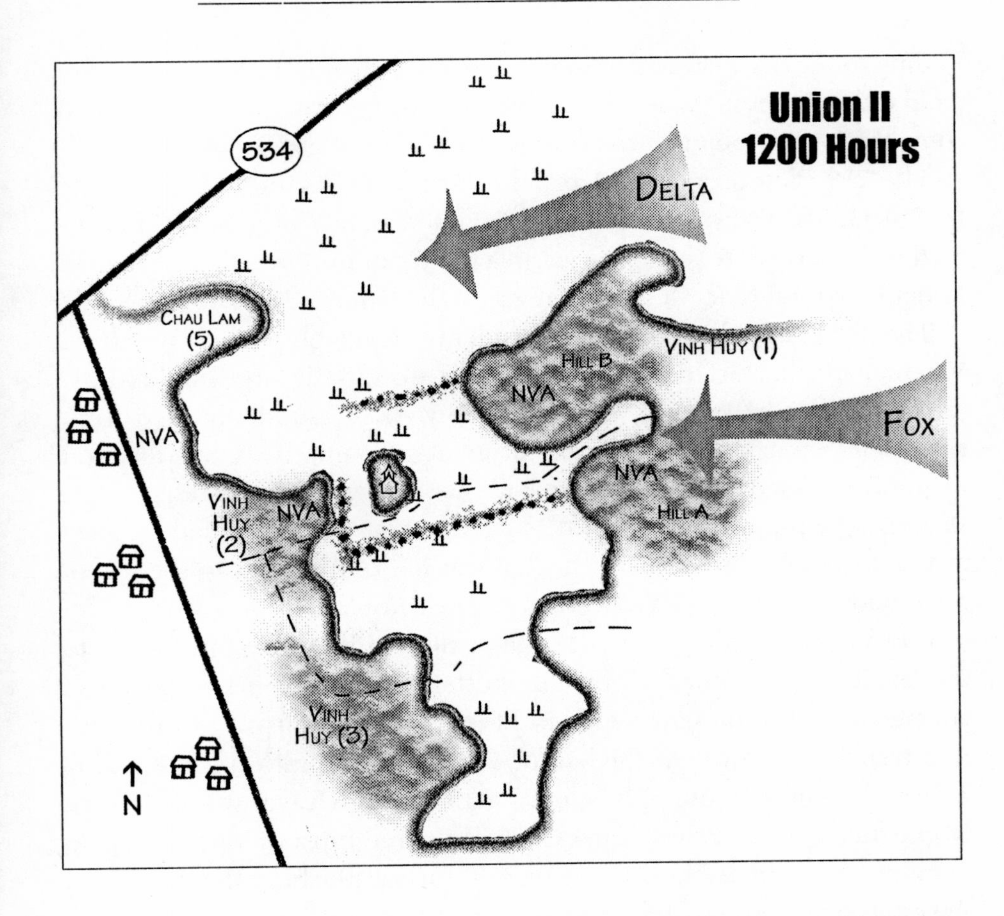

"Roger One, Fox Two will be behind you," Graham explained. "You follow the path between the two hills, then bear right when you hit the paddy. If it's possible, tie in with Delta Company. Fox Two, you are on the backside of Hill B. I want you to move down the face of that hill and when you get to the paddy, cross behind Fox One and come on line on their left flank. Fox One and Two, I want you to make your final assault with both platoons on line. Fox Three will be in reserve. Everyone copy that? Over."

"All right. Let's move out," Graham stated with resolve.

1205 hours. The 1st Platoon marched down off of the high ground between Hill A and Hill B. Steady in their descent, they followed a path leading to the rice field settled in the conclave between the hills. At the rice paddy, the platoon turned forty-five degrees towards the northwest to allow the 2nd Platoon to cross behind them when it arrived in the field.

The 2nd Platoon's descent proved tougher. They moved across the face of Hill B. The drop was only forty meters, but large boulders covered its face. Despite the obstacles, in a matter of minutes, the lead squad under Corporal Mac McDonald reached the field.

The 2nd Platoon's second squad under the leadership of Corporal Ted Varena had just started climbing over and around the large boulders littering the face of the hill when an enemy AK-47 suddenly fired from their left. Amazingly, the firing originated from the same location through which the 1st Platoon had just passed. Private First Class Werner, gasping from the painful, sucking chest-wound he had received in the onslaught, cried out with what was left of his lungs to the rest of his squad, "They're in NVA uniforms! Their not VC!"

Instantly, along the southern edge of rice field seventy-five meters to the left, Lance Corporal Gobrecht spotted ten to fifteen NVA regulars covered with camouflage which hid their khaki uniforms, running out of a trench line, through the bamboo tree line and into the rice paddy below. The enemy wore pith helmets with bamboo leaves stuck in them. Gobrecht's gunner, Private First Class Mills, and most of Varena's squad opened up on the backs of NVA troops, further flushing them out into the open rice field.

Corporal Mac McDonald's squad—already in the field, and, by this point on the company's far left flank—immediately turned and assaulted the enemy soldiers. Mac's attacking squad, consisting of Lance Corporal Art Byrd, Private First Class Mike McCandless, Lance Corporal Mike Hernandez, Private First Class Legere, Private First Class Wainscott, and Corporal Thom Searfoss, fired their weapons as they charged into the enemy. The Marines overpowered the unwitting group who were more interested in escaping than fighting. The bodies of the wounded and dead NVA were scattered from the edge of the tree line nearly forty meters into the paddy.

"Hey, Sheehy, tell Fox Six that the 1st Squad just bagged fifteen NVA in the paddy in front of Hill A," Second Lieutenant Straughan Kelsey mentioned the radio operator. With that, the last of the 2nd Platoon began entering the dry flat rice field to begin searching the fallen NVA soldiers. The soldiers appeared to be quite young. Heavy, their packs were filled with rocket-propelled grenades, RPGs, AK-47 munitions, and 82mm mortar rounds.

By the time the entire 2nd Platoon was fifty meters into the rice paddy and had peeled off to the left, the company command group entered the scene. The rice paddy, now clearly visible to Graham, was 350 meters deep. It ran left to right about 450 meters across. The tree line directly in front was obviously the hamlet of Vinh Huy (2), Fox's objective. Along their entire left flank was a hedgerow of bamboo trees. On their right was another hedgerow of bamboo trees, but, unlike the first, this one did not enclose the entire field. This hedgerow stopped about seventy-five meters shy of the hamlet and exposed another 600 to 800 meters of rice field, somewhere close to where Delta was fighting. Graham recognized his company's huge vulnerability, and it pressed down upon him like he was Atlas, the weight of the world on his shoulders.

Finally joining the 1st and 2nd Platoons, Graham directed First Sergeant Lee to move the wounded prisoners to the rear of the company column to the 3rd Platoon's location and get the POWs ready for choppering out to the rear. "Top, stay with Staff Sergeant Marengo. I'm taking Painter and LaBarbera with the CP. If you need me, call me on the radio."

"Aye, Aye, Sir. Good luck."

1310 hours. The pitched battle up in Delta Company's area continued. As Fox moved forward cautiously, Delta's fight served as a gruesome omen for the men of 2/5. Rounds that strayed from the Delta Company engagement flew overhead or landed in the rice field near the Marines. Fox's unit leaders shouted orders, "Stay down if you are not involved with the POWs!"

Despite the dangerous and sporadic small arms fire Kinh, the Kit Carson Scout, had wandered up near the 1st Platoon's position. His eyes studied the rice field. Slowly and methodically, he scanned back and forth as though looking for something lost. Raising his weapon, he pointed the muzzle at the ground thirty to forty meters ahead of him. Lance Corporal Gobrecht observed the scout and motioned to his gun team leader, Corporal Rick Barnes, "Hey, Rick," he whispered. "Look at that VN over there behind the 1st Platoon."

Rick had no sooner turned when he witnessed Kinh fire six rounds without hesitation into the field. Severed straw flew into the air as the rounds impacted the ground. Kinh moved purposefully towards the impact area, firing three more rounds.

Gobrecht headed toward the scout. Now he too spotted another patch of recently cut grass. Carefully, he approached it. It was a spider trap. He peered at it intently then opened up with a short burst from his tracer-filled M-16 magazine. He and Barnes crept up to it. Barnes nudged the grass that covered the spider-trap-hiding-place with his M-16 and found two dead NVA.

1330 Hours. With the 1st and 2nd Platoons maneuvering on line for their final assault, the 3rd Platoon began entering the rice paddy using the same path between Hills A and B that the 1st Platoon had taken. Corporal Conley's squad had the lead. Lance Corporal Ken "Big Eyes" Reynolds was the squad's pointman because he could see better than any one else in the platoon. In the paddy, he skirted the base of Hill A but was careful not to move out into the field. On the short side of forty meters he stopped, turned back to Conley, held his M-16 over his head with the barrel pointed toward the top of the hill, and with a hoarse voice, whispered, "Hey, Chuck, we got company. I saw movement up there."

Conley motioned for his fire team leaders to get back through the bamboo tree line, the same one that the fifteen NVA had moved through not one hour earlier when they were gunned down by the 2nd Platoon. He called Marengo on his squad radio, "Fox Three, this is Three Alpha. We saw movement on the hill, and we're going to check it out."

Instantly, Marengo relayed the message to the company commander, Fox Six. Graham replied, "That's a negative. The hill is already secured, and I don't want you to get far behind us."

"Roger, Six. I'll pull them back, out," Marengo acknowledged.

1350 hours. The company began its trek across the rice field. The 1st and 2nd platoons were on line each with two squads forward. The Marines readied themselves for resistance as they grew closer and closer to the line of bamboo trees masking Vinh Huy (2), their ultimate objective. Due to the shape of the paddy on the left, the 2nd Platoon neared the tree line from almost 200 meters away while the 1st Platoon, perhaps 250 meters from it, approached from the right.

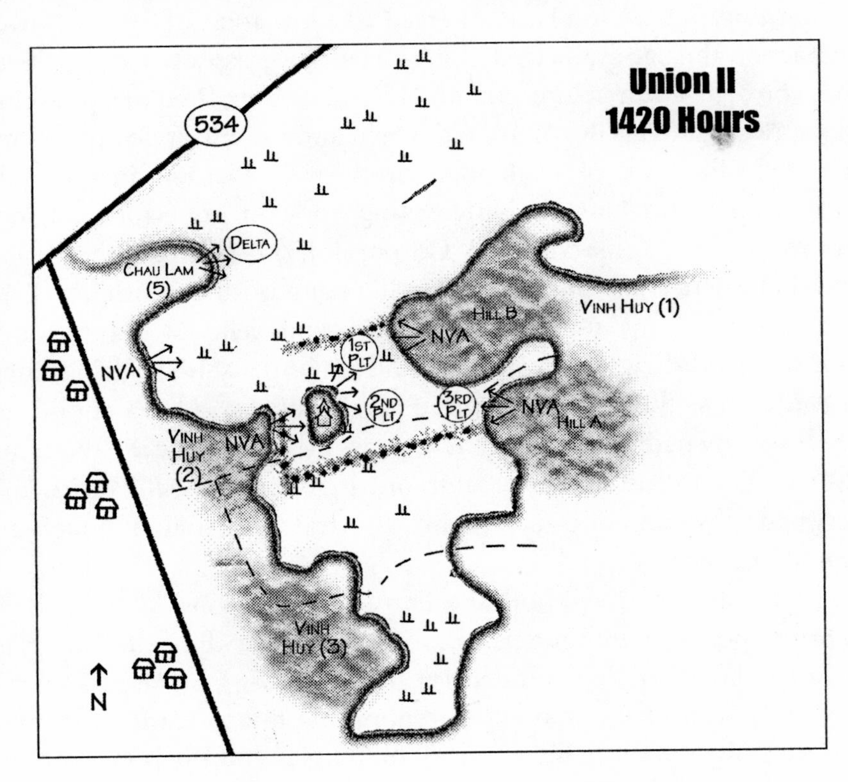

1420 hours. In the heat of the tropical summer afternoon, the NVA initiated their attack with unrelenting bursts of machine gun fire from the tree line that stood directly in front of the 1st Platoon. Another machine gun fired from an area with a small pagoda on it located in front of the 2nd Platoon. Within a millisecond, fifty to one hundred automatic and semi-automatic arms were unleashed upon them from the bounding hedgerows in front. A machine and two automatic weapons on Hill B fired on them from behind. B-40 rockets roared four feet above the paddies impacting on the far side. Another .51caliber NVA machine gun, located on Hill A, opened up twenty seconds later. Mercilessly, it fired into the backs of the 2nd Platoon. A torrent of 81mm mortars rained onto the rice field and the trapped Marines. The enemy machine guns in the Vinh Huy (2) area had a low angle of fire that failed to impact on the paddy, instead, they grazed the grasses twenty to thirty inches above it. The machine gun on Hill A, however, fired in a plunging angle, spraying bullets down upon the field and the entrapped company.

Through the wall of lead, men of the 2nd Platoon instinctively launched their final assault attempting to gain superiority. Lance Corporal Gobrecht marveled at Corporal Jerry Westfall, the squad leader on his left, who charged the machine gun position with his M-16 at his hip while making some wild charging yell. Racing forward, Gobrecht glanced right toward the other infantry squad. Firing, men dropped even as they ran. He glanced left. Westfall had been cut down. Large holes opened in their line. The brave men from the 2nd Platoon, no longer able to sustain any assault, one by one, dove belly down and hit the paddy as they continued to fire. The deafening snap of bullets ate the air above them.

The NVA mowed down both the 1st and 2nd Platoons. Many made it to a prone position without being wounded. Some did not. The dead were still. The mortally wounded lay helpless, dying on the rice field. The slightly wounded remained frozen, calling out to see if their buddies were still alive. Only the two-foot high dikes and the poor angle of fire provided any safety from the deadly guns.

The killed and wounded littered the field. Second Lieutenant Shulz, 1st Platoon Commander, lay mortally wounded. Shultz's platoon radio operator, Corporal Lloyd Woods, realized that his lieutenant was exposed to the intense enemy machine gun fire, and jumping up, made a mad rush through the splattering of lead projectiles to reach him. Once there, he hoisted the lieutenant onto his shoulder and lumbered both of them to a safe position behind the dikes.

Then, rallying his four companions, Woods sprinted across the open rice paddy attempting to evacuate another wounded Marine he saw lying near an enemy machine gun. When he reached the wounded man, Woods realized moving him would be impossible because of the enemy gun fire. Ignoring a spurt of inaccurate machine gun rounds, the corporal crashed into the tree line towards the enemy. The gunner, in total awe at Woods' reckless aggressiveness, failed to shoot at the charging Marine.

Woods fired his M-16 until he was out of bullets, killing the stunned NVA. He picked up the NVA machine gun and leapt into the adjacent emplacement taking out the second gunner. Using the enemy gun on other hostile positions, he provided cover for his companions to allow the other Marines to evacuate their wounded men. Corporal Woods wasted no time returning to the field where Fox's wounded lay and organized their evacuation.

The two machine guns in front of the 2nd Platoon continue to spit rounds at the men. Second Lieutenant Kelsey, trapped under a blanket of bullets, could do little to aid his men or lead a counter attack.

On the left flank of the platoon, Corporal Victor Driscoll's squad was the closest to a machine gun that fired from an island of bamboo trees that seemed to jut out from the tree line masking the objective Vinh Huy (2). This area was conspicuous because a small Buddhist pagoda used by rice farmers to pray during the harvest season was located there. Driscoll's squad could not assault the gun because the machine gun they were up against supported a lethal trajectory and was well fortified. Overwhelmed, the Marines leapt up to their feet and fled back towards Corporal Ted Varena's squad. Lance Corporal Art Byrd was gunned down while he made his escape. Private First Class Mike McCandless followed him to the ground. Two bullets hit Sergeant Gerard Ackley, one in the back of his head and one in his neck forcing him to the dirt instantly. The only man who made it back was Corporal Thom Searfoss.

Corporal Varena, lying against a low paddy dike, stretched flatter than a blade of grass as his platoon was systematically cut to pieces. Live rounds popped in his ears as they flew by his head and helmet. Bullets tore into his helmet and shirt. Then, to his immediate left, an American M-26 grenade exploded. A machine gun round had impacted with a grenade a Marine had stored in one of his pockets. Pieces of human flesh covered the ground, dying it red around Varena. He lost control, stood up, and grabbed a M-60 machine gun off of a dead Marine lying on his other side. He fired two bursts in the general direction of the enemy gun position before an enemy's bullet hit him in the head and knocked him off his feet. Blood ran into his eyes. Blinded by his wound, the corporal tossed back and forth in the loose dirt as he succumbed to the searing pain. Mercifully, numbness set in over his entire body, and the sounds of the battle faded far from his consciousness.

Gobrecht and his section leader, Corporal Rick Barnes, remained prone in the relative safety behind the two-foot high dike wall during the air strike. Two F-4 Phantoms took turns strafing and bombing the enemy tree line. Perhaps to avoid any attention, the enemy firing from the hamlet ceased during these strikes. Gobrecht was able to survey his surroundings for the first time in almost thirty minutes. Spying Westfall, still exposed with no dikes nearby and moving, Gobrecht yelled, "Hey, Rick!"

"What?" Corporal Barnes returned.

"I'm going to get Westfall! He's moving."

"No you're not. I'm going!" Barnes countered.

"No way, Man. You're married, and I'm not." Upon those words, Gobrecht pounced forward and ran the fifteen meters to the fallen corporal.

Once there, Gobrecht grabbed Westfall around the chest and began dragging him back across his dike. Gobrecht slowed. Am I crazy doing this? he thought.

Barnes's voice snapped him back to reality, "John, let me help!"

Suddenly, Barnes's hands grabbed Westfalls's shirt and, under fire, they crossed the to the safety of the protective dike. Westfall was unconscious but breathing. Blood smeared in his hair and covered his cheek. His head wound severe, Barnes cried out, "Corpsman up!"

There was no response. Either Doc Donovan had been killed, or was busy tending to someone else, or just didn't hear Barnes's plea.

One minute later, Westfall gasped for air, his body shuddered, and he stopped breathing. His face became pale gray. Gobrecht and Barnes watched the death of their friend, looked up into each other's eyes, and then stared away in disbelief.

The 3rd Platoon was stuck some fifty or so meters in the paddy in front of the base of Hill A. Corporal "Water Bu" Haley listened to the firing near the other two platoons, and he knew he had to do something. He crawled to a dike and heard his ammo humper, Private First Class Cliff Nolan, calling for him. Haley called out, "Get your butt over here!" As Nolan reached Haley, Marengo shouted for them to join him. Marengo had been clipped by a close round and was wounded but was still very much in charge.

Lying low below the dike walls, Corporal Haley and Private First Class Nolan, near Staff Sergeant Marengo, heard Doc Martin shouting to two wounded 3rd Platoon machine gunners. He was crawling to assist them. Suddenly, Doc Martin shouted out, "I'm hit!"

Haley yelled, "Stay there. I'll get you!"

Martin countered, "No don't. You'll get hit too. I'll crawl to you."

Haley waited two minutes. The firing never stopped. Two more minutes passed. "Doc, you okay?" Haley shouted. He never received an answer. Finally, he stuck his head over the dike only to spot Martin dead on the battlefield. "Sergeant Marengo, Martin never made it! Damn

Doc," he slurred, anger and hopelessness welling in his chest. "Why didn't you let me come?"

Marengo barked commands for his 3rd Platoon to remove themselves from the rice paddy and get to the bottom of Hill A. From there they would be safe from the enemy above them on the hill, and from there they could return fire to alleviate pressure on the other two platoons.

As the platoon crawled below the plunging fire from Hill A, under the safety of the dikes at the base of the hill, enemy mortars began exploding in the battlefield.

From nowhere, Captain Graham and his runner dove into the 3rd Platoon's CP area. "How's that arm, Tony?"

"It'll heel, Skipper? How 'bout your shoulder?" Marengo asked, noting the captain's bloodied wound.

Their enemy intensified its crippling fire not allowing the two men more time to catch up. "Not a big deal. Tony, I want Long's squad to get behind Hill A and silence that machine gun up there," Graham ordered. "He's got to move in front of this hill, then envelope it from the south because Alpha Company is moving to the junction of Hills A and B; and the Battalion Command Group and 81s are already on Hill B."

Shaking his head affirmatively, Marengo said, "Aye, aye." Among the squad leaders, Long had the best reputation for getting the job done. His tactical skills were superb, and his fearless demeanor inspired his squad to the point of believing they were invincible.

"I need another squad to accompany me back out to the 1st and 2nd Platoons positions to start bringing casualties back here!" Graham panted.

"Right away, Sir."

"Corporal Nutt," Marengo ordered, waving his tanned hand toward Graham, "go with the skipper to help with the casualties. Oh, and bring enough ponchos. Haley, send someone to get Long."

"Sure," Haley nodded.

Graham interjected, his voice amazingly calm despite the severe losses Fox was taking, "Water Bu, only shoot those rockets when you have a definite target. There's plenty of M-16 ammo, so use that for any suppressing fire."

"Yes, Sir!"

The enemy's heavy volume of fire became sporadic as a result of the counter-fire by the 1st and 2nd Platoons. At the next break in the firing, Graham, his runner, and Nutt's squad took off for the center of the battlefield. Graham held up at an area behind an embankment where Gunnery Sergeant Green and other company headquarters Marines remained and shouted, motioning, for Nutt to continue to begin evacuating the 1st Platoon's wounded first. With that, Nutt's squad veered left. Graham yelled over to his new gunnery sergeant, "Gunny, you take three men, and I'll take three. We'll fire and maneuver up to the 2nd Platoon's area."

Air and artillery fires struck Vinh Huy (2) with only modest success. For most, the enemy's tunnel system had provided speedy safety to those NVA on the line. The Marines knew that after the air and artillery fires lifted, the enemy would slip out of their tunnels and resume their slaughter of Fox.

"Doc, you tell me who to carry out first," Corporal Nutt cried to Hospitalman Third Class Wodja.

Pointing to one Marine, Wodja yelled to Anderson, Groch, Linstrom, and Rizzo, "You guys, work with Corporal Woods. He's got the whole thing organized."

1500 hours. The battalion radio crackled to life. "Fox, this is Millbrook Six, over," Lieutenant Colonel Hilgartner radioed for Graham.

McKinnon answered, "Millbrook Six, this is Fox, over."

"Roger, Fox. Is Fox Six available? Over."

"Fox Six is organizing an assault group from remnants of Fox Two and the Charlie Papa group that's out there with him," McKinnon explained.

"Roger, Fox, keep me informed, out."

1515 hours. Marengo assisted with the triage activities for the wounded brought back by Corporal Nutt's squad. As Long's squad assaulted the NVA entrenchment at the summit from the back of Hill A, automatic weapons fire rang out from on top of the hill. They killed six enemy. All of Long's Marines in Fox sustained at least one wound. While his men were setting up a hasty defensive position, Long spotted another machine gun that was firing on the 2nd Platoon further down the face of the hill. He charged the gun. Two Marines attempted to stay up with their magnificent, athletic squad leader as he again led an assault on this second gun. Bullets ripped across the heavy air, now laden with gun smoke. Long ignored the racing projectiles as he would have ignored flies. Two more enemy went down. Long, along with the other two Marines, was wounded again. The Marines at his side crumpled from their respective wounds. Long rushed forward, attacking as he moved. He fired, overcoming the NVA manning the machine gun nest.

Long stood alone as Hill A fell silent.

Below, Graham and his eight men, their lungs heaving with their effort, reached the 2nd Platoon area. In front of Graham, existed an island containing the pagoda. From the far side of the rice field, the bamboo trees on the island, particularly with its long axis paralleling the hamlet, made the island appear to be tied into the hamlet.

"Skipper, Hill A's machine guns are quiet," Gunny Green panted.

"Great. Long must have taken the hill, Gunny."

"All right, men," Graham said to all, "when that next air strike comes, everyone who can, get up and assault that gun near us on our right. That's the one right past the pagoda. We have to yell as loud as we can to scare them." The men nodded at his idea, "Okay, I hear a jet coming in, so get ready on my command."

The Marines steeled themselves and awaited his command. "Let's go!" he shouted.

1535 hours. With gusto and much bravado, a group of eighteen Marines and one corpsman began their charge. Their war screams frightening, Graham led the way. Within forty-five seconds, Captain Graham, Gunnery Sergeant Green, Lance Corporal MacKinnon, Corporal Dirickson, Lance Corporal Painter, Private First Class LaBarbera, Second Lieutenant Kelsey, Corporal Barnes, Private First Class Jack Melton, and six others crammed themselves into the left side of the bamboo tree line near the pagoda. Green took the front of the charge, killing ten NVA himself.

Lance Corporal Gobrecht and a two others from the 2nd Platoon pushed onto the right side of the island while firing at the retreating enemy. A sniper hidden at the base of a nearby bamboo tree dropped the two Marines running beside him. Gobrecht ran through the tree line firing his machine gun at all bamboo tree root systems until he ran out of ammo. Grabbing three grenades one at a time, he threw them in any other location he thought might hold a sniper. Freshly dug fighting holes and tunnel entrances seemed everywhere. Out of ammo and deep inside the underbrush Gobrecht came face to face with two armed NVA solders. Instant fury shot from Gobrecht's eyes. Panting like a wild bull, his breath came in short, almost shallow bursts. His teeth gritted as if he was about to devour the two Communists. Shocked and staring at the fearless Marine, they backed away quickly, fading into the brush. Gobrecht turned slowly assuring himself they were truly gone, then hustled back to the pagoda.

The ruins of a French-built home lay near the pagoda. Its intact structural walls served as the protective barrier for one of the machine guns that had all but wasted the 2nd Platoon. Now, thanks to the stalwart efforts of the brave men of Fox, the gun position had been overrun and captured. Some of the 2nd Platoon busied themselves with rendering the gun useless. Corporal Barnes and Gunnery Sergeant Green organized the able and wounded men and formed a hasty defensive position. They had gone without water since noon. Gunny Green knew he couldn't do anything about their dehydration; instead he had the platoon redistribute their ammunition.

Graham finally made radio contact with Lieutenant Colonel Hilgartner to announce that he had taken a portion of the objective.

Dirickson was by his side. Barns, Gobrecht and Corporal Gary O'Brien, another 2nd platoon squad leader, rested nearby. Graham claimed the opportunity to call First Sergeant Lee and directed him to send more men and ammunition.

"Lieutenant Kelsey, get a group together to silent that other gun," Graham ordered.

"I need some volunteers to go with me to get that other gun. Who's interested?" Kelsey asked.

Immediately a chorus of "Count on me, Lieutenant!" sounded from the remaining Marines. Among the volunteers were Corporal Francis, Private First Class LaBarbera, Lance Corporal Painter along with five other Marines. They left the pagoda area, traversing safely on the rice paddy side of the island to its end. From there, they hovered nearly twenty meters away from the hamlet's true tree line. Kelsey charged first as Francis, Painter, and LaBarbera stayed with him while the others from the 2nd Platoon veered right. A sniper round killed Kelsey before he entered the tree line. LaBarbera never had a chance to discover where he was hit. Kelsey's body toppled backward, halfway through the bamboo trees. Francis, Painter, and LaBarbera hit the ground five meters in front of him. Francis got to his knees telling the rest of the men to "spread out!" and waving his arm in a gesture to back up his command. A round seared into his forehead making a neat hole covered with a deep, fresh, maroon splatter that sprayed outward from his face. Only Painter and LaBarbera, the two admin clerks, remained in the group to the left. They became one with the trampled underbrush upon which they had flattened themselves. Moments later, after the sniper that took out Kelsey adjusted his position, Painter was shot in the face.

LaBarbera, lying there feigning death, flinched as a mortar exploded back at the pagoda. The pungent, iron-filled blood of the fallen men around him invaded his nostrils. He registered jets approaching his position; and still, he did not move.

The mortar that LaBarbera had heard landed in the middle of the Marines near the pagoda. Corporal Dirickson seemed to be hit the worst. He was immobile. The remains of his tattered uniform exposed Dirickson's shredded skin.

The explosion had impacted in front of Gobrecht. His face felt ripped like torn material. His right thigh muscles were severely cut by the concussion alone. The corporal limped over to the French building's foundation where Doc Donavan, out of morphine for the past two hours, was providing comfort to Barnes and O'Brien. Gobrecht could see Graham was wounded again having taken some shrapnel to his stomach and legs. Gobrecht, believing he would not make it home, pushed his diary onto Donavon rasping out, "Whatever happens, don't let this fall into enemy hands. Send it back to my parents." The Marines could see the F-4 Phantoms darting through the sky as they began their ordnance drop on the hamlet's tree line close to the vicinity of the Kelsey-led patrol.

If flying in a helicopter had been an adventure for him earlier, now LaBarbera, in a disjointed marvel, realized that he had never been bombed before either. While the NVA slunk back into their tunnels, LaBarbera lay immobile with his dead buddies. The point detonating bombs burst on the treetops above him, showering the area with shrapnel, tree branches, leaves, and dirt. Still, he did not move. The four sorties of bombs lasted twelve minutes, though to Tommy LaBarbera, twelve turned into forever. When it stopped, he stood up, untouched, with rifle in hand. Calmly, he glanced around. An NVA soldier stood twenty feet from him. The smug bastard smiled as he looked at the lieutenant's body. Just as calmly, LaBarbera raised his rifle up to his chin, squeezed his right eye shut, aimed and fired his rifle. He emptied his magazine. When he looked up over the rifle, the NVA was gone.

Out of nowhere, Private First Class "Smedly" Butler from the 2nd Platoon yelled, "Let's get the hell out of here!" He ran by LaBarbera with his knees reaching for the sky as he raced toward the hope of relative safety outside of the bamboo line.

LaBarbera turned and both Marines sprinted back to the pagoda area while rounds dug into the dirt near their dancing feet.

First Sergeant Lee radioed back to Graham and related the news that the five men he sent from the company headquarters had only made it half way across the rice paddy before they had been cut down.

Ammo was almost gone.

The radio cracked and popped as one of the F-4 pilots broke into the rapid chatter. He relayed to Graham that a large enemy force was moving in the captain's direction along an unpaved road north of Fox's position.

LaBarbera could hear multiple shouts from the enemy approaching him from the direction he'd just left.

Finally, the men at the pagoda ran out of ammunition.

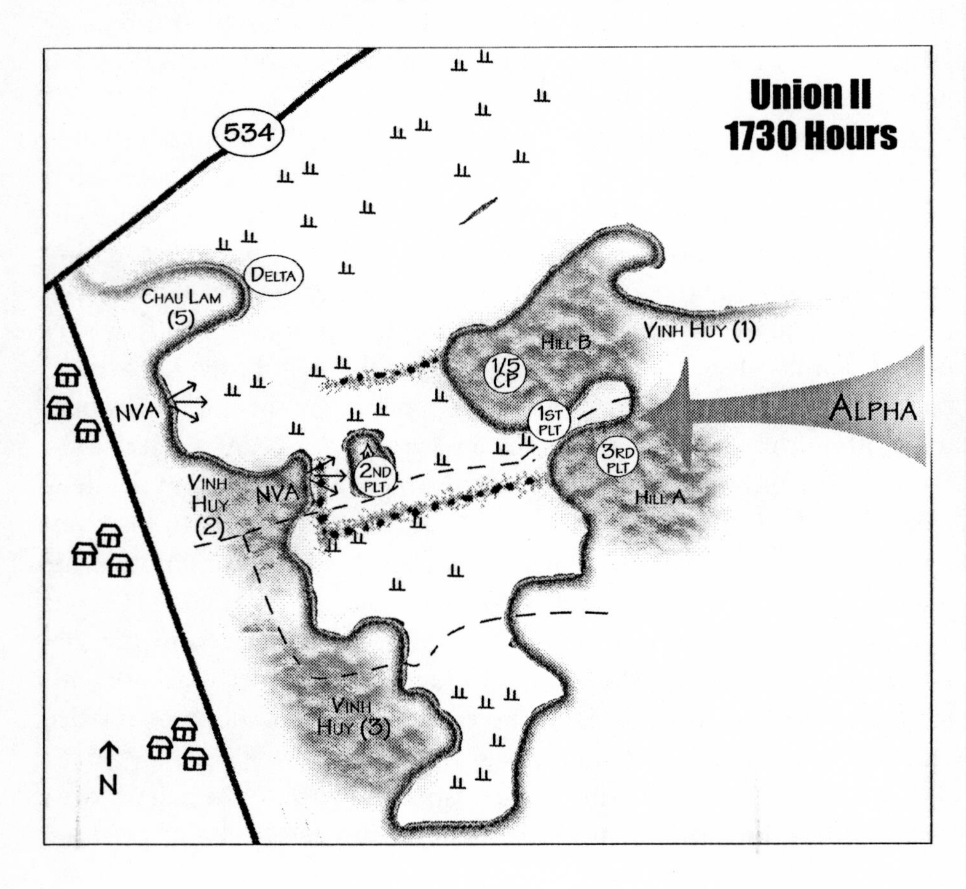

1730 hours. Above the din, Graham ordered, "Everyone who can move, get back to the rear! Gunny, you take Mac and the five not wounded, and get over to the 3rd Platoon area pronto!"

Before leaving with Green, Corporal Karl Richie turned back to the ragged Marines choking out, "I am so proud to have served and fought with each of you."

Gunny Green grabbed Richie's shoulder and squeezed it. Richie's watery eyes found his; the young corporal nodded. Green and Richie turned away and departed with the four other Marines Graham had ordered to the 3rd Platoon. None of the men left behind responded to Richie's broadcast. How could they? There was nothing left to say.

"You wounded," Graham went on. "Go back in pairs to help each other. Get as far as you can from here because we're going to bomb this place. If the enemy gets close to you, fight with everything you got. You don't want to get captured, tortured, and executed. I'm going to stay here with Dirickson."

The men doubted Dirickson would survive.

Doc Donavan worked to support Barnes, Gobrecht, and O'Brien. Corporal Barnes told Gobrecht and O'Brien, "John, you go left. O'Brien you go straight ahead, and I'll go to the right. That way one bullet ain't gonna kill us all. Doc it's your choice who you go with." The men limped and hobbled the best they could over the bodies of their friends and the discarded remnants of the battle.

LaBarbera announced he would stay with the skipper and help him with the mortally wounded Dirickson.

"All right," Graham's tired voice responded to LaBarbera. "Get up there," he pointed, "and hack a hole in the hedge, so we can drag him out of here." Graham, whose ever-present crisp, tidy appearance was gone, replaced by the torn, bloodstained, dirt-riddled leftovers of his uniform, wrapped his hands as gently as possible around Dirickson.

The two of them tried desperately to wedge Dirickson through the hedge line to no avail. Without morphine, he screamed in pain with every jolt. Finally, Graham sighed, deciding, "LaBarbera, you get going and try to make it back to safety. I'm going to stay with him."

LaBarbera's face contorted in horror as he registered the impossibility of his captain's situation. He caught the determined gleam in Graham's eyes as he opened his mouth in protest. Graham's quiet, "Go," spurred life into LaBarbera's limp limbs. He ran, ran as fast as he could—through the rice field—all the way back to the hedgerow growing on Hill A.

1745 hours. The moment Graham watched LaBarbera bound his way back toward the rest of Fox, Graham called to Lieutenant Colonel Hilgartner, "Millbrook Six, this is Fox Six, over."

Hilgartner must have been waiting for the call. He answered directly, "Roger, Jim. What's your situation?"

"I've moved as many of my men back to the rear as I could. I'm here with one kid that's probably not going to make it. I'm out of ammo and about twenty-five NVA are making an assault on my position, out."

The silence mounted. Hilgartner stared mutely at the radio.

"Fox Three, this is Fox Six, over," Graham called for Marengo.

"Roger, Six, go," Marengo responded within moments.

"Tony, can you help me?"

Marengo shook his head as though Graham could see him. His gut wrenched over, "Skipper, I just arrived at a high ground behind Hill A and am consolidating what's left of the company. We have one squad and they are assisting the wounded in establishing a defensive position," he replied efficiently, keeping the big picture in mind.

"There's nothing we can do…" Marengo explained to his radio operator; both sharing feelings of helplessness.

The pain tearing at him evident in voice, Marengo's entire frame shook with rage and regret as he depressed the button on the handset once more, "Recommend you stay where you are, Skipper; we've been in touch with Alpha Company and they're trying to get to your position. They should be up there soon."

"It's a little late for that," came Graham's shrinking response.

Marengo closed his eyes in a useless effort to blot out the meaning behind the captain's understatement.

Abruptly, the captain's voice took on the resolved and commanding tone it normally held, "You stay where you are. The NVA are firing and maneuvering against me, and they are looking pretty good..."

Graham's last transmission broke off. The radio fell silent.

Gobrecht, Barnes, and O'Brien hadn't made it thirty meters into the paddy when the enemy overran Graham's position and began firing at the retreating wounded. Barnes and Gobrecht found the safety of a paddy dike. O'Brien was shot in the back before he could join them. Doc Donavon, who ran near O'Brien, was shot in the head.

The air exploded above them as the engines of an F-4 Phantom burned the sky. Moments later, it began strafing the area with 20mm cannon rounds. The enemy retreated into their tunnels. Then the ground in the paddy shook as 250 and 500 pound bombs and napalm obliterated the hamlet's tree line. Only forty meters away from the target area, Barnes and Gobrecht, though wounded, had a front row seat. During a lull between the bombs, Barnes, whose arms had been wounded from the mortar blast that had taken Dirickson, called to Gobrecht, "You okay?"

Gobrecht, though weak from his many wounds and suffering a stiff right leg, raised his arm in the air and gave Barnes a "thumbs up". Both men continued to crawl their way back toward Fox's position. Barnes failed to notice that despite his wounded arms, he made much faster progress than Gobrecht.

1750 hours. Gunnery Sergeant Green and McKinnon arrived at the 3rd Platoon's Command Post position. The skies darkened. Staff Sergeant Marengo had left Corporal Long on Hill A until the last chance of hope for Graham's survival and his rejoining the surviving Fox Marines had vanished before moving him back to higher ground, some 600 meters behind Hill A. The new position was chosen as a safe area from where the medevacs could take place throughout the night. Green caught up with Marengo, "Hey, Tony, I need a squad to assist any of the wounded who might be able to make it."

"Right," Marengo acknowledged. Addressing Corporal Perry Jones he said, "P.J., hook up with Conley, and see what you can do."

"Gotcha, Staff Sergeant. I'm on it now," Jones affirmed. "Hey, Gunny, did you see Corporal Barnes or "Hanover" Gobrecht?" Jones asked.

"They had both been wounded and the skipper," Green paused, not wanting to think about the brave commander, "was getting them to leave the pagoda as I was leaving. That was forty-five minutes ago," Green answered. "Stay along the hedge row as you go out there."

"Right, Gunny," Jones confirmed.

"Gunny, I just heard that Alpha Company is trying to take our objective," Marengo commented.

"Yeah. Well, good luck to them because the enemy has not run out of troopers yet! How many wounded we got here?"

"We have to evac at least another twenty wounded. At this point, we have seventeen bodies as well. I already evac'd twelve wounded after Long took Hill A. The first medevac bird crashed enroute to Da Nang, but I don't have any details," Marengo mentioned.

"You've seen the first sergeant?"

"Yeah, he was down at the base of Hill A with me earlier. He should be up here before long," Marengo nodded.

"I want to get the whole company here before dark so we can circle the wagons before anything else happens," Green mumbled, clenching a tight fist.

Darkness came. Gobrecht was now alone in the battlefield. He had lost sight of Barnes and hadn't heard from him since Barnes had asked if he was all right. About an hour earlier Gobrecht heard Alpha Company attack the enemy about 250 meters away. But now the shots and explosions from that battle had receded, and all he could hear were Vietnamese voices.

They must be searching for their casualties and weapons, Gobrecht thought.

Wounded Marines they found would be shot. The NVA were posing as a Marine patrol looking for injured men, "Any Maleens? Are you hurt? Have you been shot?"

One Marine on the field yelled out, "Oh, God. Help me! Please help me!"

As the wounded men cried out, Gobrecht kept repeating in his mind: shut the hell up kid; you'll get your head blown off! A single gunshot rang out, and the young Marine fell quiet. It was time for Gobrecht to get out of there.

"Barnes, I told you not to bug me any more tonight about Gobrecht. We haven't seen him. Now you're getting on this next bird! P.J. will keep you informed," Gunnery Sergeant Green directed.

"All right, gunny." Barnes looked at P.J. Jones and said, "You hear him, don't you?"

Jones nodded. He wouldn't stop looking for him.

1940 hours. The 2nd Battalion was committed to the battle to bolster the hard hit elements already engaged in Union II. First, Echo Company began landing on Route 534 just north of its junction with the dirt road to Chau Lam (5), D/1/5's objective. Following Echo was the 2/5's Command Group headed by Lieutenant Colonel Jackson and his operations officer, Major Dick Easau. 2/5 brought along D/1/7, another rifle company chopped to 2/5 for this operation.

The last helicopter carrying these reinforcements landed at 2015. By 2230, Echo 2/5 became heavily engaged with enemy forces now defending their own terrain south of Chau Lam (5).

For the next few hours, though it seemed like years, Gobrecht hauled himself along from one dike to the next. Every time he heard enemy voices, he'd hobble on his left leg while pain stabbed at every inch of him. Finally, he heard other wounded Marines grunting and dragging themselves as they tried to get back to Hills A and B. Here, NVA and Marine bodies littered the battlefield. When artillery flares floated in the sky, the eeriness of the dead around him intensified. Gobrecht caught up with the other Marines at last, and begged them for water. After inspecting his stomach injuries, they refused his request believing shrapnel may have torn his intestines.

2400 hours. Between fifty and sixty NVA 82mm mortar rounds fell on the newly arrived 2nd Battalion units as they waded onto the deadly battlefield. Heavy casualties were inflicted.

0130 hours. Echo 1/7 was committed and joined Lieutenant Colonel Jackson's 2/5 command. Consequently, the enemy withdrew as Marine reinforcements seemed endless.

0230 hours. Gobrecht reached the evacuation point. A passing CH-53 swooped in and picked Gobrecht and six other wounded Marines up. One of the wounded finally evacuated was the twice-shot Corporal Long who reluctantly left what remained of his squad. As they were lifting off the LZ they began receiving heavy mortar and small arms fire. The CH-53 sustained numerous bullet and shrapnel hits causing the bird to thrust left and right during the lift off. Given the mission and the immediate dangerous environment, the courageous pilot chose to fly the battered aircraft to Da Nang instead of landing and waiting for another evac aircraft. The chopper shuttered and lurched the entire twenty-minute flight, finally sputtering to a crash landing as it descended onto the 1st Medical Battalion's helo-pad. All survived the crash.

0235 hours. Echo 2/5 entered the defensive perimeter of the 1st Battalion and relieved Fox Company. That shift allowed Gunnery Sergeant Green and Staff Sergeant Marengo to huddle together. Their minds tumbled through terrible reflections of the day's events. Hardly a word was spoken.

In an angered, low tone Marengo blurted, "You know, John, the skipper and most of those Marines didn't have to die today."

After a minute, Green's head raised, "Yep. You're right. What was wrong prepping that objective with air and artillery?" Green asked emphatically, rhetorically. "We could have overpowered them! I swear 1/5 doesn't know what it's doing."

A deafening silence spanned nearly fifteen minutes. Marengo finally added, "Yeah, and those flak jackets…I can't believe that 1/5's policy was not to wear them. When we had to turn ours in, I felt naked. I felt like I was losing a close friend."

Colonel Houghton, who had asked for 2/5's most aggressive company, flew at first light to visit Fox's few survivors. Most had been wounded but not evacuated. To those who were left he said, "Marines, I put Fox into the center of the breach and your company was the lynchpin in defeating an enemy regiment. I had always heard of your fighting ability…your braveness. Today you have exceeded your reputation. You men exemplify the heroic character of the 5th Marine Regiment and the United States Marine Corps. With you, I mourn your losses. We can never bring them back. They were brave Marines who did not die in vain. Men of Foxtrot, I salute you and your magnificent fighting company." The colonel gave a hand salute while turning to all ensuring every Marine and corpsman had been recognized.

Houghton paused and pulled Lee, Green, and Marengo aside for a few minutes to give them personal praise before flying away to recognize others.

In the end, Alpha Company killed thirty enemy with another probably thirty-three killed. They captured twenty-seven NVA. Alpha lost five Marines killed with ten wounded.

Delta Company killed forty enemy with another fifty approximated. Delta's losses were seventeen killed with twenty-two wounded.

Fox had 170 confirmed enemy kills and another 310 enemy probably killed. Fox lost thirty Marines killed and sustained sixty-one wounded. Many Marines attached to Fox Company during the battle were killed and wounded as well.

CHAPTER 5: NONG SON

Following Union II, Fox Company's resolve had weakened and its moral fiber grew frail. Over ninety Marines from Fox Company had been either killed or wounded. Of the sixty-four others, many did not report small wounds. Nevertheless, the battle had taken its toll on even those who had not been a casualty. Fox Company would have to rebuild.

The reconstruction began the very next day. First Lieutenant James B. Scuras was assigned to command Fox Company on the basis of his combat experience with Fox. Scuras had been the 3rd Platoon Commander and company executive officer until he had been wounded for the second time in late March. During that period, Scuras had earned two Silver Star medals for gallantry in combat. After March he acted as the battalion's logistics officer. Scuras joined the company at the battlefield twenty-eight kilometers southwest of An Hoa.

Scuras's job seemed insurmountable. He was replacing one of the finest infantry captains in the Marine Corps—a man, who had on the previous day sacrificed his own life for his men. Short at 5'8" and prematurely bald, Scuras did not posses Graham's classic commanding presence. Yet the men knew and respected him as a no-nonsense, tough Marine Corps leader who was deeply devoted to their well being. For them, he possessed every thing that mattered. It was a relief to the men that Graham's replacement was a commander with a history in Fox.

Flying in with Scuras was Sergeant Richard "Pappy" Pennell, the new Weapons Platoon commander. Sergeant Pennell had joined Fox Company in late May but had not gone into the field. He remained back at the base working on acclimating to the tropical heat, familiarizing himself with the use of his personal weapon, and becoming otherwise indoctrinated into the war. With six years in the Corps, Pennell carried the hardened physique and gravelly voice of a non-commissioned officer coming, most recently, off of the Parris Island drill field. Without knowing any specifics about his background, his voice garnered immediate respect from his peers and seniors. His time spent in charge of troops was instantly obvious. For the troops, however, his voice reminded them of their own DI. Even though they had not seen that drill instructor in the last three to ten months, immediately, it commanded their full attention.

As the helicopter landed in the mid-morning of 3 July on the sacred soil of the Union II battlefield, Scuras and Pennell began processing the full effect of the violence that took place the day before. Smoldering trees and other shredded vegetation told part of the tale. All else proved overwhelming. Troops, scattered throughout the 1000-meter-square, dry, rice paddy, silently placed their former compatriots or whatever parts they could find of them into body bags and searched for weapons and equipment.

Before all the equipment could be collected, helicopters arrived at 1400 to lift the Fox company survivors back to An Hoa. The men's minds remained locked on the battlefield, so no one anticipated a reception as they landed at the airstrip. Over one hundred Marines and corpsmen from Echo Company, Hotel Company, and their supporting elements gathered around the landing choppers. Silence greeted them. The muted salute bespoke the profound respect, most sincere admiration, and love felt for their fellow Marines as the men of An Hoa welcomed the heroes home.

Over the next two days, the Marines from the 1st Battalion finished clearing equipment from the battlefield. Helicopters brought the equipment to An Hoa, and Fox Company working parties hauled the packs and helmets and other field equipment from the airstrip to the company headquarters.

After recovering from pneumonia, Gunny Jones was transferred to the Battalion Staff. This change served to intensify the discomfort of the survivors.

Many of the Union II vets were sent to China Beach to help them recover from their lives' most traumatic event. There, they wrote to family and friends. Perry Jones wrote to his buddy John Gobrecht:

June 4, 1967

Dear John,
Well here I am alive and in pretty good health, but I wish I could be with you!
After the battle I tried to find you, but they told me that the whole second squad of guns had been wiped out and I'll tell you now I felt like crying!!
I guess your home by now or at least in good care by a nice looking nurse and I sure hope you feel good or at least better!
I lost two men, but the rest'll be all right and that's all I could ask for, right?
O'Brien was killed and Barnes was wounded pretty bad and the rest were wounded, but we had 34 killed and I was sick!!
If I ever have to pick up another dead person I'll go crazy as a bat and that's no lie!!
Boy I was sure glad to know you made it and I'm glad to know you're going back to the states; I only wish I could be there with you.!!
I'm supposed to be Section Leader now, but all we got left are eight men and three machine guns??!!
Well enough of this place; I've got your records and record player and if I get enough money, I'll send them to you as soon as possible, alright?
I guess I'll say good-bye old buddy; take care of yourself and write me soon from life alright? May God Bless and keep you safe and I hope to see you soon.
A friend always,
Perry

PS: They found your diary on Doc Donavon and now Cpl Hull has it. I'll get it and mail it to you.

Reminders of the Union II tragedy remained fresh in the minds of all Fox Company Marines. For weeks following the battle, anyone going into the company office would have to weave his way through the piles of blood-stained 782 gear, like cartridge belts and other web items, of the guys who didn't make it back from Union II. During that time many newly joined Marines walked through these piles, up the three steps, and entered the tin roof building with the crimson-colored sign bearing the yellow letters "CO F" hanging next to the front screen door. These replacements felt a hollowness in the pits of their stomachs generated by uncertainty and fear.

First Sergeant Cleo Lee and Gunnery Sergeant John Green were part of the rebuilding process. Their recommendations were passed to First Lieutenant Scuras for final approval. Lance Corporal McKinnon became the battalion radio operator. Lee had Dave Anderson promoted to lance corporal and assigned him to replace McKinnon as the company radio operator.

LaBarbera, the erstwhile company clerk who survived being bombed and shot at, was glad to be back in the rear and was far less anxious to go on the next operation if they were all like Union II. He did, however, provide good insight into the men joining Fox.

Approaching First Sergeant Lee, LaBarbera cleared his throat, "Excuse me, First Sergeant."

"What' cha got, LaBarbera?"

"Yesterday a corporal joined us, guy by the name of Brown. He seems like a real mature guy, married and all. Spent his first three years at Marine Barracks, Brooklyn. Hey, you know that's my hometown, so he must be all right." LaBarbera reflected on the previous night when he'd met Chris Brown. LaBarbera had been sitting in his hooch, playing an oldies album "Down Memory Lane" with Allen Freed. This lanky, new guy, Corporal Brown, came by and asked if he could join LaBarbera and the other admin clerks with whom he shared a hooch. They were drinking "Gook" whiskey and said, "sure". He told LaBarbera his wife was from Brooklyn. Turned out she went to LaBarbera's high school. The men got good and drunk. That was a good night. LaBarbera was glad Brown joined Fox. "I believe the 2nd Platoon could use someone with Brown's maturity."

"All right, LaBarbera, anything else?" Lee asked almost reluctantly.

"Yeah, First Sergeant, one thing. There's another guy."

"Well?"

"There's this old lance corporal that showed up at battalion last night waiting for assignment to a company. He's an 0311, a grunt, like Brown. Real mature," LaBarbera said, his voice deep, adding emphasis. "Name's Thomas Burnham, goes by 'Bernie.' He was in the Corps between '54 and '57," LaBarbera paused letting that info sink in. Green, who had just come into the admin hooch, started listening too.

"Burnham was making big bucks in the city, ah…New York City, doing something with construction. Seems that he was walking through Central Park and some hippies were burning an American flag. Well, it pissed him off enough to go to the recruiting center, cut a two-year deal with the recruiter, arrange a leave of absence from his construction company, and here he is."

"John, you may want to go to the S-1 and check him out," Lee said to Green. "He sounds interesting."

"Oh…and, Gunny," LaBarbera interrupted, "because of Fox's need for replacements from Union II, Bernie and others bypassed Vietnam orientation in Staging Battalion back at Pendleton." For added caution the clerk from Brooklyn threw in the fact that the last weapon Burnham had fired was an M-1.

In the mid-afternoon on 6 June, newly joined Sergeant Willard S. Scott III greeted a compact lieutenant leaving the An Hoa battalion adjutant's office. "Sir, are you Lieutenant Martin?"

Tom Martin, surprised that anyone in this Godforsaken outpost knew his name, raised his eyebrows and answered in a crisp, yet baritone voice, "I am, Sergeant."

"My name's Scott, Sir. First Sergeant Lee sent me over to meet you and bring you over to the company office. Can I get that bag?" the young sergeant asked with enthusiasm.

"Well, thanks, but I drug it over from Okinawa, guess I can carry it the rest of the way. You the Admin Chief?"

"Oh no, Sir. I'm going to be your platoon sergeant, and I'm sure glad you're here."

For most of Fox, the daily routine in a rifle company started to ease the pain caused by horrific memories. But for a good man from Georgia, remanded to his lonely existence in An Hoa, which once held so much life and teamed with playful Marines, reflections of the traumatic battle began to scar Perry Jones. He wrote again to his wounded friend:

June 7, 1967

John,
We finally got back to good old An Hoa and it seemed as if everyone was gone and I felt like a lone wolf!!
Well I just got through inventorying your seabag. I put your record player in it and also your letters. I didn't send your records because there wasn't much room for anything else.
It looks like we're getting back to normal. We're supposed to go on another operation the 15th of June. I think they are trying to get me killed.........
Your old buddy,
Perry

"Hey, Sergeant Pappy," Private First Class Melvin Newlin called out as he approached the Weapon Platoon hut.

Now becoming somewhat comfortable with his new handle, "Pappy", the twenty-seven year-old Pennell looked up from inspecting one of the new replacement weapons. After all, most of the troops were seven to eight years younger than him. "What's going on, Newlin? I thought you were on mess duty," Pennell questioned the lead machine gunner of the 1st Section.

"I have an hour off before I have to get back to the mess hall. But, Sergeant Pappy, the gunny wants to see you up at the staff hooch," Newlin responded, referring to the hut that housed the company's staff non-commission officers.

"What's bugging him?" Pennell questioned the private first class from Wellsville, Ohio. Newlin, whose reputation in Fox ranged from "shit-bird" to "nonchalant" to "happy go lucky".

"Beats the crap out of me, Sarge. Besides I only have six weeks to go before I rotate out of this jungle, so I can't waste time questioning Gunny Green."

"Yeah, yeah, yeah," Pennell grumbled and took off for the staff hooch.

As he opened the door to the staff hooch, Sergeant Pennell could see that Gunnery Sergeant Green was alone in the tent. Pennell thought that Green was the perfect company guns. "Troops first", the always sharp-looking, black veteran of the Korean War, would preach to his junior leaders.

"Gunny? You wanted to see me?"

"Yeah, sure. Have a seat, Pennell."

Sergeant Pennell looked around and didn't see any chairs. He chose the first cot and sat down on it.

"Pennell, Lieutenant Scuras asked me to get your thoughts on the troop morale and readiness. At least as far as the Weapons Platoon is concerned," he added.

Without hesitation, Sergeant Pennell blurted, "I got to tell you, Gunny, the men who were on Union II really surprise me. They seemed a bit tired, but they also have hinted at getting back to the field," he paused then added, "for revenge, I assume. The replacements seem like normal replacements, quiet and a bit skittish. All that said, I'll assure you that the Weapons Platoon is ready to go," he said.

"Well good, Pennell, that's what the three officers told the company commander. I will report just that to the Lieutenant Scuras. By the way Pennell, Fox's going to be on its first operation tomorrow since Union II. Operation Arizona is going to be fairly short, only four days. It should be over by the 18th of June. Get the men ready."

After two weeks of recovery in An Hoa, Fox Company found itself back on a combat operation. Fox served as the battalion reserve during Operation Arizona. It's only action came on 18 June at 1100. Fox Company was alerted for possible deployment to support the 369th Regional Force Company, a local Vietnamese unit, taking fire at that time somewhere in the Arizona Territory. At 1300 Fox Company deployed by helicopter across the Song Thu Bon and simultaneously chopped to the 3rd Battalion, 7th Marines. At 1915 hours after not finding any enemy, Fox Company flew back to An Hoa and was chopped back to 2/5.

From 20 June to 22 June, Fox Company conducted search and destroy operations south of Alligator Lake. Then, from 25 June to 29 June, Fox Company participated in Operation Calhoun along with Company G and the 2/5 Command Group. This operation took place about three to five kilometers south of Alligator Lake. The purposes of the operation were to search all the valleys and draws in the nearby foothills for hidden weapons and supplies and to relocate indigenous personnel desiring to move to the Duc Duc District town of Phu Da, adjacent to An Hoa.

During that operation Corporal Bob Bowermaster felt an emotional clinging from his best friend, the only one in his squad who had survived the deadly battle earlier that month, Corporal Thom Searfoss. Bowermaster had gone on Union II, but due to an insect bite that swelled his face so grossly he couldn't see, was evacuated two days before the devastating battle.

"Bob," Searfoss asked Bowermaster, "How is it I survived Union II? Doc Donavon? Sergeant Ackley? And even the captain!" he said pausing for a minute to reflect on his "skipper". "Remember when he gave me a pound cake the day I turned eighteen? You know there must have been something I could have done to save his life!"

"You were just lucky, Thom. Hell, if I didn't get evac'd cuz of that bee bite, I probably would have bought it as well. Our time wasn't up. That's all."

"Well, Bob, I'm not gonna lose you like I lost the skipper!"

"Okay, Thom, okay. Nothing is going to happen to us. We'll be okay." Bowermaster reassured him while thinking to himself that when Searfoss takes over Sergeant Clark's squad, they'd be far apart. If the shit the fan, he would have a hard time even trying to get to Bowermaster.

Following their own losses after Union I and II, the NVA and VC busied themselves with recruiting throughout the province. As July began, the regional communists were attacking isolated villages with small units in attempts to undermine the American effort.

Fox's parent organization, the 2nd Battalion, continued to protect the An Hoa valley by themselves while the rest of the 5th Marines remained in the Que Son basin. As a result, the battalion was stretched thin, guarding the northern entrance to the An Hoa valley at Phu Lac (6) above Liberty Bridge, the An Hoa combat base, and Nong Son, the active coal mine complex twenty kilometers southwest of the base.

On 1 July, Fox was notified that the company would be going to the Nong Son coalmines on 3 July to relieve Echo Company. Nong Son was referred to as a "permanent outpost" since it had an US Army spot light team and a section of USMC 4.2", four-deuce, mortars constantly located there. Thanks to the men of Fox Company and the other 2/5 companies, the top of the hill, referred to as the "Upper Nong Son" had permanent bunkers, machine gun firing positions, and an LZ on it. As for the troops, Nong Son was considered to be R&R. Nong Son was a defensive stronghold, which meant plenty of time to recuperate.

Lieutenant Colonel Jackson, the battalion's CO, thanked First Lieutenant Scuras personally for his enthusiasm to take the company to Nong Son. The Lieutenant Colonel knew full well that Scuras had only one week left in country before he was due to rotate back to the States. Scuras's replacement, Captain Lennartz, had arrived in Da Nang but was still processing through the Division's orientation program.

The two-day warning gave the men time to fire their personal and crew-served weapons in order to calibrate them and prepare otherwise for a few weeks away from An Hoa. The company had built back up to ninety-three men, obviously better than the sixty-four that had returned from Union II, but nowhere near the 154 men that had embarked on that operation.

"Newlin," Sergeant "Pappy" Pennell called.

Near his rack, Newlin was cleaning his gun. Newlin looked up and responded, "You want me, Sergeant Pappy?"

"Newlin, the first sergeant told me you only have three weeks to go in country. He said I could hold you back at An Hoa 'til you rotate. You earned right of not going to the field."

"Sergeant," Newlin responded while shaking his head left and right. "No way I am going to stay here and be on a three-week working party. Man, I'm going out there, set my gun up on the top of the mountain and catch some rays. I can't imagine rotating back to the world without a tan."

"All right, it's your call. Plus, I can truly say that we're better off with you behind a gun at Nong Son than having you here on a work detail."

Early on the morning of 3 July, half of Fox Company mounted on top of three amphibious tractors, amtracs. The amtracs followed four Marines on foot who searched for mines on and just off of the road. The fifty-some others trailed the amtracs on 6x6 trucks. A Marine Corps unique anti-armor vehicle with six 106mm recoilless rifles, called an "Ontos", trailed.

The vets were quiet, gazing into the mountains that surrounded the An Hoa valley. Most minds were reliving the surreal horror they faced a month ago. With each lurch of the amtrac as it climbed over bumps in the dirt road, their consciousnesses would snap back to reality. Each man resolutely stared at and firmly gripped his rifle as if someone might take it. This maneuver was immediately followed by a double check of magazines ensuring that, earlier, they had been filled with rounds.

Many of the new men wore a non-virile look. Even now in the middle of summer, their skin appeared almost ashen, especially the few wearing the black-rimmed glasses issued by the Marine Corps. Many of the new Marines' helmet covers and flak jackets were faded and bloodstained—an unspoken reminder of the cost of this war on the men of Fox. The replacements made light talk about the environment and the two nights they had spent in the bush to reinforce the fact that they were, in some way, real veterans too.

By 0930 the amtracs slowed at the crossing point of the Song Thu Bon. The fleet of sixty to seventy small oriental houseboats rested on the bank seemingly waiting to ferry the Marines across the river as they had done before. This time, however, the amtracs turned right and began crossing the river. Kids emerged from the back of the houseboats after hearing the amtracs' diesel engines leave the road and splash into the river near the houseboats. Marines on the outboard edge of the amtracs waved hello and gave a "thumbs-up" in response to the enthusiastic reception offered by the children as the amphibious tractors crossed the river.

Those Marines not on amtracs had to wait nearly an hour for the houseboat fleet to take them over. That delay didn't matter to the stranded as they traded the locals cigarettes for bananas and cold orange soda. The villagers had a good relationship with the Marines from the 2nd Battalion who had been constantly there or across the river at Nong Son since Fox Company first arrived last December. Their village economy had blossomed. Many Marines had photos taken of the villagers and themselves so that, someday, they could show them to their grandkids.

As the men looked up towards the hills, some pointed at the commanding one without vegetation at the very top overlooking the river's crossing point: the Upper Nong Son. The thought of hanging out up there or down here with these friendly villagers seemed appealing and caused a mood change replacing the men's expressions from a gruesome alertness to confident smiles.

Once across the river the amtracs continued for a few hundred meters, passing by many Vietnamese carrying satchels on sticks traveling north. As the amtracs crossed over the road bordering the western side of the Song Thu Bon, First Lieutenant Jim Scuras looked at his map. They appeared to be coming from the hamlet of Ninh Hoa (3). After stopping at the offload point, Scuras directed Gunnery Sergeant Green to take the company's interpreter back to the river road to ask the Vietnamese travelers where they were going. The few men from Echo Company who greeted Fox's arrival hadn't reported anything unusual.

At Nong Son, Scuras assembled his platoon leaders and organized the manning of established defensive positions for the rest of the day. In July, the defenses on Nong Son were organized around three strong points situated along the spine of the hill, which stemmed near the river and extended to the summit. Actually, the first 275 meters of land stretching from the river consisted of a small village occupied by the European and Vietnamese engineers who operated the coalmines. The first defensive position where the occupying rifle companies established their command posts was beyond the village, about one hundred meters up the hill.

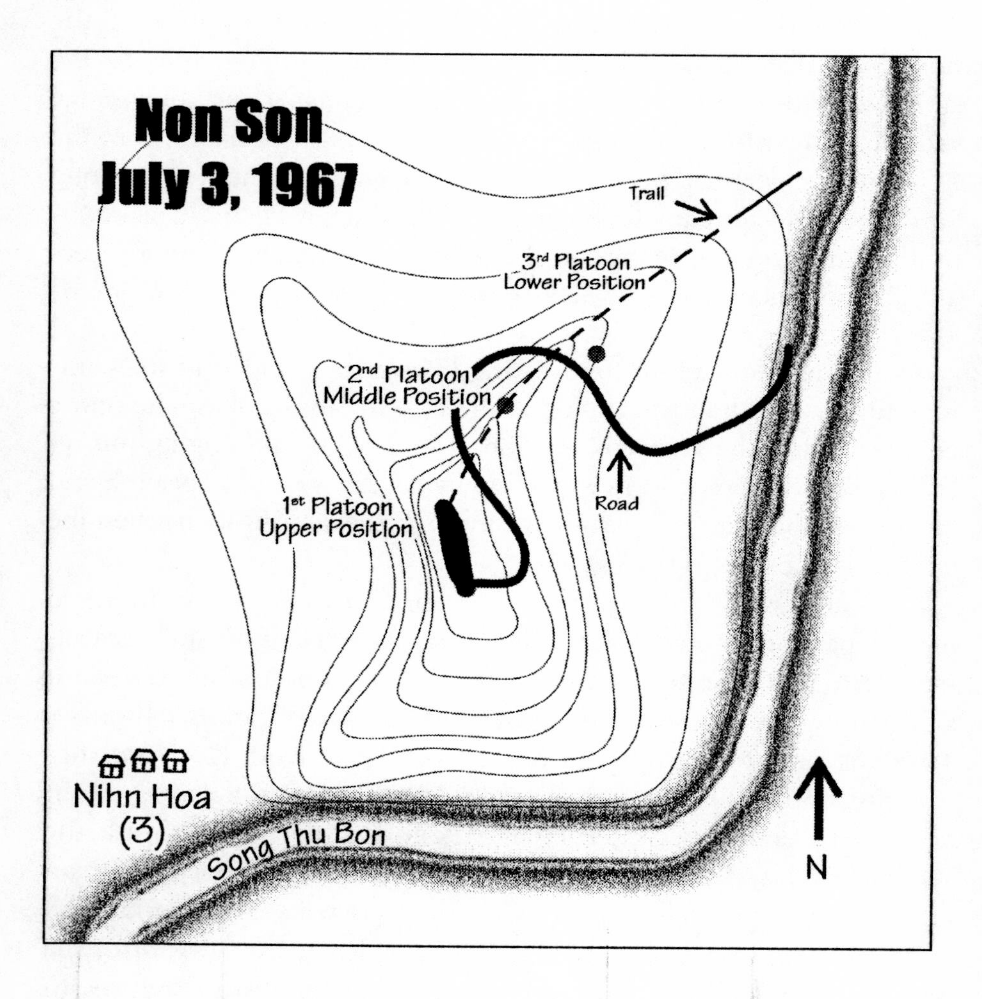

The second position was informally rcferred as the "Middle Position." This was another 400 meters further up the hill and was generally where the semi-active mining took place. One platoon would occupy this position, more or less along the spine of the hill.

The last defensive position was further up at the top, another 500 meters climb. From there, Marines could look down on the river below and at the village where the houseboats were. To the southwest, they could also observe the hamlets from which the Vietnamese with satchels on sticks appeared to be coming.

This upper position had several facets. First, it had the bunkers and trench lines dug under the direction of Captain Graham and Gunnery Sergeant Jones in February. Months ago, working parties of Fox men also filled sandbags into the early morning hours. The Upper Position also consisted of the end of a road that began at the village below and snaked back and forth over the hill's spine, finally terminating at the top. The road had been cut through the trees and brush by Marine engineers and was used to resupply the units on the top. On one side of the highest elevation was a cleared area used as a small helo pad. Last, slightly below the top, was the "106 position". Stationed at this position were 106mm recoilless rifles and 60mm mortars. The mortars provided defensive cover of the entire hill. The 106s fired on any enemy using the river to the south; they would also fire into the eastern end of the Antenna Valley through out the night. The activities were termed harassment and interdiction, "H&I", fire missions.

Scuras directed the 1st Platoon and their Weapons Platoon attachments to occupy and improve the existing fortifications at the upper position. The 2nd Platoon and the rest of the Weapons Platoon would occupy the middle defensive position. The 3rd Platoon would remain at the bottom with Scuras's CP. Before the platoon leaders left the valley floor, the platoons were to take enough munitions, water, and rations for two days. To reach the upper and middle positions, the 1st and 2nd Platoons would use a trail that went essentially straight up the hill's spine and not use the dirt supply road that wound its way circuitously around to the top.

About the time the platoon leaders began returning to their units, Gunnery Sergeant Green and the interpreter came hurrying up to group. He asked the men to stay so that he could brief them on what he had just learned. Gunnery Sergeant Green began to speak in a soft, distinct manner to ensure full comprehension of his report. "Villagers from Tu Xuan (2) and Ninh Hoa (3) are evacuating their villages. They are terrified. Several people we interrogated reported at least 200 NVA crawling from their villages up towards the top of Nong Son. Further, the NVA's reported mission was to attack Marines at Nong Son and seal off the heavily fortified Tu Xuan area to the south of here." Turning to First Lieutenant Scuras, he said, "Skipper, looks like we're in for a busy night!"

Scuras didn't have to tell the platoon commanders about the danger they were facing. If the reports from the villages were true, Fox Company, including the fifteen attached artillerymen, had only 108 men and actually less than forty at the summit. The NVA had 200 men moving up to attack their positions. The NVA could pack satchel charges, rocket propelled grenade launchers, RPGs, and automatic weapons.

Scuras hurried the 1st Platoon to begin occupying the hilltop. He gave the 2nd and 3rd Platoons directives to be prepared, on order, to reinforce the 1st Platoon. Under no circumstance would Fox give up the Upper Nong Son position.

Scuras reported the situation to "Texas Pete", the call sign for the 2nd Battalion. He requested artillery and fixed wing support to strike the enemy, who were at the time believed to be between the hamlet of Ninh Hoa (3) and the Nong Son mountaintop. The arty mission was fired. The requested air strike did not take place. Fox received no explanations for the lack of air support from Da Nang although tensions mounted as memories of Union II pervaded once more.

By the time the 1st Platoon and their Weapons Platoon attachments departed for the upper position, the afternoon was well underway. Once up there, the view was breath taking and the breeze felt like an air conditioner against the Marines sweated, camouflaged uniforms. Sergeant

Pappy Pennell set up the machine guns at already established emplacements, one between the US Army spot light team and the road entrance and one at the other end of the top position overlooking the top of the trail that led to the middle position. Most of the 1st Platoon occupied the bunkers and trenches. Sergeant Bill Clark's five-man squad that included his replacement, Corporal Thom Searfoss, occupied defensive positions at the "106 level."

Despite the current threat condition, many of the men were still planning to set off flares at midnight and have a few libations, well hidden in their packs, in celebration of the arrival of Independence Day.

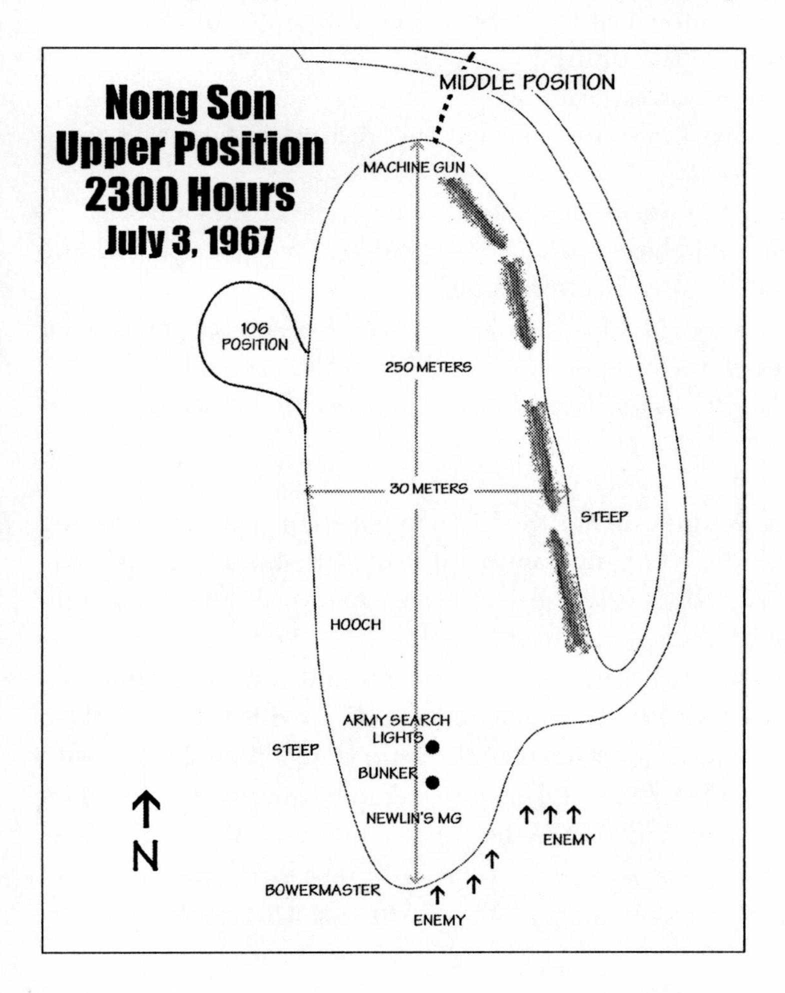

Pennell went half way down the hill joining up with his new friend, Lance Corporal Bernie Burnham, who was a fire team leader in the 3rd Platoon. Burnham's fire team was the furthest up the hill at one of the places where the road cuts across the trail. Burnham tied in with the 2nd Platoon at that location. First Lieutenant Scuras's command group and the many others in the 3rd Platoon remained at the Lower Nong Son position.

After closing the barbed-wire gate at the 106 position for the evening, Corporal Searfoss said to Sergeant Clark, "Well, Bowermaster was in the trench line and wanted 'Flames' to burn a clearing in front of his position to improve his 'field of fire'."

"What'd the platoon sergeant say?"

"He said he wasn't in charge of the flames section, so he wasn't going to do anything."

"So, why didn't Bowermaster just chop down the bushes himself?"

"Eh, well, he could have. Instead he moved his fire team to a listening post below 'Loosy-Goosy' Newlin's gun."

"You know, Thom, Newlin's an okay gunner. You just can never tell if he's serious about anything. That's probably why he's still a PFC."

"Bob told Newlin that if Newlin hears anything, he's not to shoot up his fire team."

1940 hours. At dusk one of the Vietnamese engineers came panting up the road to the company command post with "urgent news". The "Bac Vietnam", North Vietnamese, were about to attack. Second Lieutenant Martin stared at him incredulously; he was the most frightened man Martin had ever seen. Martin hustled him to Scuras and Green. The man recounted the information he provided, was thanked, and sent on his way. While Green and Martin stared at each other with eyes wide open and eyebrows raised, Scuras's only comment was, "Okay, that's one comment and there's the info Gunny picked up this afternoon. We get scoop like this all the time." The very experienced combat commander paused, then added. "We have to take it seriously, Tom," he said, trying to relax his fellow officer. "But, trust me, we get information like this once or twice a week and then nothing happens."

Martin wasn't convinced that this was "routine scoop". He returned to his platoon and directed his new platoon sergeant, Staff Sergeant Beniezo, to have the men keep their helmets and flak jackets on all night, stay at fifty percent alert until 2300, and then go to one hundred percent alert until 0100. From 0100 to 0300, the 3rd Platoon could return to fifty percent alert. From 0300 until dawn, they would be at one hundred percent alert. "Each man is to receive an extra bandolier of ammo and two grenades," Martin added.

Martin checked the lines, then returned to his platoon position. After dark he, Beniezo, and later Gunnery Sergeant Green played cards and waited.

2200 hours. Pennell, in this strange environment, remained alert, and listened for any noises. His radio operator, Private First Class Vickers reported "all secure" every thirty minutes. Vickers had two hours before he was due to be relieved at midnight by the new private first class from a 60mm mortar section.

2225 hours. "Rouzan! Hicks!" Bowermaster whispered loudly seeking the attention of his new fireteam members. "You guys hear anything?" he asked.

Private First Class Don Rouzan whispered back, "Sounds like someone digging!"

Hicks added, "Yeah, and cans rattling!"

"That's what I heard!" Bowermaster agreed. "Hey, Newlin," he called, "we hear a lot of noise just below us. Get the spot light on it!"

"Okay, I'll pass the word," a voice whispered from above.

2255 hours. More digging sounds erupted, this time closer. Bowermaster, growing agitated, pleaded for illumination again.

The voice from above explained, "They said it's probably rats or something, and you ain't gonna get any light."

2300 hours. Gunnery Sergeant Green stood up to leave having broken even. Beniezo, on the other hand, owed Martin forty dollars. Lost in thought, Green looked back at the lieutenant for a few seconds. Then, he merely said, "See you later, Lieutenant."

"Roger, Gunny," Martin said realizing the gunny was also anticipating an enemy attack.

2320 hours. Flares from the top of the hill were popped prematurely celebrating the 4th of July despite orders to the contrary from Scuras. Martin had been out on line and was annoyed by the lack of discipline no matter if it came from the Marines on top or the contingent of army soldiers operating the searchlight.

2325 hours. "Fox One, this is Lima Papa Alpha," Bowermaster began his transmission from his listening post to the 1st Platoon. "All right, now I see lots of lights from matches. They're below the road entrance to upper position, and they're headed your way, over."

2330 hours. The Marines and soldiers on the upper position went on one hundred percent alert. "Fox Six, this is Fox One, over," the 1st Platoon radio operator called to the company headquarters.

"Six, go"

"Roger, Six, we have significant movement in front and to the east of our position, over."

"Roger, I'll get Six Actual," Lance Corporal Andy Anderson, the company radioman, responded.

2335 hours. Explosions on the top of the hill could be heard from below, distant at first, but growing louder every ten to fifteen seconds. Immediately, the sky above Pennell and Burnham lit up like a twisted fire-works event.

The first two enemy 60mm mortar rounds went over the hill and exploded just outside the defensive trench line surrounding the cleared top. The third mortar round landed inside of the 4.2" mortar ammunition storage pit. The resulting explosion and concussion that followed rocked the hilltop.

A fifth satchel charge exploded above Bowermaster's squad less than a minute later near Newlin's bunker. Bob Bowermaster's eyes popped wide as he observed what seemed to be an endless stream of screaming men in pith helmets. They were silhouetted by the light of the now pulsating blasts of satchel charges being hurled at Marine bunkers above his team. He opened up his gun on the dozens of target opportunities. The two men with him followed suit.

VC sappers, the worst of the enemy soldiers leading attacks, continued lobbing satchel charges into the Marine bunkers and other fortified positions. One satchel hit Newlin's bunker. Shrapnel tore into Newlin's left arm and shoulder. His body slammed against the trench, yanking his breath from his lungs. Melvin, alive but dazed, twisted his head toward his four buddies. Their bodies were still.

Instantly, Private First Class Melvin Newlin's adrenalin kicked in full force. It masked any pain from his wounded arm and shoulder. Training, now instinctive, took over. Newlin fired his M-60 machine over 200 rounds per minute, far exceeding its sustained rate of fire, into an area where he had heard noises five minutes earlier on the road below his bunker.

In trace of the sappers were shouting Vietnamese, some in pith helmets, some bare headed. In twelve-man teams, the VC made two screeching enemy assaults on Newlin's gun. He cut the first team down one man at a time. Past its limit, his barrel over-heated. The weapon jammed. Newlin was reaching down for the spare barrel, when one of the enemy in the second assault team attacked him with a grenade, further inflicting wounds and rendering him unconscious.

Before First Lieutenant Scuras could respond to Fox One, the company radio net carried the final message from the 1st Platoon. The handset on Vicker's P-25 radio carried the transmission. A panicked voice carried the message, "We being overrun! We're being overrun! They're all over the place!" Then the handset fell silent.

After loading his third magazine, Bowermaster called to the platoon to announce his urgent need for ammunition.

No answer came.

The "106" level was seventy-five meters below the location where the satchel charges continued to explode. From there Corporal Thom Searfoss had heard his good buddy's plea for ammunition over the squad radio. With no radio response from the platoon, Corporal Searfoss told Sergeant Clark, "Bill, load me up with ammo. I need to get it over to Bowermaster!"

Bowermaster's fire team continued to fire on the enemy. Five enemy were killed before six others turned to assault the Marines. Within seconds, the exposed Bowermaster was hit hard in the chest, fell backward, lost consciousness, and lay bleeding on the road. Four of the enemy had closed to within ten meters of him. Rouzan and Hicks nailed them and the other two enemy attackers ran back to the larger force. The two young Marines, overwhelmed by their first violent combat experience, looked for help from Bowermaster. After seeing his motionless body, they looked at each other for a second to be certain of their next move. It was a no brainer. They turned and scurried up the hill.

Martin's 3rd Platoon was chomping at their bits to get into the fight. The slaughter of the 1st and 2nd Platoons in Union II incensed the men into fury. There were too many similarities taking place this night. He shouted to Green twenty meters away, "Gunny, I'm taking the platoon up to the top of the hill!"

"Outstanding, Lieutenant!" came Green's reply. Then Green added, "Lieutenant, take the trail, not the road."

Second Lieutenant Martin told Staff Sergeant Beniezo to take the rear before he started up the spine of the hill directing his men to fall in behind him as he went. When Martin reached the 2nd Platoon's position on the road, he blew by it and continued up the hill. His men, huffing and puffing, joined their former-football-player lieutenant who was merely nine months removed from his collegiate gridiron. Martin was not winded. He paid no attention to Sergeant Pennell's shouted warning as he ran by. Among the men were Sergeant Scott and two squads.

First Lieutenant Scuras had delayed the third squad, led by Sergeant Tinson, to lead them on a different path to the top of the hill.

The 2nd Platoon and Weapons stood ready to attack the hill. Private First Class Vickers relayed a transmission from the company commander's radio operator for Sergeant Pennell. "Hey, Sarge, the skipper is on his way here. We should be prepared to move up the trail with him."

"Bullshit," Pennell cursed. "Give me that radio, Vickers," Pennell ordered. "I couldn't divert that young Lieutenant Martin before he'd started up the trail, but I am sure going to redirect the skipper! Hell, I put one of the machine guns at the top of the trail pointing down here. We'll be cut in half!"

"Fox, this Fox Whiskey Actual, over." Pennell, the Weapons 'Whiskey' Platoon commander, announced.

"Ah…ah…this is Fox Six, go," the panting radio operator acknowledged.

"Let me speak to Six Actual, over."

"Ah…this is Six Actual, go," Scuras responded while he and his men raced up the trail fast as they could go in the dark of the night on a path cut into the jungled canopy.

"Sir, we lost radio contact with Fox One. If we move up on the trail, I believe the gun at the top will cut us down. Recommend we go off the trail soon after we leave my position and work our way up through the bush and away from the gun's kill zone, over."

"That's a negative, Whiskey. Ah…plan to go up the trail. Ah…I'm not worried about the gun now," Scuras's panting continued. Scuras believed that Pennell hadn't heard the transmission from the overrun 1st Platoon.

Minutes later, Scuras's command group, Sergeant Tinson, and his squad from the 3rd Platoon arrived at the middle position where the trail cut across the road. "Have 'Weapons' fall in behind, Sergeant Pennell," the company commander directed. "2nd Platoon, stay here and hold this position," Scuras added in the dark night to their gray silhouettes along the road. The lieutenant never saw his Weapons Platoon commander's tight-lipped face; Pennell was still furious that the skipper decided to ignore his advice and stay on the trail.

Martin and his two squads reached a place above Pennell's position where the serpentine road crossed the trail again. Martin glanced left and saw the road turn upward into the trees and then right to see the road disappear into the canopy. Gunny Green's admonishment, "Lieutenant, take the trail, not the road," flashed in his mind. To hell with Pennell. Martin, still leading his men, crashed into the jungle lining the trail.

Forty meters north he was greeted by a burst from a machine gun covering the top of the hill. Martin yelled, "Marines! Marines!"

Whoever was still alive on top of the hill wasn't convinced and fired a second burst. A Marine immediately behind Martin yelled, "Them's gooks, Lieutenant!"

Martin leaped to the left. His men followed. The thick waist-deep underbrush of bushes and grasses swallowed their camouflaged frames. Men were sliced by stray branches, wounds that went unnoticed in their hunger for revenge.

Assuming Private First Class Newlin was dead, the enemy poured over his position and proceeded to destroy the Marine and Army artillery weapons. They cut down the crews located in the middle of the cleared area sixty meters behind Newlin. An enemy flamethrower fired on the artillery pieces.

Rising out of the Song Thu Bon directly across from Nong Son was Cua Tan Mountain. From there, a Marine reconnaissance team observed the assault on the Upper Nong Son. They called An Hoa for an artillery fire mission on the attacking enemy.

At the same moment, with cloth bandoleers crisscrossed around his neck, Searfoss raced up and over the top of the hill firing at the attackers to his right. Enemy mortars falling behind him were but a minor distraction in contrast to the dozens of out-of-breath enemy soldiers moving in clumps toward the top of the hill. Searfoss fired his way through them, dropped the three NVA that he could see, and made it unscathed across the top of Nong Son to a collapsed bunker near the trench line. He hit the ground near Corporal Jack Melton now half buried by the collapsed bunker. Melton, a fearless flamethrower, was wounded and unable to move, futilely yelling for his rifle. From out of nowhere, Corporal Mike Bird jumped in beside Corporal Searfoss and both began giving some physical relief by scraping dirt from Melton's head and shoulder area. They found a rifle and munitions and gave them to him.

"Jack, you should be all right, I'm going off to Bowermaster," Searfoss said.

Bird added, "Yeah and I'm going to try to make it over to the platoon CP." As an afterthought he pointed, adding, "Thom, about thirty minutes before they hit, Bob moved to the other side of the road!"

A satchel charge exploded tossing Bird and Searfoss into the air. Both men were only slightly wounded. Searfoss landed near Melton who was now further buried. Again, Searfoss wiped the dirt from his face and arms. Miraculously, Melton was able to fire his weapon as cover for Searfoss as he ran for Bowermaster.

Under the protective fire of the half-dead Melton, Searfoss reached the bunkers on the other side of the entrance road. On the road below, two NVA soldiers were dragging Bowermaster back to the point where they had crossed below his position. Bowermaster, in terrible pain, thought that two Marines were dragging him to safety. "Take it easy, you guys. Can't you see I'm wounded! I'm wounded!" he kept yelling.

Searfoss never hesitated. Anger welling inside him, Searfoss fired two quick shots and two NVA lay dead beside Bowermaster. Searfoss charged down the hill to his wounded friend. Thom could see that Bowermaster had a sucking chest wound. His hand was bleeding as well. Bowermaster's face contorted as he gasped for air and pointed to his mouth. Searfoss began mouth-to-mouth resuscitation for thirty seconds until he stopped to spit out Bowermaster's blood.

Bowermaster pleaded, "More, more." Searfoss complied. Bowermaster started to look better and struggled to his feet.

Searfoss grabbed an AK-47 by his friend's feet then stripped two magazines off the bodies of the two enemy soldiers. The enemy was now being beaten off the top of the hill and was massing on the road thirty yards away. Both men fired at the horde of enemy, lit up by the continual artillery illumination rounds fired from An Hoa. Initially, the enemy didn't react. But soon the NVA saw enough of their compatriots fall; they returned fire at the two men in the road.

Bowermaster faded as blood gushed from his hand as fast as it left his chest. Both men dropped down onto the road. Thinking they were dead, the enemy stopped firing as the two Marines lie there. Searfoss gently rolled Bowermaster off the road and into the brush for safety. Searfoss performed mouth-to-mouth again to revive his sinking friend, and warned, "Don't you die on me, Bob!"

Awakened by the artillery rounds called in moments earlier by the recon team, which now impacted one hundred meters below his position, Newlin spotted the enemy back on the far side of the hilltop. Newlin completed the barrel exchange he had begun before he was knocked unconscious. Standing with the gun at waist level and holding it with his wounded shoulder and arm, he unleashed a barrage of rounds at the ten VC across the perimeter, cutting them down. In his peripheral vision, he caught movement next to one of the Marine four-deuce mortars. Gook, his mind flashed. Newlin swung his gun toward the enemy who was already attempting to wheel his rifle at him. Newlin fired first. The VC kicked back into the air and landed, motionless, nine feet away from the mortar.

While Newlin fired back across the hilltop at the enemy on the far side of his position, more NVA rushed up from the cover of the dense vegetation. They attacked as they ran. Bullets ripped into Newlin. Hit three times in his legs, he spun back toward the assaulting enemy. Firing continuously, he took out four, then five of the NVA soldiers. Three NVA ten meters away from him fired their AK-47s on the fearless

Newlin. Eight more bullets tore into the Marine before he succumbed, his defensive firing stopped, and he finally fell in death.

Corporal Mike Bird slid on the road next to Corporal Searfoss and Corporal Bowermaster like a baseball pro stealing first base. An NVA had determined their position and had maneuvered until he was on top of them. As he glided to a stop, Bird shot him in the chest with his .45 caliber pistol. Another enemy watched Bird's dramatic entrance and opened up, firing on Searfoss and Bowermaster again. Corporal Melton, three quarters buried, witnessed the whole scene and yelled, "Come on up; it's open!"

Bird and Searfoss half drug and half carried Bowermaster on a poncho up to the top of the hill. In front of them was a confused group of thirty enemy milling about on the top of the hill. When Bird and Searfoss opened fire on them, the enemy fled.

Searfoss turned around. Bowermaster lay unconscious with his weapon still in his hand. Mouth to mouth resuscitation did the trick again. This time Searfoss placed his pinkie into the hole in his friend's chest and waited for the corpsman.

The 11th Marines' 105mm howitzers and 8" guns did not catch the enemy unprepared. Anticipating such support coming from the An Hoa artillery batteries, the enemy positioned near the base fired eighty 82mm mortar rounds onto the artillerymen back at the base. Golf Company Marines guarding the An Hoa perimeter and US Army advisors at the adjacent Duc Duc District Headquarters observed the enemy mortar position. Ignoring their own danger, the Marine artillerymen counter-fired on the enemy mortars while continuing to support Fox's thinning lines.

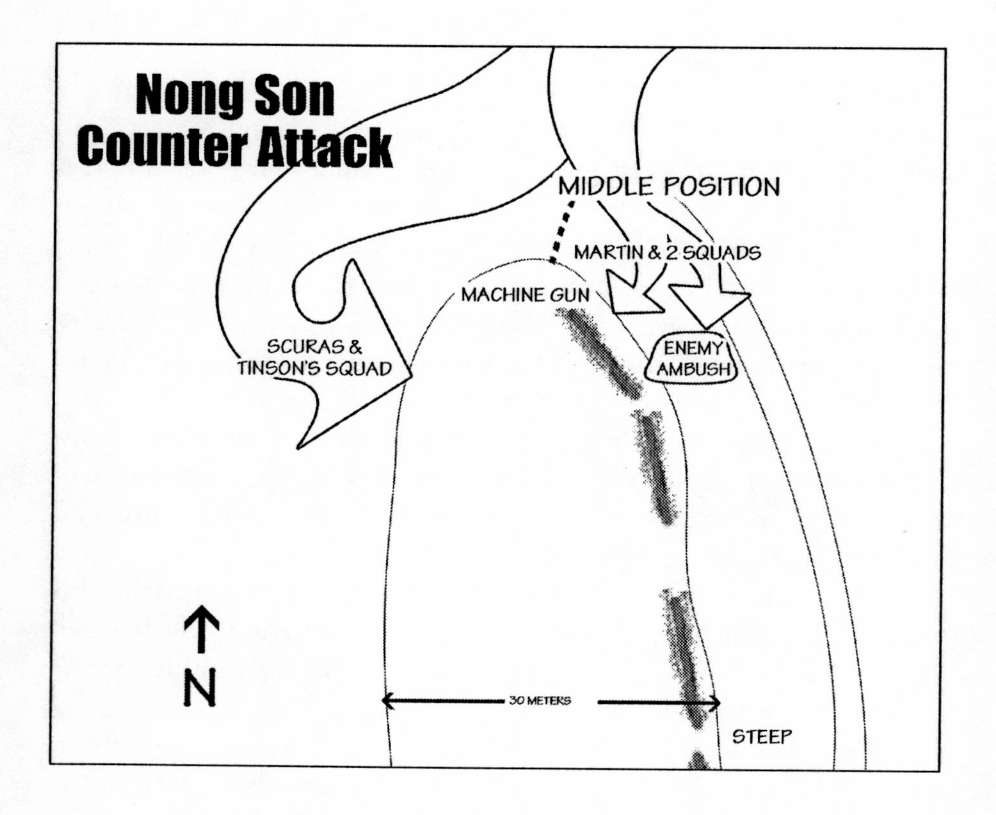

0035 hours. Scuras, with pistol in hand, veered to the right off of the path before assaulting the hill. His squad fired on more than twenty plus enemy soldiers they found on the top of the hill who were consumed in destroying artillery pieces.

Delayed by the machine gun, Martin's two squads arrived on top minutes later and were instantly embroiled in the fight.

The survivors of the 1st Platoon began firing from the trenches as the 3rd Platoon surged over the top of the hill.

Now with the two platoons firing at the NVA, the odds had shifted in the Marines favor and the enemy immediately began withdrawing from the hill. Pennell put Newlin's M-60 machine gun back into action and fired at the enemy disappearing into the jungle below the hill. The

60mm mortars were set up once again, and they too began lobbing mortars on the enemy withdrawing down the mountain.

0045 hours. Searfoss's heroic triage efforts paid off. In between plugging up Bowermaster's chest wound, watching his friend lapse into and out of consciousness, giving him mouth to mouth resuscitation, spitting out his friend's blood, and yelling for assistance, he had to shoot a huge man, who looked more Chinese than Vietnamese, five times before he fell. He and three others managed to reach the LZ where the wounded were being taken for evacuation. Searfoss deposited Bowermaster safely into a corpsman's hands.

0047 hours. Echo Company minus one platoon arrived at the lower base camp after having been notified less than one hour earlier they were needed to reinforce Fox Company. Their very much-appreciated effort had been spectacular. Echo had traveled nearly 3,000 meters, met the amtracs, crossed the river and came ready to fight within one hour. Echo took over the lower base camp and middle position, while the remainder of Fox moved to the upper position.

With wounds in his forearm and hand, Second Lieutenant Martin began to assess the need for security. The enemy had withdrawn to the south, off the mountain using the same route that they had taken to get onto it. Security had to be placed there just off the hilltop to warn the Marine defenders of a possible counter attack. Standing beside Newlin's bunker and looking at the enemy bodies below on the road, Martin turned around and spotted a Marine from his platoon. "McCloud! PFC McCloud!"

"Sir," the young Marine answered.

"Oh, McCloud, I want you and your fire team to establish an LP, a listening post, on the other side of the road and down about twenty meters," the lieutenant said pointing in the direction of the enemy withdrawal.

Even in the night Martin stared in amazement at the change in the private first class's face. His eyes grew from normal size to the size of fried eggs in a period of seconds; McCloud comprehended the full meaning of his lieutenant's order. "You want me to go where?" he stammered.

"Down there," Martin answered casually, pointing again. "Don't worry, I'll be right up here. If anything happens, I'll come right down and get you."

Under aircraft and artillery illumination, the men of Fox Company remained on full alert while evacuating their wounded throughout the remaining four hours of darkness. The only significant noise came in twenty-minute intervals from the grenades Private First Class McCloud and his fire team lobbed at the enemy as they attempted to retrieve their dead.

0500 hours. The black sky lifted. The toll from the fighting had been heavy. Six Fox Company Marines, four other supporting Marines and three US Army soldiers had been killed. The Marines suffered forty-three wounded. Irreparable damage was inflicted on one of the 4.2" mortars. One of the US Army spotlights was completely destroyed. Pennell and others visited Melvin Newlin to pay their final respect.

"Bernie," Sergeant Richard Pennell called to Lance Corporal Burnham. "Look at Newlin. Don't he look like he's just taking a darn nap. Kid's even got a pleasant look on his face."

Burnham nodded.

"And look at this," Pennell continued, pointing at an obviously warped machine gun barrel. "His first barrel melted down. Jesus, he must have been wounded and changed barrels before they got him!"

"The guys watching Newlin from those trenches over there," Burnham said, pointing, "saw he was trying to change his barrel when a grenade knocked him out. That's when the gooks came across the hill. Newlin somehow got up and saved our butts by firing on the gooks from behind. The son of a bitch is really a hero," Bernie replied.

Pennell added, "You know Doc Sawyer said he had a lot of wounds. God, it's hard to believe anyone could sustain three wounds and continue to be effective, let alone nineteen."

They walked by in silence for the next moment, just looking at the fallen hero.

"Bernie, did you see the number of gooks he stacked up below his position?"

"Must have been more than twenty. Seems to me he ought to be put in for 'The Medal'. Don't you think?"

"Well, that's what Lieutenant Scuras and the 'Battalion' were talking about on the battalion admin net a few hours ago."

"Damn incredible!" Burnham concluded. "By the way, Rich, what the hell are we going to do with all these gook bodies?"

"Don't know. I'll get back to you, Burnham."

Within an hour, Corporal Burnham had his answer.

"Bernie."

"Yeah, Rich?"

"Burn 'em!"

The 2nd Platoon and Weapons Platoon dragged the thirty-nine enemy bodies to the adjacent landing zone and burned them.

CHAPTER 6: THE CALM BEFORE THE STORM

Later on the morning of the 4th of July, First Lieutenant Scuras was medevac'd from the top of the hill with his third combat wound and the very best wishes from his men. Scuras's leadership plus the heroism and sacrifices made by Private First Class Newlin, Corporal Searfoss, First Lieutenant Martin, and Corporal Bowermaster were instrumental in holding this strategically important terrain. However, the Upper Nong Son would no longer be considered a defensive "stronghold" for its vulnerability had been laid bare. Improvements became a top priority.

After the wounded and dead had been evacuated, Fox could count less than seventy men at that position. That very morning, those seventy with the help of combat engineers flown in from An Hoa, and Echo Company Marines, began clearing the fields of fire Bowermaster had requested cleared eighteen hours earlier. With shape charges and bangalore torpedoes, eventually the top eighty meters of the tree canopy was removed. Naturally the first trees to be removed were those that shielded the 200 NVA troops on the evening of 3 July. Once cleared, the men found a neatly cut set of stairs dug into the side of the hill over 1,000 meters in length, the path that had contributed to Fox's devastating losses the night before.

During the next six months, the enemy activity level in the An Hoa valley was present, although almost dormant in contrast to the previous eighteen months. Fox Company rotated assignments with the other three 2/5 rifle companies, Echo, Golf, and Hotel. These tasks included: Nong Son defensive duties; manning the lines at the An Hoa combat base; patrolling and minesweeping Liberty Road from An Hoa to the outpost at Phu Lac (6) that overlooks Liberty Bridge; and occupying and conducting patrols from that outpost. While the activities were similar to what they had been for the past year and a half, there was a marked difference in the pace of training.

Battalion-directed training tripled during the month of September. The men knew the extra classes went way beyond those required in previous months such as calling in fire missions, patrolling, mines and booby traps, familiarization firing of weapons, and leadership. The three new courses that provided the most chuckles from the Fox Company Marines during the month of September 1967 were titled:

- Is the Marine Corps Going to "Pot"?
- Sex
- Who Pilfered My Playboy?

From July 1967 to the end of January 1968 Fox Company lost 160 men for various reasons. Five Fox Company heroes were killed during this six-month period. Another fifty-two were wounded, mostly from mines and booby traps. Those wounded for the third time would transfer out of Vietnam. Many Fox vets left after responding to a request for experienced combatants to join the Combined Action Platoon program. These Marines would live with and support local popular forces in the defense of friendly villages. Finally, many vets simply rotated "back to the world" when their twelve to thirteen-month tour was up.

Fox joined 237 new men during that period while building up from its post-Union II strength of nearly ninety men to over 200 with attachments by late January 1968. Not all these men were "newbees" fresh in from the States.

Replacing Scuras was Captain Frank J. Lennartz, an innocuous man of short stature who had little interest to go to the field. That was fine with the troops as their romance with Captain Jim Graham's aggressiveness mostly died with him on the battlefield. Lennartz was an excellent administrator. The captain brought First Sergeant Johnson with him to Fox. By no coincidence, Johnson, who also had a distain for field operations, was administratively proficient. Together, they reversed the reputation Company F held at the 1st Marine Division headquarters of being one of the worst administratively run organizations in the division. Lennartz was also credited with making a Foxtrot vet of nearly three years, Sergeant Robert Hernandez, the company supply non-commissioned officer. Hernandez squared away the somewhat shaky supply records and made sure supplies were readily available. In Lennartz's short ten-week command, one noteworthy combat event took place on the next three-week occupation of Nong Son.

The date was 1 October, and by that time Lance Corporal Burnham had proven LaBarbera's forecast to be a correct one. Burnham was indeed a fine acquisition for Fox Company. At thirty-one years of age, he was not only eight to ten years older than his rank contemporaries but he was far more mature. Socially, he had a natural fit with sergeants and staff sergeants and considered them to be his real peers. Beyond that, Burnham never paid heed to any rank in the company, from private to captain. He would speak his mind any time he wanted and would take on any issue but always for a cause he believed was right and just. He thought of himself as a tax-paying civilian more than a Marine, and by God, he wanted to get his money's worth out of the conduct of the war.

Adding to his personality was the fact that Burnham was a chain smoker, so his scratchy voice boosted his reputation as an older guy. Thus, it was to no one's surprise that he was quickly elevated to the billet of fire team leader. On the night of 1 October, Burnham and his fire team were at the Middle Nong Son position, the place where the connecting trail crossed the resupply road. Again, as on the night of 3 July, he was with Sergeant Pappy Pennell. Most Marines were on full alert as the company's positions had been probed during the past few days.

Up the one road from their position was a road junction that veered to the west and dead ended after seventy-five meters in the vicinity of four abandoned mine shafts. Sometime before midnight one of Fox's defensive trip flares ignited in the vicinity of the abandoned mines. The glare from that area was accompanied by a variety of noises. The platoon sergeant scurried up to Burnham and directed, "Take some men up there, Bernie, and find out what the hell's going on!"

"Okay," Burnham whispered in his scratchy voice.

Private First Class Rizzo was Lance Corporal Burnham's automatic weapons man and stood watch ten meters from Burnham. A new private also in Burnham's squad, was sound asleep near Rizzo. "Hey, Rizzo,"

Burnham called in a soft voice, "get Sleeping Beauty up. We're going on patrol!"

"Hey, Pete, Pete! Get up and put your gear on. We're going to check out some gook sounds," Rizzo said shaking his new mate, Private Lloyd Peterson.

"Bernie," Sergeant Pappy Pennell called, "mind if I tag along?"

Burnham shook his head and answered, "Don't mind at all, Pappy."

Within five minutes on a very overcast night Burnham led the three others up the hill. They passed by the platoon command post and headed for the road junction fifty meters ahead. Slightly crouched, the four men crept slowly up the road. Their helmets buckled, flak jackets unzipped, Burnham, Rizzo, and Pete held their seven-pound M-16 rifles in their right hands ready to hit the deck and fire or attack, whatever Burnham directed. With his .45 caliber pistol drawn, Pennell took up the rear.

As they neared the road junction, Burnham stopped, putting his hand in the air, and clenching his raised fist, which signaled the others to hold up. At that precise moment a VC stick hand grenade, commonly known as a potato masher, landed between the stunned privates. Burnham instinctively grabbed Rizzo and threw him to the right, pushed Pete backward, took a guess where the grenade was and hurled himself on top of it. He could feel the ridged device press into the soft skin of his stomach.

He waited.

Nothing happened.

Pennell ordered Rizzo and Peterson to take security positions up and down the road, while he and Burnham worked out what to do next.

"Jesus, Bernie!" Pennell started. "What the hell did you do that for?"

"I don't know. I just did. Damn it!"

"You know, Burnham, if you roll over slowly that pin could easily pop and up you'd go," Pennell stated the obvious.

"Yeah, Pappy, and what do you think we ought to do?"

"Well," Pennell began as he looked around, spying a ditch next to the road. "I say when I count to three, you roll over, and I'll pull you into this ditch behind me. What do you think?"

"I guess that's the plan."

"So, are you ready?" Pennell asked.

Burnham nodded his head.

Pennell stated, "All right, then."

Like a vice, his left hand slowly but ever so firmly curled and tightened on Burnham's flak jacket and utility collars while his right hand gripped the back of his cartridge belt. Pennell paused five seconds, took a deep breath, then said, "One!"

Instantly, with all his strength, Pennell yanked Burnham into the air, flipped him over himself like a rag doll, and they both rolled into the ditch.

Ducking low, they paused, steeling themselves.

They waited…and waited.

"The fuckin' thing didn't go off!" Burnham exclaimed.

Both men burst into laughter. "Jesus, Bernie that was a close one!"

"Yeah! and where's your damn 'Two and Three?'"

With their hearts beating at a sprinter's pace, still chuckling, the two Marines stayed put in that ditch for the next ten minutes to ensure there wasn't a delayed detonation.

Finally, Burnham said, "We'll stay here tonight, Pappy. You go back and don't let any one up here 'til dawn. Then we'll blow the damn thing."

"All right, Bernie. See you in the morning."

Burnham's selfless and extremely brave act could have saved the lives of his men had the grenade gone off. Pappy began to tell the tale the minute he reached the 2nd Platoon's position. By the morning briefing at 2/5's headquarters in An Hoa, Lieutenant Colonel McNaughton had directed that Lance Corporal Burnham be written up for a Navy Cross Medal.

On 11 October, Captain Mike Downs replaced Captain Lennartz. They met in the company office that afternoon, shook hands, and said a few brief words before Downs left with Gunnery Sergeant Pilchner to inspect the troops manning the lines at the An Hoa combat base. The men quickly learned Downs was a "Gung Ho" leader, who cared passionately for the well being of his men. He was highly intelligent. Although, with justification, he could get riled up; but overall, the men of Fox were greatly pleased to be led by the "Fiery Irishman" from Massachusetts. Problem was, for most, his strong Bostonian accent took a lot of getting used to. There was always a "What-he-say?" after he'd talk to the men.

By 28 October, Downs and Gunnery Sergeant Pilchner were hiking back to An Hoa from the Phu Nhuans having completed Fox's third operation in two weeks. "Gunnery Sergeant Pilchner, correct me if I'm wrong," the captain began, "but two days after I arrived, we were chopped to the 1st Battalion, 5th Marines to participate in Operation Onslow. Then we went on a search and destroy operation from the 18th to the 21st to help secure the Vietnamese elections. Now, we've just finished another three-day op with Echo Company."

"Well, yes, Sir," Pilchner said agreeing with the captain's facts.

"Is it normal to go on three separate operations in a two week period?"

"I wouldn't say it's normal, Sir. Sometime we're out on a long operation for more than a week at a time, like Union II, and sometime we're at the coalmines for three weeks at a time. Why are you asking?"

"Ahhh, it's occurred to me that one of the indoctrinations for new company commanders in 2/5 Marines must be to test him by sending him and his company out on several operations just to see what he does with the company."

"Maybe so, Sir; but I heard from the Ops Chief that we're slated to go to Nong Son soon. So, we ought not to have to go on so many ops like this'n."

"By the way, Gunny, do you have any idea when Gunny Green will return from his temporary duty?"

"Not really, Sir. I did hear that he might be back in December for a couple of weeks prior to his rotation. But you ought to be getting a permanent gunnery sergeant at the end of November or the beginning of December."

November 1967 could be characterized as a continuation of operations in the An Hoa valley. It came and went almost without notice. Fox was slated to join the rest of the battalion on Operation Essex during the period 6 November to 17 November in Antenna Valley. Instead, at the recommendation of the battalion surgeon, Dr Tom Viti, who believed Fox was too tired and had not sufficiently recovered from the Union II and Nong Son battles, Lieutenant Colonel McNaughton kept Fox back to provide security for the combat base at An Hoa.

Fox joined forty-eight new men during the month, sustained one booby-trap death, and had three men wounded. One noteworthy joinee was a corpsman by the name Ahrens. Hospitalman Third Class Rob Ahrens was formally assigned to Headquarters & Service, H&S, Company. Later, he would be attached to a rifle company for a period of six months.

Ahrens who had been in country for two weeks had been begging the Chief Corpsman to be assigned to Fox Company because of its need for a second corpsman in the 2nd Platoon. "Bu-bu-bu-bu-but Ch-Ch-Ch-Chief, I don't know why you think my stu-stu-stu-stuttering will prevent me from being a f-f-f-f-field corpsman."

"All right, all right, Ahrens. You can go to Fox's 2nd Platoon" the chief relented.

For all his bravado about wanting to get to the field and go on patrols, stand the line at night, and kill the enemy, Ahrens struggled mightily with low self-esteem due to his stuttering. While waiting for a flak jacket, helmet, and jungle boots in An Hoa, he was walking back from the mess hall after predicting he was going to kick some VC butt.

Hospitalman Third Class Mauricio Aparicico, who was the well-respected senior corpsman attached to Fox's 2nd Platoon, approached him commenting, "Hey, Ahrens, you'll do well not talking so tough. Don't be so aggressive. It won't help you!"

Without thinking, Ahrens turned around and slugged Aparicico, his closed fist impacting with the man's jaw. Stunned at his own reaction, he stared at the fallen corpsman. Extending his hand to help Aparicico up, Ahrens muttered, "I'm s-s-s-s sorry. I'm just str-str-str stressed out."

"Yeah and you can go screw yourself too," Aparicico grumbled, refusing Ahrens' hand while rubbing his jaw, "Good luck when you get to the field."

Building battle skills and conquering fears for these "combat Marines" did not come automatically for the "newbees". On the night of 1 December, the 2nd Platoon was to set up in a platoon-sized ambush nearly two miles away from An Hoa along Liberty Road. Their objective was to surprise any VC setting up road mines. Staff Sergeant James Smith, the platoon sergeant, was in charge. Clouds covered the An Hoa valley and blocked any moonlight. The platoon arrived at their ambush position where they could see only a sparse eight to ten meters in front of them. As the men began moving into their positions, cautiously, Private First Class Earl Miller, a newly joined replacement, crept beside a bush. He tripped a booby trap. The men sucked in the dirt-filled air while reacting to the deafening noise. Miller was killed instantly. Seven others, including Staff Sergeant Smith, were wounded.

New men were normally scared to death on night patrols and ambushes, even when nothing happened. After the booby trap exploded, they realized just how vulnerable they really were. The men took the time to successfully guide the evacuation helicopter into their position by a strobe light and the wounded Marines were placed on board. The VC would surely have seen this from miles away. Under normal conditions when an ambush site has been compromised, the unit would move to an alternate site for the remainder of the night.

That was not the luck of these new-in-country, wide-eyed Marines. Due to a weight problem, the chopper could not take Miller's body and the platoon was forced to stay in its original position for the remainder of the night on one hundred percent alert. Corporal Chris Brown, now second senior Marine in the platoon, exerted his seniority by keeping the men sharp all night. He made the rounds—checking to be sure all Marines were alert, prepped, and ready to fight. Heavy drops of rain splattered intermittently on the ground signaling that within moments a blanketing, monsoon rainstorm would add to their night's tension.

The drenched platoon began their trek back to An Hoa in the pouring rain the next morning. Miller's body was wrapped in a poncho, and the men took turns carrying him. Due to the downpour and the resulting mud, the men slipped several times dropping the litter with Miller's body on it. His dispirited, ashened face stared blankly upward as water continued to beat them without mercy. The men grieved, realizing now that boot camp had been easy.

Once back in An Hoa, First Sergeant Johnson called the emotionally drained platoon to the Fox Company office to tell them that all the wounded were all fine. However, Staff Sergeant Smith would not be able to take his R&R in Hawaii due to the wounds he'd received. Corporal Brown immediately volunteered to take his place even though he really counted on taking his R&R later in his tour. After Miller was killed Brown believed taking R&R now was better than possibly never.

"What's bothering you Tom?" Captain Downs asked Second Lieutenant Tom Martin who, by this time, had quickly elevated himself in Downs' eyes as a top notch professional young officer.

"Oh, 'Dark' John Salvati, err Major Salvati, Sir…just called and made me turn in the Stoner," Martin replied glumly, referring first to the tough-as-nails battalion executive officer and then to the prototype weapon Martin was never without.

"Tom, I've been meaning to ask you about that weapon," the captain commented.

'Well it's gone now, Sir. Sam Hall blabbed the fact that I still had it. Hell, Division thought it was lost."

"What did Sam do?" Downs asked about the lieutenant who had been transferred to the Division G-4 from Fox's 1st Platoon during the previous week, putting the story into context.

"You see, Skipper, the Stoner Weapon System may replace the M-16 one day. You can exchange major parts of the weapon and convert it from almost a pistol to a sub-machine gun. Four prototypes came in country last year. One found its way to Fox Company and Captain Graham had it when he was killed. The Division thought it was lost then; only Gunny Green picked it up, and when he left, he gave it to me.

"Ohhhh, I see."

"Well, anyhow, Major Salvati was at least nice about it, Sir."

Looking at Martin's M-16 Downs suggested, "You ought to FAM fire that this afternoon, I just got the word that we're headed out to Nong Son tomorrow.

On 8 December Fox Company was sent in two different directions. The 1st Platoon went to Phu Lac (6) to guard Liberty Bridge, while Captain Downs and the 2nd and 3rd Platoons went to Nong Son.

Ahrens finally joined the 2nd Platoon at the Upper Nong Son position. Nothing seemed to go right at first. Thanks to his cold-cocking Aparicico, he received a cold shoulder from the Marines. He blamed his reception on his stuttering or the fact that he was new and an outsider. His indoctrination took place on his first day. The Marine engineers attached to the company played a game where he was blindfolded, given an ax, and directed to chop up a tree stump. The other Marines had seen to it that he had removed his soft cover. They positioned his comfortable hat on the tree stump, and chopping away, he obliterated it. Once the blindfold was removed, the frustrated and insecure Ahrens riled; he was ready to fight the culprits who tricked him into cutting up his only soft cover. However, after a few minutes, he joined the rest in laughing about the good-natured joke and the payback played on him.

The 6' 2", somewhat-gangly and newly-joined Second Lieutenant "Rich" Horner was the 2nd Platoon's leader. Two days after the company arrived at Nong Son, at Down's request, Second Lieutenant Horner walked down the trail to the CO's hooch at the lower position to talk about the troops and tactics. Fox's newly assigned Gunnery Sergeant Ed VanValkenburgh, who was sharing the hooch with Downs, greeted Horner. "Good morning, Lieutenant. How's life up in the penthouse?"

VanValkenburgh, who had replaced Gunnery Sergeant Pilchner during the previous week, had the athletic build of a basketball player and an always pleasant, if not cheerful, disposition.

"Morning, Gunny, Skipper. We may have a much better view than you but the accommodations are like an early Howard Johnson's, not near this plush."

Downs had his business hat on, so he seemed serious, "Have a seat, Lieutenant."

"Thanks, Skipper."

"I want the gunny to stay while you give us an assessment of the defenses of the upper position. He may provide some insight to troop mentality on night defensive positions."

"All right, Sir," Horner acknowledged. "Well, first of all, the men who had survived the July 4th attack know Nong Son is far safer now than it had been before the big attack. That's because the top has been cleared and the vets are confident that their improved fields of fire will stop any major enemy assault on the position." After pausing, Horner went on, "On the other hand, the new guys are terrified at night. Since the legend of the enemy assault is frequently repeated, the number of the enemy seemed to have doubled. When I send a Marine to the listening post, beyond the brush pile, you know the one on the far side of the landing zone; invariably he'll hear something—probably a rock ape—and he opens up. Then everyone opens up."

"I know, Lieutenant. That's why I keep calling you at night to find out what in the hell's going on."

"You heard about what our new corpsman, Ahrens, did last night, didn't you, Skipper?"

"No, but I'll bet it's going to be interesting," Downs smiled.

"Well, not only does he stutter like all hell but Doc Aparicico, our other corpsman, had told me he's so gungy we'll have to keep an eye on him. Somehow he woke up and wandered over to the platoon's security post near the trail entrance to the upper position to see what standing watch was all about. You know, it's the position next to the 106 that's up there," Horner added. "I even told him corpsman do not participate in war fighting."

"I understand," Downs said approving the warning Horner gave to his corpsman about not taking part in the fighting.

Horner continued. "So, like all nights, we're firing random H&I fires. After a while the 106 gunner wanted to fire a single round as part of them."

By this time Gunnery Sergeant VanValkenburgh could anticipate where Horner's story was going and started grinning ear to ear.

Horner continued, "The gunner yelled 'Fire in the hole!' and fired a round. Well, on that hilltop, you can imagine the amount of dirt and stones kicked up with the back blast! Doc Ahrens sucked up a about a ton of dirt and thought we were under attack.

"So, for about the next five minutes he starts running all over the hilltop, waking everybody up yelling, 'In-In-In-In-Incoming! In-In-In-In-Incoming!' before he realized it was the 106. You should have seen it. Corporal Brown, PFC Campbell, and Lance Corporal Gasparini harassed Ahrens all day long today. Needless to say, he feels pretty foolish about it."

Captain Mike Down's mood lightened as he chuckled at the story. "Look, Lieutenant, you get your non-commissioned officers together and discuss fire discipline. Without it, you can't tell what the enemy's doing. You can't communicate because everyone is busy firing, and you're wasting ammo."

"Aye, aye, Sir."

"Okay Rich, how about staying here a minute before you go back up and taste some of Gunnery Sergeant VanValkenburgh special blend of Nong Son coffee," Downs offered.

Fox's 3rd Platoon, located on the "middle position" was led by a very youthful, fun-loving second lieutenant, Donald Hausrath. Many thought he belonged in a fraternity rather than a frontline infantry company. In some sense, the atmosphere in the 3rd Platoon could be considered lighter than most. Corporal Rich Carter, a serious Marine who loved a good story, was assigned as a rocket man in the 3rd Platoon. Joining him the day before and fresh from the States was a handsome young machine gunner from El Paso with a strong Mexican accent, Private First Class Pablo Contreras. At the Middle Nong Son position while dining on a can of C-rations, Contreras made a confession to Carter starting with, "You know what, Man?"

"Yeah, what?" Carter asked.

"Like last night I was on watch…and scared shitless, Man. You know?"

"Yeah, I know."

"They gave me a frag grenade, man. I only threw one before at Pendleton. So, last night I saw the bushes moving. You know, like they taught me, I looked away for a second. Then I looked back. The damn bushes were still moving!"

"What did you do?"

"Well," Contreras cocked his head to one side to meet his shrugged-up shoulder signifying the only logical thing to do, "I took out the grenade, pulled the pin, and threw it at the bushes."

"Well, good, Contreras," Carter responded.

"I forgot about the wire and netting running in front of the bunker and the grenade got caught the stinking stuff, and it fell straight down the side of the bunker," Contreras waited for the dumbfounded look that sprang to Carter's face. "I didn't know what to do so I yelled, 'Fire in the Hole!'"

"What happened then?" Carter pressed, leaning forward.

"Everyone came running and firing like it was a free for all."

Smiling and remembering, Carter said, "Yeah…I was one of them."

"I wasn't about ready to fess up, so I told everyone that a fuckin' VC threw a grenade at me!"

Carter laughed and said, "You made out better than that other new kid; I can't think of his name, a kid in the 1st Squad."

"Why what happened to him?"

"Well it was about a week ago and our platoon was here at the middle position. You know the two-hole 'shitter' near the platoon CP?"

"Yeah."

"Well, you came out to the field too quick and probably never learned how to burn shitters back in An Hoa like the other newbees."

"You're right, but I heard about burning shitters."

"You know each hole has a half of a fifty-five-gallon drum under it. To burn them you have to wait until the drum gets three quarters full," he explained. "Once that happens, some new guy gets to drag the drum away from the shitter, fill it with two to three inches of kerosene, stir it with a big stick, then light it."

"Okay," Contreras nodded slowly.

"Well, this new kid was assigned the shitter-burning detail," Carter pointed his thumb in the direction of the spot on the hill where it took place. "But no one told him how to do it, see?" Contreras nodded with interest. "All he heard was to pour the three inches of kerosene in it. Nobody tells him he had to stir it in with the crap."

"Right."

"I was about twenty feet away talking to another Marine and not paying too much attention to him when he threw in a match."

Eager to hear the rest of Carter's story, Contreras's eyebrows raised upward.

"Flames shot about twelve feet up from the 'honey pot,'" Carter exclaimed; his tone indicating his surprise at the sight. "I ran over, and the kid was in total shock. He only had his trousers on and they were rolled up to his knees. You wouldn't believe it! His skin was burned red except where the crap splattered him. He was really roughed up! The flame had burned all the hair off his arms and legs. It even frizzed and singed the hair on his head It was amazing!"

"Was he okay?" Contreras blurt out.

Carter went on, "Someone yelled, 'Corpsman up!' and Lieutenant Hausrath came running up to see what was going on."

"I'll bet someone got in trouble!"

Carter shook his head. "Once the doc got the kid stabilized and ready to be medevac'd, Hausrath was laughing like heck. He told the kid, 'Don't you even think you're going to get a Purple Heart for this!'"

That night Second Lieutenant Horner sent out Corporal Lynch's reinforced squad on a night ambush. He ordered the squad to set in at a specific location about 300 meters to the west along a trail. This was Doc Ahrens's first ambush and he was truly excited. The squad arrived at the spot designated by Horner. Lynch and his fire team leaders believed the position was unsafe because, there, they were vulnerable to an enemy attack. Without radioing back, they moved their location 200 meters further down the trail.

In about three hours, the big guns from An Hoa began firing illumination rounds in support of Nong Son's upper position. Like a fireworks display, after the rounds are fired, canisters carrying the parachutes with the illumination travel most of the distance toward the area to be illuminated. At some point the canisters release the parachutes and fall to the ground.

That night the large canisters began raining on the squad. Lynch radioed back to Horner, "This is Two Bravo, request you have arty shift their fires; the illumination canisters are coming down on us."

"Two Bravo, I coordinated with the 'Foxtrot Oscar' and he assured me that they would not fall on you!" the skeptical lieutenant pointed out referring to the company's forward observer. "Request you give me your position, over."

Lynch reported his new position. It was different than the one assigned. Horner questioned whether the person on the other end of the radio was Lynch or possibly an NVA who could speak English. The eeriness of the dark night pervaded even the most seasoned Marine. Horner would not allow Nong Son to be overrun on his watch. Marines out of place, unconfirmed radio reports…"Give me your position again!" he demanded.

Lynch repeated their approximated position.

Horner grew determined, "Authenticate. I say again, authenticate!"

Lynch's head slumped, "I don't have the authentication code, Sir." Corporal Lynch shook his head in disbelief; why didn't the lieutenant believe him? They were getting bombarded out here.

"I need your authentication code ASAP," Horner barked into the radio once more.

"We don't have it, Sir," Lynch responded, fear creeping into his voice.

Horner debated for a minute. He could detect the pitch of desperation in the voice at the other end of the handset. Finally, he ordered, "Let me speak to your corpsman, over."

Lynch, wholly confused at this point and almost frantic, gave the handset to Ahrens and said, "The lieutenant wants to speak to you."

Ahrens, who had never held a handset before, stared at it.

"Squeeze the damn thing and talk into it!" Lynch ordered.

Ahrens complied. "S-s-s-sir, this is D-D-D-Doc Ahrens."

Horner closed his eyes in relief. No NVA would be able to imitate an American accent with a true stutter, "All right, Doc. Give the phone back to Two Bravo and tell him I'll shift the arty fires!"

Lynch smiled, patting Ahrens roughly on the back, "You saved the…night, Doc. Thanks."

Ahrens' face lit. He laughed at their close call with the rest of the platoon while the men made a point of telling him just how glad they were that he had been assigned to the 2nd Platoon.

Fox saw very few enemy engagements during the rest of November, and the time passed quickly for them.

Christmas 1967 found the 1st Platoon of "Fighting Fox" at Phu Lac (6) guarding Liberty Bridge. They weren't as busy fighting as they were bent on enjoying the Christmas spirit. The platoon's mood was light. Many of the men spent time relaxing and getting to know one another. 1st Platoon's fearless Arizona Indian, Lance Corporal Roy "Chief"

Rascon, and resourceful French Canadian, Lance Corporal Reginald "Frenchy" Gautreau, even enjoyed a few light moments during the morning hours. They were often found with their squad leader, Corporal Bobby Smith, laughing and cutting up, particularly when he put on shaving cream and played Santa Claus.

CORPORAL BOBBY SMITH PLAYING SANTA CLAUS
(Photo courtesy of Bobby Smith)

Fox missed the change of battalion command ceremony on 2 January 1968 where Lieutenant Colonel Ernie Cheatham took the flag from

Lieutenant Colonel McNaughton. A week later the company returned to An Hoa to participate in Operation Checkers. "Checkers" was the name given to the tactical movement of the 5th Marines to the coastal area near Phu Bai. Fox flew by C-130 aircraft on 13 January. Their mission was "...to displace to the Phu Bai Area of Operations," and, "On or about 15 January 1968, be prepared to conduct offensive operations in an assigned area of operations as directed."

By 15 January, Fox Company had dropped their seabags near the four tents set aside for them at the Phu Bai base and moved to conduct search and destroy operations near a railroad tunnel, twenty kilometers south of Phu Bai and four kilometers north of Phu Lac. Fox also provided security for a US Navy Seabee road construction team that needed to establish a "rock-crusher" site for improving Route 1 or QL1, the provisional highway. This highway connected the ancient capital of Hue to the country's second largest city, Da Nang.

Things were back to normal by 18 January. In fact, they were better than normal. The new operating area was free of mines and booby traps. As a result, troop morale inflated. On that date First Sergeant Johnson called Corporal Burnham to come in from the field to correct a few administrative entries in his service record. The next morning, after a two-truck convoy dropped off several cases of C-rations, water, mail, and ammo, the older and more somber appearing Burnham caught a ride to Phi Bai on a 6x6, two and one half ton truck from the field amidst a hail of cat calls thrown his way by the younger 2nd Platoon members.

"Don't get too drunk, Bernie!"

"Even if she's pretty, you don't have to kiss her!"

"Hey, Bernie, tell the first sergeant I need to get out on R&R!"

As the driver shifted gears the intermittent roar of the 6x6 drowned out the youthful heckles, and Burnham was instantly disengaged from combat, enjoying the built up surroundings along the road. He viewed the military encampments at Phu Bai as he traveled north. The U. S. Army camp was on the coastal side of the compound dominated by the large airstrip, while the Marines were on the western or mountainside.

Burnham realized that the green tents scattered on the west side of the road had to be the Marines. Hell, the Army couldn't work from tents in a camp, he thought. They had to construct those nice Butler Buildings with the portable air conditioners hanging from every other window, he mused.

"Thanks, guys", Burnham yelled to the driver and his "shotgun" after jumping off the rear of the truck and walking forward to its cab. "And where was 2/5, again?"

The driver pointed to a group of tents and Burnham nodded "Okay," he said, signifying he understood.

Nearing the 2/5 area Lance Corporal Burnham spotted Private First Class Andy Anderson. After buying booze from the battalion surgeons back in An Hoa before Christmas and getting blitzed without permission, he had been reduced to that rank. In his inebriated state, Anderson projected in added decibels his uncensored and deep-felt opinions. Fox's new captain had changed Anderson's duties from company radio operator to company property non-commissioned officer. Anderson carried a seabag on his shoulder and was moving it around a tent filled with other seabags that obviously warehoused the personal belongings of the men of Fox Company.

Burnham, who didn't know Anderson all that well but had heard he was older than most of the troops and had been some sort of a Federal Police Officer in Panama prior to getting in the Corps, greeted the sweaty man, "What's up, Andy?"

Anderson dropped the bag, never smiled and mumbled in his deep, slow-clipped Arkansan voice, "Some of these son-of-a-bitches think they're going to need everything they own when they get to Vietnam. Like it's some kind of damn camp! You know one maggot from Weapons even had one of those small TVs in his bag. Like he was gonna be watching it at night in the bush. What's say, Burnham?"

"How's your new job going?"

"Great. I'm working by myself; the first sergeant can handle my crap, and I get to drink more than being out in the bush. Whatcha' here for?"

"First Sergeant wanted me to sign some papers," Burnham explained. "When's chow go around here?"

Anderson looked at his watch and announced, "It'll being going in 'bout half an hour. Go in and sign your papers than come look me up."

"Okay, Bud."

Burnham chose not to go back to the field that afternoon, although the opportunity was there. Instead, with Top's okay, he planned on catching the resupply run in the morning.

At lunch, Anderson complained about the Marine's "slop-chute" only selling Old Milwaukee beer. "Burnham, I get off 'bout 1500. Why don't me and you grab our rifles and wander over to that Army base. 'Heard the 1st Cav built themselves a nice NCO club over there. They got mixed drinks and all. We can get back before nightfall."

"Sounds good. I wasn't interested in going back to the field today anyway," Burnham offered. "I'm going in to read the paper. See you 'round three."

In broad daylight the two Marines, M-16s slung on their shoulders, walked across the highway from the Marine gate to the Army's gate, which was about 150 meters away. The camps were surrounded by barbed wire for security. An enemy attack had never occurred, but precaution prevailed. At night, pedestrian traffic was prohibited; only vehicles were considered safe in that no man's land between the two camps. Once at the Army gate, an air force guard pointed the way to the club.

"What's that flyboy doing in a place like this, Anderson?"

"Oh they split the base duties with the Army guys. Look, they got that new check-in contraption for your rifle outside the club. Seen 'em before. Never used them. Damn, can't be that hard."

After wrestling with the new device for a few minutes, they stowed their weapons. Anderson and Burnham entered the Army club with the keys to the rifle-locking device in their jungle utility pockets. They ordered a drink at the bar. The bartender told them each drink was thirty-five cents and asked if they wanted to run a tab. Both Marines had over fifty dollars with them and quickly agreed. The two started catching up with each other. Burnham was fascinated with Anderson's Panama counter-drug stories, while he told Anderson all about the ol' Corps.

The soldiers and airmen also relaxing in the club became fascinated with the two seasoned Marines and their stories drifted to Fox Company adventures. With a substantial crowd gathered around them, the Union II and Nong Son stories were re-canted once more.

Finally, Anderson looked at his watch and realized it had already been dark for an hour. "Bernie, it's 2000 and we better get our asses out of here!"

"Whoa…You're right. Hey, Guys, it's our Cinderella Hour, and we have to split. Good talking to you," Burnham's scratchy voice ground out in his New York accent. They exited the club into the dark of the night. As they proceeded to unlock their weapons, Burnham turned to Anderson and asked, "Didn't you say we can't cross back over the street at night?"

"I did.'

"You know, Andy, if we stay here tonight, there's a good chance I'll miss that morning resupply tomorrow. We ought to get back tonight."

"Come on with me," Anderson said, "I have an idea."

Within minutes they were in an area of cottage-like homes. A sign at the entrance to the street indicated that this was a restricted area and the quarters for "senior non-coms". At the first house Anderson stopped approximately thirty feet from the front door, pointed to the ground, and told Burnham, "Pretend you've been wounded in the leg." Burnham tossed himself onto the ground, hunched himself over, and grabbed his right leg with both hands. He was careful to face away from the door, so that his "wound" would be hidden from obvious sight.

Anderson braced himself, and then knocked on the door as hard as he could. Soon, a slightly overweight, middle-aged man appeared holding a beer. Anderson heard the Armed Forces television in the background. Having looked at the nameplate beside the door, he began, "Master Sergeant Turley, my name is O'Hara, Major O'Hara, from the Special Forces."

"Yes, Sir," Turley responded. He looked Anderson over, but as wearing rank insignia was uncommon in Vietnam, took the private first class at his word. "What can I do for you?"

"I've just come in from a secret mission and I need to get this wounded man to the helo pad, ASAP," Anderson fabricated, pointing to the now-moaning Burnham. Burnham rocked back and forth ever so slightly for effect.

Turley hesitated at the bizarre situation. He observed Burnham and then took in Anderson's grizzled appearance before responding, "Right, Sir. I have a vehicle; do you want me to drive, Major O'Hara?"

"No, that will be fine, Master Sergeant Turley," Anderson countered jerking his head in Burnham's direction. "He's come in and out of being delirious. I'm afraid he'll compromise our mission."

"Oh, yes, Sir," Turley agreed, nodding his head vigorously. "I understand. The jeep's right over there," Turley acknowledged, pointing to the only vehicle in the street.

"Thank you, Master Sergeant."

Anderson spun back to his accomplice. He leaned over to pick Burnham up off of the ground, whispering, "He's watching. You better make this good!"

Burnham groaned with extra emphasis this time. He writhed so much in Anderson's grasp that the private first class almost dropped him. Having left the keys to the jeep in the ignition, Master Sergeant Turley waited in his doorway and watched the two Marines until they had driven out of sight. The two friends laughed heartily the entire drive back. Within five minutes, they were safely inside the Fox 2/5 area. Anderson turned off the vehicle and looked at Burnham with a deadly serious face. "Shit, Bernie."

"What?"

"I left my damned rifle back at that master sergeant's house. We gotta go back!"

Burnham, after hearing Anderson's problem, asked, "Why in the hell did the Skipper make you Property NCO? You can't keep hold of your own…Oh, never mind, let's go get the damn thing."

And off they went…

CHAPTER 7: HUE CITY

After returning to their position near the "rock crusher" site in the Phu Bai area in mid-January, Fox Company had encountered no significant enemy contact since their arrival. Despite the monsoon rain, both the officers and men were ecstatic about the new location. Safe from constant VC rifle and mortar fire, free from mines and booby traps, operating near Highway 1 was a walk in the park when compared to the An Hoa valley to the south.

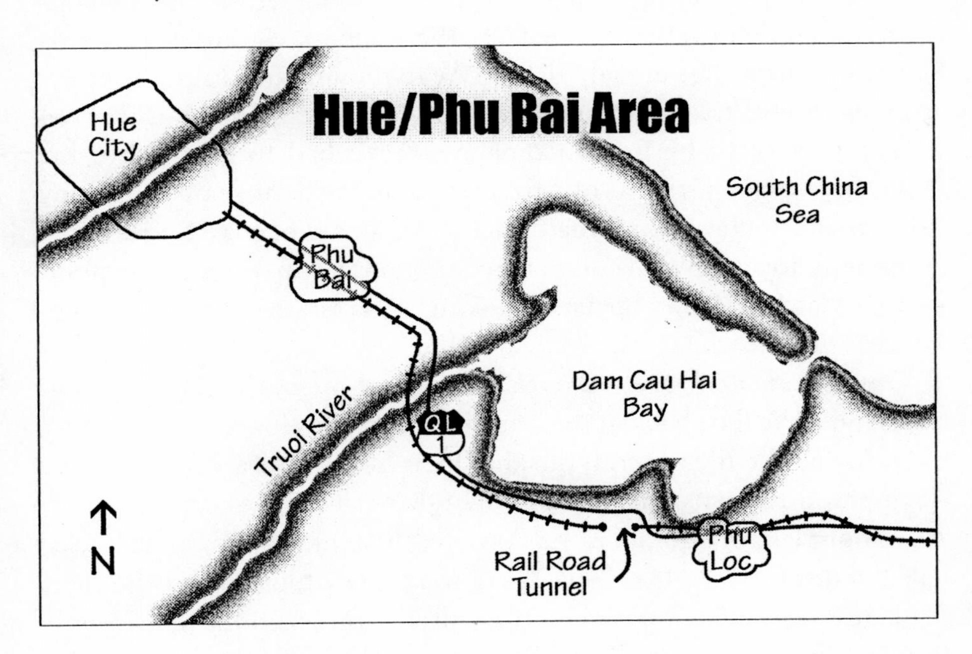

The 2nd Battalion, 5th Marines' Tactical Area Of Responsibility, stretched from Phu Bai to Fox's position west of Phu Loc and in the vicinity of the railroad tunnel. The 1st Battalion was located four kilometers south of Fox's position in a valley beside the village of Phu Loc. The width of the TAOR depended on the proximity of the mountains west of the Dam Cau Hai Bay and the bay itself. At some points there were ten to twelve kilometers of rice fields; however, where Fox was located, the rugged mountains precipitously fell into the bay and there was very little operating area.

The night of 30 January was drizzly and dark. Corporal Rogers, Downs' battalion radio operator, handed the handset to the captain. After a couple of "Rogers" and "Aye, Ayes", Downs finished the brief conversation with "Right away, out." Without pausing Downs directed his company radio operator to assemble the platoon commanders, "Corporal Violett, get the actuals up here ASAP."

In minutes, First Lieutenant Wranovitz and Second Lieutenants Horner and Hausrath reported to the captain. Gunnery Sergeant VanValkenburgh was already there. "We're moving out in the next ten minutes to Phu Loc," the captain began. "We're to fill the positions in 1/5's lines vacated by Bravo Company. Bravo had to go up into the mountains to support a reconnaissance team. We'll move in a company column and follow the railroad tracks. The order of march will be 1st Platoon, followed by the company command group, then 2nd Platoon and 3rd Platoon," Downs paused, looking at Hausrath.

"Sir?" the lieutenant asked.

"You'll bring up the rear. We really have to move out, so I want you to travel light. We'll be back in the morning! Any questions?"

Watching the men silently shaking their heads indicating there were no questions, Downs finished, "All right then, let's move out!"

An hour later the company had traveled 2000 meters along the tracks, half the distance to 1/5's lines. There were a few foothills on the right flank, just beside Highway 1 and the railroad tracks; on the left side was the shore of the bay. Just where the tracks made a slight bend to the left, the point squad from the 1st Platoon stumbled into an enemy ambush. In their path, an unknown number of enemy lay in wait. The NVA hit fast. Bullets whizzed by the Marines from several directions, killing the squad's radioman, James Jones, Jr. Immediately, five other 1st Platoon men were hit and injured in the attack. Each man fell where they once stood, unable to defend themselves. When suddenly, the firing stopped; all was quiet.

By the time choppers could evacuate the five wounded men and Jones's body, Bravo Company had returned to their lines and Fox's mission was canceled. The company who had just experienced its first "Tet" encounter was ordered to do an "about-face" and return back to their positions near the rock crusher. The bitterness of losing six good men needlessly remained unspoken.

Tet, the Vietnamese holiday, celebrating the Buddhist New Year, would begin in one day. In recognition of their largest and most important holiday of the year, North and South Vietnam had struck a truce or cease-fire period, a circumstance that thrilled the men of Fox. The Marines felt delighted by an opportunity to relax and let their guard down for a few days. At the time Fox had been ambushed no one in Fox Company, the battalion, in fact no Americans were aware that vanguard units of the North Vietnamese Army had already begun infiltrating the ancient capital city of Hue, just to the north of Phu Bai. Carefully plotted, the North Vietnamese deception caught everyone in its trap. Most South Vietnamese had returned to their ancestral homes in preparation for the ensuing celebration. Cities, like Hue, were bursting with civilians, friends, and families, all gathering in peace. Those same cities enjoyed only a skeleton crew of U.S. and ARVN troops due to the cease-fire.

That same night, just to the north of Fox, an NVA company-sized unit attacked Hotel Company units guarding the bridge where Highway 1 crosses over the Truoi River. Hotel Company fought them off bitterly causing the enemy to withdraw, but this was seen as an ordinary act of aggression as bridges were often targeted by the NVA.

Instead of returning to their packs and gas masks, Fox Company met trucks along the highway that took them toward the Truoi River Bridge to join up with Hotel. As they rolled northward, they passed a Vietnamese Army compound that had also been hit that night. On the defensive wires of the ARVN compound were the bodies of enemy dead who attempted to seize the fortification, a foreshadow of the scenes that would become prevalent in days to come.

Earlier in the morning, the two companies began chasing the enemy along the southern bank of the Truoi east toward the mountains. Both companies soon began to receive small arms, rifle grenade, and mortar fire. Fox and Hotel began routing the enemy. Approaching a heavy tree line, Fox's lead element was Corporal Chris Brown's squad. That morning as Brown's lead fire team led by Lance Corporal Louis Gasparini swept into the tree line, the NVA sprung an ambush on the team. Private First Class Jerry Barksdale was raked by rounds and killed instantly while Private First Class Richard Schultz was seriously wounded. Other casualties mounted on both sides with Fox suffering one killed and four wounded and Hotel losing another killed and three wounded. The companies slowed, evacuated the casualties, and prepared to attack the trapped enemy.

Out of nowhere came an order for 2/5 to halt the attack and prepare to return to Phu Bai. By noon Golf Company had been chopped from 2/5 and was now under the operational control of the 1st Battalion, 1st Marines. Although there was no concrete intelligence, there were reports that 1/1 was heavily engaged in combat in Hue City and needed reinforcements. Golf Company, who had been the alert company in Phu Bai, would be trucked into Hue City that afternoon to reinforce 1/1. With Golf gone, Fox was needed to strengthen the security for the base at Phu Bai. These orders "from above" had frustrated the battalion's commanding officer, Lieutenant Colonel Ernie Cheatham, as he had the enemy just where he wanted them: trapped along the Truoi River.

Cheatham was not a lightweight in many ways. He was a huge man towering over 6'4" and as a former professional football player, had the physique to fully flesh out his frame. His mind benefited from his scholarly pursuit of tactics, fast wit, energy, and intuition. Within the month of his command assumption, the Marines in the 2nd Battalion had learned to appreciate the fact that "Big Ernie" was their commanding officer.

One of Fox's 2nd Squad leaders was also frustrated. After nine months in combat, Corporal Chris Brown's handle, "Salty", suited him because he constantly looked out after and supported his fifteen-man squad much like an old sheep dog would look out after his flock. He filled an "older brother" role, as the bonds between his men grew ever stronger under his leadership. Two things happened on 31 January that frustrated Brown. First, was the loss of Barksdale. Barksdale, who had one month to go on his yearlong tour, had a reputation of being one of the nicest men in the company. A friend to everyone and a superb Marine, Barksdale's loss tore deeply into the entire 2nd Platoon. Second, when they arrived at Phu Bai and received their mail, Brown's best friend in the squad and a fire team leader, Corporal Christobal Figueroa-Perez, received a "Dear John" letter from his wife in Puerto Rico.

Brown and Figueroa-Perez had arrived in country together, and they were the only two in the platoon who were married. Brown saw Figueroa-Perez struggling over his letter. "Hey, Fig, what's up?"

"Oh, Man, I don't know. Maria said she wants to split. She doesn't tell me why. I mean what's up with this? I gotta get my butt home to find out what's happening. I'm stuck here fighting this stupid war, Chris. You have to talk to someone to get me out of here!" Figueroa-Perez clammed up. He wouldn't say another word for the rest of the night.

Brown wasn't sure how to handle Figueroa's remorse. He knew something big could be happening soon and did not believe Figueroa could fight at the level he needed for heavy combat. Staff Sergeant Tinson, now platoon sergeant of the 2nd Platoon, suggested Brown see the battalion chaplain to ask him to hold Figueroa back, but the chaplain believed it best for Figueroa to be with the rest of the men.

"The Lord works in mysterious ways, Corporal Brown. If we let him stay back, he may do something rash. I really think he'll be better off with you and his buddies than here in the rear."

That night the company became the Phu Bai reaction force and the men were allowed to sleep on cots in tents while they waited to be "called on", if necessary. The only complaints were: "God, when are we going to get our packs? I haven't brushed my teeth in two days."

"Man, I have my wallet in my pack and I can't buy any cigarettes."

"Yeah, I kept my extra bug juice in with my gas mask pouch. I'll be needing that soon enough!"

"I don't have my photo of that Australian chick who swore she'd wait for me!"

1000 hours. On the morning of 1 February 1968, Fox was told that its operational control would be passed to 1/1 later that day. Under a canopy of gray clouds, Fox was broken into flight teams ready to be choppered into Hue. Fox Company's Captain Downs received a couple of briefings, one from "Task Force X-Ray", the code name for the 1st Marine Division Forward, and one from the 1st Marine Regiment. Following his short briefings, he knew that the combat situation in Hue fifteen kilometers to the north of them was sketchy at best. Nevertheless, he updated the Fox unit leaders on what he had just learned. He also passed along a promise he'd received that the men's packs would catch up to them soon.

The company had 213 Marines and Navy corpsmen that included a section of two 81mm mortars, a section of 106mm recoilless rifles, and an engineer squad. At 1430 hours CH-46 and UH-1 helicopters began the airlift. Downs flew in the first wave of choppers with the entire fifty-three-man 2nd Platoon. Eight reporters and photographers from various news agencies also shared his ride.

Enemy ground fire greeted the choppers as they landed in an open field 150 meters north of a military compound east of the river Song Huong and adjacent to Highway 1. Bordering the fifty meter by fifty meter compound was barbed wire; guard towers stood at each corner. Inside the wire was an impressive two-story, stone structure, obviously constructed by the French; each floor had large arched windows. Prior to Tet, the small fortress housed the advisory team for Hue City's Military Assistance Command, MACV. It was now being shared by Lieutenant Colonel Gravel and his 1st Battalion, 1st Marines staff.

Downs passed by one small, barracks-looking building just outside the MACV compound and proceeded across a small street and through a gate to report to Gravel. Wounded Americans and Vietnamese soldiers awaiting evacuation lined the walls of the small open area inside the compound where eight to ten military vehicles had been haphazardly parked. Downs entered the command center expecting to witness a busy, yet orderly, field war room. What he found was a touch more chaotic. An older, somewhat nervous US Army colonel with a MACV patch sewed on the top of his left sleeve and a Marine lieutenant colonel huddled together in conversation. At a table that was covered by a map, a Marine Corps captain was engaged in a conversation with two enlisted men, both ranking staff non-commissioned officers by their appearance. A couple of radio operators, sitting near the walls of the room, monitored their PRC-25 radios.

"Sir, are you Lieutenant Colonel Gravel?" Downs asked the tired Marine officer, noting the dark circles that were prominent on the man's face.

Gravel fixed his eyes on the intruder and announced, "I am."

"Captain Mike Downs reporting in with Fox Company, 2nd Battalion, 5th Marines, Sir."

"Ahhh, Captain Downs, you're here at a most crucial moment," Gravel greeted Downs, his enthusiasm over Fox's arrival evident. "Meet Colonel Adkisson," Gravel added with no noticeable connotation of respect toward the officer who headed MACV in Hue and the Thua Thien Province.

"Pleasure, Sir."

"Downs," Gravel continued, "get your men set up in that empty building you passed as you came into the compound," he pointed in the general direction. "Report back here in about fifteen minutes for your first task.

"Aye, aye, Sir," Downs acknowledged, nodding his head affirmatively.

Outside the compound he found Gunnery Sergeant VanValkenburgh standing by the building he passed on the way into MACV. "Gunny, apparently this building is going to be our home tonight. Check it out and get the men ready to occupy it. Even though it will be good to get out of the rain, we don't want to be sitting ducks in there, so figure out what local security we need once most of us are inside."

"Gotcha', Skipper."

"Did you get any word on the rest of the company?"

"Sure did. They're airborne. Should be here any minute now."

"How about Lieutenant Horner? Have you seen him?"

"He's over there with his platoon," VanValkenburgh answered pointing to a group of men. Downs looked past the gunny's square shoulders and sturdy frame to a distance nearly twenty meters away.

He walked over to the gathering 2nd Platoon, many of whom he knew by name, and caught Horner's eye. "Lieutenant, have your men ready. I'm going back to get our mission," the captain informed the tall lieutenant.

Downs returned to the compound and immediately spied a familiar face on the small street outside the gate, Captain Charles Meadows, the commanding officer of Golf Company. "Hey, Chuck, how goes it?" Downs asked extending his hand to greet his friend.

"Hi, Mike," Meadows greeted Downs, shaking his hand at the same time. "Not worth a dime. I had fifty men wounded or killed yesterday! The NVA and, I guess some VC, are here in much greater strength than us. They have the Citadel across the river over there," Meadows jerked his head to his right, referring to the walled fortressed across the Song Huong that the Americans referred to as the "Perfume River". "I darn near lost the whole company yesterday trying to cross that bridge getting over there. On this side of the river it's no better. Every time we try to go down these streets, we get our butts shot off! Hell, yesterday we couldn't even cross Highway 1, fifty feet from where we're standing right now. Bottom line is they're set in every nook and cranny, and I'm glad to see Fox Company. I've been working with Alpha, but they are pretty well shot up too."

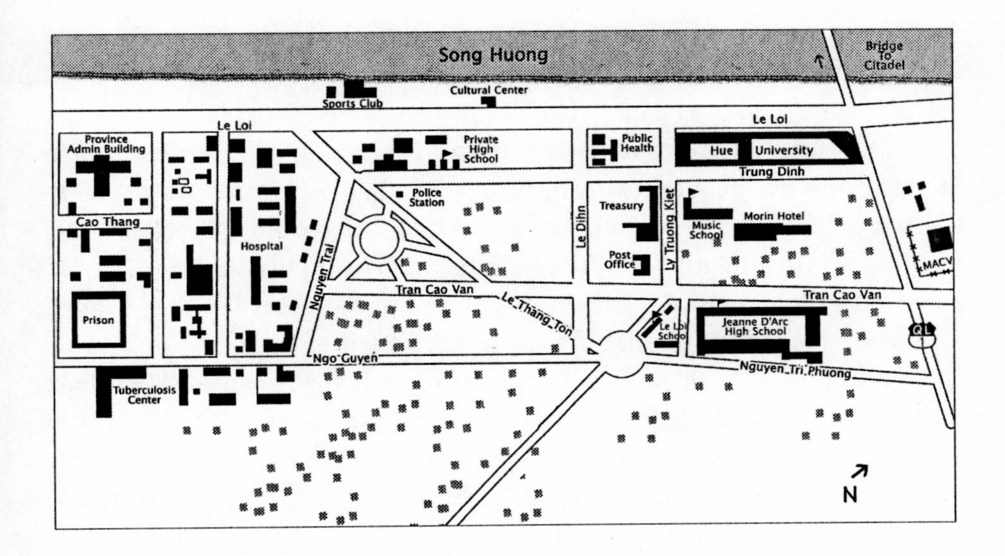

Downs and Meadows were joined by Gravel. "Captain Downs, there's an Air Force sergeant out in the courtyard who knows where a few Americans are trapped. He's the only one. I want Fox Company to escort him and bring them all back here."

"All right, Sir. What kind of support can we expect?

"There are no supporting arms available. Matter of fact MACV doesn't want us to destroy any buildings. You're on your own."

Downs looked incredulously at the man who started to return to the command center. As the two captains got ready to join their companies, Meadows turned to Downs and cautioned, "Mike, soon as you cross Highway 1 and turn up any of those streets, they'll have you in their sights, so be careful."

"Yeah, Chuck. Thanks. I guess that's the Air Force guy over there," Downs murmured while mulling over Meadow's warning and turning his head toward a mild looking man in his mid-twenties. "See you later."

1500 hours. Corporals Richard "Smitty" Smith and Chris Brown were called over to Horner. He introduced the Air Force sergeant as Sergeant Smailey. Horner told them that the platoon was to escort Smailey across the street and down several blocks to rescue a few

Americans who had been trapped for two days and bring them back to the MACV compound.

The two squad leaders left Horner to ready their squads. Their mission was simple: cross Highway 1 and proceed down Tran Cao Van Street to rescue the trapped Americans. Smitty's 3rd Squad would take the left side of the street and Brown's 1st Squad would take the right. Smailey would go with Brown. Staff Sergeant Tinson was sent to accompany the 2nd Squad to the intersection of Nguyen Tri Street and Highway 1, ready to support Brown and Smitty if needed.

Walking back to Brown's squad, Smailey asked Brown, who, at that minute, was contemplating the squad formation for moving down the street, "What makes you guys think you can get down the street? It'll be suicide! Hell, we've been trying to rescue them all day," the sergeant grumbled, his frustration clear in his voice.

"Don't know, Sarge. They tell Fox to go and we go."

Spotting one of his fire team leaders, Lance Corporal Louie Gasparini, and a member of that team, "C.C." Campbell, Brown called out, "Hey, Louie! C.C.! This here's Sergeant Smailey who's going to lead us to rescue some Americans. Talk with him a minute. I want to ask the lieutenant a question."

"Lieutenant Horner," Brown's tone was challenging as he synopsized his conversation with Smailey, finally asking, "What's the story here?"

"Brown, you have to go. That's our orders! We're moving out in five minutes," Horner uttered, twisting his wrist and noting that his watch read 1555 hours.

Returning to his fifteen-man squad, Brown clarified, "All right, Louie and C.C., you two can have point. I'll be right behind you. Smailey, you follow me. Fig," he started, referring to Corporal Figueroa-Perez, "you and the rest of the squad follow us."

1600 hours. The men nodded and steadied themselves. Gasparini and Campbell slid around the corner facing Tran Cao Van street. Smitty's point men dashed across the intersection to the left side of the street and clung to the side of a home. These jungle-and-rice-paddy

Marines quickly surveyed an asphalt street lined with curbs and large shade trees. Immediately, on the right side were walls ranging from three feet to five feet high that were used to delineate small Vietnamese properties. A ten-foot wide sidewalk separated trees from walls. The beginning of a large building complex that visually continued for one hundred meters lined Smitty's left side of the street, sixty meters from the intersection. The men would soon know this property as the Jean d'Arc High School.

The squads had crept no more than sixty meters into the empty street, when a hail of automatic weapons fire greeted them. Rounds ricocheted off the street, walls, and buildings. Gasbarrini fell behind a tree, wounded. Campbell dove over one of the small walls for cover. NVA rounds continued to pound on the courtyard walls. The men answered the well hidden snipers by firing blindly back in their general direction.

Brown, pressed against the back of one of the large trees, yelled, "C.C., you okay?"

"Yeah."

Jim Gosselin, the platoon corpsman, having heard that Gasparini was wounded, ran forward. The NVA strafed the right side of the street killing him instantly. Private Stanley Murdock, Brown's new radio operator went down at the same time. Sergeant Smailey took a round in his leg and fell, needing assistance before he could move again.

Brown cried out for the rest of the squad to lay down a base of fire in order to rescue the wounded Gasbarrini and Campbell. Any rescue attempt seemed hopeless. With no radio available for Brown, Horner and Brown communicated on the street.

"Lieutenant, this isn't logical. We have to get the wounded!" Brown shouted.

"You get back up there with your lead fire team!"

"All right, Sir." And with that Brown raced down the street with his helmet flying off his head, rounds bouncing off the pavement at his feet, and dove over the wall to reach Campbell. Two more men were wounded watching Brown's back while he made his mad dash.

Downs radioed Horner urging him to move the platoon forward.

Figueroa-Perez, his "Dear John" letter long forgotten, cut through the center of the block, through small homes, fences, and back yards in his attempt to reach Campbell from a different direction. From a neighboring yard Figueroa-Perez shouted, "Brown, you over there?"

"Yeah," Brown answered, "don't come over here. We're pinned down!"

Figueroa-Perez ignored the warning from his best friend. Thinking only of making a rescue attempt he leapt over the wall. A shot rang out, hitting him through the head where he fell mortally wounded. Brown heard the chaplain's words in his head and thought, yeah,...in mysterious ways.

The rounds making Brown's squad an easy target were coming from the high school. Across the street, sliding along the school wall, Smitty and Delariva Vara were making better progress. They had actually snuck half way down the high school wall and were about to come under sniper fire. However, without the mutual support of Brown's pinned down squad, they were halted in that position.

At Downs' direction, Horner and Smitty attempted to come up with a different strategy to end the enemy's grip on the street. They broke into a house on Smitty's side of the street to determine if they could break through the interior walls and attack the enemy from inside instead on of the street. Their infantry weapons were useless.

At 1725 hours the light-gray clouds began to darken. Horner radioed the results to Downs. "Skipper, we're not making any progress. Brown's lost almost all of his men,"

All afternoon, Captain Downs had steadfastly drove his men to accomplish their mission. Now, torn between the inability to accomplish his mission and the need to care for his men, Captain Down's swore under his breath. Soon the 'caring' portion of his psyche responded, "All right. Let's work at getting the men out of there."

Out of nowhere, two M-48 tanks churned around the corner. Horner darted over to the lead tank determined to retrieve his casualties. He was focused on saving his men. Corporal Dave Collins, his radio operator, hightailed it with him. Horner opened the radio box at the rear of the tank. It didn't work. Collins climbed aboard the tank and asked for their frequency. He turned off the company frequency and radioed the tank commander.

After Horner sent men to recover Smailey and Murdock, both tanks began cranking forward together forming a shield across the street with Horner and Collins in trace. Horner put the right tank in the lead. "Move three meters. Stop!" "Left tank, move three meters. Stop!"

The tanks provided a new threat. B-40 anti-tank rockets now exploded off the tanks' armor, wildly spraying shrapnel on the meager protection being used by the men of the trapped squads. In the first B-40 salvo, Horner was hit on his left hand, arm and side. He bled profusely but not enough to stop him on his rescue mission. Horner bellowed to Smitty's 3rd Squad on the left to fall in behind the tanks.

Collins, who had reluctantly left Brown's squad to become Horner's radio operator after Horner lost his operator, caught the spirit of being a "go-get 'em" grunt again and yelled over to Brown's trapped men, "We're coming!" Deafening, the sounds of the battle raging on the street, rounds ricocheting off of the pavement, rockets exploding off of tanks, and men shouting to and fro, drowned out everything else for the men of Fox.

Holding the radio handset while talking to the tanker, Horner was staring into the eyes of Collins when a sniper's round passed through Collins's neck. Killed instantly, he fell to the street outside of the tank's protective shield.

Lance Corporal Jimmie Palmo, witnessing his buddy's death, dashed over to the tank. Looking at the lieutenant, Palmo said, "I'll take the radio." Together they pulled in Collins's fallen body, and stripped him of his PRC-25 radio.

Twenty meters passed. The armored shield had collected eight Marines from the 2nd Platoon. Two were walking wounded. Private First Class Henshaw's body was placed on the tank's hull.

The street darkened as night approached impeding the vision of the snipers and the enemy rocket men. Soon the forward men in Smitty's squad had been collected. Smitty told Horner that Private First Class

Delariva Vara, who had been lying in the street motionless for over an hour, was also forward of them.

Pinned into their flattened positions on the street, Brown and Campbell laid low. Rounds zinged over their heads on regular intervals missing them by mere inches. As the minutes passed and the light faded the attacks lessoned. Campbell shrugged himself even lower. He twisted his body until he was able to reach a pack of cigarettes from his pants' pocket. Campbell slid his hand carrying the nearly full pack over his chest. He shook a cigarette out of the pack, tweezed it within his fingers, and slithered it between his lips.

Campbell repeated the process to retrieve a lighter from his other pocket. He peered sideways at Brown, who had used his peripheral vision to watch the entire process. Campbell hesitated before lighting his cigarette; every Marine knew that you didn't light a match or lighter lest it give away your position. Both men cringed and squeezed their eyes shut as concrete bits and dust sprayed down on them. Bullets trapped them in their prone positions as snipers continued to chip away at the three-foot wall they hid behind. Campbell offered Brown a lop-sided smile, cigarette flopping between his lips, "I guess it's not like they don't already know our position."

Brown responded with a small chuckle, "Guess not."

Campbell took his time, lit the cigarette, and savored the first long drag. He tossed the pack onto Brown, who tapped another cigarette out, eventually getting the stick into his own mouth. After Brown's was lit, Campbell stuffed the cigarettes and lighter back into his pants. In the distance, they heard the approach of the tanks. They could hear the shouts of their fellow Marines, "Fall in behind the tanks!"

"We're coming!"

"Hold on!"

Brown braved a peek over the wall, stretching his spine and neck until he was almost doing horizontal headstand. He released his position and fell back into place as another round buzzed him, missing him by the smallest margin. Campbell and Brown knew they would have to run for it, even though the enemy had their position made. "Not yet," he breathed.

"You know what I heard, Man?" Campbell asked.

"What?" Brown asked.

"I was at one of those classes we had to take about smoking, remember?" Campbell continued.

"Yeah…something about Marines and pot?" Brown responded.

"But they also said something about cigarettes." Campbell shrugged, flipping his hand that held the cigarette toward Brown, "They said, according to the Surgeon General, that these things could kill you."

"Naw," Brown started, "cigarettes?"

"Yeah," Campbell harrumphed. "The docs recommend we quit smokin' 'em."

Brown's ears perked as the tanks creaked closer. "Why?" he asked, prepping himself to jump up and run.

"Seems they don't want us doing anything dangerous," Campbell laughed, flicking the remains of his smoke aside.

"No kidding?" Brown laughed.

"And you thought the Corps didn't care!" Campbell accused.

"Yeah," Brown started. "Ready?"

"Yeah!" Campbell yelled.

"Go!" Brown shouted.

With Campbell in the lead, the men hurled themselves off of the ground and over their protective wall. Bullets impacted around them as they sprinted toward the tanks. Pieces of the streets kicked up at them, but Brown, and Campbell reached the safety of the armored shield. Gasparini joined them, and all living Marines were collected. The dead were placed on the tank hulls, weapons and equipment were retrieved.

LANCE CORPORAL C.C. CAMPBELL DASHING OUT FROM THE WALL TO AN M-48 TANK
(PHOTO LICENCED BY CORBIS)

Horner talked briefly on the radio to Downs explaining the situation. Downs told the exhausted lieutenant that they had to recover Delariva Vara's body while there. The tanks ground forward another twenty meters. As they moved three meters at a time down the street the enemy B-40 and RPG attacks intensified. One hit the lead tank just above the hull platform and the explosion knocked Henshaw's body off the tank. Henshaw lay in the street, now missing a leg and screaming.

"Hey, Lieutenant, look at Henshaw! He's alive," one of the Marines shouted.

"Someone keep him near the tank," Horner responded in a weakened voice. His blood loss was taking its toll.

Once in view, Delariva Vara began moving his arms letting the tankers know he was still alive. While the tanks fired madly to provide cover with their .50 caliber machine guns, Smitty and one of his men rushed out to the immobile Delariva Vara and dragged him back behind the tanks' armored shield. The tanks began slowly backing up to the corner of Highway 1 and out of the enemy's line of sight.

On the way, Horner finally succumbed to his injury and fell unconscious; his men carried him back the rest of the way. The blackness of night had completely enveloped the streets by the time the 2nd Platoon returned to the MACV compound. A veil of hopelessness shrouded Brown. From a robust squad of fifteen he was down to six effective Marines. He, Private First Class Keif and Private First Class Odom were all that were left and not wounded. Gasparini and Campbell were wounded although they were expected to return to the squad. Corporal Brown's best friend, his in-country buddy, Figueroa-Perez had been mortally wounded and wasn't expected to live until morning.

1935 hours. Downs was summoned to the command center. After personally checking on his men, he reported in to Lieutenant Colonel Gravel. In response to a Task Force X-Ray directive relayed to them by the 1st Marines, the lieutenant colonel ordered him to seize and occupy the provincial prison that night in order to prevent prisoners from escaping. Fox was to advance by means of Le Loi Street. Gravel added, "We were ordered to do the same thing yesterday with Alpha and Golf and could only get a half block along Tran Cao Van Street. Since then, as you found out today, I'm sure the enemy has improved its positions along that route."

Gravel had never worked with the fiery Irishman before and was unable see anything but an intense professional infantry officer with a Bostonian accent. Downs' blood was boiling. "Excuse me, Sir," Downs interrupted Gravel while gesturing to the radio operator as he tried to compose himself, "I want to alert the gunny."

Gravel and Captain Jim Gallagher, the young operations officer, waited patiently, looking at each other while Downs went back and forth on the radio with "Fox Seven", Gunnery Sergeant VanValkenburgh. The prison was the mission assigned to them by Task Force X-Ray. If Fox was successful, Task Force X-Ray would be successful. Gravel would be successful. Downs' problem lie in the fact that his company, now exhausted from the day and the loss of many men, possibly lacked the confidence to immediately go on a not-so-very-well-thought-out mission. Also, they were the visiting contingent and they would be the ones going in harm's way, and not Gravel's own company.

Downs completed his radio conversation and returned to the waiting pair. Gravel couldn't see the flushed pigment under Downs' dust-covered face. "Sir, what's between MACV and the prison?"

"We don't have any information on the enemy between here and there, Mike, except what you know they have at the high school."

Downs, studying the map and fuming inside, asked, "What's this large building complex between the prison and Le Loi Street?"

"Sir," Gallagher answered, "That's the Province Administration Building; MACV refers to it as the "headquarters for the province chief."

"Has anyone contacted the province headquarters to let them know we're coming through?"

"All we know is that an NVA flag is flying and two North Vietnamese 12.7mm machine guns were spotted on the roof," Gravel replied. "We're not sure there is anyone left to contact."

Downs snapped, "My God almighty, this is getting crazier yet!" He received a knowing look from Gravel before continuing, "Who ordered us to do this?" Downs demanded, already knowing, but forcing an answer.

Gravel noted Downs' growing temper. He listened as Downs continued, "Sir, you know this is suicide. X-Ray thinks we can stroll down Le Loi Street and waltz into that prison with minimal casualties. For all we know the only prisoners maybe the Province Chief and his staff! I visited X-Ray's headquarters and they have no clue what's going on up here in the city!" Downs paused for control, and then went on, "Let me write a message laying out the facts and ask them to reconsider."

Knowing Downs was correct, Gravel acquiesced.

Downs outlined the deadly condition of the streets, the sniper fire, and the fact that the North Vietnamese controlled most of the city. Gravel sent the message to Task Force X-Ray headquarters and within two hours received a reply.

Downs' men were to stand down for the night. He called VanValkenburgh and let the gunny know their orders. His men never knew the slaughter he spared them that night.

When facing southwest, looking across Highway 1 from the MACV compound, to the far right one block away was Le Loi Street that ran along the Song Huong or the Perfume River. On the other side of Le Loi Street was Hue University. To the immediate right of the compound, was Truong Dinh Street. To MACV's left front was Truong Cao Van Street where Fox had been bloodied on their first day in Hue. Directly across from MACV, between Truong Dinh and Truong Cao Van, were the small houses Figueroa-Perez had used during his attempt to reach Corporal Brown yesterday and a building the map identified as the Morin Hotel. Beyond the hotel was a music school and chem lab associated with the Jeanne d'Arc High School. That block measured 110 meters wide and 170 meters from MACV to the street on the far side of the music school.

The presence of the 2nd Battalion, 5th Marines grew larger the next day, 2 February, when Hotel Company, commanded by Captain Ron Christmas, fought its way into the city. The momentum of the battle for Hue was about to change. The single missing ingredient was the command presence and stellar leadership of "Big Ernie" Cheatham.

Golf Company seized and occupied the university that afternoon. Hotel relieved Golf there prior to 1700 hours. Before they were fully settled, Hotel Marines were attacked but quickly repelled the attackers.

1900 hours. As the tide of the battle turned, Fox Company was ordered to conduct a night attack, join up with Hotel, and continue a two-pronged attack to, once again, seize the prison.

2000 hours. Led by the 3rd Platoon, Fox moved across the street. The plan was to skirt around to the left side of Hue University then, with the same two tanks that rescued the 2nd Platoon, follow Truong Dinh Street to the next intersection where they would come abreast of Hotel.

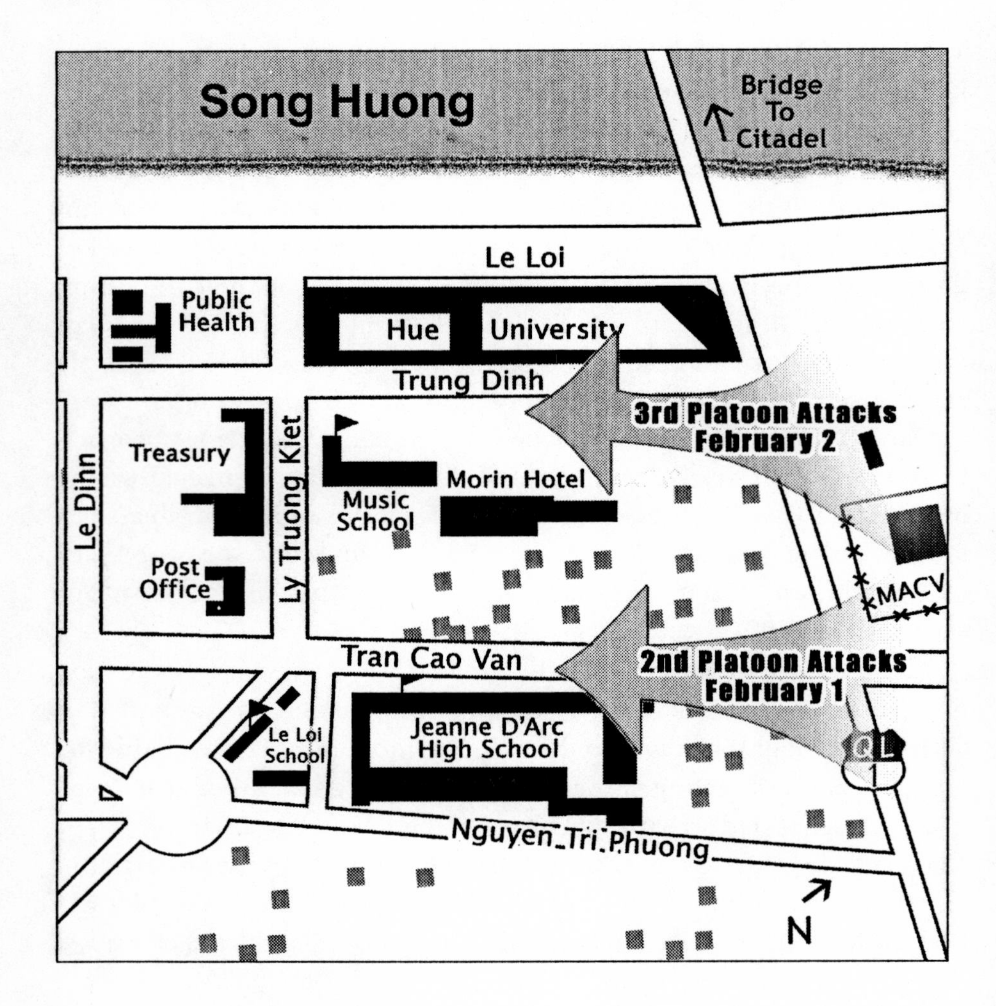

Led by Sergeant John Mahoney and Lance Corporal Ernie Weiss, the leading 3rd Platoon passed the hotel and began slipping in and around the two and half-feet high walls separating private properties. They slithered through small gardens and under the suspicious eyes of a few chickens still roosting there. They were three-fourths of the way down Truong Dinh Street when they could hear that the tanks had turned the corner and had begun coming up the street behind them. The other two platoons began crossing Highway 1 behind the tanks.

Moving cautiously around a property wall at a gated entrance, Mahoney was shot in the chest. As his body toppled over, rounds started flying wildly from both the 3rd Platoon and the NVA. In spite of the explosive clatter, Weiss led the recovery of Mahoney's body. Confusion ensued. The company pulled the 3rd Platoon back amid the shouting of small-unit leaders attempting some semblance of control.

A B-40 rocket hit one tank. Immediately both tanks reversed their course, backing up and returning to the corner. In the middle of Truong Dinh Street, the lead tank rolled over barbed wire entangling its treads. Its motor strained at the driver's hopeless attempt to free it from its entrapment. The rear tank crossed back over Highway 1 and into the safety of the MACV compound, leaving the other unsupported.

When the company reached the MACV side of the street, all firing stopped. Downs assumed responsibility for the stranded tank. Staff Sergeant McCoy, the 3rd Platoon Sergeant, was positioned next to Downs. "Sergeant McCoy, I want you to outpost that tank; so if they attempt to attack it, we can counter their attempt with a squad from here," Downs ordered pointing across the street.

"Aye, aye, Sir. I have the perfect two guys…"

After placing Contreras and Schuett at their listening post by the tank, McCoy returned to the building they were staying in that night and was greeted by Sergeant Chuck Ekker, one of his 3rd Platoon squad members. Ekker showed him the side of a C-ration box.

"Staff Sergeant McCoy, isn't this the place that the lieutenant said we were at?" Ekker said pointing at the letters "HUE". "That's pronounced 'who-ee', isn't it?"

"Yeah. That's what Lieutenant Hausrath said it was. Why?" McCoy answered.

"Well, while you were out there with the tank I was listening to the Armed Forces Radio Station, and they said there was a Marine unit heavily engaged in a battle in 'Way City'."

McCoy whistled, "Chuck, if they are fighting as hard as we are, then they're in a world of shit! Now get the men rested. I just had my canteens shot through by those bastards out there and I'm going to MACV to scrounge one of those new "doggie" canteens apparently the Corps don't seem to want us to have."

While the others regrouped, Private Jerry Schuett and Lance Corporal Pablo Contreras were on guard through the cold, damp night. Finally, somewhere between 0130 and 0200, Schuett asked, "Pablo, what's a couple of grunts doing here guarding this tank all by ourselves?"

"Schuett, don't even think that way. We're staying here. And if you even come close to falling asleep, I'm going to stomp your butt!"

Luckily, the VC and NVA forces ignored the tank and its two sentries that night.

"Big Ernie's on his way up!"

"Things are gonna' start happening!"

That was "the word" passed around on the morning of 3 February. The Marines knew that Highway 1 would be dangerous all the way from Phu Bai to Hue City, a total of fifteen kilometers. However, with the concentration of NVA forces south of the river, the final three kilometers would certainly be the most dangerous. Specifically, that dangerous terrain stretched along the segment of Highway 1 where a bridge crosses the Song Phu Cam south of Hue, all the way into the MACV compound. Lieutenant Colonel Gravel directed Fox to clear and occupy the buildings along the final leg of Cheatham's journey to ensure the safety of the convoy.

Charged by the arrival of their esteemed leader, Fox had the job done by 0915. The 1st Platoon went almost as far as the Song Phu Cam Bridge. Fifteen minutes later they began taking sniper fire from a huge cathedral 400 meters west of the highway. Gunnery Sergeant VanValkenburgh, who had accompanied the 1st Platoon to that distant point, initially ducked from the fire with the platoon members but immediately okayed the counter-fire on the church. They had lost more than a few good men to earlier snipers, so why not fire on these, even though they would hit the cathedral? After a few hundred M-60 and M-16 rounds the sniper's weapon fell silent.

Minutes later Mademoiselle Leroy, a French reporter who had been interviewing the NVA earlier, approached VanValkenburgh and in a distinctive French accent asked, "Are you the company commander?"

VanValkenburgh spun around, caught somewhat off guard by a woman's voice, the accent, and the perceived challenge, looked down at the short woman whose pencil and tablet were at the ready, and corrected, "No, I'm not."

"Do you know that you're not supposed to be firing at a cathedral?" she demanded.

VanValkenburgh squinted at her and countered, "Listen, Lady, you take this down: we'll fire at anybody when they're firing at us." He added, "We don't care where they're shooting from!"

Leroy, her French pride now in jeopardy and perceived control of the interview vanished, spun away and was seen no more.

By 1030 Fox was called back to the MACV compound based on information they'd received that Cheatham wasn't coming after all. They had all returned to the compound by 1130.

1145 hours. Downs glanced questioningly at VanValkenburgh as they heard firing, south on Highway 1, "What the hell's that?"

"Don't know, Skipper. We just cleared that area."

Ten minutes later an armada of trucks and jeeps roared to a stop along Highway 1 in front of the MACV compound. This convoy, carrying Colonel Hughes who would assume command of the Hue City Task Force from Lieutenant Colonel Gravel, also carried "Big Ernie" Cheatham. With their .50 caliber machine guns, the lead vehicles had conducted a "reconnaissance by fire" into the very buildings Fox had vacated minutes earlier on the way into MACV.

Lieutenant Colonel Cheatham brought with him all of the infantry building-busting tools, such as 106mm recoilless rifles and 3.5-inch anti-tank rocket launchers, he could find back at Phu Bai. These would be needed to remove the NVA from their strongholds. If they didn't work completely he brought enough gas masks for his rifle companies and tear gas munitions to make the entire North Vietnamese Army cry. Cheatham wasn't called "Big Ernie" for nothing.

Cheatham established his forward command post in the university buildings with Hotel Company. The "2/5 rear" in Hue City, including the medical aide station, supply and munitions dumps, and motor pools, were set up across the street, in and around the small building occupied by Fox Company for the past two days.

Colonel Hughes directed Cheatham's three-company battalion, 2/5, to attack along the Le Loi Street axis to the Song Phu Cam, and seize key buildings along the way, among which were: the Treasury, Post Office, Public Health Building, Provincial Administration Building, hospital, and prison. Gravel's battalion, 1/1, now had two companies: the battered Alpha Company and the newly arrived Bravo Company. Together, they would advance on the left flank of 2/5. Hughes summarized, "On one hand, Ernie, we have been asked to save as many of the buildings as possible, so we'll be holding back prep fires. On the other hand, we have to secure this side of the river as soon as possible in order to attack the Citadel on the other side of the river; so do what you have to do to make it happen. I'll back you up."

With Hotel occupying the university, a complex of connected buildings with two large center courtyards that covered the entire city block, 2/5 had finally established a presence one block away from the MACV compound on Le Thuong Kiet Street. Directly across Le Thuong Kiet were the three relatively small Public Health buildings. Diagonally across the intersection from the university was the Treasury building, an awesome, two-and-a-half-story, concrete structure surrounded by a small concrete wall with a five-foot high wrought iron fence. In the center was a large, wrought iron swinging gate. It resembled an elegant, fortified castle. Next to the Treasury was a less daunting building, identified as the Post Office.

After explaining 2/5's mission of clearing out the NVA from the south river all the way to the Song Phu Cam, Cheatham gave out interim objectives. He ordered Captain Ron Christmas' Hotel Company to hold the university, and on order, be prepared to attack and occupy the Public Health buildings across the street in support of Fox's attack on the Treasury. Downs' Fox Company was ordered to fight its way along Truong Dinh Street and attack and seize the Treasury and Post Office buildings. Captain Chuck Meadows' Golf Company was held in reserve.

Cheatham wrapped up his briefing by saying, "Look, I don't have to tell you three what we're up against. We'll have our hands full as we attack forward. We can't count on the understrength 1/1 to secure our left flank even though they'll be there trying to do so. So I just want to make sure every enemy soldier behind us is dead! Any questions?" The room was still. "All right then, we move out at 1545; and we're not stopping 'til we get to the river!"

1545 hours. On 3 February the next phase of the operation began. Downs ordered the 3rd Platoon to lead the attack along Troung Dinh Street. As soon as they passed the hotel building, the 2nd Platoon was to swing left so that when it reached Le Thuong Kiet Street it would be able to attack the Post Office and, simultaneously, the 3rd Platoon would be ready to attack the Treasury. They'd attack together. The 1st Platoon was held in reserve.

Within minutes, automatic weapons fire, B-40 anti-tank rockets, and 60mm mortars stopped the 3rd Platoon, led by Second Lieutenant Hausrath. A B-40 rocket hit each of the two M-48 tanks moving down the street with the 3rd Platoon. Immediately after that, an RPG, rocket-propelled grenade, hit one of them again, taking it out of the attack temporarily. With casualties from the day before and men now being wounded one after the other as the platoon attacked down the street, the 3rd Platoon needed support.

Second Lieutenant Hausrath focused on getting that support. "Carter!" he called for Lance Corporal Rich Carter, his rocket man, yelling loudly over the rifle fire.

"Sir?" Carter, who was standing nearby ready to deploy his gun team, responded.

"Oh," Hausrath exclaimed, recognizing Carter's proximity, "didn't you tell me a month ago that you had an experience with 3.5 rockets?"

"Yes, Sir."

"Look, Carter, we ain't going down that street and get our butts shot off. I want you to run," he said pointing back to the battalion armorer across the street, "and get all the house-busting, anti-tank weapons you can carry because we are going through the houses, not beside them!"

"On my way, Sir!"

Carter yelled to his machine gun buddies with whom he had been working, Lance Corporal Roger Warren and Private First Class Ron Frasier, "I'm off to get some 3.5s. Pay attention to Staff Sergeant McCoy!"

After retracing his steps from the battalion armorer who was working out of a 6x6 truck, Carter began his one-man destruction of gates, doors, walls, and buildings. The men quickly adjusted to the twenty-five foot back blast of the 3.5-inch rocket launcher. Every time Carter fired one, a member of the 3rd Platoon would hand him another rocket, while the rest of their squad entered the destroyed building, waiting for him to blast the wall in the back courtyard. As the 3rd Platoon neared the intersection of Troung Dinh Street and Le Thuong Kiet Street, the tanks began rolling again; and Carter used them as a shield.

The 3rd Platoon penetrated the music school just after 1640. Lance Corporal Burnham's squad moved forward across the front courtyard seeking the safety of the two and a half-feet high concrete wall that had a decorative wrought iron fence protruding upward out of it another two feet. The wall separated the street from the school's front courtyard. Corporal Dan "Arky" Albritton's squad remained plastered to the right side of the school building. Captain Downs, his radio operators, company corpsman, and forward observers from the 105mm arty battery and the 81mm mortar platoon, set up in the kitchen in the rear of the school.

The once seemingly invincible enemy now had neighbors across the street. The NVA opened up in earnest. From windows in the second floor of the Treasury, a third-level ventilation space in that building, and the Post Office roof, the NVA had streamlined fields of fire on the men crouched tightly beside the low wall of the school. Lance Corporal Roger Warren, his machine gun at the ready, arrived at the edge of the courtyard on the left-hand side of the school just behind the lead squad. Thirty minutes earlier, he had received shrapnel in his arm; torn and throbbing, Warren ignored his wounds and continued on. He saw one Marine fall inward toward the open courtyard; the Marine was unable to move. Warren dashed into the courtyard, exposed himself to the NVA's intensive fire, and expended two belts of counter-fire allowing other Marines to bring the wounded man to safety. He hustled back, passing the gun to his assistant gunner, Private First Class Ron Frasier. Warren charged back to the battalion for more belts of machine gun ammunition.

The music school's courtyard gate was located in front of the right side of the building for easier access to the street intersection. A second hole in the courtyard wall was necessary in order to get across the street to the Treasury. Hausrath called for his wall buster again, "Carter! Get up here!"

While receiving cover from the 3rd Platoon, Carter fired five rockets into the courtyard wall, making a four-foot wide hole. He quickly went to the breach he had just made and fired five more rockets directly across the street into the Treasury's eight-foot wall. Through that hole he saw directly into the Treasury's courtyard. As Lance Corporal Carter scrambled back for safety, one of the M-48 tanks rumbled around the corner and was immediately targeted by a B-40 rocket fired from Le Loi Elementary School one block away and across the street from the Post Office. The tank withdrew back to the intersection. Carter, now inside the music school, grabbed six Light Anti-Armor Weapons, LAAWs, barked to Second Lieutenant Hausrath for more 3.5s and LAAWs as he bounded past him, and climbed the stairs.

Private First Class Frasier, who Warren had presented the M-60 plus two belts of ammunition, dashed into the building, witnessed Carter racing up the stairs, and tore up the stairs after him.

Carter bolted into the middle room while Frasier chose the room to the left. Frasier skidded up to the open window. Glancing through it at the Treasury building, he spotted the smoke from enemy weapons that had been taking out the men in the courtyard below. He immediately opened up with no reservations, spraying a steady stream of fire on the enemy. His belt emptied. After changing belts, he had just returned to his position at the window when suddenly a B-40 rocket impacted the wall next to the window. The concussion blasted Frasier back into the room, knocking him unconscious and wounding him in both legs.

"Someone get across the street!" Downs ordered. "We need to find out if we can get into the Treasury." Hausrath relayed the captain's order across the courtyard to Burnham, "Bernie send someone across the street to see if we can get in there!"

Burnham turned to Lance Corporal Bo Borunda, his 1st Fire Team leader, "Are they fuckin nuts? Bo, you stay here. You have the squad because I probably won't be coming back!" He crouched down, clutched his weapon and disappeared through the hole. In less than five steps, a bullet struck his left foot, knocking him down. He rolled under a damaged Vietnamese Army truck for a modicum of safety. The rounds ricocheted off the street, kicking up around him. Temporarily, he was safe; but as the enemy shot the tires flat, Burnham twisted, spinning himself toward the wall, escaping just in time. He stood up and limped quickly through the breach straight to the corpsman in the back of the school.

As Burnham lay there with Doc trying to remove his boot to get to the bullet, the firing out front intensified. Hausrath had sent Burnham's and another squad across the street to take the Treasury. Burnham also heard the back blast from Carter's 3.5-inch rocket launcher as he fired from the second floor.

A hail of bullets devastated the two squads in the street. They retreated back through the hole in the wall. Two Marines placed Private First Class Dankworth, now badly wounded, next to Burnham. Burnham stared at the wounded Marine. His leg was nothing but mangled flesh. Burnham implored, "Doc, take care of him he's much worse than me!" With that the corporal sat up, removed his boot that had slowed the penetration of the round, dug a half an inch deep hole and removed the bullet from his foot, wrapped gauze around it, replaced his boot, and ran back to his squad.

Borunda greeted him while summarizing the results of their futile attack, "Wayne is still out in the street. I think he's still alive," Borunda referred to Lance Corporal Wayne Washburn, another of Burnham's fireteam leaders. "At least I saw him breathing. Yeah, and that new replacement, Barnes, just went out there to bring Wayne in, but I think he bought it…At least we can't see him moving."

By this time little light remained. Burnham peered at the sky and scanned the nearby buildings. The street was vacant of long shadows as there hadn't been any sun since their arrival in Hue. Processing the information he'd just received, without expecting an answer, Burnham muttered out loud, "Washburn? God, I love that kid!" He turned to Borunda, "Bo, cover me."

Burnham dashed through the hole in the wall, by the now totally burned truck he'd hid under earlier, passed Barnes's still body, arriving at the near-lifeless Washburn. Borunda was right, Washburn was still breathing, barely. He grabbed Washburn's wrist, yanked him into a fireman's carry, and ran back through the jagged opening in the wall. Burnham passed by his good friend and the platoon's third in command, Sergeant Willard Scott, III who stood exposed in the middle of the open courtyard firing his M-16 to cover Burnham's heroic rescue. "Follow me, Scotty!" Burnham grunted as he disappeared beside the side of the school.

Upstairs, Carter had the other infantrymen assigned to help him deliver his 3.5 rockets. The men stacked the rockets below the second floor windows facing the Treasury. When he fired a rocket, he could shift positions to deceive the enemy across the street as to his location. During this rotation, he entered the far left room to find Private First Class Frasier firing his machine gun through the window. "What the hell happened to you?" he asked the assistant gunner who appeared totally disheveled and dust covered.

"Ah nothing. A B-40 damn near came through this here window."

Eying the blood on his trousers, Carter declared, "You need to get evacuated!"

"Nah. Warren will be here soon with some more ammo. We're just starting to have fun."

"All right, I'm off to the other end of the building with Jones here, and I'll fire from there," Carter relayed.

"Okay, Rich, but watch out for those B-40 rockets," Frasier chuckled cynically.

Carter and his new A-Gunner, a kid who went by "Jonesy", had been getting a good rhythm moving into a window, identifying a target, loading the launcher, firing it and leaving for the next window. Despite the fact that there was barely enough light outside to see the targets across the street, Carter chose a side window he hadn't fired from before so he could aim almost directly at the Post Office building. "Ready, Jonesy?"

"It's ready to fire."

The rocket impacted on the first floor of the Post Office

"Load a second one, Jonesy. Make it quick before they fire back!"

"Loaded."

As Carter focused on his second target, a B-40 rocket exploded in the window frame. Its force blasted Carter into the classroom behind him. Carter lay still for nearly five minutes, his breathing shallow. When he awoke he stared blankly at lingering gray smoke, wounded Marines, and corpsman yelling triage instructions. Shrapnel pierced his left forearm. His face painful, he rose and discovered Jonesy had been blown through glass partitions separating the classrooms. He knew the young kid was in sad shape. Shards of glass were buried in Jonesy's eyes.

While Carter regained his posture and assisted carrying Jonesy to the company medevac staging area, Burnham and Scott carried Washburn back to the Battalion Aid Station on one of the classroom doors. Washburn stopped breathing before they reached the station and, by the time they returned to the nursing school, evening had dug in.

That night, Lieutenant Colonel Cheatham, his staff, and company commanders, diligently planned the attack for the morning. They now knew the strength of their enemy. With appropriate fire support, the principal objectives would fall easily and with a minimal number of casualties. They had gained ground this day. Key assumptions about the enemy were: most were professional NVA soldiers who had carefully planned their occupation and defense of the buildings months prior to the Tet Offensive; the machine gun from the Le Loi Elementary School provided their most effective fire power in delaying Fox's attack on the Treasury; and, if the Public Health buildings were defended, they were not defended in force.

With the support of 106mm recoilless rifles, 81mm mortars, and the two tanks, Hotel would take the Public Health buildings first. Once secured, Hotel could support Fox's attack on the Treasury. 81mm mortars could be fired from the secure courtyard of the university onto the Treasury prior to Fox's attack even though the range was only 170–190 meters, and perhaps the tanks could expose themselves long enough to launch a 90mm round into the Le Loi Elementary School.

0700 hours. Hotel initiated its attack on the Public Health buildings. Machine gun and automatic weapons fire burst from the Post Office and Le Loi Elementary School. Sniper fire targeted the Hotel Marines from small buildings located on the river-side of the university. Hotel's attack stalled. Golf Company, in reserve, was able to lay down suppressing fire on the snipers near the river. Fox continued firing automatic weapons and rockets at the Treasury. Courageously, Lieutenant Colonel Cheatham and a 106mm recoilless rifle crew blasted the front of the elementary school building, forever silencing the NVA machine gun that, yesterday, had prevented Fox's 3rd Platoon from reaching the Treasury.

Hotel Company overcame all three public health buildings by 0855. Together, the suppressive fires enabled Hotel to capture the day's first objective with only two men wounded. Since the Public Health buildings sat farther back from Le Thuong Kiet Street than the Treasury and the Post Office buildings, Hotel Company Marines began firing on the rear of the larger buildings.

0930 hours. While the action with Hotel occurred, the Battalion Executive Officer, Major Salvati, visited Captain Downs to grasp Fox's situation. Salvati saw the gas masks strapped to the legs of the men along the wall. He knew the NVA didn't have any. Then he remembered seeing E-8 tear gas launchers back at the MACV compound. An idea leapt into Salvati's mind. Downs jumped on Salvati's idea, which was to gas the enemy across the street. Cheatham instantly approved it. Salvati drove back to MACV to collect one or two gas launchers.

Marine Corps' 81mm mortar rounds originating from the university courtyard began pounding the Treasury building at about 1000 hours.

1105 hours. The XO returned to the rear of the schoolhouse and began setting up the heavy launcher. Forty minutes later, he raced to the school's kitchen finding Downs, "Mike, are you ready to go?"

"Give me fifteen minutes!" Downs shouted to Salvati, then turned and yelled for Hausrath.

When Hausrath reported, Downs explained, "I want you to get Carter or someone else to blow open the gates to the Treasury's courtyard and then the front doors of the building. Immediately afterwards fire a "Willie Peter" round into the street to allow your platoon time to attack under the cover of white phosphorous. Wear your gas mask. The XO is going to start gassing the Treasury. Can you do all that in the next ten minutes?"

"No problem, Sir," Hausrath assured the captain.

"Well then, get on with it."

Captain Downs passed the word to the platoon commanders to get their gas masks on. The men did so without hesitation.

On a second attempt to fire the gas launcher, Salvati finally launched canisters over the schoolhouse and onto the Treasury building. The wind drifting from the river blew the gas onto the Post Office as well.

Carter, from a one-knee firing position at the breach in the school's wall, fired a High Explosive Anti-Tank, HEAT, round with his 3.5-inch rocket launcher. It sped across the street hitting the heavy gate guarding the Treasury. The one side of the gate heaved over. A minute later he sent a second HEAT round over the Treasury's wall and blasted open the decorative and immense front doors of the building that stood fifteen steps above the street.

1200 hours. As planned, Staff Sergeant McCoy and Sergeant Ekker's 3rd Squad charged the Treasury. Corporal "Arky" Albritton, Ekker's 1st Fire Team leader, plowed his way through the newly torn entryway. He and his men charged through the white smoke and arrived unnoticed onto the street. Private First Class Frasier integrated his machine gun into the squad. From their hips the men fired at probable targets while running. As the squad stormed into the Treasury's courtyard, Frasier remained in the middle of the street, pouring lead at the face of the Treasury building.

Albritton charged up the steps and by the blown doors, the rest of his team on his heels. As one, the Marines tossed everything they had at the positions they believed their enemy to occupy. They fired their rifles, distributing lead across the gigantic banking center, and into the walls at the far end. Through his gas mask Albritton looked around. At his direction, they intensified their fire at the area behind a long, wooden, teller's counter, not allowing the stream of fire to break. Albritton's team leapt over furniture and raced their way toward a door at the far end. Tossing more canisters of gas, Albritton motioned for his gunners to advance toward their objective: a door leading to the second story. He tried the door only to find it jammed. The gunners took aim, and obliterated the wooden barricade. They climbed over the rubble that the NVA had piled behind the door to jam it and began their careful ascent up the staircase. They slowed to a cautious pace; it wasn't until they were all safely within the protective confines of the stairwell that they realized the enemy hadn't fired a single shot.

Lance Corporal Ray Stewart charged through the same Treasury doors, leading his fire team. He passed by a wall that separated the entrance from the large room. Across the room stood a counter that ran the length of the back wall. He couldn't spot any of Albritton's men; and barely had time to perceive desks littered throughout the remainder of the large, open room when suddenly, a "ChiCom", Chinese Communist made grenade, landed twenty feet in front of him. Stewart and his men stumbled back behind the wall they had just passed. The grenade exploded harmlessly on the other side of the wall.

Stewart peeked around the corner toward his opponents. Several NVA, having recovered from Albritton's fire team's initial assault, popped up from behind the counter like jack-in-the-boxes, each tossing grenades. The Marines ducked back behind the wall as three more grenades blew. Stewart's men returned fire all the while the successive concussions rang in their ears.

More grenades answered their attack and Stewart's fire team dodged the detonations. Shards of wood, wall, and furniture flew past them. "Thank God they're lousy at throwing grenades!" Stewart muttered under his breath as he braced himself to counter-attack. He poked his head out once more and the enemy soldiers sprang up again. This time, they were further away from the Marines while still behind the room-length counter. The NVA lobbed more grenades as the men sought shelter again. Stewart counted one, two, three, four, four, five grenades. The wall they hid behind was now threaded with holes. Hard on the smoke of the final explosion, Stewart and his team charged forward, spreading out within the room. They fired instinctively, but this time, no one was there.

The NVA were retreating to the stairs on the right side of the room, the same path Albritton's men had taken. Stewart and his men assailed the NVA from behind. Exposed, with nowhere to hide, the NVA were caught. The enemy turned, boxed between the Marines and the stairwell, attempting to retaliate with more grenades. One landed near the fire team, and Stewart's team dove away from the exploding device. Shrapnel tore through a few Marines nearest to the grenade. The rest of the fire team cut down the NVA, killing them all.

While Albritton's men cleared the second floor, Staff Sergeant McCoy and the other fire team that arrived at the tail end of Stewart's battle, turned to the left to rush toward the left stairwell. Instead of finding the stairwell, McCoy ran into the same battle-scarred wall that had saved Stewart and his men. McCoy and the fire team turned and followed Albritton's path while Stewart's team received medical attention from the corpsman.

Second Lieutenant Hausrath and Burnham's squad entered the front door shortly after McCoy. Resistance continued at a diminishing rate as each room on the first floor of the large Treasury building was searched and cleared. All three levels of the two-and-one-half story building were searched. The Marines would fire down the hall, then duck for cover into each new, consecutive room. In the end, six enemy soldiers were killed and eight Marines were wounded. As if on cue, the moment the building was secure, refugees began pouring into the building from the back courtyard and were immediately ushered out the front door.

Now that Fox had taken the Treasury, Burnham, newly nicked in the other leg, had formulated a plan to blow up a couple of safes and take home whatever spoils of the war he could. These plans were dashed when Downs arrived and observed the corporal placing C-4 explosives around the locking mechanism of a safe. "What the hell are you trying to do, Burnham?" Downs demanded.

Thinking quickly, Burnham responded, "Uh, trying to find out what the Communists were hiding, Skipper." He paused, noting the doubtful look on the captain's face. "May be good for intelligence," he added for effect.

"Burnham…" Downs warned while staring a hole through man. Downs had thought it through, even if no once else had. Whether or not his men would have liked to take spoils home, they didn't have their packs. They wouldn't have anywhere to carry whatever they managed to steal. In the end, he would not have Fox acquire a reputation for looters and pillagers. Captain Downs took great pride in the integrity of his company.

"All right, Sir," Burnham relinquished. "I'm on my way out of here." Burnham abandoned his quest for riches and fortune and reported in to the doc to have his wounds tended instead.

The Marines of the 2nd Platoon encountered no resistance when taking the Post Office. The platoon took its time exploring and clearing the building. The building had two floors. The first floor extended into the rear of the lot another fifty feet as a single floor. Throughout the afternoon, any time one of the Marines approached a window in the back of the Post Office, the enemy would spray the outer wall with bullets.

As they searched, the 2nd Platoon soon discovered a large cigar-shaped, concrete bunker in the courtyard behind the Post Office. The bunker had two, steel doors, one on each side, and four air vents. Any time an enemy would spot a Marine, he would slip out of the bunker, fire on the Marine, and retreat back into the bunker.

After withdrawing from the Post Office, the enemy had escaped to the concrete bunker where they were temporarily safe. However, now trapped inside the bunker, they tried to break out. Again and again their futile attempts failed. Corporal Brown's four-man squad kept the NVA neatly enclosed within their cement prison. Private First Class "Hawk" Hawkins, the rocket man attached to the squad, boldly stood up on the first floor roof with a LAAW resting on his right shoulder. Hawk ignored the occasional sniper fire and waited for the steel door to open. On a five-minute interval the door would slowly open about three inches. The NVA were obviously probing their ability to safely leave the bunker.

Each time, Hawk would fire his LAAW into the breach. On one occasion the squad did hear a secondary explosion. The truth was, however, that the LAAW wasn't getting the job done.

Downs ordered the platoon to attempt capturing the North Vietnamese. "Invite them out to join the 'Chu Hoi' program or the Government of the Republic of Vietnam's surrender program," he suggested.

The two attempts at gassing them and yelling, "Chu Hoi, Chu Hoi" produced one NVA warrant officer who emerged with his hands up. He was hustled to the MACV compound. Without gas masks, the other brave NVA soldiers, remained buckled up and moaning. Their resistance called for more drastic action.

The company's forward progress had been halted at the street behind the Treasury and the Post Office, Le Dinh Street. Since his objective, the Treasury, had been secured by 1700, Second Lieutenant Hausrath was able to go to the Post Office to observe the building from where yesterday, the enemy had fired B-40s at the university. Hausrath soon learned about the additional problem with the large concrete bunker. They were not able to fire a 3.5-inch rocket at the bunker's steel doors. Specifically, blasting the doors at the ground level did not allow enough space for the 3.5-inch rocket man to avoid his own back blast.

"Sergeant Mayhall, how about going back over to the Treasury and getting Carter, his 3.5 launcher, two or three HEAT rounds, and meet me up on the second floor?" Hausrath asked.

Mayhall took off immediately.

Fifteen minutes later Carter reached the second floor. "What can I do, Sir?"

"Carter, I want you to get out this window and go across the flat roof to the left side over there," he said, pointing. "Below there is a concrete bunker with steel doors. Blast them off. The 2nd Platoon is ready to cover you. Can you do that?"

"Should be able to."

"Okay, wait 'til I give you the word," Hausrath nodded.

Hausrath called on Staff Sergeant Tinson and the 2nd Platoon to provide cover fire. When the platoon's rifles began firing at the bunker doors, Hausrath ordered, "All right, now!"

Round after round sprayed out in every direction. Chunks of buildings chipped off as the bullets pulverized the concrete into powder. With the exception of a pesty sniper firing from a couple of blocks away, who turned out to be a bad shot, Carter was completely unmolested. He fired his HEAT round. The round blasted the door from its hinges. It fell sideways blocking the tunnel's entrance. His job done, Carter dashed for safety back inside the Post Office's second floor.

1900 hours. Any light that had existed was all but gone. The enemy inside the bunker had run out of time. The task fell to Brown's squad. They decided one man would have to sneak out in the open, get to the bunker, and throw open the blown door. Another Marine would toss a couple of frag grenades inside.

Donning their gas masks, armed with flashlights and .45 caliber pistols, Private First Class David Keif and Lance Corporal C.C. Campbell were "volunteered" to lead the attack. After Campbell lobbed the grenades inside, Keif and Campbell waited for them to go off. The grenade caused a series of rapid explosions. With gas masks on Keif and Campbell entered the room. Keif went in first. The large bunker contained stalls filled with four and one half-foot wide spools of communications cable. Systematically, Campbell and Keith crept toward each stall tossing a grenade in each one. They neared the rear of the large bunker. Only three stalls remained when they received orders to fall back for the night.

During the night Marines from Fox Company in close proximity to the bunker heard moaning indicating that there were some other NVA still alive in the bunker. At first light on 5 February Lance Corporal Pablo Contreras was ordered into the bunker. He entered the door, pointed his machine gun down the long axis of the bunker and fired half of an ammo bandolier towards the back of the bunker. As he did bodies bounced around the other end of the bunker. The moaning and groaning ceased.

Ten minutes later Contreras left the bunker silent. When he did he caught the eye of Corporal Brown, "How to go, Pablo?"

"Man, Corporal Brown," the nineteen year-old machine gunner said, "I just saw those gooks I shot fly straight up in the air! That really freaked me out."

For the dirty job of removing twenty-four dead enemy soldiers, the Marines tied comm wire around their ankles and pulled them out. That worked for about sixteen bodies. The others, due to the number of grenades that were thrown into the bunker, fell apart as they were pulled out. Fox was forced to pick them up piece by piece. After the clean up, five AK-47's, two SKS carbines, two old M-1 Carbines, one RPD light machine gun, five B-40 Rocket launchers, and three satchel charges were recovered.

5 February 1967. The 2nd Battalion pressed the retreating enemy toward its next interim objectives, specifically, the prison and the Provincial Administrative Building. To seize these two objectives, the three companies would have to attack through a variety of buildings, such as the sports club along the river, the nearly forty multi-sized hospital buildings in the next two blocks, and eight hospital annex buildings south of Ngo Guyen Street. Lieutenant Colonel Cheatham's scheme of maneuver had Hotel Company attacking along the river; Golf would attack through the northern hospital buildings; and Fox would attack through the southern hospital buildings on both sides of Ngo Guyen Street.

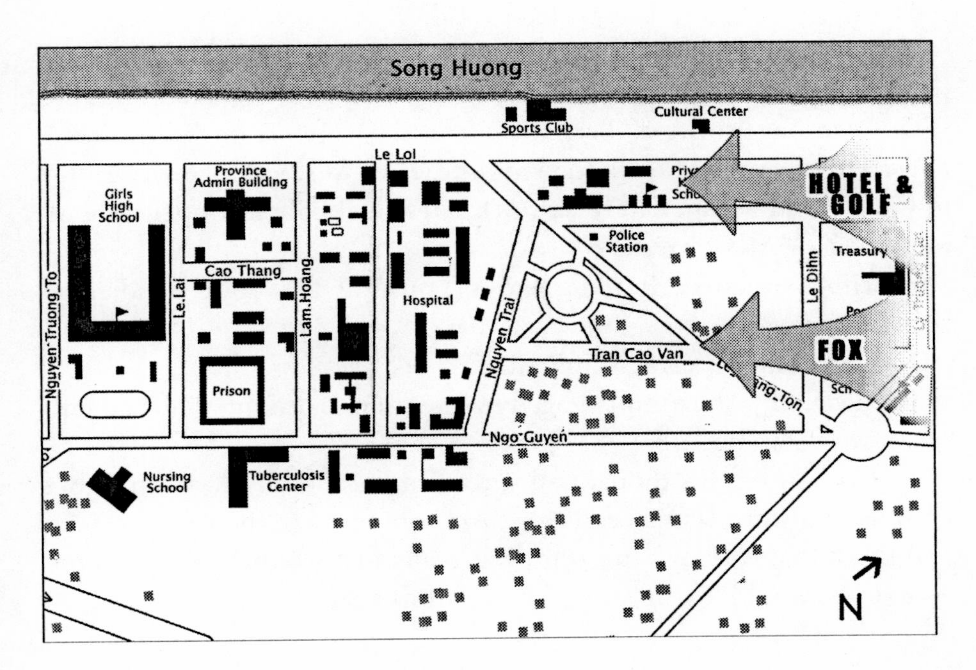

After Hotel seized the Sports Club in the early morning, the hospital complex was next. The complex stretched 300 meters from Le Loi Street to Ngo Quyen Street. In depth, the compound occupied two blocks, each about one hundred meters. The complex was filled with snipers and NVA firing rocket propelled grenades and automatic weapons.

Second Lieutenant Hausrath approached his platoon sergeant.

"Sir?" Staff Sergeant McCoy asked when Hausrath reached him.

"Skipper wants the platoon to free those Air Force guys," Hausrath informed him. "They're supposed to be hiding in one of two buildings in the hospital area. I'm going with Bernie's squad to look for them in this building," Hausrath said indicating a hospital building on the map with a circle around it. "That should be behind that little shed over there to the left," the lieutenant said, pointing.

"All right."

"You check out this one with Ekker's squad," Hausrath said referring to a second circle on the map, then immediately pointing to a small building standing thirty meters from the others.

"Got it, Sir. I'll keep you posted by radio."

After repeated fire team rushes spanning across 200 meters of a city park and a large traffic circle, McCoy reached the designated building with Corporal Albritton, Sergeant Ekker's 1st Fire Team leader. They paused to catch their breath for a minute. Then McCoy looked Albritton in the eye and whispered, "Okay, Arky. Try the knob; if it opens, I'll go in. Got that?" McCoy checked.

Albritton nodded. But, instead of turning the door handle, he knocked.

McCoy flashed a silent, "Holy shit!"

Immediately, Albritton twanged in his Arkansas country-boy accent. "Anybody to home?"

McCoy shoved his thoughts down from his throat. Albritton didn't even use a normal sentence. If those Air Force guys in there were armed and think that McCoy's fire team was really just a bunch of gooks, the Americans would fire first and ask questions later.

"Are you Americans?" The timid inquiry barely penetrated the door.

McCoy turned the knob and opened the door.

Four partially bearded men in camouflaged utilities walked into the first light they had seen in one week. Each covered their sensitive eyes. One looked at Albritton and said, "God, I'd kiss you if you didn't smell so bad."

By mid-afternoon on 5 February, the Marines began occupying building after building of the complex, but their work wasn't complete.

Clearing one building at a time was tedious, time-taking, and consumed the Marines with conflicting emotions ranging from anger to compassion. As Staff Sergeant McCoy and Sergeant Ekker's squad crept through the buildings, the NVA soldiers would vacate them one at a time and withdraw toward the prison.

One large building Fox maneuvered through had a sign reading "Périmètre du Lepre" on it.

"Uh oh," McCoy mumbled, "Leprosy Ward!"

Silently, Ekker pointed for Private First Class "Slow Poke" Rigolett and Lance Corporal Montabias to provide security outside while he, McCoy, and the rest of his squad entered the building. It looked like any other hospital ward they had seen so far.

Outside, Montabias and Rigolett started firing. Immediately, an RPG, rocket guided grenade, slammed into the far wall of the ward. The sole patient was an old, feeble-looking, Vietnamese woman with splotchy skin who reclined on a nearby bed. She waved her hands fearfully, half covering her face for protection while she begged the men to carry her out of the building. Two more RPGs impacted the far wall lethally hurling pieces of concrete at them.

Ekker yelled for Private First Class Amos, his radio operator, and the others to get out. He directed them to the same door they had used to enter the building.

McCoy looked at the helpless deserted old woman, "Ohhhh, what the hell!" he slurred. With that he reached down, picked her up, and darted for the door.

Montabias and Rigolett had been wounded slightly in the exchange, but had forced the NVA's retreat. The rest suffered only a blood pressure surge that they were getting used to. McCoy placed the sixty-pound woman gently down on the ground. He smiled at the little old lady, who mumbled, "Cam on, Ong..." or "Thank you, Sir."

McCoy bolted to the corpsman taking care of Montabias and Rigolett. "Doc! Doc!" he cried. "Can I catch Leprosy from her?"

Doc Vojda looked up and laughed, "Sarge, you'll probably catch a bullet way before that!"

1862 hours. The 2nd Platoon under the leadership of Staff Sergeant Tinson seized a portion of a large building and freed the Thua Thien Province Chief and the major of Hue City.

As the daylight started to fade, the battalion had most of the northern portion of the hospital complex under its control. Fox assaulted and seized most of the hospital buildings on the southern portion of the hospital complex before night fell. One Marine had been killed and forty-three wounded and evacuated. Another one hundred had been wounded but not evacuated. The enemy lost seventy-three killed with thirty-one taken prisoner. Some of their POWs had been wounded and occupied the hospital beds.

0741 hours. On the morning of 6 February, Hotel and Golf Companies began their half of the battalion's two-pronged pincher movement to seize control of the remaining hospital buildings in their sector. By noon Hotel had seized the Provincial Headquarters. Supporting arms, tear gas, and infantry bravado accounted for the tactical victory with the enemy losing sixteen killed. They retreated from Hotel and Golf Company to the Prison and girl's high school across Le Lai Street. The companies sustained four killed and eleven wounded during the morning battle.

Fox's mission was to clear the southern portion of the hospital complex, on both sides of Ngo Guyen Street and then, on order, be prepared to seize the buildings to the west of the prison. Building by building

Staff Sergeant Tinson led Fox Company's 2nd Platoon assault south of Ngo Guyen Street. Despite the Marines' progress, the enemy resisted ferociously. The last building was beside the nurses' training center. This building was positioned 200 meters across from the girl's high school and the adjoining boy's high school. The Marines skirted the outside of the building as they prepped themselves for the dash across the street toward the schools. Small houses provided some cover. The Platoon held up, daunted by the danger facing them. Crossing the street would be suicide.

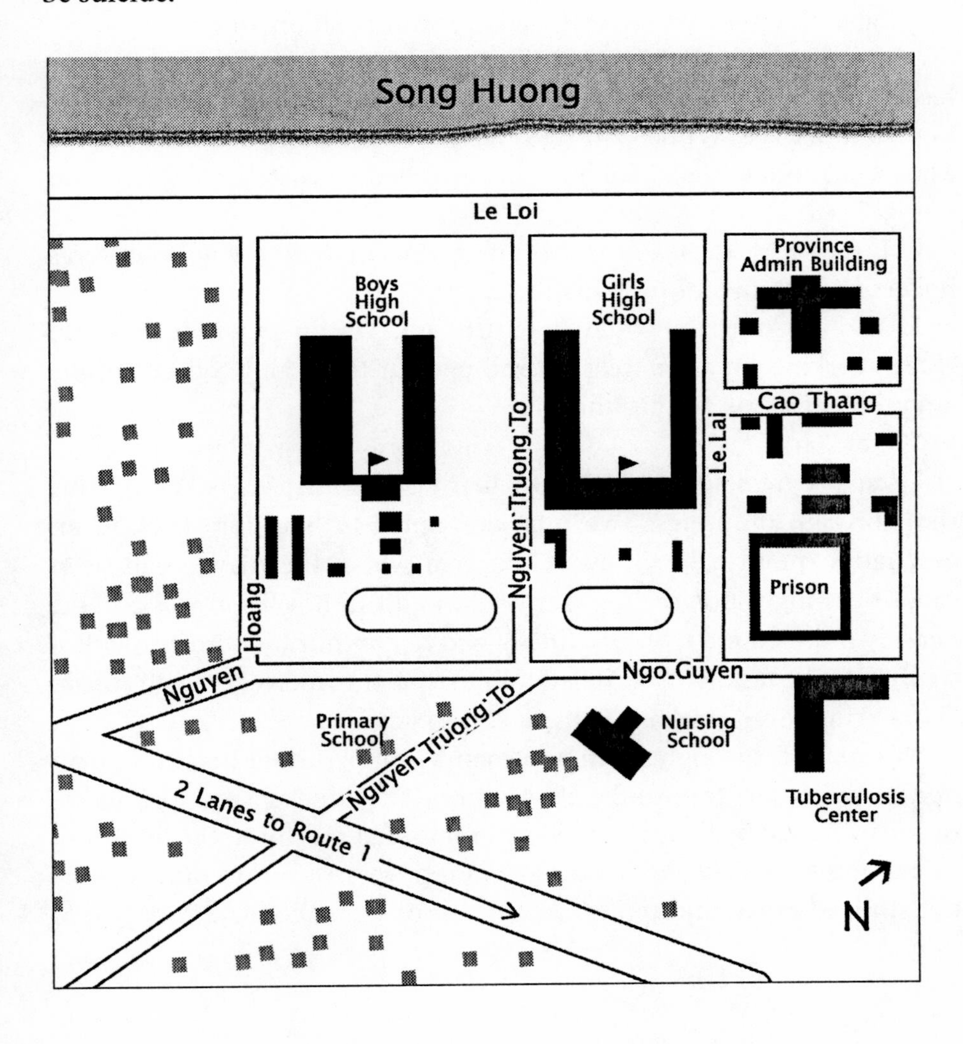

After ten minutes Downs' radio operator, Corporal Jim Violett, called for Tinson, "Fox Two, this is Fox Six, over."

"Roger, Six, go."

"Six Actual," Violett said, referring to Downs, "wants to know what's holding up the attack, over."

Over the sound of constant, nearby rifle rattling, Tinson explained, "Tell Six that we're pinned down. They are firing from one of the school buildings north of us. We're nearly out of ammo and have sent back for more."

"Roger, Fox Two. We're on the way to your position, out."

The radio quieted while Lance Corporal Contreras struggled to clear his jammed weapon. The rest of the men ducked zipping bullets and flying window glass. While Contreras ignored the danger around him, the Marines counter-fired. "Pablo," Tinson yelled. "What the hell are you doing?"

"My damn M-16 is jammed! I can't get the magazine out!" Contreras hollered with frustration in his voice.

Realizing Contreras couldn't return fire, Tinson put him to work, "Stop working on your weapon and get out there and collect up any ammo you find on the ground."

"Okay, Sarge."

Their progress slowed at 1130 when Private First Class Wilson was shot through the lungs. Two men attempted to haul him back to an evacuation point a block away, the area where the mayor had been caught the night before, but they couldn't lift him. Wilson was a huge, densely muscled man. Smitty finally had to commit his whole squad of six men to the task. Tinson yelled to the departing men carrying Wilson, "Hey, bring some ammo when you come back."

Downs and his eight-man command group rushed across a small open area in pairs toward the 2nd Platoon. They ducked and sprinted as rounds whizzed by their heads. Corporal Violett was hit in the head by a sniper and fell fatally wounded. Corporal Rogers, the other radio operator, stooped down and pulled Violett out of the street, laid him beside the closest building, removed his radio, and ran to catch up with Downs.

Corporal Smith and his squad returned to the platoon with adequate ammunition per Tinson's request and immediately started distributing it.

When Down's finally reached the 2nd Platoon, lead impacted all around the men. "Staff Sergeant Tinson," Downs called, panting, "I want you to get ready to assault the building where the fire is coming from. We'll give you cover."

"Aye, aye, Sir." Tinson replied.

Downs called for 81's to fire on the school outbuilding. As soon as the fire mission began he glanced at Tinson and asked, "You ready?"

1305 hours. Tinson gave a thumb's up, then led Sergeant Mayhall, Private First Class Palmo, and Doc Morrison onto and across Ngo Guyen Street with the rest of the platoon firing cover for them.

Tinson's four-man unit crossed the athletic field charging directly for their objective. As soon he had passed beyond Fox's effective fire support range, NVA soldiers opened up on Tinson and his men from the top of the prison and the school's outer buildings in front of them. The return to the nursing school was sixty to eighty meters behind them. Tinson knew that continuing toward his target would mean running the gauntlet through enemy soldiers firing automatic weapons. The flanking fire aimed at them from both directions increased. Tinson and his men were trapped in the middle and out in the open.

From the small administrative buildings in front of the Provincial Headquarters complex, Sergeant Ted Varina, who had recovered from his Union II wounds and now led a supporting 106mm recoilless rifle section, was seventy-five meters from one of the enemy's defensive positions. Varina and his men fired at the NVA. Tinson was caught in the crossfire. Ten meters to Tinson's right was the nearest building on school grounds. Tinson charged to the closest door for shelter. His men followed in his wake. It was locked. He yanked, pulled, jiggled, kicked, but it wouldn't budge. The enemy began firing on Tinson and his Marines. As the NVA marksmen found their range, the men of Fox

Company and Varina's 106mm recoilless rifle section watched in horror as, one by one, Tinson and his three men were cut down. The loss of the 2nd Platoon Marines thinned out the Fox company ranks measurably. Tinson's leadership and the bravery of the others could not be replaced.

1415 hours. Golf Company, with Varina's two 106mm recoilless rifles, two of the Marine Corps-unique tracked vehicles equipped with six 106mm recoilless rifles, called "Ontos", and 81mm mortar support attacked the prison. The prison fell when the Marines blew a hole in the wall one hour later with a satchel charge. When the dust settled Golf had one man wounded. Thirty-six enemy bodies and many weapons were found in the prison as a result of Golf's attack. They also found fifteen enemy bodies outside the prison, many of whom had killed Tinson and his men during their futile charge. Seven soldiers of South Vietnam's Army and two prison guards were freed.

With the capture of the prison, 2/5 had completed "Phase One" of the operation. Fox had 213 combat-ready Marines and corpsmen when they arrived in Hue City less than a week earlier. On the evening of 6 February, the company was down to ninety "effectives". As a result, Cheatham placed Fox Company in reserve to allow its troop strength to fill up with replacements.

Golf and Hotel Companies moved rapidly past the high schools and primary school seeking a foothold on the river some 800 kilometers away. Along the way they discovered numerous graves, recently dug by the enemy, containing weapons.

In its reserve status Fox dealt with the "mopping up" duties. The 1st Platoon occupied several positions from the Treasury Building to the MACV compound in order to hold the costly won ground. On 7 February Fox used two jeeps to evacuate the wounded men, who had not been removed earlier, back to the relative safety of the MACV compound. Lance Corporal Thomas with Sergeant Francis Garnsey riding shotgun drove one jeep. Gunnery Sergeant VanValkenburgh drove the other vehicle. He was alone. The gunny came under automatic weapons fire from enemy snipers as he navigated the still treacherous streets.

Undaunted, VanValkenburgh heroically made trip after trip, rescuing the wounded and reappearing each time with replacements for the strung-out, tired men of the 1st Platoon. After multiple trips and his final retrieval, he returned once more providing ammunition for the 1st Platoon. Apprised of the gunny's actions, Downs realized the company would be better served with VanValkenburgh in a leadership role rather than a logistician role and assigned him to take command of the 2nd Platoon.

While the gunny made his selfless runs, Hausrath was ordered to clear the boys high school.

1530 hours. Lieutenant Hausrath seized one of the smaller two story buildings outside the huge school. The lieutenant accompanied Burnham's squad. Up on the second floor Hausrath and the men searched for enemy hiding in closets and behind furnishings. When the lieutenant slowly opened a door off the main room with great caution, to his delight he discovered a porcelain toilet.

Despite the fact that running water in the city had been cut off since the start of the fighting, Hausrath commanded Burnham, "I don't want any one to use this toilet before me. Is that understood?"

"Sure, Lieutenant," the salty corporal said to the twenty-three year-old lieutenant.

"I'm going to see McCoy, and I'm coming back!" He turned back, briefly so that Burnham barely noticed and thought nothing of it. The lieutenant swore he had seen the slightest smirk on the corporal's face, but it had vanished so quickly that Hausrath second-guessed his own eyes.

Thirty minutes later the lieutenant returned with a map for an extended visit to the restroom.

Finally finished with his business, Hausrath departed the building again, this time to see Captain Downs. Upstairs, the men wasted no time lining up by rank to use the unflushable toilet.

By dark, the men were set into their night defensive positions around the building. Using a flashlight to navigate his way around, the lieutenant innocently returned for a second visit to the head. Upon reaching the porcelain potty the lieutenant gagged, his guts heaving upward as he retreated back away from the bathroom. The toilet was so full, almost to the seat that its contents looked like a twisted Dairy Queen ice cream cone. The stench was overwhelming! His cry of horror echoed throughout the school building.

"Burnham! Get up here, now!" he shrieked.

"Sir!" Burnham barked arriving at the lieutenant's place of disgust.

In a quivering, yet quiet voice Hausrath rasped, "You better take care of that, Burnham!"

McCoy's situation was no better. He was just across the school grounds in the horseshoe shaped main school building. The two wings pointed toward the Perfume River while the middle portion, connecting the wings, was obviously the formal entrance of the school. McCoy and Ekker's squad entered at dusk with the lieutenant's instructions that they were to occupy it until morning. There was only enough time to clear the central portion of the building. The wings would have to wait until morning.

In a low voice, Sergeant Ekker quietly murmured, "Hey, Jim, after all the RPGs we've taken, the guys are a bit skittish about staying on the first deck tonight."

"All right, let's get upstairs; we'll see what we can do," he relented.

The stairs had a beautiful spiraled shape and sat in the center of the cavernous room. The squad climbed the stairs and cleared the second deck without incident. McCoy gathered the men together by the top of the stairwell. "Stewart and Krisel, you'll cover any thing coming down the right wing. Rocet, Chek, and you two machine gunners, you cover the left wing. Sergeant Ekker, Arkie, and Amos will be at the top of the stairwell here with me. Any questions?"

Chek was a paranoid Marine with pure Chinese blood in him who constantly feared that other Marines who didn't know him would mistake him for a "gook". He hated that word. Chek asked, "What if they sneak up the stairs and you don't hear them and they throw a satchel charge?"

All right, I want you, Rocet, and Krisel to go downstairs and break every window, break the glass in those trophy cases, collect the glass, and put all the small pieces on the stairs on your way back. That way, if any gooks try to sneak up on us, we'll be able to hear them. I don't want anybody cutting himself and looking for a damn Heart; so be careful! Now move out; we don't have much time 'til it's pitch dark in here!"

Addressing the remaining men, referring to Ekker, McCoy said, "Chuck...you, Arky, Amos, and I are going to stay up here around the top of the stairs. With this railing around the stairwell," McCoy indicating and pulling back and forth on the sturdy railing, "If we hear any one trying to come up here I want you to pull the pin on a grenade, stick your arm through the spokes, and just drop the grenade. Don't throw the damn thing. You all got that?"

The glass was spread on the stairs. Then Chek, Rocet, and Krisel positioned themselves as McCoy instructed.

Over three hours later Albritton slid over to McCoy and whispered, "I hear something on the stairs."

McCoy, still awake, leaned closer to the vertical spokes of the railing for nearly thirty seconds, then turned to Albritton and whispered, "Naaah...'taint nothing. Go back over there."

Fifteen minutes later the insistent Albritton crawled back over and whispered emphatically, "I really hear something!"

"All right, Arky. I'm going to alert the others, then you drop the grenade."

McCoy was no more than ten feet from the stairwell when a concussion behind him blew him into the wall. For a half minute McCoy saw only stars. Then he saw sparks from something burning and figured it must have been a satchel charge. McCoy yelled, "Satchel charge, not grenade!" He dove on Private First Class Amos, the radio operator, to protect him from a secondary explosion.

The troops shouted, "We're getting rocketed! We're getting rocketed!" The men braced. In their defensive stances, they readied themselves for the brunt of the attack.

Nothing happened.

In the aftermath, McCoy felt warm liquid running his leg. He thought, shit…I've been hit in the back. If I tell the men, they'll panic.

Albritton announced, "I think I'm hit." He paused feeling his waist. "I think my cartridge belt caught on fire."

"How the hell did that happen, Albritton?" McCoy demanded.

"I threw the grenade and it must of hit one of those spokes."

"Well, you dumb fool," McCoy murmured quietly. "I appreciate your honesty, but when I said to pull the pin, reach your hand through the spokes, and drop the damn grenade, what in the hell did you think I was talking about?"

"Sorry, Sarge," Albritton mumbled.

"Even if you are wounded, don't you even say anything about a Purple Heart!"

McCoy went back over to his radio operator. His loosely tied right boot was filling up with liquid. "Amos," he begun in a muted tone. "I've been hit. Strike a match and tell me how bad it is."

"No, they'll see us!"

McCoy bent over near Amos's face, "Strike a damn match!"

Amos struck his lighter and as he looked the staff sergeant over, remarked, "Hey, Sarge, your new canteen is blown all to hell!"

McCoy marched over to Albritton and asked, "Arky, is your canteen okay?"

Albritton, glad his platoon sergeant was no longer mad at him, answered, "Yeah, Sarge, why?"

McCoy thrust his recently acquired, though now tattered, US Army canister at Albritton. Albritton, good to his word, raised his canteen to his platoon sergeant. McCoy yanked Albritton's undamaged canteen from the corporal's outstretched hand and growled, "Great, I'll use yours. You can use mine."

During the period of 7 February through 10 February, Fox moved from building to building clearing the remnants of the enemy force until they reached the Song Phu Cam. The river was so uniformly narrow, about thirty-five meters wide, that the men frequently referred to as the "Phu Cam Canal." Enemy snipers from across the river kept the Marines on their toes when they were outside the buildings. Along the northern side of the river, the side Fox was on, the international community possessed embassies and occupied upscale apartment buildings. The buildings totally evacuated, Fox Company Marines had the area to themselves. Souvenirs were bountiful and the German Embassy was the site of a couple of all night parties since the Europeans evacuated leaving cases of liquor to be enjoyed by the liberating force.

At noon on 11 February, the team of Second Lieutenant Don Hausrath, Corporal Bernie Burnham, and his squad were in an apartment building along the canal when the platoon radio sprang to life. "Fox Three Actual, this is Fox Six, over." It was Captain Downs' radio operator, Corporal Rogers, calling for the lieutenant.

"This is Three Actual. Go."

"Roger, Three Actual. Hotel Six," Rogers replied referring to Captain Ron Christmas, "...is looking for some fire support so that Hotel Marines can attack a building. RPGs and B-40s, being fired from the building, are slamming them. We believe you'll be able to call the fire mission in from the roof of your position, over."

"Roger, give me the grid of the gook's building, over," Hausrath agreed.

"That will be Yankee Delta 7720206, over."

"Roger, we'll go up on the roof and give Hotel a holler, over."

"Roger, this is Six, out," Rogers acknowledged.

"Bernie, let's go up on the roof," Hausrath called. "This ought to be a piece of cake."

In the second floor hallway Burnham, in one movement, stepped on a chair and pulled himself up to the roof through a three-foot square opening. The roof, covered with a black tar-like substance, had two skylights and two three-foot ventilation towers, one above the first and second floor bathrooms and one above the kitchen. The ventilation towers provided concealment from the snipers across the canal. Burnham reached back in the opening for the two PRC-25 radios and hid beside one of the towers. Following immediately, the lieutenant was up on the roof with his map and binoculars.

"Hotel Six, this is Fox-Three. Is your building the one about 300 meters from the canal along Ly Thuong Kiet street and next to the railroad tracks?...The one that doesn't have part of the roof and has a smaller building ten meters to the right of it?" Burnham asked in his very distinguishable, gravelly, New York accent.

"That's a roger, Fox Three. Got us in your sights?" Christmas asked.

"Roger, Sir. This is Burnham," he said in response to Christmas's question. "We'll call in the mission. Let us know when you want us to lift the fire," he said to the captain. "Okay, Lieutenant Hausrath," Burnham signaled as well as yelled. "Call in the arty!"

The energetic, youthful lieutenant contacted the 105mm howitzer battery located in the field next to the MACV compound with the other radio. Burnham thought that the lieutenant was really getting good at fire missions. He regularly hit his target on about the third round. Hell, Burnham thought, Hausrath was as good as any arty FO.

After the third round, the lieutenant gave a "Fire for Effect" command and rounds from all six howitzers flew over the Jean d'Arc High School, the two high schools, and the canal, obliterating the targeted building.

"Roger, sir. Mission complete." Burnham reported to Christmas. Then to Hausrath, he relayed, "Sir, the captain said that was the best fire mission he's seen. Good going!"

The lieutenant stood up jumping like a cheer leader and started toward the edge of the roof in his excitement when a sniper's bullet passed below his right shoulder, through his heart and lodged itself inside the back of his flak jacket. Hausrath's knees buckled. Burnham reached up to catch his toppling body. The lieutenant managed ten labored breaths and died in Corporal Burnham's arms.

Burnham yelled out to no one, "Lieutenant, what the hell did you get up for?" He looked down at the young Marine officer he held in his arms, shook his head, and said to the fallen man in a soft, tearful voice, "God damn it, Lieutenant."

On 12 February Fox, after being brought out of reserve, continued the attack, with the 3rd Platoon pushing across the Song Phu Cam. From 0900 to 1500 hours the enemy resisted retaliating with B-40 rockets, small arms, automatic weapons, and 60mm mortars.

1530 hours. The day's final objective, the railroad station, was in sight. Prominent in the station complex was a large wooden-framed warehouse adjacent to the tracks with a partially rusted tin roof. Marine howitzers had already destroyed much of the right side of the building. A four-foot high platform stretched the length of the building in front of the warehouse.

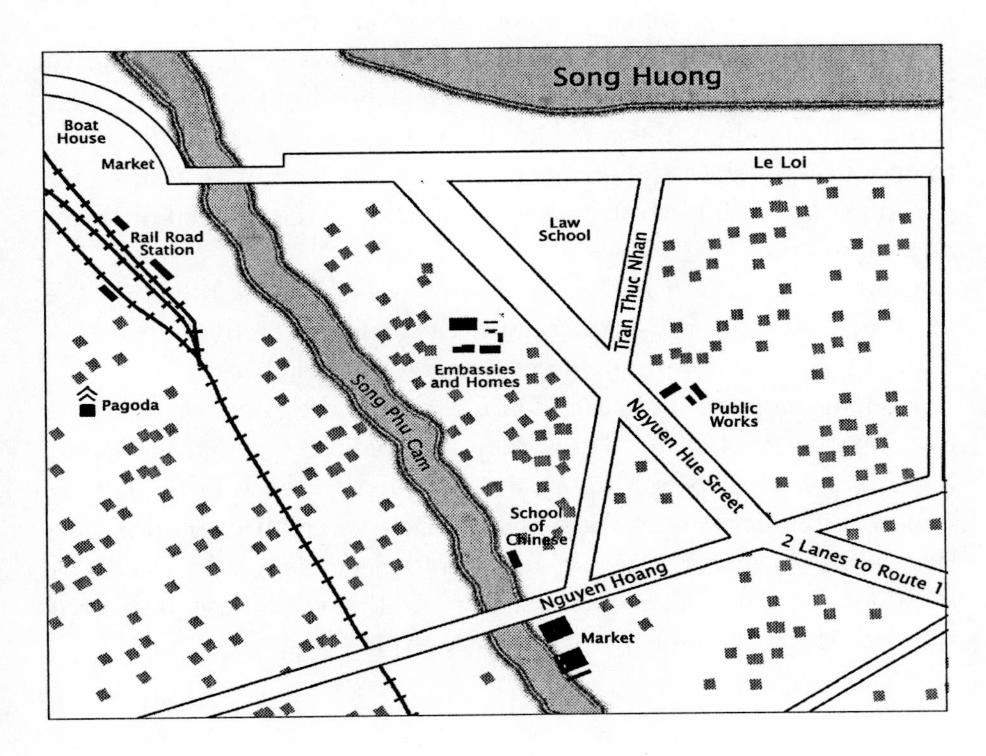

Corporal Charlie Lynch and Lance Corporal Contreras with the rest of Lynch's squad reached the empty boxcars in the rail yard. Enemy mortars pummeled the ground near them while chunks of metal ricocheted off the boxcar sides and wheels. Sniper rounds shot from inside the warehouse building, "pinging" off the tracks. From behind them they could hear Staff Sergeant McCoy, the acting platoon commander, yelling, "Some one get to the warehouse! Blow open the door and get the hell in there!"

One of the Marines fired an M-79 "blooper" from the right front. Ten seconds later the warehouse's front doors buckled and blew inward. Contreras scrambled around the left side of the boxcar that shielded him, hurdled over the car's coupling device, and leaped onto the platform. The squad's covering fire intensified as he made his assault. Contreras pitched one frag grenade at the partially damaged doors and one inside the opening. He dove for cover. Waiting only moments after the explosion, he tore the damaged door open wide enough to gain entrance. An enemy grenade exploded near him as Contreras climbed through the opening while reaching for a third grenade. It hurled Contreras back through the doors, and he landed outside on the platform. Still conscious, the grenade's flash of white fire had blinded him temporarily. Stunned and unable to move, he gasped for air waiting for the sniper to finish him off. Sniper rounds zinged the wooden platform all around him.

Contreras's survival instincts suddenly took over. He rolled off the ten-foot wide platform landing hard but safely on the tracks below. A new corpsman anxious to tend to Contreras was held back.

Dodging sniper bullets, each Marine entered the doors ripped open by Contreras. Professionals now, they systematically cleared the building. Marines cleared one room, then covered for each other as they moved methodically down each hallway. Doors were thrown open; bullets ripped through the air; snipers were killed. The battle lasted one hour longer. The last snipers hidden in the warehouse had been silenced. McCoy and the platoon took control.

Night fell and the platoon set up in defensive positions in and around the warehouse. McCoy and Amos, his radio operator, established the platoon CP near a pile of rubble on the right side of the warehouse. After a couple hours in the dark, Amos whispered, "Staff Sergeant McCoy?"

McCoy, who had been dozing, jerked awake. "Yeah?"

"Do they have rats in here?"

"Maybe. Why?"

"I feel something furry beside me. I don't want to get bit."

McCoy thought about that. "Okay, ask the other squads if they hear any rats moving. We don't want to lose anyone to a friggin' rat bite."

Amos made his dilemma clear to the rest of the platoon, reconfirming his situation every fifteen minutes by feeling the "fuzzy" thing next to him. "I can still feel something next to me. It must be a dead rat!" he would complain.

As the daylight began to illuminate the inside of the building the men roused. Much of the platoon gathered around the CP to witness Amos's "fuzzy" thing. By 0615 the entire platoon had left McCoy and Amos laughing. Amos looked at the pile rubble with the "fuzzy" thing he had petted every fifteen minutes throughout the night with disgust. The head of a dead NVA soldier now stared at Amos. McCoy, chuckling, got on the radio with Downs to enjoy the light moment.

Downs informed him at that time that First Lieutenant Dove was expected in as a replacement for Lieutenant Hausrath.

On 13 February the 1st Platoon's mission was to cross the Song Phu Cam, swing left away from the railroad station, and seize a group of buildings that had a large Buddhist Pagoda nestled among them. As soon as the platoon crossed the bridge, it fell under enemy small arms and B-40 rocket rounds being fired from a concrete building immediately across the far side of the railroad tracks about half the distance to the pagoda.

Corporal Bobby Smith's squad was ordered to seize the building. Sergeant Pappy Pennell, the platoon sergeant, trailed the squad to provide support should it be needed. The remainder of the platoon was held back in the homes on the south side of the river waiting for Smith's squad to secure the enemy-occupied building.

Smith's men crossed the tracks in fire team rushes. As one fire team ran from a relatively safe spot across the railroad tracks into the open, the other two fire teams poured suppressing cover fire onto the enemy positions. They all made it safely across. The fire teams took refuge in a small structure immediately beside the concrete building occupied by the enemy. While they were glad to be out of harm's way from the sniper fire, they were unaware the building's roof and walls were only constructed of tin. Smith knew that they needed help securing the concrete building next to their position, which was also inconveniently surrounded by a four-foot high concrete fence.

Smith called for armor and mortar support. Almost instantly, two USMC tanks rolled around the corner of a structure on the northern side of the river, fired their 90mm guns twice, and blasted the entire top floor of the enemy-held house into oblivion. From the railroad station, the Fox Company's 60mm mortar men watched the building smoke. They used "line of sight" firing to accurately lob their mortars. Not to be outdone, the enemy, 500 meters to the south from a building complex within the large Buddhist pagoda, fired 60mm mortars at the tin building in support of their own troops under the Marines' attack. Corporal Smith, now fully realizing that he and his squad were in a tin shed, called off his friendly fire support, and barked to Lance Corporal Krueger to take his fire team and secure the building.

Krueger's fire team consisted of Lance Corporal Roy Rascon, the Arizona Indian who was Krueger's best friend, and a new replacement, Private First Class Butch Richard. The three rushed to the safety of the four-foot concrete wall next to the tin building. Krueger led the threesome while Rascon trailed. They crept below the wall, turned the corner, and headed for the three-foot wide front gate. Cautiously, Krueger and Richard slid into the front courtyard focusing mostly on the remains of the first floor of the house that, thanks to the M-48 tanks, was filled mostly with what had been the second floor. Rascon had not yet passed through the gate when enemy soldiers on both sides of Krueger and Richard suddenly popped out of "spider traps" that had been dug in the courtyard. Each rapidly fired three or four rounds from their SKS rifles at the two exposed Marines taking them down.

Smith thought the two were dead until he heard moaning. Rascon, still outside, crouching by the front wall, heard the wounded men moaning as well. While Smith and Pennell yelled, "Lay still, lay still," Rascon tore through the gate and dragged the two Marines to safety. Smith ordered the rest of the squad to charge into the courtyard and throw grenades at the spider traps killing the three enemy soldiers inside.

The 1st Platoon outposted the building complex with the large Buddhist pagoda that evening. With no contact, they returned to the company command post area in the morning only to learn that Captain Downs wanted them to turn around and occupy the building complex they had just vacated.

1300 hours. 1st Platoon neared the pagoda, unaware that the NVA had snuck back into the complex. The Marines managed to re-cross the street in front of the pagoda before the NVA launched a massive assault. Caught off guard, the Marines were cut down. Six men were wounded immediately as they were taken by small arms fire.

They shielded themselves with nearby buildings, walls, whatever they could find. Rockets cratered the street. Chunks of buildings and roadway tore into the Marines' limbs as Fox pressed forward.

Resolute, the young men defended themselves. They fired their magazines at the enemy positions, and the horrific battle was silenced by Sergeant Pennell's superb direction of an 81mm mortar fire mission plus the arrival and back up of the 3rd Platoon. Two Marines were killed and thirteen wounded in that two-hour encounter. Ironically, only one dead enemy soldier was found.

During the remainder of February, Fox Company was relieved of its city street patrols. Fox continued fighting further south of Hue City with Golf Company for a day or so until Golf was called back into the city. Fox swung to the east then back north remaining five miles east of the city. Fox followed and patrolled a 5,000-meter trench line that the NVA and VC had dug a month earlier to stop ground reinforcements from Phu Bai. By 2 March Fox arrived at Co Co Beach and had cleared an area twenty-five kilometers from the city.

On this two-week sweep, Fox suffered three men killed and fifty-nine wounded. Fox Company Marines killed thirty-six NVA and VC soldiers during the same time period. Fox left the Hue City area by 8 March.

CHAPTER 8: GUARDING THE STREET WITHOUT JOY

Early in the morning of 8 March 1968 a convoy of trucks rumbled out of the Hue City on National Highway 1 carrying the men of Fox Company to a familiar area of operations twenty miles south of the city. Over the past five and a half weeks the resilient company had suffered twenty-three men killed and 180 wounded. However, with the steady stream of replacements and the return of the lightly wounded deemed "fit to fight again", the ranks filled almost as fast as the casualties occurred. The trucks slowed, then stopped while crossing the bridge over the Song Phu Cam just south of Hue, allowing a convoy carrying US Army troops from the 101st Airborne Division to enter and clean up the city. A few macho Marines mocked, "It's safe to go into now!" laughing at their own irreverence.

On the back of an open two and a half-ton truck, Corporal Bernie Burnham reflected as he glanced at his squad. All five vets had been wounded at least once in the past month, patched up, and returned to the squad. They would be ready for anything that lay ahead. The three replacements that had lasted more than a week in Hue City were, not only lucky, but already had solid combat experience—at least in city fighting. The other three he just picked up had no combat experience whatsoever and would have to be trained and tested. All in all, his squad was glad to get away from Hue and was ready to do something different.

Burnham's normally effervescent 1st Fire Team leader, Corporal Raymond Borunda, who was sitting next to him on the green-painted, wooden seats, was the only exception. Not only was he somewhere distant, he was visibly upset about something. In his quiet, constantly raspy voice Burnham demanded, "What the hell's bothering you, Borunda?"

"Nothing, Bernie," was mustered as a response.

"Yeah, nothing?"

"Well, I been so loyal since I got here," Borunda uttered before falling silent.

The trucks passed by Phu Bai. Some new men pointed at the Marine side of the complex reminding each other where they checked into Fox Company. Burnham stared across the street and smiled to himself as he recalled the night he and Andy Anderson had partied at the 101st Airborne NCO Club. He wondered just how well "Major O'Hara" was doing. He hadn't seen Anderson since they flew into Hue.

"All right if you gotta know," Borunda blurted his confession five minutes later, "My fiancé broke up with me and is dating an old friend of mine."

Burnham peered at Borunda with his steel blue eyes. He looked deeply into the face of the twenty year-old man of Italian descent whose courage in combat was now a matter of record. Borunda had hardly flinched while bearing the pain of two separate wounds, one from a bullet and one from shrapnel. Now, however, the young man was emotionally crushed just when he should be enjoying their Hue City victory. Taking his eye off Borunda for a split second to light a cigarette, Bernie glanced up again, inhaled deeply, and simply uttered, "Damn."

The men's heads swiveled left and right as they enjoyed the scenery. When they crossed the Song Troi River Bridge, Corporal Albritton pointed toward the foothills to the west and began telling a newbee next to him about how Fox and Hotel Companies had kicked an NVA company's butt on the day before they flew into Hue. The others waved to children. Ten minutes later the convoy slowed; Bernie heard two of the vets laughing at something just before they stopped at a familiar railroad tunnel. All he heard was "packs and gas masks" and he knew the subject. The Fox men remembered all too vividly that they would "not need" those items according to their orders before their "short trip" to Hue City.

The convoy pulled off National Highway 1 and into a parking lot at an area the troops called "the rock crusher." This was the spot where Seabees were mining limestone. The actual reference pertained to the huge machine that turned big rocks into gravel. The gravel was used to maintain the highway tying Hue City with Da Nang, a dangerous piece of coastal highway for which Bernard Fall named his classic book: Street Without Joy.

Gunnery Sergeant VanValkenburgh was busy directing the men in the lead trucks to dismount, assemble, and get ready to do something. None of the actions were clear to Burnham. He watched Captain Downs talk on the radio to someone while wearing a pleased expression on his face. Downs nodded his head and gave the handset back to his new radio operator, Lance Corporal Dave Harrison, a vet from the 1st Platoon. Harrison had taken the place of Corporal Timothy Rodgers who was selected by the battalion commander, Lieutenant Colonel Cheatham, to be his own radio operator.

"Gunny."

"Yes, Sir?"

"Pass the word to the platoons, Lieutenant General Cushman, III MAF," he started, referring to the Third Marine Amphibious Force, "will be here at 1500. There's going to be a battalion formation. Corporal Burnham and Private First Class Keith are getting decorated. Burnham's getting meritoriously promoted to sergeant. The executive officer, Major Steele, and the sergeant major are coordinating the show."

"Yes, Sir!"

"Oh, and Gunny, make sure those two have good uniforms."

The event went off without a hitch. Burnham was meritoriously promoted to sergeant. He was awarded a Navy Cross Medal for jumping on a grenade at Nong Son that didn't explode, a Bronze Star Medal for his many acts of heroisms in Hue City, and two purple Hearts, both earned in Hue. Private First Class Keith received a Silver Star Medal for his braveness in assaulting the bunker behind the Post Office on 5 February. Other Marines were decorated. The ceremony was a classy touch for the end of a costly battle that would never be forgotten in the laurels of the Marine Corps.

For the first few days after Hue City Operations the men of 2/5 could relax a bit. This was true of the officers as well. Fox moved to a location equidistant from the rock crusher and the village of Phu Loc. During this timeframe, Lieutenant Colonel "Big Ernie" Cheatham, while making the rounds, visited Fox Company. Captain Mike Downs asked Cheatham, "How's Rodgers working out?"

Cheatham replied, "Quite well. Why, did you expect any thing different?"

"No, no, Sir," Downs began, pausing to compose his words. "Sometimes he'd annoy me."

"What do you mean, Mike?"

"Well, particularly during the evening hours he'd pass along instructions to the platoons saying I wanted them to do this or that," Downs explained. "Despite the fact that I did not give the orders, he'd direct the platoons to execute certain defensive maneuvers that I had no idea they were carrying out! Later, I'd find out and ask the platoons about it. They say, 'you wanted us to do it; at least Corporal Rodgers said so.' It was just a bad precedence, and it bugged me a lot." Downs amplified his tone and sounded a bit disturbed thinking about it.

"Well, how did you handle it?" Cheatham asked Downs.

"Of course he'd always deny any of it. So to keep him in line, I'd get up some mornings and chew his butt out 'just for a drill,'" explained Downs.

Cheatham laughed at Downs' story, aware that any good radio operator did his best to look after his boss as Rodgers had Downs, then explained, "After I selected Rodgers, he told me that he would miss Fox a lot and even miss you, but he could never figure out why you would chew him out occasionally in the mornings for nothing."

Downs joined him in laughing, "All right, all right, I guess what goes around, comes around!"

In Vietnam, it seemed like no activity above the battalion level could be conducted without a name. The activities that commenced on 8 March were no exception. The troops rarely knew the name of the operation they were on until they read the Stars and Stripes newspaper or the 1st Marine Division's Sea Tiger a couple of weeks later. They simply didn't care. For the men, it was one foot at a time and one C-ration can at a time. However, on 8 March when the 2nd Battalion left the Hue City Task Force and rejoined its parent command, the 5th Marine Regiment, they began participation in Operation Houston. This operation lasted until 30 April. Their activities were comprised of patrols to keep Highway 1 safe and provide security around the Phu Bai air base, the village of Phu Loc, and two or three key bridges.

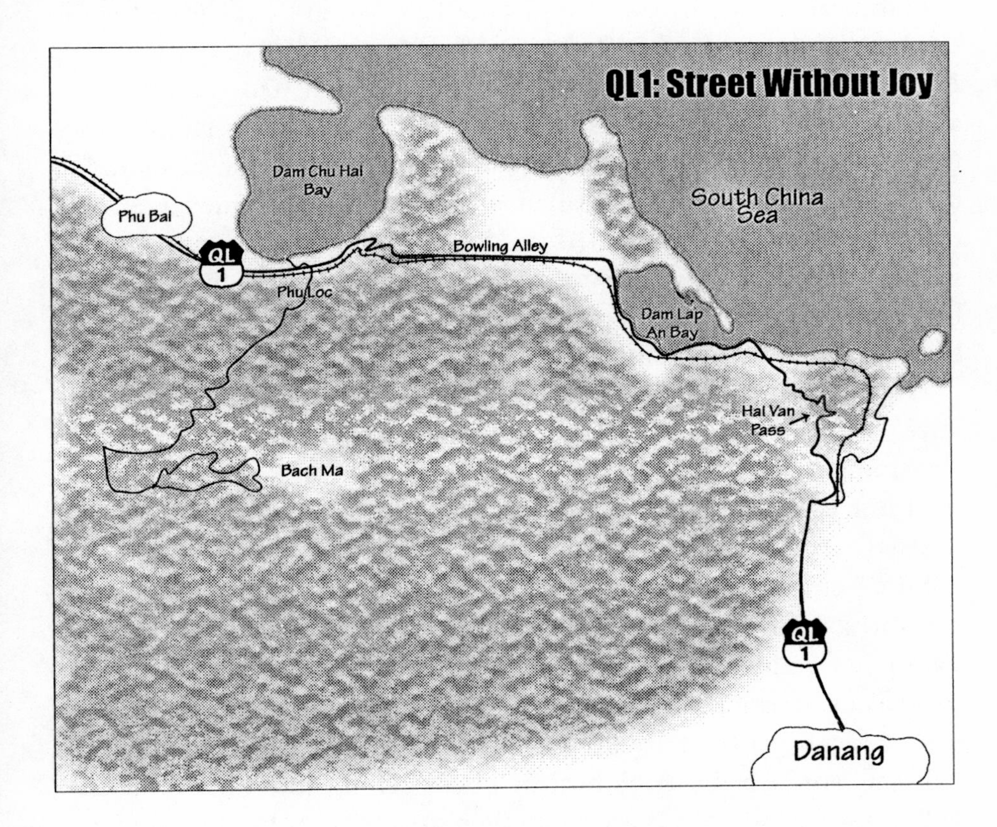

On 18 March, as part of Houston, the 2nd Battalion took Fox and two other rifle companies on a battalion-size patrol to the peak of Mt. Bach Ma, about 1,450 meters above the South China Sea and a eighteen kilometers to the east. Even without binoculars, houses could be seen dotting the top portion of the mountain. The French had built Bach Ma as a resort and rumor had it, or at least "intelligence" thought so, the

enemy may be using it as a safe haven. To reach Bach Ma, the battalion planned on a three-day march. That meant following narrow trails over two small mountains as they marched to the base of their objective. Each company would have its own route. The battalion would follow on the only road after the mountain-climbing grunts would secure various off-road terrain features.

Corporal Rich Carter's second Hue City wound had healed sufficiently, and he was back with the 3rd Platoon in charge of the Weapons Platoon attachment. Lance Corporal Jim Hanson had recently been assigned to be the 1st Squad's radio operator; Hanson was taking Lance Corporal Jeff Shay's place as the squad radio operator. "Hey, I shouldn't be humping this radio; I'm a rifleman; I haven't been trained as a radio operator," Hanson complained to the unsympathetic group of men strung out on the mountainous trail. Shay, now a fire team leader who had been Burnham's radio operator in Hue City, gave Hanson instructions and silenced his complaints.

On the second evening Carter was liberally dousing himself with bug juice. "Hanson you better put some bug juice on or you'll get eaten up alive tonight," he suggested.

"I don't need it, Corporal. I'm impervious to insect bites," Hanson boasted.

Staff Sergeant McCoy and Corporal Carter did nothing but laugh and shrug their shoulders. McCoy pulled Carter aside and remarked to Carter in an unusually quiet tone, "You know, Carter, that guy doesn't seem like a Marine. You see anything different about him other than his hair's a bit longer than usual?"

"Yeah, you're right. Look how he's belly aching about humping that radio." Carter paused for a minute then asked, "And, has he asked you any strange questions?"

"What do you mean?"

"Well, he's asked a bunch of guys about us taking the Treasury."

"Yeah."

"You know, were any of us lucky enough to have gotten away with any gold or other souvenirs…stuff like that."

"That bastard! I don't trust him. Tell you what, Carter, keep an eye on him. If I hear any more shit like that, he's gone. I don't care if he's Naval Intelligence Service or the friggin' CIA; we ain't having a shithead like that in this platoon!"

"Got ya, Sarge."

The following morning Staff Sergeant McCoy, with a C-ration cup of coffee in his hand, looked at Corporal Hanson and said, "Hanson you simple turd! What tree did you fall out of?"

Carter whipped around to see why McCoy was admonishing Hanson.

Hanson looked like the "Elephant Man!" He had slept on one side of his face. Insects had attacked the exposed side all night. Every inch of that side of his face was horribly swollen. His one ear, forehead, one cheek, and nose seemed to form half of a bowling ball. Normally the men would find some humor in a newbee's woes; only on this morning, at the grotesque sight of Hanson, they didn't.

Hanson's struggles continued during the final of the hike up to Bach Ma. About two hours into the climb, the men came to a stream and stopped to fill their canteens. From then on the trail paralleled the stream a few yards away and, on occasion, crossed back over it. At times the trail was so steep that the men slipped backwards.

Carter had his eye on Hanson who was about twenty meters ahead of him. He struggled all morning. Near the top, the perilous trek overcame the new radio operator. He slipped and fell into the stream, tumbling like a weed in the wind. His helmet flew off and his head bounced off of each rock in his path. Carter reached down and yanked the frightened man out of the water. All Carter could say was, "Not a good day, eh?"

McCoy would have no part of sympathy. The word came down that the platoon sergeant wanted Hanson to stop screwing around in the water and get his butt up with him.

Soon after Hanson moved forward, Carter saw the skeleton of a rock ape about three feet off the trail partially covered by some ferns. Being in a good, somewhat mischievous mood, he plucked the skull off of the rest of the framework. He waited until Corporal Glover, the 3rd Squad leader, approached. "Hey, Tom," Carter said handing Glover the skull,

"Sergeant McCoy wanted you to take this and give it to him up at the top."

"Just what in the fuck for?"

"Don't know. He just wanted you to give it him tonight."

"Gad Dang his ass!" Glover swore.

Two hours later Glover carried the skull on a stick. Other platoon members wondered, out loud but out of earshot, "What the hell's going on with Glover?"

Carter's only reply was, "Don't know guys. Last night he was talking something about voodoo; supposedly the skull is to bring good luck." The men looked on, some nervously, some in annoyance. Discussions sprang up: why was Glover messing with them? Why was he pulling this crap? He seemed so normal!

Glover ignored the comments and jeers alluding to his use of voodoo. He had no idea why the rest of Fox seemed so disturbed that the Sergeant wanted him to tote the skull around for the day. The trail was narrow all the way, so Glover never could catch up with McCoy. Finally at the top of Bach Ma, the platoon settled into its night position adjacent to one of the lower resort homes, which actually seemed more like a one room bungalow. Glover had carried the skull for past six hours and couldn't wait to be rid of it.

The highly agitated Glover made his way up to the platoon position at about 1800 hours. "Hey, Sarge, here's your fucking skull!"

McCoy, busy opening his pack and looking for some chow responded in kind, "And just what in the fuck am I going to do with that?"

"Well, you wanted me to carr…" Glover never finished his sentence. He knew he'd been had. He did, however, smash the skull up on the side of the building and glared around for Carter who witnessed the whole scene, laughed uncontrollably at a distance, and decided to spend the night with his buddies in the 2nd Platoon further up the hill.

Fox did not encounter any enemy at the summit of Mt. Bach Ma. They conducted patrols up and around the mountain looking for whomever "intelligence" thought may have been there. On occasion, the patrols would observe enemy soldiers on nearby ridges, fire on them, and later, after much effort traversing to the next ridge, find no trace of the elusive enemy when they arrived.

The company returned to their old position between the rock crusher and village of Phu Loc during the first week in April. Strangely, the now platoon-wide ostracized Hanson simply disappeared from Fox Company while the men were taking off their packs. They never heard any more questions about the Treasury nor saw him again.

Fox did not fly south with the rest of the battalion for Operation Baxter Garden on 19 April. Rather they "held the fort" in the rock crusher area, sending out day patrols and night ambushes. In the afternoon of 24 April, Downs assigned nine ambushes, one for each squad. They had all departed by 1900 hours, leaving the company CP, a group of about fifteen men, and a few of the weapons platoon members back near the Navy's construction battalion camp.

"Hey, Skipper, hate to bother you," Gunnery Sergeant VanValkenburgh said at about 2130 hours. VanValkenburgh had gone over to the Seabee camp to play cards for the evening with some of the chiefs. The gunny's good rapport with the chief petty officers had resulted in extra provisions that were much appreciated by all.

"No problem, Guns, I'm just writing a letter. What's up?"

"I have this VN guy here from Phu Loc who claims one of our ambushes had left their site and were "interacting" with a VN woman in a nearby village. Giving her cigarettes in exchange for…well, you know what."

The fiery Irishman flared. This time he didn't have to be diplomatic as he had been with Lieutenant Colonel Gravel in the MACV headquarters at the start of the Hue City campaign a few months earlier. "Damn it, Gunny! We just can't have a breakdown in discipline like this."

"Yes, Sir. What do you want me to do, Skipper?"

"I want you to go out and tell Lance Corporal Harrison to radio each ambush to freeze in place. You and I are going to be making the rounds!"

Second Lieutenant Horner's 2nd Platoon checked out fine. Each of their squads was at its correct ambush site. Downs and VanValkenburgh, with Lance Corporal Harrison following in trace, took off for the 3rd Platoon. At the first site, they found Staff Sergeant McCoy with his squad at its correct site.

"What's going on, Skipper?" McCoy naively inquired.

"Staff Sergeant McCoy, we have one of the squads on the loose visiting the locals for some sex. How about you lead us to your next squad's ambush?"

"Yes, Sir, Skipper. Let's just go to the 1st Squad. Ever since Borunda's fiancé broke up with him he's got 'sex on the brain.' I'll bet a thousand bucks it's his squad!" McCoy stated, putting on his helmet and grabbing his rifle "It's just down this path. Which also leads to the vil," he added.

Within one hundred meters, the foursome led by McCoy and Downs entered the 1st Squad's ambush site area where they found two intensely nervous replacement Marines guarding a PRC-25 radio and M-16 rifles.

Downs turned to one of the men and demanded, "Where's the rest of your squad, Marine?"

Stammering and reverting to boot camp third-person speak, he answered "S-s-sir, Privates First Class McMillan and Jones were told to stay here and not leave, Sir!"

"Private First Class McMillan?" Downs asked, his voice gentler this time.

"Sir!" McMillan fired back in the same manner as he had three months earlier to his drill instructor.

"I merely asked 'Where the rest of your squad was,'" Downs mentioned continuing in his soft tone.

McMillan pointed with his right index finger toward dim lights coming from a few huts down the path and then stammered, "D-d-down there, Sir."

The squad had been busted.

Justice came swiftly. Operation Baxter Garden terminated on 26 April and Lieutenant Colonel Cheatham landed at LZ Rock Crusher by 1230 the same day. By 1600 Captain Downs had the ten men in the squad who had left their ambush site lined up at attention ready for them to receive "Battalion Commander's Office Hours."

"Attention!" Downs ordered as Cheatham approached. Then performing an about-face, he looked at Cheatham saluting sharply.

Due to his large frame, Big Ernie emanated a more wizened, avuncular persona by returning the salute in a less crisp manner. Of course he and Downs had talked at length the night before on the radio about this issue and fully agreed with the captain's recommendations. The men would all be reduced in rank one pay grade and docked one month's wages.

"What have we got here, Mike?" Cheatham asked in a comfortable tone as if he would be receiving this information for the first time.

"Sir, on the night of April 24th, 1968 at 2015 hours, these men left their ambush site in violation of the Uniform Code of Military Justice. Though nothing happened, except that three of them are needing medical attention, I recommend they be reduced in rank one pay grade and docked one month's wages."

Lieutenant Colonel Cheatham stepped around Downs to address the men. The young men were instantly intimidated by his huge stature, level tone, and mature face. "Who was the squad leader last night?"

"Sir, I was." Borunda said in a moderately high-pitched Brooklyn accent.

"Is what the captain said true?"

"'Fraid so, Sir. I take all the responsibility. These are good men. It's all my fault," Borunda replied resolutely.

Moving to his left and looking directly into the squad leader's eyes Cheatham said, "Corporal Borunda, I decorated you for your heroism in taking the Treasury back in Hue City. At that time I promoted you to the rank of corporal, for I believed you were mature enough to lead a squad of Marines in combat. Captain Downs had doubts about your maturity at the time and told me so. I guess I was wrong."

Cheatham stepped back again to address the rest of the men. "You men know what you did was wrong. You failed to remember just how much other Marines, good Marines, rely on you at each hour of each day. This is true always, but especially here in combat. I'm going to accept Captain Down's recommendation for each of you to be reduced in rank one pay grade and docked one month's wages. I am also going to recommend Captain Downs replace Borunda as your squad leader."

"All ready done, Sir." Downs interrupted.

"Very well, Captain Downs, carry out the demotions."

With that, Lieutenant Colonel Cheatham turned a filled, twenty-inch, C-ration box on edge, sat on it, and witnessed Downs reducing the men in rank one at a time.

Maintaining discipline after the horrific battle of Hue City kept Fox Company officers and staff non-commissioned officers busy during the spring of 1968. The 2nd Platoon had its own close call shortly after Borunda's squad was disciplined.

"Yes, Sir," Corporal Chris Brown, 1st Squad leader of the 2nd Platoon, said announcing his presence as he joined his platoon commander, Second Lieutenant Rich Horner.

Horner, who had fully recovered from his wounds sustained on 1 February, greeted his veteran squad leader on that very warm, humid morning, "Good Morning, Corporal Brown. Is your squad ready to go on a patrol?"

"Sure, Sir. Any time."

"All right," Horner agreed, handing Brown a 3x3-inch sheet from a message pad with four annotated lines. "Here's the patrol route the company wants you to take. There are four "smokestacks" or check-points. Using these as a reference, you can identify your position in case you need any fire support."

Brown studied the paper for a minute. In Horner's handwriting he could read:

CP #1-A U 812048
CP #2-A U 816049
CP #3-A U 839003
CP #4-A U 808009

Brown reached into his right thigh pocket, pulled out a laminated military map, and correlated the handwritten checkpoints with terrain features on his map. The patrol route would take his squad out of the camp, pass by a small village, up a trail 1200 meters long to a ridge dotted with small hilltops, then return by following National Highway 1 back to the base camp.

"See any problems, Chris?'

Shaking his head, Brown said, "No, Sir."

"All right, why don't you plan to leave here at 1000 hours. Make sure you have enough ammo, get a new battery for your radio, and eat chow here before you leave. Take at least two canteens of water since the temperature ought to hit the mid-nineties today. I figure you'll be back here around 1530. You can rest up then before you go on a night ambush."

Brown continued to nod his head, comprehending the familiar patrol order.

"Oh, and, Brown, don't forget to check in at each smokestack. Make sure you take green smoke grenades."

"Yes, Sir." Brown barked, then departed for his squad.

At 1050 hours the lead man of Brown's patrol reached Smokestack 1, a hamlet 1500 meters beyond the platoon's location. The hamlet looked to be the main one for the village. Football sized coconuts hung down from trees surrounding the fifteen to twenty hooches. Three of the buildings nestled in the center were constructed on concrete slabs, unlike the others built on bamboo platforms. Coming from the other hamlets, wide trails meandered into this larger one. A bike with two 15"x15" wire baskets attached to the seat and the rear axle, was leaning against a tree. This singular mode of transportation obviously served the hamlet's logistical needs as the local pick-up truck. It carried out the important tasks of bringing chickens to town and moving beer.

As the squad began filling the hamlet center, kids first, then a couple of mama-sans who had risen from their mid-day rest, emerged to greet the visitors. The shaded hamlet center seemed to be ten to fifteen degrees cooler than the trail they had just left.

"C.C., hold 'em up," Brown yelled to his good buddy, Corporal Charles Campbell, who was on point with his fire team twenty meters in front of Brown.

Brown then turned to his radio operator, Private First Class Dave DeGroat, and said, "DeGroat, tell Fox Two we just reached Smokestack 1."

The momasons disappeared then reemerged with large unmarked brown bottles of locally brewed beer.

While DeGroat was on the radio, C.C. Campbell walked up to Brown. Looking in the direction of the next checkpoint, Campbell questioned, "Salty, you serious about going up on that hill trail?"

"Yeah, why?"

"Hey, we could stay down here, drink some beer, write letters, eat some local food, and cool it," Campbell proposed.

"What about us going to the checkpoints and reporting in?" Brown asked. "Remember what happened to Borunda's squad?"

"We'll just stay here and report in every half hour or so. They'll never know," Campbell countered.

"Okay, let's give the guys a break," Brown relented.

Brown and Campbell posted two of the new men as lookouts for local security. The rest never questioned the comfortable change of plans. Some began writing letters home, others tried the local beer and talked to the kids and mom-a-sons, and a couple just slept on their packs.

Precisely at 1245 hours Corporal Brown said, "Okay, DeGroat, call Fox Two and say 'We're at Checkpoint 2.'"

DeGroat complied, "Fox Two, this Two Alpha, over."

Degroat waited a minute until Fox Two responded, then said, "Roger, Two. We're at Checkpoint 2, over." DeGroat paused then announced, "Two Alpha, out."

DeGroat looked over at Brown who was closely watching the whole exchange and turned his hands, palms upward, and said simply, "Piece of cake."

For over thirty minutes the men enjoyed themselves until DeGroat answered the radio. "This is Two Alpha, go." DeGroat listened for a few seconds and responded, "Roger, over." He handed the handset to Brown, "The lieutenant wants to speak to you."

Brown took the handset, raised his eyebrows anticipating the lieutenant's question, moved the handset to his ear and said, "This is Two Alpha Steel Leader, over."

The communication went quickly. None of the men gave Corporal Brown a second thought as he spoke to the lieutenant. In a minute Brown assured the voice at the other end, "Everything's fine. We're taking a break. That first hill was steeper than it looks, Sir, over."

A brief response went unheard by all except Brown who concluded his transmission with, "Roger, out."

Then he yelled, "C.C., get every one up! The lieutenant has binoculars and can see Smokestack 3. He told me to pop a green smoke grenade when we get to Smokestack 3!"

The 1st Squad of the 2nd Platoon scrambled to their feet, grabbed their packs, and made hasty goodbyes to their hosts within the village. Then, they began a four-kilometer run up the hill several hundred meters on a bright, sunny afternoon in the 95° heat. Their path continued up and down a bumpy hill trail. Brown cursed Campbell every time the fire team leader asked to take a break.

Horner greeted the squad upon its return. Their uniforms were thoroughly soaked with sweat. He scanned them closely and approached Brown, who fully anticipated a butt chewing. Horner commented matter-of-factly, "Brown, it sure must have been hotter than I thought it was."

He never said another word about the incident, but the 1st Squad, 2nd Platoon had more than learned its lesson.

On 8 May Captain Carl Fulford became Fox Company's commanding officer. Captain Downs transferred to the regimental staff where he became the assistant operations officer. Downs, who was as emotionally devoted to the company, told Gunnery Sergeant VanValkenburgh that he wouldn't be very far. If for any reason he was needed, he'd be there.

Nine days later with the 101st Airborne Division no longer required to be in Hue City, one of its battalions was able to assume the duties of the 2nd Battalion in the Phu Bai/Phu Loc area. Thus, on 17 May, III Marine Amphibious Force moved the 2nd Battalion's area of operations twenty kilometers further south to protect US Army convoys moving supplies from Da Nang to Phu Bai.

The battalion headquarters was located at the Phu Gia Pass. Fox Company was situated at the southern portion of the battalion's sector at the Hai Van Pass. The Hai Van Pass was cut through the mountains north of Da Nang. Fox's command post was positioned just below the highest part of the pass, and the platoons were stationed along the highway on either side of the pass guarding culverts and other key terrain features.

Near the summit, there were five distinguishable groups or activities occupying separate areas. At the very top was a small US Army club. Just below the club was a compound for US Army engineers who maintained the highway. Then on a fifty by fifty meter piece of terrain stood Fox Company's CP and some members of the Weapons Platoon. Immediately below Fox's CP was a Vietnamese Regional Forces Company. Finally, on the opposite side of the road and down about seventy-five meters was a semi circle of six structures. In the center was a Vietnamese police station; on either side of the police station were five active brothels.

One Vietnamese man, always in civilian attire, managed Whorehouse City. He had the busy task of keeping the funds flowing from, not only each of the five houses, but a "carry out" or "curbside service" where the women would be taken by motor scooter to service units on either side of the pass.

Captain Downs returned in a jeep four days after the company began occupying the Hai Van Pass. He found the new Fox Company commander and the two distanced themselves from the others. In a few minutes they asked for the gunny to get Sergeant Burnham, who now held the position of "right guide" for the 3rd Platoon.

Ten minutes passed until VanValkenburgh's jeep rolled to a stop near the two captains. As the others removed themselves, Downs approached Burnham who was hopping off the side of the vehicle.

"Bernie, I need to talk with you."

Burnham simply said, "Sir," and walked away with the captain.

Downs started softly, "The XO has just informed me that your younger brother, Joseph Francis Burnham, died of wounds two days ago. His unit was fighting in Quang Tri Province." Downs stopped, faced Burnham, placing his hands on Burnham's shoulders, and said, "I'm sorry, Bernie."

Burnham stared mutely at the captain, his mind flashing back to better times when he and his younger brother were kids in New Jersey, and exhaled the name, "Joey…"

Corporal Burnham suddenly appeared much older than his thirty-one years. His mouth opened slightly as if he was about to say something. He remained silent but his lower jaw slid slowly to the right and outward about a half an inch, then locked. He waited for the captain to finish.

"Your mother has requested you escort his body home and not return to Vietnam." Downs waited for Burnham to digest the fact that he would be leaving the men he loved under such traumatic circumstances. "Major Steele told me that's the government's policy, so you'll be going. I'm going to go with you to Division headquarters to assist with the paperwork and get you the appropriate uniform for the escort duty. The first sergeant will ship all your personal gear to New York."

Downs compassionately placed his hands on Burnham's shoulders while looking him in the eyes and murmured, "I'm truly sorry, Bernie."

"Thank you, Sir," Burnham whispered.

While Downs remained with Fulford and VanValkenburgh, the company jeep carried Burnham back to his platoon. The men had gathered for a C-ration lunch and were laughing and joking around. Each of them grew quiet and stared at Burnham as he went over without a word to pick up his pack. His shocked and sunken gaze took in his fellow Hue City veterans, the guys who had come from An Hoa with him, one at a time, but words choked him. Then he quickly looked at the replacements. With his rifle in his left hand and his backpack straps gripped in his right hand, Burnham backed away, distancing himself from his platoon before speaking, "My younger brother was killed, and I'll be leaving. Don't you give your squad leaders any crap!"

Without another sound, Sergeant Bernie Burnham marched back to the vehicle and departed. Lance Corporal Borunda and the men stared dumbly after the vehicle as it disappeared around a sharp mountain turn. Their sudden loss left them feeling empty. They had been abandoned.

By 18 July Captain Fulford was due to rotate back to the States and Cheatham turned the company over to First Lieutenant Tom Martin. Martin had extended his tour of duty to command Fox Company with whom he had served with distinction as far back as the attack on Nong Son a year earlier. In the past six months he had been in the operations section on the battalion staff, and most recently, was the headquarters commandant, responsible for the defenses of the battalion command post at the Phu Gia Pass.

"Tom, most of my casualties are not coming from combat," Fulford stated. "They are coming from those damn whorehouses down there! Our guys are picking up VD faster than is imaginable. I hate to turn that problem over to you, but it seems to have gotten worse in the past two-three weeks. I've been on the non-commissioned officers to control their men, and I think they are trying; but the results are still not showing."

Martin fit in immediately. He knew the men, and they knew him. He was an athletic, no nonsense, fearless leader who could be counted on in battle. His first task was protect his men and knock out the VD problem. In his first daily situation report, SITREP, he told the battalion about his problem and his intent to correct it.

The next day Lieutenant Colonel Cheatham and the battalion sergeant major drove up in a M-151 jeep. It was a courtesy call so that the men could see Cheatham's personal approval of their new company commander. When he read Martin's first SITREP, Cheatham learned he faced a potentially battalion-wide problem after reviewing the information about Whorehouse City's "carry out" services.

Martin briefed Cheatham on the platoons' disposition, and then they visited the men in the CP area. The Sergeant Major had already gathered Gunnery Sergeant VanValkenburgh and the two staff sergeants to get their perspective on the men.

"Would you like to visit Whorehouse City, Sir?" Martin offered the lieutenant colonel.

"You bet, Tom," came Cheatham's reply. With that the two commanders gathered their principals and set off for the semicircle of buildings seventy-five meters down the street. They knocked on three doors to be greeted by young Vietnamese women who greeted them with a "Hi, GI, what can I do for you?"

In two buildings, after nobody answered their knock on the door, they opened the door and caught a couple of soldiers and women in bed together *in flagrante delicto.* "Tom, you're right. I want you to shut them down," Cheatham directed in his customary broad-brush manner.

"Aye, aye, Sir. I'll take care of it!"

Round one began. With the help of the local police who spoke English, the first item of business for the next day was to serve notice to each of the five brothels. First Lieutenant Tom Martin and First Lieutenant Mike McNeil did so within an hour. By this point the entire thirty-five-man contingent at the Fox CP was anticipating the forthcoming challenge between the will of their new boss and the Whorehouse City establishment. Side bets were made on the winner and the outcome. Soon, the US Army engineers who the Marines had befriended joined in the wagering.

There was no overt action of any kind made by the brothel group on that first day.

Round two commenced. Dozens of men witnessed this round from the hill above. At 1000 hours on the second day Martin and VanValkenburgh revisited the "City". This time Martin gave them a twenty-four hour notice to evacuate or "face the consequences". To most of the young, scared, Vietnamese women, this warning had sufficient credibility. They'd be welcomed back at home in Da Nang by their families, and it would be good to get away…Especially if there was going to be trouble.

A lot of activity took place on that second day. Many cars and mopeds arrived to pick up the women, who, by now, had changed from their black and white pajamas into good-looking, high-necked, colorful dresses that went to their ankles, called "au dias". Now they would be appropriately attired to return to the nation's second largest city. By late afternoon Martin concluded that all but one house was empty. Would he have a stand off tomorrow? He decided to go to the US Army club that evening and solicit the thoughts of the soldiers. After all they, as the long-term residents, had an interest in this situation.

And then came round three. At 0950 Martin and McNeil began their short trek to the only occupied house in Whorehouse City. There, in front of the small framed building with arms crossed in utter defiance, stood the civilian manager of the brothel business. The troops, both Marines and soldiers, had gathered in mass to look down at the spectacle that was sure to be a memorable highlight in their tour of duty.

Martin glared into the man's face, "I warned you yesterday you had twenty-four hours to clear out of here. Now you have five minutes." He stood back and waited a few feet from the civilian, who remained motionless with his feet spread and his arms crossed. Five minutes later as Martin looked at his watch, the clinking rattle of a very heavy Army bulldozer was heard rumbling down the road toward the object of the confrontation. The gauntlet had been thrown.

Within three minutes the bulldozer traversed the distance, stopped in front, and turned to face the building and the once defiant manager. During the bulldozer's one hundred meter journey, the defiance on the Vietnamese man's face was replaced by curiosity. Now, confused by the sinister laughing of army sergeant behind the controls of the bulldozer, concern replaced curiosity in his expression.

The bulldozer operator looked to Martin for guidance. Martin cast his right hand loosely in the air toward the cliff immediately behind the building. As he did, the manager's facial expression changed rapidly from concern to shock to total fright. The bulldozer began inching toward the house. Immediately Vietnamese women in various stages of dress fled out of the front door and a small front window. Once cleared, with one push, the building was hoisted from its foundation and unceremoniously plopped off of its cliff-side perch.

A huge cheer roused from above as debris from the crashing building spread one hundred meters down a second hill. The five Vietnamese women and their "manager" began running down the road toward Da Nang. One Vietnamese policeman emerged from his station feigning ignorance and asked Martin what was going on.

Martin told him, "Nothing, just go back inside."

The young policeman raced back inside unwilling to irritate that particular Marine officer. In that single moment, Fox Company's readiness had taken a positive turn and Martin was universally accepted as its commander.

CHAPTER 9: FOX RETURNS TO AN HOA

No member of the battalion stood out more prominently for the men of Fox Company and, as a matter of fact, the rest of the 2nd Battalion, 5th Marines, than did their battalion commander, Lieutenant Colonel "Big Ernie" Cheatham. Big Ernie was a giant of a man who had courageously led the battalion to defeat a vastly superior enemy force during the Battle of Hue City in February. This battle earned 2/5 a commendation by the President of the United States. When the time came to turn over the command of the battalion, the men felt the loss of a legendary leader. Nevertheless the change of command ceremony took place in the battalion forward location at the Phu Gia Pass on 24 July 1968.

First Lieutenant Tom Martin, who had extended three months to command Fox Company, was the only Fox representative able to attend the ceremony. He returned to the company area at Hai Van Pass shortly after noon feeling excited about what he had witnessed. There to greet him was Gunnery Sergeant VanValkenburgh.

"Well, Skipper, what do you look so cheerful about?" the gunny asked.

"You know, Gunny, we've been out here in a combat zone so long I darn near forgot just how great some of our traditional 'pomp and ceremony' activities are," Martin answered. "That change of command ceremony was absolutely superb."

"You're right. I miss Marine Corps parades, the drum and bugle marching bands, and all that spit and polish."

"'Big Ernie' was as magnificent as possible. We'll sure miss him."

"How did the XO look?" the gunny inquired, referring to Major O.K. Steele.

"Guns, he's our CO now, and I'm sure we have a great one." Martin replied. Then after reflecting for a minute on what he had witnessed, Martin continued, "You know, I have never seen a man as excited as Major Steele when he received the battalion colors from "Big Ernie". He looked like a kid getting his wish for a new bicycle on his birthday. He was all but quivering when he accepted the colors."

"That's great, Sir," the gunny interrupted as Martin paused.

"What's even more remarkable is that "Stainless" Steele seems like a really a cool guy. He's unflappable, precise, measured in tone, and action." Martin paused, "Tell you what, Gunny, with Steele's demeanor and imposing appearance, he's a poster board replacement for Big Ernie Cheatham."

"I'm only sorry I missed it, Lieutenant."

On 27 July, three days after 2/5's change of command ceremony, Captain Dave Brown arrived in Da Nang. He had been an advisor to Vietnamese regional forces the year before and was returning to Vietnam following a month's leave. Upon stepping off the plane he felt the oppressive heat, saw the drab industrial-like military surrounds, smelled the stenches of a typical underdeveloped countryside, and thought to himself, good, I made it. I'm back in the war!

After processing through the III MAF welcoming center with the masses, Brown struck out on his own as quickly as possible without waiting for assignment orders. Those orders would have been a mere non-personal directive that probably would not have reflected the fact that he had extended six months in Vietnam to command a Marine Corps rifle company in combat. No greater assignment was available for an infantry Marine officer.

Though he did not know it at the time, Fox Company would be his destiny.

Brown scrounged a few rides, and then soon climbed up the hill where the 1st Marine Division headquarters was located. Unassigned Marines don't normally go to the headquarters to assure their assignment, but he would take no such "luck-of-the-draw" chance. He didn't extend his tour of duty in Vietnam for a staff position!

Brown reasoned that the 1st Marine Division headquarters wouldn't be very different than that of the 2nd Marine Division, where he had worked about eighteen months earlier. He sought the adjutant's office in his effort to ensure his rifle-company assignment. After asking one corporal for specific directions, he found the office of First Lieutenant Tom Baker, 1st MARDIV adjutant. Baker, in starched jungle utilities, frameless glasses, and salt-and-pepper hair clearly had the look of a super-sharp admin clerk who had been picked up for a limited duty officer, LDO, commission. On the desk was a triangular-shaped wooden nameplate. Laser-carved, it had his full name in the middle, a single silver bar signifying a first lieutenant's rank insignia on the left corner, and the Marine Corps emblem on the other. This type of nameplate was a popular item and only available in the Philippines, and obviously the lieutenant had spent at least one R&R there. After knocking on the adjutant's doorframe, Brown said politely, "Excuse me, Lieutenant, are you the adjutant?"

"Yes, Sir, what can I do for you?"

"My name is Dave Brown and I just arrived in country. You don't happen to have a list of division officers, do you? I want to see if one of my old friends is still here."

Baker shrugged his right shoulder while forming his response. He realized Brown was merely being formal and knew he had a current list of officers assigned to the division, "Sure do," he replied. He began rifling through his orderly desk.

"You sure have some good digs, Tom," Brown offered, referring to the adjutant's nicely appointed office and trying to warm up to the cooperative officer.

Within a minute the accommodating adjutant gave him the list of officers assigned to the division. On the second page of the somewhat dated report Brown spotted "Major O.K. Steele, 2nd Bn., 5th Mar". Bingo!

"Ahhh...Tom, would you mind if I used your phone to call 2/5?"

"Sure, go ahead," Baker complied.

Six years earlier Major Steele, then a captain, was Brown's rifle company commander when Brown first reported into Company C, 1st Battalion, 4th Marines as a raw second lieutenant. Brown had been assigned to the 3rd Platoon.

About an hour later, Captain Brown sat in a jeep heading north on National Highway 1 to Phu Bai on his way to join 2/5. Orderly confusion best described what he observed upon arrival. Marines were crating up supplies and tents, placing them on pallets and then onto trucks. The battalion, less Fox and Echo Companies, was preparing to motor march to Da Nang the very next day en route to An Hoa.

Fox and Echo Companies had been chopped to the 7th Marines late in the afternoon of 27 July and were ordered to move by truck at first light to the 1st Recon camp in Da Nang. They were to be helo-lifted into An Hoa later on 28 July to reinforce the beleaguered 7th Marines' garrison. 2/5 would continue its motor march from Da Nang into the An Hoa valley on the morning of 29 July, join up with Fox and Echo companies at An Hoa, relieve the 7th Marines garrison, and hold the valley until their regiment, the 5th Marines, arrived on 31 July.

The motor march on 28 July to 1st Recon began as planned. Echo was picked up at the "sand spit" just north of the Hai Van Pass, and Fox loaded onto the trucks at the pass. Together, both companies arrived at 1st Recon's helo pad about noon. They waited all day for the helicopters to show up. Fox's company strength was 188 including attachments. Echo had a similar end-strength. Both companies planned on flying in CH-46 Sea Knight helicopters that had a lift capacity of fourteen combat troops and organized their sorties accordingly.

"Sir," First Lieutenant Tom Martin greeted Captain Hans Heinz, the CO of Echo Company. "We ought to firm up our plans for our activities once we get to An Hoa."

"You're right, Tom. I haven't any new information from Battalion, have you?"

"No, I just know the 7th Marine garrison has been under attack for three days now."

"You operated in An Hoa prior to Hue City, didn't you?" Captain Heinz asked.

"Yes, Sir, for about seven months."

"Since we still don't know when the birds will get here to pick us up. We ought to plan on securing the airstrip tonight and then check in with the garrison in the morning."

"I agree, Sir, unless the base is under attack when we get there," Martin offered.

"We won't know that 'til we get there. I think Fox ought to go in first since you operated in An Hoa before Hue City. You'll be oriented right away. What do you think?"

"All right, the base is adjacent to the airfield on the southern side. We'll land first," Martin agreed, "and set in on the northern side of the runway. I'll meet you when you land and point you toward the southern side." He paused, "Of course if the base is under attack, I'll move instead to the northern side, and wait for you to land. Then we can link up and counter-attack together."

"That will work," Heinz agreed. "Assuming they will not be under attack, we'll talk with the 7th Marines first thing in the morning."

"Okay, Sir. See you in An Hoa," with that comment, Martin departed.

The troops of both companies were massed in twelve to fourteen-man helo teams ready to lift off. Activities ranged from playing cards, writing letters, eating some of their C-rations, to sleeping with their heads on their packs.

After dark the short, repeating, "whup, whup, whup" of large helicopters' blades, much louder than CH-46s, could be heard approaching the landing pad. When CH-53 Sea Stallions, with a lift capacity of thirty-seven troops, began kicking up ten times as much dust as a CH-46, both commanding officers and their gunnery sergeants, scrambled to reconfigure the helo teams into the best combat lifts as possible. Still, it looked like a Chinese fire drill. On top of that confusion, making a helo-borne assault into an unfamiliar area in the middle of the night was going to be a huge endeavor!

They packed into the CH-53s and flew off.

As it turned out, the flight was uneventful. Both companies settled in around the airfield, dug defensive positions, received a few probing bursts of gunfire, and awaited the morning to begin their offensive operations.

While Fox and Echo Companies were flying to the An Hoa airfield, Captain Brown was traveling with the remainder of the battalion when they stopped along Da Nang's northwestern border. There, in Da Nang that night, Gunnery Sergeant Al "Robby" Robitello found Brown. Robitello had been the platoon sergeant of the 3rd Platoon, Company C, 1st Battalion, 4th Marines when Brown was that raw lieutenant and O.K. Steele was the company commander. Brown never knew how Robitello found him, but he was certain Steele had something to do with it.

"Well, Captain Dave Brown!" Robitello grunted in his heavy Bostonian accent as he came up from behind and surprised the captain.

Brown spun around and looked at the black hair and into the dark eyes of the gunnery sergeant. "Robby!" he exclaimed with excitement.

"I knew the war wouldn't keep you away too long."

"God, Robby, great to see you," Brown smiled, still not believing his eyes.

"Well, Skipper, let's not stand here slobbering over seeing each other," Robitello said lifting a six-pack of Old Milwaukee up to his chest. "Let's pull up a stool and work on this."

The two old friends had a few evening-temperature Old Milwaukee beers and talked about the early years when they knew and mutually respected each other about as well as any salty sergeant and naive second lieutenant were allowed. The "3rd herd" hadn't been perfect but it did have more character and spirit than the rest. Steele would have sent them anywhere. So, under the southeast Asian stars, they talked in depth about their families and careers for a few delightful and memorable hours.

Brown's destiny with Fox would wait for two more days.

In January 1968, just six months earlier, the 7th Marine Regiment took over responsibility for defense of the An Hoa Combat Base after 2/5 pulled out and headed north toward Hue. Even at full strength, the

7th Marines became stretched from the An Hoa Combat Base to Da Nang. As a result the regiment was forced to outpost the combat base with a small garrison of troops. Now, in July, they were defending the base with only a single rifle company and some "cats and dogs" units of support personnel. An Hoa had been under attack for a few days by the time Fox and Echo Companies were called to reinforce the base.

Sometime before first light on 29 July, First Lieutenant Martin and Captain Heinz found their way to the underground bunker that passed for a command center. Later, when nearly 5,000 persons would call An Hoa their home base, the compound would look more like a mini-city.

They met a major just outside the bunker who introduced himself as the "coordinator" for the An Hoa Combat Base. This poor soul hadn't slept for three days and sported at least a week's worth of growth on his face. The man's eyes were sunk back in his head from dehydration and a lack of sleep, and Martin worried about the quality of information they were about to receive. The major looked like the proverbial forty miles of bad road. According to the coordinator, he didn't coordinate much of anything as he had no real authority over anybody and seemed eternally grateful that Echo and Fox showed up when they did. He believed the enemy was concentrated north of the base and south of the "Old French Road"

Martin and Heinz made a plan to conduct a clearing operation around the base. They assumed communications would be established by 2/5 when the remainder of the battalion arrived later that day. Until then, they would be on their own. Their concept was to let the locals know the "first team" was back, and to familiarize the men in the companies with the terrain and the likely enemy approaches to the base.

Specifically, Fox would push out eastward from the perimeter of the An Hoa combat base in a series of platoon-size patrols. At the same time Echo would move rapidly up the road leading from the base to Liberty Bridge, sometimes referred to as

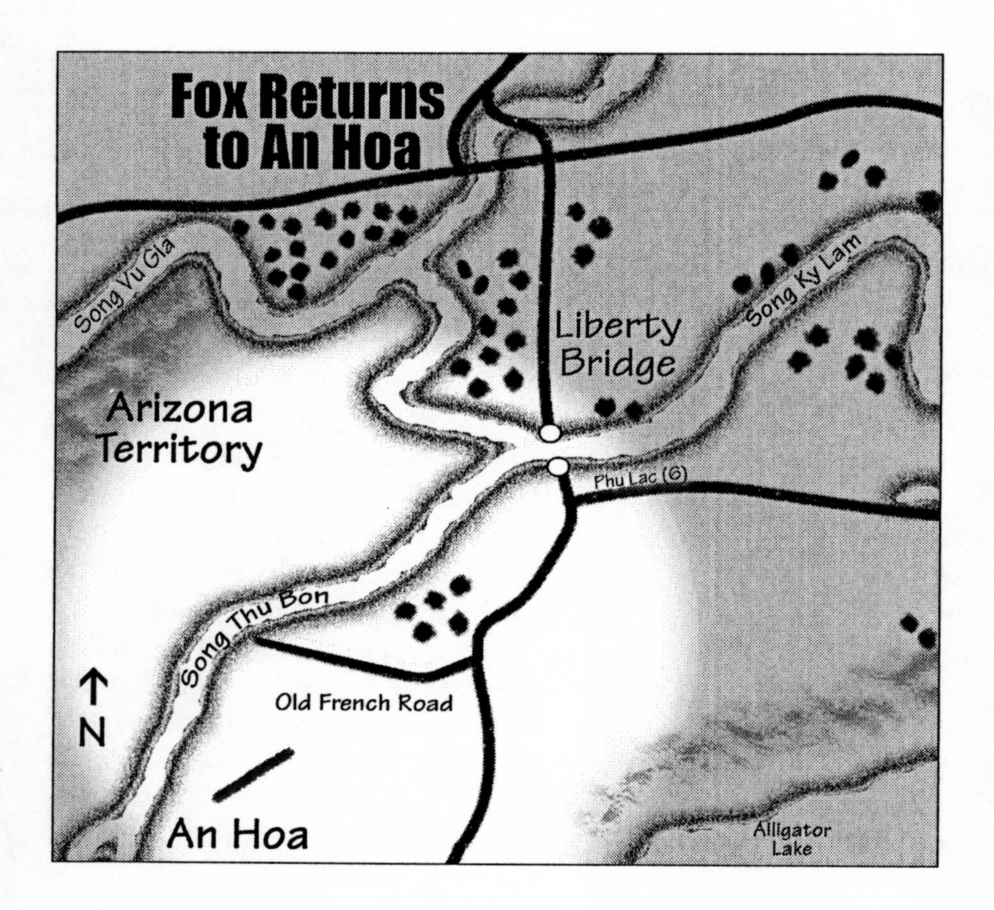

"Liberty Road". At the "Old French Road" Echo would turn west, travel toward the Song Thu Bon then sweep back south toward the base to close with Fox's patrols. According to the Coordinator, the enemy force was between the Old French Road and the base.

A platoon of five tanks, a platoon of amphibious tractors, amtracs, and a couple of trucks were among the 7th Marine assets available at An Hoa. Echo acquired three tanks and two amtracs, while Fox took the remaining two tanks and three amtracs. Fox's three amtracs would be used as troop carriers to reinforce Echo should they encounter a significant enemy force.

0815 hours. Fox began securing the combat base's perimeter and then set off to patrol northeast toward Liberty Road. Securing that road was Echo and Fox's first priority since the rest of the battalion would be crossing the river near Liberty Bridge and moving south to either join them in battle or end up safely in An Hoa. Echo, by virtue of its rapid movement up the road, would have secured the immediate vicinity of the road; Fox, once it reached the road, would clear the flanks out to three hundred meters while it patrolled north.

Echo reached the Old French Road and wheeled left toward the Song Thu Bon. Shortly after, they turned left again to use the road as their line of departure and attack south toward An Hoa.

As Echo began moving toward An Hoa, Major Steele led the rest of the battalion, less Headquarters & Service Company, across the river at Liberty Bridge two miles away. Steele and his mobile command group had no sooner crossed the river when Echo reported enemy contact that rapidly developed into a major engagement for them. Soon all other 2/5 elements that had crossed the river reported receiving enemy mortar fire.

Not formally assigned a position yet, Captain Dave Brown secured a spot on one of the H&S vehicles carrying the battalion's rear element. Thus, in relative safety nearly ten miles behind his friend Gunnery Sergeant Robitello and Major Steele's attack toward An Hoa, Brown experienced a fairly uneventful trip.

Prior to arriving at the Liberty Bridge crossing, as the H&S company relayed battalion messages, Captain Brown intercepted a message stating that Robitello had been killed by a mortar round as he fought his way into An Hoa. He read the message over and over thinking there must have been a mistake. They had spent one hell of an enjoyable evening reminiscing just one night ago. He had been so happy to find a friend and someone he respected here in the middle of Vietnam. No, he had read it correctly. In a war zone combatants live one day at a time. Captain Brown compartmentalized the sacred "regretting" in an area deep in the back of his mind to be reflected upon later. Regretting now would get him killed, too.

Echo's engagement thwarted the enemy's advance towards Liberty Bridge and allowed the support elements and rear command group to reach and begin crossing the Song Thu Bon in the early afternoon. The direct support 105mm artillery battery had already crossed the river and was set in on the high ground above Liberty Bridge. From there it provided supporting fires for Echo Company.

From the time the battalion rear began crossing the Song Thu Bon, at the burned out remains of Liberty Bridge, Brown began to hear artillery and mortar fire. The enemy was not giving the An Hoa valley back to the Marines without a fight. At that moment, Echo was attacking through the Phu Nhuan and Thu Bon villages along the Song Thu Bon to reach An Hoa.

The crossing was made on a non-motorized barge in the same manner rivers were crossed prior to the invention of powered boats—although two dump trucks were used instead of mules. On the back of one truck was attached about 600 meters of cable, long enough to cross the river. The same amount of cable was attached to the rear of the second truck on the other side of the river. The truck on the southern bank would drive forward on the dirt road beside the river in low gear pulling the cable through an anchored pulley and thereby the loaded barge was pulled across. On the north side the second truck would be pulled backwards along the river's bank to the crossing point. This activity would then reverse itself to get the empty barge back for more vehicles making the crossing to An Hoa.

Patiently, Brown watched this operation for a couple of hours as he waited for the 6x6 he was riding in to drive onto the barge. By the time his truck and two jeeps rolled on, the fascination of this clever, though primitive, procedure had become monotonous and no longer captured his attention. He wondered which job Major Steele would assign him. And when? Frankly, Brown felt bored being stuck in the "rear with the gear", particularly when he could hear the distant gunfire from the still attacking rifle companies about two miles away.

His truck rolled onto the barge and soon they began to move across. The drivers remained in their seats and most of the troops in theirs. Curious, Brown got off the truck and began studying the river's width, depth, and clarity of the water. The temperature that day exceeded ninety degrees so the tepid water from the shallow, slow-flowing river felt pleasing to his fingers.

Brown observed the first enemy mortar round exploding on the river's surface about fifty meters from his barge. They had crossed approximately one-third of the 600 meters. After thirty days in the States between assignments and a week spent peacefully getting to the middle of the Song Thu Bon, it took him about five to ten seconds to realize that his barge was under attack. By that time the second round hit at almost the same distance away.

"Everyone off the trucks! Hang close to the edge of the barge ready to get in the water! We'll have a better chance of surviving if we get hit," he yelled. The men leapt from their vehicles and scrambled into low and flat positions, hugging the side of the barge. After a few moments no more rounds fell. Brown's adrenalin continued surging through his veins. Only a few minutes later they were across, back on the trucks, and moving again along the river's edge.

Fortunately, Echo Company was not split up into platoons or even worse, squad-size units as companies normally did when the battalion previously operated out of An Hoa prior to January. Then, Marine squad-size units had patrolled the area and would, on occasion, encounter small enemy units in transit from the mountains west of An Hoa to the populated areas along the coast. Echo was unaware that the area was swarming with an enemy estimated to be at regimental strength. Echo was outnumbered by over four to one and clearly in trouble.

As he monitored the battalion radio net, First Lieutenant Tom Martin perceived that Echo Company didn't know its own location. The area in which the battle was taking place was characterized by open rice paddies interspersed with islands of tree and brush hillocks that often contained huts and communal living areas. There were no appreciable landmarks. The most prominent terrain feature was the "scar face" mountain to the east, but that was so far away it appeared on another map. However, Martin, with his months of experience operating in the An Hoa valley, figured he knew exactly where Echo was positioned.

Major Steele and the Jump Command Post, or Jump CP, a most conspicuous group of about fifty men and ten five-foot long antennas, arrived at Fox's position in a caravan of fifteen vehicles. Steele approached Martin at the junction of Liberty Road and the Old French Road.

"Sir," Martin said, "I take it you have been listing to Echo's transmissions."

"Sure have, Tom. How do you assess their situation?" the major responded.

"I believe they may be disoriented due to their unfamiliarity with the terrain. We need to get to them ASAP so that they can break off from the enemy."

"What sort of assets do you have to reach them?"

Martin outlined a plan for Fox to join in Echo's battle. Steele approved. The plan had Fox utilizing two tanks, three amtracs and a couple of 6x6 cargo trucks. Fox would place .30 caliber machine guns on the amtracs' sand-bagged, hardened tops. The five armored vehicles would provide supporting fire for Fox Company while it passed through Echo. After that, Echo could be evacuated and re-formed behind Fox.

First Lieutenant Martin called Staff Sergeant Dick Palmer and his platoon commanders, Second Lieutenant Jeff Martin and First Lieutenant Mike McNeil to give them his order.

"All right guys, we're going into the breach to help Echo get clear of the enemy." Martin explained. "We'll move in column to Echo's vicinity by the three amtracs and the tanks on the Old French Road. We'll go almost as far as the river, dismount, then turn left towards Echo's rear, and begin our attack. I believe that if we attack through Echo and hit the enemy with all the supporting fires we have at the same time they'll back off. I needn't tell you it won't be easy." He paused to eye each man meaningfully, "Already, Echo has sustained thirty casualties."

"Mike," First Lieutenant Tom Martin addressed First Lieutenant McNeil, "you'll load in and travel with the lead tracs and dismount closest to the river. Your platoon will pivot the most, sweeping counter-clockwise in a southerly direction. You'll be the extreme right platoon covering the river and protecting our right flank. I don't want any enemy coming around our rear to flank us or to escape. Okay?"

Lieutenant McNeil nodded in affirmation.

"Jeff," the commanding officer said to Second Lieutenant Jeff Martin, "you'll travel behind Mike's platoon and assume the center of the company's assault through Echo. Maintain contact with Mike's platoon at all times."

"Roger, Sir," Jeff Martin acknowledged.

First Lieutenant Tom Martin turned to Staff Sergeant Dick Palmer, "Sergeant Palmer, the company command group will follow the second platoon, and you follow us. Once we start our attack, you won't be moving too fast since we'll be pivoting counter-clockwise, and you'll be the base."

He continued, "Now it's darn near dark. I want to be able to adjust arty fires on the enemy when we get there. Let's move out."

The men joined their respective platoons. Fox formed on the road. The sergeants and corporals organized the troops for their move. Troops loaded into the three amtracs; some troops climbed on top of the tractors. Even the tanks had an external load of troops. In addition to the tanks and amtracs, Fox had two trucks and used them. Finally loaded, Fox Company headed down the Old French Road for its first major engagement since Hue City.

1800 hours. The attack began. By this time Echo Company's commanding officer, Captain Heinz, had become an emergency medevac.

Nothing went as planned. Both First Lieutenant Tom Martin, the company commander, and his platoon commander, Second Lieutenant

Jeff Martin, became casualties from mortar fire almost immediately. Jeff Martin was killed after a booby-trapped M-60 mortar round hit him in the stomach. Tom Martin was on top of a ten-foot high amtrac calling in supporting fires when a mortar round hit the vehicle severing the arm of the driver and wounding Martin. Martin sustained a more severe injury when he fell from this platform onto the ground as the explosion lifted him off the amtrac.

Fox fought on outside the An Hoa perimeter throughout the early part of the evening. Back at the An Hoa base, 2/5 had relieved the 7th Marine garrison and had taken over the sandbagged command bunker formally occupied by the coordinator.

In the command bunker, the radios crackled throughout the evening. Radio operators filled reams of message pads with casualty reports. Fox Company lost two men killed and sustained many wounded. Confusion reined inside the dimly lit bunker. Tom Martin's death, not Jeff Martin's was incorrectly reported. The notice of Tom's death caused many incorrect reports to be sent that would have to be reversed in the months ahead.

Captain Dave Brown was eager to do anything he could. More importantly, he wanted in on the fight! He tried to relieve one tired-looking radio operator and take a few casualty reports to let the man have a short break. However, not impressed with his good intentions, but aware that Brown continually asked: "Say again all after..." Steele's radio operator finally jumped on the other end and demanded, "Put someone competent on the radio!" Hell, Brown just couldn't keep up with their continual rapid use of the phonetic alphabet! From that point on, though, his respect for radio operators soared as Brown began to understand the tasks they had to perform in darkness and danger.

The following morning on 30 September, First Lieutenant Tom Martin was evacuated. By late afternoon the enemy had withdrawn and the An Hoa valley was under the control of the 5th Marine Regiment. Major Steele directed both Fox and Echo Companies to An Hoa. He also assigned Captain Brown to command Company F, 2nd Battalion, 5th Marines.

While he waited for the arrival of the troops, Brown gathered his personal gear and went into the company's newly erected admin tent to meet the first sergeant. First Sergeant Curry was a small, thin man with a quiet voice who, in his earlier career, was an admin chief. This would be perfect. The first sergeant would stay mostly in the rear to muster troops in and out of the field and manage the company's rear-area logistics. Brown could remain in the field with the gunny and fight the war. Everyone was happy with this arrangement and over the next six months the first sergeant showed up in the field on only about two to three occasions with papers for Brown to sign.

Brown immediately learned that the company had only one officer, First Lieutenant McNeil, beside himself; and the company only had three staff non-commissioned officers, SNCOs; the first sergeant; Gunnery Sergeant VanValkenburgh; and Staff Sergeant Palmer. It had lost two officers and one staff non-commissioned officer in yesterday's fight to secure the An Hoa valley and, thus, was stripped of seniority.

Fox finally arrived back in An Hoa at dusk. Brown approved the gunny's request to let them chow down, clean their weapons, and sleep in. The company would do some administrative things in the morning, eat lunch, and then meet at a noon formation. At the gunny's recommendation Fox planned for fire-team training in the afternoon.

All morning long Brown tried to concentrate on administrative tasks such as: signing "Unit Diaries"; checking out classified documents; drawing his weapon, canteen, cartridge belt, ammo; writing a quick letter home; and meeting the new commanding officer of the battalion, Lieutenant Colonel James Stemple. He also stopped by to say hello to Major Steele who had reverted to his former job as the battalion executive officer.

After meeting his new boss, Captain Brown had the distinct privilege of meeting Captain Mike Downs who was the assistant operations officer for the 5th Marines. Downs' job was to ensure Brown had the "big picture" from the regimental viewpoint. However, Brown didn't miss the main thrust of his briefing, which was to tell the new Fox skipper that Downs had commanded the heroic group of men of Company F during the Battle of Hue City and that, as their new commanding officer, Brown should ensure they received the very best. Clearly, that is what they deserved.

At noon, First Sergeant Curry assembled the company. They wore flak jackets and helmets. Their M-16 rifles were slung on their shoulders. Many were the actual, living, remaining heroes of the Battle of Hue City. Among them were Gunny VanValkenburgh, Corporal George Blunt, Corporal Gus Grillo, and Lance Corporal "C.C." Campbell. These were men who had also just cleared the An Hoa valley of the enemy. They were true hardened combat troops!

No one read the disappointment in Brown's face as he gazed out at the three undermanned platoons comprised of about seventy-five tired-looking troops in their dried, mud-coated, jungle utilities. Was this the magnificent Fox Company that Captain Downs was talking about? Man, Brown thought, I have a lot to learn!

Brown saluted the first sergeant, put the company at ease, made some remarks that moments later even he couldn't recall, called them back to attention, and ordered, "Right face; Forward march!"

They hiked out three miles, conducted fire-team training, and sped-marched back to the camp. So many straggled that Gunny VanValkenburgh and what few non-commissioned officers Fox did have couldn't keep them together.

Upon their return, Brown reassembled the company—now looking worse than ever—and addressed all, "Hue City is behind you!" he admonished. "If you don't get your acts together, I'll replace you. You'll all be killed if you don't immediately improve!!!"

Turning to the gunny, he said, "Gunnery Sergeant VanValkenburgh!"

"Sir!"

"Dismiss the troops!" Brown commanded.

CHAPTER 10: FOX GETS A "MAGGIE'S DRAWERS"

The first couple of days in August were really an adjustment and orientation period for the company. Fox participated with the 2nd Battalion Command Group, Echo, Golf, and Hotel Companies, in Operation Mameluke Thrust II, an operation that would continue until 23 October. The primary mission of the operation was to locate and destroy enemy forces, base areas, and cashes of materiel and supplies in the An Hoa valley. As it had been in the past two years, its secondary mission was to keep the main, and only, road between Liberty Bridge and An Hoa open. The enemy consisted of the local main force Viet Cong and small North Vietnam Army units.

Initially, the day-to-day operations were not unlike training exercises back in the States: saddle up in the morning, go on company-sized or battalion-sized patrols, find nothing, and return to the An Hoa base camp. This was not strenuous for the men of Fox. As a matter of fact, the period was mostly fun, somewhat exciting, and overall a fine opportunity for the men of Fox to get to know one another as new troops seemed to be joining at the rate of five per day. The troops enjoyed a hot meal for breakfast and one after they returned to the base in the late afternoon. They would take a cold shower; drink a warm beer; write a letter home, and, for those not on watch, sleep on a cot. Each day when Fox would return from the field, replacements were there to greet them.

First Lieutenant Mike McNeill had the command of 1st Platoon for the time being. The company had no executive officer and Captain Brown, the new skipper, was contemplating assigning McNeill to that billet. Brown assigned Staff Sergeant Dick Palmer to the platoon sergeant's job in the 2nd Platoon. Palmer had been Brown's platoon right guide six years earlier in 1962 at Kaneohe Marine Corps Air Station, Hawaii, when Brown was a second lieutenant. Brown knew Palmer to be intelligent and a true gentleman. He was also aware Palmer could be relied on for speaking freely whereas other officers and staff non-commissioned officers would be more hesitant to speak up until they felt more comfortable with the new captain. A salty corporal by the name of Rich Carter led the 3rd Platoon. Though an anti-tank assault man by military occupational specialty, Carter's battle experience in Hue City caused Brown to put Carter in charge of that rifle platoon.

On the morning of 1 August, Fox and Echo Companies went on a two-company sweep. The objective was to locate enemy forces near An Hoa. The two companies moved north through the Duc Duc District Headquarters and the only government protected village in the An Hoa valley, Phu Da. They split on the north side of the village separated by 600 meters with Fox moving immediately along the Song Thu Bon's southern bank and Echo Company moving inland and parallel to Fox. This "stroll in the park" started out with the men of Fox admiring the river while weaving in and out of now-destroyed French farm homes. These homes retained remnants of their once ceramic—tiled floors and wonderful views of the 400 meter-wide river. As a matter of fact, since the battalion had planned for the companies to return to An Hoa, this sweep seemed even better because all of their packs were left back at the base. The temperature was rising into the mid-nineties under the sunny tropical skies; though with the humidity, it seemed a bit warmer. Still, all considered, it was quite pleasant.

On the north side of the river was the vast, enemy-controlled, Arizona Territory. During this period, units of the 5th Marines would raid that area, but mostly it was a safe haven for their enemy. Similarly the VC and NVA, based or operating from the Arizona Territory, now yielded the An Hoa valley to the Marines, although occasionally they would venture south across the river in boats for supplies or to raid a village or two. From an informal viewpoint, the protocol of "you stay on your side of the river and we'll stay on ours" seemed acceptable, at least at the company level.

It was about noon when Fox stopped in place for a C-ration lunch. Twenty minutes later the men began the slow pace dictated for their five-mile sweep. Palmer's 2nd Platoon had the lead. Only a few moments later the word was quickly passed down the line to "Get down!"; the enemy had been sighted. The men, stretched over 300 meters, did so quite obediently without knowing where the enemy was, how many there were, or what they were doing. Captain Brown crept forward cautiously to find answers to these questions.

Palmer, crouching low, slipped down the line to update the captain. With their weapons pointed outward in various directions, all Marines were in a prone or crouched position. Muffled whispering could be heard as their excitement level rose.

"Sir, our lead squad spotted six enemy about ready to get into two small boats and cross over here," he whispered, pointing. Continuing, Palmer said, "I recommend we move the company about 200 meters forward from this spot." He then motioned to the exact location, "The enemy will paddle over, and we will fire on them when they are half way across."

Brown concurred and directed his radio operator instruct the trailing platoons to move cautiously inland and remain unseen. After about 200 meters the company would crawl forward to the river's bank and get on line. All weapons would be pointed toward the river. Fire would be held until the 1st Platoon, in the rear, got into firing positions. The 3rd Platoon would initiate the firing.

The whispered instructions were passed along the column and the forward movement began. Brown was quite pleased with the display of discipline and professionalism. Soon the mighty firepower of the 120 Marines would wipe out the lives of these six, unsuspecting enemy soldiers. Somehow, it didn't seem fair, but it was war.

Within ten minutes the bulk of the company was at the river's bank observing a far less organized group of six enemy casually loading weapons and other items into two narrow boats. Whatever they had to move across, required them to make several trips into the jungle behind them. They would put one load into the boat, disappear into the jungle, and then reappear with another load. Finally, after about ten minutes the hapless half-dozen Cong got into the boats and began paddling across the river right into the Fox ambush.

Only the infantryman lying next to each Marine could hear the sound of rifle safety locks being moved to the semi-automatic position. Fox was fully ready to "commence firing."

This was just like the rifle range at Marine Corps Recruit Depots at Parris Island or San Diego. Only, now, the range officer and the shooting instructors did not have on their "Smokey-the-Bear" hats and were not pacing up and down behind the firing line and the Marines of Fox. Now, they were on the line under helmets, in flak jackets and also in a prone position. All waited as though loud speakers would say, "*Shooters, when your targets appear, commence firing.*"

This surreal event was going to be a cruel one. Yet, thirteen months earlier in Operation Union II, Fox Company Marines were placed in a similar disadvantaged situation and the enemy showed absolutely no mercy in the slaughter of thirty Marines. Now, once the eighty somewhat new M-16 rifles, four M-60 machine guns, and the two LAAWs, opened up on the six enemy soldiers, they would die quickly and suffer little.

The Song Thu Bon was about 250 meters wide at the point of the ambush. From the Fox side of the river, it flowed perhaps two to three miles per hour to the right or east toward the South China Sea. The hapless Cong had no problems paddling across. In order to control the current's gentle pull on their boats, they paddled slightly to the southwest, ironically, looking squarely into the lead wall they would soon face. Fox was perfectly positioned.

The first distinct crack of a weapon firing came from the 3rd Platoon. Immediately its distinction was lost when the line opened up fully. The collective noise was deafening. The view was spectacular. Even though the enemy's lead boat was only a third of the way across, not half way as planned, both boats were caught in a hail of incoming bullets. Every fifth machine gun round had a red tracer showing its trajectory to aid the gunner in firing his weapon. As these rounds, mixed those of the 120 M-16 rifles, entered the water in an area twenty meters around the boats, splashes of water leapt above the river's surface three feet into the air. Soon the boats seemed to disappear in this shower of river water.

Abruptly, as the first rounds struck the water's surface, the boat's passengers jumped for their lives into the river. No longer did their cargo's delivery hold any importance. Survival was their only raison d'etre. The scene could have been easily plopped right into the middle of a "shoot-em-up movie," perhaps The Keystone Cops series. Arms and legs kicking and flailing added more splashes to the shower set initiated by the hail of bullets. If ever North Vietnam or the VC had planned to enter the freestyle swimming competition in that year's 1968 Olympics in Mexico City, this would be the winning team.

Flipped upside down, both small boats were now out of the impact area drifting lazily toward the South China Sea. One after the other the enemy soldiers managed to reach the river's bank and rapidly climb onto its grassy edge before disappearing into the jungle. The firing continued until the last, once hapless swimmer vanished.

The weapons fell silent. The adrenaline rush still filled the Marines' senses. Suddenly, it seemed that the only insult missing would be for the six enemy to re-emerge from the jungle, form a line, turn around, and moon the Marines who, at this point, were still in shock at what they just witnessed. In awe, many jaws hung low and eyes blinked wide open while the men looked to one another trying to ensure themselves that they were not crazy. Hadn't they just witnessed the most dramatic escape from an ambush ever? Surely they should have had one kill. But they didn't. All six escaped! Whoa! This was a monumental moment…for surely this was the biggest "Maggie's Drawers" ever earned in the history of the Marine Corps. The infamous red flag that was waived across targets at the rifle ranges when shooters missed their target was otherwise known as a Maggie's Drawers. Yet, this Maggie's Drawers felt ten times more humiliating than any earned on a rifle range.

Gunnery Sergeant VanValkenburgh was overwhelmed with the total misses by Fox's marksmen. His frustration rarely showed for he was always a true gentleman. His anger didn't explode. He did steam however, and clearly, he was steaming now with a massive Maggie's Drawers symbolically waved across the river at Fox.

VanValkenburgh initiated an investigation upon the company's return to base. The battalion armorer found out that most of the new M-16 rifles had not been properly calibrated prior to them being issued to Fox Company—hence the Maggie's Drawers. The word was passed along about VanValkenburgh's initiative and soon the other rifle companies of the 5th Marine Regiment benefited.

CHAPTER 11: NAPALM

Fox's first major attack into enemy territory began on 5 August 1968 after the weapons had been calibrated. As part of Operation Mameluke Thrust II, the battalion command group with Echo and Fox Companies were to attack eastward from a point along the Liberty Road 1000 meters south of Phu Lac (6). Fox Company would lead and was to attack, seize, and occupy the small hamlet of La Thap (4), 1200 meters from the main road down a gentle slope and across mostly open fields. Artillery from the 105mm howitzer battery located on the high ground overlooking Liberty Bridge would provide direct support for 2/5's attack. The battalion's 81mm Mortar Platoon was fully dedicated to the mission. Fixed wing attack and fighter aircraft, A-4s and F-4s, were available on call from Da Nang.

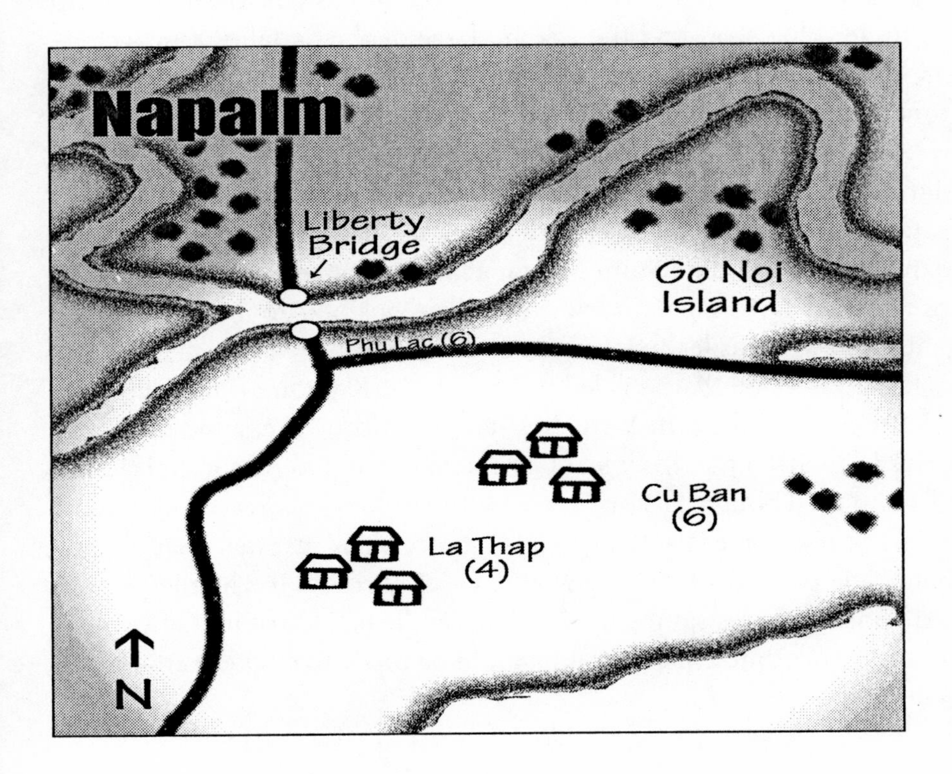

The men of Fox knew they were about to face a challenge. They could meet stiff enemy resistance in either La Thap (4) or the second objective Cu Ban (6), a higher-elevated hamlet one kilometer further northeast than the first objective. Fox had suffered over a dozen casualties seven days earlier while fighting to reoccupy the An Hoa valley. On 3 August, the artillery forward observer's radio operator was killed when he sat on a booby trap by the ruins of an old French-built farmhouse. Then, on 4 August, one of the more popular squad leaders from the 2nd Platoon, Corporal Richard Hellard, was killed after he tripped a booby trap while going through a hedgerow. First Lieutenant McNeil was wounded that day too and had to be evacuated. Fighting hard-core enemy soldiers face to face seemed acceptable; booby traps were not. Finally, Fox vets would have to bear up to the fact that this would be the first real operation under their new skipper. It would expose his command abilities as well.

1330 hours. After a C-ration lunch, Fox moved out toward La Thap (4) under blue skies and the watchful eye of the battalion's new commanding officer, Lieutenant Colonel Jim Stemple. Stemple, a veteran from the "Old Corps", had served in China in 1946. His expectations were high and Fox would be the first to be watched by this China Marine. The cloudless sky let the summer's sun shine down on Fox's two platoons up and one platoon back attack formation. Stemple, his command group, and the 81mm Mortar Platoon, located near the elevated road, would have a great view from their position looking down the gently sloped fields leading toward La Thap (4).

The 1st and 3rd Platoons led the attack, 1st Platoon on the right and 3rd Platoon on the left. With McNeil gone, Brown assigned a newly arrived blond-hair staff sergeant by the name of Ted Easton to lead the 1st Platoon. Though Easton was new in country, his recent east coast Fleet Marine Force, FMF, experience more than justified that assignment. The plan was that they would sweep through the hamlet should there not be any resistance and hold up on the far side of it. If any resistance was encountered, a decision would be made to stop the attack, call in supporting fires from the battalion's mortar platoon, and then make a final assault through the hamlet.

Captain Brown was pleased. The company's formation looked smart. As a matter of fact, the Marines' individual dispersal for such open terrain seemed as good as he had seen during his seven years in the Corps. Thus, the enemy did not cause any causalities as Fox moved to a point about 400 meters from the hamlet and received twenty to thirty shots from a pair of semi-automatic weapons. The Marines took firing positions, returned fire, held their ground, and waited for the fire support.

Soon the 81mm mortar forward observer, Corporal Pete Novak, looked at Captain Brown with the PRC-25 radio handset raised to his ear and said, "First round's away, Skipper."

The round landed and Novak made a small correction. Satisfied with that round, he then gave the "Fire For Effect" order signaling all eight mortars to fire a set number of rounds established for the fire mission.

Twenty-four mortar rounds, shot from the high ground behind the company, began raining down on the small hamlet. Their immense explosions were almost immediately followed by the assaulting platoons as they leapt into action using the hailstorm of rounds as a shield of fire. The Marines reached the hamlet, bounded by palm trees and other vegetation, and were rapidly swallowed up as they stepped through the hamlet's facade.

The 81s had shifted their fires to the back edge of the hamlet. The plan was to continue shifting these fires outward away from the hamlet toward possible escape routes in the rice fields.

Corporal Rich Carter and Corporal Jeff Shay, the long-term 3rd Platoon radio operator, had just entered the hamlet and were at a small cemetery consisting of burial mounds. Immediately, they could see that the fires were shifting, instead of away from the hamlet, back toward the middle of the hamlet.

"Shay, call the company and tell them to 'Cease Fire,'" Rich Carter directed.

"Already did, Rich," he paused. "They're on it, but there are five shots in the air."

Carter yelled as loud as he could, "Incoming! Incoming! Everyone hit the deck!"

Carter, Shay, and the platoon's new right guide, a corporal, helplessly observed the first three rounds explode within the 3rd Platoon's position, each round closing in on them. Then they too dove to the ground. The fifth round landed perilously close to the three of them.

"Fox, this is Fox Three, over," Shay called as he followed Carter to an area where a Marine's bicep had been badly injured by mortar shrapnel. Shay went on. Carter lingered to stuff battle dressings on the man's wounded arm. Shay finally connected with the company. "Roger, Fox we have several casualties. We'll need a medevac."

Carter caught up to Shay.

"Sam was hit," Shay murmured.

Shay was referring to, Lance Corporal Lupe Monsebais. Monsebais, commonly known as "Sam", arrived in Vietnam nearly a year earlier with Carter. They had been in Nong Son on the night of 3 July 1967, Hue City, and the Hai Van Pass operations together. Sam had just returned from R&R.

Shay called Fox for the second time. Soon, the company's radio began crackling away. "Fox Six, this is Fox One. We have one Priority One Whiskey India Alpha, two Priority two Whiskey India Alphas and one Kilo India Alpha in the vil. They were hit by 81s, over," he informed, referring to the wounded and killed men.

"Roger, One. We'll notify Texas Pete." Brown's radio operator replied using the battalion command group's call sign. "Texas Pete" had control of the 81mm mortar platoon.

Brown and the company corpsman, Hospitalman Second Class, HN2, Andy Rackow hurriedly joined the 3rd Platoon in the vil. Carter led him to the spot where the fourth mortar round landed. The high explosive, or HE, round had detonated and had stripped the leaves and small branches from a cluster of twenty-foot high bamboo trees creating a small clearing. Lance Corporal Monsebias' headless body lay in the middle. Two Marines from his squad were readying his remains for transport. Carter could not disguise his discomfort. One of his closest friends had been brutally and needlessly killed.

Captain Brown sensed heart-wrenching pain from the rest of the men too as they stoically went about their gross and grim duties. Monsebias had been a well-liked Marine in 3rd Platoon. The irony of the death of this Texas Marine at the hands of their own people tore at the men's sense of right and wrong. He had been killed by friendly fire, a mortar round from the battalion's own 81mm platoon, and that knowledge alone had dampened the fighting spirit of the 3rd Platoon.

Captain Brown called Texas Pete and demanded an explanation. "We're looking into it," came the answer. Instead of the company occupying this six-hooch hamlet as Texas Pete ordered earlier, Brown directed the 1st Platoon to outpost the hamlet with a squad and pulled the rest of the men back to the knoll 250 meters away overlooking the hamlet. He rationalized that the company could react fast enough if needed to support the squad and the fresh air on the knoll that night may calm any troops still spooked by the 81mm mortar rounds and the unnecessary death of one of their own.

That night Brown received the explanation he sought earlier about the errant 81mm rounds. The stray rounds were classified as accidental with the implication that there was some sort of manufacturing deficiency. Brown, who had been an 81 mm platoon commander in 1963, thought that was utter bull. A higher probability remained that an error had occurred either on the part of 2/5's Fire Support Coordination Center or the Fire Direction Center of the 81mm Mortar Platoon. He vowed not to use the battalion's mortar platoon unless it was absolutely necessary or until the platoon had better proven its abilities.

0600 hours. The night had been pleasant and uneventful. Daylight began thirty minutes earlier on the morning of 6 August. At the Fox Company field CP, the battalion radio could be heard: "Fox, this is Texas Pete, over."

"Roger, Texas Pete. This is Fox, over"

"Texas Pete Six wants to speak to Fox Six, over," the radio operator communicated, indicating that Lieutenant Colonel Stemple wanted to speak to Captain Brown.

"This is Fox Six, over," Brown responded in a cheerful and confidant voice, having received the handset from the radio operator.

Then the admonishment of the China Marine began. "Fox Six, what is your position now? Over."

His tone flashed Brown back to any of the dry, professor-led lectures he'd endured in college. Brown would have preferred a "Good Morning" or anything else like that. Concern tinged Brown's gut. While stretching to get his hands on his map, Brown suddenly felt like a school kid about to get a reprimand.

There remained an uncomfortably long pause on the radio traffic.

"Errr, we're at Alpha Tango 935518, over," Brown replied annunciating each letter and number with care, wondering what the hell Texas Pete was getting at? Brown knew Stemple could see Fox's position from his location up on the hill.

"I thought I ordered your company to 'occupy' the hamlet to your front?" "Professor" Stemple accused.

"Errr, You did, Sir. We outposted it with a squad."

"Fox Six, there's a big difference between 'outposting' and 'occupying.'" "Professor" Stemple instructed.

"Aye, aye, Sir!" "Sophomore" Brown responded.

Then Lieutenant Colonel Stemple dropped the subject and continued with the plans for the next attack as if the location of Fox was a long forgotten matter.

Despite Lieutenant Colonel Stemple's disapproval, Brown knew the outposting decision was the right one. His company was up and getting ready to move out. The unfortunate death of Lance Corporal Monsebias was a memory and was no longer a lingering cloud; the troops were ready to go. However, next time he'd inform Texas Pete Six of any change of plans, particularly when Fox was in plain sight of the China Marine.

0830 hours. After Stemple's wake-up call, the main body of the company had been joined by a section of two USMC M-48 tanks that Stemple assigned to Fox for its attack on Objective 2: the hamlet of Cu Ban (6). Fox began moving through and around La Tap (4), yesterday's objective. 1000 meters up-hill and across the barren, dried, rice fields, lay Cu Ban (6) with its numerous, tall bamboo trees.

"Hey, Campbell," Lance Corporal Dave DeGroat of the 2nd Platoon called to his squad leader, Corporal C.C. Campbell. The two had been together since April. Both had been in Corporal Chris Brown's squad then. "What the hell are we doing today?"

"Damned if I know," Campbell replied. "I was checking on the listening posts, seems like all night long. Hell, I don't think I got four hours sleep." Thinking about the question again, Campbell added, "If Palmer passed on any scoop, I must have missed it. I guess we're following the 1st Platoon, and if they get in any crap, we'll bail 'em out like we always do."

DeGroat's fire team was the lead element for the 2nd Platoon and followed generally in trace of the 1st Platoon. Mindful of the death of their squad leader, Corporal Hellard, two days earlier from a booby trap, Campbell and DeGroat were carefully selecting each step as they traversed one dry rice paddy after another. A half hour later, DeGroat called out to his buddy, "C.C., you got any candy bars left? I'm starved."

Campbell reached into the baggy pocket on the side of his thigh. After sorting through several items rat-holed in the pocket, his hand emerged clutching a C-ration chocolate bar. He flipped it over to DeGroat.

"Man, you're a life saver!" Dave DeGroat said while catching the candy bar "Hey, anyone heard any thing from Chris?" DeGroat asked referring to their former squad leader again as he peeled away the wrapper.

"I thought I told you that I got a letter at the end of June and Chris said he would be starting school at the end of August. Man, hard as college must be, it sure beats this shit."

0915 hours. The sporadic chatter, taking place among squad members on their "stroll in park", ceased abruptly that morning when the noise of a single rifle shot rang out from the tree line in front of the 1st Platoon.

Soon Fox began receiving scattered small arms and automatic weapons fire from the high ground at Cu Ban (6). Scattering dirt, dried rice stalks, and men, a 60mm mortar and a 75mm recoilless rifle began firing at Fox from a distance of 500 meters. Instantly, the forward platoons held up, a pre-planned 105mm artillery mission was called in, and an area around the men of Fox exploded with noise as the attached tanks returned fire.

The hamlet ahead of them was spread out along a high ground. The few grass huts or hooches that existed were built in and among a few bamboo trees on the right. A concentration of trees was to the left of the company's front. 105mm high explosive rounds bombarded the hilltop for four or five minutes. The air grew silent indicating that the arty fire mission was completed. The lead platoons, 1st Platoon on the left and 3rd Platoon on the right, initiated their assault. The massive firepower of Fox and its two tanks had its desired effect on the withdrawing enemy. One of the 3rd Platoon's 3.5-inch anti-tank rocket launchers demolished a hooch on the right portion of the battlefield. The explosion left the structure on fire. Its burning, damp, straw-thatched roof sent a large, lingering, cloudy-colored smoke trail skyward.

The enemy's fire, though temporarily stopped, seemed to have ended in the vicinity of the concentration of trees to the left of the company front. Counting on the tanks' "shock effect", Brown directed the two tanks towards the thicket to support the assault of the 1st Platoon. The tanks' shock effect came from their speed and mobility, and the loud rumbling of their two diesel engines that powered the tanks up the last bit of the hill combined with the clamor of the gunners firing their main guns at will.

Corporal Robert Fante, a squad leader with the 1st Platoon, led the ground assault on the 75mm recoilless rifle. The NVA crew manning the gun fled in the face of Fante's fearless charge. Now without their seven-foot long weapon, the enemy dashed into a bamboo thicket twenty-five meters behind them and ran for their lives.

Brown's command group slid behind the 1st Platoon and reached the hill's summit near the concentration of trees. The tanks cranked to a stop in front of the seven-foot long NVA 75mm recoilless rifle.

Fante, leading his squad, savagely pursued the enemy into the thicket. Throwing hand grenades at spider holes, Fante pressed on until one of his men was wounded. He covered the wounded Marine until the platoon corpsman could reach him. He then turned and assaulted a camouflaged bunker with hand grenades killing two enemy soldiers. He chased the six retreating enemy out of the right hand side of the thicket and into an open field and was suddenly exposed. Fante was mortally wounded by an automatic weapon fired on him from the bottom of the hill.

Further to the left, an unstoppable racket of gunshots resonated from the trees as the battle raged. Hand grenades exploded. The men ducked and crouched, fired and sprinted using the thin bamboo trees for whatever cover they provided. Amid the explosive sounds of rifle fire shouts of Marines chasing the enemy out of the thicket and off of the hill toward their safe haven, Go Noi, Island. That sanctuary was some 1500 meters northeast of their current position. The calls for "Corpsman up!" could be heard. The company corpsman, Doc Andy Rackow, rushed to answer the call.

Rackow had been the company corpsman for several months. Coming from the "Mainline" in the Philadelphia area where his dad was a physician, Andy was a natural as the senior field medical technician. His professional knowledge was absolutely astounding. He had a physical appearance and disposition of a young handsome college professor with longish wavy hair, some freckles, thin horn-rim glasses, and a crisp soft voice.

The noise of the fight continued for a few minutes after Doc Rackow disappeared into the thicket. Soon the firing subsided as the 1st Platoon, now joined by the 3rd Platoon, pursued the enemy from the hilltop. Gunnery Sergeant VanValkenburgh immediately sent Marines from the

Weapons Platoon in to assist with the dozen or more wounded. The 2nd Platoon Corpsman, Hospitalman Third Class Lonnie Connelly, began coordinating the triage activities.

The Weapons Platoon Marines brought Corporal Fante's body out of the thicket first. He was carried back out to where the company command group was located. Then, the wounded began straggling out. On a stretcher two Marines carefully carried out Doc Rackow who had been shot in his abdomen.

Captain Brown was aghast to see that Rackow had been severely wounded. "How is he, Gunny?" Brown asked after seeing Rackow's somewhat ashen face.

"Don't know, Skipper. It looks pretty serious."

Brown went over to his senior corpsman. He could hear Rackow painfully giving instructions to the Marine kneeling down beside him on how to apply the morphine. "Andy," Brown said after the young trooper began putting on the morphine, "we have a bird inbound to pick you up. You hang in there."

Rackow nodded.

The 1st and 3rd Platoons stopped their pursuit of the enemy at the topographical crest of the high ground to defend against a possible counterattack. This crest was nearly at the limit of the regiment's TAOR. The pilot of the Army O1-E "Bird Dog" aircraft, who had been the eyes for the Marine's attack that morning, kept a visual track on the retreating enemy and called artillery and air strikes in on them.

Fox's performance that morning was quite noteworthy as the 5th Marines had had no sizable contact since the day after it entered the An Hoa valley one week earlier. This morning Fox had engaged a reinforced enemy company and combined with supporting arms, killed twenty-three enemy and captured their 75mm recoilless rifle. However, Fox did not come out unscathed. Corporal Fante had been killed and Doc Andy Rackow had been mortally wounded. Seventeen other Marines had been wounded and were evacuated. Four others earned Purple Hearts, but were not evacuated. Stemple concurred with Brown's recommendation for putting Fante up for a Navy Cross Medal.

1040 hours. During the next hour, the battalion sent two amtracs with supplies and ammunition forward as well as a platoon from Echo Company to recover the 75mm recoilless rifle. They would also assist in the evacuation of the wounded. Munitions and water were distributed. The 1st and 3rd Platoons stayed forward, ate their noon meal, and remained alert as they stared onto Go Noi Island. Everyone remained silent.

1145 hours. The 2nd Platoon had assisted earlier with evacuating the wounded. Brown gave an order for the platoon to lead the company off the high ground and back to Liberty Road. While waiting to take off, they gathered in a small clearing. Most were sitting and relaxing. Staff Sergeant Dick Palmer was in high spirits; the company's victory had boosted the morale of his men. The captured prizes created heroic feelings in the men; the feeling was not unlike the one football players, despite being covered with bumps and bruises, experience in a locker room after winning a game.

The men of the 2nd Platoon dropped their backpacks, flak jackets, helmets, and weapons, opened their cartridge belts, and preceded to dig out cans of C-rations from their packs. The usual horse-trading commenced while some of the guys tried to procure food that was more palatable to their taste buds. After a little bartering everyone settled down and ate. Some Marines gulped while others savored each bite. It simply felt good to just sit back and relax a little from the war and reminisce about things back in the "World".

Brown, with the company's command element and the two tanks, had remained in the open field. This was the same site where the amtracs recovered some of the wounded and the 75mm recoilless rifle. The company command group was separated from the 2nd Platoon by a ten-meter thick bamboo hedgerow. While the company was waiting for the word to move out, Staff Sergeant Dick Palmer, the 2nd Platoon Leader, visited with Captain Brown as they coordinated details of the movement. Following his meeting with the company commander, Palmer returned to his platoon and met with his three squad leaders to finalize their movement back to the Liberty Bridge-An Hoa road.

1215 hours. "Black Ace 14, this is Front Runner, over," the Marine F-4 Phantom fighter pilot called to the Army aerial observer over the air net as he was flying south from Thua Thien Province at 8000 feet above the An Hoa valley.

"This is Black Ace 14, over," the Army captain responded from his Bird Dog O1-E observation aircraft loitering in the An Hoa airspace.

"Black Ace, TacAir Da Nang told me to check in with you. I have a couple of napalm canisters that I didn't use on my mission up north and need to get rid of them before I land back in Da Nang. Got any targets of opportunity?"

"Roger, Front Runner. I have several on Go Noi Island east of Liberty Bridge. Over."

"Roger, Black Ace, show me the way."

"Okay, Front Runner, I'll mark the enemy troop position with a 'Willy Peter' rocket."

Three, perhaps four, minutes passed until the Bird Dog pilot fired his white phosphorous rocket. "Rocket's away, Front Runner, over."

"Copy, Black Ace."

1220 hours. "Roger, Fox Six, we're moving out," the 2nd Platoon radio operator responded then nodded to Palmer. Palmer casually pointed to his 1st Squad leader who had been looking back at the staff sergeant for the signal. Without a word spoken, the lead squad began moving out from the small field surrounded by bamboo trees. Marines of the other two squads remained seated on the ground next to their packs waiting for the final word for their squad to "saddle up and move out." In the distance, the noise of a jet circling above could be heard. No one paid any attention to the sky.

The sky was clear without clouds. The sun's brilliance reflected upward sharply from the rivers surrounding Go Noi Island some 1500 meters north of Company F, 2nd Battalion, 5th Marines.

"Splash," the Army pilot announced in an even-toned voice. "Front Runner, do you see my smoke? Over."

Both the Marine pilot and his rear-seat radar intercept officer, RIO, looked around. Their heads jerked alternatively left and right. At times, even at 8000 feet the sun's reflection from the river was blinding. The RIO's head snapped right again: white smoke, five miles away, their target of opportunity! At this altitude the RIO naturally thought it was the "Willie Peter" marking rocket shot by the Army pilot.

He was wrong. The smoke he'd found was coming from the small hooch, still smoldering from Fox's advance in the morning. The RIO pointed out the smoke to the pilot. "I have it, Black Ace," the pilot announced to the spotter. "I'll be diving in at the target on a heading of 080."

His smoke already deployed, the Army spotter never saw the smoke from the smoldering hooch. Confirming the attack angle the spotter announced, "Front Runner, you are clear to come in hot."

"Many thanks," the pilot replied as he banked his Phantom right, bearing down on a group of men, clad in greenish uniforms.

The plane increased its speed during its sharp dive. As the jet got closer and closer, the pilot saw several targets of opportunity. Had he had anti-tank munitions as a payload, he would have chosen the two tanks. But he didn't. He had just the two napalm canisters, so he chose the most devastating target.

His attention focused on a gathering of approximately thirty men in the middle of a bamboo patch about one hundred meters from the white smoke. He shared his plan to napalm the group of men in the small clearing with his RIO, "They'll never know what hit them."

The RIO released the payload announcing, "They're away!"

Instantly, the pilot hit the afterburners for both engines, banking back toward Da Nang.

1230 hours. Dave DeGroat looked desperately at his close buddy, C.C. Campbell, to confirm what he was hearing. The jet's rumbling grew louder and louder. As one, the men of the 2nd Platoon turned, swiveling their collective heads, instantaneously assessing the direction of the incoming Phantom. Everyone in the platoon looked to see which direction the noise was coming from. Horrified, the men realized the F-4 was flying low towards their position. Too late, they reacted.

Anticipating an easy trip back, Captain Dave Brown's pack landed on one of the M-48 tanks in a secure place between the strapped-on five-gallon water can and the turret.

Seconds later, the bellow of the F-4, now only 150 feet above Brown's head, erupted. He hit the deck. The jet's thrust into the air space above Brown felt like a sharp thunderclap. Instantly the dual afterburners of the Phantom roared, then blasted two ten-foot long cones of yellow and orange flames that propelled the great war-machine skyward. The afterburner noise quieted in less than five seconds when they were extinguished by the Da Nang-bound aviator. In those seconds the jet was already one-half mile away, 2000 feet in the air and climbing.

The canisters' path was certain.

His breath arrested, limbs frozen, his gut wrenching, Brown watched the incendiary bombs speed to earth. Surreally, their progress appeared as if in slow motion to him. The captain watched in agony as they tumbled silently over his position, and over the twenty-foot high, ten-foot thick wall of bamboo trees that separated him from his 2nd Platoon. These cans of death slammed directly into the thirty-five Marines clad in their greenish uniforms. Most were sitting next to their packs waiting to lead Fox Company down the hill.

As the bombs struck the ground, firing pins detonated their explosive elements thus igniting their principal contents—a jelly-thick chemical known as napalm. A multi-layered, bubbled, red and orange fireball, edged with inky black smoke, rose over forty feet into the air and spread across the ground. As it did, it consumed all the oxygen in its path and replaced it with burning chemicals. At the top of the fireball was the opaque black smoke of a chemical fire that seemed to reach out after the fast fading gray smoke of the jet's cooling afterburners.

Before the realization of what was happening sank into his brain, Lance Corporal Dave Degroat's position burst into an inferno of scorching flames. He could feel the napalm jell as it splattered his body and ignited into life destroying fire. He tried to run, but kept bumping into Corporal C.C. Campbell. They continued knocking each other down as they tried to flee the hell all around them.

There was no place to escape. Fire consumed everything. DeGroat watched the pictures of his life dance in front of his eyes. It was like watching a video played on fast forward. Even the minor events of his life leapt forward from the recesses of his brain. For DeGroat, the pain stopped. He felt at peace, ready for what would come next, which surely would be death.

Then as quickly as it started, in a matter of seconds, it seemed like it was over. Time froze for a brief moment, yet DeGroat had no realization of how much time had passed. As the flames died down, men were running all around trying to escape the pain of their burns, but to no avail. Other Marines came running to help, but there was not much they could do. By the time they arrived some of the men's burned flesh was covered with huge water blisters, some flesh was charred, and hair was burned away where it had not been covered. Several Marines that came rushing to Degroat's aid hardly recognized him. They kept asking each other, "Is that DeGroat? Is that DeGroat?"

When they poured some water on his disfigured hands and arms the cooling sensation only helped for a brief moment. The excruciating pain returned quickly now. DeGroat was helped down to the ground so that the Marines could take his gear and equipment off and cut the jelly splattered, tattered, jungle fatigues away; once done, he was naked except for his boots.

Brown rushed through the three-foot wide pathway inside the wall of the bamboo. He halted abruptly, viewing the carnage. Steam-like smoke rose off of everything: the packs and rifles on the ground, the bandoleers of linked machine gun ammo, the scattered helmets, the grass, the bamboo and, most vividly and most horribly, the Marines. All but about six or seven Marines were hit by the napalm. Those not hit were on the opposite side from where the napalm had spewed. Its fiery poison stripped the smoldering camouflage uniforms from their friends' bodies. The survivors screamed and cried in pain. No one burned escaped the water blisters. Those distinct blisters ranged in size from a four inch by twelve inch splattering on someone's forearm to a bowling ball-sized blister covering one young Marine's scrotum. Doc Lonnie Connelly, who fortunately had been thirty meters away from the impact area, was consumed with the magnitude of the disaster and only had time to tend to the most severely burned.

Brown's mind was spinning with prioritizing immediate actions. He withdrew from the carnage. Before leaving, Brown spotted Corporal Eddie Stallings. Stallings, whose squad had started to lead the company off the hill, avoided serious burns and was now assisting the burning victims. "Hey, Stallings," Brown yelled.

"Yeah!" Stallings hollered not knowing who was calling for his help.

"Make sure you get all the ammo and C-4 away from the fire, we don't need any cooking off!"

Now, recognizing the source, Stallings acknowledged, "Aye, aye, Sir."

Brown then spotted his old friend Staff Sergeant. Palmer also helping his men, "Dick!" Brown called.

"Yes, Sir!" Palmer blurted intently.

"Dick, take care of this mess for a few minutes," Brown shouted. "I am going to check on our security and get some evac birds! Oh, I told Stallings to remove any C-4 that may be in the packs."

"Got you, Capt'n," Palmer nodded, turning away.

Brown then ran back through the bamboo opening and yelled to his company radio operator, Lance Corporal Bilski, "Ski, call battalion and give them a SITREP!"

"Already done, Skipper."

"Tell them we need to evac at least thirty guys."

"Roger, Sir!"

"I need to speak to One and Three," the captain declared. He referred to Staff Sergeant Easton and Corporal Carter of the 1st and 3rd Platoons.

"Here, use this phone," Bilski offered.

"Fox One and Fox Three, this is Fox Six. Give me your actuals, over," Brown commanded.

Once they came on the net Brown warned them just how vulnerable the company now found itself from any counter-attack. Operating independently, they were to ensure the perimeter was safe.

As Brown directed his platoon leaders, Bilski announced that Battalion had snatched a CH-53 Sea Stallion flying out of An Hoa to Da Nang, and it would be there in about five minutes.

Brown rushed back through the bamboo tunnel to assist Palmer. C.C. Campbell stood in the jungled path blocking his passage. His blackened-face, blistered torso and burned uniform trousers spoke volumes. The two stared at each other without a word for what seemed an eternity. Finally the burned man rasped, "Skipper, why did you let it happen?"

Brown stared at the young man. He was without words. There was no comfort to give him and no answer. Brown shook his head slowly knowing he couldn't answer. The simple question encompassed the totality of combat leadership's awesome responsibility.

A minute later, never breaking eye contact, Brown said gently, "Come on, Marine. I'm going to help you get home."

DeGroat was carried to the helicopter, which arrived only minutes after the accident to medevac the men of the 2nd Platoon. Twenty-six burn casualties were loaded onto the aircraft. Some were carried, but the majority limped, walked, stumbled, or ran into the huge cargo bay. Once under the slowly spinning blades of the CH-53, the air offered temporary relief from the pain caused by DeGroat's burning skin. However, upon entering the chopper, the airflow stopped and the temperature rose. As the helicopter lifted off and headed for Da Nang, the hum of the helicopter's engines failed to drown out the screams and moans of the Marines in pain.

1415 hours. The glory of capturing the recoilless rifle had long been erased. Fox limped towards Liberty Bridge in silence and arrived that night to begin a rebuilding period that lasted nearly five weeks.

CHAPTER 12: AMBUSH NEAR LIBERTY BRIDGE

Private First Class Dennis Cadigan felt strained as his plane flew away from Newark, NJ. He looked out from the plane down onto the city and prophetically thought, I'll never see this city again.

After arriving in Da Nang on 6 August 1968, he walked out onto the sweltering tarmac feeling overwhelmed by the heat, the smells of gasoline, and the nearby rot. He saw Marines waiting to go home who were sitting on their "sea" bags. Cadigan failed to understand the conflicted emotions of anger on their young faces as they knew they were leaving their war buddies behind, punctuated by smiles because they knew they were about to go home.

Shortly, he found himself riding in the back of a USMC 6x6 truck heading westward from Da Nang to An Hoa, Fox Company's home base. By the time he completed the forty-mile trip, he was covered in red dirt from the dust covering the dry roads and kicked up into the air from the truck's tires. Cadigan reported to the company's first sergeant to check in. Nearly forty-five minutes passed until he met one of the few men still in the 2nd Platoon, the platoon to which he was assigned. The Marine's name was Lance Corporal J.D. Moore. From J. D., Cadigan learned the ominous news that Moore was one of the seven or eight platoon members who survived the "napalm" attack earlier that day. Moore introduced him to others, including Corporal George Blunt, Private First Class Rene Salazar, Private First Class Ken Murray, and Private First Class Juan De La Rosa.

That night in his ten-man tent, Cadigan was alone, desolate. Frustrated, he ventured out of his quarters, pleased to meet and visit with other Marines. He met a nineteen year-old veteran that had achieved his "vet" status as he had survived nearly four months in "Nam." He seemed friendly enough, but before Cadigan could learn his name, he heard shouts from another nearby Marine, "Fire in the hole! Fire in the hole! Fire in the hole!"

The shattering noise from the Marine 8-inch Howitzer firing 300 meters away sucked Cadigan's breath away. Instantly, he dove into the nearest ditch. Only moments later, the Fox "vet," chuckling, reached down and yanked Cadigan out of the hole. Soon they were both laughing at Cadigan's over-reaction to the dominant booms of that night's Marine Corps' fire mission. Their laughs ended abruptly as three Viet Cong counter-battery mortar rounds whistled in and impacted, exploding within one hundred meters from them. Before he knew it, Cadigan was back in his hole. This time, having been pushed by the once-laughing veteran, Cadigan found himself covered by the wily Marine. Laying face down, smelling urine, garbage, and other filth, Cadigan wished he could go home more than anything else in the world.

Second Lieutenants Bill Melton and Earl "Woody" Lott reported in to the company shortly after Fox arrived at Liberty Bridge. Melton had received a field commission after having served as a sergeant two years earlier in Vietnam. He brought a wealth of experience and insight to the company for which Captain Brown was extremely grateful. Melton was assigned to the 3rd Platoon. Lieutenant Colonel Stemple and Captain Brown referred to Second Lieutenant Bill Melton as "Mustang Mike." A "mustang" is the nickname given to a former enlisted Marine who attained a commission. The name is wholly complimentary. Without a doubt these officers bring to their units wisdom, identification with the troops, a devotion to the Corps, and a high degree of professionalism. They are not known to BS anyone, and nobody would BS them.

Lott was a reserve officer with a lot of enthusiasm that occasionally required harnessing. Brown was glad for the boost in energy brought in with Lott and assigned him to the 1st Platoon.

Before the NVA blew up Liberty Bridge three months earlier, trucks carrying supplies had driven across it regularly. Now, all that was left were charred pilings that looked like big burned kitchen matches sticking up from the muddy water.

Supplies of all sorts from Da Nang were trucked southeast to An Hoa. The last seven miles, beginning at Liberty Bridge, was dubbed "Rocket Alley."

Convoys of six to eight trucks ran every other day, stopping at the northern compound just long enough to check for bullet holes in the radiators or engine parts and to check their tires before crossing the river. A barge ferried them across the water one or two vehicles at a time, the same way they had with 2/5 when the battalion returned to An Hoa in July.

The trucks would then drive off of the barge's flat, wooden deck and chug slowly up the steep sand and rock bank. As they topped the slope, every driver hit second gear and with a burst of speed drove the cargo the hundred meters through the small defensive enclosure that Fox shared with a USMC 105mm howitzer battery at Phu Lac (6). Shifting into third gear, they accelerated out the barbed wire back door of the compound at over fifty miles per hour on a dirt road that was designed for thirty. They would drive as fast as they could these final six and a half miles and only in daylight, because the last leg of the trip was more treacherous than any stretch of ground on earth.

Speed kept them alive. A mine buried in the road would blow a slow moving vehicle into a million pieces with little chance of the driver surviving such a massive explosion. Rockets were often fired at convoys from the hills on either side of the red dirt road. Snipers fired from small groves of trees two hundred to three hundred meters on either side of this dusty rock and earth highway. Stopping to change a flat tire could be fatal.

Fox Company had three primary missions at Liberty Bridge: to protect both sides of the bridge; to prevent the enemy from setting in mines on the road from Liberty Bridge to a point two and one half miles in the direction of An Hoa; and to provide mutual support for the 105mm howitzer battery that occupied about one-third of the high ground with Fox. To accomplish these missions, Fox sent one platoon to the north side of the river, kept one platoon at its hilltop location on the south side, and sent its third platoon out on night ambushes along the first stretch of the road to An Hoa. These tasks would rotate between the platoons every two or three days.

Fox's command group had undergone a significant change. By mid-August, the pleasant and efficient Gunnery Sergeant Ed VanValkenburgh had been transferred to An Hoa to become the battalion logistics chief. Taking his place as the company's senior field enlisted Marine and Captain Brown's principal combat advisor was Gunnery Sergeant Vernon Dierdalh. Both were big men with combat experience, but Dierdalh was different than the effervescent VanValkenburgh. Dierdalh, while handsome with salt and pepper hair, had a gorilla-like physique with powerful shoulders and longer-than-normal arms. When Dierdalh talked, he stared deeply into the other person's eyes. To Brown, this was assuring. To the troops, that visual penetration brought fear and perhaps intimidation. His conversation was measured. His voice was low pitched and scratchy. His words were whispered. The pleasant days with

VanValkenburgh were gone instantly. Under Dierdalh, the ultra-serious, never-ending preparations for combat lie ahead.

With that change, the men of the 3rd Platoon executed Fox's missions without complaints and, as a matter of fact, with gusto. On 20 August Corporal "Bo" Borunda, who had again become a squad leader and attained the rank of corporal, and his squad had taken a few casualties while on patrol away from Fox's hilltop. After the injured had been evacuated, Borunda and his men had to bring all of the gear of those evacuated back to the company position, on the hilltop at Phu Lac (6). Borunda grabbed a pack, which weighed sixty to eighty pounds, and slung it over his shoulder with his own pack. The squad started back to the hilltop. Halfway there they had to cross a large body of water that came up to the neck of Borunda's long-time buddy, Corporal Rich Carter.

Once Carter emerged from the water he looked back at the men still crossing and saw a gap in the column were Borunda should have been. He looked closer and he realized that Borunda was crossing under the water! Only the top of his helmet and his forearms could be seen. One was holding his rifle and the other was holding the strap of the extra pack he was carrying. He had crossed thirty feet of water holding his breath. When he finally came out, all he said was "Jesus! I didn't think I could hold my breath any longer!"

That evening the 3rd Platoon had been assigned to place night ambushes to the east of the Liberty Bridge. Second Lieutenant Melton, Corporal Borunda's and Corporal Carter's platoon commander, ordered all the squad leaders to his bunker where he was going to discuss the ambush plans for that night. When Borunda didn't show, the lieutenant ordered Carter to locate him.

Corporal Carter found Corporal Borunda's squad by the concertina gate and asked Lance Corporal Westfall about the whereabouts of Borunda. Without saying a word, he pointed to a bicycle lying on the road. The bicycle belonged to a "cyclo" girl or prostitute who was peddling her wares in the area.

Just beyond the bicycle Rick spotted a section of elephant grass waving to and fro. Carter yelled out, "Hey, Bo! Is that you?"

A voice came back from the grass, "Yeah! What you want?"

Rich yelled back, "We have a squad leaders meeting at the CP. The lieutenant is waiting for you."

Borunda yelled back, "I'll be right there!" The grass swayed faster and faster.

Corporal Carter returned to the platoon CP. Second Lieutenant Melton asked, "Did you find Corporal Borunda?"

Carter replied, "Yes, Sir. I did."

Melton asked, "Well, when is he coming?"

Carter replied, "From what I could see when I left, I say about now, Sir!"

The 2nd Platoon, to which Dennis Cadigan was assigned, recovered from the accidental napalm attack suffered in early August. By 11 September it had grown to its full strength of about thirty-five Marines plus one corpsman. Cadigan's platoon commander was a second lieutenant by the name of Jim Glum, who seemed to be a quiet, likable person. Mostly, though, Cadigan hung around Jerry Evans, another machine gunner who he'd met at Liberty Bridge. Nightly, Cadigan and Jerry would play "Wisk" with J.D. Moore and Ken Murray.

1800 hours. On 11 September the night ambush mission rotated to the 1st Platoon. Private First Class Rod Gurganious, another Fox Company Marine, assigned to the 1st Platoon, was prepared for the mission. Their very enthusiastic platoon commander, Second Lieutenant Woody Lott, had them ready to go early. As Gurganious, with battle gear on, stood looking down the road they were about to travel to set up their night ambushes, Captain Brown emerged from his sand bagged-covered hole he called the "command bunker." He spoke briefly with Lieutenant Lott then disappeared. It seemed to Gurganious that there had been a change of plans. He thought this was highly unusual.

Apparently, two trucks, loaded with ammunition, had arrived at the river-crossing point too late. They would have to wait until morning to cross. This ammunition needed to be guarded at all cost. What was unknown to Gurganious was the fact that the captain felt more comfortable with Lieutenant Lott and his platoon sergeant, Staff Sergeant Easton, protecting the vital supply load than he did with Second Lieutenant Glum, who did not have a staff sergeant in the platoon sergeant position. Without knowing this, the captain's decision that the 1st Platoon should cross the river and guard trucks with its high-value contents all night seemed surprising to Gurganious and most of the men.

As a result, the 2nd Platoon would take on the ambush mission that night. Cadigan was one of two machine gunners in the 2nd Platoon. That morning a senior corporal by the name of Rominski or "Ski" returned from R&R. Cadigan would have normally been attached to Ski's squad. But, for no particular reason, Ski asked Jerry Evans if he wanted to go on the ambush with his squad. Evans said, "Yes."

Thus Private First Class Cadigan would, by default, go with Corporal George Blount's squad. Neither Corporal Evans, Private First Class Cadigan, nor Corporal Blount minded the switch since the whole platoon was leaving the Fox Company CP on the hill overlooking Liberty Bridge and setting up squad-sized ambushes at different sites about a mile and a half from there.

1900 hours. The 2nd Platoon lingered in the B-ration chow line apparently unaware of their deadline to depart. Captain Brown grew visibly upset with the fact that they were not already saddled up with their gear on, and that they had not left earlier. He signaled Second Lieutenant Glum into his command bunker. The lieutenant followed him quickly and the two men were swallowed inside the structure. The sound of a raised, muffled voice was barely audible as the captain chewed on Glum for his late departure. Proceeding Glum's hasty departure of the command bunker, Captain Brown's final words rang out noticeably, "Lieutenant Glum, I don't know, and I don't care what your hold up is! You get those men out there, pronto!"

Glum, along with most of the platoon believed they could get out to the ambush site and set up before any enemy could dig in land mines on this main road to An Hoa. After all, this was a nightly mission that alternately each one of Fox's platoons had been doing for the past month while experiencing no enemy contact or sightings.

1920 hours. The Second Lieutenant hurried away from the command bunker, and twenty minutes later, moved the platoon out. They departed the Fox Company position at the mid-point of dusk with only a few minutes of dim, evening, nautical light remaining until dark. Moving smartly, Ski's squad took the lead. Ski and his squad would set up furthest from Liberty Bridge, while Blount's squad would set up near the "lone tree at a big turn in the road." All Marine ground units in the An Hoa valley would patrol by this landmark at some time or another. They knew it well. Even truck convoy drivers and engineers sweeping the road had its location memorized. It was the only tree of any size between Liberty Bridge and An Hoa.

2005 hours. Blount's squad arrived at the turn in the road with the tree. Ski's squad was somewhere in front of them, perhaps 250–350 meters ahead. It was all but dark, yet fairly good visibility remained for about 150 meters. Suddenly, from nowhere an old farmer appeared, frantically babbling in Vietnamese. Glum, who was traveling with Blount's squad, attempted to talk with him. Blount directed the squad to begin setting in at the site.

2010 hours. Lieutenant Glum called Fox Company and asked for "Fox Six Actual". Captain Brown was the only member of the company who could speak more than the three or four phases of slang the troops had memorized: "Ba Mui Ba," or in English, "33," the brand name for Vietnam's national beer, "Di di mau!" "Move quickly!" and, "You want to boom-boom?" This fairly obvious question, of course, is not translatable in Vietnamese, but it made many young Americans feel as if they became part of the international cultural scene. Brown had been an advisor and, according to most of the Marines in the company, was fairly fluent in Vietnamese.

Dusk finally ended. Glum was engaged with the captain on the radio, the babbling farmer by his side. He held the phone to the farmer's face trying to get him to speak to the captain. The farmer, unfortunately, wanted no part of the technological device. Brown, still frustrated by the 2nd Platoon's late departure, told the lieutenant that he could not understand the colloquial babble and once again, ordered the platoon to get set in.

2015 hours. From seemingly everywhere at once, bullets began kicking up all around Cadigan and the rest of Blount's squad. Then, from the vicinity of Ski's squad, about 300 meters ahead, mortar explosions and gunfire filled the air. Abruptly, a "willie peter," white phosphorus flare, lit up the night. The men could tell that the firing emanated from a tree line about 1000 meters in front of them extremely close to a hamlet called Phu Lac (3) and from the south across a now visible rice paddy. Cadigan answered with his gun. Against all he had been taught, he shot without taking his finger off the trigger. This stream of fire partnered with Cadigan's surging adrenalin. His gun began to glow. Still angered, he knew he must stop to let it cool down.

Yelling into the radio, Blount shouted, "They're getting hit! They're getting hit! I think they're getting killed!"

All around him, Blount's squad hollered back and forth to combine their efforts. The riflemen coordinated their fire on the distant tree line across the rice paddy. Cadigan's gun finally cooled enough to let him shoot short bursts toward the area where the enemy flashpoints had appeared.

2030 hours. Instantly, the night was still. The Marines' eyes opened wider than normal to pick up any movement. The moon, now shining light on the tree at the bend in the road, cast a definite shadow. All ears listened keenly for any unknown noises that would alert Blount's squad to more enemy action. The babbling Vietnamese farmer, who had seemingly tried to warn the Marines of danger, had vanished.

"Fox Two, this is Fox Six. SITREP over." The voice of the company radio operator broke the stillness. Captain Brown's radio operator, Lance Corporal Bilski, requested a situation report from the 2nd Platoon.

"This is Two, wait," Private First Class Nonami, the 2nd Platoon radio operator replied, stretching the handset over to Lieutenant Glum.

Glum grabbed the handset and began with a harsh, trembling voice. "Six! Our lead squad got ambushed! They took casualties, that I'm sure! I'm not sure how many. The squad is about 200 meters in front of us." He paused to verify his next statement; "I believe most of the enemy fired from across the rice paddy somewhere to our left, over."

Captain Brown, who received the handset from Lance Corporal Bilski, replied, "Roger, Jim. Hold where you are, and I'll send the tanks up." A hard edge entered his tone as he continued, "Don't go up to that squad until the tanks get to your position. We'll use the tanks to get the wounded out. I'll send out a squad from the 3rd Platoon to remain there for the rest of the night. You bring your platoon back with the tanks, over."

"Roger, Six, out."

Second Lieutenant Glum and the rest of his men waited miserably for the arrival of the tanks. The knowledge that they could not help the Marines hit by the ambush pressed down on all. The moans of the wounded and dying Marines ahead of them eventually faded and the survivors knew only too well what that meant.

2040 hours. A total of ten minutes later, the clicking and cranking of the two M-48 tanks attached to Fox Company could be heard leaving Fox Company's hilltop location. The rumbling, a most welcome sound to the waiting Marines, roared loudly in the now-still night. Twenty-five minutes after the ambush, the immense machines ground to a halt on the road by the lone tree. Blount's squad, the lieutenant, and his radio operator, fell in behind the tanks and jogged up to Ski's location.

Rominski, looking wholly disoriented, was turning over a body. It was the body of Jerry Evans. Jerry's head held three bullet holes. Another bullet hit his willie peter flare, and had burned his body black. Cadigan, who had hustled forward behind the tanks, watched Ski turn the body back over and begin throwing up on the road.

Cadigan's stomach tightened and he fought back his nausea. Rage overtook him. Cadigan's mind repeated...He's dead! He's dead...over and over until an even more horrifying and guilty thought invaded...It could have been me!

Cadigan spun his gun at the distant tree line and began firing all his rounds while screaming at the top of his lungs, "You mother fuckers! You mother fuckers!"

He began to process polar feelings: one that he was glad the other guy was dead and not he; and an overwhelming guilty feeling for feeling any joy whatsoever.

Seven Marines from the 2nd Platoon were killed and another eight were wounded that evening. The Marines from the 3rd Platoon that accompanied the tanks to the ambush site assisted the eight wounded from Ski's squad onto one tank. On the other, they piled the seven slouching and bloodied bodies of their buddies. Blount's squad and the remnants of the platoon accompanied the tanks back to Fox's hilltop position on foot. The Marines of the 2nd Platoon were back by 2300 hours and were ordered to fill the defensive positions vacated by the 3rd Platoon.

The hours of the night ticked along like days. Most 2nd Platoon Marines stayed in bunkers and were chilled as the cool night air dried their sweaty, blood-drenched, and torn camouflage uniforms. Private First Class Cadigan remained in a bunker alone for most of the evening. From Da Nang, choppers arrived around 0200 to evacuate the wounded. At that time, Captain Brown, the rest of the 3rd Platoon, and the two tanks returned to the ambush site.

The sun rose that morning at about 0530. The 2nd Platoon Marines tried not to stare at their dead compatriots whose bodies were lined up ready for evacuation. They failed in their attempt. J.D. Moore, Ken

Murray and Cadigan looked at the stiffened bodies of their former friends. Very few were inside the body bags the company had on hand that night. The others, Cadigan's good friend Jerry Evans, and another Marine who had been there only a week, were badly mangled and needed the heavy rubber bags the evac choppers would bring.

Cadigan thought to himself…we'll get them for you…We'll get them.

0630 hours. Lott, Easton, Gurganious, and the rest of 1st Platoon returned from the north side of the Song Thu Bon with the two ammunition trucks. They experienced no incidents that evening.

0730hours. A Huey from An Hoa brought a chaplain to Fox's position. The chaplain completed a five-minute service, then departed on the waiting chopper.

0815 hours. The 1st and 2nd Platoons marched the one and one-half miles to join the rest of Fox Company now located near the lone tree at the curve in the road. The defense of the hill above Liberty Bridge was left solely to the artillery battery. Immediately, Captain Brown called the platoon commanders to his position. His order centered on the hamlet that had launched the previous night's ambush. They would attack Phu Lac (3). The lieutenants in turn, gave orders to their squad leaders. Private First Class Cadigan, Lance Corporal J.D. Moore, and a Marine by the name of Private Bobby Martinez were to move with their machine guns to a small knoll above a rice-paddy. This knoll was 500 meters north of the lone tree and about one hundred meters off of the road toward the Phu Lac (3).

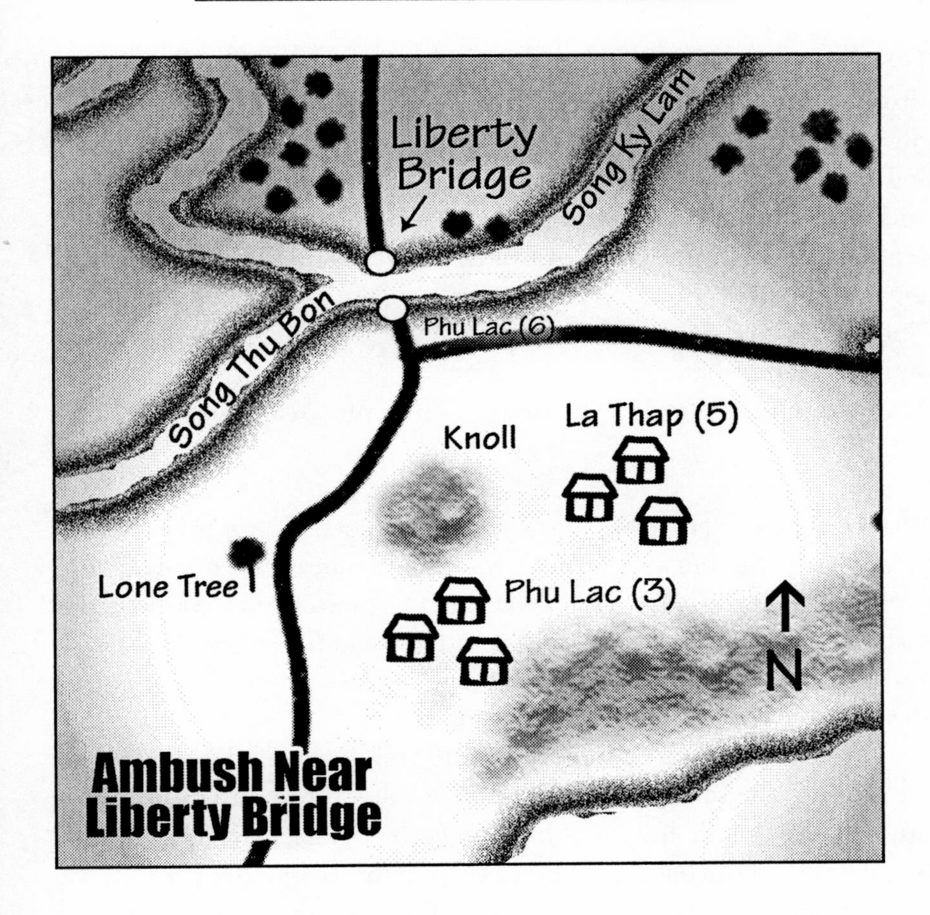

While Cadigan's and Moore's guns laid down a base of fire, the 1st Platoon would envelop the area left of Cadigan's position and occupy the high ground just to the east of the hamlet. With the high ground taken, the 1st Platoon would lay its own base of fire on the hamlet and allow the 2nd and 3rd Platoons to cross the rice paddy and assault into the heart of Phu Lac (3).

0915 hours. Cadigan and Moore began setting up their guns on the knoll. From their position they observed eight VC escaping to La Thap (5), the nearest hamlet more than 500 meters away. The VC were carrying a mortar tube, machine gun, and two AK-47s.

J.D. Moore got on his radio and barked, "Gooks in front of us! Gooks in front of us! We can see mortars, machine guns, and AK-47s." Cadigan's nostrils flared as he watched the men escape. Their weapons belied the truth; they were the same that were used the night before. Those were the very weapons that had so violently, and irrevocably stolen the lives of his friends...of Evans. Pouncing like a lion on its prey, Cadigan jumped on his gun ready to fire.

"Hold your fire! Say again, hold your fire!" someone barked over the company's tactical net.

Moore's tone dropped with disappointment, "Yeah, we're holding fire."

0920 hours. Private First Class Cadigan watched the enemy fade into the rice paddy, the muscles in his jaw clenching and then unclenching. Lance Corporal Moore tried to explain that Captain Brown was worried that the 1st Platoon could get caught in the cross fire when, "Crack!" a round snapped over Cadigan's head.

J.D. mumbled a softly uttered, "Aarrrghh."

Stunned, Cadigan turned to see Moore roll down the knoll into the rice paddy on the safe side of the hill. He yelled, "Corpsman up!" and scrambled down the hill catching up with J.D. He wrestled out of Moore's uniform the bandage Moore carried in his 1st aid kit.

Crying and somehow swearing at the same time, J.D. writhed as Cadigan's hands looped, then fastened the bandage around Moore's shot up leg. Knowing his bandage would suffice until J.D. could be medevacuated, Cadigan pushed himself off of the ground. Anger didn't quite cover his feelings at that moment. Cadigan's vision blurred as he squinted and grunted his way back up the hill to his position. They wouldn't get away this time. He wouldn't let them; he couldn't let them.

Grabbing his machine gun, he let it rip. Lying on the ground where Moore dropped the radio's handset, a voice screamed out, "Hold your fire! Hold your fire!"

Private First Class Cadigan's toughness and ire had yet to be harnessed during his first month in country. He knew his machine gun could win the war. Captain Brown's plan included more than just Cadigan's machine gun, however. The hamlet of Phu Lac (3), consisting of twenty some odd straw hooches, would be prepped by air and artillery prior to the company's assault. Cadigan's gun would be used in a fire-support role during the ground assault.

Temporarily exhausted, Cadigan was forced to extend the gun's bipods and place the machine gun on the ground to wait for the air show.

An F-4 Phantom aircraft swooped down on Phu Lac (3) dropping bombs and firing its 20mm cannon. The hamlet was all but dismantled. Only about eight to ten damaged straw hooches were left standing. After the jet's last pass, a Vietnamese woman, naked from the waist up and bleeding from multiple fragment wounds, came running out of a hooch carrying a small child. The child, also bleeding from multiple wounds, was crying over the shouts from the Vietnamese woman. Private First Class Cadigan stopped firing immediately to allow the woman to run to the Marines behind the knoll for safety from the VC who had previously occupied the village. Doc Stork, whose nickname befitted this tall blond-haired kid with a prominent nose, was the 2nd platoon corpsman. Stork, who had been working on Lance Corporal Moore, immediately met the woman and began applying sulfur and bandages to her wounds.

One of the Vietnamese interpreters followed Stork, and grabbing the woman, interrogated her in Vietnamese. From afar, the thundering blades of a CH-46 medevac chopper whipped up dirt as it landed on the road. Cadigan, Stork, and Martinez hustled to the plane carrying Moore with them.

Cadigan continued to watch the shrinking chopper with a heavy heart. Moore had taught him more than he'd ever learned at Camp Lejeune or Camp Pendleton. From Moore, Cadigan learned unpublished techniques about the gun, how to keep pace with the riflemen, and how to conduct himself on patrol. Now he was gone. In five weeks, Cadigan witnessed guys leaving faster than he could learn their names.

1015 hours. While Moore was in the air and on his way to a Da Nang hospital, the 2nd and 3rd Platoons swooped into the hamlet of Phu Lac (3) with one thing on every Marine's mind—revenge. This was the spot where the firing had come from the night before. Cadigan pressed in to join them, observing the Marines fragging the bunkers and underground tunnels that connected the hooches, but the enemy was gone.

Cadigan, standing but a few feet away, watched the angry captain screaming in Vietnamese at one woman they found. The woman had been hiding in a tunnel below her hooch. Cadigan soon learned that this woman and the two or three beetle-nut chewing women with her not only told Captain Brown that they did not know where the VC had gone, but they claimed they never even saw any VC. Brown's ability to curse so freely in Vietnamese shocked Cadigan, who had pushed closer, pleased to watch his captain at work.

Brown's anger boiled within him. He had watched Fox take nineteen casualties a month earlier while capturing the 75mm recoilless rifle, seen thirty-three men burned an hour later by a napalm bomb, and last night witnessed the dead bodies of seven of his Marines killed and eight wounded. The memory of those fine Marines stacked on the two tanks was still etched clearly in his mind. While everyone watched him in awe, he slammed his helmet onto the ground. His hands clenched at his sides, Brown stomped over to the idling tanks, which had been part of the ground assault and yelled, "Sergeant Haley!"

The sergeant, who had observed Brown's interrogation, had removed his green motor cycle-like helmet and said loudly to ensure he was heard over the diesel engines, "Sir!"

"Those lying bitches!" Brown snorted. "They didn't know anything about the VC who killed our men last night. Well, fuck 'em. Take those tanks and flatten this whole damn place. I don't want anyone to live here again!"

"Aye, aye, Sir!" Haley chirped with a broad grin on his face. Haley felt like a kid in a candy store with a five-dollar bill in his hand.

Dennis Cadigan stepped back in shock as he watched the company's two attached tanks run over the remaining hooches.

Fox changed. From that moment, a deep, pervasive, enveloping need to destroy their enemy set in. The men of Fox Company exemplified a condition described in a WWII book, entitled Bloodlust, in which, "Killing the enemy" was a natural, good emotion after traumatizing events.

Fox patrolled steadily in the Phu Nhuans for most of the month of September. For three days each month the rifle companies rotated to the rear at An Hoa to change uniforms, shower, drink beer, eat regular food called A-rations, or almost regular food called B-rations, and get paid, etc. For the other twenty-seven days, rifle companies patrolled and ambushed one area for about three days, then moved ten kilometers, six to seven miles, away and began patrolling and ambushing again. All the while, they were conducting search and clear operations. During these twenty-seven days in the field, the troops stunk up their tattered camouflaged utilities. Most had running sores from infected scratches on their forearms. The men not on patrol during the day would be resting for all night ambushes. Often the Marines could be found without boots and socks while drying out their feet. None wore skivvies.

While moving, all wore issued green bath towels around their necks, flak jackets unbuttoned, against the orders given by the battalion commander, and helmets with chin with straps open. Dennis Cadigan displayed two five-foot bandoleers of linked machine gun rounds around his neck crossing over each other at his navel and at the back of his neck. Lieutenant Colonel Stemple hated this. But since Stemple would only see the company once a week for a ten to twenty minute visit, Captain Brown, now known as "The Skipper," allowed these small idiosyncrasies betting that his non-commissioned officers would be able to instantly get the MG links boxed, jackets snapped, and helmet straps hooked should the requirement arise or Stemple show up unexpectedly. Even with the more relaxed field atmosphere, there was never a loss of their "blood lust", which countered the continuous negative contributions brought on by the heat, rain, insects, mines, and booby traps.

CHAPTER 13: FOX COMPANY WANTED DEAD OR ALIVE

By the end of September, Fox and Hotel Companies had been chopped to the 1st Battalion, 5th Marines, 1/5, while 2/5 was conducting an operation away from the An Hoa valley. Hotel was operating about two kilometers east of Liberty Bridge, while Fox was operating about seven kilometers southwest of them. Both were on search and clear operations. On Sunday, 29 September 1968, the men of Fox were feeling relaxed after having completed a week's worth of search and clear operations without incident. A chaplain was in the field at 1/5's command post. Fox was nearby. Captain Brown and others attended the chaplain's service.

Captain Brown expected the recently promoted operations officer and old friend, Major Marty Brandtner, to give him a new operating area later that afternoon for next week's search and clear operation. Brown, who often enjoyed taking the initiative, talked briefly to the battalion commander, Lieutenant Colonel R. F. Daley, and recommended Fox be sent to a position seven klicks to the east and near Go Noi Island, somewhat closer to Hotel Company, but still in 1/5's area of operations. Brown used to refer to this area as "Marlboro Country". Every time Fox had a contact with a VC unit, the enemy would escape in that direction, and Fox wasn't able to pursue because that would be going out of the regimental Tactical Area of Responsibility. Marlboro Country not only contained the VC Fox was anxious to settle the score with, but it also held neither mines nor many booby traps.

In Vietnam, by means of the radio, Marines could monitor the actions of the other companies. Such was the case on this particular Sunday afternoon. Radio transmissions revealed that Hotel Company had come under heavy fire at a bunker complex near the hamlet of Cu Ban (4). Cadigan listened to their radio traffic indicating they were getting beat up from snipers in dug-in bunkers. Within minutes Fox's "blood lust" started to grow. The skipper, spurred on by his men's hunger, visited his friend, Major Brandtner; within the hour Fox was making a seven-klick speed march toward "Marlboro Country" and Hotel's rescue.

1530 hours. Private First Class Cadigan's new platoon sergeant, Staff Sergeant Marshall, was a self-confident and wiry African American. Marshall was replacing Second Lieutenant Glum who was in An Hoa on a temporary assignment.

Before his injury J. D. Moore taught Cadigan to never walk on the flank with the machine gun. "Stay in line," he used to always say. "Don't let anyone put you on the flank."

Accordingly, when Marshall said, "Cadigan, it's your turn to take the flank!"

Cadigan replied, "Sir, a machine gunner always stays in the column!"

To which Marshall responded, "Bullshit on that crap. Get out in the flank!"

Cadigan countered, "I ain't going, Sir."

Until Marshall finally said, "Get out on the flank, or I'll court martial your ass!"

Cadigan grumbled, "Okay!" and went out on the flank.

Cadigan moved into the rice paddy. The others marched on top of the dike while he soon found himself up to his waist in water holding the gun over his head for the next quarter mile. The company's pace was nearly double-time while Cadigan plowed through the paddy's deep water getting further and further behind. Finally, Cadigan climbed out of the paddy and onto the dike. He squeezed the water from his boots and screamed at his sergeant, "What a friggin' asshole you are!"

Marshall was pleased with himself for getting Cadigan to follow orders. Cadigan never saw the slight smile on Marshall's face.

1800 hours. At dusk Fox began entering the perimeter of Hotel Company. The march had taken nearly three hours. The hasty move had disrupted the planned resupply for Fox Company, but Hotel was thrilled to see another company and gladly shared their provisions. By this time Hotel had suffered six KIA and twelve to fourteen WIA from the enemy.

2130 hours. Although the men of Company F were dead tired, the skipper received an order from Major Brandtner to conduct a predawn attack on a hamlet named La Bac (1) some 1500 meters away on the edge of Go Noi Island.

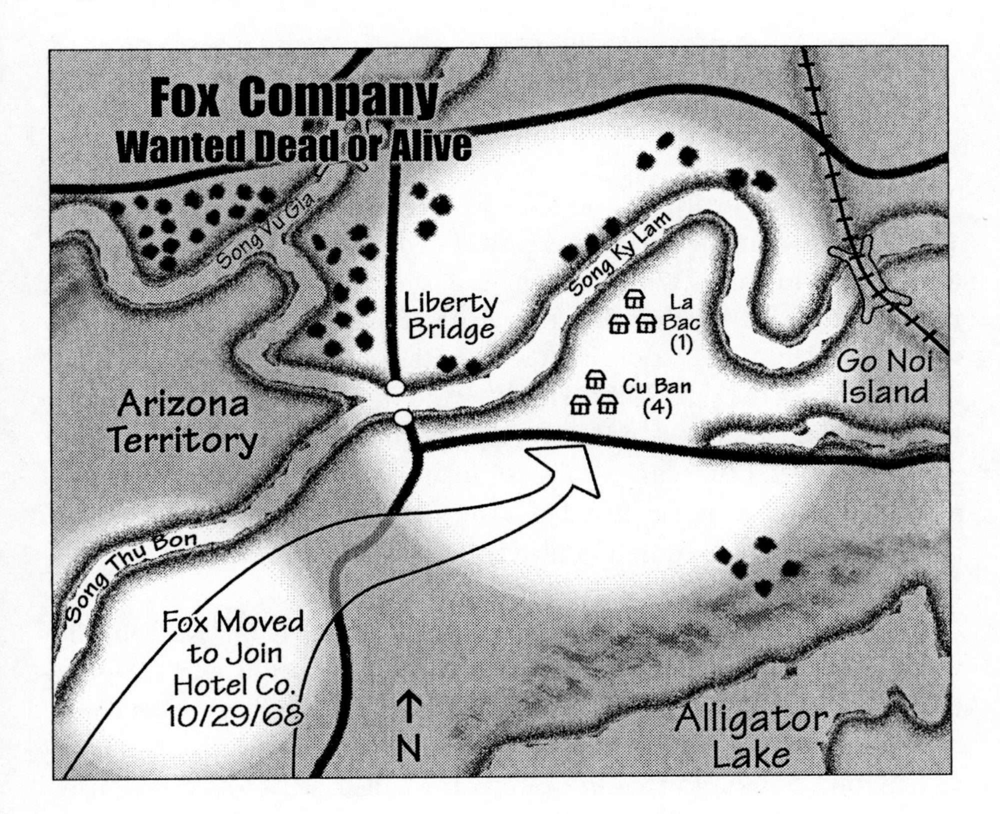

0300 hours. This was just what Fox had waited for! Fox departed Hotel's position in the pre-dawn hours of 30 September. Since this was away from the An Hoa valley, there were no mines to worry about. Nevertheless, the movement of the 120-man Fox Company proved difficult and slow in that there were no established paths to follow and the night was moonless. Fox had no experience conducting night maneuvers because they only operated during daylight in the mine-infested area of An Hoa. They moved as silently as possible toward the probable line of deployment, which was a dry creek bed 200 meters south of the hamlet. Medium to loud whispers from these inexperienced night warriors could be heard the entire way. Comments were made like, "Hey, tell those guys in front to slow the hell down!" and "You can bet your sweet ass when I get back to the world, I won't be doing shit like this in the middle of the damn night!"

Every now and then the non-commissioned officers would chime in with something like, "If someone doesn't tell Smith to keep his damn trap shut, I'll come up there and shut it for him!"

0530 hours. Finally, just before dawn, Fox reached the dry riverbed. The platoons, actually silent this time, lined up from left-to-right: second, first, and third. Without signaling, the company crossed the dry riverbed on line looking like they had rehearsed the maneuver for weeks. Suddenly, a burst of fire from a withdrawing VC's carbine could be heard along the right flank. The 3rd Platoon responded with counter-fire for about twenty seconds, then, all was quiet as the company moved into the hamlet. Dawn greeted the company's arrival. By 0700 Fox began a detailed search of the village. This took about three hours as there were approximately one hundred huts in this large hamlet.

0715 hours. During the search, Second Lieutenant Bill Melton, the veteran 3rd Platoon Commander, visited the Captain Brown. "Capt'n, Fox's fire discipline was really impressive during that assault; most companies would have gone wild if they were getting shot at! I hate to have to tell you, though, our earlier return fire killed a baby and seriously wounded its older bother and sister. Doc Connelly and Doc Stork are trying to save them now but it doesn't look too good. The kids must have gotten scared and ran when that gook opened up on us. It breaks my heart."

Captain Brown, accompanying Second Lieutenant Melton, tried to comfort the weeping mother, giving her his condolences. Images of his wife and young son filled his thoughts. He shook his head to clear his loved ones out of his battle-ready mind. When his repeated attempts failed, Brown racked his brain for a way to help the sobbing woman. He decided to give her 200 piasters, which wasn't a whole heck of a lot of Vietnamese money, but the mother took it and instantly stopped crying.

Stunned, Melton asked, "Why the heck did she stop crying?"

The captain responded, "Beats the crap out of me! They're funny people." Although they did every thing possible to save the children, both died.

1030 hours. Fox, north of Cu Ban (4), prepared to continue the attack to the northeast along the edge of Go Noi Island. Meanwhile, Hotel, south of Cu Ban (4), began receiving sniper fire from the hamlet. Hotel's return fire began impacting harmlessly around Fox. Brown loved it when a plan came together. The two companies had the enemy just where they wanted them: right in the middle. The VC had been successful before with Hotel, but this time they miscalculated the fact that the Fox Company tigers, with blood lust in their hearts, were about to spring upon them.

1100 hours. Fox moved out of La Bac (1) and returned across the dry creek bed to close in on the enemy while Hotel held the same position it occupied the evening before. Hotel would remain in place as a blocking force. This would allow Fox to squeeze down on the enemy while moving in on Hotel. Notwithstanding this simple concept, Hotel was pinned down and its company commander couldn't determine the enemy's exact location. Fox believed that the enemy was about 450 meters southeast of its lead squads in Cu Ban (4). Fox was unaware that they faced almost sixty enemy, both North Vietnamese Army and Main Force Viet Cong. Their foe was armed with AK-47 sub-machine guns, anti-tank rocket launchers, and other weapons.

1135 hours. Reaching a stalemate with Hotel Company, the enemy turned its attention toward the pressure they felt from the Fox Marines bearing down on them. Captain Brown ordered the platoons on line and called for a napalm strike on the enemy's flank from where Fox was taking fire. The company maintained its cover in a high, dry creek bed embankment, large and long enough to hold most of the men. While Fox waited for the F-4's approach from Da Nang, the enemy's defensive fields of fire raked lead that impacted at the edge of the embankment for thirty minutes without ceasing. Leaning against the creek's bank for safety with rounds cracking overhead, all felt as if they were back at a Marine Corps rifle range pulling butts during marksmanship training.

1200 hours. While Fox was temporarily immobile, unremitting and unrelenting enemy fire continued. The excitement seemed to overwhelm the men. They became hungrier and hungrier for their chance to strike. Captain Brown did not want to attack the 450 meters across an open field, leaving his men exposed and easy targets, so he shifted the three platoons left along the creek bed and immediately below the tree line defining the northern edge of Cu Ban (4). The 2nd Platoon, already on the left flank, moved further west. The 3rd Platoon remained directly in the center. The 1st Platoon tied into the 3rd Platoon taking up positions below four spider holes containing enemy soldiers.

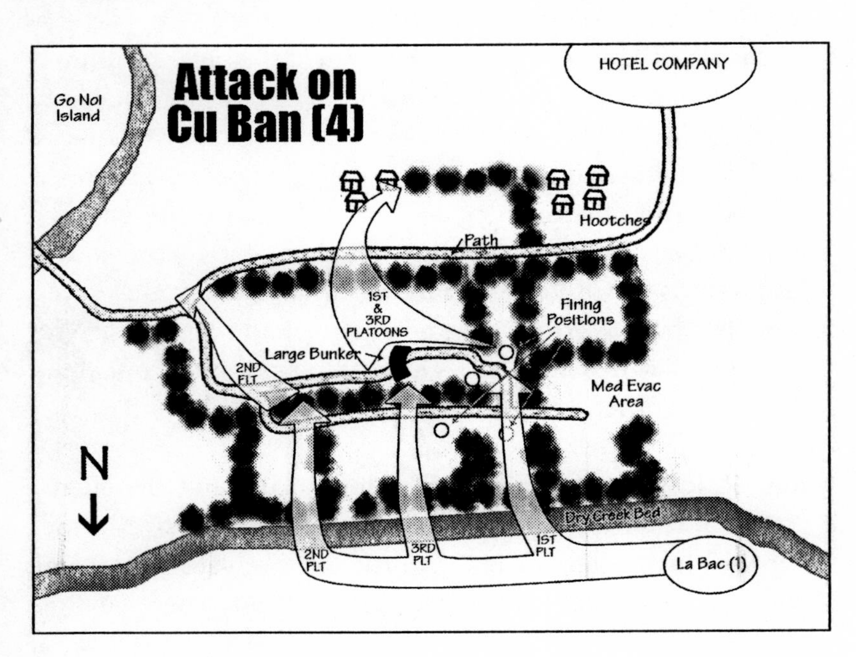

The Marine Corps OV-10 Bronco aerial observer reported seeing several enemy soldiers run into a large bunker about seventy-five meters in front of Fox Company.

Lieutenant Colonel Daley, the 1/5 Battalion Commander, called Brown on the radio. "Fox Six, this is Millbrook Six, over."

Bilski looked at the captain handing him the handset and yelling over the gunfire cracking overhead, "Sir, the colonel wants to speak to you."

"This is Fox Six, over."

"Fox Six, what are your intentions, over?"

"We have good contact with the enemy, and I'm planning to assault them before they slip away, over."

"Fox Six, you ought to wait for the air and arty to prep the village before you begin your attack."

"Sir, we've done that before and by the time we made the assault they had gotten away. I'll soften them up with the Bronco, over," Brown countered.

"Roger, Fox Six, It's your call, out."

1220 hours. With enemy firing in front of the company from within the tree line, Captain Brown had the OV-10 prep the area around the large bunker with 2.5-inch rockets. He canceled the Napalm at the same time. He motioned a predetermined signal to Second Lieutenant Woody Lott with the 1st Platoon and Second Lieutenant Bill Melton with the 3rd Platoon and catching each man's attention, didn't have to say a word. They were ready to go.

Within seconds after the Bronco's last rocket hit, Fox was roaring through the intermittent, but thick hedgerows. To maintain control Brown immediately shadowed the assaulting platoons with his small command group. Eight enemy sub-machine guns intensified their fire, but the assaulting platoons' momentum would not be stopped. Within a minute of their initial charge, Brown passed over three dead enemy soldiers in their spider holes still clutching weapons in their hands. This was the same ground covered in the 1st Platoon's assault. Brown held that platoon's progress there.

1230 hours. Staff Sergeant Marshall and Corporal Blount led the 2nd Platoon's charge out of the bank on the left flank of the company. They burst through the tree line and began firing across the open field in front of them.

Private First Class Ted Lush was on the 2nd Platoon's weapons-section radio. Ted was the new guy in country. He'd been in Vietnam for a short two weeks. Private First Class Cadigan looked at him and Lance Corporal Ken Murray to his right, saying, "We've got to go!"

The machine gun team exchanged glances with each other, "Yeah!" came their ready replies. Together they yelled above the din, "On one!" They moved. Charging through the tree line that bordered the dry creek and maneuvering, they fired continuously as they bolted the 250 meters while zigzagging back and forth across the open field.

Before the 3rd Platoon could begin its assault on the large command bunker in front of them they had to penetrate two tree lines. They moved toward the first, only to discover a seemingly unbreechable barbed-wire fence. The right squad found a hole in the fence and the platoon funneled through it. The squads aligned for a frontal assault. Corporal Borunda's squad was left. Corporal Carter was with the center squad and Second Lieutenant Melton was with Lance Corporal Scott Sampietro's squad on the right. The bunker, designed as a shelter against bombs and artillery, resembled an igloo with a grass top. It had a front entrance, a tunnel entrance at the rear that led to an escape trench, and a few openings for firing weapons and throwing grenades. An estimated enemy strength of eleven soldiers had barricaded themselves inside the bunker, all armed with automatic weapons. The enemy outside the bunker lobbed over forty plus grenades during the next ten minutes using the back of the bunker for safety.

1245 hours. During a hail of gunfire impacting near him, Sampietro saw a hand grenade land two meters from one of his wounded men being treated by a corpsman. Shouting, "Grenade!" Sampietro intuitively threw his body across his two compatriots as the grenade exploded. The shrapnel miraculously passed over him but the concussion severely bruised his back and legs. He arose calmly as if nothing happened and, with gritted teeth, continued his attack.

The Marines and their enemy continually exchanged fire during the assault. Clumps of dirt, vegetation, and men exploded into the air with each grenade blast. Slowly, steadily, purposefully, the men of 3rd Platoon pressed in on their prey. At the front of the fray, Second Lieutenant Bill Melton, pistol in hand, led the final assault and overran it. Seven enemy hurried out of the rear entrance of the bunker attempting to escape, but Corporal Borunda's squad cut them down forming a pile of bodies high along the trenched rear path. Unknown to the men involved at that time, amid the explosions, constant fire, the charge on the bunker, and the general heroism of the Marines of the 3rd Platoon, the capture of the large bunker earned them two Silver Star Medals, two Bronze Star Medals, two Navy Achievement Medals and five Purple Hearts during that one assault.

1330 hours. Captain Brown arrived and began reorganizing the 1st and 3rd Platoons to continue the attack when, without warning, two enemy who had been hiding just outside of the bunker, launched out of their position, darted out of the tall grass, and made a run for it. The captain didn't need to react; forty Marines, their weapons still on automatic and adrenalin still pumping, allowed for a very short run. Brown pressed Fox's momentum. He had the 1st and 3rd Platoons follow the blood trails of their retreating enemy that led toward a set of hooches between the bunker and Hotel Company. He had the gunny begin coordinating the evacuation of the wounded then moved over to join the 2nd Platoon.

1400 hours. The lead Marines of the 2nd Platoon saw yet another thick tree line masking what look like a bombed out village ahead of them. Those few hooches turned out to be the eastern portion of Cu Ban (4) and the escape door to Go Noi Island, the enemy's safe haven. About twelve enemy, some retreating and others holding their positions, fired on the attacking platoon. Radio traffic picked up as the 2nd Platoon's radio operator, Private First Class Morrison, reported in, "Fox, this is Fox Two. The gooks have NVA helmets, over!"

1415 hours. Half way across the field, Dennis Cadigan's machine gun double fed and jammed. He knelt down while the men from the 2nd Platoon ran by firing and yelling. He tried to clear the double feed. It wouldn't budge. Cadigan's eyes cast frantically around him until he spotted a ditch. He bolted for it, hurling himself into the ditch to find cover. Desperately, he tried to pull the jammed rounds from the chamber to clear his gun. Suddenly, Cadigan heard a voice above him. He looked up to find a Vietnamese soldier in black pajamas, a half smile on his face, pointing his AK-47 into the ditch. The VC let fly with a burst right at Cadigan. Somehow, the burst tore over his head as the barrel of the AK-47 rode up into the air. The gook must have fired fifteen rounds all at one time. Cadigan swung his gun up at him. The VC didn't know the machine gun wouldn't work. Taking just one look at the machine gun, the VC spun on his heels and sprinted away. Instantly, Cadigan heard himself screaming for anyone to come help him; he had no weapon at all. Unexpectedly, a Marine by the name of "Huey" came flying back shouting, "What are you doing?"

"My gun double fed," Cadigan yelled. "I don't have any thing to shoot with."

Huey handed Cadigan a .45 caliber pistol. Grabbing the pistol and the jammed machine gun, Cadigan leapt out of the ditch and charged toward the tree line with only the hand gun working as the battle raged on in front of him. Cadigan suppressed the terror that rose in him as he faced the ferocity of the firefight with a pistol instead of his machine gun in his hand.

1420 hours. Over the radio Corporal Blount's voice rang out distinctly, "Mo's been hit! Mo's been hit! We need support. NVA are all around us!" Private First Class Cadigan and Huey hustled to join several Marines ahead of them on a nearby trail. Private First Class Morrison was on the ground. A round had shattered his leg. Lying around him was a couple of dead NVA. Corporal Blount had shot them with an M-79 grenade launcher at almost point-blank range. Together the squad collected Morrison and began running down the trail. Miraculously, the jam popped and fired, clearing Cadigan's machine gun.

1450 hours. Cadigan and the 2nd Platoon, now in columns, observed six to eight enemy soldiers running by some hooches toward Go Noi Island. Cadigan grabbed his gun and began firing at the hip. It double fed again. He flung the gun on the ground, and turned, snatching a rifle from the grip of a redheaded Marine next to him. The Marine blurted, "Hey!"

Cadigan barked back at him, "There are gooks over there, running by those hooches!" He started firing. The rest of the 2nd Platoon joined in and soon everyone was firing. One enemy lurched forward, arms swinging out unevenly at his sides, as a round slammed into his retreating form.

1515 hours. Brown held up the 2nd Platoon's progress at the edge of Cu Ban (4). The platoon had taken four casualties, two required an emergency medevac. Brown knew the wounded had to be moved back near the bunker for evacuation where the gunny was locating a secure area for the medevac chopper to land. He quickly interrogated several nervous women fleeing the area who reported that over thirty enemy had just fled carrying their wounded toward Go Noi Island. That area would be out of the regimental TAOR, so Brown directed the Aerial Observer in the OV-10 to locate the retreating enemy and call in an air strike.

1535 hours. The 2nd Platoon returned to the large bunker with the company command group, near the chosen medevac landing site. The bunker area was not only filled with the dead enemy and their equipment, but some of the missing packs, mail bag, weapons, and a tactical radio the enemy had taken off of Hotel Company the day before. 2nd

Platoon Marines were sitting around taking their first break in nearly four hours, drinking water and smoking cigarettes. Cadigan, sitting on a tree stump, was about to light a cigarette when he saw the face of a VC staring at him from inside the large bunker about twenty-five feet away. Cadigan stared at him stupidly. The Vietnamese stared back. Suddenly, Cadigan screamed, "Gook!" rolling right off the tree stump to duck behind it.

The Marines scattered. Cadigan picked up the .45 caliber pistol and crawled around the stump towards the bunker. With his back safely away from the bunker's apertures, Cadigan peeked inside while taking his pack off. He figured he'd climb down into the tunnel and hopefully get the VC by tossing a couple of grenades into the hole in front of him. Before he had a chance to react, their gung-ho sergeant, Marshall, ran up, demanding, "What's going on, Cadigan?"

Cadigan answered, "There's a gook, Sir. He's down inside the bunker. I guess the 3rd Platoon must have missed him when they assaulted the bunker."

"Here!" Marshall grunted, taking the gun and a couple of grenades from Cadigan. He slung off his pack and descended into the bunker entrance.

A grenade exploded.

Cadigan immediately identified the rapid fire of a pistol. As he searched for another pistol, Marshall reemerged from the tunnel entrance, having killed four enemy soldiers. He carried with him the pack of a NVA major who was a surgeon. Marshall also had a powder blue and red flag with the large yellow star in the middle, the national flag of the People's Democratic Republic of Vietnam. Several stars and other fringes hanging from it signified the combat decorations of a NVA battalion. Fox had scored a good hit.

1605 hours. Thundering blades of the medevac chopper echoed in the distance. The enemy, hidden in a group of hooches in front of the 1st and 3rd Platoons, let loose its firepower on the chopper. Captain Brown faced a new challenge. One set of enemy was withdrawing east toward

Go Noi Island and the other now fired on the chopper even though trapped in the half dozen hooches on the western side of the small hamlet. Brown held the attack of the 1st and 3rd Platoons in order to prevent the company from being too spread out and to concentrate on the medevac.

1610 hours. The corporal radio operator for the forward air controller, FAC, came running up to Brown. "Sir, the medevac chopper is refusing to land because they were getting fired on."

"What?" Brown roared, "Two of my guys are going to die if they don't get out! Give me that handset. What's their call sign?"

"Sir, its 'Safety Zone Two Alpha,'" his FAC responded, giving Brown the handset.

"Safety Zone Two Alpha, this is Fox Six, over," Brown barked, watching the chopper hover safely almost 500 meters to the north but within eyesight.

"This is Safety Zone Two Alpha, go."

"Safety Zone Two Alpha, did you locate the medevac site?"

"Errr, roger, Sir, but the site's too hot for us to land."

"Safety Zone Two Alpha, if you approach low from the west, you won't get shot at, over," Brown informed the pilot, his patience running out.

"Still too hot, Sir. We won't be able to come in until the LZ isn't hot," the lieutenant aviator replied. He had used "Sir" twice, revealing his relatively junior rank; Brown quickly matched it with his youthful voice.

"Safety Zone Two Alpha, we got a couple of men dying," he ground out slowly. "We have another fight ahead of us to kill those gooks that were firing on you and that will take until dark. So, you better get in and pick those guys up now!"

There was no response from the chopper.

"Tell you what, Lieutenant!" Brown growled. "I have sixty weapons and sixty dead-tired Marines. We have no patience for any one not picking up our wounded," Brown declared in the clearest terms. "One damn word from me to them and you'll be crashing in that rice paddy below you. And frankly, I don't give a rat's ass! Now you get into that site, and we'll be giving you some God damn cover!"

A significant pause followed Captain Brown's declaration.

"Errr, roger, Sir."

The chopper landed and the wounded were evacuated. Brown ordered the 1st and 3rd Platoons to prepare to make a two-platoon frontal assault on the set of hooches between Hotel and Fox. Meanwhile, Gunnery Sergeant Dierdalh was completing the redistribution of ammunition, captured and recaptured equipment, and supplies. He and the rest of the command group were saddling up to follow the 1st and 3rd Platoons' assault. The 2nd Platoon was on call; they would assist the walking wounded, cover the rear and join the company when needed.

1700 hours. Brown knew Fox had another fight ahead. Some wounded during the fight would need to be medevac'd before nightfall. The 1st and 3rd Platoons were primed, in position, and ready to finish off the enemy. There could be no delays. He raised the Hotel Company Commander on the radio, "Hotel Six, this is Fox Six, over."

After a moment Brown got his response, "Fox Six, this is Hotel Six, go ahead, go."

"Hotel Six, we're ending this fight here and now, over," Brown announced.

"Roger that, Fox Six, what'd you have in mind? Over."

"We're attacking straight toward you, so keep your heads down! We'll be coming in firing!"

The reply was immediate, "Fox Six, that's a roger! Come on in, over."

With that, the 1st and 3rd Platoons launched their third and final assault at the end of what turned out to be an exceedingly long day. Nine enemy soldiers had taken over the dozen or so hooches in that part of Cu Ban (4). Each hooch was separated by approximately ten meters and had underground tunnels that connected several hooches together. The tunnels had entrances both inside the huts and outside between them. These were designed to protect the indigenous from both US and VC fire. This configuration and the fact that the enemy were popping up at hooch windows like "pop-up" targets on a rifle range allowed the two lead platoons to maneuver up to the hooches. For nearly forty minutes Fox endured what seemed to be an endless rounds of hand grenades being thrown at them.

Even though Fox was technically under the operational control, OPCON, of 1/5 during this fight, word of its exploits and its incredible triumphs while facing a decorated NVA battalion unit soon prompted Lieutenant Colonel Stemple, the 2/5 commanding officer, to contact Brown for a Situation Report. Lance Corporal Bilski, Brown's radio operator, crouched beside the captain and pressed the handset toward Captain Brown, "Sir! It's Texas Pete Six!"

Brown and his radio operator were crouching low to avoid grenade shrapnel. Bilski turned around, handing the captain the radio handset. Explosions impacted and erupted all around them. Straw and thatched roofs scattered through the air as the attacking Marines fired at the enemy ahead of them. The M-16 rifles rattled in Brown's free ear as he reported in over the radio, "Sir! Fox Six, over."

"Dave, this is Texas Pete Six, how 'bout a SITREP? Over."

An explosion from a few feet away rocked Captain Brown. He regained his composure as Gunny Dierdalh released a shout, "Get down!"

Enemy soldiers popped up out of the tunnel holes behind the hooches. Bullets from the VC whizzed past Brown's ear, and the rifle fire from his own men caused Brown to breathe into the handset, "Say again, all after Texas Pete Six, over."

Two more grenades blasted in front of Captain Brown as the Lieutenant Colonel responded, "Dave, what's your situation? Over."

Showers of sand raining down upon the ground caused Brown to respond, "Say again, over."

Preoccupied, his adrenalin pumping, Brown was far too busy directing the Marines' fire as more VC popped out of hiding then to respond to his boss's question. An explosion from yet another grenade shook the ground again and Brown, while comprehending what his CO was asking for, did his best to respond. "Sir, 1st Platoon…"

Brown lowered the handset as he crouched away from another grenade detonation. As they adjusted their position slightly, Brown tried again, "We're moving toward Hotel. The enemy..."

Captain Brown ducked again as more enemy popped out of the holes in the ground. The rifles of the men with him echoed in his ears. Without thinking, he murmured into the handset yet again, "Say again, all after SITREP."

Finally, in frustration, Stemple ordered Brown to give the handset to Bilski, his radio operator, "Damn it, Dave. Give me your radio operator!"

Lance Corporal Bilski caught the handset as the captain threw it toward him. Brown yelled, "Ski, tell the colonel what the hell's going on,"

Brown advanced with the Marines as the platoons methodically cleared each hooch with their own grenades and eventually blew the tunnels with C-4 explosives. The result of the immediate battle was six enemy dead with three wounded POWs.

Their aerial observer, AO, in the OV-10, ever on the alert, spotted eight NVA soldiers moving in to block Fox's path back to Hotel's position. The bird dog pilot called in artillery fire within only 200 meters from Fox killing seven of the eight additional enemy.

1830 hours. With the hooches secured, Brown wanted the 2nd Platoon to come up, pass through the other two platoons and lead the company back into Hotel's lines. He motioned to his radio operator, "Ski, order up the 2nd Platoon. Let's have them lead the way back to Hotel."

Marines loaded up with Hotel's weapons, one of its PRC radios, and its mail pouch, plus about fifteen enemy weapons, and enough enemy documents to keep the "Intel" folks busy for a month. Now, in addition to their own packs and the medevacuated Marines' weapons, each exhausted Marine was carrying at least one other item. Brown was no exception.

Five minutes turned into ten when Brown wondered out loud, "Where in the hell is the 2nd Platoon?"

Gunny Dierdalh shrugged. The gunny knew his captain was concerned with his decision to leave the platoon under the new leadership of Marshall. Granted the large bunker was about 500–600 meters away, but surely their lead man should have reached the command group's position near the rear hooch in ten minutes. Then, in the distance, Brown's ears caught a low hum. He tilted his head, allowing himself to better interpret the sounds drifting up from the woods below his position. It was at that moment that Brown understood what he was hearing. With Marshall's booming voice leading the men, there emerged from the tree line the words "…of Montezuma to the shores of Tripoli." The song rang out clearly in the late afternoon light. There, from the 2nd Platoon, came the most thrilling and inspiring sound, heard by these combatants in months: the confident tones of twenty-five young Marines singing, of all blessed things, "The Marine Corps Hymn".

From the Halls of Montezuma
To the shores of Tripoli
We fight our country's battles
In the air, on land, and sea.
First to fight for right and freedom
And to keep our honor clean;
We are proud to claim the title
Of United States Marines.

Chills ran up Captain Brown's spine. He had never heard the "hymn" sung better. Fox had clearly fought in the sacred boots of their predecessors who richly distinguished themselves at Belleau Woods, on Guadalcanal, and at the Chosin Reservoir. Marine Corps lore and its sacred traditions gave Fox Company an edge in battle on that day. Brown looked at Gunny Vernon Dierdalh, smiled, shook his head, and quietly said, "Un-Damn-Believable!"

1900 hours. On the way back to Hotel's position, one of the wounded POWs moaned excessively from the shrapnel in his back and arms. At least one tired, young, twenty year-old Marine, concerned about the loud groans signaling other enemy, pleaded to shoot him. Brown interceded and the injured POW was ignored.

1930 hours. They reached Hotel's trapped position, and Fox entered their lines. Second Lieutenant Denny Lister, a Hotel platoon commander, approached Captain Brown with a wide smile on his face, "You guys came in, and I swear each of you seemed like you stood twelve feet tall. You were scary-looking as hell!"

During that seven-hour battle, Fox had one man killed and fourteen wounded. Twenty-seven enemy were killed and Fox brought back three POWs. The number of enemy wounded was never recorded. Fox's exploits were significant enough to get written up in the Stars and Stripes newspaper. This article was the source for Hanoi Hanna, North Vietnam's equivalent to World War II's infamous Tokyo Rose, to place Fox Company on her "Wanted Dead or Alive" list.

CHAPTER 14: PISSING OFF AN NVA PRISONER OF WAR

In early October 1968 Foxtrot remained under the operational control of the 1st Battalion on Operation Mameluke Thrust. Fox Company with the rest of 1/5 was helo-lifted to the mountainous Arizona Territory for one week, a short trip across the Song Thu Bon.

Still working with Staff Sergeant Marshall's 2nd Platoon, Private First Class Dennis Cadigan was tired after hiking for three days in a row. One afternoon, he stumbled going down a hill with his machine gun. Along the way, he crashed into other Marines. With his knee cut, he stood up, shaking. Doc Connelly came up, looked at Cadigan's knee and announced, "Doesn't look too bad, can you stand on it?"

Cadigan whimpered in a great deal of pain, "No, no, Doc! I fell down like a Raggedy Andy doll. I have to be medevac'd!" Then, after looking at Connelly's questioning face, he thought…well, that didn't work! So, he picked up his gun and pack and got himself ready to move out.

Staff Sergeant Marshall observed the scene from a distance. Private First Class Cadigan was a great machine gunner, but his attitude reeked of belligerent independence too often. Marshall had a growing concern that his lack of responsibility would end up getting him or another Marine hurt.

The night after Cadigan's failed attempt to procure a medevac, Marshall jumped on Cadigan's case. The company set up a perimeter and Marshall advanced toward Cadigan saying, "You have to give me a fire plan."

"A what?" Cadigan responded.

"Yeah, a plan with interlocking fields of fire with the other gun units from the 2nd platoon." Marshall explained, adding, "Do it!"

Cadigan stated flatly, "I don't understand what you're talking about."

Marshall replied, "Didn't you take machine gun training at Lejune?"

Cadigan answered, "Yes, Sir, but they never taught us about fire plans!"

"Use geometry!" Marshall barked.

With the other machine gunner, Private First Class Ted Lush, who had some limited experience with fire plans Private First Class Cadigan drew the terrain. They drew the interlocking fields of fire and corresponding angles. They turned it in, and Marshall was quite impressed. Cadigan regretted even more the fact that Lance Corporal J. D. Moore was not with him to complete his mentoring.

Due to the mountainous terrain of the Arizona Territory, the company was not able to be re-supplied for the first two days. Finally, the company climbed up to the top of a hill to receive their re-supplies by helicopter. The climb took almost three hours. Once on the top, they found the peak covered with trees. The rifle platoons had been immediately sent out on patrol. Cadigan's machine gun section, the forward air controller, the FAC's radio operator, and Gunnery Sergeant Dierdalh were left on the top of the hill.

"Lance Corporal Cadigan," the gunny called out.

"Yes, Sir, Gunny."

"Staff Sergeant Marshall told me you were upset because we didn't have any food for a couple of days."

"Yes, Sir, Gunny."

"Well, we need a re-supply bird to land right here on this hilltop."

"Right, Gunnery Sergeant."

"Do you know what to do, Cadigan?"

Cadigan looked around at his fellow machine gunners for any kind of support he may get. None was offered. "Yes, Sir, Gunnery Sergeant."

Cadigan took on the task of preparing the landing zone for the helicopter. With no machetes, Cadigan's rusty "K-Bar" knife, and Ken Murray's and Ted Lush's bayonets, the three men chopped enough trees down to allow a chopper to drop a pallet of re-supplies on top of the hill. The space they cleared was nearly twenty feet wide by forty feet long. The rifle platoons were returning as the last drops of sweat fell from Cadigan's forehead.

By 15 October, Fox was called back to An Hoa. On that same day Lieutenant General Lew Walt, the Assistant Commandant of the Marine

Corps, was scheduled to visit the base. Fox became part of that visit. Specifically, the regimental commander, Colonel James Van Ord selected Fox Company to be the single rifle company to meet the general. In preparation for the visit, Fox company was issued the relatively new and non-regulation "jungle hat". Other than that, the only guidance that Captain Brown received was: "Be standing tall by1400 hours."

Staff Sergeant Marshall, who had quickly become a continual thorn in Private First Class Cadigan's side, ordered Cadigan and the rest of the 2nd Platoon to wear their jungle hats rolled up like a cowboy hat with the sides up. That was the manner prescribed for the entire company. Cadigan religiously wore his in a "Pancho Villa" style with the front brim up. Marshall did not stop there. He ordered all 2nd Platoon members and attachments to polish their jungle boots. As a result of Marshall's order, Cadigan suggested to Marshall that if all hands were in the formation, the personal gear might be stolen. While the Staff Sergeant considered that event, Cadigan volunteered to watch the gear. He claimed to lament skipping both the formation and talk by General Walt. Truth be told, he would have felt like an "idiot" with his hat folded on the sides.

VARIOUS COVER STYLES WORN BY FOX 2/5 MARINES IN 1968
(Photo courtesy of Marc Waskiewicz)

After their visit from esteemed General Lew Walt, Fox was air lifted onto Go Noi Island on 23 October 1968 as part of Operation Henderson Hill. By this time they were back under the control of the 2nd Battalion. That operation was being conducted in the central and western half of

Go Noi Island. The object of all search and clear operations was to rid an area of the enemy. In this operation, 2/5's command element, consisting of about fifty to seventy-five men, was established on the high ground to the south of the island. Its rifle companies were on the island executing the "searching and clearing" with many patrols. Fox specifically was operating near the railroad berm, near where they operated during Operation Tuscaloosa. Over the long run these patrols tended to be repetitive, becoming dangerously monotonous.

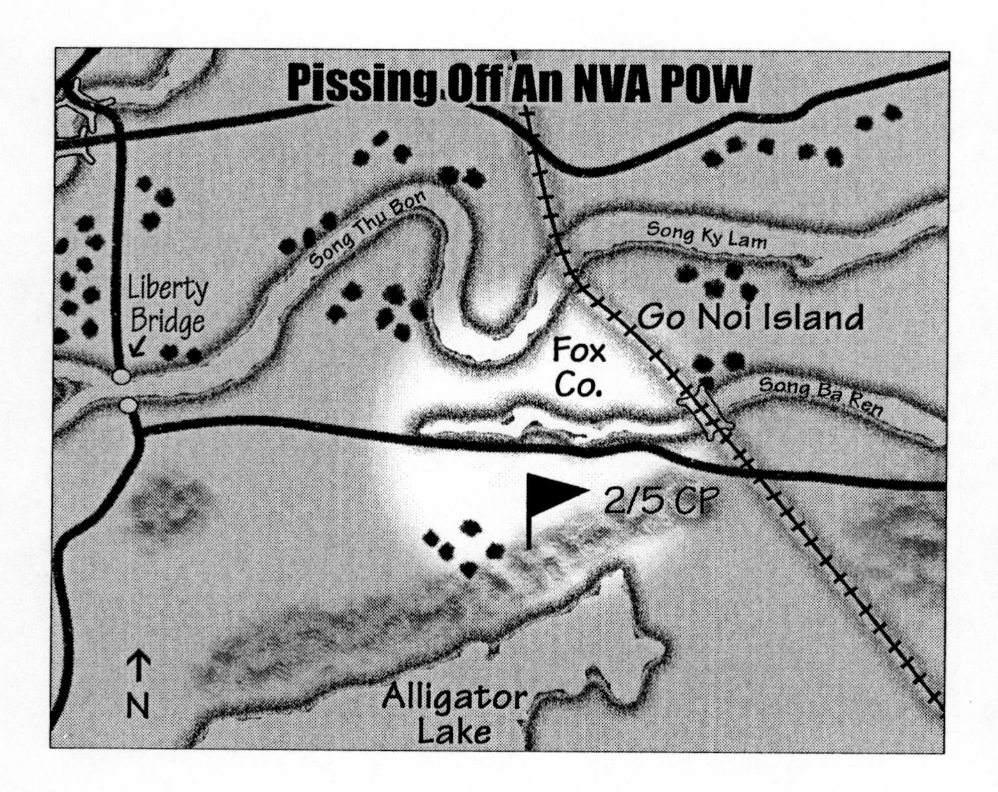

And so, the search and clear operation began with Fox's platoons patrolling back and forth sweeping the area near the railroad berm constantly alert for enemy they may stumble upon. While the sweeping was taking place, one of the platoons stayed with Captain Brown and his fifteen-man command group. The proximity enabled Brown to get better acquainted with members of Fox. Brown was also able to talk on the radio to his first sergeant in An Hoa about administrative matters. During the day, Gunnery Sergeant Vernon Dierdalh busied himself working up re-supply requests for C-rations, ammunition, camouflage utilities, batteries, and C-4 explosives. Doc Connelly contacted platoon corpsmen to identify their medical supply needs in order to forward the requests to the gunny. Corporal Waskiewicz, the new, savvy artillery forward observer, who was quickly earning the respect of Brown, was coordinating fire plans for daytime patrols and night defensive operations. Waskiewicz though, once finished with his fire-support planning, would occupy his extra time by planning and executing some kind of practical joke on his buddies.

The 2nd Platoon was patrolling near the railroad berm. Private First Class Cadigan and others wandered through some bunkers and burned out hooches finally approaching a hedgerow. Lance Corporal Ken Murray mentioned, "Hey Cadigan, do you know why I don't like walking by a hedge row?"

Cadigan responded, "Why?"

Murray replied, "Well, if you're walking by a hedgerow and a gook is in there, they'll shoot you because they can see you, and you can't see them."

Cadigan asked, "So, you want me to do a 'recon-by-fire' on the hedge row?"

Murray stated, "Yeah."

Cadigan raised his gun and began to fire. Immediately, the hedgerow exploded with counter-fire. Marine small arm rounds and grenades ripped into the hedgerow. Cadigan leapt into a ditch and continued shooting at the hedgerow. Both men shouted for reinforcements. Other 2nd Platoon Marines raced up, firing M-79s over the top of the hedgerow. The enemy fire ceased. Marines charged the hedgerow and discovered blood trails. The platoon followed the trails for almost a mile along the raised railroad track to a bunker hidden near a tree line. Cots and food were in the bunker, but no VC were found.

Just beyond the bunker was a hamlet consisting of a pagoda and about fifteen hooches. As the 2nd Platoon approached the hamlet to search for enemy, Cadigan noticed that most of the hooches appeared to be intact. Eerily, the silence and absence of any activity caused a certain degree of edginess. His senses rapidly heightened. Something was about to happen.

Suddenly, a black-pajama'd man darted from behind the small pagoda carrying an AK-47 sub-machine gun. Cadigan fired immediately. As the bullets struck the man's body, they appeared to lift him up. Cadigan continued to fire. The bullets spun the enemy in a continuous circle. It was a scene, seemingly, straight out of the movies. Cadigan, mesmerized, kept firing. The enemy soldier kept spinning. Finally fifteen feet from where Cadigan's first round entered the VC's torso he fell to the ground. Everyone, seeking to reach Cadigan, yelled, "Cease Fire! What are you doing? Cease Fire!"

Cadigan's fire could be heard at Fox Company's command post area. Gunnery Sergeant Dierdalh looked at Captain Brown and stated, "Sounds like its coming from the 2nd Platoon's area."

"Yeah, it sure does," Captain Brown responded. Looking toward his company radio operator, Lance Corporal Stan Bilski, Brown said, "Hey, Ski, picking any thing up?"

"Sir, looks like Two Alpha has got some action," Ski announced. Two Alpha was the 1st Squad, 2nd Platoon's call sign.

Private First Class Mike Castilletto, with the 2nd Platoon, and others ran over to the VC Cadigan had shot. Amazingly, he was still alive. They finished him off. Mike came back with the prized AK-47 and handed it Cadigan. "This is yours," he said. "You got him!"

Staff Sergeant Marshall, sprinted up to the scene. Trying to regain control, he quickly directed, "Castilletto, you carry the rifle back to the gunny, and he'll get it back to An Hoa. Now, let's move out and search the rest of this place!"

Cadigan was still in a post-adrenalin, somewhat traumatic, state of mind. He felt disoriented. After three months in country this was the first time he actually witnessed himself killing somebody.

The sweep of the hamlet took about one more hour. When completed, Marshall commanded, "Saddle up and move out!"

The platoon moved out of the hamlet on a narrow dirt path walled by four- to six-foot high elephant grass. On the trail in front of Cadigan was a new kid they called "Johnny". 200 meters away from the hamlet Johnny exclaimed, "Oh my God!" Cadigan jumped to the right, away from where Johnny was looking, thinking the new kid had just tripped a booby trap. Johnny was saying, "Get up! Get up!" to someone near him.

Crawling out of the elephant grass was a young enemy soldier. He looked no more than fifteen years old and wore soiled black pajamas. He neither had a pack nor a weapon. His bush hat indicated he was an NVA, not a VC, though that identification was irrelevant to the men of the 2nd Platoon. His hands were raised above his head, and he was jabbering nervously in Vietnamese. Johnny spun him around and forced him down on his hands and knees. Staff Sergeant Marshall came up and announced, "Johnny gets three days R&R!"

Jealousy danced through Cadigan's mind. He shot an enemy and got nothing while the new kid almost tripped over one got three days R&R. It just wasn't right! What a joke! His envy lasted the rest of the day.

Captain Brown had an instinct for injecting excitement into these operations. He knew enemy prisoners were a rich source of information for both intelligence and psychological operations. A dead enemy could be used for body-count purposes but was far less useful in winning this already protracted war. Brown established a reward for capturing enemy soldiers: three days R&R in Da Nang and leave on the next chopper. Company F was believed to be the only company in the battalion with such an award system in the battalion. This system was successful even though it was established without the battalion's authorization. Under Lieutenant Colonel Stemple, the battalion operated well within National Guidelines for conducting warfare, and establishing a "Three days R&R in Da Nang and leave on the next chopper" award system pushed the envelope, an activity Fox Company enjoyed doing. Brown knew his Fox Company bloodhounds would enjoy the sport of running down a prisoner, rather than simply squeezing a trigger—well, most of them.

"Sir," Bilski chirped, getting the captain's attention, "Two Alpha has had a good day. This afternoon they killed one gook with an AK-47, and now they've captured one. They think he's an NVA and they are bringing him back to our 'pos'. Should be here in twenty minutes."

"Great news, Ski. Thanks," Brown shot back. "Hey, Gunny why don't you figure out the best place to keep the POW and figure some kind of guard schedule," Brown subtly directed.

"Don't you think we can get him out tonight, Skipper?" the gunny asked.

"Nah," Captain Brown reflected negatively. "It's already 1600 and most of the wing's birds are involved with some kind of maintenance check after 1700. We'll probably get him out first thing in the morning. I'll get the air liaison officer to check on it."

Captain Brown marched over to Corporal Manuel Villa Gomez, "Hey, Pancho, how about checking on the Admin Net to see if the ALO can frag the POW out in the morning?" he asked. Brown directed his question toward the battalion radio operator attached to the company. Martinez, from Texas, had Mexican parents and wore his "Pancho" handle proudly. He and Lance Corporal Bilski were always within yards of each other: Martinez communicating with the battalion and Ski with the company.

Gunnery Sergeant Dierdalh went out to the edge of the 1st Platoon's defensive position and waited for Staff Sergeant Marshall's platoon to return with the POW. Soon the platoon's point man emerged from a clearing fifty meters away. Marshall followed immediately with the "prize" in tow, an emaciated ninety to one hundred pound Vietnamese clad in black pajamas. His black hair was matted and his pajamas weren't exactly black, rather a mix of gray and tan dust covering what was once black cloth. As he walked closer to the waiting Marines, all could see that he was quite sick.

At 2000 hours after debriefing his platoon commanders, Second Lieutenants Lott and Glum, Captain Brown left his immediate campsite with a canteen-cup of coffee and walked forty yards to where a young Marine was guarding the now-sleeping prisoner. Brown studied the thin young man lying in a pre-natal position on the dry dirt under a camouflage blanket that the guard had given to him, no-doubt out of compassion.

Brown's expertly made coffee came from C-rations. Most C-ration boxes contained a coffee packet. Some had hot chocolate packets. Young infantry men preferred the hot chocolate, while the coffee drinkers, continued their "after-evening-chow" one or two cups of coffee ritual. Since younger Marines didn't drink coffee, there were always plenty of coffee packets to spare, even in the field in the middle of a tropical war zone. For anyone who liked coffee, C-Ration coffee is probably the worst imaginable. That said, a canteen cup with two packets of coffee mixed with canteen water was probably as good as it would get in the bush. In the field coffee drinkers could heat coffee to a boil in about twenty seconds with a half-inch pinch of match-lit C-4 explosives. If C-4 was not available, "heat-tabs" supplied with the C-rations would be used. With heat tabs, after about three minutes the temperature would be just above warm. This was the method prescribed by the battalion and its parent organizations. It was not the preferred method for Fox coffee drinkers.

The aroma of Brown's coffee woke the NVA prisoner. He sat up, startled, and lost. He was unaware of the condition of his capture. His eyes bespoke his confusion. Would he be killed? Or would he be taken and held elsewhere? The Marine guard and Brown increased their defensive alert. In a war zone, anything could happen. But, nothing did; and all three relaxed. Brown's outgoing nature broke the silence. "Ong muon coffee, phai khong?" Which translated literally in English, yet correctly phrased in Vietnamese resembled, "Mister want coffee, yes no?"

"Da phai, cam on ong," the prisoner replied. His response translated to, "Yes, definitely. Thank you, Sir."

"Private, how about getting the gunny to make a cup of coffee for this guy. I'll keep an eye on him," Brown ordered.

"Aye, aye, Sir," the young Marine replied and hurried away for the gunny.

Brown looked into the young North Vietnamese's face. It was dirty and pale, even under the bright star-filled night. His eyes were somewhat sunk back into his head. His cheeks were sucked in, making his oriental cheekbones more pronounced. Like most North and South Vietnamese, he had three to five inches of jet-black hair parted on the side and all but covering the opposite eye. This guy's hair, like many of his mates, was well tapered on the sides and exposed his ears.

He was an exhausted young man who, for some reason, Brown respected instantly. For he had hiked, most likely, over a thousand miles along the Ho Chi Minh trail in sandals, carrying weapons or logistics to end up on this swampy island with malaria, no water, and starving. Damn right he wanted some coffee, Brown thought. Unlike, their young American counterparts, most Vietnamese drank coffee at an early age, so accepting the coffee offer was natural.

"My name is Mr. Brown," the captain said squatting in Vietnamese fashion he had learned how to master the year before as an advisor. "Are you well?" Brown asked in Vietnamese.

"Very tired," came his response as the young man sadly shook his head.

"Do you want a cigarette?" Brown offered.

"Yes, Sir." He reached for the Salem offered by Brown.

The captain took one, held it in his lips and struck a match for his prisoner before lighting his own cigarette.

They studied each other for a moment in silence, each enjoying his first couple of drags on the cigarettes. About that time, Gunnery Sergeant Dierdalh with the Marine guard in trace arrived with a steaming hot cup of coffee, obviously C-4 heated, and offered it to the prisoner. Brown could read the snarl on Dierdalh's face. The gunny was not up for delivering coffee to a young enemy POW as much as he was making sure his skipper was okay.

"Cam on ong," the Vietnamese said softly, which caused the gunny's head to turn abruptly to his skipper for a translation.

"He said, 'Thank-you,'" Brown offered, reading his gunny's expression. "I'll join you in a few minutes. Leave Private Smith here, we'll be all right."

The gunny left and Brown initiated a dialogue in Vietnamese with the prisoner, none of which the Marine guard understood.

"What's your name?"

"Tam Ky."

"Are you from North Vietnam?"

"Yes, Sir."

"Hanoi?"

"Yes, Sir."

"Are you married?"

Tam Ky's eye lit up and a smile grew on his face. "Yes, Sir, I have two children. Do you have any?" he came back to Brown.

"I sure do. I have a son who just became five years old." Brown paused before adding, "My doctor believes you have malaria. You'll get some medicine tomorrow. We do not have any here."

"Thank you, Sir."

"Are any of your friends sick with malaria?"

"A few."

"When's the last time you saw them?"

"Yesterday. I went for water, I got lost going back to them."

"Here's your wallet," Brown said giving back the wallet to Tam Ky.

"Thank you, Sir."

"You have photos of your children?"

"Yes. Look at this photo."

"They are pretty. I hope the war is over soon so you can go back to your house in Hanoi to be with them."

"Thank you, Sir."

"All right. Go sleep. It will help."

Thirty minutes later the command radio to battalion began the familiar "shhhhh," hissing sound breaking the silence. "Fox, this is Texas Pete."

"This is Fox, go."

"This is Texas Pete Three Alpha. Is Fox Six available?"

"Roger, Texas Pete Three Alpha," Lance Corporal Bilski replied, "Sir, Lieutenant Pace is on the radio and wants to talk to you," He stretched the phone wire and handed the receiver to the captain.

"Hey, Three Alpha, this is Fox Six. Having a good night?"

"Roger, Sir. We're all set up here on this hill. View is beautiful. Nice breeze. Hope it's as nice down in the marshes. Get any scoop from your POW?"

"Not much, Says his name is Tam Ky. He's from Hanoi. Got a couple of kids. He's got malaria and so do a couple of his buddies."

"Roger, Sir."

"Apparently he went for water and got lost on the way back. One of our patrols darn near stumbled over him on a trail near the railroad berm. He surrendered without a fight."

"Did he say how many buddies he had, Sir?"

"Don't know, didn't ask."

"Are they on Go Noi?"

"They were yesterday."

"Appreciate the scoop, Fox Six. If you get anymore, let me know."

"Sure enough, Pete. Fox Six out."

Brown looked at Gunny Dierdalh who had heard half of the exchange and asked, "Do you think I should have asked Tam Ky anything more?"

The large man turned and said, "Nah, Skipper. He'll fess up more details after they get him out of here."

The night was perfect. Those in Fox Company not on watch got a good night's sleep. Go Noi Island had comfortable dirt and sand to sleep on and the night sky, though moonless, was filled with stars. The enemy platoon nearby was malaria-stricken and, now with Tam Ky gone, was also one man shy. The battalion's PSYOPS, Psychological Operations, team had set up an amplification system and was playing soft Vietnamese music and broadcasting things in Vietnamese that Brown could not understand.

Some time just before midnight Tam Ky began moaning and then screaming at the top of his lungs. The noise masked the chatter from the PSYOPS loud speakers. Brown bolted into a sitting position, looked up at Gunny Dierdalh who was already putting on his boots, and said, "What the hell has gotten into the POW?"

"I don't know, Skipper, but he's pissed at something. I'm going to check with the guard."

Dierdalh walked over to the Marine guard. "Jackson, what did you do with this prisoner?"

"Nothing, Sir, he was sleeping and all of a sudden he started moaning, then yelling. He's been pointing up at those speakers. You want me to shut him up?"

"No," said the gunny as he went over and lifted the ninety-pound NVA soldier off the ground with one immense hand raising him to nose level.

In plain convincing English, Dierdalh muttered, "Shut your mouth!" After which he unceremoniously tossed him back down on the ground into a weakened heap.

Jackson's eyes popped wide open upon witnessing the whole scene. The eighteen year-old, 145-pound Marine decided to never cross the gunny! He'd make certain his buddies knew not to mess with gunny either!

"What the hell was that all about, Gunny?" Brown asked as Dierdalh sat back down beginning to loosen his boots.

"Oh, something coming over those damn loud speakers up at the battalion's position pissed him off," Dierdalh replied.

"Whoa, really must have!" Brown said. "I'll check with Texas Pete to see what they were saying." Brown leaned over, "Ski." He addressed his radio operator who was now monitoring two handsets with Pancho sleeping nearby. "How about asking Texas Pete what they were broadcasting that pissed off our little buddy?"

"Okay, Skipper. I'll let you know in the morning."

The rest of the night did not pass without incident. The second platoon was dug in along the company perimeter facing the hills. Cadigan had his gun set up at the edge of the hamlet. Twenty feet in front of the position was an insignificant tree marking the junction between a small path leading from his position to the main trail outside the hamlet. At about 0230 Cadigan took the watch. While sitting behind his gun, he saw a movement to his right. Silently, he lowered himself into a prone position behind his gun sights. He strained to see what had been moving without success. He remained confident he had seen something move. He had been told that there were no Fox patrols out. He knew the location of Fox's listening posts. Again he saw something move.

Cadigan, no longer a newbee, squeezed his sometimes "itchy" finger on the trigger. The machine gun's burst caused those nearby to begin firing. Apparently he was not the only one to have heard movement. Soon a loud voice resonated, "Cease fire! Cease fire! Who the fuck opened up and started that shooting?" Corporal Blunt, the squad leader, came along whispering, "Don't start firing again. Marshall's pissed."

Cadigan began to doubt himself. Maybe he was getting spooked. Out loud he contemplated, "Too much war in three months?"

Possibly.

At 0600 hours Brown questioned the radio operator who was now monitoring the two radios Bilski had been guarding six hours earlier, "Any scoop from Texas Pete, Pancho?"

"Sir, Ski left you this note," he said, handing a 3x5-inch paper from a message pad.

The note read: "Sir, the loud speakers were saying, 'Your comrade, Tam Ky, turned himself into the Marines and is getting treatment for his malaria. He wants you, his sick brothers, to turn yourselves in and receive good treatment. Tam Ky is glad to get out of the war and is looking forward to returning to Hanoi to see his children. Please Chu Hoi, surrender, like Tam Ky did and you will be treated well!!'"

Brown felt an uneasy feeling for betraying someone else's confidence. But he smiled, almost laughed, and instantly let that feeling dissipate into the marshes of Go Noi Island. This was the enemy, after all.

While Brown may have felt uneasy, Cadigan fumed. The 2nd Platoon sent out a patrol at first light to check out what caused Cadigan to fire his machine gun. They returned within minutes with another NVA soldier. The NVA soldier's whole chin and lower face had been shot off but amazingly he was still walking on his own. Bandaged from his nose to his neck with a small parachute from a flare, the patrol sat him down next to one of the hooches to wait for evacuation. Though Cadigan took a photo of the man, once again another member of the platoon, Private First Class Johnnie McAllister, was sent on R&R. He was credited for bringing in the prisoner.

"Gunny, is McAllister and the new A-gunner, what's his name? ready to fly out with the POW for his R&R?" Captain Brown asked.

"They are."

"I know Stemple won't be popping in on us since he's up on that hill." Reaching in his pocket Brown asked, "How about having them take this $20 bill and bring us some booze when they return?"

"I'll take care of it, Boss."

Three nights later, the company's command group moved into a large hooch in a nearby hamlet. The hooch, only about two miles away from the railroad berm yet still on Go Noi Island, was a perfect place for Brown, Dierdalh, Melton, Bilski, Martinez and Waskiewicz to sit and consume the couple of bottles of Crème de Mint that McAllister and the new A-gunner had brought from Da Nang. They passed them around swigging from the mouth of each bottle, savoring, then gulping down the syrupy sweet emerald liquid.

"No, no, no!" Melton rushed. "It's 'An old COWBOY went riding out one dark and windy day', not soldier."

"Are you sure?" Brown teased. "How can you be so sure?"

"Yeah, what's the name of that one there?" Dierdalh asked while reaching for the bottle out of Melton's hand.

"Ghost Riders in the Sky"," Melton offered. "It's one of my favorites."

"That's one of my favorites too!" Bilski chimed in. "'Yippee yi sky…no wait…Yippee yi yaaaaay, Yippee yi Ohhhhh, Yippee yi sky."

"What?" Waskiewicz asked.

"No!" Bilski exclaimed. "It's 'Yippee yi Ohhhhh, Yippee yi yaaaaay, Ghost Riders in the skyiiiiiiiiiii…'"

"What?" Waskiewicz asked again. He looked around for help, "Is it me?"

Dierdalh gave Waskiewicz a sharp, measured look while the captain patted Bilski on the shoulder. "Okay, Ski," Brown started. "That Crème de Mint is going to hurt tomorrow." He deliberately skirted around Bilski as he passed the bottle on.

"That Crème de Mint is going to hurt all of us tomorrow," Dierdalh stated firmly, pointing accusingly at the first empty bottle now discarded on the ground.

Ignoring them Melton began again. "It starts like this…'An old cowboy went riding…'" With that he began leading the gathering in what seemed like endless verses of "Ghost Riders in the Sky". As the night flew by and each man enjoyed the singing and drinking, the clamor grew so loud that one of 3rd Platoon's listening posts sent an urgent request to, "Keep it down!"

CHAPTER 15: OPERATION HENDERSON HILL: THE MCGOO EPISODE

A day or two after the Crème de Mint was consumed, the company was choppered five kilometers over a 900-foot ridge line to a valley nestled in the small foot hills southwest of Go Noi Island. Unlike the An Hoa valley dotted with one hamlet after another, roads, trails, kids, mama-sans, and a noisy war, this valley was in the virgin-like territory of the NVA and was quiet. Fox landed near a lake surrounded by a grassy field, perfect for camping and swimming. The lake's 500 by 4,000 meter, irregular shape dictated the informal name given to it by Marines, "Alligator Lake". For two wonderful days, the men of Fox camped, swam, and searched for an NVA hospital that "Intelligence" claimed existed in the hills nearby.

L/CPL DENNIS CADIGAN AND HIS A-GUNNER AT ALLIGATOR LAKE

(Photo courtesy of Dennis Cadigan)

After finding absolutely nothing but one discarded NVA canteen, Fox was ordered back to An Hoa. Back to the mines and booby traps and away from this serene valley. The plan was to climb back up the south side of the foothills. Fox would patrol along the hills heading westward on the same ridgeline the choppers took the Marines over only a couple days earlier. Then, back to An Hoa for hot chow, a cold shower, and a warm beer. Once on the top, the view of Go Noi Island and the An Hoa basin would be dramatic. The patrol was anticipated to cover about twenty-five kilometers or about fifteen miles and take the better part of three days. If enemy were found, Fox may be out there longer. In this war, seldom was length of time an item of any particular consequence.

Fox Company's top field staff non commissioned officer, Gunnery Sergeant Vernon Dierdalh, was a mammoth, iron-like Marine from Wisconsin. With speckled white hair and cat-claw lines by the side of his eyes, he commanded the respect of seasoned veterans. Dierdalh claimed his mettle came from the requirement of all farm boys of Norwegian decent: lifting stray calves over fences after they had wandered away. "Norweegie strong," he would frequently say. His size and quiet demeanor were accompanied by a persona that made the troops both leap like children to follow his orders and yet made them his avid pupils at the same time. While Dierdalh was the field logistician for Fox, he also served as Captain Brown's tactical advisor when the need arose. Prior to the long trek back from the serene valley to An Hoa, the need arose.

Dierdalh warned the skipper that two years earlier, he had patrolled that very ridge. Along the top was a trail—the only trail—littered with mines and booby traps. His unit had suffered numerous casualties. The admonishment was passed along to the platoons.

After about two hours of movement north, the lead element of Fox had yet to begin its climb out of the valley. Gone now was the serenity of Alligator Lake and the men's camouflage utilities began showing signs of sweat. As the hill grew closer and the sun baked them, an explosion punctuated what was left of the remnants of tranquility. Adrenalin raced, body muscles tightened, and the visual and hearing senses sharpened as all sought intuitive answers to "Location?" "What's next?" "Cause?" "Results?" In this case, the explosion rocked the entire company.

Should another one or two blasts and bursts of higher-pitched cracks of rifle fire follow the first, men would yell, "Hit the deck! We're being ambushed!" Should the explosion be followed, first by silence, then by a young male voice or voices shouting "Corpsmen up! Goddamit, Corpsman Up!" their adrenalin would subside, the muscles relax, and remorse would soon saturate the spirit, as their lung-held air slowly escaped.

With the exception of the wounded Marine, nearby Marines, and the devoted corpsmen racing to the wounded, the others, amazingly in unison, quietly spat out, "Ffffucken booby-traps!"

Thirty seconds later a flurry of well-rehearsed activities began. The Marines closest to the blast went immediately into action. They had practiced this drill too many times. As with all booby trap incidents, the guy next to the wounded Marine shouted for the corpsman, and was doing his best to provide comfort. The squad leader of the wounded Marine directed the Marines of the squad, particularly the newly arrived privates and privates first class, to be aware of other booby traps and simultaneously to take defensive positions almost in the very place they were standing. Now, anticipating an injury like a leg severed below the knee with blood pulsating from the stump, the platoon sergeant raced over with the corpsman to begin triage activities. The platoon commander then simultaneously received a damage assessment from those nearby the wounded Marine and communicated the information by radio to "Fox Six." The gunny, forward air controller, and the FAC's radio operator began "fragging", fragmentation air order, for an evac chopper.

Beyond this horrifying, if not daily routine, the remainder of the company with unspoken, yet heightened awareness of other booby traps in the vicinity, assumed defensive positions because the incoming bird was vulnerable from small arms fire as it approached the forward air controller's chosen landing site. Fox's progress to reach the hilltop ground to a halt and was delayed by almost two hours.

All waited nearby in silence after this initial surge of activity subsided. The skipper directed his company radio operator to apprise the battalion commander of the situation and inform him that Fox would be late in reaching its next predestinated check point, the top of the largest hill where the company would take an abrupt left turn and begin it's trek along the booby-trap laden trail. A casualty report, CASREP, with an assessed priority of evacuation was sent over the battalion's administrative network.

"Priority One" was reserved for life-threatening wounds, such as head wound, a sucking chest wound or a lost limb; "priority two," was given to a fragmentation or gun shot wound not considered to be life threatening; and "priority three" was for those killed in action, nicked, or suffered from severe medical situations such as dysentery. Marine—trained dogs occasionally attached to the company were treated the same as the Marines. Thus, if a dog was wounded and considered to be a "priority one" medevac, he would fill the last spot on a medevac chopper should that be the only one left. A wounded Marine with a bullet in his leg and tagged as "priority two" medevac would have to wait for the next chopper.

Within fifteen minutes the whirring and thumping of the blades and sight of the lone medevac chopper was evident as it crossed the crest of the large foothills to the north. The gunny popped a green smoke grenade and the valley suddenly filled with noise and activity.

On this sunny morning the helicopter slowly settled near the site where the colored smoke marked its landing location. Four Marines carried their wounded friend toward the bird on a hastily made field stretcher made of rubber poncho rolled around two M-16 rifles. The four Marines carrying their wounded buddy were moving, not in a sprint, but as fast as they feasibly could toward the chopper that landed about 150 meters from the booby trap. Thirty meters from the waiting chopper, fate dealt its second blow.

One of the lead stretcher-bearers tripped a nearly invisible wire, attached on one end to a small bush and approximately four to five feet away attached on the other end to the pin of a grenade. This was the most common type of booby trap. The grenade holding the pin was hidden and attached to another bush near by. Its explosion seemed muffled when compared to the first and collapsed the stretcher party, slightly wounding all of the men. Nevertheless, it affected the emotions, adrenalin, muscles, and senses for all nearby. Fortunately, the chopper escaped damage and the other wounded Marines were evacuated along with their buddy.

Fox began its march out of the valley and up the hill. The relaxed, peaceful lake seemed like a distant memory. Non-commissioned officers cautioned their men to stay far apart knowing that Gunny Dierdalh's earlier admonishment was now much more than just that.

The 2nd platoon had the lead as the company moved northward on the trail up the nose of the ridge. The recently promoted, Lance Corporal Cadigan, with the 2nd Platoon, carried his machine gun up the switch-back trail. When he reached the top, he looked back at the rest of the company climbing out of the valley on the non-vegetated hillside. "Hey, Berry!" Cadigan shouted while taking a short break to catch his breath. "Look at those guys down there. They look like a bunch of ants." Dennis Cadigan and Private First Class Bob Berry reached the summit and crossed it together.

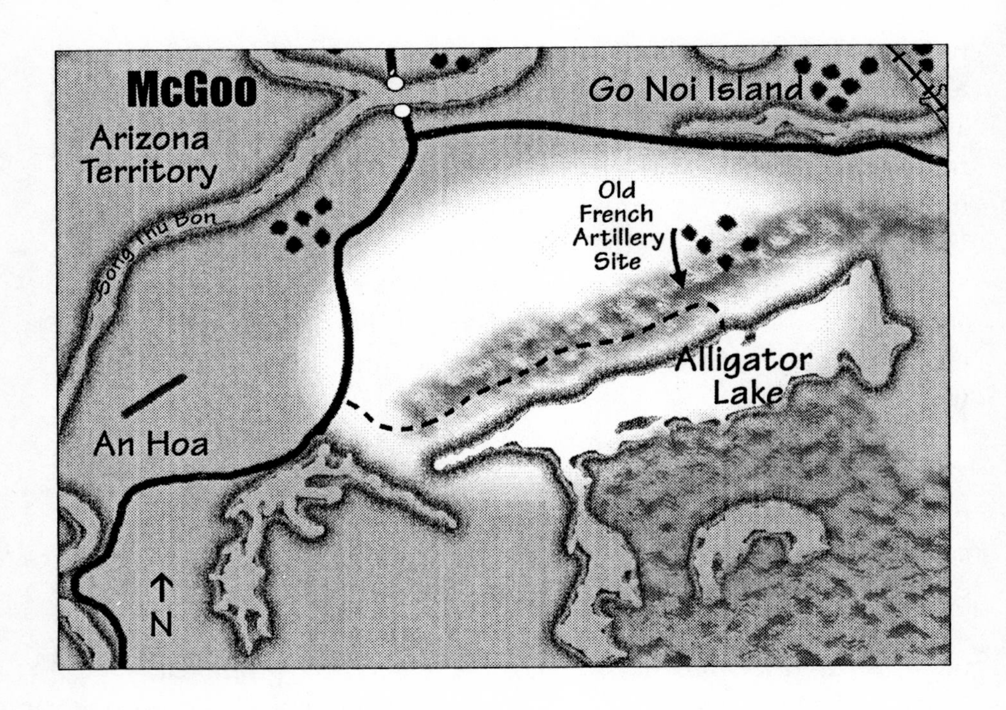

"McGoo" was the handle given to a newly arrived young 2nd Platoon member who wore black, military-issued, thick-framed glasses. In this case "McGoo" who was following Cadigan and Berry, had been grumbling all the way up the hill, "Man, I hate climbing these stinking hills."

Cadigan laughed, "This is just a walk in the park, McGoo."

"Yeah, well in the park back home, we don't have no hills!" McGoo panted.

"Could be worse," Cadigan responded. "Could be raining…"

McGoo rolled his eyes and slowed down a bit to catch his breath. Cadigan and Berry moved on ahead, their pace quickening as they moved further and further down the hill. McGoo, lingered as long as possible taking in his surroundings. He spotted an engineering stake. He smiled to himself murmuring, "Hey, this is a great stick to make a hooch out of, later on."

The view north to Go Noi Island and Da Nang beyond that was spectacular. Following Cadigan and Berry, the last platoon was just leaving the valley, and the lake had vanished behind other smaller hills. The top of this hill was sandy and flat. Only scrub bushes grew on this summit. The wind was a cooling contrast to the warm sun. The crossing point stood at the site of a French artillery emplacement in a war that occurred more than fifteen years earlier.

Cadigan's gun team followed the lead squad of the 2nd Platoon, which had turned westward or left toward An Hoa at the old artillery site and was descending down the hill's peak along the trail approaching the next hill. As Cadigan walked no more than five steps off the hilltop, the hill erupted behind him. He turned, catching sight of a shower of sandy dirt rising into the air, temporarily masking the blue sky.

As dirt and debris rained down on the men of the 2nd platoon, they crouched for safety. "What the hell was that?" Lieutenant Glum shouted as the last piece of debris settled back on the hill. It turned out to be a fifty-pound box-mine that had been booby-trapped.

A member of the trailing squad, called out, "Sir, I think I saw McGoo pulling on an engineering stake from the ground before the explosion."

Again, Fox was halted and the medevac choppers were called. This time they called a Priority Three medevac since McGoo's body had to be collected and placed in a body bag that the chopper provided. The evac bird came and went by 1600 hours. At that point Captain Brown moved the 2nd Platoon another 500 meters so that the company was then stretched out from the 2nd Platoon's forward position to a point near the hill where the old French artillery emplacement stood. Defensive positions were established as the sun began setting over the western mountains. As they dug in for the night, Brown reflected on the French who fought in the very same spot…Well, they didn't win their war. And, after today, Fox didn't feel much like winners either.

Following Marine Corps procedures, the company called for a count of all men. The 1st and 3rd Platoons reported all men accounted for. After a protracted half hour, Captain Brown turned to his radio operator, Lance Corporal Stan Bilski, "Ski, raise the second platoon and find out where their report is."

Minutes later, Lieutenant Glum asked to speak to Captain Brown on the company net. Glum reported, "Actual, we are missing a Marine named Cooper."

"Roger, Jim," Captain Brown responded. "When was PFC Cooper last seen?"

Glum reported, "Best estimate, he was seen about seven hours earlier around when McGoo triggered the box mine."

"Perform a recount, Fox Six out," Brown directed.

Brown lowered the handset, turning his head toward Gunny Dierdalh and others in his company's command group. "Well, what do you think?"

"I think it's highly unlikely that he's AWOL," Dierdalh smirked.

Doc Connelly, the company corpsman, a highly intelligent and compassionate man, mused silently for about ten minutes before addressing the company commander and gunnery sergeant. "In hindsight, I think I remember, perhaps, packing three shoulders into the body bag." Doc confessed. "It's just possible we placed the body and both shoulders of Cooper in the bag with the head and one shoulder of McGoo's in the same bag."

Captain Brown immediately called Lieutenant Colonel Stemple to discuss the next course of action. Stemple, having conversed with the battalion surgeon, directed that at first light a sweep of the entire hill be made and body pieces collected. He informed Fox that the surgeon would visit the company on the first flight to inspect the body parts collected.

The surgeon arrived by chopper shortly after 0800 the next day. The gruesome sweep had begun an hour earlier. Finally, after a jawbone and a blown-up, yet somewhat intact, backpack with Cooper's mail were found, the surgeon was convinced both Marines had been killed in the explosion. Much sobered, yet resilient, the young men continued their march toward An Hoa.

While along the ridge they were able to see Liberty Bridge nearly four miles to the north and An Hoa over six miles to the west. Again the sky was blue and the sun pleasantly warm. The plan was for Fox to hike for about four more miles, get re-supplied in the late afternoon, establish a bivouac for the evening on the ridge, and finally descend into An Hoa valley in the morning. Fox's command group followed the lead platoon.

After about two hours, Brown noticed artillery "willie peter" rounds hitting the ridge about 1000 meters ahead. They landed on the top of the ridge near the An Hoa side. Others noticed as well but with all the many activities being conducted by the 5th Marines in that area of operations, these occasional explosions were not unusual. Still, the proximity of the marked area seemed a bit unusually close for comfort.

"Corporal Waskiewicz," Brown called back to the artillery forward observer.

Corporal Marc Waskiewicz had suffered with dysentery-like problems all morning that had caused him to fall out of the march every ten minutes. Subjected to catcalls from the passing Marines as he relieved himself, Waskiewicz put up with the harassment as best he could. But when his skipper summoned, his stiff upper lip took over. Waskiewicz charged forward past Bilski and Villa Gomez, Brown's radio operators, and reported boldly, "Sir!"

Eyeing the somewhat pale-faced forward observer warily, Brown asked, "How about finding out what those guys are firing at? Our lead platoon will be there in about fifteen minutes."

"Roger, Skipper," Waskiewicz acknowledged.

After looking at his map Waskiewicz squeezed his radio's handset. "Head Cold, this is Beechnut 64, over."

Since Waskiewicz was a corporal serving in a lieutenant's billet, he tended to be as professional and as serious as possible when he called artillery units. This façade belied his normally playful personality. After getting a response from Head Cold, he continued in an accentuated deep voice, "Interrogative, Head Cold. What do you know about the fire mission at coordinates Alpha Tango 972473? Over."

Brown's attention was piqued enough for him to follow Waskiewicz's one-sided responses.

"Err...Roger, waiting," Waskiewicz responded.

A long pause followed Waskiewicz's reply.

"This is Beechnut 64; go," he said, finally.

Another significant pause followed the first. Captain Brown shifted his stance as he waited for an answer.

"Well, Head Cold, you better have them cease fire now because we'll be moving through that area in about ten to fifteen mikes," Waskiewicz said referring to the ten to fifteen minutes it would take for Fox to be in harm's way. "Also, request you check with the Foxtrot Sierra Charlie to find out why they don't have our movement plotted."

The Fire Support Coordinator Center was dubbed Foxtrot Sierra Charlie. Yet another pause ensued.

"Roger, this is Beechnut 64 Actual," Waskiewicz acknowledged.

A short pause occurred until Waskiewicz gave his final reply, "Roger. Thanks for the scoop. I'll pass the word along."

Corporal Waskiewicz concluded his transmission, turning to Captain Brown. "Sir," Waskiewicz started, "That damn 8-inch battery down there was registering their friggin' guns. Can you believe that? Adjusting their guns while we're walking right into the middle of it? They're stopping now."

Brown, looking up ahead said, "Right, I can see that. Who the hell said they could do that without checking first?"

"I asked them to check on it. I'll let you know when they get back to me." Waskiewicz answered. "Oh, by the way, Sir?"

"Yeah?"

"The Head Cold radio operator said that the base has been out of beer for the past two days. They have been unable to get any shipped from Da Nang. The cargo trucks are being used for something else. Whatever. He said some may be in tomorrow or the next day," Waskiewicz added.

Sometime after a noon break, Captain Brown approached Gunny Dierdalh, "Gunny, you heard about the beer?"

The gunny nodded.

"I want to send a sergeant in on the re-supply chopper this afternoon, and have him join up with Sergeant Hamilton in the rear."

Dierdalh's large mouth found yet another smirk. Hamilton was Fox's incredibly resourceful supply non-commissioned officer at An Hoa. He listened as Brown continued, "Then have them catch a morning flight to Da Nang, buy some beer and have it iced down for us when we get back tomorrow afternoon. Here's $200," he said, thrusting the money into Dierdalh's outstretched hand. "That ought to cover us. Don't you think?"

Dierdalh's lips parted into a wide smile, "Sure should be, Skipper. Is this your treat?"

"Hell no, Gunny! Just sell it to them so I get most of it back! My wife'd kill me for spending it on beer without her!" Brown laughed, "Oh yeah, and Gunny…"

The gunny guffawed loudly. He knew better than to expect this Berks County, Pennsylvania-boy captain to spring for all that beer. But, he liked this man who knew how important cold beer back at the base was for the morale of the troops, "What's that, Skipper?"

"No Crème de Mint!"

The next afternoon after several long, hot miles later, Fox trekked into An Hoa. Their trip lasted longer than expected making them arrive later than the rest of the 2nd Battalion's rifle companies.

An Hoa was dryer than a desert.

While the rest of the companies settled in without beer, Captain Brown ordered Fox to assemble in front of the first sergeant's General Purpose tent. This tent, proudly displaying the Fox flag held erect by a cut-off, fifty-five-gallon drum and sand, was where the captain had decided to dismiss the company. Lately, the tin covered buildings had become known as the Fox headquarters. Behind Captain Brown stood two sergeants armed with .45 caliber pistols. They were guarding twenty-five cases of ice-cold beer—the only beer in An Hoa.

CHAPTER 16: OPERATION MEADE RIVER

Less than two weeks had passed since Fox had enjoyed the only beer in the regimental camp. By Wednesday, 20 November 1968, after one mini-operation in the Phu Nhuans still searching for the elusive Cong and their supplies, Fox was back in An Hoa getting ready to participate in a super-secret cordon and search operation dubbed Operation Meade River.

Operation Meade River was planned and run by the 1st Marine Regiment. The 2nd Battalion, 5th Marines' operational control was transferred for the operation to that regiment. In military jargon, "2/5 was chopped to the 1st Marines". In addition to 2/5, the 1st Marines had their own 1st Battalion and "opcon" of 3/5 of the 5th Marines, 1/7 and 2/7 of the7th Marines, and 2/26 and 3/26 of the 26th Marines. All total, this force consisted of seven battalions and their twenty-eight rifle companies.

The 1st Marine Regiment TAOR during this operation was an area called Dodge City near the city of Hoi An. The Marine Corps battalions would literally ring the Dodge City area, and then the southern-end battalions would press north and east, forcing their enemy into 2/5 and the other Marine Corps battalions. In this way, the enemy would be squeezed out of the area. The estimated total enemy strength was one hundred to 150 VC infrastructure personnel with a possible 900 NVA or VC regular forces. The R-20 VC Battalion and the 1st Battalion, 36th NVA Regiment had been confirmed in the area. Their numbers were placed above 630 combat troops.

Sequentially, Fox was to be inserted in the middle of the companies that would cordon off the operational area. The men were ready to go even before the morning meal at the regimental mess hall. At 0635 Company F was instructed to go to its predestinated lift point along An Hoa's airstrip. This location was no more than one half mile from the mess hall and inside the defensive wires. Upon arrival at the site, the troops were told to relax and stay with their helo teams. Then the wait began. One hour passed. The second hour came and went, but still there were no birds for Fox. The regimental planners had executed an impeccable "hurry-up-and-wait" phase of the airlift operation.

WAITING TO FLY OUT ON MEADE RIVER AT THE AN HOA AIRSTRIP
(Photo courtesy of Marc Waskiewicz)

To get to and surround the Dodge City area, the Corps flew in four battalions and trucked in two others. One battalion marched into their initial position along the corridor. The 1st Marine Aircraft Wing's helicopter aircraft group, MAG 16, had been turning the blades of their CH-46 Sea Knight helicopters and their much larger CH-53 Sea Stallion helicopters since before the crack of dawn. That morning they had to airlift more than 3000 infantry Marines.

By 0930, after waiting nearly three hours, Fox was airlifted out of the An Hoa valley in two flights of six helicopters each. Finally, they were on their way to land on the eastern portion of the entrapment area a distance of sixty kilometers from An Hoa.

Aviators never understood this, but grunts, or infantry Marines, were most happy when they were on the ground. The ground may often be wet and dirty, but infantry combatants are more in control of their own environment. Flying in a chopper wasn't bad as long as they were at least 1500 feet in the air where they were safe from ground fire. However, descending to landing zones in enemy-controlled or unsecured territory made the transported grunts highly vulnerable to ground fire. Boxed in only a light metal flying container and unable to hit the deck and return fire a grunt loses that controlling edge he had on the ground. Descending was a major pucker factor for grunts. While descending, it is hard not to imagine a bullet from an enemy firing below ripping up through the metal and passing through the leg of a buddy sitting across from you or ripping through your own skin.

Landing occurred abruptly, as usual. Once on the ground the pucker factor reversed itself. The grunts were happy to get on the ground and away from the chopper as fast as they could while the aviators were equally desperate to get as far away from the ground as fast as they could. Instead of saying, "We'd like to thank you for selecting the 1st Marine Aircraft Wing for your flight to LZ Baldy. We hope you had a pleasant flight and hope you will select 1st MAW the next time you choose to fly." Crew chiefs were barking commands like, "Move off the plane! Hurry up! Get off! Get off!" All this happened while the co-pilot monitored the deplaning to tell the pilot exactly when to, "Lift off!"

No operational scenario was ever the same for combatants in this war or any war. This was assuredly true in Vietnam for helicopter operations. A map reconnaissance prepared the company leaders for what general direction each platoon would move in after deplaning in the primary landing zone. Of course if the LZ was hot, meaning the enemy was shooting at the choppers as they land, alternative landing zones were planned and other options put in place. The decent into the LZ was still a mystery for the Fox Company passengers landing to form a part of the cordon on Operation Meade River; still, the Fox Marines were ready for anything.

Lance Corporal Cadigan was flying in a CH-46. He saw the scenery change from rice paddies and rivers to actual houses and one wide, paved road. As the first group of helicopters approached its intended landing zone, a rice field next to a village with a single road running through its middle, the men wondered if their welcome would include the same exciting hot zones experienced in Go Noi Island and the Arizona Territory. At seventy feet off of the ground, Cadigan's helicopter slowed to about forty knots. The men tensed, ready to deplane into the rice paddy. The noisy, though uneventful, trip ended abruptly as Cadigan witnessed small holes appearing in the side of the chopper. All hell broke loose. The men had their "welcoming-question" answered. Seconds later, now at twenty knots and height of forty feet, the door gunner returned fire with his machine gun. He fired on enemy hidden in a tree line on the other side of a single road while the crew chief pressed tightly on the button lowering the offload ramp. Seconds later, now hovering at ten feet, the crew chief began screaming, "Get off! Get off! Get off!"

Cadigan blindly followed the Marine in front of him off the ramp and ten feet down into a knee-deep, water-filled, rice paddy. Other combat-equipped Marines poured down on Cadigan like rain. Mud slurped unnoticed over the uniforms and weapons onto men of the 2nd Platoon as they dashed noisily through the paddy to the safety below the elevated road. By the time they reached the embankment, rockets from the AH-1 Cobra gunships escorting the CH-46 choppers began exploding in the tree line near where the enemy had fired minutes earlier.

Then there was only silence, save for the fading chopper blades beating the November air. From above a Marine yelled, "All clear. All clear." With that, the 2nd Platoon, led by their "in-your-face" Staff Sergeant Marshall, climbed to the path that led out of the dike and onto the single road. Once on the road the men stared in amazement. As they gazed in the direction of the South China Sea about eight kilometers to the northeast, they saw a real village which was actually the hamlet Vinh Dien (2). There were no thatch hooches connected by underground escape tunnels that could hold VC munitions here.

These were nice homes, many made of cement-like walls and red-tile and tin roofs. Homes had colored cut-glass pieces imbedded in the cement walls for decoration. Some had porches. The fact that the homes still had dirt floors was of little consequence. There was a small school and, a bit down the road, a Buddhist temple.

The single road was about 800 kilometers in length. At one end were rice fields, the villagers' main source of income. The South China Sea end of the road and far edge of the hamlet was at the intersection of the seventy to one hundred meter-wide river, called Song Vinh Dien, and the National Highway 1, the main inter-provincial artery in I Corps.

The people were friendly. They appeared to welcome the presence of these field Marines who had come there to rid the area to the west of the village of local and main Force VC who taxed and harassed them constantly. Apparently, at some time prior to Fox's arrival, the villagers must have been briefed about the operation. Most were gone.

For their own safety ARVN soldiers and Vietnamese police assisted the Fox Company Marines in evacuating additional refugees from hamlets within the cordoned area. On 21 November and 22 November Fox assisted 1,968 refuges, who had gathered at the edge of the hamlet, and moved them through it to the transportation point on Highway 1 and then on to a government-controlled village.

After the evacuation, the men of Company F had the hamlet to themselves. Each platoon had two squads in the field facing the center of the cordon. The rest were inside homes and away from the onset of the Monsoon season. Gunnery Sergeant Dierdalh and the rest of the staff non-commissioned officers ran a "tight ship" and the area remained spotless. Fox had no concierge service, but the next few days seemed like an in-country R&R.

While the troops were relaxing, Captain Dave Brown hoped Fox would be able to stay in the village past Saturday, 23 November. The Armed Forces radio network had promised that they would carry the Big Ten Championship football game between Ohio State and Michigan. Ohio State, then 9–0, needed to get by the Wolverines to get to the Rose Bowl for the National Championship. Most others were not into the game with as much enthusiasm as Brown. But Brown had played football at Denison University, a small school in Ohio where earlier Woody Hayes had coached. Hayes was now the legendary coach of Ohio State University. His leadership style was brutal. In 1959, nine years earlier, Denison's season ended the week before Ohio State's season and Brown was able to go to Ann Arbor, Michigan in late November and watch Coach Woody Hayes employ his intensity against the University of Michigan. With the temperature in the upper thirties, Hayes paced the sidelines, as always, in a short-sleeved shirt. The crowd could sense that his emotions were ready to explode at any moment. One play pricked that emotional bubble. Hayes, furious, turned around and kicked a folding chair over the track surrounding the football field. The chair finally landed in one of the front rows, ten feet above the track. Now that, Brown thought, is the intensity needed to win. Brown compared his own experiences in combat with football games. Battle thrilled him. He maneuvered Fox's fighting units under fire like a coach moves players on a field; and the method had been extremely successful for Fox. They hadn't lost a fight yet.

The best thing that can be attributed to Fox's stay in Vinh Dien (2) was that there were no casualties. 22 November passed uneventfully. Lieutenant Colonel Stemple paid a visit. The men had their flak jackets on, were shaved, and told him they were ready to go. Right look, right words. He left pleased. "Go get 'em, Fox!"

Finally, 23 November arrived. Fox was still holding their positions in the nice little hamlet. The monsoons had set in by this time: cloudy half the time, and light rain showers the rest. Brown's one wish came true. He was able to listen to Ohio State University take the Michigan Wolverines apart. Coach Woody Hayes had shown no mercy. Ohio State beat Michigan 50–14. After the game the commentator asked one of OSU's coaches about the high score. His comment was, "If we would have let up they could of come back to life and turn the tables on us."

Good advice, Brown thought, taking the game to heart.

By 24 November the easy life at the village coupled with constant light rain had caused a downturn in the overall company mood. The squads out on the perimeter began focusing more on building superb all-weather hooches than they did on the enemy that had yet to be seen or heard. Instead of being half-hungry, half-thirsty, always tired, ready to fight, the young Marines were enjoying life. A dangerous ease to their way of life had settled over the company. The music from the Armed Forces radio was even played a bit louder than normal. More drawings on uniforms popped up, particularly on helmet covers. Many of the troops had carved small branches from local trees to make "short-timer sticks". They began brandishing them in front of other Marines, particularly the newly arrived ones, to show how few months or weeks they had left to serve in country.

That night, Fox was ordered to get ready to move out the next morning. The noose was about to tighten. The enemy must have sensed it. Cadigan had set up his gun about half-way down the main street of Vinh Dien (2) behind a set of cinder blocks which he and his A-gunner gathered and constructed for their protection as soon as they arrived. They faced rice fields away from the inside of the corridor covering the rear approaches to Fox. Just past midnight Cadigan was looking toward the rice paddies beyond his defensive position. A company from the 26th Marines, 400 meters to his right, opened fire on the enemy. Cadigan waited in anticipation for action in front of him. Instead, he began taking fire from his rear that was coming from across the narrow river on the cordoned side of the hamlet. With others he scrambled into a home across the street. Immediately they began looking out of the windows to see where the fire was coming from. The enemy, close enough to see them, fired at them. Bullets started hitting the outside rear wall. The Marines hunched down to avoid being hit. Cadigan quickly placed his gun on the window sill and fired on the enemy's muzzle flashes. Minutes later, air support silenced the enemy and the night remained quiet until dawn.

By 0700 on 25 November, the entire company left their little oasis and left it in immaculate shape. The battalion was to move to blocking positions along the shallow Song La Tho by evening. To get there the battalion would have to travel through non-secured terrain. The battalion's map showed a few hamlets between the jump off point and the blocking positions. "Intelligence" believed the hamlets once supported or were the homes of local VC. However, no activity had been seen in the past few days, and now the intel-community believed the hamlets were deserted. The rifle companies believed that hamlets supporting the VC with food, munitions storage, and sex were expendable, simply because, if they were not taken apart, they could "turn the tables on us."

Lieutenant Colonel Stemple called his four rifle company commanders together for a conference before kicking off their movement through the non-secured area. The plan was that each company would travel different routes to get to their blocking positions. All companies would tie in together at the river. Fox, on the battalion's far right, would tie in with a company from the Battalion Landing Team, BLT 2/26, and with Golf Company on Fox's left.

Stemple, the China Marine, asked if anyone had any questions. Hotel Company's new company commander, Captain Drez, asked, "Sir, what sort of enemy resistance can we expect?"

"There are only two confirmed units in the area: the R-20 VC Battalion and the 1st Battalion, 36th NVA Regiment."

"What's their strength, Sir?" he probed.

"Well, they had a approximately 630 men when we kicked this thing off," Stemple answered. "Since then with 2/7's big fight in the Horseshoe sector on 22 November and other attempted break outs, they are probably down to about 300–400. Those battalions have been squeezing down on the enemy for five days and now it is our turn to tighten the noose."

The lanky Golf Company Commander offered his thoughts, "We will have to watch for any dangers lurking in front of 2/5's movement." He paused for a moment while reflecting. Then in his deep-toned voice he continued his gloomy prognostication, "The enemy has mortars, recoilless rifles, snipers, and automatic weapons. We are dealing with trapped, perhaps desperate enemy forces. We better be prepared for a major fight."

The Golf Company CO's half-empty glass of water view irritated Captain Brown. Hell, the enemy was almost finished! This was Lieutenant Colonel Stemple's show, but Brown had no wish to have the new Hotel CO walk away with shaky knees. The last thing Fox needed was a weak link in their battalion chain. Provoked, Brown felt his emotions swelling, "Desperate, maybe. But doomed, certainly." Brown's adrenaline pumped as he went on, "Our Marines are tigers! Their training's so superior! We're rested and in far better condition than those under-fed, malaria-stricken, and scared, poor bastards." He continued, "The enemy may have a few light support weapons, but they are of absolutely no equal to the vastly superior supporting arms that we have. Jesus, they may have snipers and mortars, but that is no match for our A-4s, F-4s, Cobra helicopters, 8-inch guns, 155mm and 105mm howitzers, tanks, and a lot more! What are rifles and mortars against us?

He paused only slightly, "Those poor gooks in there are about to get their asses kicked. There is absolutely nothing to be concerned about. We'll rip 'em up!" Now, out of any thing else to contribute, Brown fell silent, so did the other commanders.

After about fifteen seconds, the China Marine said, "All right then. Let's move out!"

Brown, fully pumped, returned to the company and summoned his platoon commanders and the gunny. "We'll move out with the 1st and 3rd Platoons up. Bill Melton's 3rd Platoon will tie into Golf Company on the left during the movement. The 1st Platoon will tie into the 3rd Platoon, while the company command group and the 2nd Platoon will follow in trace of the 1st Platoon. The 3rd Platoon's route should be the slowest, so they'll set the pace."

The combined cordon movement began around 0930 under partly clouded skies. Beyond the few unoccupied hamlets that stood 1,000 meters in front of them was dense terrain. Corporal Gus Grillo of the 2nd Platoon reminded a few of his men to pay attention to his instructions.

Corporal George Blunt of the 1st Platoon was working equally as hard with the movement of his squad. These were two of the best squad leaders in the company, perhaps in the battalion. All, particularly their own men, respected them. Squad members hung onto their every word.

Captain Brown, having given his "half-time pep talk" to the other commanders and not Fox Company, observed the too relaxed men of Company F. They weren't hungry. Psychologically, they were still lulled by the five-day stay on unofficial R&R. Where were the Ferocious Fighting Fox tigers? Where was their blood lust? Brown thought. There was no place for a 3rd quarter slump in this game.

Within an hour, the lead squad of the 1st Platoon, led by Corporal Jerry Witforth, began receiving a few rifle shots from a withdrawing enemy soldier or two. No Marines were hit. The shots acted as a wake up call for the troops.

Witforth's squad entered the hamlet looking anxious. Their instincts were returning. Along with the rest of the platoon, the squad immediately began a house-to-house search. They did find stores of rice and small arms munitions in one of the first hooches.

"Skipper," Gunny Dierdalh said, "there's no time to search all the hooches. We'll need a couple hours. I'll bet they have a lot of supplies here the local Cong could use."

Fox had to move out to keep pace with Golf Company and the rest of the cordon, so there was no time to continue to search the other fifteen to twenty hooches.

"Guns," Brown replied nodding in agreement, "let's torch it!" Then, he provided his justification, "There won't be any more Vietnamese coming back here. They all went to the refugee camp or, if they were VC, they went into the middle of the trap, and we'll get them soon enough."

The troops, like grade school boys being let out for recess on a warm spring day, embraced their task with utter abandonment. Soon, white and black smoke billowed upward. With smiles on their faces that came from ridding the area of any enemy support, Fox Marines returned to their squads and made ready to move out.

The order to move out was delayed as Lance Corporal Bilski, Captain Brown's radio operator, approached the captain with urgent message. "Sir," Ski said, "Texas Pete Six wants you to call him ASAP! Colonel Stemple is going to ask you about the fire. Apparently he's riding around in a chopper with the regimental CO, and he's demanding an answer."

Oops. It's Professor Stemple again, Brown thought, and this time I'm going to get zapped!

Bilski, after being with Brown four months, could read his boss like a book. He knew Brown was about to fess up to his boss that he had ordered the troops to torch the hamlet. Instead of placing the radio handset into Brown's outstretched hand, he pulled it back away from him. "Skipper," Bilski started, demanding the captain's attention, "Don't tell him we torched the vil." He paused for time, "You can't do that!" When it was clear that Brown was listening, Bilski explained, "You got to say it happened some other way. Like we shot a rocket at those guys that shot at the 1st Platoon as we were coming in here. Anything!"

Brown, honest to a fault, reluctantly nodded as he agreed with his savvy Chicago-bred radio operator and the sage advice he had just been offered. Bilski had Brown's best interests in mind, but more importantly, he liked this gung-ho, fearless captain; and he protected him whenever possible. Bilski passed the handset to the captain.

"Texas Pete Six, this is Fox Six, over," Captain Brown finally responded.

"Fox Six, I want to know exactly what the hell is going on down there!" Stemple demanded.

"What do you mean, Sir? Over."

"The fire where you are standing!" Stemple demanded again.

"Oh," Brown murmured which sounded something along the lines of 'Oh, THAT fire!' "Well, when we entered the vil we took fire, Sir. We fired a couple of 3.5 rockets at them. The enemy withdrew, but a couple of hooches caught on fire. It spread fast," he continued. "The troops were trying to put it out, but the gunny and I thought that was too dangerous, so we pulled the troops back; and now we're ready to move out, over."

"Fox Six, that better be the story! Out."

Brown looked at Bilski who wore a large, lopsided smile on his face for saving his boss's butt, which of course he had. By this time the gunny had joined the two of them in time to catch most of the radio conversation. Brown squinted his eyes, "Ski, I'm going to skin you alive if Stemple ever finds out the truth!"

Lance Corporal Bilski laughed heartily knowing he would die before any one in battalion ever found out what happened. Gunny Dierdalh chuckled as well. Then in his gruff voice he asked, "Are you ready to move 'em out, Skipper?"

Brown looked at his two friends and said, "You assholes. Yeah, let's get going."

On the way to the river, the Golf Company CO complained to Brown that his platoon was at the correct coordinates where it should have tied into Fox's 3rd Platoon, but Melton's platoon was missing. Brown asked Bill Melton to affirm his position. "Mustang Mike" Melton assured Brown that he was at the assigned coordinates.

Brown reported this information to the Golf CO. Five minutes later, Stemple intervened, demanding an explanation. When Brown asked, "Are we going to question whether or not Mustang Mike can read a map?" Stemple dropped the issue.

Fox arrived at the river by mid-afternoon and finally tied in with Golf Company and a company from 26th Marines. The companies set up along the river's serpentine bank as a blocking force. The noose was tightening around the large, trapped group of VC and NVA. Fox was part of the blocking force while the other Marine units drove the enemy right towards them.

While the 1st and 3rd Platoons easily dug two-man foxholes in the sandy soil along the river's bank, most of the 2nd Platoon manned a trench line behind them for rear security. No one quite fully comprehended the trench's origin. A few of the Marines said it was a former NVA trench, proving the enemy was here in mass! Others said that maybe the ARVN or US forces had dug it earlier during the past couple of years. The more imaginative among the Marines, men like Corporal Marc Waszkiewicz, suggested it had to have come from the French, long ago. Its origin aside, most of the 2nd Platoon Marines rejoiced that they did not have to dig a foxhole!

Fox settled in for a long night. Brown, Waszkiewicz, Dierdalh, Bilski, and the rest of the company command group slept near the 2nd Platoon. Waszkiewicz was sleeping in a two-man hooch consisting of two snapped-together ponchos. Early in the morning, sometime about 0400, he was awakened not fully but to a level of half-awareness common for infantrymen in Vietnam. There was an annoying yet ever-so-gentle finger-prodding sensation to the portion of his torso contacting the ground. Not sure if he was dreaming, Waszkiewicz repeatedly ignored the nearly imperceptible "finger-poking". Finally, in a thrashing, spinning motion he arose, rolled back the ground-covering poncho on which he had been sleeping, and directed his red lens-covered flashlight onto the dirt. His face soured as he looked at what appeared to be an asparagus farm! The poking had come from huge earthworms. They had feasted for years on the corpses buried below the 2nd Platoon in an unmarked cemetery. Now they sensed his body heat, and were seeking entry to his warmth only micro-inches away! Disgusted, he moved to another location twenty-five meters away.

The morning was sunny and pleasant. Fox was set in waiting for the enemy cattle drive to cross the river and come their way. There was nothing to do but wait and watch. Spirits were high despite the rounds occasionally being shot over their heads by Marine Corps companies as they drove the enemy towards Fox. The men played cards, wrote letters, and shot the bull. However, as the day wore on, boredom set in.

Corporal Waszkiewicz, and Sergeant Donny Serowik, a 2nd Platoon squad leader, grew tired of playing cards when their attention turned toward finding a victim to harass. They noticed Staff Sergeant Marshall sleeping in his hammock about twenty feet away. Despite respected and repeated acts of braveness, Marshall had gained a reputation of being a dedicated, over-serious disciplinarian. They referred to him as a "lifer"—a Marine who would stay in the Corps for at least twenty years. Marshall, like many Marines, had acquired an NVA hammock and used it for sleeping off the ground. At that moment, he was sound asleep in his olive green canvas hammock, strung between two small, tipping banana trees. He almost looked like a banana in his hammock...How peaceful...How vulnerable...How tempting...How irresistible!

Waszkiewicz had a smile on his face and a twinkle in his eye. He looked at his buddy and said in a mock British accent, "Don, did you know that that fine "lifer" is totally obsessed with a phobic fear of creepy-crawly things, especially slithery snake-like ones?"

"No, Mr. Waszkiewicz, I was wholly unaware of that fact," Serowik replied with his own mock propriety. Serowik was now also beaming ear to ear.

"Secondly, Mr. Serowik," Waszkiewicz announced, "have you observed the most ingenious creation made by our fine 'lifer'? That is, the stringing of a clothesline directly over his body from which is stretched a poncho, tied down at the spread-out corners, and thus making a shade covering over his hammock?"

Serowik looked at Marshall then back to Waszkiewicz and responded, "You know the man is quite clever."

The two nearly burst out loud with impish laugher. Serowik dug up some of the foot-long worms that had awakened Waszkiewicz the night before. Each was as thick as a man's index finger. Waszkiewicz carefully and quietly untied the ropes holding the pegs of the poncho corners. Then with the same nylon ropes he tied the grommet eyes of that poncho together underneath Marshall's hammock encasing the sleeping staff sergeant within his own poncho.

Giggling, Waszkiewicz said, "He looks like a sausage, or a tamale, wrapped in corn husks."

CPL MARC WASZKIEWICZ (RIGHT) AND HIS RADIO OPERATOR ENJOYING A LITTLE LEVITY ON OPERATION MEADE RIVER

(Courtesy of Marc Waskiewicz)

Serowik added, "Perhaps a hot dog in a bun. Or a 'lifer', right where we like him to be."

The two poured literally dozens of the hideous, flesh-seeking giant earth worm body hunters into both of the tiny, restricted openings at the head and foot of Marshall's hammock encasement. They then retreated back to their area twenty feet away and pretended to be busy doing "Nothing in particular, Sir" after motioning to all the surrounding troops to "hush" and say nothing.

Time passed. Occasional chuckles from numerous Marines threatened to blow the surprise, but no, Marshall slept on. Quietly. Peacefully. Until…

The poncho encasement and canvass hammock began to move. The Marines observed what appeared to be an elbow poking the material followed by stillness. They knew what was about to happen! More rustling. More tossing. Slow at first but with a rising tempo and intensity that gave way to screams and curses! Wailing! Flailing! Ripping apart the entire banana-taco-tamale-hot dog in one final magnificent thrash, Staff Sergeant Marshall exploded from his encasement and drew himself up to full height and "command-rank" stature screaming, "Who the fuck did this!!!!!"

Everyone was "busy doing nothing, Sir" and ignored his rage. The occasional chortlings and choking sounds of stifled laughter only heightened Marshall's commitment to seek the perpetrators and deliver justice! Justice, however, did not prevail because Marshall never did find out who it was.

The 1st and 3rd Platoons held their positions on the evening of 26 November along the river, while the 2nd Platoon guarded the company's rear. The entrapped enemy with the noose tightening around their necks could cross the shallow river at numerous points so an attempted escape was anticipated. Fox's rear defense was closed in tightly as numerous trails leading to the river meandered into the 2nd Platoon's position. The 2nd Platoon had established listening posts seventy-five meters on those trails away from the platoon's main position. The sun set, and vigilance began.

Sometime after 2100 hours "Puff the Magic Dragon" or just plain "Puff", the AC-130 aircraft equipped with Gatling-like machine guns, a 105mm cannon, and a flare-dropping system went to work inside the corridor. Most grunt warriors loved this sight. The jet-black night became a distance backdrop. Puff lit up the stage with flares that gently floated with the wind. Each flare, held aloft by a parachute, would oscillate back and forth like a clock's pendulum and illuminate the "stage" for almost a minute. As one flare began to dim another would replace it. The light was continual. Then the invisible protagonist, "Puff's" rapidly firing machine guns would roar as only a dragon could. The guns spewed bullets so fluidly that every fifth one equipped with a red burning tracer joined the previous tracer to look like a solid red stream of dragon fire poured out from above. The sky was aglow. The night came alive. Fox Company could easily see across the sixty-meter river and into the scrub bushes beyond. This was pure entertainment for the troops, not so for the trapped enemy.

Within an hour, Fox's neighbors from the 26th Marines became the site of the attempted break out. Their machine guns started blazing. Artillery HE rounds began exploding across the river from friendly lines. Hand-held flares poured additional illumination in front of their position less than a half-mile away. Lance Corporal Dennis Cadigan turned to his assistant gunner, a newly arrived Marine. Cadigan constantly doubted the young man's ability to "assist" should it be necessary, and softly murmured, "Looks like the gooks are going to make a break for it. Better stay alert."

The action died in twenty minutes. All was silent. The night grew pitch dark. Cadigan felt as if he were walking down a dark alley alone. This is when combatants quietly steal a feel for their weapons. Riflemen check that magazines are fully inserted while their safeties are on. Machine gunners ensure links are fed and ready to chamber. Marines were trained for this moment. Some welcomed it. Most didn't.

0215 hours. Still quiet except for occasional snoring, the night waned on. Dennis Cadigan had taken over his portion of the watch fifteen minutes earlier after being awakened from a deep sleep. The night was still black and silent. The temperature had fallen. Cadigan could hear up to thirty to forty meters away. He could see for fifteen to twenty meters.

A sudden, large explosion ripped from the 2nd Platoon's Listening Post #1, seventy-five meters away from Cadigan and along one of the trails that meandered into the rear of Fox Company. Heard by those on guard who immediately woke their foxhole mates, the company silently went on full alert. After a couple of minutes following the explosion, the 2nd Platoon radio operator whispered to Cadigan that, "Milligan's LP had a couple of gooks coming at them and they fired off a Claymore that 'cut 'em in half'."

When the sun rose, the 2nd Platoon reported that the gooks killed the night before most likely were married. He had an SKS rifle and she had been seven or eight months pregnant.

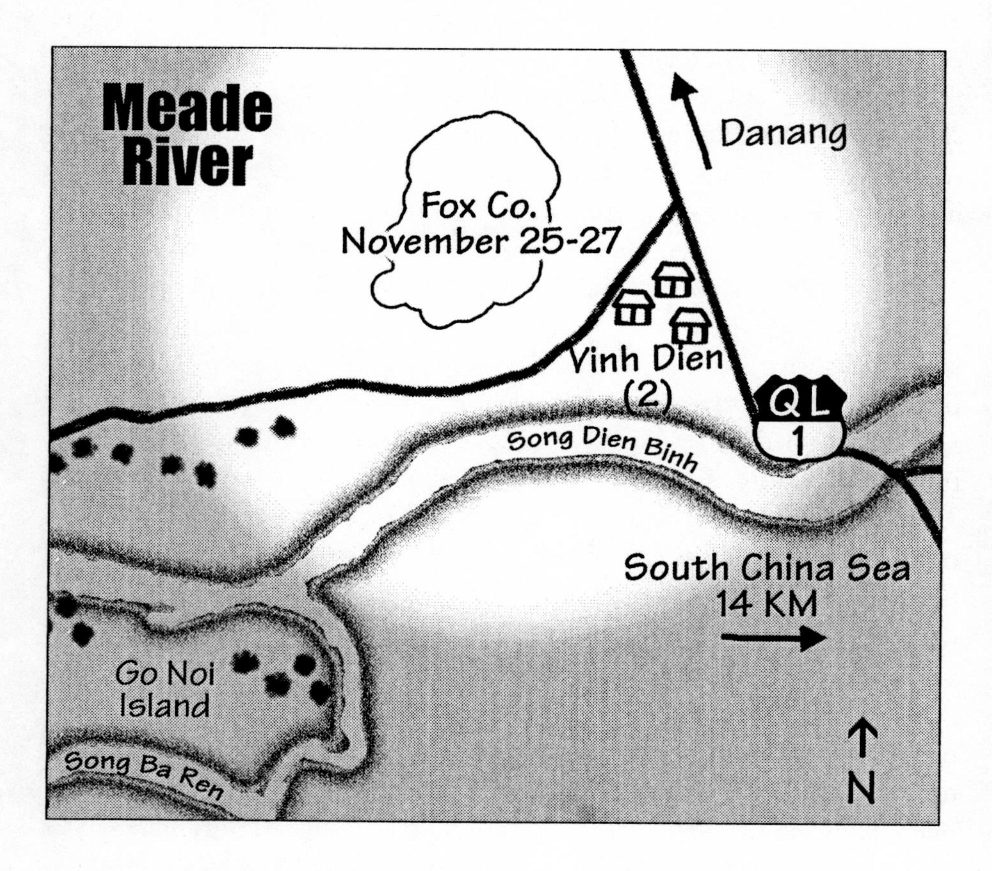

Fox Company held their position along the river with two platoons. Captain Brown and the 2nd Platoon conducted a sweep of the hamlets immediately behind the company's position away from the corridor. Cadigan anticipated some resistance given all the action the night before. He was nervous but excited as usual about the prospect of moving around and a possible engagement. The platoon began its movement across a large rice field toward a tree line. Fox started taking some sniper rounds from the distant trees. The platoons spread out further as the men began hustling across the open field.

At 1430 Fox entered the tree line that had concealed a small deserted hamlet. The 2nd Platoon started throwing grenades into bunkers in and around the five or six straw huts. They set up perimeter security for the platoon and company command group.

Before long, Cadigan's A-Gunner came over to him, pointed at a hut with roof-like canopy that created an appearance of a front porch and said, "Lance Corporal Cadigan, there's something strange looking about an M-60 ammo can over there."

Convinced his A-Gunner was totally useless, Cadigan demanded, "Here, give me your damn rifle." Cadigan walked over to the hooch all the while preoccupied with the inabilities of his A-Gunner. Up to that point, Cadigan had never touched anything that even looked like it might be booby-trapped. However, on that afternoon, 27 November, he walked up to the ammo can and without thinking, bent down and with the tip of the rifle flipped up the lid of the can.

He watched the explosion shoot right at him and instinctively tried to turn away. The speed of the detonation outstripped Cadigan's instinctive head turn and its force flung him back ten feet from the blast. The impact of the blast ripped through his left arm, chest wall, and the left side of his face. Both his eyes were blown right out of their sockets and lay dangling on Cadigan's cheeks. His right side received other permanent injuries, but not as severe. The explosion threw grit and gun powder into his face. It lacerated his chest wall and shattered his left arm. Even though he felt no pain, he rolled over knowing he was badly hurt. Cadigan said an act of contrition for his foolish impulse then. He heard the platoon corpsman, Doc Stork, running up. Cadigan felt the corpsman pushing on his chest. Cadigan groaned, "Get off!"

Stork said, "Quiet." Cadigan then tried to wipe the dirt out of his eyes but the corpsman grabbed his hands and said, "No. Don't do that. Let the dirt alone. I'll clean it up."

Acquiescing, Cadigan finally said, "Fine, Doc, do your thing."

The last sight Cadigan ever saw as his optic nerves died were the dim shadows of Marines standing round. These were his best friends. How many times had he stood where they were standing looking down on a buddy who had been badly wounded? He wanted to ease their pain and said with a smile, "Well, I guess I'm going back to the world, and you guys have to stay here."

He was upset to leave these guys, the Marines Corps, and the combat actions that had begun to reshape the somewhat bitter psychological profile he had brought to the war in August: one of anger towards his nation and its many political actions including its involvement in Vietnam. He knew he was hurt and probably was not coming back, and this crushed him more than anything else at that moment.

The men left one at a time in silence. Cadigan was now finally bandaged and alone with Doc Stork. Deep in thought and still without pain, Cadigan cursed. He would miss these friends. He wanted to be able to stay with them forever. He would miss not being able to fight for his country. He would miss being a Marine.

Captain Brown softly asked for Cadigan's attention, "Corporal Cadigan?"

"Sir?" Cadigan responded, recognizing his skipper's voice with false hope that there would be just one more, tough mission he would be ordered to do for Fox Company.

Brown held Cadigan's right hand that somehow escaped the blast and looked down at his bandaged head. "I'm going to miss you. You are an outstanding Marine." Brown paused collecting his thoughts while looking at the bloodied Marine. "You have been an inspiration to us all. We'll survive without you, but it won't be easy."

"Thank you, Sir," Cadigan responded with humility. "I'm going to miss you all."

Not wanting to close the door forever, Brown said, "You're from New Jersey, aren't you?"

"Yes, Sir."

"I'm from Pennsylvania and believe I'll be stationed in Quantico in a couple of months. I'd love to visit with you again."

"That would be great, Sir."

"Sir," Doc Stork interrupted.

Brown looked at Stork.

"The medevac bird is almost here."

"Right, Doc. Get Cadigan home safely."

On 4 December Fox and the rest of 2/5 left the cordon as the perimeter continued to tighten. 2/5 was no longer needed. They swept southwest toward Go Noi Island.

CHAPTER 17: CHRISTMAS IN THE MOUNTAINS

The transition from Operation Meade River to Operation Taylor Common was seamless. Returning to An Hoa via Go Noi Island, 2/5 participated in Meade River through 6 December 1968 under the operational control, OPCON, of the 1st Marines and was chopped back to the 5th Marines at 1800 hours on 6 December. The battalion and its rifle companies swept a portion of the An Hoa valley from Liberty Bridge to the combat base on 7 December and 8 December. The objective was to push the enemy generally westward and into the mountains. That sweep was Phase I of Operation Taylor Common.

The OPCON transition was not only the only thing that appeared seamless. There seemed to be no break in the monsoon rain falling from the omnipresent gray skies onto the muddy six-inch to six-foot deep rice paddies as well. Thus, on 7 December and 8 December, Fox Company Marines patrolled with ponchos over top of their flak jackets and water dripping from their helmets. Marines were restricted to travel on slick trails and rice paddy dikes, easy areas where the enemy could place mines and booby trap trip wires. Their fingers possessed the white, wrinkled look of those on a body pulled out of a river. Their feet looked the same when their "jungle boots" were removed. Cigarettes became harder and harder to light and hot C-ration coffee started tasting better. The monsoons would last until February.

From 9 December through 12 December, Fox stayed inside the battalion area that had been moved to just outside the main base's fence. There was a certain degree of ambivalence regarding the "comforts" of a large combat base. Taking a shower required wrapping a fairly soiled towel around the mid-waist, getting into rubber "go-aheads", walking one hundred meters in the chilly rain on a slippery, muddy road that led to the showers. The showers were in large general purpose tents. What grass that may have been there before no longer grew, and wooden pallets now provided the flooring. Since soap racks were non-existent, the many pieces of partially used bars of soap that had slipped from the wet hands of showering Marines fell irretrievably between the pallets and emitted a wretchedly-sweet perfumed odor. The shower water was unheated. Other than the concept of a shower being hygienically a plus, the shower experience was awful.

Phase II of Operation Taylor Common was designed to prevent NVA regulars' use of the mountainous trails west of An Hoa that connected the Ho Chi Minh trail to the rice paddies and urban areas south of Da Nang. According to intelligence reports, the caves and camps were used by transient NVA soldiers and not used as base camps.

The concept of operations was for the Marine infantry battalions to establish Fire Support Bases, FSBs, on mountaintops with artillery batteries from the 12th Marines. Once established, the battalions would send their rifle companies out in a 2,000-meter radius of the FSB to locate and destroy the enemy along the trail networks in the valleys. Throughout the operation, after a period of a few weeks, the battalions would begin leapfrogging westward towards the Laotian border. 2/5's mission was to establish a FSB on Hill 214 and conduct combat patrols within its 2,000-meter radius. Hill 214, operationally named FSB Pike, was ten kilometers west of An Hoa and six kilometers northwest of the Nong Son coalmines.

On the drizzly morning of Friday, 13 December, combat engineers supporting 2/5 rappelled from helicopters through the triple canopy of trees onto Hill 214. The engineers rapidly cleared the mountaintop's trees with explosives. Golf Company landed immediately after and secured the perimeter. Lieutenant Colonel Stemple's Jump CP, or forward command post, followed. Fox Company landed in the next choppers some time around 1100.

Fox expected an easy trek that day. They had been ordered to move from Hill 214 to Hill 258 approximately 1800 meters away or just a bit over a mile to the south. The stream, 114 meters below and halfway between the hills, would serve as a nice breakpoint. Despite the fact there were no trails on the map, Captain Brown anticipated arriving at Hill 258 by late afternoon in time to clear it with explosives for Fox's resupply choppers the next day.

After thirty minutes of hacking with a machete, the lead platoon had traversed about 150 meters down the hill. Most of the last platoon waiting to start down the tunnel trail cut by the machete hackers still remained up on Hill 214. Brown worked his way to the front to assess the situation. He found the jungle density so thick that the Marines with the machetes could last only about eight to ten minutes at a time. Those that were finished chopping lay sweat-soaked and exhausted in the brush along the trail. Other Marines worked their way forward until it was their turn to grab the handle of the three-pound cutting tool. They would step over those resting.

The company snaked its way downward for about two and a half hours. By then doubt crept into the minds of the leaders, fueled by fear that those on point maybe going in an unwanted and lengthy direction. Within the dense, triple canopy, the sky could be seen above their heads only occasionally, but they had had no views of terrain in front of them. The platoon commanders, gunnery sergeant, and artillery forward observer met with the skipper to confirm direction and location. No one was wholly confident as to Fox's precise location.

Brown updated his command group, "Okay guys, we've been at this path for almost three hours. I know we've been going downhill all that time and that we are generally going south. But we may not be going the most direct way to the stream, and if we're off by five degrees, it may end up costing up to an extra two hours of chopping. Hell, in here it's hard to tell. Anyone got an idea?"

First Lieutenant Melton responded first, "I'm about eighty percent sure we are going the right way."

First Lieutenant Lott added, "I have been tracking with my compass. A couple of times, because of the ridges, we were heading southwest. But mostly we are going south, so I think we are close to being on track."

Gunnery Sergeant Dierdalh put in, "Well, I heard the battery registering their guns when we were up at the top. Then, I was confident where we were. Now the gun noise seems to be echoing off different hills, and I am no longer as sure as I had been."

Corporal Waszkiewicz asked, "You want to mark a target, Skipper?"

"Yeah, go ahead, Marc. They may as well hit this side of the top of our objective, Hill 258. Have them fire an HE instead of a Willie Peter. We'll be able to hear it better," Brown answered.

Corporal Waszkiewicz replied, "Roger, Sir." Then speaking into his radio handset he said, "Head Cold Echo, this is Beechnut 64 fire mission, over. Request spotting round grid Zula Charlie 203439, shell HE, orientation round. One gun adjust. Azimuth 2955 mils. Request splash, over."

Everyone waited silently with compasses in hand looking in a south by southeasterly direction as specified by Waszkiewicz with his Azimuth 2955.

"Shot away," Waskiewicz announced just in front of the noise of the single howitzer firing from FSB Pike behind them.

About thirty-five seconds later the noise from the exploding round could be heard. It confirmed the route's general correctness. With that, Brown said, "All right, let's move out again."

Ironically, just like a plot in a bad comedy show, within ten minutes the lead men reached the streambed, so of course by then, they all knew exactly where they were.

The 3rd platoon crossed the waist-high, twenty-meter wide streambed and took the point chopping their way up toward Hill 258. The 1st and 2nd Platoons patrolled in different directions upstream and downstream along an already established NVA trail that crisscrossed the stream every one hundred meters or so. The stream weaved in and out so rapidly that the jungle swallowed up the men of both platoons within twenty to thirty meters after they split. Captain Brown and Gunny Sergeant Dierdalh sat along the stream, where the 1st and 2nd Platoons split, discussing options should the company not reach the top of Hill 258 by nightfall. Lance Corporal Bilski and the new battalion radio operator, Private First Class Mike Malanowski who had replaced Corporal "Pancho" Gomez, were receiving routine messages and responding on occasion "Say again all after........."

Twenty minutes passed. Unexpectedly, the sound of a man running noisily from the direction of the 1st Platoon suddenly silenced all discussions. Was it a Marine from the 1st Platoon or an NVA who had hid from the platoon until they passed his location? Brown's right hand slowly reached for his M-16 leaning against a nearby tree. Dierdalh moved his index finger of his right hand down along the upper portion of his .45 caliber pistol holster, catching it, and lifting it up silently enabling him to withdraw the weapon.

Then, a 6-foot Marine seemed to be propelled from the jungle and appeared: eyes wide open and gasping for air. Corporal Bill Higgins, a squad leader with the 1st Platoon and an absolutely handsome twenty-one year-old with a chiseled physique, red hair and freckles, stopped running when he reached the command group. Searching rapidly for Captain Brown and finding him standing ready and waiting for the news, Higgins panted, "Skipper, are there any 'slopes' up here?"

"No, Corporal Higgins, only NVA," Brown answered.

"Shit! We were about to cross a stream and they were about to cross from the other side," Higgins panted as he turned and ran, disappearing as fast as he popped in.

Brown smiled at Dierdalh. He felt pride in his aggressive men but even more pride that they had judgment enough to verify the absence of innocent civilians prior to harming any.

An hour later, the 3rd Platoon reported easier going up to Hill 258. Corporal Bill Higgins had radioed to report that, by the time he returned to his squad, the enemy had run back the way they had come. He and his squad were unable to catch up with them. With that information, Captain Brown directed First Lieutenant Lott and his 1st Platoon to establish night ambush positions along the stream and be prepared to join the company on Hill 258 in the morning. Brown, the company command group, and the 2nd Platoon would follow in trace of the 3rd Platoon up to Hill 258.

No significant action occurred following the first encounter. By 16 December, Fox was becoming familiar with Hill 258 and its surrounding area. The hill, rising 150 meters up from two streams below it, was generally configured like the top half of a football resting on the ground. It was sloped reasonably well on its 2000-meter north-south axis but was dangerously steep on its west side. Actually, the northern side had three navigable ridges allowing access to the valley below. The platoons had been patrolling during the day from the hilltop down to the large stream that they had first crossed three days earlier. The stream, Khe Gio, ran along the hill's western side and flowed northeastward towards the Song Thu Bon ten kilometers away. A no-name dry stream ran along the valley floor along the hill's eastern side, where patrols found no signs of enemy activity. Night ambushes were set along the Khe Gio stream at various positions.

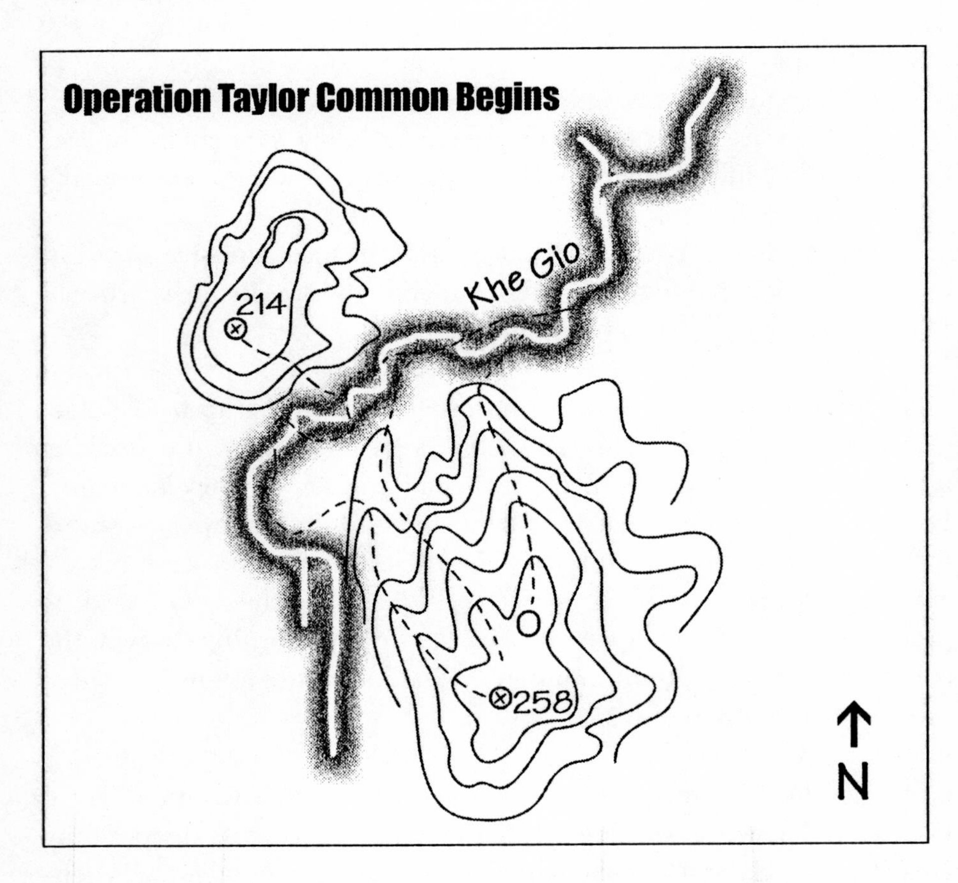

At 0830 on 16 December, Melton's 3rd Platoon was ordered to patrol the trail network beside the Khe Gio from the point where the north side's western ridge touched the valley floor and return by way of the center ridge. Melton selected his 1st Squad led by Corporal Bill Baumgardt to make the patrol. Baumgardt had been a 140-pound state-wrestling champion in junior college and, with almost two years of college under his belt prior to joining Fox Company ten months earlier, he was quite savvy and highly trusted by First Lieutenant Bill Melton.

"Sergeant Baumgardt," Melton called.

"Sir," Baumgardt acknowledged, never understanding why Melton called him "sergeant" instead of "corporal".

"Baumgardt, I want you to take your squad down this western finger to the stream and look for any signs of enemy," Melton said while pointing at his map. "Then return here to Fox's lines by way of this center ridge."

"Yes, Sir," barked Baumgardt, fully comprehending the mission.

"You'll be on your own down there, so be cautious, because if you get in trouble we won't be able to bail you out right away."

"Sir!" the soft-spoken Baumgardt sharply replied.

"Oh yeah, last night a couple of scout-dog teams were flown in, and I'm giving one to you for this patrol."

"Very well, Sir."

"Any questions?"

"No, Sir."

"How soon do you think you'll be ready to move out?"

"About twenty minutes," Baumgardt answered.

"Good. That will give me enough time to work up some checkpoints and artillery fire missions you can use. Pick them up on your way out."

By 1245 Corporal Baumgardt's squad had reached the dense valley floor and had picked up a trail leading to the stream. Lance Corporal Gary Conner's three-man fire team had the point. Baumgardt assigned the dog and its handler to Conner. Baumgardt and his radioman, Lance Corporal "H. C." Constantine, followed. The remaining two fire teams were behind the radioman with the attached two-man machine gun team taking up the rear.

Lance Corporal Conner's fire team consisted of himself, Private First Class Romero, Private First Class Williams, and the canine team. Still hidden by the brush along the trail, Conner soon began to hear the babble of the mountain stream as it rushed the monsoon rains over rocks toward the Song Thu Bon. He held his men up and worked his way to the point. Like most experienced combatants, Conner principally trusted his own instincts when danger was present. He crept forward cautiously.

LANCE CORPORAL CONNER APPROACHING DANGER ZONE

(Photo courtesy of Gary Cooper)

Upon reaching a clearing, Conner saw the rapidly flowing stream ten to fifteen feet below. Large boulders separated the trail's end from a small sandy beach beside the water. Conner could see across the thirty meter-wide stream to a four-foot bank cut out by the water. Rocks the size of bowling balls were being washed in the middle of the two-foot deep stream. Again Conner held up his fire team. He was reluctant to cross as he suspected they would find themselves in a "kill zone" for any enemy who may be set into the bushes beyond the far bank. Their vulnerability would only increase while they were in the middle of the stream. Conner checked left and right of the clearing only to find out the stream was too deep and too swift to cross anywhere but at the present site. Reluctantly, Conner ordered the dog team across first. When dog and its handler reached the middle of the water, Conner singled for Romero to cross, believing that he would be in the middle of the stream by the time the German Shepard dog reached the far bank and was able to sniff out any enemy. Forty seconds passed. Conner nodded to Williams to go. Thirty seconds later, Conner moved into the stream himself.

Lance Corporal Connor did not want to alert the enemy of the squad's size and formation, so he suddenly turned back to inform Corporal Baumgardt of the situation.

At that moment, Baumgardt had just reached the large rocks at the top of the clearing and had seen Gary Conner, below, abruptly turn around and walk toward him. The lead fire team had already been committed and were in the water. By then it was too late for him to bring the machine gun team to the edge of the clearing and have them recon the far bank by fire.

The enemy opened up with a machine gun and automatic weapons fire. Lance Corporal Conner dove back towards the beach and was immediately hit by an AK-47 round. He instinctively looked for his men only to see Private First Class Romero lying in the river trying to crawl to the beach. He could not find Private First Class Williams.

"Williams," Conner called out hoping to find his other fire team member. But he could not make any noticeable sound. The bullet had ripped through his chest cavity and punctured his lung. Instinctively, he got back on his feet ran forward three, perhaps four, steps before passing out at the bottom of the large rocks.

Baumgardt's eyes scanned the scene. Bullets were filling the air from the brush thirty-five meters away. Initially, the dog looked wounded, but it was merely disoriented by the exploding weapons fire. The dog jumped off the bank joining its handler who had fallen back into the stream and was now tightly pressed against the far bank safely below the trajectory of the enemy's fire.

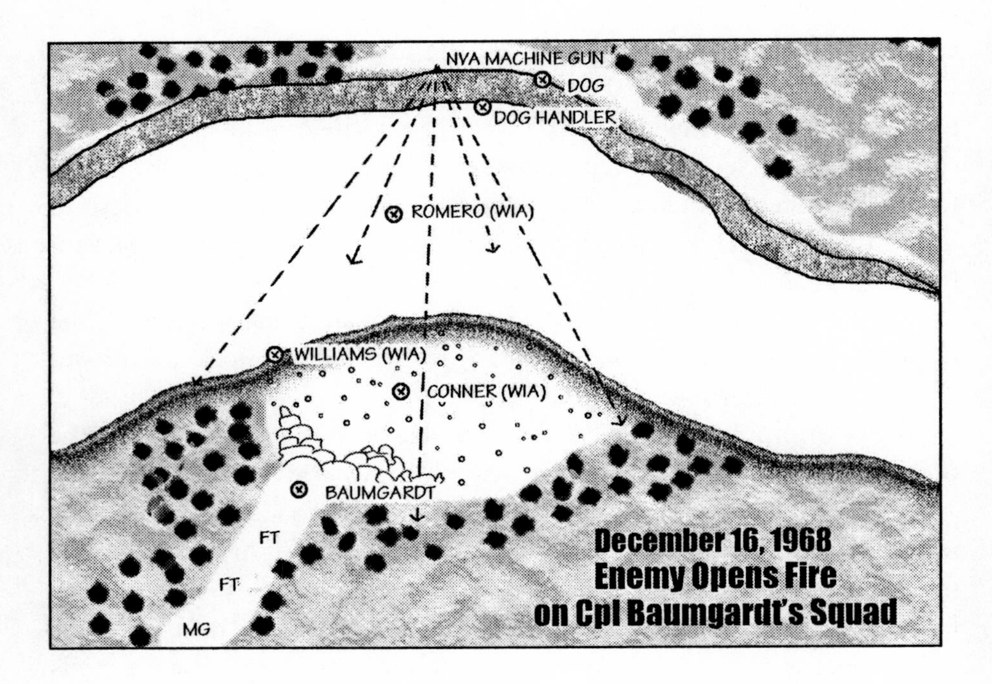

Baumgardt yelled, "Jonesy, get the gun up here!"

Baumgardt, still scanning, saw Romero trying to get back. He was in the center of the two-foot stream, obviously unable to stand and struggling to keep his head up even in the shallow water. "He's not going to make it," Baumgardt concluded.

The enemy's rounds continued unabatedly, filling the air with noise, water, and sand.

Baumgardt looked to the left and right. The other fire teams reached the jungle's edge and began firing. The machine gun was setting up and would fire in a few seconds. Firing his M-16 rifle at the enemy,

Baumgardt leaped upward and ran down the hill over the rocks and through the sand.

Continuing to fire as he entered the stream, he reached Romero before the wounded Marine went under. Baumgardt slung his rifle strap over his head. Applying wrestling techniques, he quickly grabbed Romero's upper right arm, ducked his head under the wounded man's chest and flung him on his back in a fireman's carry. He began racing back to the rocks. The enemy, luckily firing their version of a Maggie's Drawers, sent bullets splashing around Baumgardt's legs and crackling past his and Romero's ears.

With adrenalin pumping, Baumgardt's thoughts for Romero's safety flashed through his mind. Then, the heroic squad leader heard a groan-like command coming from his wounded passenger, "Run faster! Run faster!" Private First Class Romero managed to order his squad leader.

He's still alive, Baumgardt thought joyfully. Baumgardt grunted in response, "If I'm not going fast enough for you, you can get the hell off!"

Baumgardt began his trek back across the beach and up the large rocks. By that time he was covered with the blood gushing out of Romero's upper left thigh. He saw Jonesy, his machine gunner, coming out of the jungle firing across the river from the hip. The gunner eased off enough long enough to let Baumgardt pass by. Baumgardt reached the safety of the jungle trail and met Doc Sonny King, the squad's corps-man, who helped remove Romero from his shoulders. They placed him beside an unconscious Conner who miraculously reached the rocks and was dragged up to safety by Doc King and Lance Corporal Constantine.

Corporal Baumgardt dropped and returned fire while Doc King began working on Romero. He spotted Private First Class Williams on the left side of the beach. How could he have missed him? Williams, a huge Marine, had been shot in one leg. He was now lizard-like moving up the beach to a small sand hill powered by only his arms. Baumgardt raced for him. He had to get over that sand hill for cover, Baumgardt thought as enemy bullets exploded in the sand all around them. His thoughts shifted, make that 'we' have to get cover! Exhausted from car-rying Romero, Baumgardt looked at the large Marine and thought, he must weigh 1,000 pounds...no way can I carry him! He stooped down and began dragging him along the ground. Soon exhausted, Baumgardt pulled Williams over the little sand hill and to safety. Doc King assisted them from there.

Abruptly, the enemy stopped firing.

"Fox Three Alpha, this is Fox Three over," Constantine's radio crackled as First Lieutenant Melton's radio operator contacted the squad.

"This is Three Alpha, go," Constantine responded.

Lance Corporal Wick, Melton's radio operator asked, "Interrogative. We're hearing firing. What's your situation, over?"

"Roger, Three. We were ambushed at a stream crossing. Break. Enemy had a Mike Golf and small arms, probably Alpha-Kilo-47s. Break. Seems like the enemy boogied. Break. We have three Marine Whisky India Alphas, over."

"Roger, Three Alpha wait."

"Three Alpha, this is Three Actual, put on your actual, over," Melton said demanding to talk to Baumgardt.

"Roger Three Alpha," Constantine replied handing the radio's handset to Baumgardt.

"Fox Three, this is Three Alpha," Baumgardt said, still panting.

"Three Alpha, what's your 'pos'? Over," Melton asked.

"Roger Three, we're at Check Point Golf, over."

"Will you need an evac, over?"

"Roger, Sir. We have one sucking chest wound who's coming in and out of consciousness and two with Priority Two leg wounds, over."

"Do you have a Lima Zulu?" Melton asked.

"That's a negative, over." Corporal Buamgardt responded. There was no available landing zone for an evac chopper.

"Roger, Three Alpha. Secure the area. I'll get back to you about the evac, out."

At the stream bank Lance Corporal Conner found himself propped up against a radio between some trees. He remembered trying to get to the rocks. He had been in tremendous pain. Now Doc King was applying plastic gauze to his chest wound. Blood was in his mouth. He saw that Constantine was also there. They must have dragged me here, Conner thought.

Lance Corporal Conner's vision darkened. Then, a pale light came into view again. "Now Corporal Baumgardt's here," Conner deduced from a somewhat cloudy dream. "Good, I don't hurt as much," Conner reflected as the morphine's effect took hold.

"Romero? Williams?" Conner slurred forcing a small stream of blood to trickle down his chin.

"They're okay. Hit in the legs, but they'll make it," Buamgardt said.

A fog drifted over Lance Corporal Conner's mind. As it did, he could hear Corporal Baumgardt telling him to, "Hang in there."

Then, he registered the noise from a helo. Conner thought, Baumgardt's picking me up again; he's carrying me now; guys are yelling; and he's laying me into a wire sled below the helicopter.

Then, Conner saw nothing but blackness.

"Is he gonna' make it, Sonny?" Baumgardt asked anxiously.

"He'll make it. I'm certain of that. But, I wouldn't expect to see him back in the war any time soon," the corpsman forecasted.

19 December 1968 was Second Lieutenant Pete Korn's second day with the 5th Marines and his first with Fox Company. Since he'd arrived in country several days earlier, Korn had become more and more apprehensive about his forthcoming assignment. While deplaning and seeing many body bags waiting to go back to the States, he asked himself, will I go back this way? During the first night at the 1st Marine Division headquarters, they received incoming mortars. Korn crouched in a water-filled shelter with some troops and wished he was somewhere, anywhere else. The next day the Commanding General called in lieutenants and told them they were to look out after their men. While all the other lieutenants trucked to their regiments, due to incessant rain, he waited two days to fly to An Hoa. After arriving at An Hoa and reporting into the 5th Marines, he felt even more isolated as he found his way to 2/5 outside the gate to the main Regimental area. Then, 2/5 assigned him to Fox Co, which was in the hills east of An Hoa on Operation Taylor

Common. The following day, he choppered into the Fox CP on Hill 258. He was greeted by Captain Dave Brown and assigned to the 3rd Platoon.

"Fox Three, this is Fox Six, over," Captain Brown called over the radio for First Lieutenant Melton.

"Roger Six, this is Fox Three," Lance Corporal Wick responded.

"Hey, this is Six Actual, put on your actual," Brown said, his manner upbeat.

"Roger, Sir."

"This is Three Actual," Melton announced.

"Roger, Bill. I have a big surprise for you!"

"Roger, Sir. What is it?"

"Your replacement is here!"

"Now that is a surprise!"

"Roger Three. I'm going to send him out to your position with some men from the Whiskey Platoon. How 'bout you send a patrol to meet them half-way there, over?"

"Roger, Six."

"Oh, and Bill, I will have the Whiskey patrol leader fully briefed on our friendly patrol-identification process."

"Roger, Six, out."

At an unfortunate incident in October, one of Fox's patrols ran into another patrol from a different platoon, resulting in one Marine killed. The officers and non-commissioned officers believed the tragedy could have been prevented. Both platoons were aware of the patrols nearing each other and they communicated their proximity to their respective patrols. However well intended, that method did not prevent the killing of a Marine, since somewhere there had been a communication failure.

A new seemingly flawless system was devised wherein at a preplanned location the platoons would pass the communication responsibilities to the patrols approaching each other, and at that point the platoons would monitor the patrols' interaction. Once done, each patrol leader would be aware of the other and could describe a specific terrain feature near him as they were drawing closer to each other, such as, "we're coming up on the stream junction." The other patrol leader, nearing the same feature could acknowledge that fact. One patrol would often make a noise and the other patrol would give a, "Roger, we hear you." The concept had worked flawlessly so far.

"Lance Corporal Wick, ask Corporal Robertson to come up here. I need to send him on a small patrol," Melton announced.

"Aye, aye, Sir."

Minutes later, Corporal John "Robbie" Robertson, whose squad was nearby, reported to Melton. "Sir, you need us to go on a patrol?"

"Right, Robbie," Melton agreed and added, "Take your squad towards the company CP, and you'll run into a patrol from Weapons Platoon who has a very special package—my replacement."

"Got it, Sir!"

"Oh and, Corporal Robinson…"

"Yes, Sir?"

"We'll be passing the communications to you almost immediately. The skipper will be briefing the Weapons patrol leader and the new lieutenant about coordinating directly with you. So, that ought to work okay. In any case, be careful. Weapons doesn't lead many patrols."

"Right, Sir."

"See you back here in about a half an hour."

After their briefing, the men moved out.

"Roger, Fox Six, we'll be looking out for them," Lance Corporal Fraser from the Weapons Platoon patrol announced into his handset.

"Fox Three Bravo, this is Fox Whiskey Alpha, over."

"Whiskey Alpha, this is Fox Three Bravo," Robertson's radioman responded. "We're looking for you now."

"Whiskey Alpha, I think we have your point man seventy meters away stepping over some trees that fell across the path."

"Roger, Three Alpha. That's him, over," Lance Corporal Fraser acknowledged, quite relieved to know just how effective the rifle squads were in coordinating patrol movements.

Fraser looked over his shoulder and said, "Lieutenant Korn, the 3rd Platoon's patrol sees us."

Looking ahead Lieutenant Korn softly called out to Private First Class "Lifer" Rockwell, who planned to make a career out of the Marine Corps and was on the point for the Weapons patrol, "Hey, Rockwell, hold it up. The other patrol sees us."

They were now approximately fifty meters apart. Staring forward, Rockwell stopped. He searched for the other patrol but couldn't see them.

Fifteen meters in front of Robertson's point man, hidden under a blanket of leaves was a single NVA soldier. He could hear both patrols approach his hidden position. His choices were to remain there and get killed, be captured, or run and possibly escape.

In front of both patrols was an explosion of flying leaves followed by a Czechoslovakian-made SKS rifle firing at Robertson's oncoming point man. Private First Class Bonnett fell instantly as a round penetrated his temple.

Robertson led the firing from his patrol on the now-escaping NVA soldier. His men joined in firing their weapons.

Korn immediately and instinctively deployed the Weapons squad until the situation became clear.

The NVA soldier was hit several times and, after about thirty rounds, the jungle became quiet once more. Lieutenant Korn called to Corporal Robertson, now in sight, "You guys all right?"

"Don't think so, Sir," he said to his future platoon commander. "We got one guy down."

As Korn approached Bonnett's fallen body, he directed Robertson to search the area for other possible hidden NVA. He asked for Robertson's radio operator to put him in touch with Fox Six Actual. He made the report feeling unsure about all that had just happened before even reporting into his platoon. At least Captain Brown's compliments about him having presence of mind for deploying the Weapons squad made him feel somewhat better.

Also arriving on 19 December was Private First Class Francois "Frank" Olivier, immediately nicknamed "Frenchy". He joined the 3rd Platoon as a rifleman. As all new men in their first combat tour, Olivier was wide-eyed focusing more on his entire environment and less on the enemy threat. He arrived to find the bodies of two Marines waiting to be flown back on the same chopper that flew him into Fox's LZ. Their bodies were still as he expected, but the four boot-covered feet extending out from the ponchos bothered him. "Will that be me?" he asked himself.

Frenchy's first patrol came later that day. When his squad came to a small clearing in the dense mountain jungle where the trail they were on intersected with another, the jungled reeked. In front of him were the bodies of two enemy soldiers killed a couple days earlier by another Fox patrol. The other guys didn't seem to mind the two bodies as much he did. But they all detested the stench. One of the bodies appeared to be moving. Looking closer Olivier realized the maggot-covered body was being devoured. Another body lay motionless in a pre-natal position. But the strongest odor came not from the two corpses ten meters away. It was much, much closer. Olivier looked down in horror to see he had been standing on a third enemy's rib cage. "Welcome to Vietnam, "Frenchy", or whatever they're going to call me!" he uttered under his breath.

Rain fell lightly that cool evening. Those, not on a listening post or on an ambush, were asleep under some sort of poncho arrangement. The radios crackled through the night about every fifteen minutes with calls from platoons to their ambush sites or listening posts as they routinely did each night. "One Alpha, this is Fox One. All secure? Over." The 1st Platoon radio operator asked. More accurately the question could have just been, "Are you still awake?"

To answer, one would squeeze the handset twice "shhhhh, shhhhh" came a hissing answer that could be heard on the platoon radio's handset if the forward position was secure, or once "shhhhh" if the forward position may have enemy nearby. If no answer was made a second attempt was made to ascertain the forward position's status before telling the platoon commander that the post had probably fallen asleep. The platoon commander, platoon sergeant, or squad leader would head out to rectify the situation. The squad leader would probably thump a new guy; the platoon sergeant would cause three days of misery for the squad; and the platoon commander would initiate non-judicial punishment or relieve an offending non-commissioned officer for his men's dereliction of duty. This routine was obviously taken very seriously. Heard on the company radio net by all radio operators, it cast a blanket of safety over the men of Fox. The feeling of safety, combined with daytime mountain patrolling earlier and the cool, evening light rain, was soothing for the remaining majority. Between 2200 and 0100 on their Hill 258 mountaintop, they slept soundly.

Harassment and interdiction fires were shot every night of the war. Their purpose was to prevent the enemy from feeling comfortable. Randomly fired through the night from an artillery position miles away, H&I fires were targeted for trail junctions, road intersections, and possible rest areas. On the night of 19 December, the 8-inch gun battery from An Hoa was firing H&I fires in direct support of the 5th Marines' Operation Taylor Common. The trajectories of the rounds, shot from ten kilometers away, would have to be elevated quite a bit to clear the triple canopy treetops on Hill 258 and land near the steam, Khe Gio, where Corporal Baumgardt had been fighting three days earlier.

At 0354 hours the sky above the company command post and 3rd Platoon exploded. An 8-inch high explosive shell with a point-detonating fuse had not cleared Hill 258's treetops. Shrapnel, propelled by the exploding shell, rained down on the radio operators and sleeping men. Falling branches elongated the deafening sound and added to the possible casualty infliction below.

Captain Brown awoke like a scared child to find himself hugging the tree trunk he was sleeping beside. Regaining a bit more consciousness to allow him to suppress his fear, he called out to his nearby company radio operator, "You okay?"

"Yeah, Skipper," a voice answered back in the dark.

"Ski, get Waskiewicz to hold any more fire," Brown directed as he began putting on his boots. And get a SITREP from everyone up here. And the 3rd Platoon," he added as an after thought.

Before Bilski could call the 3rd Platoon, they called him. "Fox Six, this is Fox Three, over," the 3rd Platoon radio operator, Lance Corporal Wick, announced.

"This is Six. Go," Bilski answered.

"Six, we have three casualties. One is a 'priority two' and two are 'priority three'. We'll be making up a CASREP, over."

"Roger, Three."

"Six, my actual wants to speak to Six actual, over."

"Roger," Bilski said handing the handset to Brown.

"Sir," Lieutenant Melton said, "that round really ripped up Three Alpha's leg. Doc says he ought to be okay 'til morning so we don't need him evac'd tonight, over."

Tying "Three Alpha" to Baumgardt, Brown acknowledged, "Roger, Bill. We'll get a chopper in here at first light. How's everyone else?"

"Ahhh, light scratches, that's about all."

"All right, I'll check with you first thing in the morning. Out."

LIEUTENANT COLONEL STEMPLE AND GUNNERY SERGEANT DIERDALH PIN ON MAJOR BROWN'S RANK INSIGNIA ON 23 DECEMBER

(Photo courtesy of Mike Malanowski)

Patrols from the hilltop continued until 24 December without any more friendly-fire incidents. In Paris, the peace negotiators from the warring countries agreed to a twenty-four hour truce beginning at 2400 hours on Christmas Eve. In preparation for the truce, the men of Fox Company began to relax in the dampness of their hilltop jungle. Christmas packages had been received from the resupply choppers during the past two days and had been shared by all. After nearly three weeks of rain, by 2000 the night sky cleared, the stars twinkled, and the temperature dropped a few degrees. The C-ration coffee seemed particularly warming. Christmas was in the air. Everyone greeted each other with a Merry Christmas. The "spirit" had settled on these young warriors, and somehow they didn't seem as ferocious as they had days earlier. Soon all, aside from the listening posts, quieted down for the evening to await a day away from the war.

The sun greeted the men on Christmas morning as it streaked through the triple canopy. "Morning, Big Ski," Brown said to Bilski as he crawled out from under the shelter-half hooch he and the gunny shared. With Bilski and Malanowski as his company and battalion operators, Brown had named the corporal "Big Ski" and Malanowski "Little Ski". "God what a great day!" Brown professed to anyone who cared to hear him as he felt the warmth of the morning sun greet him. "And Merry Christmas to you, Little Ski," Brown wished his other radio operator. "Ski, where's the gunny?" Brown asked.

"Merry Christmas to you, Major," Bilski responded to Brown who had been promoted two days earlier. Little Ski nodded in agreement. "The gunny is up at the LZ waiting for our 're-supply' chopper and the chaplain who's slated to give us a service. The chaplain's going to one company at a time, so we don't know exactly when he'll get here."

"Well that's great," Brown said, "I'm going up to the landing zone and wish that old Marine a Merry Christmas!" Brown stated, fully appreciating the temporary peace, the warmth of the morning sun; and, even though it surely did not look like Christmas in the middle of a jungle, the spirit of the day.

As he walked up the narrow, muddy trail passing Ron, the scout dog, his Marine Corps handler, and other pockets of Marines who had been bivouacked immediately beside the trail, Brown greeted one and all by their first names or nicknames with a Merry Christmas. He thought of Scrooge opening his window on Christmas morning wishing the best of Christmases to everyone. For a second he wished he was home with his wife and young son watching one of his favorite movies, "A Christmas Carol". Instantly, a cloud of regret cast a dark feeling on what was once a bright and cheerful morning. God, was I crazy to extend these six months in Vietnam? Was commanding a rifle company that important? He kept on walking.

Soon the dark trail brightened as the major approached the cleared LZ. His spirits leaped again as he saw his large friend smoking a cigarette at the far end of the 100'x100' stump-laden hilltop. By the grin on the private first class's youthful face who was standing with Gunnery Sergeant Dierdalh, Brown could see that the gunny was entertaining the young Marine radio operator from the Helicopter Support Team, HST, who had joined the gunny to bring in the choppers.

"Merry Christmas," Brown called out as he walked up to the two.

"To you too, Skipper," Dierdalh responded.

"Yes, Sir," Private First Class Cornman added, feeling uncomfortable in a strange officer's presence.

"Welcome to Fox Company, Private," Brown said. "What's your name?"

"Cornman, Sir."

"When did you get here?"

"About 1700 yesterday with the mail bird."

"Well then I owe you a big 'Thanks!' for the nice weather. We just might dry out in a couple of days."

"Yes, sir," Cornman offered his safe response.

"Gunny, what is the scoop on the two birds?" Brown asked.

"Looks like we're going to get the resupply bird in about twenty minutes and the chaplain ought to be here around 1030."

"Well, Cornman, don't let Gunny Dierdalh tell you too many stories."

"Yes, Sir!"

"Guns, I'm going back to write a letter."

"All right, Skipper. I'll wait here for the chopper."

Brown worked his way back down the path to his hooch and his backpack in which he had a small box of stationary sealed in a plastic bag. As he did, his mind wandered to the letter he would compose to his wife. After being out of the Marine Corps for ten months in 1965, Brown rejoined the Corps soon after the war began. His marriage had been somewhat rocky before then. He went on to Camp LeJeune while she and their son, Billy, remained in Pennsylvania. They had not lived together except for visits since November 1965, a bit over three years. Half that time he was prepping for Vietnam and the other half of the time he was here in the war. He was due to rotate home in two weeks. Their reunion, he believed, would be frosty at a minimum. So what was he to say to her in the letter?

"*Oh, hi. We're having a good time here in the mountains on this sunny Christmas morning. Hope Christmas is good for you and Billy. Got to go now before the chopper comes. Don't want the troops to see me depressed. Blah blah blah blah blah blah blah blah…*"

Nah, that wouldn't work, Brown thought, feeling about as down as he ever had since he joined Fox. What were his depressed feelings all about? Missing Christmas with his family? Going home and facing the music for extending? Being divorced from his high school sweetheart? Batching it?

Hell no. Those would be bad, he reflected as he walked up to his radio operators and his waiting stationary. His deepest regret was, three days from now, leaving the Marines he had come to love right here in Fox. They had done so much together. Six months of battles, booby traps, and bullshit bugs! Twenty-seven Marines had been killed. Over 150 Purple hearts had been earned.

They were so tight. Never had he been closer with any others, never in high school, never in his college fraternity, and never anywhere else in his first six years in the Corps.

"Skipper, want a cup of coffee?" Bilski offered snapping Brown out of his funk while extending his right hand that held a canteen cup with steam rising from its top.

"Yeah, sure. Thanks, Ski."

"Merry Christmas, my good Major," Corporal Waskiewicz cheerfully offered, neatly balancing respect with continuous humor.

"To you too, Marc," Brown replied. "And, Doc, Merry Christmas," he added to Hospitalman Second Class Jacobs, the company corpsman. Turning he asked, "Little Ski, you got more of those cookies your mom sent? They'd go good with this great coffee." Then, almost in the same breath he added, "And Big Ski, how'd you fix this coffee? It's better than the stuff back in An Hoa."

"Yes, Sir," Corporal Malanowski answered Brown's first question with enthusiasm as he turned and began digging in his backpack. Soon Brown was reaching into Malanowski's paper bag, taking a couple of cookies and saying, "Thank your mom for me, Little Ski"

After a few minutes of chit chat, Bilski removed the handset of his PRC-25 radio from his ear and said, "Sir, the gunny wants you back at the LZ when the re-supply bird gets here. He didn't tell me why."

"Okay," Brown said noting the gunny's request.

That instant the low-toned rapid drumbeat of a distant CH-46 could be heard closing in on Hill 258. Brown murmured, "Well, looks like the gunny beckons." He stood up, returned Bilski's canteen cup and grabbed his rifle.

Brown meandered back up the trail. He passed the point where the poncho-covered bodies of two Marines killed were kept next to the trail for three days. They were there while the Marines waited for the clouds to lift long enough to allow an evac chopper to fly them out. He also passed the point where Ski's practical joke had darn near given him a heart attack.

Brown flashed back; boy, did he remember that night! A couple days after Fox took over the hill, 15 December, the two German Shepard Scout dogs and their handlers joined Fox. Naturally it was raining and they landed about 1600. With the weather and time of year, darkness fell about forty-five minutes later. The handlers found a niche of terrain three yards off the trail between the LZ and the company's command post, CP. They tied their dogs to a tree next to them with their seven-foot leashes and prepared for the night. Brown had only a verbal report about the dog-teams arriving. Three hours later, about 1900, Ski said, "Sir, Lieutenant Melton wants to see you up at the LZ. Melton's 3rd Platoon was guarding the far end of the LZ. So, in the darkness, Brown slowly worked his way up the fifty meters to the landing zone. No enemy could ambush me here, Brown thought. It's too damn dark! Nevertheless he listened attentively as he cautiously moved forward. His hand held his M-16 ready for anything. Without notice, neither visual nor sound, a huge mad dog silently sprung from its crouched position and its fangs landed within one foot from Brown's neck. Restrained only by the length and strength of its leash, the dog was barking, almost screaming, at Brown's invasion of its trail. When he returned, clear that Melton had not requested his presence and fully intending to nail Bilski, Brown found it difficult to chew his butt in the midst of eight laughing Marines. In the end, he'd let the matter drop. It was a good joke, after all.

But now, nearing the LZ, Brown heard the chopping sound of the CH-46's engine boom lower in tone and slower in beat. Hmmm, he thought. The pilot's turning off its engines; what the heck's going on?

The sun was pouring down on the aft end of the dull, green, painted helicopter, which was comfortably coming to rest on top of the cleared mountaintop. Silhouetted against the rare blue sky and the canopy of darker-green trees covering the smaller hills below Hill 258, the now-quiet bird was the star of show. Its audience was the gunny, Private First Class Cornman, the eight-man working party, and now Major Brown. Its first act was to lower its tailgate. Then, emerging from the darkness of the bird's interior, as big as you please, was the most dramatic sight Fox Company veterans had seen in many months.

Stepping out was a six-foot man with a long white beard and a red hat drooping down to his shoulders. He was dressed in a red and white suit cinched up with a four-inch wide black belt. The thoughts behind the smiling faces of his greeters were obvious. My God, there is a Santa Claus! And, he came here to this humble mountaintop home to visit us. If there ever there were any doubters among the eleven who remained motionless, they surely became believers at that moment.

"Ho! Ho! Ho!" roared Master Sergeant Jenkins, the maintenance chief with HMM-161. His Santa Claus outfit fit perfectly. "Come over here and help old Santa take some presents from his sled."

With that Gunnery Sergeant Dierdalh, still laughing, said to his working party, "Okay gang, let's give ol' Santa a hand."

CHRISTMAS IN THE MOUNTAINS

(Photo courtesy of Mike Malanowski)

Then, while the men were unloading almost twenty cases of soda, four cases of beer, bags of sandwiches, fruit, and mail, Brown went up to Santa to thank him for coming. By this time at least thirty other Marines had come to see the sight and pitch in to help off load the goodies. Jenkins removed his hat and beard and was laughing with the rest at the fun of it all. He said, "Well, thanks, Sir. I love doing it. This is my second year I have played Santa in Vietnam. Say, we're used to delivering beer, but your Colonel Stemple…is that how you pronounce his name?…said no alcoholic beverages for 2/5. My guys were able to find you a few cases though, hope you don't mind."

"The beer will be well appreciated," Brown said. "But your coming was the best present anyhow."

Then, like the poem, he soon got back in his "sleigh", waved a big arm, and said, "Merry Christmas to all." And, in a minute, Santa flew away.

The chaplain, Friar Glenn Powell, showed up thirty minutes later and reminded the forty some odd Fox Company Marines who attended his service that they had much to be grateful for even though they were in a war zone.

Despite the fact that he was slated to leave the company on 29 December, Major Brown had been bothered by what always seemed like missed opportunities at and near the stream junction that formed the Khe Gio Stream immediately to the west and below Hill 258. On 14 December the 2nd Platoon found an enemy canteen near a freshly-extinguished cooking fire; Baumgardt's ambush on 16 December was less than 500 meters north of the junction; and on 22 December an encounter at the junction with an enemy squad resulted in two Marines WIA and one of the two scout dogs killed. Clearly, the enemy inhabited or constantly transited this area near the junction. A company-sized operation was definitely needed.

On the morning of 26 December, Brown gathered his platoon commanders, Lott from the 1st Platoon, Marshall from the 2nd Platoon, and Melton and Korn from the 3rd Platoon together to announce the next day's operation. The company gunny, Dierdalh, and artillery forward observer, Waskiewicz, were also present. Brown summed up the enemy situation to the small group for the record and announced his intention to conduct a hammer and anvil operation on the morning of 27 December.

"Staff Sergeant Marshall, I want you take your platoon off the backside of the hill late this afternoon and form a blocking position at dusk 200 meters south of the stream junction. It's essential you get in and set up between the two streams without notice. The rest of us will be moving south toward your position along the stream's trail in the morning and will be trying to drive the enemy towards you. Make sure that by 0800 all your men have good cover as we may be shooting in your direction. Got it?"

"Yes, Sir."

"Bill," he said referring to the First Lieutenant Melton, "your 3rd Platoon will lead the company command group and Woody's 1st Platoon off the north side of the hill at 0600. When you get to the stream trail turn south toward the junction. You'll be the hammer driving the enemy toward the 2nd Platoon. Any questions?"

"No, Sir."

"Good. Keep Pete Korn in the planning loop. Next week he'll be on his own with the platoon."

"Woody," he turned toward Lieutenant Lott, "you'll follow us off the hill and, when we turn south, assume the role of rear security and also be prepared to move into the attack if we need you. Okay?"

"Sir!" Lott signified his understanding.

"Gunny, you'll stay up here with the 60s," he said, referring to the 60mm mortar section, "and be prepared to provide on-call fire support."

"Corporal Waskiewicz, I don't want any enemy ambushes as the 3rd Platoon moves south along the trail. Plan supporting fires about fifty meters on either side of the stream. Coordinate with Staff Sergeant Marshall so you know where he'll set in tonight and what kind of fire support he may need tomorrow before we get to his position."

"Anyone have any questions? All right. Good. Let's get going."

About 1800 that evening, Lieutenant Melton, approached the major and said, "Skipper, I've got a problem. We need to talk."

The two walked away, each with a cup of coffee, and Melton began. "It's Lance Corporal Westfall. He's refusing to go on the operation tomorrow."

Brown looked at Melton without saying anything.

Melton continued, "We all talked to him. I told him both you and I were leaving the company sooner than he was and that we were not worried. I told him that the operation was not particularly dangerous. But that did no good. He's been wounded twice before and has a bad feeling about this operation."

Brown, still listening, was thinking about the ramifications such a situation like this would have on the rest of the men.

"Sir, he's been a real fine fire team leader and, on occasion, he's been acting as a squad leader. He's really a good Marine. I just don't know what to do."

"I agree, Bill. We don't want to rake him over the coals. I know him, and he's not only a good kid, but he's been a good Marine. Yet we can't condone him taking himself out of an operation without us taking some sort of action. Hell, everyone will be wanting to do it."

"Yes, Sir. That's the problem."

"Tell you what, you go back to him and give him a direct order. When he refuses to go on the operation, bring him up to me. I'll send him up to Colonel Stemple for battalion commander's office hours. What do you think about Stemple only reducing him to private first class and reassigning him to some lousy job in the rear?"

Melton thought a moment before responding, "That ought to work."

"Oh, and Bill, tell you what, after he refuses to accept your direct order, have your platoon sergeant escort him up to the gunny, and I'll have the gunny send him back on the next bird. Is that okay?"

"That will work. Thanks, Skipper."

"Right. And, good luck on the operation tomorrow."

"Yes, Sir. Good night."

The operation on 27 December went remarkably well. The 2nd Platoon moved into position at the stream junction the night before without a hitch. In the morning the remainder of the company moved south along the trail bordering the Khe Gio stream's trail. The 81mm mortars on Hill 214, now more trusted by Brown, lobbed mortar rounds fifty to seventy-five meters away from the trail, into the jungle. No enemy were in the vicinity and thus the 3rd Platoon made contact with the waiting 2nd Platoon without a hitch. The hammer and anvil idea was a good one, but the timing was such that it yielded nothing. Perhaps the NVA were still enjoying the twenty-four hour truce.

The evening of 28 December was the final night Major Brown would spend with the men of Fox Company in the field. With no executive officer, First Lieutenant Melton would remain as the senior officer and in charge of field operations. Together they visited all the Fox units as much for Brown to say goodbye as for him to ensure they knew Melton was going to be in charge. Brown was scheduled to go on an in-country R&R and would be back in the rear at An Hoa by 4 January or 5 January.

Captain Brown remained the nominal company commander while waiting for his RTD, Rotation Tour Date, scheduled for 13 January.

CHAPTER: 18 BUGGED, BOMBED and BEATEN

Most of the Fox Company Marines knew that they would be getting an intermediate company commander on 29 December, the day Brown departed. He left on the morning resupply run and immediately left behind, at least in the company command post area, a perceived void in direction. However, by 1400 hours Private First Class Malanowski received a message from the battalion that the new company commander was expected in around 1500 hours on an administrative flight along with the chaplain. Fifty minutes later, the static coming from the battalion radio's handset broke, and Malanowski answered, "This is Fox, over."

Bilski headed for Malanowski and reached him just in time to hear, "Roger, out." Malanowski turned to Corporal Bilski and announced, "They're five minutes out!"

Bilski notified the gunny and the platoon commanders. Soon forty-five men circled the hilltop LZ. The CH-46 landed without incident, its tailgate opened and two passengers emerged. Bilski pointed to the first man off the plane and announced to Melton and Dierdalh, "There's our new skipper!"

The first man was in his late twenties and wore a new pair of camouflaged utilities. He had a square jaw, strapping physique, and high and tight or close-cut haircut. A chubby-cheeked, youthful looking lieutenant followed him. Melton, the senior officer present, strode out proudly to meet the new company commander. Gunnery Sergeant Dierdalh followed closely by his side. As Melton extended his hand to the welcome the bigger man he spotted a small brass cross on his left collar. His beaming face fell instantly and almost apologetically he uttered, "Good afternoon, Chaplain."

Melton eased over to the first lieutenant and sheepishly asked the younger man with the cherub face, "Are you our new CO?"

"I am." On that day First Lieutenant Robert L. Wing took the reins of Fox.

First Lieutenant Melton greeted Hospitalman Third Class Norwick the next morning, then asked, "What's wrong with Lance Corporal Gunderson?"

"Don't know, Lieutenant. He has the same symptoms that Heath and Jackson had. Seems like they get the flu for a couple of days, you know…fever and throwing up. Then we have to send them to 1st Med Battalion in Da Nang."

"Well that's not a good way to celebrate New Year Eve, Doc. Think I'll report it to Lieutenant Wing."

"Who's he, Sir?"

"Oh, he's the officer who came in yesterday as our interim skipper 'til we get a new one to replace Captain Brown…err rather, Major Brown."

"Yes, Sir. I heard the major went on in-country R&R."

"He did, back to his old Advisory Team to say goodbye," Melton confirmed, pausing to reflect on the feverish trooper. "Doc, why don't you report the sickness up your chain as well? The 2nd Platoon has a couple of guys sick also. I'm off to see Lieutenant Wing about it now."

Melton approached the company CP group saying hello to Bilski and Malanowski. "Where's the Lieutenant?" he asked, referring to Wing.

Never hesitant to be a comic, Bilski chuckled while picking a C-ration toilet paper package from his upper left shirt pocket and waving it toward some bushes thirty meters away, "He's over there voting for his favorite sailor, Sir."

Melton, helmet under his arm, smiled back saying, "Bilski, you're getting a bit salty. Don't you think?"

Emerging from the woods with his entrenching tool, Lieutenant Wing greeted Melton, "How's it going, Bill?"

"Good. How are you enjoying your new accommodations, Bob?"

"They're not bad. What's going on?"

"Well, I'm really bothered by the amount of men getting sick. I know it only seems like a few, but if it keeps up, we'll really be hurting." Wing frowned giving deep thought to the meaning in Melton's message.

Melton continued, "I told Doc Norwick to pass my concerns along to the battalion surgeon."

Wing finally replied, "You're probably right, Bill. I'll give Stemple a call later tonight."

"You know, if it is malaria, we've been taking the pills every Sunday. As a matter of fact, the company policy is that the platoon corpsmen personally places the pills in the men's mouths and keeps a record."

"Well, that's good. I'll call the colonel and get back to you tomorrow. Hey, you'll be here tomorrow, won't you?"

"Why?"

"You don't look so well yourself, and you're sweating like a hog." Reflecting for a few seconds, Wing asked, "How's Pete Korn doing?"

"Pete's doing a fantastic job! The men have really taken to him. I already feel like a stranger."

On the following day, 31 December 1968, Fox Company humped from Hill 258 to a new position one and a half kilometers south—part of Operation Taylor Common's leapfrog concept of operations. Along the way a fire team split away from the company and escorted the almost delirious Melton, the company's thirty-first Malaria victim, to Fire Support Base Pike for his evacuation. Now, two days later, at the new company position, the command group was getting adjusted to its new environment.

Interrupting Lieutenant Wing as he was explaining his recent assignments to the ever-curious Malanowski, Bilski said, "Excuse me, Sir. Seems like Fox One has received some sniper fire on their patrol, 400 meters from here below the hill. They have a guy shot up pretty bad."

"Right, Bilski. I thought I just heard some shots," Wing responded pointing to the west. "See if you can get a report when they get settled down."

Fifteen minutes later, Bilski handed his handset to Wing, "Sir, Lieutenant Lott wants to speak to you."

"This is Fox Six Actual, over." Wing responded.

After Lott's briefing, Wing acknowledged, "Sounds good, Woody, keep on searching. I'll have Fox Seven and the helo support team guy come down to your position and give you a hand, out."

Wing turned and with a slight increase in volume called, "Gunny Dierdalh!"

The large man, canteen coffee cup in hand, answered, "What's up, Skipper?"

Wing liked hearing that. It was the first time he'd been called that name…made him feel good!

"The 1st Platoon needs your assistance."

"What's going on?" Gunnery Sergeant Vernon Dierdalh asked as he approached the youthful-looking, smaller man.

"Lieutenant Lott just told me that the sniper that fired on them about an hour ago must have been protecting a good sized weapons cache. They killed the sniper, although we have one Marine who was hit pretty badly. I told him I'd send you down with a helo support team guy to assist getting the wounded man and the weapons out through the canopy. We have an HST man don't we?"

"I'm waiting for a new one. Cornman, the kid we had, came down with the flu yesterday, and I sent him to the rear. But I'll go down with the forward air controller's radio operator and a couple of 60mm mortar men who've been bugging me to go on a patrol…particularly since Madrid, the flame thrower kid, went with the 1st Platoon this morning. How'd they find the cache, anyway?"

"Well, seems like after the sniper fired from some heavy brush, the platoon used Madrid to burn out the brush looking for other snipers." Wing paused and asked rhetorically, "Smart move, eh?" After pausing, "Anyway without the bushes, Dixon, a young PFC from Tennessee, discovered the cache."

"Okay, I better get going. I'll give you a SITREP after I get there, Skipper."

The cache yielded 185 new weapons ready for use by the many North Vietnamese Army soldiers nearing their final destination in South

Vietnam. There were 166 K-44s carbines and nineteen SKS semi-automatic rifles.

Four days later, the 2nd Platoon went out on a planned two-day patrol, despite being undermanned due to malaria. After moving to the south, they walked up a trail and found a position that had been used by an NVA sniper when shooting at the artillerymen on Fire Support Base Pike. Lance Corporal Bill Martell led his fire team cautiously following the trail that curved at the top of a small hill. The Marines spread out into a cleared area and found a recently used NVA base camp. Martell said, "Hey, Sarge, look at these slit trenches. They're full of fresh crap! The gooks must be close by, so stay alert." The men on point were very happy to find the position vacated. They did not want to engage a significant enemy force with their understrength platoon.

The platoon searched the area and found weapons, ammunition, and mortar rounds. Rain precluded the evacuation of the munitions. Medevacs were able to take a few more malaria victims. Even Staff Sergeant Marshall had been stricken and evacuated. After two days of waiting for the skies to clear, they took all the machine guns and blew up the remaining items. Looking like a squad of machine gunners, they set off on a different route. On the way back to Fox Company, the NVA probed the platoon, now laboring with heavy loads. The few, weary men returned to the Fox Company area soaked and exhausted after staying awake for ninety-six hours.

Melton's earlier concern about the health of the men was validated. By 9 January, Fox Company was down to fifty-five men in the field. Over sixty men had come down with malaria. The investigation that followed also supported his contention that the company policy of the corpsmen administering the malaria pills was more than adequate, and though many of the other companies actually used a similar procedure, it became a battalion-wide policy. The investigation revealed that the creek below Hill 258 where Fox operated during the latter half of December was highly infested with malaria-carrying mosquitoes. In fact, the area was so bad that an intelligence report further revealed many NVA soldiers, having passed along the same stream, were similarly infected. Unfortunately, Private First Class Cornman, the Marine from the HST, passed away from the illness.

Captain Brown, after enjoying his brief R&R, thought all went as he planned until the evening of 9 January when Lieutenant Colonel Stemple requested to speak with him. Brown, by this time, was getting comfortable in An Hoa, sleeping on a cot, enjoying hot chow, and waiting for his flight home. The "battalion rear" switchboard operator caught up with Brown in the hooch of Major Jess Owens, the Battalion Executive Officer, where the two majors and a couple of others were enjoying dry martinis, even though they had no olives.

"Texas Pete, this is Fox Six, over," Brown announced.

In his rich, professorial voice Lieutenant Colonel Stemple started motivating one of his favorite students to "go the extra yard." "Dave, I hope your R&R was enjoyable, over."

"Roger, Sir. It was, over." Brown replied, trying to figure out what the "old man" wanted.

"You know I'm going to need your insight into Lance Corporal Westfall's office hours," Stemple stated referring to the non-judicial procedures that he administered. "He's coming out here tomorrow, and I want you to escort him."

"Sir, that doesn't make a lot of sense. I'm out of 'Nam in three days. I've turned in all my "deuce" gear," he explained, referring to a supply category in existence since Chesty Puller was a private. "782" gear, the "two" in 782 transfers to "deuce", includes a canteen, cartridge belt, shelter half, medicine pouch, and five or six more items, "...and my weapon. I'm sure you'll do fine without me."

"Well, I think I really need you. Besides I want to say goodbye. You only have to stay for an hour or two."

"All right, Sir," Brown gave in with a slight bit of hesitation in his voice. "I want to say goodbye to you as well. See you tomorrow with Westfall."

"Good, see you tomorrow. Now let me speak to Jess, over."

The trip to Texas Pete on Fire Support Base Pike was due to lift off at 0930. Brown anticipated no delay as the day was beautiful and the flight was a mid morning one. Also, there were no major engagements on-going and, thus, no emergency medevacs to divert the mission. So, Brown had the company driver, Lance Corporal Juan Ortiz, drive both him and Lance Corporal Westfall to the airstrip at 0920. Ortiz, a short, muscular and handsome Marine who had come from Columbia, South America, the year before as a stow away, could hardly speak English and always greeted the Captain with, "Hey, Skeeeper." Once at the An Hoa airstrip, Ortiz drove the jeep to the only helicopter with its blades idling, a CH-46, and Brown and Westfall jumped out.

"Gracias, Juan," Brown waived.

"Adios, Skeeeper," Ortiz said as he drove away.

The flight was considered to be a "milk run" in that eight replacement troops, supplies, mail, and an eleven-foot, 461 pound, 106mm recoilless rifle would be on the flight beside Westfall and Brown. The passengers sat on green nylon benches without safety belts; the "no belt" custom was developed in Vietnam to evacuate helicopters rapidly. The 106mm recoilless rifle rested on its tripod also unstrapped. The door gunner occupied his standing position at one door window next to the mounted M-60 machine gun. The crew chief raised the tailgate that the passengers used to get onto the helicopter, walked back to his door window, and let the pilots know they were ready for liftoff.

A CH-46 helicopter lifts off the ground and flies because of the camber-design of its six blades, three of which are on the front propeller and three are on the rear propeller. As the blades rotate, the higher velocity air passing over the curved top of the blades creates lower air pressure above the blades and lift occurs. The flight, expected to take about twelve to fifteen minutes, lifted off with no difficulty and within a minute, was racing west towards FSB Pike at 2,000 feet.

On 10 January all the passengers looked silently across at each other or through one of the four small windows at the hills below. The roaring thwump, thwump, thwump of the whirling blades prevented any conversation. They would be offloading in minutes.

Offloading a helicopter onto a hill top position where there is no landing zone is done by the chopper approaching from the downdraft side of hill, flying over the hill, and hovering over the updraft side of the hill. Then it lowers its tailgate so that only the aft portion near the ground. The nose of the aircraft hovers twenty to thirty feet away from the hill's offload spot.

CH-46 LANDING IN A "RAMP HOVER" ON A FIRE BASE
(Courtesy of George T. Curtis)

As Brown and Westfall's helicopter approached FSB Pike, high in the mountains, it slowed its forward speed. The men gripped their weapons and seat firmly, ready to spring off the chopper when its forward motion stopped, tailgate lowered, and the crew chief directed the exit. Still seated, the passengers looked out the windows to view Marines, many bare-chested and without helmets, moving away from the dust kicked up by the chopper which passed five feet over their mountaintop base.

That morning a shift in the wind direction had occurred. Whether it was a pilot error or misinformation by the forward air controller, the chopper had approached from the wrong direction. By the time the craft passed the mid-point of the hilltop it reacted to a downdraft and was propelled down into the valley 300–400 feet below.

Attempts to recover on the part of the pilot only caused the helicopter to wobble out of control. Nearing the bottom of the hill, the pilot regained a modest amount of control and lifted the craft sufficiently to attempt a second offload. The wobbling never stopped. Again, the helicopter approached the wrong side of the hilltop. This time they were at ground level. And this time the fear stricken men inside could now see the same bare-chested, helmetless Marines running for their lives away from the impending crash.

The aft propeller struck the ground of the hilltop causing the chopper to begin plummeting down into the valley. While the path of the chopper was different than the one Fox Company Marines cut one month earlier off the top of that hill, the vegetation was the same. Almost instantly, the chopper turned sideways, rolling down the hill like a cigar. Three times it made a complete turn, and three times the eleven-foot, 461 pound recoilless bounced against the side of the craft. The Marine passengers were not only tossed around, but also beaten by the heavy weapon. While they were flopping on top of each other. The chopper abruptly stilled at the bottom. It lay on a sixty-degree angle with its tailgate at the valley floor, its nose pointed up the hilltop.

All was silent.

After what must have been no more than sixty seconds, the crew chief intuitively began to focus his energies. He was all right. He had to get the passengers off. They remained motionless mostly from shock. His voice became commanding. He began grabbing Marines, Brown included, and throwing them off the CH-46, "Get off! Get off of the chopper!"

Major Brown was about the sixth man to find himself tossed like a rag doll on top of the broken vegetation at the bottom of the valley. His mind became alert enough to smell and see the helicopter's fuel steadily spilling from the back of the crumbled chopper. His body, however, was not as responsive. His shallow breathing was so rapid that oxygen failed to fill his lungs. His was the same reaction as anyone's would be when jumping into frigid water. He began stumbling away from the wreck. At fifteen meters away, a large, beat-up Marine was trying without success to climb over a tree that had been knocked down. The tree's trunk was only two feet off of the ground. Intuitively, Brown wanted to seek safety. Professionally, he knew he had to help the Marine. He reached down and grabbed the Marine's flak jacket. His grip was strong enough to maybe lift a belt or tie.

"Come on, Marine. We got to get going," Brown pleaded.

As he struggled to help the weakened Marine, his breath returned. His grip strengthened, and the Marine began responding and moving on his own to safety, 300 meters up the hill. The men crawled, grabbed limbs, and pulled themselves along. They helped themselves and each other. When they neared the top of the hill, the helicopter burst into flames. Machine gun ammo began cooking off. Rounds zinged in all directions. Like the others, Brown found shelter behind one of the several large rocks on the hillside that he shared with another Marine. The cook-off lasted for five or six long minutes. All that while Brown and the young Marine with him laughed. A little at first, then realizing he was only bloodied and bruised, Brown laughed heartily with joy.

Once the area quieted again, all looked down through the path of the broken trees to a small, smoldering pile of metal. The forty-five foot long, green bird was a quarter of its size and totally black!

The injured finally reached the hilltop after approximately fifteen minutes. There to greet them were Marines ready to help. There to meet Brown was a laughing Stemple, "Damn it, Brown. If anyone could survive that, I knew you could!" Stemple's battle-hardened Fox company commander had survived, again.

Below his lip, Brown's lower teeth had cut through his chin. He wiped at it, looked at the blood on his arm and smiled back at Stemple comprehending his boss's reaction. "You son of a bitch, Sir!" Brown said smiling while shaking Stemple's hand. "This was your idea that I come out here, wasn't it?"

They both laughed.

The injuries of that morning's crash totaled a broken collar bone, a broken arm, a nose that had to be surgically removed, Westfall reduced to private first class, even though both Brown and Stemple agreed the crash should have been sufficient punishment; and, for Brown, more bruises than he'd sustained from ten years of playing football and six months of the war, together.

As he moved the PRC-25 radio near Fox's new boss around noon on 10 January, Lance Corporal Malanowski said, "Lieutenant Wing, Colonel Stemple wants to talk to you."

"This is Fox Six, over," Lieutenant Wing answered.

After five minutes, Corporal Bilski, the company radio operator, shrugged his head toward the lieutenant and asked Malanowski, "What the heck's going on? The colonel's been talking to him for five minutes."

"Don't know, Stan. Something about a helo crash and Westfall."

First Lieutenant Wing, in his mellow voice, finally closed the conversation with an "Aye, aye, Sir, out." He looked at the two radio operators and declared, "I want you two to pass the word that Major Brown and Westfall were in a helicopter crash, but they're all right. As a matter of fact, everyone survived the crash."

"What crash, Lieutenant?"

Now realizing that the radio operators, who always seem to get advance information, had not in this case, Wing summarized the helo crash story. Later, changing the subject, Wing said, "Ski?"

Both Bilski and Malanowski in unison responded, "Sir!" as if it had been rehearsed.

All three men were still chuckling as Wing defined, "Corporal Bilski. Hey, what's the scoop with this guy Corporal Grillo?"

"What do you mean, Sir?"

"Well, two weeks ago, the day before I came to the field, he was the company's Supply Sergeant. I went to get a new pair of jungle utility trousers and all he did was give me the meanest stare and pointed to his home made sign:

IF YOU NEED IT, WE MAY HAVE IT.

IF WE DON'T HAVE IT, YOU DON'T NEED IT.

Bilski smiled and said, "Sir, Gus Grillo's on his third or fourth six-month extension. He'd never make it in the rear. He's the most savage killer we have! He's originally from Argentina. Doesn't swear, loves his mother, the Catholic Church, and killing gooks. And I'm not sure in what order. You know he came back to the field right behind you," Bilski explained, "'The Greek', Lance Corporal Kostopolos in the 1st Platoon who's a buddy of Grillo's, told me about you not getting your trousers. I guess he felt pretty bad about not having trousers for you. 'The Greek' says Grillo's not smart enough to make that sign, anyway. Grillo quit the job back there to get out here. Although I heard the first sergeant was about ready to fire him anyway."

"He sure is a character! I'm glad we have him out here with us, particularly with the clerk's out here taking the squad leader jobs to replace our malaria losses."

"Yes, Sir. With these thirty-some replacements we just joined, they need all the field leadership they can get."

"The battalion XO told me that there is a Captain coming out here to take the company in a week to ten days. You all hear any more about that?"

Both men raised their eyebrows in total surprise.

"I've been the company commander for almost two weeks. Too bad, I was actually getting to like the job."

"What's his name, Sir?"

"Kingrey. They told me its pronounced 'King-ray' or 'King-ree'...Something like that."

"I sure hope he's as good as you and Major Brown," Bilski offered, soliciting a comment.

"Don't worry about that, Ski. Heard he was a mustang, so he'll be sensitive about the troops needs."

"What's gonna happen to you?"

"I figure I'll be the XO for a while."

The new captain actually arrived in the field on 21 January 1969, about the same time the malaria-stricken troops started returning. Immediately he seemed different. He constantly had a kerchief tied around his neck. He carried a "Grease Gun" instead of a .45 caliber pistol or an M-16 rifle. He didn't mind telling anyone he grew up poor, enlisted in the Marine Corps, and went to Eastern Carolina University on the GI Bill. While there he was the "Tumbling Pirate", the mascot that would lead the football team onto the field doing flips in the advance of the players. ECU had a reputation as being a "party" school. Kingrey did not mask that reputation. Pretty soon his command group knew he was inclined to nip on an occasional bottle.

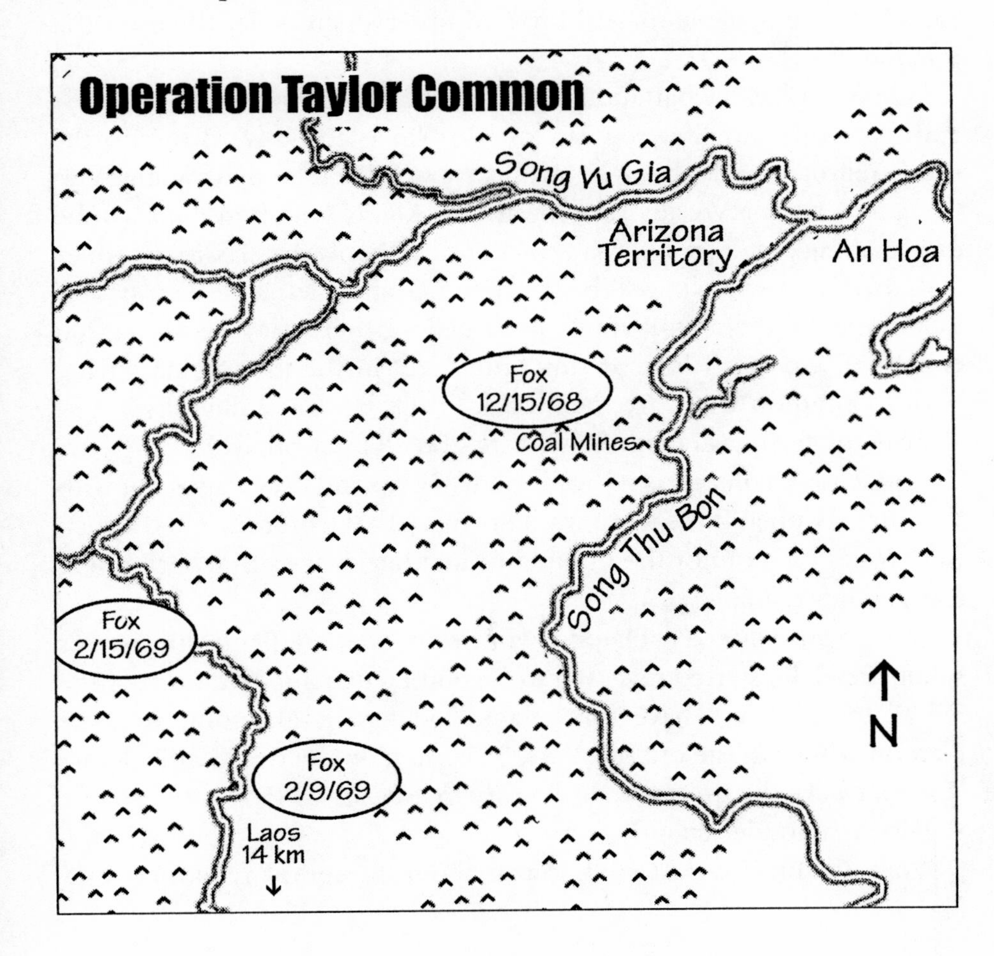

In the next thirty days Fox went back to An Hoa to dry out for three days; was airlifted back to the mountains near the Laotian border to Hill

1061; had a chopper crash into the company headquarters during a resupply run on 30 January with no injuries; and left the mountains for good on 18 February to return to An Hoa for "rehabilitation and refurbishment." Lieutenant Colonel Stemple called the company commanders together on 20 February to have his staff brief them on an operation that would commence on 22 February. Briefed, Captain Kingrey returned to the Fox company office and had Gunnery Sergeant Dierdalh round up the lieutenants and forward observers to brief them on the mission.

"On Saturday, the battalion is going to be trucked out to Phu Lac (6) and from there we'll sweep east on Go Noi Island toward the north-south railroad track about eight klicks away. We'll be driving any Viet Cong and their NVA advisors toward an ARVN battalion who will be dug in along the raised railroad track. You all know the classic "hammer and anvil" tactic. Well, we'll be the hammer and Vietnamese army battalion will be the anvil. "Intel" folks believe there may be about 200 enemy on Go Noi Island at this time. Hell, in the mountains during Taylor Common we drove them back to the Ho Chi Minh Trail, now we're going to squash them down here. You all up for that?"

There was a consensus of heads nodding up and down agreeing with their new skipper. If the truth was known, both the officers and the men were glad to get out of the mountains and begin operating back in the rice paddies again.

"McDugal, your 2nd Platoon will be on the left flank during our sweep. Pete," he started referring to Second Lieutenant Pete Korn of the 3rd Platoon, "You'll have right flank. Lieutenant Newsom, your 1st Platoon will be in the middle. We'll be getting on the trucks at 0600, so, Gunny, I want the troops fed and ready to leave by 0545."

Dierdalh nodded silently.

"Also, Gunny, I want to talk to you about the company radio operator."

"Yes, Sir."

"Are there any questions?" Kingrey looked around. "Alright, let's start getting ready."

Dierdalh hung around after the rest had gone. "What's the matter, Sir? Bilski still annoying you?"

"Gunny, I want him replaced today. If he tells me one more time how things were done in the old days, I think I'll beat him up!"

"Got you, Captain. Consider it done!"

The battalion began their sweep onto Go Noi Island at 0800 on 22 February under a partially cloudy sky. Fox's position was in the center of the battalion formation. First, they were going to clear the same hamlet, Cu Ban (4), where Fox had invoked the displeasure of Hanoi Hanna five months earlier.

Before an hour had passed, one of the machine gunners tripped a booby trap and had to be evacuated. As a matter of fact, the booby trap knocked out the entire three-man machine gun squad. The 2nd and 3rd Platoons continued in order to stay in line with Golf and Echo Companies. After waiting thirty minutes for the medevac chopper, the 1st Platoon began to move out with riflemen carrying the gun and its ammo. With two platoons forward and the 1st Platoon behind, the company moved in a two up and one back formation.

The company command group was positioned immediately in front of the 1st Platoon. While moving, the captain coordinated with the artillery and 81mm mortar forward observers. The gunny provided advice to the company's 60mm mortar section leader. Lance Corporal Malanowski busied himself instructing Lance Corporal Kostopolos, who had replaced Bilski, on radio procedures.

Private First Class Dwight Anderson from the 1st Platoon had been assigned to help out the "baddest corporal in the entire United States Marine Corps" who was now carrying the machine gun, Tommy Byrd from Grapeland, Texas. His handle was "T-Byrd." Byrd was Anderson's squad leader before the booby trap, but due to his longevity in the Corps Byrd was quite adept at firing the M-60. However, being an assistant gunner was a new job for the young replacement who had been trained only as a rifleman. Now he was carrying his rifle, one 60mm illumination mortar round in his pack, and a large box of linked ammo. His best new friends, Bud Canada and Donny Clough, remained with the rifle squad.

All the men believed they would be in a fight before long. The view was excellent as they closed on the twenty-foot high railroad berm about four klicks ahead. An OV-10 Bronco kept a steady stream of white phosphorous rockets flowing, marking targets of opportunities for two F-4 Phantoms dropping bombs not too far in front of Fox Company. That smoke lingered on this cloudy day. One of the huts hit by the Willie Peter rocket was still smoldering and billowing its own smoke skyward.

Had Foxtrot's history been written and read by then, surely someone would have known and compared the situation Fox was stumbling at that moment into with that of the napalm strike on the unfortunate 2nd Platoon in August. The warriors of Fox did not regularly pass on its oral history as they fought day-to-day just trying to survive this surreal war. For only seven months earlier, less than 500 meters to the south of their location at Cu Ban (6), a pilot error cost the 2nd Platoon thirty-three burned Marines. Yet in seven months, not one of these currently active field Marines were on the rolls of the company on that fateful day.

Lance Corporal Bill Martell walked behind a tank with his rifle, three rocket rounds, and a 3.5" rocket launcher. Earlier, his 2nd Platoon had taken fire from a hut which he and several others rapidly destroyed.

Near the hut with a flag flying, the platoon advanced toward NVA soldiers in a trench. The tank in front of Martell fired at the flag, but the defiant NVA hoisted it right back up. An air strike was called to prep the area before the assault by the platoon; however, aircraft were not available, so the strike did not materialize.

Second Lieutenant Pete Korn temporarily held up his 3rd Platoon as they, on the left flank, were getting too far forward of the company command group and the 1st Platoon. Korn looked forward at Lance Corporal Frenchy Olivier, the forward fire team leader, to ensure he had received the "Hold it up," order. He had.

Olivier showed a lot of promise. For that reason, Korn had promoted him to Lance Corporal and made him a fire team leader.

"Hey, Victor", Olivier called over to his best friend and member of his fire team, Private First Class Victor Jouvert. Frenchy always believed his buddy had a strange name for a Puerto Rican from New York City.

"What d'ya got, Frenchy?"

"Nothing. Just checking on your water. Do you have enough?" Olivier asked, inquiring about his team's welfare as any good fire team leader would do.

Silence followed as they both took a swig from their own canteens.

All of a sudden the noise of an attacking aircraft echoed in the distance. At that precise moment, a 500-pound bomb hurtled toward the 3rd Platoon.

"Hit the deck!" The call rang out. No one reacted at first. Again the voice of warning cried out, "Hit the deck!"

Olivier stared into Jouvert's eyes before they dove for the ground, canteens in hand.

The ground exploded upward in white smoke. Spike after spike raced toward the sky. An orange fireball laced with black smoke followed and floated away from the devastated platoon.

Olivier felt his head being squeezed like a wet sponge from the concussion of the 500 pound bomb exploding. His lungs seemed to be collapsing. Convinced he was dead, he stayed still, thinking that death was not as painful as he had imagined.

After a minute, Olivier's eyes opened. All was gray. His eyes closed. Rocks and other debris began to fall all about him. It sounded like rain hitting a parked car. He opened his eyes a second time. The view was now gray mixed with brown. His eyes closed again. Soon the faint sound of voices became audible.

His eyes opened a third time. Now he could see figures moving around. He looked for Jouvert and could not find him. Struggling to his feet, the dust covered fire team leader searched for his only friend.

The bodies of Marines were flung and scattered everywhere. Olivier called out weakly with a tinge of hopelessness in his voice. Finally, he witnessed other Marines standing by a motionless man. He rushed over.

It was his friend. With a look of peace masking his face, Jouvert looked fine until Olivier realized that he had been nearly cut in half by the blast.

Olivier and Martel, behind the tank were lucky, but many of the others were not. In addition to Jouvert, the explosions took the lives of Lance Corporal Daniel Margrave-the cross-country champion from the state of Montana, Private First Class Rhena Webster, and three men from Headquarters and Service Company. Twelve others were wounded.

At first the men blamed the two Phantoms. Later they learned that the two bombs might have come from an A-6 Intruder, an all weather attack aircraft, on a "Beacon Hop" mission. They never found out for certain.

The rest of the day was consumed in evacuating the casualties and rebalancing the company's combat power. Evening fell and all prepared to resume the attack in the morning. Everyone except the Viet Cong who probed Fox's positions, and who, throughout the night, were trying to mess with the minds of these men back in the paddies for the first time in a few months. Bamboo sticks clattered with a hollow, repeating "pop" "pop" "pop" sound; rocks banged off the bottom of cooking pots with a "poing" noise; and death-defying screams that, anywhere else would hardly cause a Marine discomfort, that night got their full attention.

"What the hell was that? That gook son of a bitch can only be out there forty meters!" Lance Corporal "Big Marve" Carpenter whispered to Second Lieutenant Korn.

"Hold your fire, Carpenter!"

"Sir, I can get them. I saw two gooks over in that clearing five minutes ago."

"Well, hold your fire any way. They're trying to find our positions. When they do, they'll attack."

Fox did nothing. The NVA continued their scare tactics and Fox kept their location secret. That same night, enemy 82mm mortar men successfully fired on two of the ammunition bunkers in An Hoa at 0130.

Their rounds inflicted heavy casualties and spread ordnance throughout the combat base and nearby rice fields outside the fence.

The 1st Battalion who had remained at Phu Lac (6) was immediately trucked to An Hoa to secure the scattered ordnance, while the 2nd Battalion had its attack mission canceled and was ordered back to Phu Lac (6).

At first light, the company moved back to Phu Lac (6) in a tactical column with the 1st Platoon in the rear. The mission of protecting the absolute rear of the column fell to Corporal Tommy Byrd's machine gun team and a squad of young riflemen protecting him. The company moved in and out of the dry and semi-dry riverbeds lacing Go Noi Island. The sandy bottoms were five-to-seven feet below the elephant grass that grew on the high ground above. Halfway back to Phu Lac (6), the six men comprising the rear guard began crossing the forty-meter wide dry creek bed.

As he rushed down the six-foot bank into the creek bed, Private First Class Anderson could feel the illumination round slip from his pack. "Corporal Byrd," Anderson called out, "How 'bout giving me a hand with this round."

Byrd spun around gave Anderson the machine gun to hold. Anderson bent over to allow Byrd easy access to his pack. At that moment, two AK-47s opened up from behind cracking into the air and breaking the silence.

"Jesus! We're getting fired on," Anderson yelled. A bullet passed overhead. Anderson watched it impact into Private First Class Donnie Clough's rucksack. Donny fell down the embankment.

"Donny, you okay?" Anderson shouted.

Clough coughed and responded, "Yeah!" and scooted back up the bank into the elephant grass.

T-Byrd with the machine gun in hand had run half way up the embankment when Anderson realized he had better get moving. He raced to catch the large, muscular machine gunner. At the top Byrd stopped, took a prone position, and began returning fire on the enemy.

Anderson finally reached the top with rounds skimming by him. He needed cover from the enemy's fire. Instinctively, he dove behind the only protective item there. When Anderson's helmet slammed into Byrd's butt, the source of Anderson's protection from the bullets, the big machine gunner reached behind and began slapping Anderson on the head, yelling, "Get your head out of my ass. I need some ammo!"

An inexperienced assistant gunner, Anderson gave Byrd the unopened ammo box. Byrd cursed and opened the box. He began to load the gun.

Anderson, in this, his first significant firefight, opened up on the enemy with his M-16 rifle—only a few inches away from Byrd's left ear. Byrd wheeled on Anderson, anger infused on his face. Anderson didn't believe it was humanly possible to create a look of that much rage, let alone sustain it. The gun finally loaded, Byrd shoved the end of the five-foot long belt of ammo at Anderson and roared, "Hold this and follow me!"

Byrd stood up and began running. Anderson trailed the gigantic man holding tight to the end of the belt of linked ammo. Byrd whipped him to the left then to the right. Within a few meters Byrd stopped, turned, and fired back on the enemy. The trailing Anderson ducked from the blast. Byrd whipped him in trace again. Then, suddenly, Byrd spun and bolted away from the enemy whipping Anderson on another left then right circuit. This comic routine, repeated several more times, mirrored the last man in a dragon outfit during a Chinese New Year parade…complete with firecrackers.

Back at Phu Lac (6), Anderson, Canada, and Clough were laughing at their good fortune. "Man, I'm glad those gooks weren't good shots!" Anderson offered.

"I don't know. Take a look at this," Clough said showing his rucksack where the bullet penetrated, passed though a five-pack of razor blades and his box of stationary, glanced off one armor plate in his flak jacket, and came to rest against a second armor plate. "I'll tell you guys something," Clough replied in all seriousness, "my friggin' back feels like I was stepped on by an elephant."

The next day, a sunny one for a change, Fox began patrolling the Phu Nhuan village area between Phu Lac (6) and An Hoa. Collectively, the Marines called the nine Phu Nhuan hamlets "The Phu Nons." With the Marines were two amphibious tractors, "amtracs". The Phu Nhuans were littered with mines and booby traps, and sure enough, one of the amtracs blew a land mine late that morning. Once the amtrac was ready to move again, Kingrey and Dierdalh passed the word for every one to "stay in the amtrac tread marks."

After an hour the company came to a halt. The 2nd Platoon stopped by a two-story Buddhist shrine that caught the eye of the platoon commander. Impulsively, Second Lieutenant McDugal said, "Hey look at that!" He took five steps and detonated a booby trap that wounded him and killed his radio operator, Private First Class John Erbs, his platoon sergeant, and two others.

Following the medevac, the company altered its strategy. "Put out flank security since we need to get back to the base to help with the ammo cleanup," Kingrey ordered.

Placed on one flank security detail was Lance Corporal Elliott who had just returned to the field after being wounded; he was a bit nervous. T-Byrd joined him. Private First Class Jim Carney was the last man in the company column and had the ultimate responsibility for the security in the rear. Carney looked to the rear for a moment, perhaps two, when the column moved leaving him all alone. The sun was setting and long shadows distorted the light. Carney hustled to catch up to the last man in the company column. Instead of closing with the main column, he ran in Elliot's direction. Elliot, in the strange light, believed he saw a pith helmet charging him. He fired one shot and killed Carney.

After the bombing, the booby trap, the landmine, and the accidental fire, Fox returned to its company area in An Hoa feeling more bewildered than glad to get back.

March 1969 came and went with, seemingly, only two significant events. On 1 March, Gunnery Sergeant Dierdalh was promoted to first sergeant and transferred to the Operations Section as the operations chief. On 30 March, the engineers reopened Liberty Bridge.

The battalion participated in Operation Muskogee Meadow from 7 April to 20 April under the new battalion commander, Lieutenant Colonel J. H. Higgins. Its mission was rice denial and security for the Vietnamese rice harvesters in the southern portion of the Arizona Territory. The Viet Cong had become rice thieves and now were not only forced to hide in the mountains, but were being starved out. Their NVA counterparts still commanded Higgins' full respect. Fox served as the regimental "palace guard" by manning the defensive perimeter at An Hoa for the first two weeks in April. Fox finally joined the battalion on 16 April. Muskogee Meadow netted five tons of rice, twenty-three enemy killed, and many weapons confiscated. Six battalion Marines were killed, and forty-four were wounded and evacuated.

Operation Muskogee Meadow was a precursor to the highly successful combat operations conducted during the month of May. The 2nd Battalion pressed an NVA battalion day and night in the Arizona Territory. For the operation throughout the month the battalion also had operational control of four other 5th Marines' rifle companies, including Bravo, Charlie, Delta, and Lima Companies. Overall, the battalion with combat arms support, both artillery and air, killed 256 enemy, most of which were NVA. They also captured eleven enemy and had five enemy surrender. All total, Fox had more than fifteen enemy encounters with the enemy during the month that resulted in seven enemy killed while losing two of their own and sustaining forty plus wounded.

Sunday, 11 May, might have been Mother's Day back home in the States but, due to the International Date Line, while moms were going to church in the US, in Vietnam the men of Fox were on the move; and it was already Monday morning. A company move to a new location, perhaps five to eight kilometers, is normally not too exciting. As a result many of the men allowed their thoughts to drift back across the

International Date Line and home to the wonderful women they loved and for whom, among others, they were fighting.

Precisely at 1235 hours, an enemy forward observer found Fox Company on the move. The 3rd Platoon had the lead. The 2nd Platoon and company command group followed. The 1st Platoon was "Tail End Charlie." The 3rd Platoon had just moved from one treeline, across a clearing and into another treeline when 60mm and 82mm mortars began raining down into the clearing. Lance Corporal Marvin Carpenter of the 3rd Platoon hustled the remainder of his squad into the tree line and some previously dug, shallow trenches. The company command group rushed back into the treeline with the 1st Platoon. The 2nd Platoon, hopelessly caught in the middle of the target zone, immediately began enduring the wrath of the enemy's indirect firepower.

To prevent further casualties, the 3rd Platoon sent men out into the opening to pull in the rapidly mounting 2nd Platoon casualties. The astute NVA forward observer, after locating the source of the rescuers, shifted his fires onto the trenches. Carpenter ordered his men away from the trenches, further into the jungled forest. Once they were repositioned, the rescue of the men in the 2nd Platoon resumed.

"Fox Three Bravo, Fox Three Bravo, this is Fox One, over," Second Lieutenant Doyle Newsom called for Lance Corporal Carpenter.

"This is Three Bravo, over."

"Three Bravo how about you send two men and I'll send two, and we'll get those mortars! Over," Newsom suggested.

"Roger One. We're on our way. We'll meet your men at the north side of the clearing, over," Carpenter agreed.

"Roger Three. Bravo, out."

Carpenter and one other made their way to the north side of the clearing and met Newsom and another Marine. As the four of them rushed up a trail toward where they believed the mortar tubes were located, the forward observer shifted his fires away from the company and onto the band of four. Everywhere they went, the mortars followed. Frustrated, the foursome was forced to return to the company. Upon reaching Fox, they turned to witness a squad of four US Army Hueys shoot deadly, precise rockets that destroyed the mortar tubes.

The "Mother's Day Massacre" resulted in Fox sustaining thirty wounded; twenty-two of them had to be medevac'd.

...But Fox did not always suffer in the field.

COOLING OFF IN THE ARIZONA

(Photo courtesy of Mike Malanowski)

MORALE NEVER DIPPED WHILE FOX WAS IN THE FIELD
(Photo courtesy of Mike Malanowski)

"You'll get to be with the men out on the lines as soon as I check you in, PFC Bullock. Now just sit down for a moment," First Sergeant Tony Marengo suggested to the mature looking new black kid from Brooklyn, NY. Marengo had been gone from the company for two years, since just after Union II. In that timeframe he had been promoted twice to his current rank. "I'm assigning you to the 2nd Platoon, but first I want you to check out your deuce gear and rifle. When you have that done, report back to me and I'll get you out on the line. Is that clear, Marine?"

"Yes, Sir, First Sergeant, Sir!"

Marengo noted the enthusiasm in Dan Bullock's tone. Marengo had only been back with the company for the past four days. In his quiet, though observant style, he noticed a huge change in the attitude of the men. As a whole they were no longer as anxious to go to the field as they had been two years ago. Their discipline seemed more relaxed. Was it the attitudes coming from the States? The leadership? Drugs? Always prudent, he resolved to get to the bottom of the problem and get Fox on the right path if necessary.

Bullock was standing at attention in front of Marengo's desk with helmet on, chin strap fastened, flak jacket on and zipped half way up, and M-16 rifle held tightly to his right thigh. Marengo looked up at him in disbelief. It had only been fifteen minutes since he sent this kid off! Maybe his initial assessment of the men was made in haste? If they were anything like this kid, there should be no problems. "Private First Class Bullock reporting as ordered, First Sergeant!"

"Very well, Bullock. Follow me." The two went over to the 2nd Platoon hooch where Marengo dropped him off with the platoon sergeant.

An hour later, Bullock's wish came true; he was on the lines with his platoon on the perimeter of the An Hoa combat base. Soon he found he was actually a member of the "Palace Guard". Bullock had been assigned to Lance Corporal Larry Eglinsdoerfer's squad that included Privates First Class Don Bunn, Jason Hunnicutt and Steven Montgomery. Their bunker adjacent to the 1st Platoon's first bunker was the farthest on the right of the four 2nd Platoon bunkers, which consisted of Lance Corporals Dwight Anderson, Paul Trenn, Bud Canada, and John Ahern.

After a night watch, the men would police up the trash, repair the fortifications and take turns going to chow, the exchange and sickbay. Most of the time, however, they could be found at their bunker or in the immediate vicinity. Bullock peppered the "salty" lance corporals in the next bunker with questions about the bush. He wasn't ego stroking them at all as his questions seemed never-ending, one leading into another. From the time he had joined the company on 28 May a week earlier, the rest of the Marines had grown pretty fond of Bullock.

On the afternoon of 7 June, Lance Corporal Dwight Anderson was walking back to the company area having bought some items at the regimental exchange. In front of him was Dan Bullock. "Hey, Bullock," he called. "Wait up."

"Yeah, Man. Did you go to the PX too?" Bullock asked.

"Right, Bullock. I'm on the way back to the company area. Are you headed that way?"

"Yeah, I have to sign something at the company office. By the way, what's them rifles doing over there stuck in those sand bags in front of Golf Company's office?"

"Well, Dan, remember when I told you the battalion was in a lot of big fights last month?"

Bullock nodded silently.

"Golf lost twenty-two men then. They must have just completed a memorial service. Each rifle with their helmet resting on top represents a Marine who was killed."

Bullock walked over and, one at a time, counted the three rows of seven rifles and the one extra one. Anderson waited silently near by for him.

Looking square at Anderson, Bullock said resolutely, "You're never going to see a rifle and helmet representing me! I'm going to be famous one day."

That night, sappers carrying explosive charges cut through the barbed wire and attacked the bunkers. For some reason the men in Eglinsdoerfer's bunker remained inside during this ground attack instead of getting into the connecting trenches, as was the practice. Bunkers were only designed to protect against shrapnel from indirect weapons fire such as mortars and artillery fire and not to be used during a ground attack. A satchel charge was thrown into their bunker. All perished, including Bullock.

Within two days Fox was trucked to China Beach. The Non-Commissioned Officer-In-Charge, or NCOIC, greeted them. "Fox Company, I have heard of your fine work in the field." Pleased with the praise, a chorus of "Ooohras" and "Aaruugas" followed. "And did y'all hear that, yesterday, President Nixon announced that 25,000 lucky bastards are going to be out of 'Nam' in August as part of a series of troop withdrawals?"

The men had not heard that. They fell silent contemplating the meaning of what the Non-Commissioned Officer-In-Charge had just said. At first there was a single shout of joy. Then slowly, all the troops understood the war might soon be over and they too may be going home earlier than expected. The joyous chorus grew into a mighty crescendo of voices.

Waving his hands to quiet the roar, the Non-Commissioned Officer-In-Charge yelled, "I have 400 cases of beer and 400 cases of soda. More hamburgers and hot dogs then you can possibly eat in the next two days, so have a good time!" The "Ooohras" started once more and the party began.

At China Beach, there was a lot of just plain-old Tomfoolery, like shaking up beer cans and squirting the beer on each other especially that day. At night a couple of inter-platoon fights broke out that were more serious than they should have been. The non-commissioned officers broke them up and soon the company slept. On the next day the band, "The Green Machine", comprised of Marines stationed in Da Nang entertained the men while they ate and drank. Their version of Blood, Sweat and Tears' popular hit, "You've Made Me So Very Happy," garnered the most attention due to the Marines' favorite lines:

"I lost at love before,
Got bad and joined the Corps,"

As the music revved the men up, more fights brewed. The most famous of which was actually classified as "boxing". The men egged the ever-popular Lieutenant Doyle Newsom into challenging their eccentric Captain Bob Kingrey. Soon, a circle of bare chested men in green shorts circled the two somewhat reluctant boxers forming what they would call a ring…and so the fight began.

It was to be the fight to the finish, until the last man was standing. Lance Corporal Buddy Canada, who personally couldn't stand Kingrey, became his "corner man". Every time Newsom would knock his captain out of the ring, Canada would catch Kingrey, pick him up, pat him on the back, and shout, "Come on, Captain! You can take him! You can take him!" Then he'd push Kingrey back into the ring, all the while looking over at Anderson and laughing silently almost out of control. Finally, Newsom was declared the winner and the two officers withdrew to put the side of a cold can of beer on their bruises.

All too quickly the company found itself on the way back to An Hoa. Lieutenant Colonel Higgins was there to greet them. He spotted the command group and waited for them to pass by his location. Anyone could tell that Kingrey had been in a fight. His right eye was blackened and swollen. Elsewhere he had yellow and greenish bruises. The lieutenant colonel's eyes widened as he stared at his Fox company commander. Kingrey, anticipating the obvious "What-happened-to-you?" question neither saluted nor greeted his boss. He merely looked at him and stated flatly, "The Battle of Amtrac Beach, Sir." Without another word Kingrey continued to the company office leaving his lieutenant colonel staring.

Within two days Fox moved to Phu Lac (6) to guard the now fully functional Liberty Bridge. They held a memorial service for Bullock and the other five Marines killed by the sapper. Shortly after the move, at mealtime Captain Kingrey called Corporal Malanowski and asked, "Hey, Ski! Did you see this?"

The corporal moved to join his captain. Kingrey showed his battalion radio operator the front page of the Stars and Stripes newspaper.

The lead story reported on the death of Fox 2/5's Private First Class Dan Bullock, who had been fourteen years old when he enlisted and was fifteen years old when he was killed. He was, and would be always, the youngest American serviceman to die in the Vietnam War.

CHAPTER 19: FOX GAINS THE UPPER HAND

Unknown at the time, the war that Fox Company Marines were fighting in June 1969 was vastly different then it had been six months ago. For the men who had served since the beginning of the year, who had endured being bugged and bombed, and who had enjoyed the "Battle at Amtrac Beach", things seemed somewhat better. Although Fox Company remained in the An Hoa valley splitting time between guarding Liberty Bridge, serving as the palace guard back in An Hoa, and looking for the enemy everywhere within a twenty-kilometer radius of the combat base, encounters with the enemy had not gone away entirely.

As far as the replacements were concerned, they were finally in Vietnam: the place where they had been told, "It's not uncommon to have daily fights with the enemy." That was their expectation when they arrived.

When they reported into the 1st Platoon of Fox Company, however, good old Sergeant Tommy "T-Byrd" Byrd would explain in his rich Texas accent, "Before the war was like supper where the cow, the chicken, and the pig were all fully committed to the meal. Now," T-Byrd went on, "it's like breakfast: the cow's just providing the milk; the chicken's just providing them eggs; but that pig, he's still very much committed!…And, here in 'Nam we don't know which of us is going to be that darn pig. So you new men, y'all pay attention to the vets!"

The character of the company had been restored in June with the arrival of their new company commander, Captain Ken R. Furr, who the troops instantly respected. As a former co-captain of the North Carolina University wrestling team, an infantry platoon commander in the 9th Marines, and an advisor to the Vietnamese Marines, Furr was in every way ready to command. The men instantly recognized him as a dedicated professional and a compassionate leader possessing high expectations. He had extended, like Brown had a year earlier, and like Brown, could speak Vietnamese. With Furr leading in the field and First

Sergeant Marengo running the rear, Fox Company discipline and standards had been significantly strengthened.

What was not as obvious to Fox Company was the fact the Viet Cong had been mostly defeated in the An Hoa valley through the Marines concentrated efforts over the past year. Their insurgency had been traumatically weakened. They were unable to recruit as they once had. The Marine Corps Combined Action Platoon concept restored the confidence of the local militia. The South Vietnamese government's surrender program, called "Chu Hoi", was repatriating many former Viet Cong. Kids were turning in unexploded ordinance for a few piasters, the Vietnamese currency, instead of letting the VC use it for booby traps.

North Vietnamese Army, NVA, units there and in the nearby mountains, though highly respected and possessing an ability to fight at a company-sized level, generally did not seek engagements with the proven power of the Marine forces operating out of the An Hoa combat base. The NVA wandered between the foothills of the Que Son Mountains southeast of An Hoa and those to the north that ended in the Arizona territory mostly at night in groups of ten and twenty to obtain rice from the indigenous population.

Due to the NVA actions, the 5th Marines added two strategic dynamics to their wartime planning. First they expanded their territory to occupy and operate from Hill 65, ten and a half kilometers due north of An Hoa. Between Hill 65 and An Hoa was the rich, rice-growing, eastern portion of the Arizona territory. To the west of the rice paddies were the mountains the NVA used as a safe haven. To the east of the fields were the Marine Corps' outposts, Phu Lac (6), and Liberty Bridge. With Hill 65 added as a combat outpost the food source for the NVA had been effectively framed and isolated.

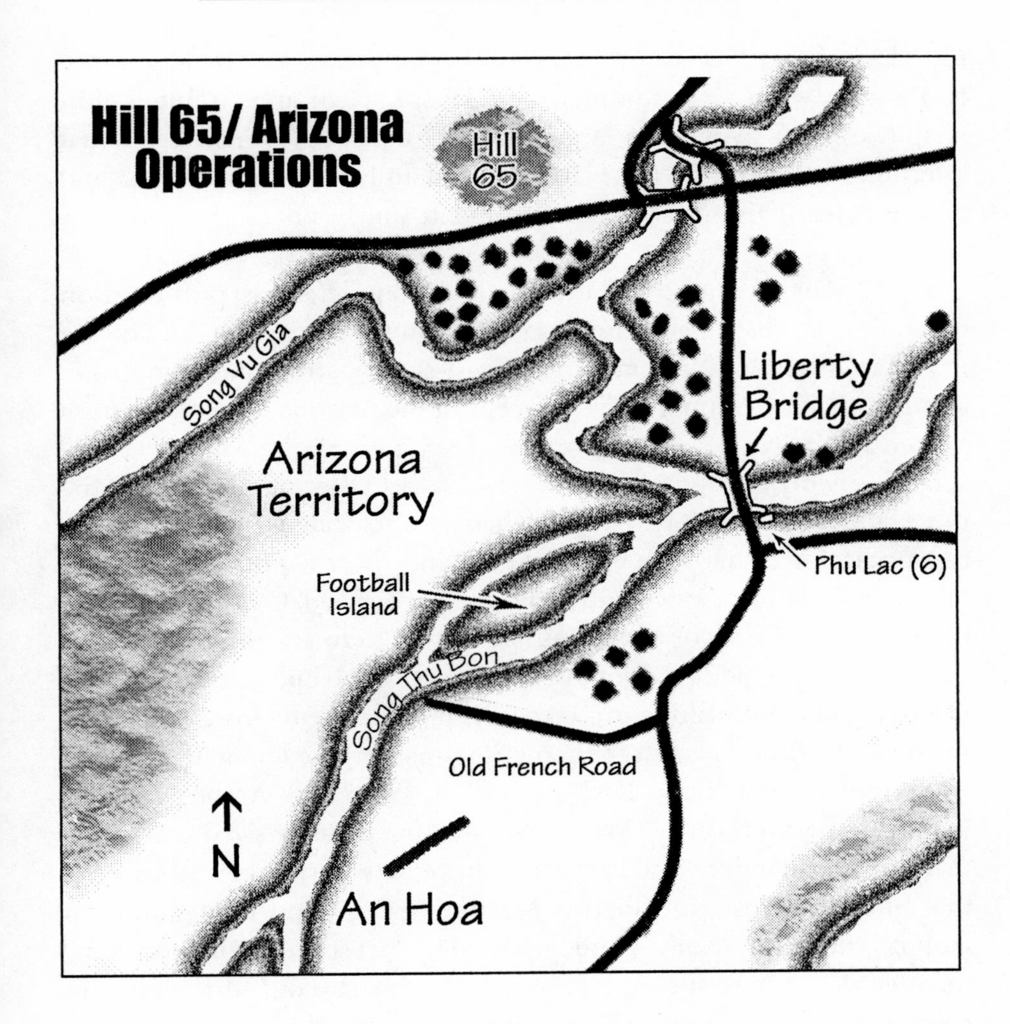

The Marines' second strategy was to begin rice denial operations. In two parts this effort included destroying the rice fields and moving the rice farmers and their families back to the Duc Duc District camps for good.

During the first two weeks in August, Fox Company Marines, along with the rest of the battalion, participated in support of the 2nd Battalion, 1st Marines. This operation, called Durham Peak, took place in the Que Son Mountains. On 8 August at 1100 hours, a platoon patrol found an enemy base camp used only a month earlier. The base camp had a deep water well, command bunkers, kitchen area, training aids, hospital, and a living area large enough for 300–400 men. Later that afternoon, at 1645, another platoon found an NVA command post and training area. This one could accommodate one hundred to150 men.

By 12 August the 2nd Battalion had completed its participation Operation Durham Peak and began the movement to Hill 65. For the next few months, platoon- and squad-sized patrols and ambushes accompanied by company-sized sweeps in the Arizona territory characterized the daily operational routine. Even with all the Marine Corps' activity, enemy encounters were sparse. As a matter of fact, during the three and a half month period when 2/5 relocated to Hill 65, Fox accounted for twenty-five enemy killed and three captured while sustaining losses of five killed and forty-seven wounded. Compared to earlier periods, the pace of Fox losses had slowed dramatically.

Captain Furr added a lot of spice to tactical operations. Because patrolling and ambushing produced the highest enemy losses, Furr had the men utilize and perfect the sometimes-earlier-used maneuver, called by various names: "Drop-Back Ambushes, "Stay Back Ambushes", and "Ambush the Ambushers". While moving on a platoon-sized patrol, the platoon commander would identify a productive-looking ambush site that afforded protection for his Marines and a good killing zone to ambush the enemy. As the platoon passed by that spot, the platoon commander would have the middle squad, unseen, slip out of the platoon column and into the ambush site. When Fox entered a densely vegetated portion along a trail or road and emerged out of it without the squad that was dropped, any enemy observing the Marines' would not notice the difference in the column. The troops loved the tactical advantage this stratagem afforded them.

Despite reductions in firefights indicating that the war was slowing tactical creativity, and field promotions for many Fox Marines, their minds stayed on that darn pig that was still very much committed for breakfast in T-Byrd's story. A reminder of the pig's commitment occurred shortly after the death of Ho Chi Minh on 2 September 1969, an event that some how raised the aggressiveness of the NVA for at least a couple of weeks. On 7 September a listening post/outpost, LP/OP, was attacked at night resulting in the deaths of two Marines and the wounding of three others. At daylight a search resulted in two VC killed, one of which was a local village chief, and their AK-47 rifles captured.

On 8 September, Fox Company was ordered to change its area of operations. After moving about 2,000 meters, the company arrived during the late afternoon and began digging in. At 1730 hours, "higher ups" concluded the company had been moved into an ARVN artillery impact area and ordered the company back to the village they left earlier that day. Lance Corporal George Garcia was sitting in his fighting hole waiting for the word to move out when an NVA officer casually strolled around the path's turn and almost walked on top of Garcia. Garcia spun and shot the unwitting enemy who fell partially into Garcia's hole, dead.

0025 hours. The company reached its destination. Visibility was almost nil on that particular dark, rainy, and overall dreary night. The 1st Platoon led the company into the village. Lance Corporal Byron "Bud" Canada's squad had the lead. Lance Corporal Donny Clough was the point man. The company's attached dog team, Canada, and his radio operator, a relatively new but ever-so-bright, skinny Marine by the name of Private First Class "Tennessee" Randall, followed him.

Halfway into the village at a junction in the main path, the dog froze in his stance and his neck hairs bristled. His handler placed a hand on the dog's back indicating he had received the message. First the handler whispered forward to Clough to, "Hold up." Then he looked back at Canada and whispered, "Gooks!"

Canada rushed forward to take the point with Randall in trace. Canada then proceeded with utter caution on the left branch of the main path.

As the word was passed back to the following squad, Lance Corporal Dwight Anderson, who was in the front of his squad, split off onto the path that went to the right. With Lance Corporal Canada moving cautiously and Anderson hustling to come on line, the two squads were nearly parallel to each other, seventy-five meters apart.

Now side-by-side, Lance Corporal Bud Canada and Lance Corporal Donny Clough were cautiously leading the squad on the left-hand path. Twenty meters later, three enemy AK-47 automatic weapons opened up on the two men. With their index fingers resting on their trigger guards, the two counter-fired immediately. Anderson's head jerked left to see his long-term mates now silhouetted like Christmas trees from the light of exploding rounds leaving their rifles. Without hesitation, he dashed through the low shrubs to join them.

Canada stopped firing seconds before Clough. He put his rifle down, simultaneously grabbing a grenade from his shoulder harness, and in one seamless move pulled the pin, ran forward, threw the grenade at the ambushers, and dove for a small mound in front of him. As Clough's M-16 magazine emptied, for just a second or two the night blackened. In the same moment, Clough grabbed a second magazine from his cartridge belt, and Canada's grenade exploded. Already in the air, a Chi Com grenade thrown by the now-retreating attackers, headed straight for Clough.

The enemy grenade exploded at Clough's feet. A lethal fragment of the device flew upward, partially severing his windpipe. His legs were ripped apart. The dog and his handler were also hit. As Anderson neared his two friends, Clough was gasping for air, spurting and spewing blood with each remaining heartbeat.

From his position on the ground Canada yelled, "My legs, my legs!"

Lance Corporal Anderson checked on Lance Corporal Canada who remained flat on his stomach as Sergeant Byrd, now the platoon sergeant, and the platoon corpsman, Doc Don, arrived. "Listen to me Bud," Anderson comforted him. "You're wounded on your backside, but your legs are intact. They're okay," he reassured his friend.

"Dwight!" Sergeant Byrd called out. "Doc and I are going to try to do a tracheotomy on Clough, you get out there and frag those family bunkers in case those bastards are hiding in one of them!"

"On the way, T-Byrd."

"Randall!" Byrd called out again as the corpsman dug through his medical bag, "Get the company to frag us a medevac. We've got two priority ones." Looking back at the dog and the dog handler who were also wounded, Byrd said, "Add two more casualties. We'll classify them later."

From a distance of fifteen meters behind, Randall answered, "All right, Sergeant." He began transmitting, "Fox, this is Fox One Bravo, over."

Anderson and two other Marines dropped grenades in to the L-shaped family bunkers, asking first for anyone in them to come out. Muffled explosions throughout the relatively small hamlet punctured the drizzly night. Finally satisfied the enemy had vacated the hamlet, Anderson returned to the ambush site.

Doc Don was now working with Bud Canada. T-Byrd was standing over Donny Clough's poncho-covered body, smoking a cigarette. Anderson, with his lingering Canadian accent, confirmed, "He's gone, eh?"

Byrd nodded his head compassionately. Then he turned in the dark toward Randall and asked the squad radio operator, "Hey, Randall, any scoop on the evac bird yet?"

"Right, Sarge. The bird left Da Nang about fifteen minutes ago, and its about ten minutes out."

"Okay, so when he's nearby, the LZ will be just behind us, near where the two paths split. You guide him in, and I'll be out with the casualties. I have a yellow smoke."

"Roger, Sarge."

Miraculously the medevac chopper landed safely in the dark night and tree-covered area allowing Byrd, Anderson, and a couple others to load Canada, the dog, his handler, and Clough's body. Task completed, Byrd and Anderson ran safely away from the thundering blades. However, it did not lift off as expected.

Moments earlier as the helicopter landed, Randall transmitted to the company to tell them that he too had been wounded. He would leave the radio in place with the squad and be evacuated with the other casualties.

His final transmission was to the chopper pilot to tell him that there would be one more casualty coming to the helicopter for evacuation.

As Byrd and Anderson stood near the chopper more or less scratching their heads trying to figure why it hadn't flown out, Randall calmly walked by them and boarded. In the dark they could not see the gauze pad tied around Randall's head which covered his left eye. They went back to his radio, found some drops of blood, and called Fox to report a fifth casualty. In the morning, they learned then that their brave, skinny little radio operator, Private First Class "Tennessee" Randall, had lost his eye from shrapnel off of one of the NVA's grenades. He had never complained, but merely performed his assigned duties until he could be medevac'd.

From one of the family bunkers later that same morning three scared NVA soldiers crawled out; they were only seventeen or eighteen years old. Two were boys and one was a girl. They surrendered two AK-47 rifles and one M-16.

Regarding the rice denial efforts, Captain Furr initially struggled with the idea of denying local farmers the ability to grow rice. Growing rice was, in fact, the most important value for this set of Vietnamese. However, when Furr understood that the rice farmers would be relocated and allowed to grow rice again in the government-protected area and only the NVA and VC would be harmed, Fox soon took the lead in denying the rice to the enemy.

Here was Fox's concept. To grow rice, farmers first begin with a seedling bed. Once the rice in the bed begins to sprout, the grass-like plants are removed and hand-planted throughout the paddy to populate the entire field. Seedling beds appear as small, richly green islands of vegetation. Furr's plan was to destroy the beds. Without rice to grow, farmers had to relocate to Duc Duc District. There were two methods of destroying seedling beds. One was with Marines on their hands and knees ripping out the plants. The other was by "Huskies", small Army tracked vehicles, destroying larger beds by pulverizing the ground with their treads.

The company continued its aggressive destruction of the rice beds in December. In December alone Fox Company destroyed a total of 269 seedling beds. Naturally this frustrated the ever-hungry enemy. One of Fox's most successful operations took place on the morning of 16 December.

0945 hours. Fox Company was conducting a company-sized sweep along the southern bank of the Song Vu Gia. The 1st Platoon was on the company's right flank and was actually patrolling along the river's bank. The platoon's formation had the newly promoted Corporal Dwight Anderson's squad and Lance Corporal Mike Farrell's squad forward with Farrell's along the river itself. The new platoon sergeant, Staff Sergeant Eddie Bryer, an older balding man, was in the middle. Just behind the staff sergeant was Lance Corporal Carl Pond's squad.

Occasionally, a small stream would cut across a peninsula converting part of the land into a mini-island by overflowing the river's bank and cutting through the sandy soil only to join with the river again. This was the case as the platoon swept along the six-foot wide stream, which divided the rice fields from an island the stream had created. The island, about 300 meters long and forty meters wide, was covered in five-feet high elephant grass.

Farrell's point man hollered back to the rest of his squad, "Two gooks across the stream! Gooks across the stream!"

Lance Corporal Ferrell fired two rounds into the elephant grass that swallowed the noise of the impacting bullets. Staff Sergeant Bryer had Lance Corporal Pond's squad move up to the center of the friendly bank to set up a base of fire. Farrell's squad prepared to assault across the stream to pursue the enemy into the long grass. Corporal Anderson had maneuvered close behind, ready to follow Farrell's squad. Because the island was about 300 meters long and closely paralleled the southern riverbank, Captain Furr sent his other lead platoon forward to the place along the riverbank where the island ended to block any possible enemy escape.

All eyes were fixed on the elephant grass ready for a counter-attack or enemy soldiers to emerge. Like popcorn popping without a lid, from out of the top of the tall grass came Chi Com grenades thrown toward the Marines. The explosive devices fell far short of the stream bank and the Marines. After the surge of grenades, Farrell leaped into the chest-high water and made it across the stream before his men could even hit the water. Anderson and his squad were close behind.

Now the sweep of the small island began. Within moments the Marines nearly tripped over the little NVA troops, some cowering in a pre-natal position, others sitting on their heels Vietnamese style, and others crawling away seeking cover.

FOX'S BIG DAY: 16 DECEMBER 1969
(Photo courtesy of Dwight Anderson)

Those resisting were killed, particularly the ten that tried to run through the blocking force. One female nurse and two others attempted to swim across the Song Vu Gia. All three were shot and killed. At the edge of the island, standing with a smirk on his face along the riverbank, was an NVA warrant officer with pistol in hand. The Marines approached him cautiously. He had no intentions of allowing his weapon to be confiscated and with a bit of bravado threw it into the water. With the same smirk still on his face and his brave act of defiance complete, he turned to a nearby Marine who was ready to apprehend him and winked at the Marine. Big mistake? Must have been because the Marine shot him, and he fell into the water and floated away.

The Marines killed twenty enemy and captured twenty-eight. All were NVA, except five Viet Cong. There were seven women in the mix. Besides the Chi Com grenades and the warrant officer's now-lost pistol, they only had seven AK-47 weapons. They had thrown the rest of their weapons in the river.

The next day, USMC recon scuba divers recovered over twenty weapons that had been thrown in the Song Vu Gia. The unfortunate enemy were on a rice-gathering mission. Their failed mission would have a great impact on their comrades left up in the mountains. It did not, however, disturb the fine Christmas Fox had planned to have back at An Hoa, nor the Rotation Tour Date Party planned by the 1st Platoon for Corporal Dwight Anderson.

Three days later Corporal Dwight Anderson traveled to Da Nang. He flew home the next day with mixed emotions. He was happy to leave Vietnam, but he was one of thirty-one men who arrived in country a year ago and only one of six who made it through the whole year. Torn, he could only think about leaving the service.

EPILOGUE

Dwight Anderson's aircraft landed at 1530 hours. His body was as athletic as it had been when he left Vietnam thanks to his workout regimen. His face remained handsome, though his full head of hair had whitened. In Concourse B the veteran spotted two people he had met at the last reunion in Reno, Tiffany and Kevin Holmes. All three were anxious to see the Fox vets and their families they hadn't seen for two years. Anderson was especially looking forward to seeing eight more men from the 1969 era who were coming for the first time.

After exchanging pleasantries, Anderson went ahead to the hotel where the reunion was taking place. Tiffany and her husband waited another twenty minutes until her dad's airplane arrived at gate B-20. The plane landed on time and Dave and Julie Brown joined them for the ride to the hotel.

On the way, Brown confirmed that Pete Korn and Chris Brown would be sharing details from their recent trip to Vietnam; that Chuck Conley was coming to the reunion and that, as always, he'd be telling his "Who farted?" story after the banquet; and that the 1970–71 history of Fox would be told by '70-'71-era vets in a panel format after the Saturday morning business meeting. After the short ride to the hotel and checking-in, they agreed to meet at Fox Company's popular hospitality suite.

In the second-floor suite, seated at a long table covered with paperwork, hats, and mugs all bearing the Fox logo, were Donna Henderson, and Margaret Jones. "So, Donna, how many are we expecting for the banquet?" Margaret, Gunny Sam Jones' wife, asked of Sam Henderson's wife. The principal job of "running" the membership typically fell to these two outstanding ladies.

"We already have eighty-five people signed up, and I know of at least 130 more who are coming. Of course almost half are wives and kids and grandkids. Then we'll have twenty to thirty who never signed up from outside of Fox coming, so we ought to have 235 to 245 at the banquet. We had 230 in Reno. Our membership keeps growing. Anyway, Margaret, the hotel said they could handle up to 250 for Saturday."

Donna Henderson, who had been managing the association's funds since the group was organized in 1990, praised Ken Kreader's wife who had just taken her place at the sign-in/orientation table with them, "Judy, these are some of the nicest polo shirts and caps we've ever had. So, when these guys come in, make sure you push the caps and shirts. I don't want to have to store them for two years!"

"Okay, Donna," Judy agreed.

Twenty-five minutes later, as soon as the elevator doors on the 2nd floor opened, Dave Brown could hear loud chatter and equally loud laughing. After waving to several Fox vets talking by the far window, Brown went to the registration desk, "Donna?"

"Dave!" Donna stood and, leaning across the table, gave him a big hug.

"Hi, Margaret," Brown said to Sam Jones's wife, "and 'Hi' to you, Judy," he turned to greet Ken Kreader's wife.

"Tiff told me you had a good flight, Dave. Where's Julie?" Donna asked.

"Oh, Julie will be along in a minute, Donna." Brown already knew where his daughter would be heading to first, so he asked, "Where is that 1966 gang huddling?"

"Dave, you know Tiff, she reports in to George Burgett, Gunny Jones, and Sam as soon as she gets to the reunions. They're over there talking to Charley Schlader. Once Marengo gets here, it's hard to separate those five!"

"He's not here yet?"

"No. He told me that he'd be here late Friday. I guess the President's in California today, and he's still setting up his security. He's still one of the President's main Secret Service men in southern California."

"All right, Donna, thanks. Margaret, what do I owe you for the reunion?" Brown asked getting down to business.

Huddled around a beer keg standing in an ice-filled trashcan, Tiffany and Kevin listened with great amusement to the men manning the distribution of the keg's contents. They enjoyed a comfortable circle as Sam Jones, now known to all non-vets as Gunny Sam, replayed his part of the night when George Burgett nearly shot him inside their hooch.

Jones wiggled his finger through a button-hole on his shirt, imitating the hole in the tent. "Jesus, Skipper! Just get your pistol qualification?"

The group laughed merrily as Jones wound down his story.

Glancing around at the large hospitality room as he left the registration table and walking up to Chris Brown, his wife, Maddy, and C.C. Campbell, Dave Brown greeted Maddy first. They hugged briefly, and made pleasantries for a moment before Brown greeted the two Hue City warriors, "Hi, Chris. Nice place."

The ever-exuberant Chris Brown responded by extending his hand to meet Brown, "Dave, how you doing? Glad you like it."

Then, meeting Campbell's eyes as he had nearly forty years earlier when the napalm victim asked, "Skipper, why did you let it happen?" Brown greeted in a softer, more compassionate tone, "Hi, C.C."

Campbell responded to Brown in his familiar, low-toned, emotionless voice, "Hey, Skipper."

"You doing all right, C.C.?" Brown asked knowing he really had never recovered from the war.

"Sure," his answer was unconvincing.

"Hey, Chris, have you seen Mike Downs? I want to see if he and Ed VanValkenburgh are playing golf tomorrow."

"General Downs won't be in until 8:30 tonight, I believe. Ed said they are playing at the Sand Hills Course tomorrow. They are playing with

Rod Gurganious and Pete Korn. He has some empty foursomes if you all are playing."

"Great. Where is the 1970–71 panel going to be on Saturday morning?"

"Right here in this room. We can arrange it any way you want."

"Thanks, I guess we'll work that out Saturday morning. Hey, are any of those '70 guys here?"

"I saw Ian Bailey and Ray Ruby. Oh yeah, Joe Finneran and Bernie Navarra were looking for you."

"Chris, you're amazing. You know all five hundred of us and when we served with Fox!"

"We're up to 575 guys now. Those '69-'70-'71 guys just keep coming out of the woodwork."

"All right, I think I'll look for my '70 guys to welcome them. You're going to have the Fox business meeting before the panel, right?"

"I was, is that okay?"

"Yeah, that's great. Where are you all going for chow tonight?"

"We're not sure. We're meeting down in the lobby at 6:30."

"Okay, see you guys then."

While looking for the panel members, Dave Brown became distracted when he saw the back of a somewhat short, muscular man holding a white cane with a red tipped bottom. Two other middle-age vets and an attractive woman surrounded him. Immediately, Peggy Cadigan saw Brown walking up to the three men who were laughing over a meaningless argument. Brown came up behind the blind man and put his index finger to his lips to have Peggy not say anything. "Doctor Dennis Cadigan," Brown called out.

Immediately, the practicing psychiatrist stopped laughing, looked into the air, and mentally analyzed the one of over 1000 voices he had in his incredible memory bank. Three seconds passed while Cadigan reflected. "Dave Brown!" he said with assuredness.

With that Brown moved around to Cadigan's front and shook his extended hand. "Hello, Dennis! And, 'Hello' to you, Peggy. My goodness, you get prettier at each reunion; what's your secret?" Brown asked to

Peggy. With the compliment, Cadigan beamed with pride. He hadn't seen his attractive wife since before he got on the plane for Vietnam. The always-modest Peggy discarded the compliment, giving Brown a polite hug, "Hello, Dave."

"Hey there, J.D. and Ken," he said to J.D. Moore and Ken Murray. "Now just what are you three old timers arguing about?"

The three men smiled as if a referee had just arrived on the scene. Finally, Moore explained, "Cadigan keeps arguing that the reason I beat him all the time in our card game, 'Wisk', back at Phu Lac (6) was because I was cheating. You know, Skipper, that I would have never taken advantage of a newbee!"

Brown laughed and responded cynically, "Sure, J.D." To the four of them he said, "Say we're meeting down in the lobby at 6:30 if you all want to join us for supper. We don't have a restaurant chosen yet."

Peggy Cadigan immediately responded, "That sounds good, Dave; we'll see you there."

Following supper, the hospitality room filled up once more. Now seventy or eighty vets, their families and friends were in attendance and were more boisterous than before as many were under varying degrees of influence from the bountiful and varied set of Class VII Supplies Sam Henderson obtained—the same he Tony Marengo managed and stored nearly forty years earlier in their "Staff Hooch". The amount of smoke lingering a half-foot off the ceiling indicated some vets were still ignoring the Surgeon General. No change since Vietnam. It seemed as if a third of the men were listening, a third were telling a sea story, their battleline, and the rest were laughing. Most of the wives, grown sons, daughters, and their spouses were listening intently.

Bernie Navarra and Dwight Anderson were busy welcoming their old skipper, Ken Furr, to his first reunion. At this point though they were having Tommy LaBarbera, the admin clerk from New York who had volunteered to go on Union II, explain exactly where in Brooklyn the "PFC Dan Bullock Way" was located. Anderson, now a retired US Army

Command Sergeant Major, was saying, "He told me the afternoon before he died that, one day, he would be famous. Geez!"

Mike Downs, Rich Horner, and Tom Martin were at the pinned up Hue City map having a hot discussion about exactly who was involved in the unsuccessful attack down Tran Cao Van Street on the afternoon of February 1, 1968.

Pete Korn, Patty Korn, and Kurt Luedtke caught up with one another in front of the pinned up An Hoa valley map. Korn and Luedtke were pointing out to Dave DeGroat and C.C. Campbell the same spot where the napalm had burned Campbell's and Degroat's bodies and where Korn and Luedtke had recently traveled to say a prayer to relieve their friend's continuing pain.

Dan "Arkie" Albritton, who Dave Brown always considered to be the actual founder of the Fox 2/5 Vietnam-era Association due to his diligent efforts to reunite the Fox veterans, was laughing with Jim McCoy while bragging about having the biggest chigger ranch in Arkansas.

The same scene with more players was replayed on Friday night while the golfers now sported red cheeks caused by the sun and those vets, who had gone swimming in the hotel pool with their grown children and several grandchildren, managing an even brighter burn. Families visited with other families. Marvin Carpenter's daughter, Carla, and her husband, Jon Boeve, had arrived. Kevin and Tiffany Holmes joined the Boeves and other friends they had made at earlier reunions around a table to hear Marvin's war stories.

Perhaps the significant difference in the two nights was the composition of the groups. On the first night the groupings were men who had fought together during their tour of duty. On Friday evening men from different time periods were gathered learning of the experiences and heroism of Marines who served during different times. The camaraderie was obvious. All had proudly served with Fox in Vietnam.

Saturday morning as Chris Brown ended the annual business meeting, he announced, "Well that concludes the business portion of the meeting. Dave Brown is going to moderate the next portion of the meeting, and we are going to learn what happened in 1970 and how Fox finally left country. Dave, you want to introduce your 1970–1971 panel?"

"Sure. Thanks, Chris. Okay, first from the left we first have Joe Finneran. Joe was the radio operator 81mm mortars' forward observer. Joe was with the company from July 1970 to January 1971, so he gained a lot of insight into Foxtrot's operations at the company level. Beside him is Ian Bailey who was assigned to the 1st Platoon as the 3rd Squad leader. Ian served with Fox from March 1970 until his rotation tour date the next February.

"Next to Ian is Joe Bibish who transferred to Fox in December 1969 from the 3rd Marine Division as a lance corporal. Joe went to the 3rd Platoon and became a squad leader right away. He was promoted to corporal almost immediately and earned a Bronze Star Medal in March 1970."

Turning his back to the panel, Brown addressed the gathering of eighty vets and forty of their wives and other family members, most of whom were sitting, although about a dozen were standing along the sides. "Before these gentlemen begin to tell you their story, permit me to paint the picture of I Corps at the start of 1970. The enemy losses in 1969 had been so high that they made a deliberate plan not to engage the Americans in any significant way. Instead, if you vets of earlier periods can possibly believe it, they increased their mine and booby trap efforts. On the US side, the 3rd Marine Division and other forces continued to leave Vietnam during 1969. Because of this, the 1st Marine Division had to take on more and more responsibility for the security for the northern part of the country. To accommodate this 'fewer enemy/larger area of responsibility' situation, the 5th Marines introduced "Kingfisher Operations" in early 1970.

"These operations consisted of a Marine observation aircraft scouting over the Arizona Territory, the An Hoa valley, and Go Noi Island for the enemy. A rifle platoon stood at the ready at An Hoa with three dedicated CH-46s and four Cobra gunships. Within minutes a platoon could be inserted most anywhere with dedicated air support. The rest of the 5th Marines conducted operations similar to the ones we conducted in previous years.

"Okay," Brown continued, "I'm going to kick things off with a few questions for the panel. But please ask them questions, if you need to clarify something or for any other reason. We have to be out of here in an hour, so let's get started.'

"First, a question for Joe Bibish. Joe, I believe you had your squad by January 1st, didn't you?"

"I did."

"Some of us have heard you men talking about the 'Daisy Chain' booby trap incident that took place on the night of the 3rd or 4th of January. Can you fill us in about that event?"

"Sure. Let' see," Bibish began, pausing to gather his thoughts. "Fox spent New Years Eve at Phu Lac (6) overlooking Liberty Bridge. You all remember where that is don't you?"

Every one began shaking their heads affirmatively when Dennis Cadigan's hand shot up in the air.

"Dennis?" Brown said, calling on his friend.

"Was the bridge still burned out at that time? I remember the bridge looking like a row of burned telephone poles," Cadigan, whose visual recollection of Vietnam was as crisp or more so than anyone else's, asked.

"No, it had been rebuilt by that time. It was real low, near the water. Not near as high as the former bridge had been." Bibish answered. Sensing no more questions, he continued. "All right, we were planning to stay at Phu Lac (6) for a few days," he paused then added, "you know, to screw off, swim, and that stuff. Sometime before midnight on the night of the 3rd, the battalion ordered Fox and Echo to go on a two-company sweep through Go Noi Island. We were to take off at midnight. Fox was to be the lead company. We were actually going to drive the VC toward the railroad berm that cuts the island in half. A company from the 3rd Battalion and an ARVN force were there waiting for the VC.

"I talked to Lieutenant Murray, our CO, err…now, retired Major General Terry Murray…a couple of years ago and he told me that the battalion commander was upset that it took us so long to begin moving out. I remember at that point it was pretty dark and we had to stage our packs on the road before we took off. It was kind of a cluster when we left. We were to parallel the Song Thu Bon. The 2nd Platoon had point. The CP group followed them. The other two platoons trailed.

"By about five in the in the morning we had gone a klick and a half and were near Cu Ban (4). It wasn't near as dark then. I was behind the CP, about fifty meters, when the first explosion occurred. The VC command detonated a 60mm mortar. Right after that, boom! boom! boom! Three more were set off. The VC must have let the 2nd Platoon pass through because they saw all those antennas. They darn near wiped out the CP group."

The faces of the vets hardened as Bibish described the event. Most every vet there had fought in the An Hoa valley, in the Arizona territory, or on Go Noi Island. Over the four and a half years Fox operated there, at some point each of them had been either wounded by a mine or booby trap, or had only been lucky and the wound happened to one of their buddies. Silence prevailed.

Bibish continued, "It was a mess. The 81 FO radio operator was killed. One of the skipper's radio operator's, I believe it was the company radio operator, lost an arm or a leg; I can't remember which. Another twelve men, all in the CP, had to be evacuated. Thankfully, the skipper and the gunny were far enough forward that they didn't get hit.

"We had radio operators flown in from everywhere. Bernie Navarra, who's sitting right here in the front row, told me yesterday that, after he left Fox and extended for six months, he was assigned to be the battalion liaison radio operator at the Special Forces camp overlooking Go Noi. With no notice, he was picked up by a chopper and dropped into Fox's position.

"It was a good thing too. Bernie had been Captain Furr's radio operator during '69 and had a lot of experience; no more than ten minutes after he arrived we were mortared. Bernie immediately directed the company's 60mm mortars and shut down the enemy. Lieutenant Murray put you in for a citation, didn't he, Bernie?"

Multiple, low-toned "Ooh rahs" broke out from the men assembled in the audience. Navarra, wearing his bright, crimson-colored Fox baseball cap with its Fox logo as were the majority of the vets, beamed and nodded in agreement.

"There's not too much more to say except I became the point man that day and the skipper and the gunny were so impressed that, any time the company moved for the rest of my tour, my squad had the lead. Oh yeah, and I know you'll believe this: by the time we arrived at the railroad berm, the enemy had vanished."

Cadigan was curious again, "You mentioned a Special Forces camp above Go Noi Island. I didn't know there was anything up there."

Bibish shrugged his shoulders indicating there had been one in 1970. "Maybe they built it after your tour," he suggested.

"Was it on a bald, large hill that once was believed to be an old French artillery firing position?" Cadigan asked.

"I believe so. In 1970 there were either Army Special Forces or USMC recon teams there."

Perceiving the reason from Cadigan's interest, Brown interjected. "You're right, Dennis. That's where the 'McGoo' incident took place."

No one else asked any questions, so Brown added, "All right, let's move on. In February, Fox spent most of time conducting patrols on Go Noi Island. But on March 11th, under the tactical title of 'reconnaissance-in-force', Fox was flown to the Arizona territory to patrol and ambush there. Three days later, on the 14th...well, I'll again ask Joe Bibish to tell you."

"As Dave said, on the 14th of March, the company was located on 'Hot Dog Hill' and my squad..." Bibish paused as a hand went up.

"Sam," Brown called on Sam Jones, the veteran of both the Korean and Vietnam wars.

"I don't recall any 'Hot Dog Hill.'"

"Oh, that's what we called it. It was in the Arizona," Bibish explained.

"Right, not too far west from where the Song Vu Gia and Song Thu Bon rivers come together...north of 'Football Island' if you recall where that was," Brown supplied.

By this time Jones was nodding his head indicating he was somewhat oriented.

"Well, my squad had to go on an ambush, some eight klicks away towards the mountains. We had only gone about 500 meters and were passing by a small cemetery on a hill when Cisco Gutierrez, who had the point, said, 'Hey Joe, there's gooks up there to the left.' He was referring to the ten to fifteen grave stones on the little hill.'

"I told him, 'I don't see them.' But just then a gook poked his head from behind one of the stones. I gave the squad a 'By-The-Left-Flank' and we all turned left and charged the hill. We wounded two NVA but one got away. I called the action in to the company. They wanted to take the prisoner back, so we had to wait for the Kit Carson Scout, an interpreter, and a fire team to come out to our position. By the time they arrived, it was late morning. Since our mission was to set up an ambush eight klicks out, I suggested to Lieutenant Murray that we go to a closer site or go there the next day. Fox Six said, 'No. Proceed on your mission.' Which, of course, we did.

"We finally arrived at the ambush site at around 1400 hours. Immediately, we shot and wounded two NVA. I didn't want to medevac the two; but Murray insisted again that they might have some good intelligence.

"While we were waiting for the medevacs, a squad of gooks attacked us. They were trying to overrun our position. It was a big gun fight. Seemed to last forever, but probably was only five to eight minutes long. My radioman was wounded and down and so was Gutierrez. My '60 team' was pinned down, so we didn't have any guns. I strapped on the radio, charged forward and fired two to three clips at the gooks. The gun team finally put their gun into action and the gooks fled. I called for air support." Bibish paused, "The AH-1s came and chased them far enough away to let us medevac our guys and one of the two wounded prisoners. The other one died.

"So now I'm down to five or six guys in my squad who are mostly newbees and we have to get back to the company. And we had eight clicks to go. It's dusk. I told my guys, 'If the gooks get me running through the paddies, that's all right. At least we're not going to be stuck out here all night with hundreds of enemy looking for us.' I ran those guys right back across the paddy dikes, right out in the open. Of course the young kids thought I was as crazy as a hoot owl.

"We finally got back inside the lines, and I passed the word for them to chow down then clean their weapons. Fifteen minutes later I heard an accidental discharge. No one was hurt, but I got those kids together and chewed their butts. I was really mad! I told them that the next time there's an accidental discharge, I'm taking that kid outside the lines and shooting him. That really got their attention."

The men in the audience were nodding their heads in full approval. Some of the younger family members in attendance had their eyebrows raised in surprise. Most children of the veterans shared one thought: this guy sounded just like their dads. Before this, each was certain that his or her dad was one-of-a-kind.

"The word got back to my new platoon commander, Second Lieutenant D. J. Kelly, and he asked me, 'Are you really going to do that? Drag them out and shoot them?'"

"I said, 'Nooooo, Sir. It just makes me so mad when an accidental discharge happens!'" Looking over at Brown, Bibish said, "That's it, Dave."

The men applauded as they enjoyed hearing his exploits and the reinforcement of their high standards.

"That's a great story," Brown offered, "Joe, thanks. Now, let's transition somewhat from Joe's story. In April, Lieutenant Murray was called up to the battalion staff to work for the operations officer, Major Hanson, because their minds were on the same track to introduce a new tactical maneuver, at least a new one for the An Hoa valley. This was a variant of the classic cordon and search operation: one company would surround a hamlet or a small village at night; at first light another company and the battalion Jump CP would charge in and sweep the hamlet."

Marvin Carpenter raised his hand and Brown said, "Marvin?"

"We didn't do that in '69. How did that work out?"

"The successes were dramatic," Brown answered. "For example, on May 13th Hotel Company surrounded Le Nam (1) which was east of Liberty Bridge, and Fox swept through and killed two, captured twenty-four, and bagged sixty-five detainees." Brown added, "As a matter of fact, Marvin, while providing security for the bridge and Liberty Road, on two occasions during the month of June, Fox conducted cordon and search operations with Golf Company. Then, at the end of July, the battalion Jump CP, Fox, Golf, and India Companies began Operation Barron Green. They conducted a cordon and search of My Hiep Village on the southern side of the Song Vu Gia. Joe Finneran was there and has been quite anxious to share his experience."

"Thanks, Dave," Finneran began in his pronounced New England accent. "I was in 11th Grade watching Fox 2/5 and other Marine units on the nightly news fighting their way through Hue City. You men were my heroes in high school! I couldn't wait to graduate. I joined the Corps and was on 'the Island' ten days after graduation in 1969. By the 14th of July I arrived at An Hoa where my NCOIC, Sergeant Bernie Navarra," he dipped his head toward Navarra, "assigned me to Fox Company as the 81mm mortar forward observer's radioman.

"Within ten days we began Operation Barren Green and that's what I wanted to tell you about. It started on the 24th of July, before the sun came up. We were lined up along the edge of the An Hoa tarmac in columns, you know…sticks of approximately twenty men each. A bunch of CH-46 choppers extended all the way down the runway," Finneran said gesturing with his hand. "Some had two AH-1 Cobra gunships, one on each side, for protection.

"I happened to have been at the head of one of these columns, immediately next to the cockpit of one of the Cobras. As a newbee, I was totally enthralled and fascinated by the pilot of that gunship and his skills. He hovered completely still and unflinching, less than two feet above the deck for what seemed an eternity. When his head turned toward us and he saluted, it was eerie. The small flashing red and white lights from the 46's illuminated, not only the painted sharks mouth design on the Cobra's nose, but also the black face mask of the pilot's helmet. It was the most memorable image I have of my entire tour.

"Our string of 46s and Cobras took off and banked south first and then northeast along the foothills of the Que Son Mountains just when the first rays of sunlight hit us. All aircraft banked west, this time across Liberty Road, and onward toward the northern Arizona territory—our intended area of operation.

"We hovered close to the ground and our rear door dropped. The men exited into what must have been a two-feet-deep, water-filled rice paddy. The air was filled with tracers as the Cobras swirled, prepping our target area. As I reached the tree line on the edge of the paddy, I noticed some corpsmen attending wounded Vietnamese apparently hit by the gunships. The grunts were busy fragging the tunnel system entrances alongside the crude hooches. This was just a very small outlying hamlet of VC-controlled My Hiep vil. Almost immediately, although temporarily, we were delayed with a number of older and very young civilians who were escorted to some other extraction point for removal to the An Hoa Combat Base for questioning, I believe.

"By mid-morning it was already sweltering. The company command group held up a after one of the radio operators confessed he had somehow lost his secret shackle code sheets. A couple of grunts were detailed to search the trail we had just traveled. They did recover the lost papers. However, unfortunately one of them triggered a booby trap, and I recall having to hurry and call a medevac for him.

"Later that day, many of us were astounded to come across Marine tanks belonging to 1st Tank Battalion. Those Marines referred to their tanks as 'Tigers'. I still don't know how those tanks got into that ridiculously wet terrain. Unfortunately, one of the tankers jumped to the ground from his tracks during a brief stop, and landed smack-dab on another one of the notorious Arizona booby traps.

"As Dave was saying, the post-Hue City operations such as Mameluke Thrust, Henderson Hill, Meade River, Taylor Common, and Pipestone Canyon had radically deflated, but not eliminated the enemy's eagerness to engage the 5th Marines in open combat. This was particularly true in the greater An Hoa corridor. Soon they started rethinking their combat strategy. The operations I just mentioned totaled thousands of enemy killed. I don't know if any of you have read R. J. Brown's book, A Few Good Men, The Fighting Fifth Marines: A History of the USMC's Most Decorated Regiment?" Some of the heads in the room nodded. "In there, he explains that the increase of the number of booby traps, especially in the Arizona, exacerbated the Marines' problems. By late summer 1970, that terrain had become so saturated with traps that even a small unit could not go a hundred yards without encountering some sort of booby trap.

"Even the enemy had it bad. The NVA's 38th Regiment must have been on somebody's 'S' list in Hanoi to be assigned to the Arizona for its duty area during that time frame. I remember a couple of stories about that regiment's problems tripping their own traps, while beating a hasty retreat after some rocket attack or ambush.

"During the late afternoon, Captain Kane, our CO at the time, made a decision for the Fox command group to set in around a very small, primitive VC dwelling for the night. A couple of Fox grunts turned over three prisoners with packs and weapons to the gunny. One guy was older, in his mid-fifties, who wore the uniform of an NVA officer; another was a female NVA nurse in her early twenties; and the third in black pajamas was a mid-thirties Viet Cong combatant.

"I was one of the three Marines detailed to guard these captives for the night. The gunny told us that we were expecting to get hit that night, and for that reason, he wanted us to stay underground in one of the hooches' bomb shelters. We complained, but it didn't do us any good. We were chosen because each of us had a handgun, making it much easier for us to maneuver in the tiny shelter.

"While we were packed in there, one of my companions on the detail attempted to explain, as best he could, his hatred toward the VC prisoner. He felt more feelings of respect toward the NVA officer, who at least went into combat in a uniform.

"After an hour down in the bunker and a load of typical Marine conversation, a fourth Marine squeezed down into our already confined space. It was almost dark, however, and I realized in the faint candlelight that I didn't know this guy. He explained he was from the 3rd Battalion. None of us had realized that any company from 3/5 was even with us on the operation. Recognizing my accent, he asked if I was from the Boston area. I replied yes and realized he was too. I asked him, 'Whereabouts?' and he replied, 'A little town you never heard of—Dedham.' Not only had I heard of Dedham, but I came from the town of Walpole only nine miles away.

"By this time we all needed a short break for fresh air. I agreed to go up the tunnel first. I had no sooner got up and out of the hole and straightened up when a noise from outside the Fox Company perimeter got my full attention. I looked up and saw a wavering, bluish halo shape coming at me through the air. It was an RPG round obviously designed to take out the Fox command group. It was a good shot. It landed about ten yards from the skipper, Captain Kane, and almost next to me about fifteen feet away. It landed in a five-foot gully and the explosion picked me up and slammed me first into the bamboo tunnel entrance, then over it. I remember being covered in what seemed like a hand sparkler that kids burn on the 4th of July, only a thousand times bigger. It wasn't until I was on my feet again and I could clear the dirt from my mouth, that I realized those sparkles were pieces of white-hot shrapnel.

"I went back into the tunnel. The guy from 3/5 looked at me as if he had seen a ghost. It turns out he had followed me to get some air. He had seen me get thrown over his head and assumed I was dead. Obviously, I wasn't. Both of us were extremely fortunate to say the least. Shortly after that he left to make his way around the Fox perimeter, and eventually reach Lima Co. I assumed he made it back; however, I never even got his name or address. To this day I regret that.

"At the end of the operation, we had to hump it back. We left the Arizona from Football Island by crossing the Song Thu Bon at probably its most narrow point. The river wasn't very deep. Nevertheless, someone had rigged a rope across the river for us to hang on while walking across. I will never forget being in the middle of that river hanging off that rope when Cobra gunships screamed upstream with their skids no more than a foot above the water. Then they rocketed the rivers banks for our protection.

"Once across, we set in for the night. The grunts established their night perimeter and we four radio operators set up our comm gear as usual. Soon our Kit Carson scout informed the skipper that we would probably be hit again that night from the north end of the island. You all know about lob-bombs?"

Many of the men in the audience shook their heads.

"Well, most of the lob bombs were made from unexploded B-52 ordinance. The gooks would wait for an opportune time to move within forty yards of a U.S. position and build a bamboo cradle against a paddy dike into which they put a large satchel charge. When the charge was ignited, the bomb was lobbed at us with unbelievable accuracy. Not long after the scout warned the skipper, we heard an unusual sound. The four of us jumped up and heard the whop-whop-whop of a lob-bomb coming into our position," the men nodded at Finneran's imitation of the noise the bomb makes as it tumbles through the air. This one exploded no more than twenty meters away. The ground shook like an earthquake. As luck would have it, a high sand dune was between us and where it went off. We survived in spite of being covered with sand and debris.

"That's what happened on Operation Barron Green. Thanks for letting me tell you about it," Finneran concluded.

Again the men smiled and applauded. A few "Ooh rahs" showed even greater appreciation.

"And thank you for the story, Joe." Brown continued, "I will say that Operation Barren Green terminated on July 27, 1970 and resulted in seventeen enemy dead. After a quick return to Liberty Bridge, the company was back in the Arizona on Operation Lyon Valley by mid-August. On this operation, Fox was one of two companies helolifted into the foothills that, acting as a driving force, moved down into the rice paddies driving any potential enemy toward a blocking force. While this operation did not have the normal results in terms of KIAs or POWs as others did, its significance was that it was the final one we had in the infamous Arizona territory.

"From August 1970 until March 1971 the whole picture began to change. Tactically, for the men, it was field operations and C-rations as usual. For example, on August 29th, Fox and local Vietnamese troops from the Duc Duc District were helolifted into Phu Nhuan (2); Fox surrounded the hamlet; and the Vietnamese soldiers killed seven enemy and picked up four POWs. But, strategically, our regiment began its an exit from the war we had fought in for five years. Actually, the 5th Marines' Headquarters Company and the rear elements of 3/5 and 2/5 left An Hoa on August 17th.

"Although a 5th Marines' presence was retained in An Hoa until the Vietnamese were ready to assume full control," Brown continued, "the operational control of the combat base was formally passed to the 51st ARVN Regiment on September 15th. The base was far too large for the Vietnamese, so they chose to occupy a portion of the old industrial area outside of our combat base. Then, and well into October, the dismantling of the combat base was the main activity of the few men remaining at An Hoa. Bernie Navarra, sitting here in the front row, can give anyone the details involved dismantling An Hoa since he was there. It wasn't particularly pretty nor fun right, Bernie?"

Narvarra's head nodded in concurrence.

"By the end of September the artillery support coming from the 11th Marines had moved from An Hoa to fire support bases on the eastern portion of the Que Son Mountains. From there they could provide fire support for operations as far as Go Noi Island to the north and the Que Son basin to the south. Fox's operational control, OPCON, passed to the 11th Marines on the 26th of September, and Fox began providing security for them at Fire Support Base Ryder," Brown informed the group.

"OPCON of Fox was returned to 2/5 on October 15th when, from then on, Fox would conduct all of its remaining operations from or within the Que Son Mountains. For those vets of the Union II, you'll recall that this was one of the principal areas the 2nd NVA Division passed through on the way to the Que Son basin, and you flew over these mountains on the way to your battle. Ian Bailey was a corporal, a squad leader by this time, and he has a couple of stories about mountain operations."

"Right, Dave. Well, Dave mentioned that our 'OPCON' was passed back to 2/5 on October 15th. We troops probably missed that fact!"

Most of the vets smiled at Bailey's cynicism. Today they knew something about "operational control" after having read enough books about the Vietnam War, the war they fought. These overview events had never been a subject the troops were briefed on while actually in Vietnam.

"But we didn't miss the fact that it had been raining for days; we were soaking wet; and," Bailey paused for emphasis, "hadn't been resupplied for three days."

Now a low rumble rose from the men in the audience who, at that very moment, were compelled to share a similar "remember-that-time-we" experience with the men next to them.

When the noise quieted, Bailey continued. "Fox went on non-ending operations or patrols up in the Que Sons at that time. We'd be mostly confined to switchback paths. Sometimes one platoon would be humping up a path going one way and my platoon would be on the same one going the other way. We would bump into a few enemy but no large units. Seems like our role at the time was to destroy their infrastructure.

"For example, at the end of October, on the 24th, one of the other platoons killed a couple of enemy, maybe three. One of them was an NVA pay officer who had a 9mm pistol and all sorts of 'intel' documents on him. On the 26th my squad was helolifted to a spot where those 'intel' documents said there had been an NVA hospital. Oh yeah, our lieutenant had to tag along." Again Bailey paused to be careful in crafting his words. "I don't know about you all but I had been in 'Nam' for about eight months and I had issues with my platoon commander from time to time. Which could be considered 'often', but don't quote me," he smiled.

Chuckles also came from the men in the audience who had shared the same experience.

"Well, we found the aid station in a cave system almost directly below where we landed. We blew it up, best we could, with C-4. Just for background..." Bailey added. "A lot of times we were up there we'd discover caves. We used to flush any gooks out by throwing in a couple bags of CS, you know...gas bags, and drop frag grenades on top of the bags. That way the gas would float all around the inside of the cave complex. So, at this aid station surrounded this thick canopy, except for the area above the caves where the chopper landed, my lieutenant orders me to drop in a CS bag and frag it. I told him we shouldn't do it because we didn't know which way the gas would drift.

"The lieutenant said, 'Do it! The chopper is expected here in two minutes. We'll be long gone before the gas drifts out of the cave entrances.' My next protest went nowhere, so we fragged the CS. The chopper came late, ten minutes late, and by this time the gas was coming out of the ground from everywhere. With a thicket of trees surrounding the cave complex, we had no place to go to. By the time the chopper arrived, we ran onto it with tears streaming down our faces.

"The crew chief who was laughing at us grunts asked, 'Why are all you guys crying?' So, we told him. About that time the chopper's blades began sucking all that gas into the chopper, and it hit the crew chief. He turned around to tell the pilot and panicked. Within a second we were in the air climbing faster than I'd ever done before.

"But on the next day, October 27th, Fox discovered an NVA regimental base camp guarded by six NVA we surprised. A man in our lead squad was killed. We ran over the defenders and discovered the most sophisticated complex I'd ever seen. It was spread out, and some of it was underground. There were lots of all-bamboo hooches with bamboo chairs and tables. We had to destroy the whole complex. My squad found the cooking area. The chimney system was amazing. They used to conceal the smoke coming from the stoves, by capturing the smoke from their fires and directing it into a long trench, about 200 feet long, that was dug from the kitchen upwards toward the mountain. They covered the trench with some sort of vegetation. This way, instead of the smoke going up from one of the fires and being visible in the sky, it dissipated before it left the treetops.

"We discovered the complex early in the morning and by noon had to request additional C-4 to complete destroying the base camp. Since the canopy was so thick, the choppers dropped cases of C-4 through the trees. We ended up running around trying to get the cases and not leave any for the gooks to find. Only one case fell off a cliff and disappeared out of our sight as it tumbled down the mountain."

Bailey waited a moment, and then looked at Brown, "Well, Dave, that's some of the things we did."

"All right, Ian. Thanks for your stories." Brown addressed the panel now, "I concluded two things. First, that while your group may have been up in the mountains, your personal experiences and insights struck the same chords with vets from other eras." The rest of the veterans agreed. "Then second, it's pretty obvious the enemy was not nearly as potent as he had been in earlier years.

"I want to share a story about the 2nd Platoon as a 'Quick Reaction Force'," Brown offered. "On November 4th the platoon was standing by on QFR alert with choppers nearby when a Marine CAP east of Go Noi Island and halfway between National Highway 1 and the south China Sea, reported being attacked by an enemy platoon. The CAP unit repelled the attack and the enemy withdrew in column toward the Song Ba Ren. The 2nd Platoon, led by First Lieutenant John Scott landed by chopper near the enemy column. The enemy had only a few AK-47s, though many had pistols. Firing on the platoon as the enemy fled, the combined NVA/VC force scattered in all directions. Some dove for the underbrush and some ran for the river. The 2nd Platoon responded viciously, Cobra gunships fired a wall of steel around the surprised enemy. That day, the enemy lost twenty killed and, unfortunately, Fox lost one Marine, Lance Corporal Ray Arnett. This was the last significant contact for Fox in the war.

"As a final note, the company was pulled out of the field during the second week in March. They were flown to a camp near Da Nang where they were all issued a new set of jungle utilities for the trip home.

Obviously, they were thrilled to be leaving. Officially, the company departed Vietnam on 12 March 1971 aboard a US Navy ship. Their destination was Camp Pendleton. Many of them flew back via Okinawa a few days before the ship set sail; others, like Captain Ed Easton, Fox's last in-country commanding officer, remained in Vietnam for a few months to complete their overseas tour of duty.

"Well that's it. Thank-you very much Joe Finneran, Ian Bailey, and Joe Bibish. We've use up our hour," Brown said looking at his watch, "and then some. If the rest of you have any questions you can ask them over a beer later today. Thanks for coming. Now I'll turn this over to Chris for any final comments."

The meeting concluded once Dave Brown finished his final comments. Free for the rest of the day, many of the veterans and their families hit the town to explore.

That night at the banquet, dressed to the hilt, the men and women enjoyed Pete Korn's and Chris Brown's terrific slide show, convinced Conley to share his "Who farted?" story, again, and welcomed all of their newest members with a standing ovation. From the lectern at the front of the room, President Chris Brown explained the significance of the one, lone place-setting next to him. It was their fallen-man table. A special toast was made honoring the men of Fox who had been lost, in Vietnam, and since.

Once dinner concluded, the veterans hit the hospitality room again. Now the party really began. Stories were shared and bonds were renewed until late, or early rather, into the morning.

Sunday, President Chris Brown stood in the center of the men of Company F, 2nd Battalion, 5th Marine Regiment who had fought in Vietnam. Beside them were their wives and grown children. There were 180 in all. He removed his cap and on cue the rest who were wearing caps did as well. "Our final event for this wonderful reunion, as it is for every reunion, is our Sunday Service. Here we can pay our respects to our brothers who did not come back from the war.

We landed in 1966, and left in January 1971. What I would like to note is that even though there wasn't much action in 1971, our final combat loss in country took place on January 28th where we lost Private Ron Rigdon.

"This list," and with that Chris Brown raised a set of four or five pieces of paper in the air, "contains the names of the men who died serving with Fox. The list is far from complete; as you know we lost many of the men attached to Fox from other companies. I will pass this list around, please read three names and the dates of their deaths, then pass the list to the man next to you. If you know of any others please say their names when it is your turn. Help us remember them, honor them, and keep them with us always."

The list was passed. In turn, each Marine stepped into the center of the circle to honor their dead, the men whose battlelines only the living were left to tell…

Private First Class	Robert Nelson	Davis	4/26/66
Corporal	George Steven	Edley	4/27/66
Corporal	Leo C.	Lawson.	7/25/66
Private	La Marr	Fisher	8/20/66
Hospitalman Third Class	Phillip Carrol	Fox	10/13/66
Sergeant	Dennis D.	Harris	10/13/66
Lance Corporal	Andrew	Chmiel	10/13/66
Sergeant	Joe L.	Ronje	10/13/66
Private First Class	Edward A.	McWright	11/15/66
Private First Class	James P.	Bauer	1/26/67
Private First Class	Kirby W.	Bradford	1/26/67
Sergeant	Thomas Joseph	Carey	1/26/67
Hospitalman	Dell C.	Geise	1/26/67
Private First Class	Allan	Guinn	1/26/67
Private First Class	William F.	Kranz	1/26/67
Lance Corporal	James E.	Myers	1/26/67
Private First Class	Dale Martin	McCauley	4/14/67
Private First Class	Richard	Hernandez	4/30/67

Sergeant	Gerard Levie	Ackley	6/3/67
Lance Corporal	Stephen A.	Balters Jr.	6/3/67
Lance Corporal	Richard Lee	Blasen	6/3/67
Private First Class	Larry Neal	Boatman	6/3/67
Private First Class	Jimmy Ray	Crook	6/3/67
Lance Corporal	William Stanley	Daugherty	6/3/67
Hospitalman Third Class	Thomas Stephen	Donovan	6/3/67
Corporal	Victor Michael	Driscoll	6/3/67
Corporal	John Paul	Francis	6/3/67
Private First Class	Lawson Douglas	Gerard	6/3/67
Captain	James Albert	Graham	6/3/67
Lance Corporal	Robert Reyes	Hernandez	6/3/67
Second Lieutenant	Straughan D.	Kelsey Jr.	6/3/67
Lance Corporal	Gary Wayne	Kline	6/3/67
Private First Class	Michael David	McCandless	6/3/67
Private First Class	Dennis Eugene	Monfils	6/3/67
Private First Class	Keith Milton	Moser II	6/3/67
Lance Corporal	John Ralph.	Painter Jr.	6/3/67
Lance Corporal	Benjamin F.	Pelzer II	6/3/67
Private First Class	Robert	Richardson	6/3/67
Corporal	Karl Balthasar	Rische Jr.	6/3/67
Second Lieutenant	Charles Joseph	Schultz	6/3/67
Private First Class	Clifford	Shepherd	6/3/67
Lance Corporal	Jereld Eugene	Westphal	6/3/67
Lance Corporal	Arthur Malcom	Byrd	6/3/67
Lance Corporal	James Jerome	Deasel Jr.	6/3/67
Corporal	Marion Lee	Dirickson	6/3/67
Captain	James Albert	Graham	6/3/67
Corporal	Gary Malcom	O'Brien	6/3/67
Private First Class	Steven Edward	Scharlach	6/3/67
Private First Class	James Allan	Weed	6/3/67
Sergeant	Tony	Ahinzow	7/4/67
Lance Corporal	James Edward	Ball III	7/4/67
Private	Andrew	Currie	7/4/67

Lance Corporal	Arthur	Lanteigne	7/4/67
Private First Class	Melvin Earl	Newlin	7/4/67
Lance Corporal	Joseph Lonnie	Hicks	7/4/67
Corporal	Francis George	Monin	7/5/67
Hospitalman	James Lee	Townsend	7/29/67
Sergeant	David Harold	Brown	9/10/67
Corporal	Jose Francisco	Acosta	10/1/67
Sergeant	Dudley Norman	Jordan	10/19/67
Corporal	Daniel John	Yeutter	11/12/67
Private First Class	Earl David	Miller	12/1/67
Private First Class	John Henry	Jones Jr.	1/30/68
Lance Corporal	Jerry Dean	Barksdale	1/31/68
Corporal	David Leroy	Collins	2/1/68
Private	Stanley	Murdock	2/1/68
Hospitalman Third Class	James Edward	Gosselin	2/2/68
Corporal	Christobal	Figueroa-Perez	2/2/68
Sergeant	John Edward	Maloney Jr.	2/2/68
Private First Class	William Carel	Barnes Jr.	2/4/68
Lance Corporal	Wayne Arthur	Washburn	2/4/68
Lance Corporal	Reginald Joseph	Gautreau	2/6/68
Sergeant	Alonzo Earl	Mayhall	2/6/68
Hospitalman	Charles Lloyd	Morrison	2/6/68
Private First Class	Jimmie Charles	Palmo	2/6/68
Staff Sergeant	Paul Drake	Tinson	2/6/68
Corporal	James Edward	Violett	2/6/68
Corporal	Gary Wayne	Holbrook	2/7/68
Second Lieutenant	Donald Arthur	Hausrath Jr.	2/11/68
Private First Class	Wayne Franklin	Crapse	2/13/68
Private	Jerome Alan	Schuett	2/13/68
Lance Corporal	Kenneth Lee	Crysel	2/15/68
Lance Corporal	Patrick Eugene	Lindstrom	2/18/68
Private First Class	Charles Thomas	Martin	2/25/68
Corporal	Stephen Lee	Huber	2/26/68
Private First Class	George Francis	Robilotto	3/2/68

Lance Corporal	Lawrence	Williams	4/27/68
Sergeant	Paul Conrad	Johnson	4/30/68
Lance Corporal	Richard Castillo	Gonzales	5/5/68
Private First Class	Charles Ray	Marshall	5/15/68
Private First Class	Darrell Dwayne	Bratton	5/22/68
Lance Corporal	Willard Loyd	Williams	5/22/68
Private First Class	Jesus Ramon	Perez	6/24/68
Staff Sergeant	James Robert	Long	7/26/68
Second Lieutenant	Jeffrey Lea	Martin	7/29/68
Corporal	Richard W.	Hellard Jr.	8/4/68
Lance Corporal	Lupe	Monsebias	8/5/68
Corporal	Robert Gerald	Fante	8/6/68
Hospitalman Second Class	Andrew Charles	Rackow	8/6/68
Lance Corporal	James Merton	Edwards	8/8/68
Private First Class	Allen Lea	Ward	8/13/68
Lance Corporal	Darrell Lynn	Trumble	8/13/68
Corporal	Robert Jay	Brown	8/16/68
Private First Class	John Kenny	Hill	8/27/68
Private First Class	James Henry	Jessman	8/30/68
Private First Class	Bruce Landon	Carter	9/11/68
Private First Class	Bruce Wayne	Crabb	9/11/68
Private First Class	Jerry Brian	Evans	9/11/68
Private First Class	Billy Joe	Scott	9/11/68
Lance Corporal	Fred Concetto	Spina	9/11/68
Private First Class	Frank	Vallone	9/11/68
Private First Class	George William	McGee	9/11/68
Private First Class	David Michael	Sowards	9/12/68
Lance Corporal	George	Sandoval	9/17/68
Lance Corporal	Gary Ray	Townsend	9/30/68
Private First Class	George Henry	Brewer	10/7/68
Private First Class	Philip Jeffrey	Taft	10/9/68
Private First Class	Howard Kenneth	Cooper	11/11/68
Private First Class	Richard Lee	Moyers	11/11/68
Private First Class	Sherl Kent	Bonnett	12/19/68

Lance Corporal	Rene Javier	Salazar	12/19/68
Private First Class	Irineo	Guevara	1/11/69
Private First Class	Charles Fredrick	Wade	1/15/69
Private First Class	Lawrence Hamilton	Moore	2/14/69
Corporal	Donald Lee	Kujawa	2/17/69
Private First Class	Victor Modesto	Jouvert	2/22/69
Private First Class	Daniel W.	Margrave II	2/22/69
Private First Class	Rhena Charles	Webster	2/22/69
Private First Class	John Henry	Erbes	2/27/69
Private First Class	James Patrick	Carney Jr.	2/27/69
Lance Corporal	David Allen	Floyd	3/1/69
Private First Class	John Edward	Shiraka	3/11/69
Lance Corporal	James Carl	Jones	4/17/69
Private First Class	James Albert	Sanders	5/9/69
Lance Corporal	Edward	Atkucunas	5/10/69
Private First Class	Dan	Bullock	6/7/69
Private First Class	Donald Wayne	Bunn	6/7/69
Lance Corporal	Larry James	Eglinsdoerfer	6/7/69
Private First Class	Jason David	Hunnicutt	6/7/69
Private First Class	Steven Hugh	Montgomery	6/7/69
Second Lieutenant	Albert Duward	Benson	7/6/69
Corporal	Michael Lee	Lewis	8/15/69
Private First Class	Clifford Michael	Gibson	8/16/69
Lance Corporal	David Michael	Hartogh	9/7/69
Private First Class	Larry Kenneth	Robillard	9/7/69
Private First Class	Donnie Joe	Clough	9/9/69
Sergeant	Albert N.	Wright Jr.	10/19/69
Lance Corporal	Ronald Lee	Spence	11/28/69
Lance Corporal	Warren J.	Ferguson	2/20/70
Sergeant	John J.	Boyd	3/15/70
Private First Class	William Francis	Brooks	3/17/70
Hospitalman Third Class	George R.	Cuthbert	3/29/70
Sergeant	Ramon	Moya Jr.	5/12/70
Lance Corporal.	Arden E.	Kersey	6/13/70

Corporal.	William P.	Arthur	6/19/70
Lance Corporal.	John W.	Brown	6/19/70
Corporal	Stephen Leslie	Boyd	8/3/70
Sergeant	Edward Bernard	Iwasko	10/10/70
Lance Corporal	James Edward	Miller	10/27/70
Lance Corporal	Ray	Arnett Jr.	11/4/70
Private	Ronald Michael	Rigdon	1/28/71

About the Authors

LtCol David B. Brown, U.S. Marine Corps (Ret.), recipient of the Silver Star medal for Gallantry in Combat, was a Captain and Company Commander in the Vietnam War. During his distinguished 20-year career in the Marine Corps, Dave Brown instructed at the U.S. Naval Academy and headed the Marine Corps Procurement Budget. Upon retirement, he was a logistics consultant for the U.S. Marine Corps and the U.S. Navy. He has published numerous articles in the Marine Corps Gazette and Amphibious Warfare Review; and has authored books on training, automated information systems, and logistics.

Tiffany Brown Holmes, author of Once Defiant and The Promise, holds a degree in English with an emphasis on Expository and Creative Writing. Tiffany is Chair of the English Department, District Curriculum Designer for 6th, 7th, and 8th grades, and an English teacher where she resides in Texas. In addition to her work on Battlelines, she is a Model Teacher for Advanced Placement Strategies.

978-0-595-67407-7
0-595-67407-0

Printed in the United States
40344LVS00004B/344